UNWILLING
DEITY

# UNWILLING DEITY

## Sufferborn Book 2

## J.C. HARTCARVER

Dorwik Publishing

Unwilling Deity
**Copyright 2020 Jesslyn Carver**

This is a work of fiction. Names, characters, businesses, places, events, locales, and incidents are either the products of the author's imagination or used in a fictitious manner. Any resemblance to actual persons, living or dead, or actual events is purely coincidental.

Cover art "Her Ecstasy" oil on linen, back cover art "Thing of Desire" oil on canvas, and all interior illustrations by Jesslyn Carver.

Fan mail can be sent to J.C. Hartcarver via the "contact" page on her website: www.jchartcarver.com.

ISBN: 978-0-9982104-7-6 (paperback)
978-0-9982104-9-0 (hardback)
978-0-9982104-8-3 (ebook)

Library of Congress Control Number: 2020918384

Dorwik Publishing
Greenbrier, TN

# Table of Contents

# The Darklands

Ilbith

The Black Mountains

Goblin Country

Hathrohskog    Wikhaihli

Alkeer

The Longwalk

Valltalhiss

Laugaulentzei    Hanhelin's Gate

Norr    Carridax

Theddir

Wexwick

# The Lightlands

# Prologue

Baring his teeth, Lehomis grabbed Gaije's lapel and a lock of his hair. Gaije yelped and tightened his lips.

Lehomis roared, "What do you mean they took her?"

Gaije could only shake his head and swallow.

Lehomis jerked him this way and that for no other apparent reason than to be rough, and Gaije stumbled. Though the pulling hurt his scalp, a lot of his senses had raced away with the night. And his sister.

"I saw it," Gaije said.

After those three words, Lehomis stayed quiet, focusing on him. His brow narrowed. "Listen to me, deserter. *You're* going to get her back."

Gaije nodded. "Grandfather, let's get everyone together—"

"Not everyone! You!"

Gaije cocked his head. "The *saehgahn*—"

"Not the *saehgahn*, just you. I don't know how many *saehgahn* are left as it is. Besides, you abandoned your company and ran home like a coward. You have to redeem yourself."

"But Mhina is a female!"

"I know. Don't you know how important she is to me?" Lehomis's voice tremored with vibrato. "She's more important than you are, but what this means for you is serious. It's life and death. If you'd like to have any chance for a long life, you'll go out there and come back with that *farhah* in your care. Alive."

Gaije's jaw trembled. He dropped to his knees. "Where's my mother?"

"Safe," Lehomis said, standing tall over him. "I'll take care of everything here. I'll tell her about Mhina. I'll also tell her not to worry. Here."

Grandfather's bow fell before Gaije, bouncing against the soil before settling. *Leho's Bow*. The bow from all his stories. The new dawn light struggling through heavy clouds and smoke from the buildings gleamed pale across its shiny, reinforced surface. Elongated horse bodies leaped along the bow's limbs.

Gaije raised his hot face in the cold misty air, his eyes squinting. "Grandfather?"

"You'll take *my* bow with you. She needs it more than I do. Do you remember when I showed you how to use it?"

Gaije struggled to swallow. His trembling fingers grazed across the inlaid silver horses. Leho's Bow. Grandfather had owned it for the past thousand years or more. He'd found it in the Darklands during his legendary adventure.

Gaije wrapped his hand around the grip and lifted the bow a smidge off the moist ground. Feeling stupid, he put the bow down again and shook his head. "I can't. Grandfather, you must come with me."

Grunting, Lehomis grabbed his hair and jerked his head back so their eyes met. "You're. Wasting. Time." He shoved the bow at Gaije's middle, forcing him to take it.

A female's voice sounded. "Grandfather?" Anonhet's voice.

Gaije scrambled to his feet, awkwardly holding the bow. A bow should've been a natural thing in his hands. Grandfather had been putting bows in his hand since he could stand. This bow he'd held at least once when Lehomis secretly let him shoot it in a meadow.

"Anonhet!" Lehomis called back.

She came around the path looking crisper than most everyone else outside, aside from a few soot marks on her *hanbohik*. After the initial glance, Gaije turned his eyes away from her and kept them away.

Lehomis continued, "Gaije is going out to find Mhina. Pack him a good inventory of food and travel tools."

Anonhet's face dropped into shock. "Is Mhina lost?"

Leaving Gaije to stand awkwardly with the bow, Lehomis turned her by her shoulder and pushed her in the opposite direction. "Yes, so hurry. I'll explain later."

"I'll tell Tirnah what's happened!" Anonhet said before taking off.

When she ran back up the path, Lehomis turned to Gaije. "Go with her. Say goodbye to your mother. You'll return with Mhina, or you won't return at all."

Any *faerhain* not inducted into the Desteer wailed; wives and mothers bent over the bodies, shedding tears and dabbing blood off the dead faces of the *saehgahn*. Members of the Desteer strolled contemplatively along the growing line of corpses. A bark in Norrian drew Lehomis's attention to the forest as a few older *saeghar* hauled in another body, bringing about a shriek from another *faerhain* who'd busied herself with a neighbor. It would take days to cremate these bodies before carrying the ashes to *Laugaulentrei*, the place where all elves retired in death.

Hours ago, Lehomis had sent Gaije off to retrieve Mhina, who'd been captured last night. At least he didn't have to look at Gaije's dead body lying among the others. And thank the Bright One no *faerhain* or *farhah* lay dead—that they'd found yet. Mhina was the only female missing. Otherwise, a young *saeghar* named Bairhen had been deemed missing too, perhaps taken alongside her. It would be best if they were together now.

To his right, a ways down the line, a Desteer maiden put her hand on the shoulder of a particularly loud *faerhain* and gestured with her other hand while shaking her head. The crying *faerhain* swiped her hand away and stood to shake a finger in the maiden's face. Lehomis could've smiled at the brazen act. The maiden must've been shushing and reminding her to keep her composure, but the *faerhain* wouldn't hear it. Sometimes the maidens needed standing up to. Maybe all clan members should practice a little more of that.

Lehomis counted the dead and ended with thirty, not counting the ones moved into houses for cleaning and such, plus Gaije, Mhina, and the other lad who might or might not return... But he couldn't entertain negative thoughts. Gaije could very well succeed. Still, thirty *saehgahn* was a lot to lose. This had happened soon after his heated discussion with the Desteer about the severe imbalance of *saehgahn* to *faerhain*.

Lehomis's heart suddenly burned. Decimating the *saehgahn* population helped nothing: the thought of making rounds with the rest of the clan to disperse them into other clans now taunted him. It no longer mattered if the Tinharri, the royal clan, came to court Clan Lockheirhen's *faerhain*. From the number of stray horses trotting around with young *saeghar* chasing them, brandishing lassos, they had also lost a lot of horses. He'd do more than trade away his clansmen, he'd also have to clear this place out, trading the village's assets to the other clans. Lehomis's clan deserved a better life than the desolation he foresaw. He faced the possibility of moving to another clan with them or staying in his ancient cave-home as a lonely hermit. He rubbed his face and shoved the dreadful idea away for now. Too much to do before that happened.

"Elder," a shaking young voice said, turning him around.

Lehomis slapped the young *saehgahn*'s face, arching his arm wide. "Don't cry!"

"Sorry, Elder." He wiped his face on his sleeve. "We found a horrible thing."

Lehomis ignored the lad's quivering lips and inability to stopper his emotion. He couldn't blame him. Lehomis would've cried too if several generations of elven life hadn't beaten that reflex out of him. "What did you find?" Lehomis resisted grabbing the lad's shoulders and shaking him.

"A few of them, of the *saehgahn*. Their...their hair is gone. Their skulls are showing."

Lehomis fought an urge to puke. He widened his stance. "How many?"

"At least four. Why, Elder? Why would they do that?"

Lehomis swallowed and wiped the cold sweat collecting on his forehead. He chose not to answer. Showing this *saehgahn* and the young future *saehgahn* strength in these days took utmost precedence. He stumbled to the side to be rid of the lad's innocent questioning face. He couldn't discuss this with such a young one at the moment. He needed the other experienced *saehgahn* and the Desteer. He'd call a meeting soon to discuss these current affairs: how they'd enhance clan security in addition to how they'd deal with the Tinharri royals' visit.

Willing himself to straighten his spine, he stumbled toward Tirnah's house, into which he'd helped her carry her husband's body this morning. Inside the door, he collapsed on the little chair in the foyer where the residents sat to take off their shoes. His head lolled to the side and his vision spun.

"Grandfather," Anonhet called from the central room. He wasn't really her grandfather, just her legal guardian while she worked as his maidservant until the day of her marriage. He'd told her on the day he took her in that she could address as him such. He'd promised to be her family member if she wanted it.

As she turned the corner to view him from the archway, her voice saddened. "Oh, Grandfather, look at you. Come in here."

She pulled his arm to make him stand, and he weakly trudged to the central sitting area. A weak fire ate at the dried leaves she'd hastily thrown onto the hearth. The smell of damp earth mingled with wood smoke. She'd clearly been trying to build the fire and boil water for a while now.

He plopped down on the pile of cushions, all hand-woven and embroidered through a few generations of Trisdahen's foremothers, then stuffed with goose feathers and horsehair. Tirnah had crafted the newest ones.

Anonhet hastily dipped a cloth in the basin and dabbed his face. "You have soot and blood all over you. You look so tired, Grandfather. I'll fix you up, and then you should sleep."

"No time," he said, though it didn't stop her work or prevent her from undoing his hair carefully from the looped knots he'd put it into last night. Little sharp pulls stung his scalp until the bulk of his hair finally tumbled down his back. She began the difficult task of combing it while the water on the hearth worked to a boil. "Tirnah," he moaned.

"She's fine, Grandfather."

Anonhet lied. Tirnah wasn't wailing like the *faerhain* outside; instead, Lehomis had entered a horribly heavy silence when he crossed the threshold. He would've liked to go into the bedroom to check on her, but was that the right thing as of now? Who could say?

Anonhet did the dual job of carefully combing his locks while wiping his arm with the cool, wet rag. He couldn't help but wince when the rag roved over an open cut disguised by dirt and blood.

"Tirnah *will* be fine," she reiterated. "She's *faerhain*; she has to be. She wouldn't let me talk her into taking a break."

"*Faerhain*...have a toughness about them, complementary to *saehgahn*," he said.

"You're right. She already told me she'll remarry quickly, Grandfather, so don't worry about the clan."

A shaky laugh burst out of Lehomis's throat, and he lowered his face to cover wiping a tear. "She said that?"

"Mm-hmm."

"She's good like that."

Hopefully, she wouldn't have to remarry too soon. Norrian propriety dictated a good mourning period, and in his last meeting with the Desteer, they had declared she'd be pregnant again soon. Praise to the Bright One if they were right. Not that it would matter to the clan at this point. For Tirnah's sake, and Lehomis's, it would be good if they were right. Any child of Trisdahen carried Lehomis's bloodline. If Gaije didn't make it back, all his hopes would ride on Tirnah's unborn child.

Anonhet's kettle finally whistled, and she struggled to her feet to pour him a cup. She'd never admit her true exhaustion. After a series of hasty sips from the fragrant steaming tea she served him, he too worked his way to his sore feet. He'd never gotten around to removing his sweaty boots in the foyer. On this bizarre and surreal day, Anonhet didn't scold him like she would've on a normal day at his own house. Ignoring the boots, he went toward the bedroom where Tirnah and Trisdahen had spent the most intimate moments of their marriage. Dear Bright One, those moments had been few. Trisdahen had spent most of his life serving the king and then the queen, coming here briefly to conceive Gaije, and later Mhina, before dying!

Lehomis stopped at the door. He shouldn't go in. He tapped on it.

The voice on the other side rang out soft and flat. "Come in."

They'd found Trisdahen around midnight, right before Lehomis discovered Gaije's return. At the dawn hour, after he had located the majority of the *faerhain* in their hiding place below the Desteer hall,

Lehomis informed Tirnah and carried Trisdahen into the house.

Now, he opened the door slowly. Tirnah sat beside the bed, tenderly combing her dead husband's hair one small lock at a time as one of the final steps of his presentation. By now, she'd already cleaned and dressed him in one of his finer robes.

Tirnah peered up with glassy eyes. "He looks all right, doesn't he?" She hovered her hand over his face, down and up. "The Bright One will be impressed. Don't you think?"

"I know He will. No doubt, lass."

Tirnah closed her toothy smile and cleared her throat with a bob of her head. "He just…he needs his weapons. His medal from the queen. And…heart leaves for his hair." She bent over as if to let out a flood of tears, and Lehomis lunged to put a hand on her shoulder. She didn't break down.

"Take a break, lass," he said. "You can't go into the forest until we've cleared it to make sure those raiders are gone. As soon as word goes around they are, I'll take you out to find the vine myself. All right?"

She buried her nose into her handkerchief, rose, and put her arms around Lehomis's neck to his surprise. He patted her back.

"Listen," he said. "I'll escort you to *Laugaulentrei* to send him into the lake. And then I'll take you straight back to your old clan, back to your mother's house."

She raised her head from his shoulder. "No."

"Why not?"

"Because when my children come back, they'll be expecting to find me here. I'm going to make sure I'm here when they do. I won't have them go a moment too long without me."

"All right, but listen." He took her face in his hands. "You'll stay at my house. It's the safest spot in the village, and it's right at the edge where they're likely to enter. They'll probably stop by my house first because it's convenient." She nodded her head between his hands. "From there, I can better protect you and Anonhet."

He looked to Trisdahen's body and then to the door. He noticed Anonhet standing there watching them. Lehomis released Tirnah. "Before we leave for the lake, I'll go get a tally of who's alive and in good fit condition to take care of you, Anonhet, while we're gone."

"Nonsense," Anonhet replied, and rushed to take Tirnah by the arm. "I'll come too. Tirnah might want my company."

"Please do," Tirnah said. She let go of Lehomis and gave Anonhet a hug.

Anonhet took his hand. "Let's go, Grandfather. I haven't finished with your hair, and you still need to sleep."

# Chapter I
## What is a Coward for a Friend

The long, iron-hard arms crossed over Kalea's bosom, pinning her limbs down. The man squeezed and pressed his lower body against her bottom. His exhalation hissed through his teeth. The long hair shimmered bluish for as long as the moon lasted before a thick black cloud of mist swallowed it, leaving her locked blindly against his hard, sultry body.

"How would you like it?" he asked again, breathing against her ear. "Hurry, or I'll choose for you."

A squeak squeezed up her throat instead of a word. Though his hands pressed carefully, she couldn't manage to talk. She was alone. Whatever his question meant, it sounded bad. She managed a whimper.

Footsteps treading through the leaves sounded and rose in volume.

"I think he went this way!" a distant voice told the others.

The man holding her grunted, and he suddenly pushed her away. She stumbled, flailing her arms, and fell into a jagged leafy bush.

The resonant voice which had whispered into her ear now roared behind her. He tensed up amidst a crackling, flashing light, like a small lightning bolt with wires dancing along his limbs. From her place inside the bush, with twigs jabbing her sides and snagging her hair, she spied a group of men from the sorcerers' camp as they swarmed around the strange blue-haired figure.

"What the shit happened here?" a hoarse-voiced man asked.

"I dunno, but…" The second man paused to chuckle. "I think he found an elf-woman. Maybe she strayed this far from one of the villages he attacked. We might'a interrupted an interesting engagement."

"It's over now. Time to go."

"But don't you think we should catch her? I'm sure the kingsorcerer would delight in an extra gift."

"No time for a chase. Let her go."

By now, they were wrapping ropes around the person they'd electrocuted after securing his wrists together. They hauled him away like a beast plucked from the wild, his legs dragging through the leaves and brush.

When their voices and footsteps became faint enough, Kalea let out the breath she held and struggled to untangle herself, her hair, and her chemise from the prickly hedge. The open wound on her leg, caused by the beast that had attacked her own camp, screamed and pulsed with each movement she made. She clamped her hand over her mouth at certain points to keep from moaning.

Once on her feet, she limped along the forest terrain in a direction she hoped would lead back to Bowaen. The shock of the stranger's hold must've made her forget about the pain, but now it returned worse than before.

"You again?" a familiar voice whispered, though she didn't know this person. The elf with red hair she'd met a few moments before approached, the one who helped Bowaen kill that horrible beast.

"Yes," Kalea whispered back, the pain cracking her voice.

"Why are you still here?"

"I tried to get away, but I'm injured."

She moaned and staggered, shifting her weight as far off her injured leg as she could. His hands landed on her shoulders, but he kept a more respectful distance than the last person to take her by the shoulders. The odd black mist faded, and she saw his figure in the restored moonlight.

He sniffed the air. "Oh. I should've known. The stench of those men must've been too strong. Look at you, you have blood on your gown." He put her arm around his neck. "Let's go." So close beside her, his hair gleamed in the soft light and contrasted with his fair skin. His ear tips shone in the light too, clearly elven. She hopped along with him. Any small strain her body made elicited more pain.

"Weren't you stalking that camp?" she asked.

"I was, but it's too late now. Something stirred them up, and I'll be found if I continue. I need to form a plan."

"Who are those men?"

A brief pause preceded his answer. "Bad men. They attacked my village and…killed my father."

"Oh, I'm sorry." She should've dealt with the pain rather than talk in an attempt to smother it.

"Will you introduce me to your friends? I may ask for their help."

"Of course. Bowaen is a talented swordsman, the best in the lower Lightlands. Why, may I ask—?"

"I need someone like him to help me kill those sorcerers," he said.

Her next word slid out breathy. "Sorcerers."

"You've heard of them?"

Of course she had. Flashbacks of her days with Chandran, his warded ropes and punishments, flashed in her head, followed by the horrible images of her novice sisters being raped and dragged through a glowing doorway leading to some other place far away, and innocent townsfolk dipping their fingers in blood as a false priest with a red glove planned to sort them into various different uses for his faction.

"Yes, I've heard of them. You and I have things in common."

"What did they do to you?" he asked.

"Besides attack me just now? They kidnapped the novices from my convent and…and an elf I'm supposed to be with."

"An elf?"

"His name is Dorhen. Have you caught any hints of his whereabouts from the camp?" Kalea didn't care what Lord Remenaxice had told her; she would continue looking for Dorhen—not Rem's brother, Adrayeth, as she'd been instructed.

"*No.*"

She hesitated after the shakiness of his voice. "Are you all right?"

"No, I'm not. Like you, they stole someone from me. More than my father's life, they stole my young sister. Alive. And I intend to get her back before I lose her forever. I believe they held her at that camp. I tried to get close to the cargo where they might be hiding her, but they guarded it well."

"Oh, dear. Kidnapping people must be their business. I don't want to try to imagine what they plan to do with my sisters. I already saw Vivene in their camp."

His pace quickened enough that she feared tripping.

"Wait, I can't go so fast."

He scooped up her legs and carried her the rest of the way. Kalea had to wrap both arms around his neck and hang on.

"I can hear your friends' voices in the distance," he said.

She strained her ears. "I don't hear anything."

"They're calling your name."

"Who's this?" Bowaen asked as Kalea approached, riding draped across the elf's arms.

"Gaije," the elf answered, letting her down. She collapsed to sit on the soft, cool earth. "Gaije from Clan Lockheirhen."

"I'm Kalea," she said in return, "though you must've heard my name already. This is Bowaen and Del."

Gaije put his palms against his hips, elbows back, and bowed formally. A bow and quiver hung from his back. The bow was short and sleekly sculpted from wood and some type of metal that twinkled in the moonlight.

Kalea pointed to Gaije. "He shot the arrows at the beast who attacked us. Did you notice?"

Bowaen nodded. "We could be a smidge worse off if you hadn't been there."

"Yes," Kalea said, "and he kept me out of trouble. I found a camp of sorcerers, Bowaen."

Bowaen wrinkled his nose. "Is that right?"

Gaije stepped forward. "They've been ravaging my homeland and must be stopped. Kalea tells me you're following the sorcerers too."

"No, no, no, she's wrong." Bowaen waved his hands and crossed his arms. "I'm following a pale-haired boy who doesn't want to go home. We didn't know we'd find sorcerers out here. Elf rangers is what we were worried about."

"But Bowaen!" Kalea climbed to her feet and staggered toward him. "They have Vivene! I found her, and they might have the rest of the novices, and Dorhen too!" She grabbed his arm and leaned on him to keep from falling. "Gaije and I are both following this sorcerer band."

"What's wrong with you?" Bowaen asked, taking her hands and looking over her form. His eyes landed on the thick, blossoming bloodstain on her chemise. "You're hurt!"

"I'm fine."

The thick muscles in Bowaen's forearms tightened. "We're just passing through here, if you don't mind," he said to Gaije. "Thanks for shooting at that unnatural beast." He and Del both wore a new collection of scrapes and dirt stains from the long night.

"Can't you see your woman is injured?" Gaije asked.

Bowaen wrapped his arm around Kalea. "That's why we're going back to our camp to get some rest."

Kalea pointed into the darkness. "There's"—she paused to wipe the sweat from her brow—"some cloths in my basket."

"I got better," Bowaen said as they began their trek back. "Lord Dax put salve and bandages in our travel kits. What happened to you?"

"The beast scratched me," she said, panting as they walked. "Let's hurry and get back to following the sorcerers. Gaije, join with us! You're welcome to. We both have people who need rescuing."

Bowaen growled out a sort of sigh.

Along the way to their ruined camp, Kalea found her filthy quilt, which had been dragged through the leaves when the beast ripped her away. Del tossed Bowaen one of the bags sent with them by Lord Dax before attempting to revive their campfire. The elf knelt beside Kalea, darting his eyes away as she raised her chemise over her leg.

"Don't worry about me, Gaije. Tell them," she said.

Bowaen tossed her a small corked bottle and a rolled strip of linen, and then crossed his arms again and waited.

Gaije rose to face him. "I helped you when you were attacked, and I helped your—Kalea—I stopped her from stumbling into the enemy's camp. I ask your help in return."

"The elves have sorcerer problems too, Bowaen. Why wouldn't they?" Kalea said, and winced as she dabbed the smelly concoction into the grates in her skin. That creature had dug its claws in deep. Impossible to tell if she'd need to stitch them up—not that she'd have the endurance to stitch her own flesh together.

Gaije continued, "We have to follow the camp and make the right move at the right instant. They have my sister, and I must get her back before they gain any more ground."

"And don't forget about my friends," Kalea added.

Bowaen huffed. "How many men are there?"

"About fifteen armored fighters that I could count, and another fifteen practicing sorcerers. And…one of them is strange," Gaije said.

Del planted himself by the struggling fire, and his hands shook as he attempted to stuff tobacco into his heavy, oversized pipe.

"Not right now," Bowaen hissed, and batted the thing down.

"Don't spill it!" Del said, and turned to Gaije. "What could be stranger than a sorcery practitioner who transforms into a huge, hairy beast?"

"The difference is the beast felt pain when my arrows sank into it. This"—Gaije grimaced—"*elf* didn't flinch."

"What do you mean 'elf'?" Bowaen said. "One of the sorcerers is of your kind?"

Gaije shook his head instead of nodding. "Makes me nauseous to use the word, but yes. Their strangest member. He's the one who stole my sister. He rode away wearing three of my arrows, one through his neck. If he is indeed an elf, he must have the Overseas Taint."

"What's the Overseas Taint?" Kalea asked, glancing up from her work.

"Tainted elves," Gaije said. "A danger in our lore the Desteer remind us to stay wary of. They work every day to keep the tainted ones out of our society."

"So it's like an illness?" Bowaen asked.

"An illness of the mind usually," Gaije said. "It has symptoms, but we believe it to be a hereditary thing. It's called the Overseas Taint because we believe foreign elves brought it from other lands. They come here, keeping a low profile, and blend in with our kind. They're bad, and they breed their badness into our population. An elf with the Overseas Taint" could easily be bad enough to join a faction of sorcerers. They wouldn't have the honor, integrity, and virtue of a true Norrian *saehgahn*."

Shaking his head, Bowaen mumbled, "I hate sorcerers."

Kalea tied the ends of the bandage around her thigh. The sting throbbed so intensely, she couldn't care less about her leg being exposed in front of three men. She'd worry about the breezy rips in the back of her chemise later.

"I'm helpless by myself," Gaije continued. "I need some capable allies to help me snatch my sister away from them. I'd like to do it under that tainted blue-haired elf's notice."

She'd tied the bandage a bit tight, hopefully sufficiently. Kalea paused in flexing her knee to say, "Blue-haired elf?"

"It's unbelievable, but yes."

"Blue-haired…" Her memory registered his hot presence at her back again, and she shuddered. "Is he the one who…?"

Gaije watched her closely. "Who what?"

"You didn't see him? He grabbed me. The one you're probably talking about."

Gaije squinted. "I didn't. I couldn't see in the dark, though you seemed to appear out of nothing but shadow, your white gown illuminated. At first, I assumed you traversed around a bend of flora."

"There was a dense smoke with no scent. It was air, but also… darkness. I thought the clouds covered the moon, but they hadn't. And you say the one who took your sister had blue hair?"

"Yes," Gaije confirmed.

Kalea buried her face in her hands and rubbed them up and down. "That doesn't make sense." She'd lost too much blood, and her muscles were weak and shaky. "Arius Medallus has blue hair. It doesn't make sense."

"What are you talking about?" Gaije asked.

Bowaen and Del were looking at each other. Bowaen said, "Look, Gaije, I'm sorry. But how can we go trackin' down a group of thirty men with fifteen sorcerers, plus one unnatural freak, when we got a girl bleeding here? We can't leave her behind."

Gaije stood up and faced Bowaen with a wide stance and squared shoulders. "There's a Desteer grove somewhere to the north of here. If we follow the sorcerers' trail, we're bound to find it. We'll leave her there and continue without her."

Bowaen cocked his head. "What's a Desteer grove?"

"It's a place where our religious leaders go to pray to the Bright One. Listen to me. They won't harm a woman. They can help her, and then the three of us can chase the sorcerers, but we must act because they're gaining distance."

"Don't leave me behind!" Kalea shrieked, and struggled to her feet.

"Sit!" Bowaen ordered.

She picked a long stick off the ground and tried leaning on it. "I can limp on this. I'll try to keep up, but don't bother yourself with me. I'll stay out of the way when you face them."

Disregarding Kalea, Bowaen said to Gaije, "I can leave Kalea with you, since it's in both your interests to follow the sorcerers, and not mine. I'm looking for a kid from Sharr and got no time to chase sorcerers."

"Fine," Gaije said. "I'll go my way and report you to my superiors if those sorcerers leave this forest with my sister. They'll—"

Kalea lurched, balancing on her stick, and grabbed Bowaen's arm. "Please, Bowaen! I just need to get Dorhen! Together with him and Gaije, we'll rescue the others. Let's go see what we can do. Gaije is good at shooting and you're good with swords and Del's good at sneaking."

Bowaen snorted. "Del's stink is a dead giveaway."

"He smells no worse than those foul men who're keeping my sister stuffed in a basket," Gaije said.

Bowaen traced his gaze across the grass.

Kalea sank to the ground again and moped. "They stuffed your sister in a basket, raped my sisters, and I saw how they groped and made a joke out of Vivene. They made her their servant."

"Bowaen." Gaije stepped forward, extending his hand. "Mhina is seven years old."

Bowaen hawked and spat, but his eyes softened to contradict the stern face he tried to hold. "You got gold? Or silver?"

Gaije scowled at him. "My grandfather is rich in jewels, artifacts, and horses. He wants her back as bad as I do—and so does her mother, whose weeping was the last sound in my ears before I departed my village."

Bowaen cleared his throat. "Let's just...start walkin' and see what's going on with this sorcerer band and their groping creep. Which way are they going?"

"Northwest."

# Chapter 2
## His Performance

"Good work," Tumas said to Vivene as she spat and wiped her mouth. The fury with which she used to spit out his white slurry had dulled over the long days of being held captive. "Come to the fire now and have some stew, then you can get to washing and mending until bed."

She lingered on the ground to rub her neck and then her eyes. She wore a layer of grime because they hadn't given her any chance to bathe since the night they raided her convent. At least he'd ordered her to use her mouth this time; she'd be damned if she'd have to give birth to this idiot's child. Nonetheless, she'd already let all the other idiots work their lusts out on her. The salty taste of his essence lingering on her lips mixed with all the others'. This combined flavor made all the sorcerers seem as one man, and they might as well have been. One evil, loathsome man who deserved to be destroyed.

Her life had devolved into a disgusting existence. If she could, she'd go back to the convent and be a good novice, like Kalea, in a heartbeat. And she'd never read Sister Scupley's love manual again. That stupid book. That putrid, lying book claimed lovemaking was wonderful. It described flowers and happiness and pleasure. How it used to tantalize her, made her curious about her body as well as men's bodies. It made her curse her existence as a future vestal. It praised "the nectar of life," which secreted from a man. Rubbish. It didn't taste like nectar to her.

She climbed to her feet, a difficult feat after such a long day of work, travel, and sin. Repetitive misery looping round and round, over and over, with no end or hope in sight made up each day, like a lifetime in Kullixaxuss, the underworld the Creator's Word warned about. She dusted her soiled kirtle off. She'd been awarded the kirtle at the outpost for good behavior, since she and all the other novices had been ripped from their beds wearing nothing but their underdresses.

These days, Vivene took it all in stride; however, she hadn't always been so compliant. She walloped a few gangly idiots in red robes when they first took her into their place, but after a while they returned her aggression. So instead of fighting rashly, she'd decided to be smart. By then, they'd already ruined her virginity, and she found if she simply lay back and did as they asked, the sex wasn't as horrible as her first impression. Being still and letting them do their business proved quicker and easier than kicking and screaming and having to be held down.

For some reason, they held a sort of creed that commanded they all get off regularly, and Vivene happened to be a woman among them—her unlucky lot. There wasn't any real spite or passion involved in their need to copulate—no leisurely enjoyment or lustful excitement, just business. She had quickly noticed how none of the sorcerers slept. After doing their dirty business with her, they'd typically go straight back to their books and their chanting. Something about sex, for them, canceled their need to sleep. Except for the one with blue hair.

As she came around the wagon behind which she'd serviced Tumas, they were dragging the blue-haired one to the center of camp, their faces red, their voices raging. The blue-haired one's face stayed solemn regardless of how roughly they treated him. If any of them got any sleep, he did, and he did it during the daylight hours, often atop the horse they strapped him to. Now, it seemed he'd tried to sneak away, and they'd caught him while Vivene did her ugly duty.

"Gettin' big for yer skirt, are ya, sir?" one sorcerer yelled. They dragged the blue-haired one straight to the fire and shoved his face close to the flames. Though his expression stayed neutral for the most part, his eyes widened with a hint of concern.

"The King of Shadow wants to join the fire in eternal bliss!"

The blue-haired one finally started to wriggle, and they held him firm.

Tumas approached, clicking his tongue. "What now? Tried to escape already? And here you've done so well until now, especially when you found that little elfling."

Vivene glanced at the large, lidded baskets bound shut with rope where they kept those poor children snatched up from the nearby towns and elven villages. They were one reason Vivene hadn't tried to slip away and make a mad dash into the night. If there was any way at all she could manage to… She sighed. What could she do to help all those kids? She didn't even know how many there were in total. She did happen to know that more than one group of sorcerers and prisoners headed to the sorcerers' home, however. She was the only one from her convent chosen to accompany this group because they said she was tough—and because of her good behavior. The only other women with them were the whores from Wexwick, more than happy to embrace one smelly man after another in exchange for cheap promises of wealth and status when they arrived to wherever they were going. To hell with them all.

The sorcerers continued their ridicule and belittlement of the blue-haired elf. "We're tying you down again!"

Another man stepped forward as they inched the blue-haired one's face ever closer to the flames. His face glistened with sweat. "Maybe we shouldn't be too hard on him. He let us catch him easy enough, and…"

"And what?" Tumas demanded.

"We found him groping some elf-woman he'd captured. Put his hands all over her. He probably wanted no more than a wet release."

Tumas leaned in close. "Is it true, Wikshen?"

The blue-haired one—Wikshen—had never bothered to speak to any of the sorcerers, as far as Vivene had heard, and Tumas's question changed nothing.

Tumas smiled. "Well, I'll let it pass for now. I guess we don't have to set your face on fire yet. But you'll spend the night strapped to the chair again. Understand?"

As usual, Wikshen didn't answer, and Tumas slapped his face, prompting him to glare. Tumas paused to glance at his hand before barking out a laugh.

"You want a wet release?" Tumas asked him. "You should've asked one of the ladies, or the fat girl—Vivene's her name." His grin spread wide, and his sudden eye contact made Vivene jump and grab the wine pitcher off one of the stolen barrels. "Don't let her appearance turn you off. That Vivene knows a lot more than a vestal should know, and I can vouch!"

At Tumas's gesture, they dragged Wikshen to the heavy chair they'd brought along because it was sturdy enough to stand against his strength. They tied a cloth around his eyes. What good did blinding him do? Seemed more like doing Wikshen a favor since he hated the fire.

Vivene played nonchalant but kept Wikshen in her sight as she went about, collecting dirty laundry from the sorcerers. They finished tying off his ropes, and Wikshen sat quietly at a comfortable distance away from the fire. He relaxed when they walked away, despite the bind they'd put him in.

At a certain dark hour, a chorus of moaning commenced from the different corners of their camp as the sorcerers performed their nightly constitutions with the whores. For now, they left Vivene alone. Though Tumas had bragged about her carnal skills, her full figure made her the last choice for most sorcerers. To her dread, her body fat wouldn't be around for too much longer on the available food rations they were all eating. If they found her more alluring later down the road, she might find herself busier than ever.

The sorcerers didn't all start having sex at once; they took turns, which allowed a good number of others to keep watch. For now, she might catch a break and focus on the chores she'd rather do. She moved about, collecting laundry, even from beside one or two very busy sorcerers. She'd seen their filthy act with the whores plenty already, and it stopped shocking her eyes long ago.

Her gaze drifted back to Wikshen. What went through his head as he sat near the cool forest shadow, listening to the noises? Vivene checked around the area. No sorcerers were paying her any attention. The ones who weren't busy with the women were totally engrossed in either a heavy book or a handful of the herbs they tended to collect from the woods as they traveled, either sorting them or stringing them up to dry.

Vivene put her large wad of clothing aside and instead collected twigs for the firewood reserve. Her heart immediately sped up as she made her way, casually slow, to the blue-haired one. He made no indication of awareness of her presence, yet somehow she felt his attention. She found a greater abundance of twigs in the shady area around him, inching closer to him. She knelt behind his chair, pretending to pick up yet another.

"Hey," she whispered, and for lack of a better idea asked, "are you the elf who came through the magic door with us?"

"Why would you ask that?" he whispered back, his voice grating and deep.

She jumped at his answer. All this time, he'd offered so few statements to the sorcerers. Why would he respond to *her*?

She took a step and lifted another stick while keeping nice and close to him. "I kept my eyes open back at the mansion. There was a blonde elf and a brown-haired one, the only two elves I could see. They sent the brown-haired one into the basement of the house, but he never came out. You emerged. Are you that elf?"

His lips drew tight, but his smile remained absent. "Maybe," he said.

"Hmm." She walked a few paces to add another twig to her growing bundle and paced back to him. "It doesn't matter if you're him or not. I can tell you don't like those sorcerers. Not at all."

He didn't respond.

Vivene cleared her throat. "You're a dangerous creature."

His mouth widened into a smile. "How would you know?"

She shrugged and collected another stick. "I don't know. There's something menacing about you, though you're the calmest person here. Why haven't you asked to use any of the whores?"

"They're not worthy."

Vivene snorted. "Well, that's menacing. Am I worthy?"

His head shifted slightly; otherwise, he hardly moved. "Hard to say yet."

"Why haven't you tried to escape? I mean *really* escape?"

No answer. He lifted his chin and inhaled deeply, his large chest pushed against the creaking ropes.

She couldn't linger around him much longer or the sorcerers would get suspicious. One lifted his eyes from his book to raise an eyebrow at her. She hastily located three more twigs but returned to whispering distance with Wikshen.

"Listen," she said, her voice becoming shaky, "I need to leave here, preferably with the children. Can you help me escape? I'll do whatever you want me to. You want a screw?"

"I don't think that's possible."

"It's not? Why can't you help me? Maybe you can make a minor, but helpful, move next time they untie you."

"Calm yourself. They're looking at you again."

Vivene shot her head up, and then remembered to act casual. She faked coughing to prolong her lingering if nothing else. She froze when she remembered Wikshen wore a blindfold. She studied him to find out how he might be able to see, but his blindfold held tight.

"At night, I can see more than ever: them, you, and all the things they do when they think they are secure."

"Th-that sounds impressive. With your ability, how come you can't help me?"

"I didn't say I couldn't help you, I meant I couldn't 'screw' you. But I suppose they don't need to know that."

Vivene repositioned her arms around the bundle. "Good. Tell me what to do."

He raised his voice to a moderately loud level. "I need you, you little tart!"

Her twigs clattered down around her feet. She gawked. Why would he speak so loud?

"Please come closer." He added a low, dragging spice to his tone. She obeyed, staring. His voice lowered to a whisper again. "If you want my help, you have to help me first. Kneel in front of me." She did. "Put your hands under my battleshift."

"What's that?"

"My *skirt*, you fool!"

A brief hesitation preceded her unsure hands sliding up his hairless, naked leg and into the slit at the front of his black, kilt-like garment.

"What am I doing?" she asked. Her hands shook in the warm space.

"You're pretending to suck my cock."

She swallowed as she listened, staring at his blindfolded face with its handsome lips and strong jaw. With no way to be entirely sure she should be doing this, she resisted the urge to look back and see if she was being watched.

"You don't have to do it for real," he said. "Make it look real. Work your head up and down, and as you pretend, move your hands to my feet and take the leather bindings off of them."

"Why am I doing—"

"Begin."

As much as he could manage, he pushed his pelvis out and raised his chin to appear like he enjoyed it. She pushed his "battleshift" upward, revealing a pair of black linen braies underneath, which matched the fabric of the battleshift.

"Put your face in my lap. Be authentic."

Authentic. Keeping that in mind, she made like she handled his genitals. He hadn't said anything about taking them out, so she didn't. She angled her head in ways to try to shield her work from the sorcerers so they wouldn't see that she didn't actually have Wikshen's body part in her mouth.

Wikshen sighed, prompting voices behind her. "What the—?" She dared not look, but she imagined the sorcerers were elbowing each other and pointing. They were indeed snickering.

"Didn't expect the freak to take my advice." Tumas's voice. The whole thing made sense to her then: Wikshen had appeared to want a release earlier when they caught him in the woods, and now he merely did what Tumas recommended he do. She just hoped they wouldn't be too entertained by the spectacle and come over to watch the whole process. She wouldn't put it past those perverts.

Wikshen took deep breaths despite the ropes binding his chest. Every once in a while, he'd let out a sigh or a groan. He had a knack for pretending to receive the sexual act, better than she could pretend with all of her nerves flaring. She hadn't been this afraid since the first time a sorcerer forced himself on her.

"Hurry, now take off my bindings," he whispered. "I have to be barefoot, or I'll remain useless."

She'd almost forgotten her real task! She worked her neck the same way as when she gave fellatio for real, and slid her hands down his legs to find the shoes he'd referred to. Why on earth would he want to walk around barefoot across all the thorns and twigs and rocks?

She couldn't waste any more energy on wondering—she had enough trouble with her nerves and concentration. She found his feet with the long strips of leather and rawhide the sorcerers had put on him. Her cold, fearful sweat intensified when she found the tight knots in a bunch behind his calves. The good news was, from her experience, bringing a man to climax with her mouth typically took a long time. But how could she ever untie the knots with her bare hands, not to mention without looking at them? Anxiety built higher than ever. Her sweat poured. She didn't have any sharp objects to use. What could she do?

"Concentrate," he whispered, and followed up with a short moan. Something about the sounds he made, fake as they were, ignited a conflicting sensation in her body. His mouth hung open with his chin high in total relaxation. Fine muscles braided all through his body. His deep voice groaned. He was too good at this act.

She struggled with the dual chore of bobbing her head and fiddling with the ties. Why didn't he want her to untie a few of the straps behind his chair?

"Make sucking sounds. Your performance is pathetic," he said, working the suggestion into sounds of pleasure.

*Who is this bastard?* She added the sucking sounds to her list of simultaneous actions.

"Don't overdo it."

The rawhide strings around his shanks were knotted well. Picking at the tight bulges hurt her fingertips after a while because of the chill in them. One string came free, but the knot remained.

Wikshen groaned, drawing steady breaths through parted lips. "We've been at it for about fifteen minutes already. Hurry."

Her hands moved faster. Frantically. Her panic impaired her progress. Surely they were all tied the same way. If she could figure out the system of the first knot, the rest should come undone with the same maneuvers.

"Hurry and finish, or else we'll go too long and someone will approach."

His urging didn't help either. The first knot finally came undone. Vivene sighed herself—in relief. Now to hurry through the rest of them and pretend to finish the fellatio. She drew her head back long and slow, as if adding some variety in her movements would make them appear more authentic. She placed a sucking sound and dipped back down.

The next knot loosened. The binding on that leg slackened, and she attempted to yank the whole thing off, but it didn't budge. The last knot needed to be removed. Her hands raced.

Success.

Wikshen drew in a long inhalation before pumping out a few fast ones. "I'm getting close. Hurry and take off the other one," he groaned.

Close to what? She wasn't touching him! His penis hid tucked away where it should be, and her head bobbed stupidly above his lap!

Nonetheless, she continued with the other leg, hoping its knots were no tighter and not much different from the first. And those sounds he made…caused her to feel strangely good.

One knot.

He moaned.

She moaned back and checked herself. *Concentrate!*

Two knots, and she inserted another wet, slobbery sound. He raised his hips slowly, hissing raggedly through his teeth. Her blood raced now.

"Faster," he panted.

She obliged despite her aching neck. One more knot remained on his second leg, as far as she could tell.

"Hurry." He spoke loud through his panting for the sorcerers to hear. Vivene's legs flared at his deep, grating voice.

The last knot loosened and, as soon as the leather bindings fell, he bucked his pelvis high and the package containing his slumbering penis touched her face. She abandoned his leg and shot her hands to his hips, surging with excitement for the show he put on. Fast, ragged breaths heaved out of him, accompanied by the sound of spittle. Settling back into his seat, he relaxed with a long sigh. She rode him all the way down with her hands on his body. Her weight was nothing to his strength.

While she pretended to put his cock back into his braies and placed his battleshift back over his lap, he offered a grin that quickly faded. "Now spit into the brush and wipe your mouth," he ordered.

She did so. Shaking off her jitters, she got back to business. "I did what you asked, so will you help me?"

"Shut up and go."

She stashed his discarded leather bindings behind a thorn bush and gathered the sticks she'd dropped beside his chair before hurrying back to the fire. The exhilaration hadn't finished racing through her core. Soreness, exhaustion, the terror of being caught, and this new carnal thrill fought each other in her system.

*What in the Creator's good grace just happened?*

After she bent to place the twigs beside the fire, a hand landed on her shoulder, and she jumped. One of the sorcerers.

"Quite a show you did, sweetum." He stifled a laugh.

Her heart sank. *Does he know? Will he beat me?*

"Ready for your next client?"

Dreadful as his question was, she sighed in relief. Despite all of her sweaty nerves, she nodded.

"Raise it, then."

He meant her skirt. This man, and several other sorcerers, didn't mind having sex publicly. She lay beside the fire and hiked her skirt past her hips. He slid inside her with surprising ease.

Her eyes wandered back over to Wikshen, who sat as calmly as before. As nerve-wracking as the ordeal had been…it excited her. The way Wikshen moved his muscular hips, especially in that last moment.

The sorcerer pushed into her, pulled back, and pushed in again with spirited force. She wrapped her arms around him and pushed back against his thrusts of her own free will. She moaned in pleasure instead of misery for once in her life. Listening to herself, she sounded as horrid and sinful as the whores, but every thrust he made, she appreciated for the moment. If her eagerness with this loathsome man happened to be a filthier thing than her cold compliance of earlier today, she'd deal with that guilt in the morning. Right now, she needed this.

Her eyes returned to Wikshen. He grinned under his blindfold.

# Chapter 3
## What is Plaguing the Kingsorcerer

A chilly breeze swept around Lamrhath after he stepped through the portal.

"No," he said as several sorcerers emerged behind him. He turned and pushed back toward the open negative space in the air. The dim candle glow of the North Lightlandic outpost winked out after the last man slipped through. No time remained for Lamrhath to dart back in.

Something had gone wrong. A vast, waving field of pale grass surrounded their group.

"One of you fools made a mistake!" Lamrhath roared, and the six other men flinched. They also turned their heads and frowned at the windy setting. "I see no mountains! Where have you brought me?"

"It must be the Longwalk, my lord," Kaskill offered. He was a promising young sorcerer but might have been responsible for this disaster due to his inexperience. He shifted his eyes around no more than the others. He'd developed the habit of fidgeting his hand, bandaged after Wikshen bit his index finger off.

They were headed home to the Ilbith tower after that disastrous incident with Daghahen, Dorhen, and Wikshen. Lamrhath might have made himself the new Wikshen if Daghahen hadn't foiled him, deceiving him with a fake holding sphere containing Wik and then throwing the real one at Dorhen. Afterward, Lamrhath's slimy twin brother had made his way out of their domain and escaped as Lamrhath's men scrambled to correct his mess.

With their limited resources, they'd arranged three parties which were to take different routes. Wikshen accompanied one party, which would travel on foot straight from the outpost. The second party would walk through a portal to some place near Alkeer and head home from there over a few weeks. That party transported the large group of young vestals they'd collected in the Lightlands to help supplement their population in the Ilbith tower. Lamrhath's own party, he and his elites, were supposed to emerge practically on Ilbith's doorstep through their portal.

"My lord," Sigmune began, "our golden implements might've been confused with the other party's. We've emerged where they were supposed to."

Lamrhath held in the rage stirring in his bones. He couldn't help clenching his fists. "How could you have made such a mistake?"

Sigmune waved his hands in defense. "*We* couldn't have, my lord. Not us. Someone must've tampered with our set-up."

Lamrhath hissed and rubbed his forehead. "Daghahen."

The group exchanged more glances and mumbled various curses and theories. Daghahen must've tampered with the golden rods and the enchantments pre-cast on them. Daghahen used to be a sorcerer too, after all. Naerezek only knew what else that smelly bag of skin had touched before he fled the outpost.

Lamrhath chose to keep his temper. After a deep breath, he said, "Well and good." He didn't smile—he hardly ever smiled—and despite his words, the sorcerers around him shrank back, lowering their heads. "Well and good," he repeated. "This means the ladies will be delivered home in good time, with less chance of anyone dying on the long journey through the mountains." A few sorcerers nodded at his logic. "We need our women, don't we?"

"Yes, my lord," a few different men responded.

"Me most of all," he growled to himself.

The others stood dumbfounded, anticipation building over what he'd say next. A great gust of grassland wind whirled around their group, whistling through their ears. That too-familiar tightness arose in Lamrhath's abdomen, the first telltale sign his ailment would flare up and scream louder and louder throughout his body until he finally found release. He scoffed in disgust at his available companionship: six clunky men with scratchy faces and repulsive body odor. He assumed a man couldn't tame his ailment like a woman could, although he'd never mustered enough interest to find out.

In his younger years, Lamrhath had never guessed what a nightmare his own sex drive would become. It was all fun and games back then. Pleasing his frequent erections became his priority from the moment his cock took its first stand. Daghahen, on the other hand, never acted quite so interested in the forbidden deed. He'd always been content to do his work, enjoy his dinner, and listen to the stories of their human stepfather.

The forbidden deed. Lamrhath could still hear their mother's voice in his head today, telling him never to engage with a woman. Ever. Her tone had taken on a grating, grey growl. Her teeth clenched, her lovely *faerhain* countenance faded away in favor of a savage beast that would prefer to kill. She had been serious about that rule. Her sons could never pair up with women. She'd warned that they couldn't marry *faerhain* either.

But Lamrhath didn't like her rule. He disobeyed her. He stuck his tool into the first receptacle that would have him—a cackling little thing with frizzy hair, missing teeth, and old pregnancy stretch marks raking up her sagging belly. How that cold whore laughed at him when he came too early.

The rest was history. He enjoyed himself, especially after his mother died. Lamrhath loved sex. He took it regularly. He took it faithfully. And eventually, he discovered how enslaved he'd become. He was addicted. His desire morphed over the years into something more like an illness. It developed harsh symptoms: a nauseous stomach, a dizzy head, piercing cramps that dropped him to the ground, and sometimes a fever. Not to mention the sore testicles and throbbing erection.

What had his mother known back then? She'd never told him, and he never asked, why she forbade the deed. In his adolescence, he sought to fight her rule, not to question it. Did she know it would come to this? Did she assume the same would happen to Daghahen? Or did she harbor suppressed Desteer talents and foresee what would happen to Lamrhath later in life? Could his reckless pursuit of sorcery have put him in this place, and she caught psychic wind of the travesty? He would never know.

"Let's go to Alkeer." Sigmune's voice shook Lamrhath out of his reverie.

"We can't!" Lamrhath snapped, his frustration at his ailment already showing through his demeanor. "The Clanless will capture us. I don't think enough of our own are staying there in secret, either."

Sigmune raised his hands. "No, my lord, I mean we'll go there as calm and peaceful as can be. We'll smear mud on our red garments and stash our sorcery implements under a hedge before entering. Whatever it takes to get you to a brothel fast."

He had a point. Lamrhath would soon reach a state of mind where anything they offered would sound good. If it took too long to find a solution, they'd have to create a makeshift stretcher out of branches upon which to carry him the rest of the way to Ilbith. His ailment lurked inside him like a hungry demon, waiting and ready to rip at his stomach and his loins until he gave it the sexual release it wanted. It wasn't fair, especially considering he'd already released twice this morning before their traveling procedures. And now his body asked for another bout? Already?

He pushed the tickling little feeling running through his blood to the back of his mind and forced himself to think of more important things. A brutal dilemma stood in their path: they were stranded far away from home or any outpost without proper traveling equipment or a woman to sleep with along the way. If only he'd brought one with him, just in case.

From now on, he would.

The sorcerers bickered amongst themselves, often gesturing toward him with heartfelt words concerning their master's suffering, and Lamrhath raised his hand to silence them.

"Listen," he said, "we won't go to Alkeer. It's too far away. We'll go to the nearest settlement, and either talk or use our cunning and our magic to slaughter the lot of them. This depends on how big the settlement is. We'll collect food, travel supplies, and hopefully gold, not to mention a woman to keep me company. If we can scrimp enough gold, we'll erect a minor portal to crawl through to get home. If not, we'll continue on foot and get a little richer for making the effort."

The sorcerers hummed in thought at his idea.

"You mean we'll sack or sway?" Kaskill asked.

"Yes," Lamrhath said, scraping together as much calm and patience as he could with his burgeoning need. "And along the way, I'll have a lay or two."

The sorcerer named Gavor groaned. "It's hard to sway the Darkland tribes! Ninety percent of each stop will be to sack—and we simply don't have enough men, sorcerers, dunces, or weapons, my lord."

"A new factor will make things different this time," Lamrhath countered.

"What would that be, my lord? We've held many meetings about this difficulty before. It's easier to worm our way into Lightlandic establishments than it is to persuade Darklandic tribal chieftains to worship Lord Lamrhath."

"If you'll shut up, I'll tell you!" Lamrhath dabbed his clammy temple with his handkerchief. "The difference is Wikshen has been reborn." He turned to Sigmune. "Did you bring the whisper stones?"

Sigmune nodded and pulled a drawstring pouch out of his satchel. Lamrhath opened it and chose a foggy crystal with a red ribbon tied around it. He untied the ribbon and tapped a pattern onto the stone's surface. When the little cracks in the stone's center put off a pulsing glow, Lamrhath cupped it in his hands and spoke into it to deliver his new plan to the sorcerers in Wikshen's entourage.

For all of the next day, Kalea and her expanded entourage tracked the sorcery caravan with Gaije leading the way, poised with his bow and focused on the trail. Bowaen and Del trudged behind him, often turning around to check on Kalea, and she waved them on with reassurances not to bother themselves over her. The task of finding Dorhen and Gaije's sister prevailed over the stinging, burning gashes on her leg.

The first branch she had chosen to help her walk broke after a while, and in the new sunlight she spotted a fresher, more suitable walking stick. Though she had fallen nearly flat on her face when the first one snapped, she waved her friends on once again. Gaije's expression showed a deep concern for her, but his anxiety for his sister's well-being dragged his attention away any time Kalea started looking pathetic. She made it a point to herself not to cry or moan when a misplaced step sent a stampede of pain through her muscles. Whatever she could do to prevent them from dropping her off and leaving her some place, she'd do it.

At twilight, they stopped to rest in a small clearing off the trail. Instead of the common trail, now they followed some narrower, foot-beaten path. They often found damaged branches and wagon tracks pressing the grass down where the sorcerers had made their way through. With all of the cargo, horses, and people making up their caravan, the sorcerers couldn't manage to take a more secretive path through the thicker parts of Norr like a few people on foot could.

Gaije continued to pace long after the two men settled down. Stopping had been his suggestion in the first place.

Bowaen approached Kalea. "Let's see how your leg is doing." He motioned for her to raise her skirt.

Instead, Kalea drew her skirt around her leg tight and put up a hand. "It's fine. No need to worry about me. Doesn't even hurt." She clenched her teeth at her lie as Bowaen returned to his seat. Her leg hurt constantly. "We don't have those pretty lights out this way," Kalea said, looking for a distraction from her pain. The forest shapes were darkening, and the crickets commenced their songs.

Gaije didn't sit, he leaned against a tree. He shook his head at her. "You won't see them this way. They're lit mostly for the travelers going along the common trail."

"So you elves *do* honor the common trail custom," Bowaen said.

"Well, you humans still tolerate our journeyman *saehgahn* in Theddir." Gaije crossed his arms and motioned to the trail they'd left behind. "Not that there's any point in the common trail now. It'll only take you to a huge fence blocking off an enormous and desolate land full of trolls."

"The Darklands," Bowaen said.

Gaije's shoulders tightened, his back still turned on them. "The sorcerers are going home. They're trying to take my sister where I can't follow."

A long silence nestled between each person.

Kalea cleared her throat. "If you can't follow, how are they going to cross to the other side?"

"They must've developed a sort of magic to make it possible."

Bowaen sat quietly beside Kalea, also regarding Gaije. Del's lips stayed clamped around his pipe, wrapped in his blanket across the way.

"How far off do you think the sorcerers are by now?" Bowaen asked.

"Not far. Every once in a while, I find their footprints and the droppings of the horses they stole from my village. The droppings are always about a day old. The blue-haired sorcerer rode one with a troop of armored men. They are swift, though. I followed them for a day before we met."

Bowaen's hand squeezed and loosened around his sword's old scabbard. "A troop, huh?"

Gaije nodded. "I've wondered myself how I could possibly take them on alone. Stealing my sister back quietly may be the best option, although I'd prefer to eradicate them and prevent any more tragedies like my village went through."

Bowaen shook his head, continuing to fiddle with the wrapped sword.

Del lowered the pipe from his mouth and said, "No way, forget it. Count me out. Bow, this is none of our business. Let's go back to looking for Damos the Grey Mage so we can go home." He spat on the ground and went back to his pipe.

Gaije fidgeted now. "Thanks for nothing." He began walking away, and Kalea and Bowaen both rose.

"Wait!" Kalea called. Rising so fast made her sway with dizziness for some reason. Fighting through the dizzy spell, she limped after him. He truly meant to leave them—he hadn't even dropped his belongings to rest yet. She stopped him with a gentle hand on his arm. "Pay no attention to him," she said. "Del is a coward. He always talks like that."

Gaije gave a weak smile, which quickly died. "He's a coward, is he? So am I."

She glanced behind her. Bowaen waited where they were sitting a moment ago. Would Gaije have said that if he'd followed too? "That's not true," she replied.

"Yes, it is." Under her hand, the muscle in his arm trembled, along with his bottom lip. "Before I left, I promised my mother I'd get her daughter back."

He sank to a squat, and Kalea followed, easing to the ground against the raging pain in her leg. "I'm a new *saehgahn*. My ceremony happened two months ago. The queen drafted me to her escort training. To make the story quicker, I deserted…right in the middle of an attack. More of those damned humans." He glanced over her from the ground up.

"Sorcerers casting lightning spells."

"Lightning spells?" she whispered. Last night's image of the strange blue-haired person being electrocuted flashed in her head.

He said, "I ran straight back home to find the blue-haired sorcerer with glowing eyes attacking my village."

"Did he"—Kalea paused to swallow—"kill your father?"

"I don't know; I didn't see my father die. And I didn't see the blue-haired one do much of anything besides ride by and swipe up my young sister. I shot arrows into his back, but he didn't seem to feel them. Mhina, my sister, should've been locked safely in the Desteer hall with the rest of the females."

He bit his lip. "After the marauders left, I saw my father dead. My grandfather, with a fire in his eyes unlike anything I'd seen from him, jerked me around—I don't know why. He proclaimed this my new *caunsaehgahn*. He told me to bring Mhina back or die trying."

"Oh." Kalea moved beside him and put a hand on his shoulder. "Wasn't it lucky you decided to run home from the attack? You were the eyewitness to what happened to your sister. Weren't you?"

He inclined his head. "Look what I have to do now. I'll die. Worse, my *sister* will die."

"Not with us around. The least we can do is try to help you. And trust me, we will try. I noticed how Bowaen caressed his sword. He'll help you regardless of what he says. He'll make a plan."

"I'm asking too much of you. Of strangers."

"Not strangers anymore. Those same sorcerers have my friends. And I want to see this blue-haired sorcerer. I need you to track him."

"Who is he to you?"

Kalea cleared her throat. "I don't know what you'd think of my story. I think maybe this 'sorcerer' fits the description of a fairy who raised Dorhen—my friend—I mean, my love. I love him. And that fairy... I may not be able to trust it any longer if they are indeed the same person. Not that I trusted it before."

Gaije stared at her.

"See, I didn't know what you'd think of me, and now I think you'll turn me away."

He huffed and turned forward to stare at the forest. "Your story is ominous and outlandish."

"I see."

"But if you think you know this blue-haired sorcerer—if he's actually a fairy—who am I to stop you from confronting him?"

Kalea spread her hands. "Regardless of whether the sorcerer and the fairy are the same, he's traveling with the same sorcerer band who took your sister and Dorhen. I know this because I spotted Vivene in their camp. The ones who attacked your village, did they wear red gloves?"

"In all that chaos, I didn't stop to study them. Some wore tabards from your kingdom." He crossed his arms over his knees. "We'll track them down."

Kalea nodded. "Let's go back and form a plan." As she attempted to stand, a huge whoosh of dizziness washed over her head. She hardly noticed the little mew of a sigh she made, or the feel of Gaije's hands steadying her.

"What's the matter?"

"Nothing," she insisted. The fire in her leg was spreading to her hip and her foot. She shoved her own pain behind all her other thoughts. Dorhen, Vivene, Gaije's sister, and all the novices needed her.

"You lie. What could've happened to them?"

Del's grave voice awakened Kalea the next morning. She slept curled in the grass, cloak wrapped around her. Groaning, she tried to close her eyes again, but the morning dew had dampened her all over, and their tones were tightening on each word spoken. Not to mention the pulsing ache in her thigh.

"Why would I lie?" Gaije asked. "You can see for yourself."

"Sounds like a problem solved. Is your blue-haired sorcerer dead too?" Bowaen asked. "What about your sister?"

"No. Hurry and follow me!"

Kalea forced herself upright and rubbed her eyes. Whatever they were talking about, she needed to see it too. "Wait for me," she said, untangling herself from her covers.

Gaije shook his head. "You might not—"

"Rubbish, I'm coming too." She still wore her shoes and everything else. They'd hastily prepared for sleep last night with the plan to get an early start so the sorcerers wouldn't gain too much more distance.

"We slept obliviously close to danger all night," Gaije told them as they trekked over the tall grass and fallen branches.

A smell glided over the air and caught Kalea's nose after a while. It deepened to more of a stench the farther they went.

"Oh my, what is that?" she asked, now tasked with balancing on her good leg and covering her nose.

"You'll see," Gaije said. "The smell is what woke me. At least I know I'm still fast on the blue-haired sorcerer's heels."

They climbed over one more tangle of shrub, and she cried out. Gaije shushed her. Dead bodies were strewn about the ground, twenty or so.

"Those tabards—they're Sharzian!" Bowaen said. The maroon-and-olive checked garments were tattered and filthy on the dead men.

Gaije put his hand up. "Listen, it's more than it appears."

"Are these the men who attacked your village?"

"Yes, alongside the blue-haired sorcerer. And there's also more to tell. This isn't really a matter of your people attacking my people. It's the sorcerers, always the sorcerers, doing their malice. Look." Gaije moved to the nearest one and leaned over him.

"No, don't touch it—" Kalea began but didn't want to waste any more breath in this noxious air.

Gaije pulled the dead man's helmet off. Bowaen and Del now also covered their mouths. The remaining skin on the carcass had darkened and dried. Only small patches of hair clung to the loose scalp flaking off the skull, and the lips had shriveled and curled back to show his deathly grin.

"And how long ago did this man pillage your home?" Del asked.

"Three days!" Gaije said. "Three days ago, he and all of this group were walking and murdering!"

Kalea squinted. "I don't understand."

"I do," Bowaen said. "They were dead even as they were pillaging. They shouldn't be so far decayed if they'd died last night."

Gaije pointed to Bowaen and nodded. "And it doesn't look like any ranger *saehgahn* finished them off," Gaije said. "They all must've expired."

Kalea leaned hard on her stick, needing to breathe but not wanting to. "Sorcery."

"Sorcery," Gaije echoed. That word held more infamy and dread now than it ever had on a normal day in Kalea's past. Gaije continued, "Sorcerers do everything behind a mask. They wanted my people to think the Sharzians were attacking us. I'm sure they succeeded in the illusion."

"But you said their leader was elven," Bowaen said.

"An elf, yes, bone structure and all. I could glance at him and confirm his elfishness, but I'm hard pressed to accept he is Norrian. My people would take it that an elf with the Overseas Taint had joined up with their Sharzian enemy. This…elf aimed to terrorize, kill, and loot. That behavior will always be sure to incite impartial emotions of fear, rage, and vengeance in the receiving party."

Kalea shook her head; the action brought all her dizziness back again. "But I still don't grasp what Bowaen said. How could they have pillaged if they were dead all along?" she asked.

Bowaen answered this time. "Does it matter to us? Besides, they're all dead now, so these goons are no longer a threat."

"Well, knowing how it works might help in fighting them if we happen to run into more," Kalea replied before placing her bunched-up kerchief back over her mouth and turning her face away from the decay.

"She's right," Gaije said. "If we keep close on their heels, we could do more than uncover their tricks—we could prevent them from completing any similar spells."

Del lit his pipe, and for once, Kalea welcomed its pungent smoke in the air. "Well," he said. His motions were jerky as he finished, placing his striker in his pocket and putting the end of the heavy thing to his lips. "You just now noticed they were smelly corpses? Why didn't you notice back when they were attacking your village?"

"I've known since they attacked my company on the trail, when no blood poured through the gashes I made on their flesh!" Gaije said. "Besides, in all the chaos of my neighbors' houses burning and my comrades being struck by harnessed lightning, time for pondering and musing escaped me." Gaije's glare made Del shrink a little.

Bowaen said, "So the sorcerers have lost their dead warriors now and their numbers have dwindled considerably, plus they are toting around your sister, Kalea's friend, and other kidnapped people."

"They have women moving about freely," Gaije added. "They may be kidnapped, or they may be as dangerous as any of the males."

"That does alter things a bit," Bowaen replied.

"What about Vivene?" Kalea asked. "She was moving around freely, but she obviously didn't want to be there."

"Other women," Gaije said. "They were…" He averted his eyes. "I don't know how you would describe them because they don't act the same as *faerhain*. They were…cocky, I suppose."

"Sorceresses?" Bowaen offered, and Gaije's brow lowered in confusion.

"They weren't quite sorcerers, unless I'm too ignorant of the sorcerers to know better—which I am. But no. They were smirking, enjoying themselves. They were decorated with flashy beads. And…" Gaije's face suddenly went red to match his hair.

"What?" Kalea asked.

"They were not shy. At all. I don't think they were prisoners. I think they would pose an added threat if we attacked. They would also have open eyes and ears, making it difficult to sneak around the camp."

Bowaen put his hands out. "Why do you think the sorcerers would attack a simple elven village? Is your village rich?"

Gaije shook his head. "No, not besides our horses. Well, my

grandfather is rich, but he's also secretive. Though he has decades of experience outside of Norr...something could be catching up to him."

"Should you have stayed home?" Bowaen asked.

"No, wait!" Gaije's eyes widened. "They did find something of value in my village. My sister!"

The other three leaned in closer.

"How so?" Bowaen pressed.

"I didn't know—of course, I've been in the army for the last three months—but I recently discovered she's a healer."

Bowaen cocked his head. "A healer?"

"I'm not talking about medicine. In our lore, there used to be healers among us, lots of them, but even in ancient history they were valuable. Elven healers are born with an ability to heal the wounded with a single touch."

"And your sister can do that?" Talking advanced Kalea's nausea.

"I witnessed her doing it."

A chill skipped through Kalea's body to add to the nausea and pain. She lowered the kerchief from her mouth, forgetting about the rotten stench. Between Gaije's account of his sister and Dorhen's magic hood, all of the fantastic oddities she had read about the elves were now hitting her in the face. Elven magic was more than just stories to dazzle children. It was all real, even the aspect of Dorhen coming out of the forest to woo her.

"That's why he scooped her up," Gaije continued. "He witnessed her heal a dying *saeghar* same as I did. We don't have healers like we used to. There were none in any of the places my military company visited. Mhina is...extremely rare and valuable."

"Well, this is good," Bowaen said. "It means they won't kill her."

Gaije firmed his jaw.

Bowaen flexed one shoulder and worked his neck. "I can help you find your sister, and maybe this issue is critical enough to your homeland that you'll lend your skills to me." He reached a hand out to Gaije.

Gaije locked his hand around Bowaen's forearm, and Bowaen returned the grip. "As long as you help me free Mhina," Gaije said, "I will continue in service to your cause as payment."

"It's a deal," Bowaen said.

Kalea stepped away from the carnage. "Well, it's settled. I'm finished standing among the dead."

# Chapter 4
## What is a Hero to Kalea

The path stretched on under the awkward silence of Kalea's re-formed traveling party. Bowaen and Del resisted most of their normal banter and whispered to each other instead. Kalea tied her captivated eye to Gaije, one of the few elves she had ever befriended. Lord Remenaxice had told her not to go looking for *saehgahn* because they were "nothing but trouble." Gaije didn't seem troublesome. He averted his eyes, ate his own food, and walked several feet ahead—as if he were alone. He cast his sight sharply in all directions as he moved, scanning for any important clues. What was he like beyond his uncomfortable politeness? She found it difficult to ask him anything, considering his personal difficulties. After losing his father and sister in one day, Gaije now walked with three strangers. Humans.

*His trust in us must go as far as my little finger!* Kalea glanced at her pinky wrapped around her walking stick as she hobbled on her sore leg, single file behind Del.

On the third day, Kalea tried opening a conversation, deciding Gaije needed a friend. She had been itching to ask him an array of questions about Norr elves. After all, she hadn't learned much from Dorhen, who lived outside of the culture. He had observed only human ways in his travels, forbidden from entering his homeland.

At first, she often found herself in silence again because Gaije didn't carry conversations further than needed. He easily obliged Kalea's questions and eventually relaxed, and their conversations became longer. He spoke Lightlandic as well as Dorhen did, and commented on how all elven children, especially males, were taught this second language. Kalea talked about her life and home too. Gaije showed genuine interest in her story, even putting in his own words of wisdom when appropriate.

"In my language, the name Dorhen means 'stranger' or 'exiled,'" Gaije said, gaining Kalea's full, shocked attention. "Names are extremely important to us. They're branded to the soul upon birth, so he is living the existence of an outcast because he is meant to. Notice the long, sad 'oh' sound. Sounds like a long walk downhill, doesn't it? Not many elves receive his name."

"Poor Dorhen," she cooed.

"My distant cousin, Togha, has that sound in his name too. *Toh*-gha. It's a good name for him. He's an odd one."

"Dorhen did mention something like that about his name when I met him. It's an…uncanny coincidence. Does it mean he's also tragic?"

"No," Gaije said. "It sounds heavy in the first half but levels off with the masculine 'hen' part. It simply means he is a stranger—an outsider."

"Well, it's right on all counts. He exists outside of both elven and human societies. A true outsider…

"Gaije, what does your name mean?"

Gaije cleared his throat. "'Hot.'"

His answer drew a lighthearted giggle out of Kalea despite the horrid pain ravaging her leg all the way up through her hip. "Because you have red hair?"

He sighed and nodded. "When we elves get our hands too close to a fire and pull away fast, we tend to make a sort of *ghaish* sound through clenched teeth, and from that sound we get our word for 'hot.'"

Kalea's lingering smile gave away her effort to stifle her laughter.

When Gaije estimated they were a mere day away from the Darklandic border, they camped once more under the pale Norrian whitewood bowing overhead.

Kalea scurried away from the camp for a bit of privacy. Hissing at the sting, she peeled away her bandage and used the last of the sun's light to check her wound, which had been feeling hot all day today and off and on yesterday. A new runny goo oozed from the raw, clawed trenches. The hotness from her leg also tended to radiate to other parts of her body.

She hastily dabbed the pus away and applied the last of the salve they carried in Lord Dax's medical kits. She finished by winding the same bandage around her leg and hobbled back to camp before anyone wondered about her.

"Kalea, how's your leg?" Bowaen asked upon her return.

She dabbed the sweat off her temples with her cloak and forced a smile. "It's fine. I checked it a minute ago."

He frowned, studying her with unblinking eyes. "Are you sure? You haven't been walking—or looking—any better. Is it healing?"

"Yes, it looks much better. Besides, this wound is nothing compared to the devotional flagellation I used to take for penance." She held the fake smile as long as she could, wishing he'd go away. She couldn't risk him, or any of them, getting any more ideas about leaving her behind. Dorhen and the novices depended on her, and no little scratch wound would stop her.

"Can I see it?"

She shook her head. "I'm tired of men looking at my leg, all right?"

Bowaen sniffed. "Let me know if anything seems wrong with it."

She waved her hand and turned her face away.

Later that night, beside the dying fire, Kalea flipped through her beloved book, *The Questionable Tales of Lehomis Lockheirhen*, which Father Liam had been sweet enough to leave for her when he departed for Sharr. Throughout all of her trials, the book had survived with only wrinkled pages from the misty air. Trying not to let her tears worsen the effect, she pored over the book's woodcut illustrations, reliving familiar feelings of her long-gone childhood.

Her favorite illustration showed Lehomis, a short and slender figure with dense black hair waving in the wind as he stood beside his beloved horse, Miktik, on the edge of a mountain. In the story, Lehomis runs away from home at a young age to find freedom—to carve out a life for himself rather than live in the constraints of his home village. Kalea had left her home too. She should be with Dorhen right now making their own bright beginning.

"Oh no. Is that who I think it is?" Gaije asked, standing over her on his way back to his bedroll from his trip to a private shadow in the forest. She hastily sniffled and composed herself before turning her puffy eyes to him, and he switched his question. "Has something upset you?"

"It's a book about Lehomis. Do you know this story?"

Gaije smiled and sighed. "More than I'd like to admit. He's my grandfather."

Her heavy mood lifted for the moment. "What?"

Gaije nodded. "Oh yes."

"Why didn't you say so sooner?"

"Should I have said, 'Nice to meet you, Kalea. I am the descendant of the famous Lehomis Lockheirhen?'"

A giggle escaped her. "Yes! And what do you mean by 'descendant?'"

"He's not actually my grandfather. He's my ancient ancestor, but he's still alive nonetheless."

"He is?"

"Maybe I should go back to bed. You're getting yourself worked up."

She reached out and grabbed his wrist, tugging it until he sat beside her. "You must tell me about him! You must!" Kalea studied Gaije's face. "Does he look like you?"

"I'm taller. And his hair is black."

"Do you see him a lot?"

Gaije laughed. "He helped raise me during my *saeghar* years because my father served as a White Owl Guard—the personal guard of the king. After the king's daughter's coronation, she discharged my father, but Lehomis lives a quiet life as my village's Elder. He's a widower and a *shi-hehen*, so he spends his days lazing about when not arguing with the Desteer about one thing or another."

Gaije was right, she could hardly sit still now. "How is it he's still alive? How old is he?"

"Oh, you didn't read that part yet? It must be written in another book. He's alive because he's cursed."

"No, that's not in this book. I must find the others." She covered her mouth. "Dorhen bought one for me, and I dismissed it!"

"His curse keeps him alive. It's not a good thing, truthfully. Like I said, he's a widower. He has to watch all of his loved ones be born and die."

"Oh, my—I wouldn't have guessed the amusing mishaps in this book are true. So is everything in the book true?"

Gaije ran his fingers through his hair. "I've never read it, so I can't say if it's different from his spoken stories. His books are banned in Norr."

"Banned? How terrible. Why?"

"They're considered smut."

Kalea's smile dropped. "You jest." She pushed his shoulder gently.

"I'm telling the truth. Those books were only written in Lightlandic. The elves tell the stories orally, and even then they're barely legal. But he brags that he can write nearly anything he wants in Lightlandic. It's full of romance."

"Well, it *is* romantic," Kalea said, "which is the best part."

"The *saehgahn* like to hear about his battles and his comical foibles. Overall, we're not allowed to enjoy romantic stories, but that's not to say we don't hear them." He gave her a wink.

Kalea smiled weakly now. "Why aren't you allowed to hear romantic stories? That sounds kind of silly."

"We have to stay focused," he said. "Most of us can't get married, so we can't count on such a thing happening to us."

"Oh." Kalea wanted to keep her smile, but didn't want it to look forced. This little book had already told her much about the state of romance in Norr. Male and female elves were born three to one. Therefore, out of a group of three *saehgahn*, only one would be lucky enough to marry—possibly less, considering some *faerhain* served as Desteer. The remaining two would be expected to live in celibacy or die honorably in battle. Part of the challenge of a *caunsaehgahn* was to find stray *faerhain* outside of Norr and bring them home. From what Gaije told her, it seemed reading about romance was too sad for a *saehgahn's* heart, considering he might never get to enjoy that aspect of life.

Gaije politely said goodnight, and left Kalea to her book and her melancholy thoughts. She would find it hard to sleep after that conversation. She'd be sure to pester Gaije about it again tomorrow if they weren't yet close enough to the sorcerers' caravan to make a move.

"Kalea, run!"

She found herself back in the convent.

*No! Never!*

Dorhen had broken into the dorm to save her. The green-painted door lay in splintered wreckage.

A snarling creature with a beastly face and a red robe grabbed Dorhen's arm. Another quickly took the other arm.

*Dorhen!* She tried to call his name, but couldn't tell if her voice sounded aloud. Too many people swarmed around and between them, keeping them separated. Novices screamed and ran around. Sorcerers planted themselves between her and Dorhen.

"Don't worry about me, Kalea!" Dorhen called, locked in his captors' grasps. He smiled even as one of the red-robed creatures bit into his bicep. The other bit his neck. Blood ran down his chest between the open lapels of his shirt. "Go!" he ordered. More huge beasts with fangs wearing red robes moved in. Dorhen took on more fatal bites to his throat, his side, his leg. Still, he smiled.

*No! Please!*

The throng pushed her farther away as Kalea reached for him. She persisted until a few more sorcerer-monsters approached, their interest turned to her.

"Hurry!" Dorhen yelled as the growing horde of creatures mauled him to the ground and covered him until she couldn't even see a foot.

She had no choice but to flee, or they'd attack her next. She ran through the doorway, forgetting about the broken green door. She tripped and tumbled to the floor. The red-robed beasts were fast upon her. As one opened its jaws to bite at her face, she raised an arm to shield herself...

And trembled awake, quaking in a freezing fit. Bowaen and Gaije were bent over her as Del paced behind them. The dim morning light illuminated a heavy mist.

"She's awake!" Bowaen proclaimed. He'd been patting her face, practically slapping it. "Stay awake now, girl!"

"M-m-my leg," she groaned. Half her body burned.

"A fever," Gaije said.

She didn't notice his hand on her head until he moved it. Her vision spun. She wanted to raise a hand to point to her leg, but she couldn't feel her right arm. Her left arm was trapped helplessly beneath her. Her head lolled, and Gaije caught and cradled it.

Bowaen lifted her skirt and grimaced. "Dear Creator. It's every color I can think of. And the blood! Why's it still bleeding?"

Balancing her head on one arm, Gaije fiddled with his belt pouch. "It's either septic or the creature's claws secreted venom. Probably both."

"She said the scratches weren't any worse than the flagellations she would take at her convent," Bowaen said.

Gaije replied, "Any open wound can go septic, even religious ones. Here." He put a leaf to her mouth. She could hardly feel or see it with her numb lips and dark, wavering vision. "Chew on this," he said, pushing it between her lips. When she managed to take it into her mouth, Gaije handed another one to Bowaen. "Put this under her new bandage. This might alleviate her fever until we make it to a clan village."

Kalea squinted at the elf above her as the colors moved and flowed around him. A sense of calm passed through her mind. She reached up to him. "I love you, Dorhen." She traced a finger gently along the side of his face.

"This isn't good." Gaije's voice emerged from Dorhen's mouth. He shook her in his arms, and it made the dizziness worse.

Bowaen clicked his tongue. "We have to try to stitch her leg or she may bleed to death. Del, the medical kit!"

After a frantic rummage, Del brought the leather pouch with needles and thread included in Lord Dax's supplies. "You know how to sew?" Del asked as Bowaen snatched it from his hand.

"'Course I do. You don't train for as long as I did in Wistara and not get an education in field medicine."

"Same for our *saehgahn* training," Dorhen said above Kalea's face as he held her. His body heat generously warmed her. She had missed him so much, and now she finally basked in all the senses of his being.

Bowaen continued as he threaded a needle, "Thank the Creator that hideous atrocity of sorcery Chandran changed himself into made only two scratch marks." He got to work pushing the needle into the side of her gaping flesh.

"I think I'm gonna be sick." Del turned away.

Kalea wailed in pain before she fainted in Dorhen's arms.

Kalea woke up soon before sunrise after another nightmare about

Dorhen, this one less clear and memorable. All three of her companions were dozing where they sat. They obviously hadn't planned to go to sleep last night. Gaije, the most upright sleeper of the three, sat beside her with legs crossed and eyes closed, his head braced on his hand.

Her fever had lifted; traces of Gaije's fragrant herb remained in her mouth, and she swallowed the last bits. Her whole leg was numb but heavy and swollen. Nonetheless, she crept away to a bush to take care of personal business. Keeping silent proved hardest, but she managed not to wake her friends.

On her way back, Gaije finally perked up. His hand shot to the abandoned quilt they'd wrapped her in. "Kalea?"

"Yes," she answered, "I'm right here." When he turned, she made an extra effort to stand tall. Hobbling as gracefully as she could, she lowered down to her knees with a tightening thickness in her bad leg, and folded her quilt over despite her weakness.

Gaije lunged to help her. "Don't overexert yourself!"

She batted his hands away from her quilt. "I'm fine, can't you see?"

"But you had such a bad…" He squinted at her.

"I'm better now. No little fever can stop me." She turned her face away from his assessing stare to cover whatever paleness or clamminess might've shown on her skin. It would pass—she just had to keep going until her leg healed. Resting be damned.

After folding and stuffing the quilt back into her basket, she roused Bowaen and Del. "If you three can find food," she said to them, "I'll cook it, and we can get back on the trail quickly."

"Kalea," Bowaen said groggily, "are you all right?"

She scoffed. "Why are you three like that? I'm fine. Now, let's go."

"Gaije already foraged some stuff for us to eat last night," Bowaen informed her. "Sit and eat."

"Oh, all right." She hobbled over to Bowaen with the help of her stick and eased herself to the ground, close enough to him to take the bundle of berries, roots, and herbs he offered, but far enough to keep him from puzzling over the state of her appearance.

"And drink this." He handed her a corked bottle which used to hold some of the medical salve that had been used up on Kalea's injury, now full of a yellowish drink. "Gaije brought back some elderflowers and put us to boiling them last night."

Kalea took the bottle.

"We're not gonna leave yet," he continued as she struggled to chew the foul, uncooked leaves of whatever plant Gaije had recommended they eat. She washed it down with the elderflower water. "We'll take the day to help you recover, and Gaije will go ahead and scout the sorcerers' trail. We'll leave tomorrow morning and meet him later as he doubles back."

"Nonsense," Kalea said, moving on to the wild raspberries, which replaced the leaves' flavor with their tart juiciness. "I'm fine, and I don't need to stop. This situation is too urgent. Dorhen and Mhina and Vivene need us."

"Kalea," Bowaen said, shaking his head.

She knew what he would say: that she was weak, that she would make too much noise, and that a big fight might break out if the sorcerers were to spot them.

"We planned it out real well," Bowaen's raspy voice continued, though she refused to look at him. "It's good for Gaije to scout ahead. You'll tell him what Vivene and Dorhen look like. If he can make contact secretly, those two might be a big help in thwarting the caravan. If he can locate Dorhen, he said he'd quote your name. He and Dorhen might be able to do some real damage. Vivene too. Two capable adult people added to our group will make us that much stronger."

Kalea moved on to the little orange, worm-like roots Gaije had foraged. She focused on chewing them and tolerating their intense flavor. Bowaen's point made sense. As much as she wanted to insist on being there to find Dorhen in captivity, it would be a childish request.

"Fine," she said, "I'll stay here with you two. I'll get some work done, and I'll eagerly await Gaije and Dorhen's return."

"No need to do any work—"

Kalea put her hand up, refusing to meet his eyes. "Our little union here could use some upkeep. I'll wash your clothes and such. We'll be better off."

When she rose again, Bowaen protested, "Kalea," but she would hear none of it.

"I have to get started now so the clothes can take all day to dry. Anyone who needs a garment washed, give it to me now."

Hiding her persistent dizziness, she gathered her kirtle and extra braies as the three men followed her watchfully toward the burbling of a creek hiding in a crevice between two slopes.

"Nah, these are the only clothes I got," Del said when she turned to him and threw out her hand. She forged the strongest expression her face could manage in her hour of pain and illness. Del perched himself on a fallen log and Bowaen joined him, borrowing a drag off Del's freshly lit pipe.

Why did they have to watch her so closely? Rolling her eyes at their doting presence, Kalea immersed her garments in the water to soak;

they'd collected quite a few dirt stains since the other night.

Gaije shed his green tunic and handed her the thin undershirt he wore beneath. Displaying the best smile she could in hopes of hiding her exhaustion, she took it. Maybe the rhythmic washing process she so missed would cleanse her mind of the horrible experiences she'd endured since her last night in the convent.

Gaije undid the rows of braids running along the side of his head, which kept the hair out of his eyes while shooting his bow. With his shoulder-length hair, the ends of the braids stuck up behind his head like a spiky rooster's tail. Kalea's eyes trailed down to his legs. She tried not to stare but could so easily trace the fine, toned muscles under his leggings. Elves wore their braies out in the open, their leggings attached with a tied cord in front and back. She could see the whole side of his exposed hip and buttock.

Her eyes darted back to her load of clothes as she sat on the stream bank, her cheeks heating up. Maybe now the color would return to her face. Her deep leg wound screamed, and she fidgeted for a better way to sit. Edging closer to the water, she reached for a garment floating within the cold current.

"Here." Gaije's voice rang out again. He tossed his braies and leggings onto the pile of waiting laundry. "Might as well do those since I brought a spare set with me."

When she looked up again, he'd stripped completely naked and headed for the water, unashamed to be seen. She gasped, trying not to scream, and Bowaen let out a storm of raspy coughs.

"Gaije!" Del said. "What're ya doing? There's a lady here!"

Kalea shielded her eyes with her hand, trying to be calm. Like Dorhen, he didn't have a speck of hair on his body, not even on his legs.

He hesitated before going into the stream. "So? It's better if I bathe so the sorcerers won't smell me coming near."

"Shouldn't you go bathe downstream?" Bowaen countered.

"Why?"

At his question, Kalea lowered her hand. He made no effort to cover himself from her view. He was as shameless as Dorhen.

"Are you offended?" he asked her.

Del responded, "*We* sure are. Yeesh."

Kalea cocked her head, forgetting about her pain momentarily. "Elves don't have any shame in their bodies, do they?" she asked.

"Should we?"

Kalea raised her eyebrows. "You mean…in your culture, a female wouldn't be offended by this?" She waggled her finger in his general direction, still averting her eyes.

"Not at all," he said. He began to shrug and step in place at all of Del's grumbling, ankle-deep in the water. "I'm sorry. I didn't know your culture didn't accept this."

Kalea couldn't help but smile. "We're quite the opposite. Boys and girls can't see each other naked in our culture," she said.

"I'll go somewhere else."

"I'm not offended, Gaije. You can bathe wherever you want."

At her word, he moved farther into the stream. "Then I'll bathe here so I can watch over you." He dunked his head to wet his hair.

She turned her blushing face back to her work. "So in your culture, girls and boys *can* see each other naked?"

"Not exactly. Only *faerhain* can look at *saehgahn*. It's somewhat related to what I told you about the romantic stories. It's forbidden for us to see them."

"But how come they can look at you?"

"So we can always be available to protect them."

Kalea kept her eyes on his swirling white undershirt in the water. "Well, how can you protect them if they have to bathe separately where you can't see them?"

"They throw a big fuss over the whole process." His voice sounded like he might be smiling. "Especially when traveling. They'll either erect a screen to shield themselves or have other *faerhain* create a people-wall, holding up sheets to hide the ones who are bathing. Not to mention the other reason they look at us naked."

"Which is?"

"To evaluate our form and pick a husband."

Kalea paused briefly to ask, "They pick husbands? Can you not…?"

He finished for her, "Pick one of them and ask her for marriage? No."

"Oh, dear. Your culture is strict, isn't it?"

Gaije scooped more water over his head. "It's all necessary," he said, combing his fingers through his drenched red hair. "We *saehgahn* have to work hard on our forms if we want to get chosen for marriage. There are many rules, and we're being evaluated constantly, so we also have to act in the absolute best manner."

Kalea giggled. "Well, you do a good job. You're so polite, unlike someone else I know," she grumbled over her shoulder loud enough for Del to hear. The other two had turned the opposite direction to keep from having to watch Gaije bathe. She concentrated hard on keeping her eyes down at the moment he stepped out of the water. "You'll get picked for a husband, Gaije, I know it," she added.

"Don't get my hopes up," he said, heading to where he had left his fresh clothes.

She allowed herself one more peek at his sculpted body, and a sudden lightheadedness made her sway. Any conversation she could immerse herself in helped to forget her illness, but it had crept up on her.

Turning back to the water to catch herself, bracing her hands on the rock beneath her, she spotted another person on the other side of the stream. His white hair waved in the breeze—like the Grey Mage Bowaen was pursuing. A grey parrot alighted on his arm from a nearby tree.

Kalea's vision darkened over the image. Her leg throbbed with a new personality of pain. She moaned.

"Kalea?" Gaije had yet to don his clothes as he turned around to check on her—not that she could see much of him anymore.

She raised her arm to point at the new person who'd approached the stream across the way and spoke back to Gaije. Her voice faded into a roar flooding her ears, as if the stream's sound rose in volume. Her vision filled with dancing sparks that blinded her.

"Kalea!"

She was falling.

He sprinted over to catch her as the water rushed over her head with a cold splash.

# Chapter 5
## What is Wrong in Kalea's Dreams

Kalea wandered, lost.

Merely a moment ago, she was washing clothes for her friends. A cold shroud of liquid had swallowed her head. And now she was…

*Where?*

Darkness and thin air. She touched her face, her arms, and reached a shaking, hesitant hand toward the gashes on her leg.

Gone. No bandage. No more blood or pain or swelling. Mobility had returned to her leg.

*Did the wound kill me? What happened? Think, foolish girl!* She called out to Bowaen and Del, and then Gaije when she remembered him. They were real, weren't they? Yes.

"Dorhen."

*He's gone.*

Was he real or a dream? That's what he felt like, a long-ago dream. She retained bits and pieces of it, but longing and doubt twisted around in her stomach.

*Me, in love? Impossible. I'm a vestal.* That wish was secret and forbidden. *I wouldn't deserve a devoted and loving creature like him.*

"No, he is real!"

She remembered his touch, his scent, and his soft, trustworthy eyes.

Where was he now? Perhaps dead after the raid on her convent. She shook her head rapidly but had no way of reassuring herself he still lived. Maybe she had died too.

*It's probably better this way.* She could search for him in this… underworld. But how could she find her way through this black nothingness? She crouched and touched the cold floor beneath her feet. Smooth and level stone. She stood again and walked cautiously with her arms outstretched. Stone again. She must be somewhere tangible after all.

She walked slowly, one hand feeling in front while the other grazed the wall. A soft golden glow appeared ahead and traveled toward her. A candle.

*I am somewhere! I'm not dead. I think…*

A hooded figure holding the candle walked by. A monk? A momentary sense of relief washed over her. The candle revealed tall, arched windows lining the opposite wall. A cathedral! She called out to the monk. How lucky to have found an agent of the Creator!

"Wait! Where am I?" He didn't answer. "Stop. Do you hear me?" She followed. Trotting ahead of him, she waved her hand before his face, and he didn't flinch.

*Wait a minute...* Walking backward, she leaned in to see his face, then screamed and jumped.

It wasn't human! It had the face of a jackal, with brown fur, a pointed muzzle, and big yellow eyes. A beast walked these halls, like the one who'd scratched her, except this one had a furry dog's muzzle. Never could she have imagined such a horrifying thing. It wore a red robe like the beasts which tore Dorhen to pieces the other night... Kalea's head suddenly ached. That couldn't be right.

The dog-headed monster remained oblivious to her. She might be dead after all. Though what could she have done in life to deserve to go to hell?

*Oh.* Her head sank in shame. *I dishonored the One Creator with betrayal. Consorted with a male elf, dashed my vows, and offered my flesh to him. The scratch wounds killed me, and I'm in hell now.*

She reached out to touch the demon's shoulder. Her hand went right through.

*Am I also a ghost?* Or was he? Even though she'd gotten herself thrown into hell, she didn't want to remain in the dark any longer. Though disturbing to behold, the demon carried a light and might possibly lead her somewhere useful, so she followed it.

The corridor curved to the left. The darkness stretched a long way before the candle's glow. No doors yet. Dense blackness hung beyond the window panes. No moonlight, no stars. Some of the windows were broken, allowing in a horrid chill that crept up her gown and nipped at her body. The morning should make things less scary, if morning existed in the underworld.

Shadows danced past. Kalea tightened her fists around handfuls of her chemise. Where had her overdress gone? And her shoes? They passed a red and gold banner hanging on the left wall; she didn't recognize its insignia.

Music? Kalea concentrated hard on the deafening silence of the place, marred by her and the demon's padding bare feet.

Yes! Fluttery music echoed, expressing hopeful feelings strangely complemented by downward notes. Its volume increased as Kalea ventured closer with the light-bearing demon in the lead. Large double doors with a soft glow seeping through the cracks finally came around the curve.

She stopped at the door as the dog-man walked on, taking the light with him. She hesitated, torn between continuing with the jackal and opening this door. Someone played the harp in there. Were her chances better with the jackal? Perhaps it could lead her to some place where people gathered.

*Perhaps, perhaps, perhaps!*

The jackal disappeared, leaving her with the glow through the cracks as her sole light. She could catch him if she ran a bit, being careful not to smack against any curved stone walls or fall out a window.

*The doors.*

She grasped one of the handles and pulled. Locked.

Kalea groaned. As she rubbed her face, a door hinge creaked, and the sharp wire of light between them expanded and softened. Simultaneously, the music slowed and the melody changed to a dragging wander of notes that would flick one or two at a time, sometimes leaving a few seconds of anticipation in between.

No one occupied the room. She took it upon herself to enter and explore anyway. Forget the soothing warmth; she should've gone with the jackal. Never in her wildest nightmares could she have imagined such a horrible sight. It was a bedroom, ugly, in bad taste, and it belonged to someone…sick.

She couldn't settle her eyes anywhere. The music fluttered from a lonely harp playing by itself. In the center of this round chamber, the bed stood on a dais with four steps. Also large and circular, it was covered in fine velvet blankets and topped with the pelt of a huge white wolf. A heavily carved headboard stood strong with numerous posts holding up layers of draping scarves and canopies that crowned the whole thing, suspended from the tiered ceiling over the bed. But the rest of the room…

A human-shaped cage hung from the ceiling, with inward-facing spikes to force its victim to stand straight, empty at the moment. Wooden platforms with large gears and handles and belts lying across them stood around the circular space of the room. There were various horrible, rusty, sharp iron contraptions the uses of which Kalea didn't want to ponder, and below them were grated drainage holes with strange sounds echoing up. Each torture contraption stood angled to view the bed. A fireplace, large enough to stand inside of, warmed the room, and next to the usual hanging tea kettle, chains with manacles hung over the fire, glowing orange in the heat. Old bloodstains splotched most of the brittle tapestries on the walls.

The only thing preventing Kalea from running back out the door was the warmth of the fire and the room's vacancy. A few lit candles were reflected tenfold by a large collection of mirrors. A grand, yet ugly, divider screen stood to the side, painted with a scene depicting winged demons carrying off screaming naked women. The high ceiling depicted a similarly demonic fresco.

She decided to approach the harp, the least disgusting item in the room, to marvel at its strings, which danced amazingly by themselves. Its depressing music suited the place. Temptation overcame her, and she slowly reached out to touch one of the strings.

"Are you lost, my dear?"

Her hand froze, and Kalea spun at the sound of the rough-edged baritone voice resonating behind her. An elf in a long maroon robe hanging open to display his shirtless chest had stepped out from behind the divider. His wavy blonde hair lay neatly over his shoulders and shone as if in competition with the pale yellow of the firelight. His eyes matched the fire's intensity in sockets darkened with soot.

Kalea's whole body went stiff. She couldn't force anything through her throat.

"This is interesting," he said when she didn't answer his first question. He walked toward her barefoot. "Look at you. Straight off a farm." His face possessed a suffocating quality of anger, though his demeanor held even.

Kalea stuttered.

"You're not so bad, though." One side of his mouth curled.

"I *am* lost," she finally said, ending his smile.

He stopped before drawing too close. "How did you come here, my little starling?" he said.

*Starling?*

"I don't know." She dropped her gaze to the floor. "Can you tell me where I am?"

He eyed her. "You're in my home. Deep in the mountains, north of Goblin Country." He continued to look her up and down.

Goblin Country? No such place existed in the Lightlands.

"So I'm not dead?" she accidentally muttered aloud.

"This seems like death to you?"

"I don't know. I only remember awakening here."

His eyes narrowed and he walked closer, arms tensed at his sides.

"I'd like to go back. Sorry I bothered you."

His voice rumbled, "You want to go back?"

"Yes, I've been separated from my traveling company."

He turned away for a moment. A large image on the back of his robe depicted another jackal-headed man sitting on a throne holding a flame in one hand and a dagger in the other. After seeing that demonic image, Kalea would seize the first chance to escape.

"Where is it you'd like to go back to?" he asked.

"Norr. We were traveling through Norr, but now I'm here and don't know where here is."

He smirked. "That's also interesting. You don't know what you've accomplished tonight?"

She shook her head, feeling like the perfect lost child.

"I'll tell you where you are, my dear. Though you may not believe it."

Kalea stepped forward. "Tell me. Please."

"You've wandered into my dream."

Kalea blinked for a moment. "Your dream?"

"That's what I said!"

"So I'm dreaming. This is all a dream, and I'll soon wake up."

"Oh no, darling, this is very real—for you." He stepped closer to her again.

"Wait, you said it was a dream—"

Without another word, he struck her across the face. She never saw it coming. She rocked back on her heels and struggled to keep from falling over. It burned and stung; her cheekbone might develop a bruise. She cried out, holding her face, now aware of his long fingernails.

"Did you feel that?" he asked over her whimpering.

"Yes!"

"Then you're real here, aren't you? For me, it's real too. It's...quite special." He combed his fingernails through his silken hair. "You're not completely to blame, however. You found my dream easily because I open them to girls like you, hoping someone special will come along."

She wiped her eyes and sniffled. "How did I get into your dream?"

"It's a magical technique called dreamwalk, my little starling." He continued regardless of Kalea shaking her head, "Our souls have met here in the mental space I've provided."

She grasped her head with both hands as the dizziness from the slap persisted. "How is that possible?"

"When you went to sleep, your soul separated from your body and took a magical journey into my dream." His tone implied what he thought of her intelligence. "Since you've found my dream, we can form an understanding. Let's also forge an alliance."

"But I don't know you. I don't think I need an alliance, but thank you anyway." She began to turn.

"Where do you think you're going?"

"I have to leave!" She left it at that and took off, dashing back toward the double doors, past the silent harp and torture devices. Her feet padded along a fine rug and then slapped against the hard floor before she exited the door.

Out in the dark corridor, she turned right and sprinted the way she came, trailing her hand along the wall to avoid hitting some other one. She squealed at the approaching light—carried by the jackal-headed man! He paid no attention to her, the same as before. She didn't follow him. If she continued in the opposite direction, she might find the exit to this place. So she ran on, ignoring the freezing sting of her feet slapping the stone. She left the jackal-man far behind and found dense darkness again.

The wall fell away, and her hand met wood in a recess. A door. Kalea panted and ran her fingertips along the grains. This door might lead her to some place useful. She trailed her touch along the door in search of a handle. Cold iron appeared in the region expected. A little line of light pierced through the crack. She pulled the door open.

The elf laughed out loud. "What did you find out there? That my dream space is small? You must be a silly farm girl born with the talent."

Kalea's mouth dropped open. She twisted to observe the dark hall behind her. A glow moved through the corridor toward her. The jackal-headed man passed her on his round. Kalea's thoughts jumbled.

When she turned forward again, she jumped to find the elf had approached her. He reached out and touched her hair. Absolute cold fear restrained her. He curled a strand around his finger.

"See what I mean?" he said. "You can run out, but you'll only wind up back here. You've accidentally found my dream, but this is fortunate for both of us."

He stroked her hair now, grazing her scalp above her ear with his nails. Kalea swallowed hard, trying not to make contact with his reflective amber eyes when his thumb touched her lips and smoothed across them as if to test their softness. She feared another slap if she made a wrong move or resisted his gestures. "You'll spend the night here."

*Not a chance!*

She couldn't quite manage to say "no" aloud. Instead, she forced out the words, "Can you tell me how to return to my body?"

"Why rush away? I never have bad dreams."

"Who are you?"

"I don't think you need to know that, my little starling." A sensual note rang in his voice. He took her chin in his hand, forcing her to look at his diamond-shaped face with skin smooth and fair even for an elf, she guessed. "I can tell you I'm a dreamer." His voice grated in her memory after he finished speaking.

"Why do you call me 'starling?'" she asked in hopes of delaying his advances.

He grasped her shoulders. "A starling is a naughty bird." He leaned in to the side of her face, brushing his cheek against hers, and lowered his voice even more. "But you'll be fine. You'll return most nights—for me and for yourself."

"How do I get out of your dream?"

"How should I know? I can't dreamwalk."

"I want to go now." Her voice shook more than ever at this point.

"Why are you frightened? It's only a dream." He aligned his lips beside her ear and whispered, "Besides, I need your ability. I've a malady you must heal, and in return I can reward you with great things."

"Why won't you listen? I want to leave."

"I'm sure you'll find your way out eventually. But for now, I need your help. If you'll shut your mouth and come over to the bed…" He leaned back, but his hands remained on her shoulders. What did he find so interesting about her?

She raised her hands to see them fading into thin air. "What's happening now?"

"I think someone is waking you." The most relieving news of the whole night. "Farewell, little starling…"

Her vision darkened.


Kalea gasped awake. A cold chill doused her from a mist thickening the air. She shivered under the layer of water beads all over her. White-trunked trees towered high—Norr. A strong smell of burning wood and straw persisted under the refreshing mist.

"Good Creator, you're awake!"

Someone unfamiliar knelt quickly beside her. She shook. Her leg throbbed with sharp pains. He put his arms around her trembling shoulders to share warmth and wiped her face and hair with his cloak. She could barely focus her eyes.

"Azrielle! Lend a wing, for the Creator's sake!" A shadow whooshed over them both, slinging heavy drops of water off giant, silver feathers. The mist swirled under the shade, refusing to be shielded. "Do you remember me? I'm Damos. We met back in Jumaire, at the…the tavern."

She groaned in response when she couldn't find any words in her sluggish brain.

He mumbled about how she probably couldn't hear him and he was making a fool of himself, yet he continued talking to her. "Your friends' voices cut through the silence of the forest near my position, and I ventured to meet you—to trade for food mostly. But you were ill and your friends spun into a panic, so I volunteered to take you away. There's supposed to be an elven village somewhere close by, but we had to land due to the mist. We might've gotten lost."

He huffed in exasperation. "You're still not waking up. Sorry, madam, but I'll have to…"

As Damos's voice faded out, she could feel her skirt lifting because the stranger meant to check her wound. She slipped back into a deep slumber against his side, this time peacefully.

Kalea opened her eyes to the darkness once again.

*Please don't be that dream again!*

"Bring her in here," a stern woman's voice echoed across a large interior space.

Footsteps tapped loudly across stone. The walking motion shook and jiggled her to the left and right; she would vomit if the endless misery didn't stop soon.

"Forgive me for the intrusion," the soft male voice echoed in the silence—the voice from earlier. Kalea struggled to open her eyes and focus them on the stranger who held her in his arms. Adding the whirling visuals to the mix made things worse, so she closed her eyes again. "I'm in a difficult position with no other options. I think she's dying!"

"Be calm!" The female's voice demanded compliance from anyone around.

"It's lucky you're here and I've found you," the male's voice continued politely. They moved into a smaller, tunnel-like space. A hallway, Kalea guessed.

"Lucky indeed," the female voice said. "My clan fled to the next village over, several days' worth of walking, but by chance, I stayed behind to find and nurse any surviving *saehgahn*. By an unfathomable strangeness, I found you carrying that human woman. Both of you are human. What are you two doing in Norr?"

The male's soft voice sounded again. "My name is Damos, and this is a friend of mine—or at least I'd like her to be. I mean, she's an acquaintance… Her name is Kalea."

"You say her name with a certain depth in your voice, as if you know her better than an acquaintance," the woman said.

"I don't know her. What do you mean…?" Damos asked.

"I was merely taking note. I'll know a lot more about you after I've given you *milhanrajea* to make sure you mean no harm to my clan."

"Milhan-what?"

"You'll find out. First we must tend to your...acquaintance. In here. Put her on the bed."

Kalea tried to move and only accomplished fluttering her eyelids. In the slight crack of light, she managed to catch a terrifying ghostly face with long, straight hair hovering over her. The sight sent a charge of fright through her nerves, and she lurched, grasping to the side for anything comforting she could find. Damos took her hand and held it close to his lips. His bright blonde hair glowed in her bleary vision.

The ghost-like woman went straight to work, raising Kalea's skirt and untying her bandage. She paused to regard Damos and study his posture with Kalea's hand. "This is an odd situation," the woman said, her voice always flat in tone. "Normally, I would not permit a male to be in here, but you are not *saehgahn*. You are both strangers, and I'd prefer you in here so I can keep an eye on you."

"I prefer to stay as well," Damos said. "I mean no harm to your village. I'm worried about her."

The ghost-woman returned to her work. "We've found agreement. The customs of my clan do not apply to human strangers. I may need your help anyway, as all of my sisters left with the *faerhain*."

Kalea tried to stay awake. She wanted to talk to Damos, to ask him questions and find out where her friends were, but her whole body pulsed with fire. If she truly was on her way to hell, its doors were opening. With no more strength to fight her impending death, she let herself drift away again.

Dreams came and went. The fire roved over her and disappeared, only to return again.

"There." The woman's voice echoed in the distance. "I've done all I can."

"Will she live?" Damos's question pealed.

"If her body can fight off the rest of the venom. The wound is clean. I recommend she stay here for a week or more."

"I'll stay with her."

"Not easily," the woman said. "I must perform *milhanrajea* now. And when my clan returns, they won't be happy to see a human man here. If I deem you pure and without malice, I can vouch for you, but there will be a string of intense meetings to decide whether you can stay for more than a day."

Damos responded, "I should tell you, there are three more people on the way—if they can find their way. Two men and an elf."

The woman's flat voice turned ice-cold. "You are slow to tell me such important details, human."

"Sorry. I was too worried about Kalea." Damos sighed.

"I'll have to perform *milhanrajea* on all of you. Her as well."

"What is *milhanrajea*?" Damos asked again.

"It's a viewing of your mind. I will see your thoughts, memories, and desires. When I know them, I'll better be able to tell if you mean to bring harm to my clan."

The room fell silent. Kalea fought to open her eyes, but for now she could do no more than listen.

His voice slid out so breathily, Kalea almost missed it. "I can't let you do that."

"Then you can't stay here with your acquaintance."

Damos stuttered. "You'll—you'll just—it won't…" He paused to breathe. His voice rattled. "I can't."

"What are you hiding, Damos?" Kalea's imagination pieced together the woman stepping closer to Damos, beyond his comfort.

"All right," he said. "Do it. But please…" A pause. "Whatever you see…please don't tell anyone. If you want to throw me out of your village, do it, but don't tell anyone. Please let me go."

The woman hummed. "Keeping harmful people out of my village is my aim. Who would I tell?"

"Just don't tell anyone. I beg you."

"If you're hiding an evil, I will simply have my *saehgahn* kill you when they return."

"I'd like that better than having you pass along my secrets."

"Kneel down. This will be quick."

Kalea wanted to see. She worked her muscles and turned her head upon the pillow. She opened her eyes as Damos knelt before the ghost-like woman. The woman wore face paint and long robes with a sash tied around her chest. They were in a cozy room with other beds and curving earthen walls. The woman—an elf!—took on an expression of concentration. She closed her eyes and reached for Damos's head. She slid her fingers into his white hair, and the two tensed up simultaneously.

It ended after a second. They lurched away from each other after a jolt, as if they had taken an electric shock. The elf-woman's face scrunched, and when she recovered, she hid her mouth behind her wrist, her eyes wide. Damos buried his face in his hands, hunched over.

"You saw, didn't you?" he said. "You know now."

The woman shuddered. "And you are now running to the Darklands?"

He nodded. The woman fanned herself. "I'm not the oldest Desteer maiden I know," she said, "but I've seen many things in the minds of my people. I've never yet seen anything that warrants the death penalty."

"And so you're going to kill me now?" Damos asked.

She took in a long breath through her nose. "This is a difficult situation."

"Like I said, I mean you no harm!" Damos leaped to his feet. "And when the other men get here, please...please don't tell them."

"Listen," the Desteer maiden said, "I'll follow your wishes. I won't tell. I'll allow you to stay the night, but no longer. To answer your question, I don't think you deserve the death penalty from us. It's none of our business. After you rest for tonight, you'll go your way. Kalea may stay here until her leg heals. You may wait for her outside the Norrian border." The elf-woman shook her head. "In all my years, I've never seen anything so explicit. So vivid."

A brief sob slipped out of Damos's throat. "Don't remind me." He covered his face with his hands again and dropped into a seat by the window instead of Kalea's bedside.

The elf-woman moved to stand over him. "I'd like to put my hand on your shoulder in comfort, but I mustn't. You disgust me."

Damos shrugged, keeping his face hidden. "I'll leave in the morning."

# Chapter 6
# What is Kindness from a Stranger

Lamrhath shot awake with a new burst of sexual exhilaration. "I don't believe it," he whispered. He brushed his shaking hands over his face and through his hair. "A healing dream."

Yet it hadn't healed him. His body trembled, more agitated than ever. His companions slept peacefully nearby, an activity the sorcerers didn't take the time to do very often. A different woman had entered his dream. He had no way to find out her identity, but he'd open himself to more of it. Whatever magical technique he could find, he'd use to lure her back. He didn't have the rare talent required to dreamwalk himself, and therefore couldn't seek out those "healing dreams." He needed another dreamwalker in his life, especially while stranded out here in the grasslands.

He shivered in the cold night mist. A walking cloud had moved in. He lay back down and threw his cloak over his head to shield himself from the soggy air. Curled in the fetal position, he hugged his aching stomach. He wouldn't last long. He hadn't taken many chances to test his endurance against his sexual ailment, but now he dared to wonder if his symptoms could kill him. He needed a woman and wouldn't find one for miles.

A tear leaked from his eye, one nobody would see under the cloak in this darkness. He was alone. But crying and acting pitiful wouldn't cure his pain any faster than a punch in the face would. He needed some distraction.

He reached into his tabard pocket for the whisper stone with the black ribbon tied around it. He knew it by its shape, at least. Removing the ribbon, he tapped the pattern required to activate this particular stone, and a soft pulsing glow from within it lit up his tiny space under the cloak.

"Kilka," he whispered, "tell me about Wikshen's magic. How does it work? What can it do for him?"

A warm glow radiated against Kalea's face. A fire.

"Look there, she's awake," said a spirited, familiar voice. Del's voice.

"We knew we'd lost you when Damos took you away."

Kalea's eyelids fluttered and reopened before she could focus her eyes on him. Damos and the elf-woman had been replaced by Bowaen, Del, and Gaije. Bowaen and Gaije weren't so cheerful, but they turned their eager eyes to see her sitting up. Each man's shoulders relaxed a bit, though her alertness didn't fix the heavy mood in the room. Bowaen stepped over to sit next to Kalea as she found herself bundled in several blankets and a wooly grey pelt to trap in a great level of heat around her. Del sat by a tiny fireplace sculpted into a smooth, plastered wall while Gaije stood watching out the little round window with a dreadful stiffness in his spine.

Del continued, "Should I tell her the tale now, or do you think she's not yet ready?"

"Tell me," Kalea said. "Where are we?"

"We're…um…in a ruined elven village. Another one sacked by the blue-haired sorcerer," Bowaen said.

Kalea moaned and tried to leap out of bed. Earning another dizzy wave, she plopped back onto her pillow.

Del went on, "Yeah, turned out the sorcerer had a good bunch of allies left after losing those decayed soldiers. Don't worry, though. There's an elven priestess here, a nice lady. She said the women and children fled to a safe place. Outside, there are just a bunch of *saehgahn* lying dead."

Rain pattered on the roof, and Kalea tried to rise again too quickly. "So you're going to leave them out there to get rained on like logs?"

Bowaen threw his arms around her and ushered her back to the floor mattress. "Stop or you'll faint again," he said. "They're dead, and there's not much we can do now. We'll let the priestess take care of 'em. We can't bury them in the rain even if we did have the time and energy."

Bowaen cleared his throat. "Anyway, it was a day in hell, you might be curious to hear. Early this morning, right as you fainted, Damos approached from across the river. He called on the magic of his pet bird, and it transformed into a huge, beautiful dragon with silver feathers."

"You mean a ravian," Kalea said. She made note of the darkness outside the window. She'd lost the whole day.

"Sure," Bowaen replied. "There Damos was, right within my reach, but you didn't look good at all. Damos said he could fly you to a nearby elven village, so that's what happened. We sent you with Damos to this village."

Kalea vaguely recalled Damos speaking to the Desteer maiden.

After barking a short laugh, Bowaen said, "I got stuck with the choice of letting him save your life or roping him and taking him back to Carridax."

Kalea snorted. "Thanks for choosing my life over his bounty."

Bowaen ignored her sarcasm. "When the two of you got here, it had already been destroyed, freshly struck by that sorcerer. Apparently, no one lingered around who could help you."

Kalea said through chattering teeth, "I'm going to catch that monster and, with Gaije, see him dead!"

Bowaen shushed her and continued, "Damos was at a loss when the air suddenly misted up. He said he hadn't seen nothing like it before. For us three, it was like walking through a large wet wall when we got to the area. Rainbows bounced all over the place. He said you were dying, but in the mist, you suddenly sprang awake. How do you feel?"

Kalea wiped her tears. "Alive, I suppose. I don't think I'll faint again. I'm tired."

"Well, by the Creator's grace, the elf priestess found the two of you and invited you in here—their village hall," Bowaen said. "This place has food and medicine. That priestess saved your life. She says it's a Desteer hall and was locked up tight during the raid, so the sorcerers didn't get anything good out of here."

"Where's Damos now?" Kalea asked.

Bowaen barked a short laugh and produced the little wooden box bearing Lord Dax's spelled ring from his pocket. "This is workin' out well for me. Damos is still here. I'll give him the ring, and then you and me and Del can turn back for home."

Gaije twisted briefly around to scowl at Bowaen.

Kalea dropped her head to the pillow. "Not so fast, Bowaen. Gaije asked you for help, and I haven't found Dorhen!"

Bowaen put his hand on her forehead. "Don't get yourself worked up."

Kalea frowned and touched the back of Bowaen's hand. Dead *saehgahn* being rained on outside, Dorhen and the novices still in the sorcerers' grasp, and now Bowaen approached the conclusion of his duty and would turn for home soon—everything had advanced too fast.

Gaije finally stepped away from the window and spoke. "I'll rest tonight." He joined them by the little fireplace. "In the morning, I'll leave here. Just as well that you've found Damos and will go back home. Kalea needs you right now."

"With all those dead bodies out there?" Del said. "If we stay, I'll find myself digging one hundred graves in the morning at the priestess's request."

Gaije frowned at him.

A new female voice entered the room. "It won't be necessary."

Kalea twisted a tad too fast for her own good to witness the first elven female she'd ever seen striding into the room with a proud starch in her back and smooth, silent steps. Kalea had seen her hours ago talking to Damos, but the memory had already hazed over.

"I'll make a case for your woman," the elf continued, "but if you two men are here when the *saehgahn* return, there'll be trouble."

Kalea assumed that meant Gaije could linger too. Nonetheless, she wasn't staying. She'd go with Gaije to track the blue-haired sorcerer, and there'd be no resting or biding any time. Dorhen and Vivene needed her. She only needed to convince Gaije to let her accompany him.

"Which reminds me," the Desteer said, "I've yet to perform *milhanrajea* on all of you."

"I don't understand your language," Del said.

Gaije piped up, "Just kneel and do as she says." His voice hummed somberly.

The Desteer approached Del. "You first. Kneel." He did, and she put her hands around his head like she did to Damos earlier. That same jolt occurred between them, and the maiden gasped. "Just as I thought, vivid...and putrid too."

"Putrid?" Del made an amused grin at her word choice.

The Desteer collected herself and smoothed her skirt and sleeves. "Not as bad as I saw earlier. I have never performed *milhanrajea* on humans before today, so you'll have to understand, this is...interesting for me."

Gaije's curious eyes darted between Bowaen and Del. Bowaen's turn came next.

"Will it hurt?" Bowaen asked.

Del answered him, "*Startle* is more like it."

Bowaen's *milhanrajea* observation looked about the same on the outside as Del's. The Desteer shook out her hands and took a deep breath.

"Good," she said. "I hope to never glimpse into a human mind again, but you are all... I won't say 'fair,' so I'll say 'passable' instead. I will not order my *saehgahn* to kill you when they return."

"What a relief." Del snorted and turned back to the fire, hugging his arms.

Gaije obediently approached her next, head hanging. He didn't need to be called on. The Desteer lifted her chin as she stood over him. Gaije's body tensed more than the men's had, yet he clearly knew what to expect. She slipped her fingers into his hair. By the consistency of her finger placement, the spell must have a lot to do with the physical body and its key points. The same thing occurred with Gaije: a minor startling jolt, and then the two separated after a mere second.

The Desteer closed her eyes and nodded deeply. "Today I've learned of a new trait the male half of my own people keep."

Everyone in the room waited for her explanation—if she chose to give one.

She continued, "*Saehgahn* are extremely disciplined in taming their thoughts. They hide their thoughts from us maidens. Humans don't practice such discipline."

"Of course not," Kalea said. "Instead, we confess our sins to a priest."

The Desteer eyed her, smirking with interest. "You willingly give your faults to your religious ministers?"

"Yes," Kalea said. "We willingly give ourselves to the Creator."

"Telling your ministers what you've done requires honesty."

"Of course it does—yes," Kalea said.

The Desteer turned her probing eyes to Gaije, who stayed miserably on the floor, hugging himself with his head bowed. "And yet my *saehgahn* refuse to tell us what is rotting their minds, and we have to pull it out of them."

Kalea winced for Gaije. "I didn't mean…" She didn't know how to finish the sentence, so she altered it. "Gaije is good. Please don't put any pressure on him."

"Good, you say?" The Desteer's voice put a blanket of tenseness over all of them at this point. "Was it good when Gaije ran away, leaving his fellow *saehgahn* to die?"

Gaije's head sank lower.

"Is it good that he lusts for a *faerhain* when he isn't supposed to? When it should be her decision alone whether he is granted the privilege of entering into marriage with her?"

"No! Listen!" Kalea pulled herself up and attempted to drag herself out of bed. Her leg screamed. It felt enormous and tight.

Bowaen put his hands on her shoulders. "Stay in bed," he hissed.

The Desteer also put her hands up to halt Kalea. "Listen to your friend," she said. "I am merely making an observation. Today, I have seen into the minds of humans and a *saehgahn* consecutively, and have seen contrast. Gaije is not at risk. In his own clan, he would face punishment, but not here. I also fathom he is working hard to right a wrong: to retrieve a stolen *farhah*. A *farhah* is worth more than a hundred *saehgahn* lives. Retrieving this *farhah* for his clan should earn him forgiveness for his cowardly deed."

Kalea settled back into her bed. Poor Gaije. More than his sister's life hung in the balance. His status as a *saehgahn* also faced jeopardy. Who knew what harsh punishment awaited him if he didn't retrieve Mhina? Is that why his grandfather had sent him alone? Perhaps his grandfather had been looking out for more than Mhina when he sent Gaije without any help from his clansmen.

The Desteer turned to Kalea. "And I won't forget you now."

Kalea partially rose and pointed to her chest. "Me?"

The Desteer bowed her head. "Females usually receive *milhanrajea* less often than males. You are human, and a stranger, so I must see into your mind too."

Kalea swallowed. "Does it matter if I feel ill? Will it harm me?"

"No."

Del waved at Kalea. "Like I said a minute ago, just a little startle, nothin' painful."

Kalea pulled her lips in and sighed through her nose. The maiden would see Dorhen in her thoughts. She'd see all the lust Kalea harbored for Dorhen. She'd see Kalea's failure to confess about her association with Dorhen—right after she told this woman about how humans were honest and gave themselves to the Creator. Kalea's face heated. She poised to give the Desteer her permission but didn't need to. The Desteer was already leaning over her.

"Stay in bed," she said, reaching out to grab Kalea's head like everyone else's.

Kalea closed her eyes and braced herself, hugging her knees on the bed. The Desteer's robes smelled like dried river water and lavender. Her hands were hot when they connected to Kalea's skin. A chill traveled across her cranium, and she and the Desteer both shuddered and split.

Kalea opened her eyes and blinked. "Is it over?" she asked.

The Desteer stood cupping her own face in her hands. "It is," she said and proceeded to stare at Kalea.

"Wh-what did you see?" Should she stare back into the elf-woman's eyes, or at her blankets and furs?

"I saw water."

Kalea met her eyes. "Water?"

The Desteer tightened her mouth. "The water…prevented me from seeing much."

Kalea frowned and cocked her head. Her companions standing around also wore confused expressions. Gaije seemed to forget his troubles for the moment.

Kalea spread her hands and returned to clasping her own wrist. "So what does water mean?"

"It means what I already said. It obscured most of my view of your thoughts."

Kalea tucked her chin. "Did you see…did you see Dorhen?"

The Desteer squinted and drew her mouth thin. Her lips were completely caked over in white paint, making it hard to tell how thick or thin they naturally were. The thick layer of paint covering her whole face shimmered in the firelight.

"You invoke a forbidden Norrian name."

"The name 'Dorhen?'" Kalea asked. "He's an elf I know. I expected you to see him in my memories…and my thoughts."

When she mentioned her thoughts, her cheeks turned hot again. Since she'd decided to run away with him, and after he'd taken his clothes off in her convent courtyard, she'd entertained more thoughts about his body than she cared to admit. As shameful as it made her feel, she couldn't deny a certain interest in Dorhen's body and what it could do for hers.

"I'm not sure if I glimpsed your Dorhen," the Desteer said. "However, somewhere in all the water and mist, lingered a figure."

Kalea nodded. She must mean Dorhen.

"This figure sent me a warning. It meant to protect you."

Now Kalea's face twisted. "What do you mean by *protect* me?"

"It's as I said. It prevented my view of your mind."

Bowaen rumbled beside Kalea, "That don't make sense."

"What did the figure look like?" Kalea asked.

"Hard to tell for the most part. The mist and spilling water obscured it. Its hair was like the water. I recall…" The Desteer put her fingers over her mouth. Her eyes spaced out. "Bluish lips. Its eyes were like a frog's."

Kalea shook her head. "Bowaen's right, that makes no sense at all."

A sudden flash of frog-like eyes stared at her from the water in her memory. As Kemp had drowned, the thing in the water grinned. Kalea's heart sped. Her air struggled through her lungs.

"I don't know what you could be talking about," she told the Desteer. Should she ask if it meant Kalea couldn't stay in the village to heal because she was dangerous or some such? Better if it did. She harbored no intention of staying in this village any longer than Gaije. Kalea avoided looking at the Desteer for now. She avoided looking at anyone.

The door swung open. "Is she awake?" a male with a soft voice ventured to ask. "Oh." A ceramic clinking indicated a tray of teacups.

"Thank you, Damos," the Desteer said. Damos had poured six cups of elven tea, and he now extended them to her. The Desteer didn't raise her hands to take his tray. "I won't take that from you, lad. Remember what I said."

"S-sorry." Damos put the tray on the little table by the fireplace and rushed to Kalea's bedside.

Bowaen patted Damos on the back with spirited firmness. "You remember Damos, Kalea?"

"Vaguely." She politely reached her hand out, and Damos kissed it.

"I'm so happy you're awake. Are you feeling all right? Are you in pain?"

"I'm fine, thank you. Damos…?"

"Yes?" Damos's handsome face and warm attention made her feel she might blush again, which didn't do well for her illness.

She couldn't quite find the words. "Thank you."

His lips spread into an adorable smile, and he gave a bow worthy of polite nobility.

Bowaen shook Damos's shoulder playfully. "This little scamp right here, this man is a hero! I don't drink anymore, but I'd certainly drink to his honor!"

Bowaen turned to the elven woman, who constantly held her straight and somber mien. "Desteer madam," he said, "what you got in this hall as far as celebration drink?"

"We have tea." She motioned to Damos's abandoned tray.

"Tea it is," Bowaen said, keeping his cheer. "Del!"

Del obliged and handed him and Kalea both a mug made of thick clay. Because the cup had no handles, Kalea had to hold it in both hands. The warmth of the clay soothed her.

"What a horrible day," Bowaen recounted, "when Kalea almost died. But Damos here, the hero, happened to be there with the power of a dragon at his aid."

"It's a ravian," Damos corrected. "Dragons are ravians, in myth as well as history. Her name is Azrielle." His face didn't show as much excitement as Bowaen's. His eyes lingered on Kalea a little too often for comfort.

"Okay, a ravian," Bowaen said. "And he and his ravian took Kalea up into the sky and they flew. A feat worth celebrating." He sipped his tea and struggled with its temperature. "You don't know how relieved it made me to find you alive," Bowaen said, slightly more soberly, to Kalea's face.

"Sorry I made you worry," she said. She took a deep lungful. She couldn't assume sleep would grace her, but she'd try. Too much plagued her foggy head. What did it mean that the Desteer saw water in her mind, plus a figure with frog eyes?

Bowaen put his hands on both Damos and Kalea's shoulders. "And soon we'll leave here and go back to our own country."

Damos stopped him. "Sorry, what?"

Bowaen gave him a smile. "You know, time to go home. You, me, Kalea, Del."

Damos blinked. "I'm sorry, sir, but I'm not going back to Sharr. I'm going farther north."

"Damos, I could use your help. More of us makes us stronger, and we're about to lose Gaije anyway. And it's dangerous out there. I think Kalea could benefit from your protection."

Damos's eyes darted to Kalea. His face stretched like a frightened deer's. Kalea stifled the panic that welled inside her.

At Damos's silence, Bowaen began fishing through the pocket where he kept Lord Dax's ring, eager to fulfill his duty to escort Damos back to Carridax, or at least give him the ring, which Remenaxice had enchanted with a tracking spell.

Kalea's hand moved before she could think about it. She grabbed Bowaen's arm to stop his gesture. She couldn't begin to guess what manner of crime Damos had committed, but she could *not* go back home now! All well and good if Bowaen could convince Damos to join their cause before returning home, but she couldn't—and wouldn't—forsake Dorhen and her sisters. Had Bowaen forgotten about her mission already? She was still waiting for the sword, Hathrohjilh, to lead her to Dorhen—an outcome Arius Medallus himself had promised her on the day the sorcerers kidnapped him. Not to mention Gaije needed help with his task too.

"Bowaen," Kalea said. She succeeded in making him abort his plan. "We're all very tired, especially Damos. Can we talk about it in the morning?" Her voice turned from a mumble to a growl. "Besides, *I* have to help Gaije track the sorcerers."

Bowaen frowned. Kalea got the impression that he wanted or expected her to accompany them. Did he worry about her meddling with the sorcerers?

Sipping a teacup, Gaije said, "I'll stay no longer than the night. I can't let the sorcerers gain any more distance."

The Desteer nodded in approval of his plan. All their clothing articles hung around the room to dry in the warm space of the fire. The priestess must've been hospitable enough to offer such a respite from the rain. Kalea wondered if they'd all be in a cage right now if not for Gaije, and if all the male elves of the village hadn't left.

The priestess glided over and refilled Gaije's teacup. "Sit," she ordered. Her expression remained frosty despite her nurturing presence.

The priestess approached Kalea again, calm and cool despite the strangeness of Kalea's *milhanrajea*. "Rest. You need it more than they do. You had an infected wound on your leg when I found you, hastily stitched and ill cared for."

Wrapping her hands around her little glazed clay teacup, Kalea turned her eyes away at the elven woman's tone.

"But the wound is clean now and you'll live." She rose from where she knelt beside Kalea, crossed her arms within her long sleeves, and took Gaije's place by the window. She continued her prior discussion with Gaije. "You can rest too. The sorcerer with blue hair... I think he stopped to take shelter. There has been thunder and lightning."

"So?" Del said.

When they all quieted, she continued in a monotone, practically rhythmic speech, "I stayed here throughout the raid, gathering children and young *faerhain*, making sure they found their way to the Desteer hall. He wasn't wearing any metal when I saw him—the blue-haired one—at all. Elves wear metal armor or trinkets, swords and arrowheads. And sorcerers like metal objects too, amulets and jewelry. But this particular 'sorcerer' wore none. He draped himself in cloth, not armor. No buckles, and no sword other than random ones he picked up. No jewelry. I don't think he wants to attract any lightning. If I'm right, he's huddling in shelter now, and you males must sleep or you'll be useless. Let your clothing dry."

"Tomorrow then," Gaije responded.

A long silence passed. No one wanted to disagree. Gaije chewed his lip beside Del, holding a teacup he'd clearly forgotten about. Bowaen fidgeted beside Kalea. His hand rested in his pocket. Damos sat right next to him, the object of Bowaen's mission. Yet he'd also told Gaije he'd help him track the sorcerers and retrieve Mhina. Damos joining them would be the best case scenario. With his aid, they could rescue all those captive in the sorcerers' band.

They were all too tense for the good of their missions, so Kalea changed the subject and asked, "What is this place?"

"It's where the Desteer maidens live," Gaije answered.

The priestess added, "And this is a room for anyone who is injured or birthing."

Gaije stood and retrieved an extra pillow from the other bed. The priestess raised an eyebrow, watching him with interest. Setting his cup down, he approached Kalea. "Need an extra cushion for your leg?"

"Thank you," she responded, and took the pillow to tuck under her knee. She couldn't guess what the priestess had done to her while she slept, but the pain was now concentrated to the gashes themselves, and the swelling had gone.

"So is this building like a Sanctuary of the Creator for the elves?" Kalea asked the priestess.

"It does serve as a sanctuary of sorts—take right now, for example," the priestess said. "But we actually worship the Bright One outside, under His strongest light. This building is simply where the Desteer live, although the villagers hold certain kinds of meetings at the center of this structure."

"That's where the elder frequently meets and argues with the Desteer," Gaije added.

"Argues?"

His smile seemed forced. "Yes. My grandfather does it all the time. It is how they reach important decisions concerning the village."

"Your grandfather is the elder?" the priestess asked, drawing Gaije's attention from Kalea.

"*Ah*," Gaije said the word *yes* in Norrian to her with a bow of his head. "*Sa* Lehomis Lockheirhen," he explained in their native tongue.

His grandfather's identity still baffled Kalea's mind, even in its unsettled, exhausted state.

"Mm," the priestess responded, narrowing her eyes. Her features were most likely beautiful, but her face paint, smudged and cracking by now, made her a fright to be near. Were all elven women this cold? "I'll send word to your clan as soon as my *saehgahn* return, informing them of your status and that you're close behind the sorcerers' trail."

"*Harranhennhi*," Gaije said. "Thank you."

Everyone except Kalea filed toward the door.

"Sleep," Bowaen said, yawning. "That's the best idea I ever heard."

Kalea reached out and caught Damos's arm as he trudged behind the group. His eyes widened at her gesture. "Damos," Kalea whispered.

"Yes, milady?"

She waited until the chattering group was all out the door and lowered her whisper more. "I heard bits and pieces of your conversation with the Desteer."

His breathing sped up. "What did you hear?"

"You are very bothered by something. I'm just very sorry for you."

His eyes darted side to side. "Thank you, but…"

"Damos, have you thought about confession?"

A pained expression spread across his face. He eyed the door. Kalea couldn't tell if he wanted to sprint out, or if he worried someone would return through it.

"You look like you have such a heavy heart," she said in a cooing voice she didn't really mean to use with him.

His eyes softened emotionally again. "Am I that transparent?"

"Not at all."

A quiet moment passed between them.

"Would you like to confess to the One Creator?" she asked.

He shook his head. "I have to go. Please heal well and quickly."

"Damos?"

He walked out the door.

# Chapter 7
## What is Left Behind

Vivene didn't like the way the sorcerers murmured to each other in the dark night. She caught wind of a stalker in the shadowy forest. She couldn't guess what manner of person, but apparently it wasn't the Norrian rangers.

She walked beside the wagon loaded with baskets. Children wept and murmured behind the wicker weavings, lonely and starved for sunlight. She checked behind her, where Wikshen walked at the caravan's midpoint with his wrists bound tightly. Several sorcerers walked around him to make sure he didn't try to escape. She wanted to send him some sort of signal to remind him to make a move. She'd already done her part of the bargain; now, she awaited his help in escaping with the children.

An arm slithering around her neck made her jump. "Hey, Vivene," one of the whores drawled in her high, syrupy voice. The paint around her smiling lips had smeared since the morning. The whores kept as busy with the sorcerers as Vivene did. "I see you lookin' at him, sweetheart."

Vivene clamped her mouth and rolled her eyes. A few of the other whores had already asked her about Wikshen.

Walking in a half-embrace, the whore, who was younger than Vivene although she acted older, pressed one breast against her arm and leaned in close. "Do you look at him a lot?"

"No," Vivene said.

"Well, I do. Why didn't he ask one of us to please him?"

Vivene held her chin high. "I genuinely don't care."

When the whore sucked in a long pull of air while staring at Wikshen, her bosom smashed harder against Vivene. "I was busy, as you know, but I caught the end of his climax. It shocked me to see the two of you. What was it like?"

Vivene grunted through her nose. "Sweaty and a pain in my neck."

"I mean his…you know." She burst into an annoying laugh. "How big was it? I imagine it's huge."

"I don't know if we're allowed to talk about this," Vivene snapped.

"Oh, *foosh*, we're allowed, Vivene…Vivene."

"Stop saying my name."

The whore wrapped her other arm around Vivene's shoulders, making their gait awkward. Vivene stumbled. She hesitated to shrug the girl off because the sorcerers were always watching. Vivene didn't have a lot of room to goof around.

"I was born in Wexwick," the whore said. "Grew up there. And my mama taught me all the tricks." She laughed again. "I serviced so many men: old, young, rich, poor, good, bad, priest, poet, bald, pretty—all kinds. But him..." She gazed at Wikshen again. "That's a stallion." She turned back and nuzzled her nose behind Vivene's ear. "Help me out, my friend. What made Wikshen ask you?"

"I talked to him."

She reared her head back. "Is that all you had to do?"

"Yeah."

"Hmm."

It occurred to Vivene how she might befriend this little harlot. What if she could set her up for a dalliance with Wikshen? Could she make this girl another ally to help her escape? Would Wikshen appreciate a moment with this raggedy, yet attractive young girl? When Vivene chanced one glance backward, Wikshen was indeed looking at them. Blinking, Vivene turned forward again.

"So what should I say?" the whore asked. "Please tell." When Vivene hesitated, more out of fear than anything else, the girl pecked a kiss on her cheek. "Please," she said again. Another kiss. "Please." Her childish play of consecutive kisses and "pleases" continued until one of the sorcerers from Wikshen's entourage caught up to them and laid a hand on the whore's shoulder.

"Wagon," he said.

The whore smiled sleazily at Vivene once more. "We'll talk again soon." And she climbed in to ride with the baskets, followed by the sorcerer, to do that ugly deed with him. The way she'd nagged Vivene had apparently bothered him into readiness. Thank the Creator Vivene didn't have to do it.

The young whore's love cries were loud and shrill—she was notorious for it, and the sorcerer clamped his hand over her mouth while he worked. He warned her of the Norrian rangers who might detect them. This happened among the baskets inside which the children were held.

Vivene hissed through her teeth, having to listen with them. After tonight, she would befriend this girl. The stupid tart wouldn't actually buy into the friendship; she'd use Vivene, and Vivene knew it. Such was the relationship of women. Vivene would use her in return. Even if they didn't become the phony friends she expected, she could use this girl to gain any sort of information, whether the girl realized she supplied it or not. Sure, she'd arrange for the girl to have a good romp with the blue-haired enigma. Vivene could possibly talk to him about it in support of the girl's desire.

Up ahead, one of the torches leading the caravan fell, and a shock reverberated throughout the company.

"It's here!" someone shouted. "Veils! Veils!"

A swell of spell-casting voices echoed among the men. The one with the whore on the wagon bed released the girl's mouth, and she let out one more long moan before he abandoned her and stood up.

He leaned over and extended his hand to Vivene. "You better ride in here," he warned.

Vivene took his hand and he hauled her, with much difficulty, into the wagon bed. Vivene was stretching her neck out, eager to see what was happening, when the man pushed down on her head.

"Stay low. Hide."

Vivene's frantic eyes met her new whore-friend's, who had lost her seductive mirth in favor of alarm. The wagon's speed increased with raucous leaping and shuddering, and Vivene lay flat to keep from flying out. The children's voices in the baskets rose in alarm too. A load of sorcerers leaped and clung to the back of Vivene's wagon for a ride. They were in a chase with someone. The caravan stretched a long way, distance gaping between each cart and person. Vivene lost sight of the cargo wagon in the darkness. Wikshen too.

"The breach is around the corner! Hurry! Get to the breach!"

A horse screamed behind her, followed by the sound of cracking wood. Men yelled. Not many of their torches remained lit, possibly two. They raced along a rock wall. The night air whistled through her ears.

Her whore-friend made her way to a kneeling position in the wagon and hung her head over the side to watch the events behind them. "Did a horse just die?" she asked Vivene, who couldn't answer, of course.

"Get down!" Vivene shouted at her, feeling incredibly unstable in her own place.

The girl didn't listen. Their wagon surpassed the men running in front, while the torchbearers kept up behind.

"Here it is," a sorcerer clinging to the back of the wagon called. "Gonna be a tight squeeze!"

The two sorcerers to the sides let go of the wagon, but the center man remained.

"Get down!" Vivene ordered again.

A denser shadow passed over the wagon and blinded everyone. The many loud sounds of rickety wagon, horse hooves, and yelling were amplified inside the musty cave they'd entered. A great *bang* rocked the wagon as it hit and scraped the cave wall. The whore fell across Vivene. They kept rolling. The horses' hooves thundered on, but slowed. Vivene shook the whore, but the girl didn't stir.

Behind her wagon, the torchbearers and a bunch of other sorcerers entered the cave mouth. The new light revealed the whore lying over her with blood oozing from her head and her dead eyes staring. Vivene shoved the dead girl off of herself. She must've hit her head on the cave wall when they rumbled through.

Though her wagon slowed, the sorcerers remained frantic. They took the wagon horses' bridles and guided them through the catacomb. The torches did no good to Vivene with the men running about, sometimes leaving her to ride in the dark with a dead woman.

Vivene attempted to calm her heart when a strange sound echoed in the stone surroundings. The sorcerers quieted to listen.

"Not good," one man whispered.

"Shut up and grab this rope," another replied.

The loudness returned with the sounds of clashing weapons. Many hits were blind slashes of steel against stone. The animal chirp continued.

"Oh no!" a man yelled. "It's got Kolmus! Kolmus, stop this! Snap out of it! Kolmus!"

Vivene didn't know what that meant. She huddled and shivered among the children's baskets. She'd stand and protect them if necessary.

"Wikshen!"

She perked up at the sound of Wikshen's name. She'd forgotten about him.

"What's he doing?"

Vivene chanced a peek over the edge of the rough wooden rail. The wagon couldn't be raced through this deep, dark catacomb, so she could accomplish the stunt. A few of the sorcerers lingered behind with Wikshen, who stood silent and stern. He showed no fear in his tall, rigid stance. He was staring into the shadow cast by the light of one of the torches. As Vivene's wagon kept moving, she lost sight of the incident around a black corner.

"Just keep moving," one sorcerer told another. "The exit shouldn't be far."

Bird calls and the smell of fresh-baked bread woke Kalea in the morning. Two berry tarts and a bowl of oats lay on the tray beside her bed. The rain had stopped and the sun graced the window instead, drying last night's droplets. The cozy earthen room in the Desteer hall loomed over her with a rounded ceiling, supported by expertly curved wooden rafters. Her old blue kirtle hung from one of them on a branch tied to ropes. Other branches dangled empty where her companions' clothes had dried last night. The brightness of the sunshine implied the waning morning.

Kalea sat up and stuffed a pastry into her mouth. They were late to leave to catch the sorcerers, and Kalea didn't need Bowaen or anyone else scolding her for sleeping in. They'd be anxious at this hour.

The Desteer maiden's voice drifted on the stirred air when the door swung open. "Pace yourself." She approached Kalea's bed, her face paint fresh and crisp this morning. Her blonde hair hung combed and spritzed with more lavender scent. She bent to pour hot tea into the cup on Kalea's tray. "You should eat slowly and sip this tea. You have been terribly ill lately, and your leg will be weak for a long while."

"Doesn't matter," Kalea said after swallowing a big bite of the sweet, fruity tart, the pastry warm, flaky, and fresh. "We have a lot of ground to cover, and I'm sure we've fallen far behind the sorcerers' trail."

The Desteer stood straight again with her teapot and regarded Kalea. "Your friends are keen on following the sorcerers and Damos, but you're not to worry."

Kalea tried to rise. "That's why I have to get dressed."

The Desteer blocked her. "Stay in bed." Kalea shot her a puzzled look. "They left at sunrise. I agreed to nurse you to health as long as you need, and Gaije will return to get you after he finds his sister. He has also vowed to look for the elf called Dorhen. Afterward, he will escort you and Dorhen out of Norr."

Kalea's jaw dropped open. "They left me?"

"I recommended it. You almost died from infection, as well as venom the claws put into your leg."

Kalea fought to stand against all her dizziness, her aching leg, and the Desteer's insistence. "I'm leaving," Kalea said. "I'm supposed to go with Bowaen because he has the sword. Besides, those sorcerers have Vivene and probably Dorhen, so I have to go!"

The Desteer stepped back. "I can't force you to stay."

"Good." Kalea pushed on, shoving a big bite of bread into her mouth. She rose from the elven floor mattress, not too different from the one she'd slept on for years at the convent, and hobbled toward her hanging kirtle. "Why did they leave me so soon?" Kalea asked.

"Damos fled in the night," she answered. "Bowaen was angry to learn of it. Gaije awoke eager to leave also. They didn't want you to take on any more injury, so they made the hasty decision to leave you here and they departed together. They were hoping to catch Damos before the end of the day."

"Why did you let Damos leave?"

"I possessed no right to hold him here. I wanted him to leave anyway."

Kalea yanked her kirtle off the branch and balanced on one leg to put it around herself. The Desteer maiden helped her get into it and lace it before proceeding on to Kalea's shoes.

"You are not being smart, lass," she said.

"When am I ever smart?" Kalea grumbled but knew the answer. She had been smart before Dorhen entered her life. After that, she'd followed the dictates of her raw emotions and her selfish longing! She used to hold her discipline, standards, and self-control in the highest regard. She used to be the one telling the other novices how to do things or what not to do. She might've grown into the human-vestal equivalent of this elven Desteer. Back then, if she had remained "smart," she'd now be tied up in the sorcerer caravan alongside Vivene. Dorhen was the sole reason she had escaped the convent raid. As of today, if she returned to being smart, she'd lose him forever.

The thought made her jaw lock and her throat go sore. Let the Desteer look into her thoughts now and see her passion and sadness and ferocity.

The Desteer stayed out of her way as Kalea hopped around the room, gathering her things. After wrapping the scraps of uneaten breakfast into a handkerchief, she packed them for later. She fastened her washing bat to her belt, its silvery grains flashing in the morning sun. Whether that meant the bat contained magic or not, she couldn't guess, but she let it be a reminder that she was more than a crazy convent girl. Arius Medallus had changed her bat and specifically told her to follow Hathrohjilh, the sword. Kalea would find Dorhen somewhere along its path.

When Kalea had all her things together and no longer required help, the Desteer maiden left her alone and exited to attend her duties outside. Kalea navigated a long, curved corridor with little round rooms on the outer wall until the path opened up to a gallery of sorts, showing a huge central space through archways. Big, dewy windows, glowing in the bright late morning, stood high at the front, above heavy double doors leading to the outside. Embers from a fire last night glowed on a big hearth opposite the doors.

She stepped outside to find a broken scene of lonely earthen buildings with caved-in roofs and shattered windows. Some of the houses' walls showed black scorch marks, and many trees lay fallen and smoldering in the humid air. The first elven village she'd had the privilege to visit, and it lay in wrecked scraps of strewn tools, household items, and broken pottery, hosted by a small rabble of motionless *saehgahn*, young and eager to die for their clan.

Kalea stifled a shocked sob under her hand at her first sight of one. *No time for respects now. I'll say my prayers as I walk,* she thought, and proceeded to look for a new walking stick to keep her from having to hop the whole way on one leg.

The Desteer maiden caught Kalea hesitating near one of the dead *saehgahn*. "They did a great service to their clan and closest loved ones. They will join the Bright One soon, if they haven't already," she said.

Kalea's aching heart needed to know if Dorhen lay among them. The priestess moved about, doing the proper rites for all the dead *saehgahn*. Her face held its coldness as usual.

"I'm worried one of these *saehgahn* could be Dorhen," Kalea explained.

"He's not here," the priestess said. "I've found all the dead that I can see, and they are all clan members."

Kalea let out a breath of relief. Her awful imagination had painted vivid pictures of him possibly trying to make his escape during one of the sorcerer raids, joining up with the other *saehgahn* who stood to defend the village. If he lived, would this clan take him in? That would be the best case scenario. He'd disappear into the hidden network of elven society, making him harder for Kalea to find, but he'd live.

"Wait," the maiden said as Kalea started to hobble away on her partially singed walking stick. "You'll get farther with this one." She handed Kalea a finely carved fighting staff. It was coated with beeswax polish to protect it from the weather, and it even exhibited little carved reliefs and decorative stains in the wood.

"Thank you," Kalea said, dropping her rough branch. "Why are you giving me this?"

"We have many, and the ambitious *saeghar* who used it won't be needing it anymore."

The Desteer didn't motion toward the young teenaged elf who lay mere feet away, dirty and motionless. She had recently fixed his pose to something more dignified with his hands crossed over his middle. Kalea flicked her eyes away fast.

"Hurry," the Desteer said. "You have a slim chance of catching up to your friends."

Kalea took her advice. All day long, she rushed, swinging on her new elven fighting staff through the brush and tangle of one of the forest's thickest areas. Before she departed, the Desteer maiden pointed the way her friends took. They'd cut across the curve of the path to gain on the sorcerers.

Every once in a while, Kalea noticed a broken limb or a bent weed and took it on faith that she still followed their trail. Her slowness was the problem. Panting for air, she swung along, having lost the ability to run. Her arms quickly turned numb. They'd be sore in the morning, but she'd have to get straight back to using them.

It took effort for Kalea to convince herself to stop and rest. She fought the burgeoning emotion inside of her. One little injury to her leg, and she was already out of the group. The chirping and buzzing of insects filled the hot air of a new summer. She sat in the tall grass, surrounded by the flowering bushes common to Norr, with thorns that grabbed her dress and poked her.

Stubbornly, she dragged herself to her feet without using her injured leg. Her muscles flared, begging not to be used again. Maybe she shouldn't have stopped. Now her reluctant arms moved weakly. In her need to catch Bowaen, she forced her body to comply. Her swinging steps shortened.

Later that night, her brain grew numb, and her body kept moving autonomously. Her lungs wheezed. She kept her steady pace, as slow as it was. Her new stitches strained tighter with every step. One more step was what she continuously promised herself. One after the other. If she weren't bent on catching Bowaen, she'd stop to sleep for the night, but no. Catching up meant she'd have to walk longer than they did.

After one last swing of her staff, she paused, standing on one jelly-like leg, and swayed. Her staff fell and gave a wooden *thonk* against a fallen tree on the ground. She dropped as her knee folded against her will to keep it straight. A thunderous pulse rushed through her injured leg. She'd gone dizzy and delirious, beyond thirsty after hours of ignoring her bodily needs.

The bushes before her rustled and parted. A bowstring tightened, but in the dark night she couldn't see who had found her. She tried to speak, but a moan escaped instead.

"Kalea?" Gaije's voice. "Is that you?"

"Oh, Gaije." She panted and smiled. She wanted to rise and greet him, but her limbs didn't move.

"What've you—? Hold on!" He lunged and caught her when she flopped over.

Voices in her ear sharpened to clarity after moments of muffled gibberish. "Dumb girl."

Water trickled over her mouth; some got in and went straight to her lungs. She coughed and found more alertness. She took the water skin and drank.

"What a dumb thing you did," Bowaen said. "Didn't the Desteer tell you to stay put?"

Kalea groaned. "She did, but she couldn't force me to."

"So you idiotically stumbled out of the village to follow us."

Kalea perused the three of them in the torchlight they'd created. "Why did you leave me there? You knew I wanted to accompany you."

Bowaen motioned to her leg. "Why do you think? You can't walk with your injury!"

"I could've shot you, you know," Gaije put in.

Bowaen continued, "Damos ditched us! And here I thought we had him as a friend."

"You implied you'd take him back home, though. He doesn't want to go back."

Bowaen swiped at the surrounding tall grass in anger. "Well, he'd be wearing the ring now if you hadn't stopped me from giving it to him."

The group fell silent.

"The sorcerers left a fresh trail." Bowaen muttered.

"Perfect," Kalea said. "Now that we're all together, I'm coming with you."

Bowaen rubbed his palm over his face and kept his eyes averted, resting his chin on his hand. His bland eyes shifted to Kalea. "They were on the move right after the rain," Bowaen said. "We gave Damos a merry chase until we lost him. He changed his bird into a ravian and took off stark north, but the sorcerers keep heading in a westerly way. Before Gaije found you, we were wondering if we should split up."

"Might as well keep our alliance," Gaije said. "If you follow Damos north, you'll only find a fence you can't climb. Help me track the sorcerers, and we may find out how they plan to cross the fence."

Kalea looked around for her walking stick. Bowaen pointed to it leaning against a tree. She said, "Whatever you three are planning, count me in. I'm going too." All three of her companions gawked, each wearing a dreadful expression for which she didn't want to hear the explanation.

"Kalea, your leg—"

"Is fine, Bowaen. I'm going too. I have to find Dorhen and the blue-haired monster. I said it last night, I want to see him punished. If we can keep this company together, we can do all of those things."

"We can't carry you," Bowaen said.

"I'm not asking to be carried or taken care of!" For the moment, she forgot the ripping pain in her leg. She tensed her arms by her sides to keep from flailing them. "If I fall, leave me behind to be eaten by ants for all I care, but by my Creator, I will walk with you as far as I can!"

And so they walked, after resting for the night. Before dusk the next day, they left Norr behind and found the desolate fields near the border of the Darklands. Eager to catch up to the ones they pursued, they ate while walking. Kalea, of course, found such a task difficult, as she needed her arms to maneuver on her staff, but she kept firm and insisted that she didn't need anyone's help.

Before long, a tall, black fence rose on the misty horizon, stretching beyond sight, east to west.

"There it is," Gaije announced. "The Darklands are on the other side of Hanhelin's Gate. My ancestors crafted it to protect us from the dread creatures who lurk there. It was a great service Norr paid to the whole of the Lightlands long ago."

"Before the elves got into a war with the humans?" Kalea asked.

"Mm-hmm," Gaije confirmed. "Back then, there were a lot of trolls."

"Trolls?" Del's smirk could be heard in his voice.

"Yes," Gaije said. "I suppose your land has no history of trolls like mine does—too much heat and sunlight south of here. But Norr is nice and shady, with trees big enough to accommodate them."

He was right: Norr's white trees were massive. They towered in the distance like a tiered choir of mountains rising above the nearby poplars.

Bowaen snorted. "The elves ran out of creatures to fight, so they fought us instead."

"Gotta fight somethin'," Del put in. "But how could it keep trolls out when they are underground creatures?" he asked. "What's stopping them from tunneling underneath?"

"Tunneling is how they got into Norr in the first place," Gaije told him. "The fence must have magic running deep into the earth."

"Your ancestors built the fence only to *stop* them? Does that mean they're still out there? I mean over there?" Del followed up.

"Of course," Gaije said. "We couldn't kill them all. As far as we know, the Darklands are crawling with them."

Bowaen grunted. "Disturbing thought, especially at a time when we need to cross over."

"I'm going, that much is guaranteed," Gaije said. "I'll go wherever I need to."

Their talking soon died down, and they could only stare at the approaching wonder. It turned out to be taller than expected, made of thousands of thin metal vines weaving around each other in intricate patterns. Kalea never thought it would be called the Darklands for literal reasons, but even the skies on the other side loomed darker and cloudier than their side—surely a coincidence, but its first impression made a fine accomplice to the Darklands' mystery.

Suddenly, Del pointed high. "Over there! It's Damos! See him?"

Damos and his massive, bird-like steed soared high on the other side of the border. The bird—the ravian—glided into the heavy clouds, speedily disappearing from view.

The "Oh, shit," Bowaen uttered next to Kalea tore through the silence of their awe-turned-dread. Now they would definitely be going into that dangerous, uncharted land with or without having to chase the sorcerers.

"Little bastard," Del spat.

"To the Darklands, then," Kalea murmured.

"He must be an idiot," Del added. "Why is he so desperate to leave the Lightlands?"

"He has a heavy heart," Kalea answered. "Something happened to him. He was so upset."

Bowaen eyed her. "Did he tell you? Tell us. It may help to know."

Kalea's arms dropped by her sides helplessly. "He didn't tell me. During my fever and delirium, I overheard his conversation with the Desteer maiden. She did *milhanrajea* on him. She didn't like what she saw."

"She didn't like what she saw in any of us," Del pointed out.

Kalea hummed. "She had a worse reaction to Damos. I hope he'll be all right."

Drawing close to the fence, Kalea couldn't control her urge to touch one of the bars. The cold and coarse texture grazed her fingers like ordinary iron, no strange sensation of magic or anything.

"What if we can't return?" she mused, after a long study of the iron.

"I wouldn't doubt it," Bowaen said, "being made of elven magic and all. No tellin' how dangerous it could be."

"This fence has kept our civilization safe for centuries. Thank the Creator for it," Kalea said, not finished marveling yet.

Bowaen also ran his rough hand along the iron weavings. "Well, I guess it would need a pinch of maintenance after all those years, considering we're crawling with sorcerers now. Either it's broke somewhere, or they've developed magic to counteract its own."

Bowaen tugged at the bars. Nothing happened. He pushed and pulled in his search for an opening, but none of them budged. They walked along it in search of a door, unable to guess how many miles might go by before they found one.

"Just keep walking along it to the west," Gaije said. "We're bound to find another clue to the sorcerers. We'll have to be swift. If it's by magical means, we could miss our chance with them."

"I have an idea," Del said. "We'll climb over it. It's high, but an easy climb."

He made a running leap toward the fence, and an array of lights flickered in that section of the bars to electrify the area he touched. A loud snapping sound echoed in all directions with a bright flash of light. Del promptly fell to the grass and remained lying on his back.

The rest of them ran over to check on him, Kalea hobbling as fast as she could. It had happened too fast, but she swore the flash of shimmering light along the surface of the bars had formed an angry face.

"He's still breathin'!" Bowaen announced, leaning over Del. "Are you all right, man?"

"Goats, that hurt." Del groaned and sat up.

Gaije couldn't keep a smirk off his face. "Thank you for eliminating that option, Del."

"Ah, shut up," he replied.

Bowaen shook his head and helped Del back to his feet.

Del scoffed at the fence. "If it can zap me, why didn't it zap Damos and his ravian?"

"Probably because it's what Kalea said," Bowaen replied.

"Makes sense to me," she said.

Bowaen lifted a fist-sized stone from the ground and pitched it at the fence in a high arc. A smaller flash of light met the rock, and it bounced backward to land on the Lightlandic side of the fence.

Del sniffed. "I guess the Darklands don't want our rocks."

"That settles the idea of Damos's magic bird's ability to fly over," Bowaen said.

Del hoisted his travel bag. "And here I thought of suggesting we build a catapult to hurl us over."

Kalea giggled at his comment, despite their frustration and her aching leg. "Gaije, don't you think…?" she began, chuckling, then noticed he wasn't there. "Gaije?"

Gaije walked on without them.

"C'mon," Bowaen said, serious once again. "No more playing. We'll let the sorcerers show us the way."

# Chapter 8
## What is Found Deep Inside

Vivene collapsed to the grass in the heavy, wet fog outside of the catacombs. The remaining four whores paced around, panting and weepy, some grabbing at their favorite sorcerers' sleeves for reassurance. The sorcerers ignored them and leaned in to each other, arguing about the horrific occurrence.

"Had to have been Chandran," one sorcerer said to the group who'd clustered around him.

"In all my days of observing and performing the summoning craft, I've never seen…" The other sorcerer's statement ended in a silent show of his jaw working up and down. Naked fear lit his eyes.

Vivene shivered and hugged herself, remaining in the grass for as long as she could before they gave her an order—although running straight across the field, away from the cave, would work too. They should all still be fleeing.

One of the sorcerers collapsed and shivered harder than she did. His loss of blood turned his skin ashy. He flopped over to the side, laying his head along the grass blades. The creature they'd found deep in the catacombs hadn't injured him; his brother sorcerers were the ones who added the gashes to his arms and collarbone with their daggers. They had attacked him with no other choice available. Now he needed some caretaking, and his brother sorcerers knelt around him.

"Kolmus," an older sorcerer said to the quivering, injured one. "Tell us what happened in your mind." The one speaking to Kolmus happened to cause the worst of his injuries.

He stuttered in his reply. "L-l-lights, a-a-nd—" He paused to swallow. "A-a voice…in my head." He exploded into a sob. "Couldn't remember who you…you all were. No longer could control myself."

When his voice rattled out of control in his flood of emotion, the older sorcerer patted his shoulder. "You want some drink, son? Maybe you can talk more after."

Kolmus attempted to nod his head but instead went into uncontrollable convulsions. At the older sorcerer's snap, the one listening to them rummaged through his robes for a corked bottle.

"Got some brandy left here," he said, and handed it over. It took skill to pour the liquid into the shaking man's mouth.

Another sorcerer stood with his arms crossed inside his wide red sleeves, surveying the lot of them with a hard expression. "Our survival is thanks to Wikshen. Did you see his exchange of looks with the creature?"

All attention shifted to the blue-haired one, standing with his hands tied in front of him, emotionless as ever. "At the moment those two engaged in a sort of…standoff, Kolmus took his final blow, and we found our break. We will inform Lord Lamrhath of this occurrence, as well as Chandran's work in summoning the creature."

Rubbing his face, another sorcerer with dirt-smudged skin said, "Thank Naerezek we have enough food to continue. Plus these two remaining horses can do as well." The younger of the horses danced around nervously.

"Lost a whore, though," another man replied. "The little fetching one."

Vivene had just endured the hardest ride of her life. The dead whore's blood left a huge stain on her dress. Huddling in the wagon bed had bruised her knees and elbows. The incident in the catacombs mirrored the intensity of her convent's raid. They'd lost two wagons, most of the horses, and a lot of crates during the chase, but retained one wagon strapped tight with the children's baskets. Thank the Creator they hadn't been left to the monster.

"I think we're fine to catch our breath out here in this mist," the older sorcerer said. "We'll sit a while and get some answers out of Kolmus. At least we've made it to the Darklands."

The whole group gave a cheer, but Vivene's stomach churned. No going back now. She'd be nothing but a memory to her parents and superior vestals. She couldn't go back to the catacomb's opening with that creature in there. As of now, her best hope lay in getting away from the sorcerers. Later, she'd see what kind of life she could make in this new land.

Her eyes trailed back to Wikshen, whose demeanor hadn't changed. She hadn't witnessed the whole scene back there, but according to the sorcerers, Wikshen made the creature stop in its tracks. He must be a higher being than that sparkly-eyed thing in the cave. Wikshen still owed Vivene help, but that better not have been it!

Among all the sorcerers' toiling, she made her way over to him. He no longer wore a blindfold, but it didn't mean he bothered to look at her when she approached. None of the sorcerers noted his lack of foot coverings. Whatever effort he'd made to help them escape the cave, if he'd intended so, might strengthen the sorcerers' trust. She didn't step too close to him. She made herself look idle, twiddling her fingers and perusing the goings-on.

"It's been days," she hissed out the corner of her mouth. "I took your boots off like you asked, and they happen to believe I answered your lustful request. Now, when are you going to help us?"

At his silence, she chanced a glance at him, standing with a firm jaw and a forward stare. He made no indication if the cooler air in this region chilled his half-naked body. Despite his imprisonment among them, he towered like a swan over the sorcerers, a strangely graceful structure of a man with blue waving hair, sculpted muscles, and long limbs. A rope dangled around his neck like a leash. The sorcerers must've used it to pull him along to make sure he didn't escape during the chaos.

"Well?" she pressed. "Do you plan to help me at all? Or are you a liar?"

"Be patient…" he said.

Another glance at him revealed how he dug his toes into the dirt like a child at the beach. Her puzzlement over why he preferred to go barefoot resumed. Before anyone could catch her talking to him, she drifted away.

Tumas took a walnut-sized crystal out of his belt pouch and tapped it before cupping his hands around it and speaking into his hands.

"It was a sanguinesent," he said. The small space muffled his voice, but Vivene could hear when she concentrated, pulling her skirt over her knee to casually adjust her stocking. "We suspect Chandran summoned it against your order. He was the only one of us who could do it."

Vivene scowled. So their terror and misfortune was brought on by yet another sorcerer? One supposed to be these people's ally?

"Wikshen displayed some sort of power or superiority over it," Tumas continued. "I will keep you posted, my lord."

He took the stone away from his mouth. From what Vivene had seen, the stones they spoke into only worked one way. Tumas would talk into it, and then later lift a different one to his ear and listen for a short period. Amazingly, this was how the sorcerers communicated over long distances. Who knew what sort of havoc they could do to her homeland with that ability?

A whole day of walking uncovered a fresher, more apparent trail from the sorcerers. Kalea found it hard to celebrate with her pain.

"A struggle happened here." Gaije pointed to some wagon wheel tread marks in the grass. They dug deeper into the dirt than before. The tread marks also began to swerve and the horses hitched to the wagons had dug their hooves in, kicking up clumps.

"Wonder what happened," Bowaen mumbled.

Kalea struggle to catch up. Her fussing had trained them to walk nonchalantly and let her trail several paces behind. They still cast glances over their shoulders at her, though.

Del said, "The sorcerers must've run into someone who didn't like them. Elven bandits?"

"Norr doesn't have any 'elven bandits,'" Gaije corrected.

Del pointed. "Up ahead." The men ran forward, once again leaving Kalea to take care of herself.

*Wait!* she wanted to yell, but it would hint at a want for special treatment, and she'd already told them one hundred times how she needed no special treatment. It hardly mattered, for she also saw the broken crates littering the ground and one wrecked wagon wedged between two trees. She also noticed the dead horse—or rather, the dead horse's skeleton with most of the meat picked off, still hitched to the stuck wagon.

"There's salted fish in this box!" Del announced, but quieted when he finally noticed the horse's remains, red and moist with bits of torn white cartilage on joints twisted around in odd ways. The head lay in the field several paces away, the eyes dulled to staring black orbs.

Kalea covered her mouth as she limped close enough to ogle, but kept a leery distance. Bowaen and Gaije gawked at the mess.

"Good Creator," Bowaen mumbled. "You know what this is, Gaije?"

Gaije's face turned paler than usual. "One of my clan's horses. I would think the sorcerers would unhitch it before deciding to eat it, though."

Del absentmindedly gripped one of the salted fish he'd found when he joined them. "The crates have mostly salted stuff. Lots of flour sacks too."

"Why didn't they just eat the fish?" Bowaen asked.

"Because humans didn't do this," Gaije said. "Can't you see?"

Del's eyes spaced and he dropped the fish. "Chandran."

"Or another creature like him," Bowaen added.

"Or something else," Gaije said.

Kalea held her nose, although the smell hadn't soured yet. The horse had died recently. "The sorcerers ran into trouble," she said.

"That blue-haired bastard," Gaije said next. "He must've turned on them. Easy to believe such a creature would do this."

Gaije darted into the nearby copse and searched around. "Horses ran off!" he reported in a shout.

"What are you doing?" Bowaen called back, standing idle like the others.

"Looking for my sister!"

At that, Kalea set off, swinging on her staff, to join him. Time to look for Dorhen's dead body again. That sense of ill dread she had come to know over the past few weeks filled her once again, now a normal part of her days. She scanned the grass, stirred gently by the wind coming from the other side of the tangled black fence. No bodies yet. She reminded Gaije to look for *saehgahn* and women too.

Their search turned up nothing. The four of them scanned together, reaching out past the circumference of the disturbed site to where the grass was not broken or bent, and no broken crates littered the ground. No dead bodies at all. Nor did they find any of the baskets Gaije had been interested in during his previous scouting missions.

They regrouped at the fence and continued to follow the trail of the escaped wagon. Despite stopping to search, they followed closely. No enemies lingered, to their relief, but they stayed wary. Even though no evidence of dead sorcerers lay around, their loss of wagons and supplies should make them more vulnerable than before.

They followed the wagon tracks and grass damaged by many feet until the terrain became rockier. The earth dipped lower, so gradually they hardly noticed until the grass thinned and disappeared in favor of compacted earth with jagged boulders. The wagon tracks were brushed away once the grass stopped.

"The sorcerers can't have my people spotting signs of their passage through the fence," Gaije said.

Little hints of their presence remained anyway, especially in their haste after whatever violence had struck them. Still no sign of the enemy. As their path dipped lower, Hanhelin's Gate rose higher along a graduating toothy ridge, the perfect setting to find a cave running underneath.

"We have a lot of anomalies in our terrain like this," Gaije pointed out. "Lots of chasms, slopes, and cliffs. It's all damage caused by troll activity long ago. This is exactly why Hanhelin's Gate is here: to stop the violence."

The farther they walked, the higher and more jagged the rocks and broken hill faces became. Many deep crevices appeared along the ridge face, showing a number of false caves to draw the four of them off the trail. The path itself stayed level, though a wagon ride would be miserable, and the carefully swept surface continued. The downpour of a few nights ago must've made sweeping the muddy tracks away difficult.

"Wait," Bowaen said before they retreated. He ventured into the deep curve along the path, which bent the growing cliff face to another angle. Marks left in the soil showed in enough places to announce certain activity. A heavy blanket of moss grew on the side of that nook. He put his hand on the moss and peeled up the edge. It came away from the rock too easily.

"It's fake moss," he nearly shouted. "A façade."

If he hadn't paid the extra attention, they would've moved on and lost the sorcerers' trail for good. He lifted the soft green façade higher and revealed the canvas underneath. The whole thing was a huge tarp covered in many small, green thread knots, like a carpet. Real moss covered most of it, as this particular spot faced northwest. The threads were in the process of losing their dye to the weather, which added to the ruggedness of the picture.

"We found it?" Del asked.

Bowaen tugged at the tarp, and Gaije helped him rip it halfway down, revealing a gaping hole wide enough to slip one wagon at a time through.

"Oh, Bowaen," Kalea said, and hugged him.

Even though a sense of relief washed over her that they might easily find their way across the fence, Gaije's shoulders and back stiffened and his jaw tightened. He said, "If Mhina wasn't in danger, I'd take this information straight to the palace."

"Wonder how long they've been using this opening," Bowaen mumbled.

"For decades," Kalea answered him, losing her smile. "Long enough to make regular visits to the Sanctity of Creation, particularly the cathedral in Carridax."

Bowaen grunted in response.

Gaije started for the cave mouth. "Let's go."

"Hold on," Bowaen said. "We gotta approach this with caution. The enemy or thing which attacked the sorcerers might be in there. And we don't know how deep the cave will go."

Bowaen went straight to work building a small fire on a bald patch of ground. "Del, gimme your striker."

Del dug through his pocket and tossed him the item he always used to light his pipe.

Bowaen said, "I'll make torches. When the first torch weakens, we'll light the next one, and so on."

"Shouldn't we wait until morning?" Del asked. He fidgeted with his pipe on its strap, in a show of craving to settle in and have a smoke like he usually did.

"Not a good idea," Bowaen said. "Those sorcerers are weakened, tired, and not too far away. Besides, it'll be dark in there whether we go in by day or night. Gonna take a minute to get the fire going. We'll hurry through the passage as fast as possible, and then decide what'll happen on the other side."

Gaije paced back and forth while Bowaen worked. "I wish we could've ambushed them before they left Norr. Over in the Darklands, we won't have the cover of the trees to stay out of their sight."

"Well, things got complicated," Bowaen said without raising his eyes from the little flames he tended.

Kalea settled to the ground to rest her feet and her sore leg. She tucked her chin and averted her eyes from the conversation. They'd failed to construct a solid attack plan because of her. She'd done nothing but slow them down from the start. Maybe she *should* stay behind and go home.

"Del! I need branches! At least three of them!"

Grumbling all the way, Del wandered off into the trees.

"Kalea," Bowaen barked in a manner similar to the way he ordered Del around. She shook out of her gloom, but couldn't keep it off her face. "We might catch the sorcerers soon."

She sighed. "I know." He was going to tell her to stay out of the way.

"What does your friend Vivene look like?"

Kalea blinked. "She's full-figured in a comely way. She has dark hair, and she's cocky."

Bowaen chuckled. "Sounds like my kinda woman. And Dorhen, you said he has brown hair around Gaije's length?" She nodded. "Eyes?"

"His eyes are bright. Greenish, with some blue."

Bowaen tightened his mouth and bobbed his head. "He'll be easy to spot among the sorcerers' band. If he really is good like you say, he's as much a prisoner as Vivene. When we get 'em out of there, they might be in bad shape, so we'll need you to tend them. They might have injuries for all we know."

Kalea cocked her head and studied his face. She appreciated his kindness, even if he wasn't sincere. She possessed no healing skills; she didn't even have enough talent to mend their clothing. The best she could offer was to wash their garments, and she hadn't managed that chore the last time she tried.

"Del saved some salted fish from the wreckage," Bowaen went on. He held a tiny cookpot, provided by Lord Dax, over the fire and poured water from his waterskin into it. Next, he added the fish from his bag.

"That'll be too salty to eat unless we let it soak for several hours," Kalea warned.

He shrugged. "It's the best we can do. Gotta eat something, and the dried stuff we got from Dax is running out. We'll save some fish for

Dorhen, Vivene, and Mhina's return, and then *you* can cook it up for them."

A pathetic laugh burst out of Kalea.

"What's so funny?"

She wiped her eyes. "You're trying to make me feel less lousy. Do I look so useless?"

"I never noticed."

"Well, it's not working," she said. "I'll stay out of your way—as I already told you."

He stirred the fish around in the hot water with a twig. "You joined my group promising to cook and wash and pray. I'm holding you to it. You'll do what I order because I'm in charge here." He ended his statement by peering up at her from his focus on the fish. A smile dug into his prickly cheeks.

When the dried fish softened in the boiling water, Bowaen handed her the pot along with a wooden spoon from his supplies. "Eat a few bites of this," he said, "but save some for the rest of us."

Kalea graciously took the spoon and broke off a piece of the dead, staring fish beneath the water. It tasted as salty as she expected, having turned the whole thing into a salt water stew. She didn't complain. Even though this meal would make them extremely thirsty, her stomach didn't care. The fish was small, so she decided to quit after three bites.

Del approached them and threw down three sturdy branches, and as he took the pot and spoon from Kalea for his turn to eat, Bowaen got straight to wrapping the ends of the branches with cloth ripped from one of their spare shirts. Afterward, he doused them with oil.

"I don't know how long the tunnel will be, so we'll use one torch at a time."

Once they'd all eaten their share of the fish, Bowaen kicked soil over the fire. "On your feet," he said to Kalea.

She hesitated and pointed to herself.

"Are you coming or not?"

She cleared her throat. "I assumed you'd tell me to wait out here."

Bowaen gave her a smirk. "You assumed, and that's all. I won't stop you if you prefer it that way, though."

Kalea climbed painfully to her feet, stifling the moans and groans she wanted to make. "I'm coming," she said.

"All right, then."

All four of them ventured into the gaping cave mouth with their first lit torch. "Take care, but be swift," Bowaen reminded them. "We don't want to spend the night in there."

The torchlight revealed jagged scratch marks on the inside of the cave where it had been roughly carved for passage, although plenty of stalactites and flowing rock growth on the walls kept its natural appearance plain. The sorcerers had likely found the cave a long time ago and carved out tunnels large enough to suit their needs. The wagon wheel tracks showed on the smoothed, dusty floor a ways in.

"We got 'em, friends," Bowaen said with a fierce grin at the tracks' appearance. He handed the torch to Gaije and unsheathed Hathrohjilh in case they ran into the sorcerers down here—or the sorcerers' enemy.

"They still have some horses," Gaije said, dipping the torch low. "One extra besides the one pulling the cart."

Several nooks came around the bend along with alternate pathways, but the wagon tracks showed clearly enough which way to go. The underground road turned out to be quite sophisticated. Wooden doors, hammered together roughly, were affixed to some of the nooks.

Bowaen put his finger to his lips. "No more talking," he whispered. "Someone could be dwelling here."

Their first torch dimmed already, and despite what he'd said, they didn't find any other light sources, not even glowing behind any of the doors.

"I can pick those locks," Del whispered close to Bowaen. "They could be stashing any kind of treasure in this place."

Bowaen shook his head sternly and reminded him to be silent.

After a time, the party eased their guard. No one seemed to linger down here. Long into their second torch, Kalea developed a doubt that this cave would end in the Darklands at all. Who knew if it even had an exit? The cave could very well stop at a dead end, where they'd find the wagon and all of the people involved. They'd either have to fight their way out of the predicament or sprint back the other way, praying to get out and escape the sorcerers' pursuit. This cave might be wide enough to accommodate wagons, but it felt like a worm's hole when fighting crossed her mind. She'd never be able to flee the sorcerers on her bad leg.

However, the thought of finding Dorhen in mere minutes put a new starch in her back. She swung along on her staff faster, taking care not to tap it on the floor too loudly. Her washing bat hung on her belt as always, ready to be used for defense if needed. She was more attuned to swinging it than the fighting staff.

The corridors wound to the left, then right before branching. The wagon trail went through the stranger option. Gold shone along the archway.

"Oh, dear sweet Creator," Del said, and Bowaen echoed him. "This is a gold mine."

"No," Bowaen countered. "Gold in a mine doesn't look like that."

Their group stopped at the shining wall. It looked as if the rock had been painted with melted gold. Thick and heavy, it glistened in their torchlight. Gaije put the torch closer to the gold, and it flashed across all the gentle hills and valleys of the stone.

"Did the sorcerers…put this gold here?" Kalea asked. The gold layer covered the rock like a painted stripe along the tunnel opening, spanning two hands thick and arching over their heads.

Del ran his hand along the surface hungrily. "Why would they decorate this doorway? I mean, nothin' else in here is as pretty. They didn't decorate any of those other passages. This place has been ugly as the Swine since we got here."

"What do you mean about swine?" Gaije asked. "Are you saying this place looks like wild boar?"

Kalea put her hand on Gaije's shoulder. "It's an expression. The Swine is actually a demon who looks like a pig. He's the greatest enemy of our God, the One Creator."

"I see," Gaije said. "Del is invoking an evil entity when he thinks something is ugly."

Kalea couldn't help but drift back to her convent. The stained glass windows, the arched ceilings, the altar. Her home. The everyday sights, sounds, and scents. The massive room with naught but two rows of floor mattresses where she had slept, an image tainted by her last memory of it. Sorcerers coming out of the air, grabbing her sisters' hair and clothing. One girl being raped in the corner. And those two eerie men in red who chanted and tapped golden poles on the floor. The sounds of their rhythm and voices echoed, burned into her ears.

Gaije placed his warm hand on her shoulder after she shuddered. "Are you all right?"

*Are you all right?* Dorhen would ask her. He cared so much about her.

*Dorhen. I'm not all right.*

"Kalea."

She blinked her eyes and finally regarded Gaije's concerned face; her frown deepened to find he wasn't Dorhen. Their shared elven heritage marked the end of Gaije and Dorhen's similarities. Gaije's eyes were narrower, less bright, and not as sad as Dorhen's. His nose was smaller too. His pale skin complemented his red hair, which hung in spiky locks with small braids and copper cuffs.

"Sorry," she said. "Did I look strange just now?"

"No." He took his hand off her shoulder and fidgeted in place.

Beside them, Bowaen scolded Del, warning him not to chip gold off the walls as he'd been tempted to do during Kalea's flashback.

*Gold.* Kalea closed her eyes and thought about the convent raid again, this time on purpose. Golden poles. Gold. A stranger named Mr. Tal had asked Father Superior for gold as she listened through the door. It seemed like ages ago already. Gold. The sorcerers wanted it. Kalea put her hand on the wall and ran her finger pads across the lumpy surface, heavily coated in the smooth treasure.

"Not you too!" Bowaen hissed. "We're not taking any gold. Now let's go before this torch goes out."

"No," she said. "Don't you see what this is?" The three men stopped talking. "It's the entrance."

They stared at her.

"The entrance to the Darklands," she elaborated. "The gold is important to the sorcerers' magic. They use it to channel magical energy. They need gold." She traced her pointing finger up the wall and across the golden archway. "This gold is holding back the magic of Hanhelin's Gate. *That's* the magic they used to cheat the fence. I'm sure directly above this arch, the fence is running this way. It's a magic-blocking arch."

"We actually found it," Bowaen said. "Well, let's go. C'mon Gaije, you got the torch."

Bowaen backtracked a few paces to retrieve his jewelry lockbox, which he'd set on the ground for the moment. "I might consider consolidating these goods and drop the box off somewhere," he said grunting. "I'm getting too damn old…"

Bowaen stopped short at a wall of black which hadn't been there before. Shining in the torchlight, two huge eyes like sparkly nuggets—diamonds—filled the eye sockets of a dry, skeletal face.

Kalea wanted to tell her friends to run, but instead a shaky nonverbal moan squeezed out. Readjusting their second torch set off a fiery shine in the eyes and illuminated the rest of the face, a face which ended in four huge fangs like a cat's. The jaws opened, and a long tongue lolled out to taste the air and release a high-pitched, rapid sound blending a bird's chirp with a cat's purr.

Kalea's arm jolted the other way—Gaije yanked it to make her follow him through the gold-covered arch. They ran deep into the corridor, barely missing the curved walls and wooden support posts found in a wider area. In the wider space, they might stand a better chance of fighting the creature. She couldn't look back as Gaije pulled her arm desperately forward, not caring if it hurt, not caring if her leg couldn't handle the running. She'd dropped her elven fighting staff. No telling if

Bowaen and Del were on her heels—she could only hope they'd reacted as fast as Gaije had.

Their sprinting feet echoed in the wide open space as they stumbled to a stop. She glanced back at the entrance and saw only shadow. No Bowaen or Del. What happened to them? Her stomach burned with dread until they both trudged in. They walked slower than expected, and Bowaen slogged behind Del under his heavy lockbox.

Kalea limped toward them with a sigh of relief. "What happened? Did you kill it, Bowaen?" she asked. His eyes were dull, and he didn't answer.

"Watch out!" Gaije tackled her to the floor as Bowaen's sword whooshed over their heads. If not for Gaije's reflexes, she would no longer have a head by the sound of the blade whistling through the air and the stirring breeze it created.

"You are both guilty," Bowaen's dull voice muttered.

Del's voice followed like a watery ripple. "The guilty must be sorted." Gaije hauled Kalea away from them.

"What's wrong with you?" she cried.

The two men walked slowly and exerted sudden bursts of energy in random patterns, but saved them mostly for attacks. Gaije dropped the torch and threatened them both with his drawn arrow. Neither reacted to the threat.

"They're bewitched!" Gaije said. "I have to kill them!"

"Don't!" She grabbed his bow, and they both toppled over as Bowaen sprang forward and narrowly missed them again. They scrambled to their feet and traced the curved wall to gain space.

Across the way, the creature entered the room, a tall thing in long black draperies, its hands hidden in the folds. No lids housed those shimmering eyes, and its head lacked skin, only a hard bony surface save for a little white fur beard on its chin and dried skin sticking up like small mousy ears at the back of its head. It let out another shrill chirp that sent painful chills through Kalea's spine. The nugget-like eyes weren't eyes at all; they were clusters of gems embedded in the sockets. They bored into her eyes, wanting her to return the gaze. She had seen them already, so why was it so important?

"Gaije, shoot the creature, please don't shoot the men. Please!"

He didn't need the instruction. The first arrow burrowed into the creature's robe accomplished nothing. The chirping sound continued in a mocking manner, and the arrow disintegrated.

Gaije inhaled slowly, drew, and blew along his arrow's shaft until the arrowhead erupted in a bizarre green flame. Kalea stared in awe. He released it.

*Twok!*

When the arrow embedded itself in the creature's robes, the flame caught and roved across every drape of fabric until it met its starting point and extinguished. The robe regenerated itself behind the flame, and the creature continued as if nothing happened.

The blood drained from Gaije's face.

"Desire corrupts. You are both guilty," Bowaen said. Then his voice and Del's chimed in unison, "Sinners must be sorted."

Kalea shrieked, having nearly forgotten about them. Gaije pulled her to him in the last possible instant as the sword's wind kissed her face. The creature watched, still wanting Kalea to look at its eyes.

*Its eyes.*

Gaije thumped Bowaen's head with his bow and drew another arrow. Kalea reached and grabbed it again.

"Don't do that, Kalea!" Gaije yelled.

"Don't kill them! They're mesmerized! We have to snap them out of it."

"I'll kill them before they kill you!"

"Be logical!"

He jerked her away from another attack. Kalea untied her washing bat and held it poised. Gaije returned his aim to the creature, so Kalea took the opportunity to face down the men as they trudged forward, waiting for another burst of energy. If not for her wound, she'd dodge and prance around them all she needed. She stood ready, knowing she might get hurt.

When Bowaen sprang again, Gaije also reached for her. She dodged Gaije instead. When she went in the unexpected direction, Bowaen's blade narrowly missed Gaije's throat.

Her leg wound ripped as she landed on the floor behind Bowaen. Del conserved his energy, brandishing the heavy pipe he both smoked from and used as a blunt weapon. She ducked under the swing of his pipe, pain raging across her body from her strained stitches. On his follow-through, she reared back and banged his head with her washing bat.

His eyes focused and he blinked at her, lowering his weapon. When he proceeded to look around, she threw her arms around his head to cover his eyes, dropping her washing bat with a wooden clatter.

"What's the goblin-cockin' idea?"

Gaije tripped Bowaen to the dusty stone floor and wrestled him to stay out of the sword's path.

"Don't look at the monster," Kalea told Del.

The creature moved around again, having lost one of its thralls. When she released Del's head, it approached too close for him not to gawk. Its glittery eyes demanded attention, and even she took a moment to stare in awe. The creature's mummified skin put off a dry must. Hot, dry breath rushed through its teeth. The chirping call whistled loudly in her ears, rattling up its throat from deep within its belly. Del's eyes clouded over again, but Kalea remained unaffected.

"Desire corrupts, and this one is pungent," Del said.

The creature's sleek tongue licked at her face like a snake. A long, scaly finger snaked out of the creature's robe, followed by the palm and one other finger. Additional barbs grew along its wrist, black and slender like a cricket's leg. She couldn't hit Del on the head again because she'd dropped her washing bat, and Del now held her arms down.

The creature's black, slender hands wrapped around her face and its bright eyes burned. Moist, flexible appendages like earthworms slithered into her ears from its palms. Exploring deep into her head, it irritated more than it hurt. The wrist barbs pressed into her jaws to hold her head steady. She stared at its eyes helplessly.

A sound rumbled in her head. *What is the purpose of this one which can't be enthralled to sanguinesent dominion?*

The mental inner voice was a crisp opposite to the creature's outer voice. Everything outside Kalea's mind froze; her body disappeared, pain and all. Those blindingly bright eyes became the center of the world.

*As is usual, the elf is immune to our persuasion regardless of the fact that the natural desires of its kind outweigh even that of the lowliest man, but this one is human and therefore puzzling. If it will hold its motions, its purpose will be known.*

The creature squeezed her face harder and probed her mind with a mental potency she could never hope to shake.

*Many lusts and desires exist as is usual with humankind, but additional factors may explain its immunity to sanguinesent dominion.*

*So are you a sanguinesent?* Kalea forced the thought into her mind, and the creature paused.

*This one mocks its conductor during its own observation.*

A rumble of other voices echoed faintly in her head. The creature communicated with others like it, though she couldn't make out what they talked about.

*One wishes to eat its flesh beginning with the face,* the creature continued, *but this one must be delivered for inspection. If it would keep stationary, the observation will be completed.*

Kalea tried to squirm—to bring the rest of her body into her consciousness. A bright light erupted around them, and the creature's hold on her head flinched. The light drowned the shine of its eyes.

*This one remains immune.* The creature's voice cracked despite its continued insistent body language.

Kalea forced thoughts of what she'd forgotten around her, and the real world materialized in her vision again. The talon-like hands loosened.

*Difficult.* The voice weakened further.

The tentacles in her ears slackened. The light brightened, and she couldn't tell if its face withered away or if the light obtruded on her vision. The sanguinesent let out a shrill physical chirp as if in pain or annoyance and released her face, and the vines exited her ear canals. It faltered away, disappearing into the fog of light.

Kalea took a moment's respite, hoping the creature had run away and left them alone. She rattled from head to toe, bursting with adrenaline for survival. She whirled around, remembering the two mesmerized men.

Bowaen was straddling Gaije with the edge of the sword against his throat, trying to force it down as if to chop an onion in half. Gaije's arms shook; the leather palms on his bracers were nearly cut through as he pushed back on the blade's edge.

Picking up her washing bat, she lunged to hit Bowaen on his head, then whirled around for Del as he poised for another attack on Gaije. Both of them snapped back to their senses with one simple hit on the head.

Gaije collapsed in exhaustion on the floor when Bowaen let up. A moist red line ran across his neck; Bowaen had only nicked the skin. The two men staggered and rubbed their eyes for a moment. The sanguinesent had retreated.

"What was I...?" Bowaen stopped to rub his face again. When he motioned toward Gaije, the elf lurched away and held his bow shaft before him in defense. "Easy, man, easy," Bowaen said. "What's the matter?"

"What do you mean, 'what's the matter?'" Gaije yelled. "Kalea, get behind me!" He kept his eyes on Bowaen and shifted them to Del, who had also lost his lethal demeanor.

"It's all right now, Gaije," she said. She admired the surface of her gleaming washing bat, an old tool, well-worn by many women before her. It retained its signs of wear and tear, but somehow, when Arius Medallus had given it back to her, it had been strengthened with some kind of silvery petrification. It had cured Bowaen and Del of their enthrallment.

"Gaije, I..." Bowaen began again. "Was I fighting you?"

"Yes, you were!" Gaije said.

Kalea made her way over to calm him.

Bowaen huffed. "I didn't... I couldn't. Dear Creator." He turned away, worrying at his nose bridge.

"You were bewitched, you and Del," Kalea said.

"I can't believe it," Bowaen murmured. "I lost myself there." He turned to meet Gaije squarely. "Gaije, I'm sorry. If I'd known, I would've..."

"Would've what?" Gaije asked. "Not attacked me and Kalea?"

Bowaen turned away again, as if he couldn't bear for anyone to see his eyes. "I didn't know."

"None of us knew, Bowaen," Kalea said. "It's okay now. My washing bat broke the spell quite easily." She tightened her grip around the handle. "I won't let that monster have you ever again."

"Don't think about it any longer, Bowaen. We should leave this cave," Gaije said.

Kalea noticed he held his palm to his neck. "Oh, Gaije." She rushed to him as fast as her aching leg allowed and patted his bloody throat with her handkerchief.

Gaije narrowed his eyes. "What's that light?" At his question, the men followed his gaze to Kalea.

She shrugged. "I can't tell where it's coming from."

"'Cause it's coming from you!" Del pointed. "What are you doing there?"

"Nothing." She inspected herself and patted her torso. At her bosom, she hurriedly fiddled for Dorhen's moonstone, which put off the bright light. As she marveled, its light dimmed. Something about it comforted her, as if it meant Dorhen still lived. He was her angel. She tapped the pendant and shook it as its glow died in her hands.

In the returned darkness, Gaije said, "Let's leave quickly."

"Can't believe we lived through that," Del said in the background. He retrieved the fallen torch.

Allowing her to finish tending his wound, Gaije informed them, "The three of us, we're alive thanks to Kalea."

# Chapter 9
## What is Lehomis's Trouble

Lehomis kept a careful distance throughout the trip to and from *Laugaulentrei*. Tirnah put aside her natural warmth and vibrancy in favor of the appearance of a mourning widow. She was a good *faerhain*. She rode quietly atop the wooly black ox, holding Trisdahen's ashes in a clay urn, with Lehomis, Anonhet, and five other surviving *saehgahn* walking alongside. She bothered not to speak, except to Anonhet for practical purposes, and somehow managed not to cry. She could've at certain points, and none would blame her. On the stretches between neighboring clans, widows were bid to keep quiet for security purposes, but Tirnah... She didn't cry at all.

A long trip they endured, winding around and over the ancient troll mounds and across the high bridges over the chasms. The damage the trolls had done to Norr in an ancient age appeared more frequently on the northwestern side of the country. The thickest section of flora grew around the heart of Norr, where the path vanished and Tirnah's ox squeezed carefully between the tightly grouped trees. At some parts, sections cut out of the sides of the trees made for easier travel. When they found the path again, it bridged over giant whitewood stumps or broken trees that clung to life. One of the clans lived in this region, having carved out their village and also trained the trees to grow in certain ways.

Lehomis had planted himself at home for so long, he had almost forgotten how difficult Norr could be. Every twenty or thirty miles, they stopped at another clan's village for the night, where the Desteer maidens greeted Tirnah and symbolically granted her an extra amount of strength to help her go farther. They reminded her to remarry and have another child as soon as the mourning process ended. Lehomis still awaited the news of her impending pregnancy. She hadn't mentioned anything like that yet, and neither did the many Desteer cults she stopped to visit. If she was pregnant, she'd catch even more advice to marry sooner, in which case Lehomis planned to step in and shut them up. He wouldn't have her rushing into such a decision. He could, and would, be her guardian for as long as she required. She didn't need anyone's superfluous pressure.

When they reached *Laugaulentrei* after nearly a week of travel, their group somberly continued their appointed duties. The five other *saehgahn* set up camp a long walk from the lake while Lehomis borrowed one of the available gondolas and rowed Tirnah out to the middle, with Anonhet sitting next to her for support.

The lake was as beautiful as he remembered. Over five hundred years ago, he'd said goodbye to his last son. The name, *Laugaulentrei*, meant "lake of the dead tree." The giant weeping tree in the center of the lake wasn't actually dead; it lived with vibrancy and long-lasting blooms. A shrine to *Lin Yilbarhen*, or the Bright One, functioned on the little island, tended by a small group of resident Desteer maidens.

On the gondola ride to the island with the tree and shrine, Tirnah emptied Trisdahen's urn into the water. The Desteer members met them on the island, and Lehomis and Anonhet were made to wait in a private booth made of wicker so Tirnah could carry out the rest of the ritual without any prying eyes.

As they sat side by side, Lehomis could feel Anonhet's curiosity. Little noticeable exhalations would exit her nose, but she refrained from asking him any questions. Lehomis had done the ritual several times, once for his wife and again for his deceased, unwed sons. This was his first mission to escort someone else and wait in the wicker hut.

Instead of talking, Anonhet listened hard for hints of voices from outside. Her youth made her curious about things she'd experience soon enough.

"Grandfather," she whispered another half hour later, "Tirnah told me the secrets of marriage. About the marriage ritual, what a wife does for a husband. She didn't tell me about this, though."

Lehomis made a smile she'd barely see in the sharp dots of light from the sun shining through the woven walls. "Not for a long, long time will you need to know about this."

She didn't say anything else for a few long minutes. Her knee bounced. "It's so sad."

"Nothing to it, really," Lehomis offered in the slightest of whispers. "You do stupid things at the Desteer's direction, like scoop up water and then pour it out. You take off your clothes and dunk yourself in the lake… Then we go home." At the end of his statement, Lehomis turned a small degree away from her.

"What after that?"

"The healing begins."

"Do you think Tirnah will remarry like she says?"

Lehomis tightened his mouth. "I wish she wouldn't. I don't like to see her like this. And she doesn't have to, despite what you'll hear other *faerhain* tell her, because she gave two children to the clan. She can retire and focus on other things from now on."

"She'll feel better when Gaije and Mhina return."

Lehomis smiled and patted her knee, now calm.

And now, they headed home. Tirnah hadn't spoken yet, but she met their eye contact and offered weak smiles at the short exchanges of dialogue.

As many Desteer maidens as they had met, none alluded to any knowledge of Tirnah being pregnant, at least not in Lehomis's earshot. His worry over that detail quieted. The Desteer would've told him about it for safety's sake, especially while traveling, since he was the one in charge of their group. Now settling on the idea that she wasn't, he could relax a bit, regardless of such a thing being a shame in this time of their clan's low population. Her slate was clean, and she could remarry as she wished. He wouldn't encourage it for a few years, but when she deemed herself ready, it would mean good news for one of the as-yet-unmarried *saehgahn,* as well as possibly any number of children added to Clan Lockheirhen.

The elves' and ox's feet were treading loudly through the old dead leaves when one of the accompanying *saehgahn* fell, his leg plunging deep into the earth. His brother lurched forward quickly enough to catch him, and Lehomis lunged to help pull him out.

"An old trap," Lehomis said at the brittle, broken limbs lying across the large pit. "You're lucky your brother's so quick!"

Collapsing to the ground, the lad hissed as he attempted to peel up one leg of his torn *sa-garhik.* Blood ran down his calf.

Tirnah slid off the ox and knelt beside him. "Poor *saehgahn,*" she cooed, and motioned for Anonhet to hand her a salve from her travel bag. While she waited for the younger lass to rummage, Lehomis didn't miss Tirnah's eyes perusing the *saehgahn*'s muscular leg. She was looking in *that* way already.

Lehomis huffed and turned away to wait for them to finish their tizzy. A few measly scratches marred the lad's leg, for crying out loud. If Tirnah hadn't acted so fast, Lehomis would've hauled him to his feet and shoved him to keep walking.

The lad limped when on his feet again. Tirnah pulled his arm toward the ox.

"*Faerhain,* that's your steed," the lad protested.

"Nonsense," Tirnah said. "The funeral is over, and you'll be of better use to me if you hold your bow ready from up there."

Lehomis approached her, motioning to the hole in the ground.

Before he could speak, she put her palm over his face, as elves do to shut each other up or block their view. "No, Grandfather, I won't hear it. If Anonhet can walk this terrain, so can I."

Lehomis scoffed. "All right, listen: ox to the outside, and you *faerhain* walk at the heart of the group. If there are any more pits, one of us will find it instead of you."

So the six *saehgahn* walked in an arrow formation, with the new bow-ready ox rider at the outskirt and the two females behind them.

Once they made it home, Lehomis longed to collapse. He never minded traveling—in fact, he used to live up north in the Darklandic wilds—but there were some trips he hated to take. He dropped Tirnah and Anonhet off at Tirnah's house and hurried to check in with the *saehgahn* he had left in charge of the village. Gaije and Mhina still hadn't returned, which was obvious when they found the house empty, but no other mishaps had occurred during the days of his absence, thank the Bright One.

Lehomis selected a different group of *saehgahn* to escort the next widow to *Laugaulentrei*. They couldn't afford to send them all out at once or there wouldn't be enough *saehgahn* left to protect the clan, so all the widows and their escorts took turns. The process was tedious, but they all understood the value of patience.

He dragged his feet over the threshold to see how Tirnah was getting along. She had agreed to move into Lehomis's house and donate hers to someone who lost their house in the raid. Next summer, they'd build a new house for her, Gaije, and Mhina to inhabit. It would be a good change for them. Widows didn't always move out of their houses, but they sometimes did for any logical or beneficial reason.

Anonhet passed him in the curved gallery encircling the sitting area with the hearth. "Just going out for some water, Grandfather," she said with a new life in her voice. They were all happy to have completed that journey.

He found Tirnah in the bedroom, packing a trunk with all the things she'd take with her. She stood quietly, staring at the armoire which housed Trisdahen's old clothes. The two doors were closed, and he could imagine how her eyes were probably not really seeing the grains of wood. Lehomis cleared his throat.

"I know you're there, Grandfather."

"How long do you think you'll need to pack? I can go get the horse hitched—"

"You know something, Grandfather?"

Lehomis lowered his chin. He didn't offer a word of response; he waited for what she'd say.

"I never thoroughly knew him." When she turned around, she cocked her head, her little frown and laced-together eyebrows giving her the appearance of a puzzled child. Still no tears. She turned back around and ran her fingers across the carved, dark walnut surface of the armoire. "In here is where he kept his clothes—the *sa-garhik* he'd wear when at home the few times he graced this house." Facing him again, she spread her fingers and counted three of them. After a few seconds, she bounced her point to the fourth finger. "What a strange existence. Don't you think?"

Lehomis shook his head and worked his jaw.

Her quizzical expression continued, her sight grazing the ceiling beams. "In my first few days as a *faerhain*, he visited my clan village. A huge landslide struck us after a particularly wet season. We lost a few lives and two houses. So the palace sent a troop of *saehgahn* to us, to help rebuild. That's when I saw him. It went about as you would expect. I watched him at work. I caught sight of him when he took his shirt off. I spied on him when he bathed. He was a beautiful young thing."

Lehomis attempted a joke. "Of course, he's from my stock."

Tirnah laughed out loud and threw a pillow at him from the bed. Her laugh came out strange, though, and Lehomis didn't try to push the lighthearted mood. Her action brought forth a child-like side of her. She was still young—extremely. To Lehomis, her birth would've felt as close as yesterday if she had been born here.

After laughing, she covered her mouth and turned her back. "Later that evening, after watching him bathe, I made sure he got a token." A fluttery giggle followed. "My little brother told our father, and he went into a rage. Trisdahen hadn't been in our village long at all."

Her serious and baffled expression had returned when she faced him again. "I didn't know him, and I didn't care. A few nights later, we were together on the marriage pelt he'd hunted. He did well. We were married. And when we returned from the forest, my father attacked him." Tirnah smiled. "I didn't expect it. Such an adventure I'd found. After a spectacular fight, both *saehgahn* were bleeding. My father calmed down because there was nothing he could do, in truth. The Desteer validated our marriage as good. We moved here, to his clan village. We didn't stay with my family as custom says, because of my father's difficulty with it all."

"I see," Lehomis said. "You never told that story. He didn't either."

"Because he wasn't around to tell it," Tirnah said, quick on the heels of his statement. "Don't you see?" Her eyes perused the room. "He was summoned back to the palace, drafted again, and added to the king's guard. We couldn't leisurely get to know each other. Now, I loved him,

Grandfather. He was kind and patient, and whenever he returned on leave for a short period, I made my best recipes, made the house pleasant, did my wifely duties."

She paused to shake her head, and Lehomis might've caught her lip quivering. "I don't think I ever learned his favorite color. But a fine *saehgahn* I chose. He gave me Gaije and then Mhina, and…" Her hand hovered in the air before her for a brief second.

"And what?"

Now her eyes finally watered. "These clothes. It's all he left in this house besides us and some of his weapons. But the palace didn't let him keep his royal garments. There's no memory of him imprinted here!"

She burst into tears. Lehomis took a step and put out a hand so she could hold it, but she threw her arms around his waist instead and sobbed into his shirt. "Grandfather!"

Hand holding would've been more proper with one such as her, but Tirnah had always been the emotional type. He stroked her soft hair and hugged back. She squeezed him. Her wailing escalated to a level he couldn't bear. His own throat closed up and his lungs shuddered. He'd never cried for any of his grandsons' deaths, nor any of his sons' deaths for that matter, but Tirnah had a way about her!

Her knees buckled, and he grabbed her before she fell. Her upper arms were so thin in his grasp. Both of them awkwardly sank to the carpet, next to the bed, where she continued to nuzzle her face into his breast, releasing sobs and tears into his clothes. He bit his lip to stop his own emotion. His fingers combed into her hair. Somewhere in the confusion, she got his long black braid and gripped it tight in her fist. Mhina would go straight for his braid when she got upset too.

He lost himself in the chaos of her weeping, hating her situation. *Saehgahn* died all the time, and it was supposed to be okay. Everyone kept their chin up and said honorable words about the dead elf's bravery; they saved feelings of despair and loss for when *faerhain* died. But this *faerhain* had lost much, not just a husband, but twenty years of memories they should've collected in leisure, not to mention two children. She'd lost her whole family in one night!

Before he knew it, his arms embraced her, crushing her in, his nose in her hair detecting the fragrant oils she used. His teeth gnashed in his effort not to cry. His eyes burned, but no tears came yet.

A door closed on the other side of the house, the sound echoing within the earthen walls, and Lehomis noticed that he and his granddaughter-in-law had wound practically into one large ball. He couldn't let anyone see them this way. He pulled away and shushed her.

"C'mon, lass, sit on the bed. Here's my cloak to wipe your nose." He wiped his own nose on his sleeve and peeked at himself in her little silver hand mirror. His eyes were red; Anonhet shouldn't judge him too harshly if she caught him crying, but whatever that was he'd gotten into with Tirnah was scandalous.

Tirnah's wailing had softened by the time Anonhet flew into the room. She hardly noticed Lehomis standing there, to his relief. He took the opportunity to slip away and see about the horse needed to haul all of Tirnah's belongings away.

The move into Lehomis's house wasn't too hard. Tirnah left Trisdahen's clothes and the wardrobe in the old house for the next family; instead, she brought his weapons, medals, hair ornaments, and all the other military accolades she'd donate to Lehomis's collection of family relics. *Faerhain* who intended to remarry didn't typically keep any mementos of past husbands. Lehomis would pass on to Gaije whatever the lad desired from the lot when he returned. If he returned. Dear Bright One, he'd beg nightly for Gaije and Mhina's return.

Tirnah hadn't broken down since that one occasion, to Lehomis's relief. Her wailing sounded a bit too much like his wife when any of their sons had fallen in war or accidents. After she died, he didn't have to listen to the wailing anymore. A good batch of his sons survived their mother, leaving Lehomis forever alive to deal with their funerals.

On their sixth day in the new housing arrangement, Anonhet came running over the hill to find Lehomis with Tirnah under the kitchen pavilion. "There you are!" She brought with her a young *saehgahn* from another clan.

"Elder Lockheirhen?" the lad asked.

"That's me, yes."

The lad panted but did the formal bow and handed him a folded letter.

"Who's it from?" Lehomis asked.

"From our Desteer."

Tirnah joined Lehomis's side as his eyes finished roving over the handwriting. He grabbed her arm tight. Her eyes widened in anticipation, matching the wideness of his.

"Their Desteer," he said to her. "One of them encountered Gaije. He hasn't found Mhina yet, but he's well."

"I'm going out, need anything?" Lehomis asked Tirnah later that day as she toiled away by the hearth, arranging her collection of tea canisters on the rough wooden shelves to the side. She hummed merrily. They hadn't spoken of what happened between them a few days ago. He didn't know exactly how she felt about it, but after the letter about Gaije, she'd bounced back from her moods quite fast.

She had seemed to settle in well. She busied herself with unpacking, and when she ran out of things to unpack, she rearranged Lehomis's kitchen and other parts of his household, and she chattered away with Anonhet. Lehomis couldn't deny he loved every moment of it. They transformed his deep-burrowed cave dwelling into a home, not just a shadowy hole decorated with rugs and pictures. Back when he and Anonhet inhabited it alone, the place could be pretty quiet; the best he could hope was for Anonhet to come into the sitting space and ask him for a story, or she'd hum to herself while busy. The soft noises ascended to energetic echoes of joy through his rocky corridors.

At his question, Tirnah peered up from her work and gave him a deep smile. "How about some thyme? You only have a pinch."

He smiled back. "Sure."

Anonhet accompanied him toward the bustle of town. Despite Tirnah's progress, an odd silence hung between Lehomis and Anonhet. She talked more to Tirnah than him these days. Something about their long funeral trip had altered her thinking. He didn't pry.

"So," Lehomis began, "are ya going to make the big decision soon, lass?"

From the corner of his eye, she shrugged. "I haven't thought about it lately."

"Hmm." Something bothered her. "Would you like to stop by the bathing pools? I'll keep watch for any Desteer."

"No thank you, Grandfather."

"Suit yerself… Hey, if you see something you like at the market, a pretty garment or trinket, I'll buy it for ya."

"Thank you, Grandfather."

He wished he could ask if she worried about Gaije, but that could be interpreted as inappropriate. *Faerhain* were burdened with making their own educated decisions for *daghen-saehgahn*. No one could do anything to sway her, which included Gaije's mother. That wasn't to say Tirnah didn't try to convince her to choose Gaije when they were locked away in private—and Lehomis wouldn't put it past her—but the consequences could be dire if someone were to find out Tirnah had been coaching Anonhet on the matter.

Before he could try to propose another conversation, another *faerhain*,

Tilninhet, burst from her house and ran down the path toward him.

"Elder!"

"What is it?" Lehomis started, opening his eyes wide. "What's the matter?"

Tilninhet thrust her hands at him, and he dodged because they were in public. He took her hands in both of his and held them instead. She whined and threw her face to his breast, similar to what Tirnah had done.

"Tilninhet, please!" he hissed.

Anonhet gaped at the scene. "Anonhet," he ordered, "go on and meet me at the market. Pick out whatever ya like." Anonhet ran off at his word.

Leading Tilninhet by her hands, Lehomis guided her back toward her house. "What's the matter, lass?"

"It's Togha!"

Lehomis paused halfway along the little footpath to her doorstep. "What about Togha?"

This was Togha's mother. Also a widow, she lived her life suspended in perpetual mourning and used to rely on her son a lot for emotional support. One of her brothers served as a partial house-guardian for her, but Lehomis helped her out a lot too. He owed it to her.

Standing together on the path, her hands went to his lapel to fiddle with it, her face red and distraught. She was older than Tirnah, but still of a fertile age and lovely by Lehomis's standards, with her dark cherry hair and lavender eyes. He took her hands away from his lapel and held them to stop their wandering.

Her words came out stuttering. "Togha, he's—he's gone."

Lehomis sighed. "He was drafted, lass. He's putting in his time, you know? *Saehgahn* duty." He disregarded her doubtful head shaking. "He has to do this so he can attract a wife and fill your house with lots o' grandbabes."

"No," she whined. Tears poured down her sculpted cheeks. "Something's amiss, Elder." She tried to fill the void between them, but he held her at arm's length. "Togha's missing!"

Lehomis scoffed. "No, he's not!"

"Yes, he is! He hasn't delivered the letters in months!"

Lehomis stopped himself before letting out another yelled word. He started walking her toward her house again, hoping to talk calmly on the doorstep. Moisture worked to fill the sky anyway, and if it rained he'd prefer to be under the awning. Although if it rained, she'd certainly invite him in, and he couldn't do that. Not again. When she got hysterical like this, she harbored a bad habit of getting amorous too. This lass was mad to a degree. She, of all people, should've gotten remarried long ago, but she had blatantly refused the advice due to her deep love for her late husband.

"Togha's gone, I'm telling you, Elder!"

He shushed her gently. "Take a deep breath."

She tried it once, but her breathing accelerated until she sobbed. "Togha doesn't come around anymore!"

"Now, now, listen. He's probably been rotated to another route. The military does this sort of thing. They might've assigned him a new position. Maybe he's a page in the palace now. Wouldn't that be nice, Tilly? He'd be all safe and warm in there every winter. And in a few years, he'll come home and get married. Won't that be pleasant? Having lots of grand-*saeghar* and a few *farhah* running around your house, giggling, fillin' it with life?"

Her mouth clamped shut as if to stop herself from talking—and breathing. When she finally opened her mouth, she gasped for air. "You don't understand, Elder. Togha... I told him."

Lehomis stopped walking, and his forced warm smile dropped. "Told him what?"

"I told him the truth!"

Lehomis's head grew light. His stomach boiled. "When?"

"Soon before he stopped showing up with the letters." She paused to swallow. "You see, my brother didn't like him. He's suspected something about my little *saeghar* all these years. You don't get hair that black from my late husband. My husband was blonde!"

Now he shushed her harshly. "Not so loud!"

"They fought, Elder! My brother punched my Togha clear across his beautiful nose. I had to reset it."

Lehomis grasped her upper arms. "Tell no one! I'll banish your brother from the clan, you understand?" She sobbed before his face. "Togha is your son, and you're entitled to him."

"Elder," Tilninhet said, wiping her face, "anger disturbed my Togha. After I reset his nose, I was cleaning the blood off his face. He wanted an explanation. His uncle was so bothered and surly all the time, and Togha deserved the truth. So I told him."

Lehomis let her go and scoffed. "You shouldn't have!"

"No other choice revealed itself! How else could I have helped him? Togha has always struggled with fitting in, especially with my brother and in-laws. He is nothing like his father—not my husband! He needed to know, not only because my brother rejected him, but for the sake of everything else in his life. He *had* to know."

Lehomis bent over to cup his face in his two hands. "This is not good."

"Well, why not?"

"What if the Desteer find out?"

"They can cut all my hair off, for all I care. I don't want to remarry anyway."

Without looking up, he waved a hand. "So you think Togha, being upset by this…news, got into a rage and ran away from his service?"

Tilninhet's hysteria calmed. "Something like that, yes."

"Did you tell your brother the same news?"

"No. Only Togha. My brother is left with his guessing."

Lehomis straightened his back. "Listen," he said, "I'll send a letter to his branch, asking for an update on him. The letter will prove you have nothing to worry about."

She clasped her hands. Her wet eyes sparkled. "Oh, thank you, Elder!" She reached for him again, and he dodged. She smiled now. "Would you like some tea, Elder?"

"I really shouldn't." Shutting off his words, Lehomis stood there and sighed, hands on his hips.

"Elder?"

"Yes, Tilninhet?"

"My roof. It's been leaking."

He rubbed his hands over his face one more time and nodded. "I'll come around and fix it this afternoon."

# Chapter 10
# What is Togha's Trouble

If he had known how bad it would be, what a horrible place the Darklands really were, Togha would never have left his homeland. He sat on the grass with his wrists tied. Pain pulsed through his bruised cheek. At least they didn't break his nose. The pain of when his uncle broke it had recently subsided.

Togha had become a lost *saehgahn*, stuck in a negative space between two worlds. He'd left behind him an uncle who hated him and a mother who… He didn't want to think it… She was crazy. For so long, she'd praised Togha's dead father. How tough, how honorable, how fierce he was! He sang, he told stories, and he painted the earthen murals in the sitting room. His father was a myth Togha could only dream of meeting, but he prized that myth like a favorite possession. He'd been wearing his father's old black poncho ever since he'd grown big enough to fit into it, and he memorized by heart the points of his father's creed. In his struggle to fit in, Togha used to believe that his father held the key to the mystery of his own identity. So he held onto his father's memory—or rather the praises his mother sang, since Togha possessed no memories of his own.

And then one day, after eating the cookies and drinking the tea Mhina had decided to serve him every day when his route brought him home, he'd popped in to see his mother. He made one smart comment in his uncle's presence, he couldn't remember what, and they both tore into a fight. Afterward, Togha's mother told him the worst news he'd ever heard. The *saehgahn* Togha thought was his father had turned out not to be his father at all. Elder Lehomis had helped conceive Togha.

He hated the elder. Always. He'd refused to believe her until he checked his nose in his mother's mirror. Reality hit, and what the mirror showed him made more sense than his mythical father ever had. How could he not have seen the resemblance all those years? How could his mother have lied? A deathly law warned elves not to lie. Togha couldn't stay in that village any longer. He couldn't stay in the military, either. He couldn't even stay in the country. So he ran away and found his way to the Darklands through a cave. And now here he sat, tied and bruised.

One of the Clanless *saehgahn*, the one with the orange tabard, dropped a carrot before him. "Eat," he said, and walked on.

Togha took it and brushed off the remaining dirt. The Clanless, a faction of Norrian rejects, boasted a fair amount of power in the Darklands. They protected several farms across the land and took a percentage of their harvests as payment. They were a ragtag group of rough-looking elves, some of whom bore the *sarakren* brand, while others had been maimed in battle.

Togha might've joined them, but he happened to have an object among his possessions they didn't like: a grass-made scroll with a human figure and odd writings all over—some kind of spell. He'd found it in a hollowed tree stump while foraging in the woods. Togha couldn't blame them: the scroll would've earned him a beheading back home.

These elves were more lax, yet more chaotic than their old Norrian civilization. A few of them traveled with a wife. Two of those wives were human and one a *faerhain*. At first, the *faerhain* had shown Togha kindness, even after his scroll got him in trouble, but her husband jerked her away and shot off harsh words in Norrian for her never to go near him. An expected outcome. Togha was more interested in the *saehgahn* with human wives and how they'd kiss and paw at each other in front of everyone. Public displays of affection were also illegal back home.

A loud donkey braying beside him tore his eyes away from one such wickedly interesting sight. Haggis, his beloved pet. At least the Clanless treated her with kindness.

A hand grasped Togha's hair from behind. It uncannily seemed as if Haggis had known that would happen and meant to warn him. Togha had pondered that theme more than once along his and Haggis's long journey north.

"Stand up, shit stain!" Riminhen, this group's leader, yanked Togha's hair until he obeyed. "Time to move."

"Where are we going?" he asked, and Riminhen jerked his hair again.

"Wouldn't you like to know?" he snapped.

Togha had already survived this treatment for a week. As hard as he'd tried to overhear his captors' conversations, he couldn't figure out if they were headed to a dungeon or a chopping block or… He couldn't think past the dungeon or chopping block ideas.

An hour later, one of those low "walking clouds" passed over them, to the curses of the Clanless. They couldn't have avoided it.

"Keep your wives close," Riminhen warned. "Bad folk like to walk in obscurity."

He was right. In the depth of the cloud, they were overrun by a band of thugs wearing yellow and brandishing long, curved knives.

"Stand down, Vandalyns!" Riminhen roared. The Vandalyns, Togha knew by now, were a faction of sorcerers. This wouldn't end well.

The Clanless raised their bows and fired. The Vandalyns used the stones embedded in their leather gloves to create glowing shields which deflected the projectiles. Their curved blades buzzed to life with swirling wires of lightning. They threw their knives, and the dangerous, cutting blades of electrical power shrieked through their opponents. After a certain distance, the curved blades swooped and returned to their throwers.

Togha leaped backward to create as much distance as he could. He couldn't go far because he was tethered to the wagon where the females and cargo rode. Braying in panic, Haggis trotted toward Togha to stand beside him. He petted the side of her hairy neck, happy to have her devotion, but he couldn't let her get hit with a stray arrow or flung lightning-knife. Thank the Bright One a horse pulled the wagon instead of Haggis.

Togha turned to the women who huddled under a thick skin tarp in the wagon. The tarp was reinforced with chainmail—an implement invented by the Clanless to help protect their female companions.

"Hey," he called to them from outside the wagon. He winced as Haggis screamed at a sorcerer who drew too close. "Ladies!"

One of the haughtier women peeked from under the edge of the tarp with a tight brow. "What do you want?" she asked.

"Cut me loose! Please!" Her eyes narrowed fiercely. "Regardless of what they think of me, I'm *saehgahn*! I'll help!"

She threw the tarp back over her head, and Togha growled. Beside him, the donkey threw out a side kick to fend off another sorcerer. She'd reached her wit's end and kicked at the air now, dancing in place and braying.

When the tarp flap jumped up again, Togha stared in shock. The woman brazenly stood and braced a foot on the wagon rail.

"Come 'ere!" she ordered. Togha stepped closer, and she bent to cut his ropes with her own knife. "Don't make me regret this, pretty boy!"

Togha shot her his best smile, and her face flushed. With his hands free at last, Togha leaped onto the back of the wagon with them and rummaged through the bags for his own belongings. She wouldn't regret her decision to free him, but he also wouldn't stick around. He threw his bag over his shoulder, unsheathed his knife, and proceeded to cut Haggis free. Now the donkey pranced around, kicking and braying. He worried for her. If his beloved pet died from one of those shocking knives, he'd never forgive himself.

That infamous scroll had been shoved back in with his things. Togha unrolled it for a quick reminder of what he'd read before. He dropped it as the wagon rattled; one of the Clanless members' bodies slammed against it. Scrambling in fear, he lifted the scroll, rolled it, and put it back into the bag.

He leaped off the wagon and practiced filling his diaphragm with the proper amount of air. The scroll's drawing showed wavy lines flowing into the outline of a human figure. Smaller sketches around the largest one showed stances to be used. Despite all his adrenaline, Togha got a handle on his breathing. He found a good spot, not too close and not too far from the Vandalyn attackers. One of them and at least two of the Clanless lay dead already. The sharp sound of lightning buzzed in the air—the loudest, most horrible sound, worse than Haggis's voice.

Togha went through the hand motions the scroll recommended, which helped to channel the proper energies and the right use of the air he'd put into his diaphragm. If he aimed wrong, or if a Clanless stepped in the way, he'd be in deeper trouble.

Togha stepped forward, extended his hands, and released a sharp, powerful, *ha!* A tremor traveled through the ground from under him into the group of Vandalyns. Beneath their feet, the ground softened. They stumbled, some falling, and most lost concentration on their shield and lightning spells. One appeared to break his ankle as his foot sank too deep and he fell wrong.

Togha's disturbance, as little as it was, gave the Clanless quite an edge. Three more Vandalyns died in the brief moment of their failed spells. Togha pumped a fist and hooted loudly. He reached for Haggis's bridle, and suddenly remembered his poncho. He couldn't leave his mythical father's poncho behind.

He returned to the wagon and rummaged some more. He didn't bother the women, who stayed hiding under the armored tarp. They had missed his amazing deed which helped their *saehgahn* to win the skirmish.

After Togha found the garment and threw it over his head, he noticed more people, these wearing black, charging in to join the fight. An older woman with a drum scurried around with them. She took her drum in hand, pounded it once with a skin-covered beater, and caused more earthly tremors to disturb the Vandalyns as well as the Clanless.

The people in black swarmed the wagon and grabbed anything they could. A tall man with a black tabard and half-shaven head threw the tarp off the Clanless women, who screamed and vacated the wagon. Leaving these three groups to sort out their differences, Togha grabbed

Haggis's bridle and took off in a random direction.

A ways across the field, over a hill or two, the people in black swarmed around him. Togha jumped with a yelp. He lurched and fell at their sudden jostle, leaving Haggis to shuffle and bray on her own. They didn't grab him. The people in black laughed and celebrated, moving on to gather on the grass ahead.

"Damn Vandalyns!" one of the men with a half-shaven head yelled. Three streaks of blood decorated his face.

Togha remained shaking on the ground until a hand tousled his hair.

"Welcome, young man," an elderly voice croaked behind him. "How lucky were we to find a friend out in this unforgiving mist?" She moved around to look at his face and gave him a smile. She wore a round, thin drum on her back with the beater hanging from her belt. "The Mastaren is always blessing us, even from his throne in Kullixaxuss. He created these mists originally, did you know?"

Staring, Togha absentmindedly shook his head. He hadn't the foggiest idea what those words meant.

"You did good work back there," she said. "Come over here. Let's enjoy a hearty meal from our spoils. What's your name, young...elf?" She finally noticed his ears.

"My name is Togha," he said cautiously.

"Togha the elf. An elven Wikshonite, now that's a spectacle I've never seen before. How magnificent!"

Grinning ear to ear, the old woman pulled on his poncho to lead him to her friends as they grouped in tightly. He let her. Apparently, these folk weren't disgusted by any of his oddities, neither his elven heritage nor the spell they had likely witnessed him casting during the skirmish. He sensed they wouldn't mind his bastard lineage if he shared that secret. He thought of asking her what a Wikshonite was, but didn't. He'd learn by observation soon enough. If they expected him to know any details, he'd feign being new to the position. For now, they had food and a welcoming presence.

The old woman with the drum nudged him right into the tight circle of black-clad hoodlums and said, "This is Togha, everyone. One of our own who escaped those snobbish Clanless."

Many faces in the group shot him smiles and enthusiastic barks of "welcome." Togha said hello back. They were a strange lot indeed. If not blood markings fresh from the skirmish, the men and women wore black paint to decorate their eyes. Some wore black star-shapes on their faces.

"Nice to meet you, Togha."

The musical voice drew Togha's stare away from the others. The woman sitting beside him held out a fluffy slice of bread. He wanted to thank her, but his throat dried. He blinked a time or two before taking the bread. Her eyebrows curved in pity. He almost couldn't see them from the odd way she'd cropped her hair across them. The rest of her black hair was braided and pinned up behind her head. The black paint around her eyes made them appear bigger and set off their rich hazel color. Her smile held his attention like a spell itself.

"You must've been through a lot." She pointed to the red and purple rope marks entwining his wrists. He nodded, still unable to speak. "Don't you worry anymore," she cooed, "I'll take good care of you." She patted his back. "My name is Metta."

# Chapter 11
# What is Growing from the Earth

Lamrhath took the whisper stone from his ear. So Chandran had managed the feat. He'd specifically ordered the fool not to summon a sanguinesent. The spell needed more testing, and the foreign creature needed evaluation and restraint. Instead, the hot-headed maniac had decided to go through with the spell. Lamrhath's authorization to make his transition into a servant of Naerezek must not have been enough for him. The sanguinesent summoning spell came out of the book of Ingnet, a whole different pixie pettygod, an untested entity.

Lamrhath sent a message back through the stone asking about Wikshen's status. It usually took a few hours for each message to reach its destination. By the time his new message was delivered, they might have more developments on the enigma of Wikshen. He also ordered them to regroup and prepare to put his plan into motion. Now that they were in the Darklands, warnings of Wikshen's ominous threat would travel far and fast, and Lamrhath would help set it off.

"Vibrations," he said into the stone cupped in his hands. "Lash him. Knock him on the head. Scream at him. Put vibrations into his body. My Wikshonite contact says it riles him. Watch what you do with any herbs," he added. "Don't burn any near him, or even let him smell them unburned. My contact warns that they cast various effects over his moods, and we don't need any more unpredictability than we already have."

Lamrhath thought fast. He could only say so much into the stone, or the words would distort as they struggled through the facets to be received by its brother from which it had been cut. "We're about to begin our campaign with the first settlement. If you come across any village not displaying a red flag, make Wikshen attack it."

Finished with his message, Lamrhath tied the red ribbon back around the stone and put it away. Now to consider the matter of the wandering sanguinesent. It might be put to good use.

Outside the caves, in the fresh air, Hanhelin's Gate loomed behind Kalea's party on the tall slope. A cooler, damper air greeted them out here on the Darklandic side. Though it was late afternoon, a mist drifted over the deep green hills. A heavier shroud of airborne water buried the horizon. Despite their exhaustion, they hurried to move away from the cave exit in case the sanguinesent stalked them.

The Darklands. Kalea never would have dared to think in her wildest dreams that she might one day step into this land. The maps at her convent showed an empty space in the Darklands' location, unlike the Lightlandic side which boasted little inked cities and trees. The cartographers had no way of knowing what lay on this side of the continent.

As depressing as the scenery appeared at first, Kalea liked it. What would roll over each next hill? An old dirt path appeared after a few rising and falling slopes of earth, ruts carved between the grassy knolls, though nothing else around hinted that life went on here. On every high point they climbed, they tried to survey the land, hoping for a glimpse of the sorcerers' caravan ahead, but found nothing except a heavy fog hanging low and growing thicker the farther they walked. Soon, they'd be walking through it and following the sorcerers' trail would increase in difficulty.

They were running out of their rations. The road became grassier and grassier until it disappeared completely. Now, they had to travel by the position of the sun and stars, but the clouds moving about overhead usually obscured their view. No new signs of the sorcerers or Damos.

Del lit his huge pipe and puffed it fast as if he needed to soothe himself. "Hold on," he responded as they waded through waist-high grass toward a forest on the horizon, discussing the earlier events. "You're saying that...*thing* in the cave...had us hypnotized?"

"Yes, I said that. And will you put that out, you knobhead?" Kalea replied.

"But you and Gaije weren't? Why not?"

"Who knows? Maybe because I'm a woman—or because I belong to the One Creator."

"Doesn't sound right," Bowaen said. "I belong to the One Creator too."

"And so, does Gaije belong to the One Creator?" Del asked.

"If the Bright One is anything like your One Creator," Gaije answered.

"But he's also an elf," Kalea said.

"So?"

"Actually, the creature's voice in my head said Gaije couldn't be hypnotized because he's an elf. Must be because I'm a woman..."

"Well, how in hell did it happen to us?" Del asked.

Kalea panted, having to work harder than the rest of them to get around with her staff and bad leg. At least the conversation distracted her from the pain. "How? Because of its eyes. What did you feel about its eyes?"

"I hardly remember much except an urge to snatch them out of their sockets and sell the bleedin' things in Dawdler's Alley. They'd bring me a fortune." He finished with a long drag.

"Exactly. You wanted the diamonds for their value, so the creature used them to hypnotize you. It wanted me to look at its eyes. It stared at me, but I couldn't figure out what it wanted."

"Why didn't *you* feel like stealing them?" Del asked.

"Aside from the fact that I don't steal? I was so scared it wouldn't have crossed my mind. All I saw were big teeth and no skin and Bowaen swinging his sword at me."

Suddenly, she could feel Bowaen's presence as he led the way. He didn't make a sound or turn, but walked stiffly on.

"I'm sorry, Bowaen. It's over now. Let's move on and be wary. The creature might've followed us outside. If you ask me, don't look at its eyes if it finds us again."

Kalea's stomach ached like it had when she used to fast in an era long ago. Their rations had run out already, including the salted fish they'd hoped to save for their three escapees.

Hope rose when they spotted a mass of trees on the horizon. Food might be found within it. The grasslands didn't offer much more to eat than a locust found nibbling on the grass, no hare or other game to catch and eat. Plenty of boisterous carrion birds mocked them, though. A forest could be hoarding anything from game birds to edible roots.

None minded the detour, as they'd completely lost the sorcerers' trail. Despite his poor sister's plight and his training in stretching hunger far, Gaije agreed to alter their course to the forest. He acknowledged the wisdom in restocking their rations while they could.

Once they reached a certain distance from the dense, towering canopy, he reported a sweet fragrance drifting over the hills toward them. The rest of them sniffed the air, but the humans couldn't detect what an elf could from so far away.

"It is fruit," he said, "good-smelling fruit." They all hurried forward.

"Gaije, you're amazing," Kalea said. "I would die if we parted ways now. Thank you for joining our group." She sent him her warmest smile but couldn't tell if he received it. He gave no reply.

As they approached the forest's entrance, the sweet fruit smell tantalized the humans' noses. Apples. None hung from any visible trees, though. Kalea and Del, the two younger humans, wanted to run, but

Gaije warned them to stay quiet. Anything could be dwelling under the canopy.

The forest offered no sounds to welcome them, no animals or even insects. Their feet sank into the soft, silent ground. The evergreen trees apparently didn't drop their needles. When Kalea grazed one of the branches, it tore her sleeve and scratched her arm, drawing blood. She ignored the annoyance, eager to find the source of the sweet smell of apples growing stronger.

At least a mile inward, the fruit trees finally appeared. Big yellow apples enticed her eyes and hungry belly. They all charged forward, picking the biggest specimens from low-hanging branches and biting into the firm, juicy meat.

Bowaen tossed one to Kalea first, and then proceeded to help himself. Kalea savored the juice running over her tastebuds and swallowed gladly.

She opened her mouth for another bite when a sudden dizziness halted the action. She swayed. "Hey, Bowaen," she said. She'd gotten accustomed to his friendly warmth; lately, she'd been turning to him whenever she felt ill or off in some way.

He let her wait a moment as he dug into his own big apple. Her vision blurred. The image of him biting into the apple, its juice running through his chin scruff, dissolved.

"Dear, sweet Mother. You live. Please awaken and live."

Kalea's stomach ached and buzzed with enough pain to make her forget her leg with its strained stitches. Her eyelids fluttered open, but it took her a while to make out anything.

"Good, good. Open your eyes. Don't close them anymore." A hand, callused but gentle, touched her face.

She tried to talk, but her voice came out as air.

"You need drink water first. The poison, it dries you out. You not live anymore. But first, you sit up. Be calm, you'll be dizzy."

A light finally flickered over her eyes and she blinked, trying to see something. Anything would do. The light bloomed, and shapes appeared and shifted. She was inside a musty building. A cool night breeze wafted through an open window. Close beside her, a shadow morphed into the shape of a person. She could tell the shape of the head, but not the face yet.

"There now. You can focus, yes? Sit up now. You drink, or bad might happen."

The gentle hands were now strong, pushing her upward. She wanted to groan, but that too only happened as air. The man's other hand put a cup to her mouth and poured water down her throat, freezing all the way to her belly. She accidentally inhaled some and coughed violently. During her fit, a voice finally resonated in her throat.

"What is—?" she got out but couldn't finish the question. She searched around the background for her friends. No one accompanied her besides the stranger. When the coughing ended, she admitted to feeling much better and snatched the cup from him to guzzle the rest.

"Bring more!" he called out, and followed up with harsh-sounding foreign words.

A door swung open and a woman in a dingy red veil entered with a clay pitcher, tiptoeing toward her. Kalea sat on a bed with her legs tucked under a moth-eaten blanket. The man rose and took the candle from the woman to set aside for more light while she poured the water. The woman kept as much distance from Kalea as possible. After the cup was filled, the man ordered the pitcher restocked and chased the woman away.

Too thirsty to puzzle or question, Kalea felt like she would never get enough water, although each gulp brought her closer to normal. When the woman returned with the refilled pitcher, the man took it and closed the door in her face.

"What did she do wrong?" Kalea asked, having finally found her voice, then went right back to chugging water.

"Nothing, just—trust go not far among us with you here." He sat beside Kalea with an air of the most serious attention that had ever been lavished upon her.

With the additional candle, Kalea could see much better. She had worried she'd gone blind, but it was evening time. Where had the day gone? Where had she wound up? A stone room. She sat low to the floor on a flat straw mattress. A few measly pieces of furniture, all old and worn down, made the room more than a hollow space. A grand headboard leaned against the wall behind her. Some of the darkening windows were broken and covered with tattered sheets waving on the cool breeze.

She could finally see his face too. His blonde, shaggy hair hung below his ears and swept across his forehead. He wasn't quite an old man yet, perhaps in his late thirties. Starvation showed on his face and in his tired eyes.

His eyes. Kalea couldn't help but stare. The irises were unmistakably red, like red stained glass in the morning.

He remained quiet for a long while, staring at her. What did he find so strange about her?

"Who are you?" she asked, prompting him to blink and smile.
"Your husband, Mother Kalea."

# Chapter 12
# What is a Long Night with a Stranger

A stutter pulled on Kalea's speech. "Wh-what?" She couldn't have heard right.

"I said I'm your husband, Mother Kalea."

Her jaw trembled. He put his hand on her forehead, and she shook it away. "How did that happen? Where am I? Where are my companions?" She gazed around the stone room full of rickety old furniture again.

He smiled and dragged air through his nose. "You are in Valltalhiss, our dying city. Your companions are dead, and our union...has not happened yet, but soon."

She shrieked the words, "What happened to my companions?"

"Same as happened to you. They ate the poisonous fruit and died."

"Poisonous fruit!"

"Shh, yes. Poisonous fruit, looks like apples but is not. Many unfortunate humans are fooled by it. We found you in time, but they were dead already. They took larger bites. I am sorry, Mother Kalea."

"No, that doesn't sound right. They can't be dead." Her teeth clenched; simultaneously, her fists gripped the smelly old mattress full of old straw.

"The poison, it is potent, I'm afraid. My people are trapped within this forest due to a curse. We can make antidote for the poisonous fruit, and a lot of water helps. It is our mission to scout and find poor souls who mistakenly eat it and rescue them. You, my lover, were a lucky one."

"Show me! I need to see their bodies. I need to...pray for—" Her sobbing brought a stop to the words too hard to speak.

The man with red eyes shook his head. "You don't want to see such things. Their remains should be mummified by now. The poison dries you out, as I say. Takes only hours for a person's body to dry out completely. My people say prayers and bury them already. Such is our duty."

He put his hands on her crown and his lips to her forehead in comfort. She batted him away.

"Don't touch me!" Her voice bounced off the lonely walls. One old tapestry remained on one of them with many loose threads dangling.

"As you wish." He sat quietly beside her until she spoke again.

"Who are you?"

"Kerlin. I am king to the Thaccilians of Valltalhiss."

She nodded at his words, but could hardly process anything beyond the image of her friends lying dead in the forest. He sat patiently as if awaiting another question. She could think of plenty to give him.

"Kerlin," she said, partially in recital, "why do you think we are married?"

"Forgive me, we are not married yet. I am too elated you have come to me; I can't help but say such words. We will be joined tomorrow on full moon night."

Kalea shook her head. "No, I can't marry you. I have to leave here, I have to go somewhere."

He nodded his head rapidly as she spoke, his eyes smiling. "Yes, good. And when we are married, I will take you anywhere you like, Mother Kalea, though don't tell my people. They think you're their goddess, and though you are, I would do anything for you, even forsake them in this isolated existence."

"You're insane!"

"Why you so cruel?"

"What are you talking about? Tell me now, why again do you think you'll marry me tomorrow?"

His hopeful expression dropped. "Mother Kalea, don't you understand?"

"No! How do you know my name?"

Kerlin stood, and the shadow fell over him as he stepped out of the candle's range. He went out the door.

Kalea didn't move from the mattress on the floor for the whole five minutes of his absence before he returned with a burning torch. She trembled in her lack of energy, aside from the fear. His torch highlighted a heavy old drape on the wall before he threw it open to reveal a massive relief carved into a wooden wall panel.

"I don't know where you have been," he said, "or why you don't know your destiny. So listen."

He raised a pointed finger toward an image of a demonic-looking deity carved immaculately into the panel, one of the largest figures in the scene. Its eyes bulged and horns crowned its head. Half a naked figure hung from its mouth as its jagged teeth stabbed into the flesh.

"This," Kerlin said, "is our god, Thaxyl. A pixie of chaos, of primal nature. An entity who despises humans. He made us, the Thaccilians."

Kerlin moved his torch across the panel, highlighting the whole intricate scene, which told a long story. A violent story! He stopped at the other end of the panel and pointed to the other large figure. This one was fish-like, and tiers of fins decorated its head. It held a tiny baby curled in its giant hands.

"This is Lusche. A pixie of water. He made your kind. Women with a blessed power. Lusche loved humans, so he made Luschians. The Luschians seduced Thaccilian men and turned them human upon the act of mating. Luschians were irresistible to my people—the Thaccilians. The Luschians proved stronger, and they neutralized my people, turning them human. Female Thaccilians can't produce Thaccilian children without Thaccilian males.

"When most Thaccilian men became human, our race reduced. The rest were chased into this old city by mages, who cursed it afterward, trapping us in this forest behind the force of an invisible wall."

Kalea worked her jaw. "This is madness." Her throat tried to close of its own will. She wanted her friends with her now. She wanted Dorhen.

"What is matter?"

"You're wrong, that's the matter!"

He cocked his head, his face menacingly dark, a stark contrast to the warmth he had displayed when she woke up. "Wrong?"

"Yes, this is all wrong! Don't you know the Creator...?" She stopped herself. He didn't know what she knew. After all, this was a real native of the untamed and mysterious Darklands. He didn't know anything about her religion and couldn't be blamed. It might be foolish to argue with a stranger when at his mercy.

"You have the wrong woman," she said instead. "I am not a lusch-an. I'm a woman from the Lightlands." He nodded, seeming only to want to please her. "I'm not a goddess either—why would you think so?"

He nodded again, though she knew he disagreed. He placed the torch on the wall sconce and said, "To us, you *are* goddess. All Luschians are goddesses because they are rare and beloved creatures. We Thaccilians have an endowed ability to hear heartbeats in our prey. We follow heartbeats when we hunt. The Luschians have a special rhythm we recognize. When my party found you in the forest, we immediately knew what you were. Your heart's rhythm told me your name because it calls to me."

Kalea shook her head while he spoke.

"We are dying, my love," he said. "There is no food here for us. We have been waiting for a Luschian to transform one of us. The people in this city think we will all be released from the curse and set free, a myth my grandfather's grandfather invented. They think I, their king, am descended from Thaxyl directly, and you, their awaited goddess, will join together with me and rescue them.

"I know better than my poor starving citizens. Since I'm king, I will claim you. You will transform me human, and then you and I will leave here together. We could do it now, but my people are excited. We hold a ceremony on the full moon, and I will indulge them what they want. They'll get their goddess ceremony, and we will escape."

Kalea gnashed her teeth. "I won't, I won't do it—no!"

Kerlin watched her silently from the shadow.

"How do you expect me to turn you human?"

"We have to mate, of course."

Kalea buried her face in her hands, nearly ready to vomit all the water sloshing in her stomach.

"When we mate, we are married; such is our custom. And for you and me, it fulfills a prophecy instilled by your maker."

She would try to run if she didn't feel so weak. The ache hadn't left her leg wound. The torch crackled in the silence in addition to her whimpering.

"I won't do it," she mumbled.

His voice softened. "It won't hurt."

"That's not a conversation I want to have right now. I'm here by accident. I'm not your goddess, and there is no prophecy. You are wrong!"

He threw up his hands. "Fine! Good. I told you prophecy is false. But there is one fact. You are Luschian and every man in this town, one hundred six of them, would all take your flower if given the chance. I tell them about prophecies and goddesses to protect you. You are highly wanted here. I promise, tonight there are men smothering their wives under pillows and plotting to sneak in here to steal you from me. The prophecy story protects you from the majority. But there will be some, no doubt. So I have female guards—who believe the prophecy—all around this building to alert me and fight off attackers. They are outside the door as well. They'll stay awake all night, and I will sleep in here with you for your protection."

Kalea's mouth hung open, her brain spinning.

He motioned toward the dark window. "As you see, it is late." He walked toward her mattress. "I am sorry you have found such turbulent days. Everything will be better after tomorrow."

He knelt on the mattress with her and leaned over to kiss her forehead; she dodged, and he wound up kissing air. He showed no annoyance for it. "Sleep now. We will talk more at sunrise." He guided her by the shoulder to lie down and trapped her under his arm.

"I'm not very—"

"Shhhh, you'll be all right so long as I'm here." Trembling fingers caressed her hair. His erection under his leggings grazed against her leg, and he pulled away as if to hide it.

Kalea froze in terror. *Oh, dear Creator, he'll rape me in the night like those sorcerers!*

Despite her tensed body, chattering teeth, and overall trembling, he kept calm, closed his eyes, and took a deep breath. She had to get out of this situation before his self-control failed.

Relaxing proved impossible so long as she remained in this aroused stranger's embrace. Besides that, his claim of her being some sort of non-human was absolutely insane. After several minutes, she fidgeted in place, pinned to the hard, flattened mattress.

The longest minutes of her life slogged by. She kept still and filled her mind with Dorhen's image in an effort to relax. Kerlin's breathing steadied. He fell fast asleep. As outlandish as his claims were, Kerlin had displayed honesty as far as she could tell. His eyes, though oddly colored, were soft and warm. Hopefully, he would at least keep his promise to take her out of this forest. But she couldn't let him mate with her! She had assumed long ago her road to finding Dorhen would be rough, but she would do anything and everything in her power to keep herself pure for him like a good wife of tradition.

When the rhythm of Kerlin's breathing developed a soft snore, she gingerly wriggled loose, begging the Creator to keep him asleep. If she couldn't turn over and relieve the pressure under her hip and shoulder, she'd scream. She didn't have to worry about falling with the mattress spread out on the floor.

After several agonizing minutes of work, she shimmied free and went straight to the window. Tiny lights and hints of movement livened the city below, though she couldn't tell its layout in this darkness. Little torches marched around, sometimes revealing dark shapes standing immobile as if staring up at her. If Kerlin had told the truth, there were men out there obsessing over her presence. Suddenly feeling vulnerable, she moved away from the window.

The torch hung on the wall, its flame barely hanging onto life. Approaching the carved panel, she studied the horrific images closer before dismissing it as heathen drivel. Whatever mythical creature Kerlin claimed she was, he was wrong.

Another huge curtain hung on the opposite wall. She took the torch and carefully drew the curtain to see what this one hid. Bookshelves stuffed near to bursting. She could not help but study them. They were old, and she feared lifting some. Many were poetry books. Against all odds, a copy of *The Questionable Tales of Lehomis Lockheirhen* occupied the shelf. Her throat tightened at the sight of it. How long ago could it have been written exactly? She twisted around and scanned the room for any of her belongings. Her basket sat near the vacant bed.

She jumped at Kerlin's presence beside her. "Are you looking for something?"

"Um, I couldn't sleep."

"You must try."

Trembling violently with no hope of stopping, she said, "Kerlin. I'm trying to understand my situation. Am I a prisoner?"

He whispered, "No."

"Then please give me some space. I don't want to be locked up in here."

"You can't leave this building, I've told you this. You are not safe until we mate. A Luschian's power only works once. Afterward, you can walk freely."

"Do you love me?"

He stared at her for a while, his face barely visible in this lighting. His hand grabbed hers, also trembling violently; the knowledge made her strangely jittery all over. "You are the goddess my grandfathers and father have waited for. All Thaccilians want a Luschian. Against all likelihood, you came to me. I will hold you close. I will die before letting you go."

"I'm not a goddess."

"Does not matter because you have already arrived. To me."

"I can't be with you. I'm looking for an elf."

He squeezed her hand. "I've not touched a woman yet, because I wait for you. You are mine now."

Kalea jerked her hand, but he held it fast. She pulled and pushed, and panic granted her new energy, so she screamed until he restrained her and covered her mouth.

"Don't let the other men hear your voice," he hissed in her ear. "It will excite them. If you go out, you will be in trouble. Why don't you look at the books more? If you read them, maybe you will relax. Tomorrow night after we mate, I'll be able to walk through the barrier, and we will go into the forest. You can see your friends' graves along the way."

She could barely stand on her own when he released her. "My friends…" Her body shook with pulsing sadness. In her confusion over Kerlin's craziness, she'd forgotten about them. What would she do without them? How could she escape this place alone? Poor Gaije. Without him, Mhina would fall victim to the sorcerers. And Bowaen and Del…

As she sobbed into the back of her hand, Kerlin hushed her gently and motioned toward the books. "Read books. Or you can tell me of the outside world."

Pushing away from him, she turned to the books. He held the dying torch while she browsed, her watery eyes glazing over. At random, she put her hand on a large one with a strong spine and a greenish color. The green fabric had peeled away to reveal its fragile wooden base. The first page inside read, "The Lung Journii hov the Sol."

Kerlin stuck his head out the door and ordered some candles brought in for "the goddess" to read by. He settled against the wall to watch her but soon fell asleep.

Several languages were present in the book, and she found her own—or rather, something close enough to it for her to decipher. She happened to find Kerlin's story about his gods, Thaxyl and Lusche, and their children, the Thaccilians and the Luschians.

One hand-drawn illustration showed Thaxyl eating humans, like on the wooden panel, as his children, the Thaccilians, sprouted from the ground under his enormous, barbed foot. Lusche, with wings like fish fins, leaned over a baby's cradle. Lusche chose his favorites among already existing children, whereas Thaxyl expelled his energy to make his children from snake bones found in the earth.

Another illustration showed a Thaccilian man and a Luschian woman in a sexual embrace which Kalea skipped over, her face warming. She checked Kerlin to make sure he still slept.

She turned to a new chapter. This book had much to talk about concerning heathen magic and mythology. A section with a list of magic spells included the heading, "DREAMWALK." Kalea's eyes popped in the candle light. She looked over the dense text, written neatly by hand in an attractive script.

She whispered the words she read on the page. "'A special ability for…communication among magic practitioners… Only for the most talented of souls.'"

The practice involved the soul leaving the body to visit another person while they dreamed. Though extremely useful, it was also dangerous. The dreamwalker had to know when and how to return, and the book showed a long list of rules for visiting the dreams of enemies. Mages and sorcerers practiced this hard-to-grasp skill, but it came naturally to creatures such as fairies, *faerhain*, and…Luschians.

"Luschians…" Her whispered voice drew long through her lips. The book laid out instructions on how to do it.

Kerlin slept soundly. His female guards murmured to each other outside the door. Trapped in here, Kalea had never felt so alone in her life, not even when Chandran had captured her. But if she indeed happened to be what Kerlin claimed, perhaps she wasn't quite as alone as she thought. Her friends might be dead, but possibly, by the Creator's grace, Dorhen dreamed somewhere nearby.

# Chapter 13
# What is Beneficial to the Kingsorcerer

Luckily for Lamrhath and his small group, they each lugged around a heavy bag of supplies and tools, including Lamrhath's kingsorcerer crown and other regalia. He carried his regalia to any outpost he visited because it was always good to inspire his followers with all the flash and pageantry a kingsorcerer could show. He had originally anticipated meeting Dorhen while wearing all of it, but he found satisfaction in the way it had actually unfolded: him displayed in his dark chamber with a load of women standing outside the door.

Today, he maintained a modest entourage of six other sorcerers due to the confusion they'd experienced with the golden portal rods. He had spent most of his recent days and nights cursing Daghahen's emergence from their mother's womb as an elf and not just a tumor with teeth. Their campaign would be brief: they'd visit as many Darklandic villages as they could, then go home richer and better stocked for the journey.

Traditionally, Wikshen's reputation preceded him because news of his coming spread fast, and for this era, Lamrhath would seize the opportunity to profit from it by becoming the bearer of that news. He currently formulated a collection of plans for how to use Wikshen for profit. The Ilbith clan had surpassed the other sorcery groups in past decades. They controlled a secure base in the mountains, many resources, outside supporters, and bustling support inside, complete with servants and soldiers. From there, they could only strengthen their hold over the Darklandic territories.

Now that Wikshen had returned, he would subdue any settlement in his path, and this was where Ilbith would carefully alter the natural course of Wikshen's campaign. This new Wikshen belonged to Ilbith. Lamrhath knew as well as any other how Wikhaihli, the pettygod's base, expected its own conquest. They would be dealt with later, if not put to use for Ilbith courtesy of Wikshen's own compliance. For now, the more settlements they could secure for Ilbith, the smoother things would be down the road to Wikhaihli. Best to claim them early because, as lore told, Wikhaihli would also try to sway the tribes and settlements before destroying them.

Lamrhath's entourage quickly found the first settlement somewhere west of Alkeer. He sat upon a small sedan they had crafted and decorated with feathers, red beads, and whatever else they could find. His next highest sorcerer, Sigmune, led the way on foot with both hands raised in friendship toward the group of elders and brash village youths bearing primitive spears with sharpened stone heads.

Lamrhath took a few deep breaths and attempted to rub the tightness out of his stomach before starting his spiel. The sedan served more purposes than simply looking impressive. He'd be too ill to walk soon. It would take great focus and all of his strength to appear strong, talk sharply, and suppress lustful thoughts. His cock was already standing, hoping to be used soon, but it wouldn't show under his belt with the cascading maroon satin and gold chains with ruby and crystal beads. The chains were not enough to cast a portal, but they'd be accounted for after Ilbith had gathered lots of new gold. The gold on the kingsorcerer's crown was forever off-limits for petty uses.

"Peace," Sigmune declared when they stopped at shouting distance.

"What's this? Sorcerers come to extort our hard-earned comforts?" the prominent elder in the group of primitives shouted back. He wasn't the chieftain, but he appeared important with his swirling green face paint and mantle woven with animal bones.

"Not at all, old one," Sigmune said. He motioned toward Lamrhath, who waited silently, hooded under his grand cloak with gold and copper threads running through the embroidery. "This is your kingsorcerer, who watches over your village from the heavenly mountain." He pointed toward the tallest peak on the distant horizon.

The old primitive crossed his arms. "Who are you and what do you really want?"

"An audience with your elite," Sigmune said. They stopped at a respectful distance, but close enough to speak without shouting. "We have an urgent warning—a thing of good faith! We are traveling around to all the tribes and settlements to deliver our message before it's too late."

After a few moments of sizing up their tiny group and eyeing the hills for other sorcerers possibly hiding, the primitives led Lamrhath's band into the village toward the big, round gathering hall. The bulk of the village's members scrambled out of the way. Men hoisted spears and the women scattered, grabbing little children and yanking them off the path.

A shock of lustful pain pierced Lamrhath's belly at the level of flesh this tribe found decent to expose. All of the women, old, young, and ripe, were naked. He kept his chin high in pride to look grand and in control along his ride on the sedan, but necessity dictated he avert his eyes. Hard to do. This village boasted a lot of fine women with long sleek legs, wearing nothing but little loincloths that split their buttocks and rawhide straps hoisting their swollen breasts proud and high. They were nicely decorated with colored stone necklaces and pierced nipples. Each one looked every bit the sensual sculpture of a concupiscent artist. Their swirling green paint suited them better than the old man who had greeted him.

A wave of nausea washed through him, accompanied by a genuine interest to explore and enjoy this village's best-endowed morsel for hours upon hours. He caught his breathing slowing and deepening to a state of sexual meditation, his mouth ready to please, his hands twitching—ready to caress, his cock *needing* to be rubbed. Many people were watching him.

And then he spotted her, one particular beauty with full lips to mimic her round breasts. This specimen had spirals to draw his eye round and round her voluptuous bust. Primitive cultures like this favored fertility over most other aspects of survival.

He resorted to narrowing his stare to the hall before him, pushing all the busty onlookers out of his consciousness. He couldn't let any one of these people realize he was in less than a business state of mind.

In the hall, rough-cut, spiraling roof supports loomed above them with a hole in the roof's center for the hearth smoke to escape. The tribe members laid out a modest feast of goodwill for them.

Dismounting the sedan and walking gracefully to his seat was a chore. A great amount of energy and aggression always preceded the pain when his ailment acted up, energy he'd use to please his partner. He had to trust his ornamentation and not worry whether his erection would show, just as he'd have to keep his temper under control and avoid looking at the bare-breasted women standing by, watching the newcomers with sparkling, doe-like eyes. By the time Lamrhath made it to his seat in the hall, his erection throbbed, sending pulsing aches across all of his limbs.

Lamrhath sat as the keystone with the other six sorcerers, three on each side. Sigmune sat with his ledger and sharpened charcoal poised. Lamrhath let his hood down, and the elders all quieted. Removing the hood revealed his crown, made from the huge, beastly teeth of an ancient scouel—a beast as rare and mythical as a ravian—and more gold chains and rubies dangling down his long golden hair. He kept his eyes sharp and unimpressed.

Across the circle, a clutch of old men with long beards, decorated mantles, and body paint sat stern-faced. The village chieftain sat at their center.

"Who comes uninvited and demanding my audience, and on a holy day for our people, no less?" The chieftain's voice boomed regardless of how old he appeared.

"As I've told your second in command," Sigmune said calmly, "this is the glorious kingsorcerer. He guards the Darklands from his high throne on the mountain. And he is here today to deliver a friendly warning so you might prepare yourselves and survive the coming dark days."

The chieftain snorted. "This *glorious* kingsorcerer brings a paltry little rabble for someone so grand."

Sigmune waved his hand. "Of course," he said. "The kingsorcerer wishes to show his goodwill and gentle intent by bringing six administrators with him to deliver this warning."

The chieftain crossed his arms and stared at Sigmune as if in contest as his fellows murmured and nudged each other.

Sigmune opened his mouth to speak again, and Lamrhath canceled him with a raised hand. "Your hospitality is pleasing," Lamrhath said. "I thank you for pausing in your holy rites to allow me into your hall and hear what I have to say." The more god-like he could appear, the better, but graciousness went a long way too. Getting them to do exactly as he wanted would be another matter. "Ilbith and our god, Naerezek, have watched over you in past years, and continue to."

"My people don't believe in this god you flaunt," the chieftain said. "Why don't you go ahead and tell us what dark news you have?"

Lamrhath drew out a moment of silence before he answered. He needed to concentrate. Keeping his hands from trembling proved hard. It felt a little too good whenever he shifted and his penis grazed against the inside of his codpiece, and he resisted dabbing the cold sweat from his temples for fear of looking weak or nervous.

"Do you believe in the legend of Wikshen? He has returned," he got out, his voice gaining a rough edge, husky the way he wished he could groan and pant heavily beside a woman's ear. Rubbing his body against...

*Damn the demon who has taken up residence in my loins!*

The elders' faces twisted, and they murmured amongst themselves again, some in an argumentative manner. The ragged, husky voice should add good effect.

"H-how do you know this?" the chieftain asked.

Lamrhath took a deep breath to prepare for a long speech. "Our scouts spotted him on the hills one misty night. For centuries, Wik couldn't be contacted through our sorcerous channels. After Wikshen the Sixth died, we assume the pixie spent all that time in a glass holding sphere, but now Wikshen is alive again. He roved in the south when we saw him. He's moving this way and will be well-equipped with a number of dreadwitches too."

"Dreadwitches," the chieftain repeated.

Lamrhath nodded. "Do you know what this is?"

Amid the fearful expressions of his fellows, the chieftain leaned back and pressed his finger pads together. "We have remembered much but also forgotten much. The way we live today is because of the terror of Wikshen, a murderous monster my generation can only imagine in our nightmares. Legend has it he tore through our cities and stole our comforts and, more frighteningly, our women.

"Today, we do not place permanent roots but leave when we feel is necessary. We have found life comforts in our reformed ways, as well as security. But we do not speak past what and who Wikshen is. We raise bonfires every night—big ones. We raise a fire over our memories of what he did to our people, and we have every intention of burning him before he can harm us again."

Lamrhath took a moment to let the chieftain's words resonate. "Good Chief," he said. "I'm afraid merely keeping on the move and refusing to remember specifics will not save you from the wild, ravenous lust that is Wikshen and his dreadwitches."

As he listened, the chieftain mouthed the word "dreadwitches."

Lamrhath continued, "I know indeed what you folk have survived throughout history. Wikshen is out there *today*, roaming the grasslands and the forests and the cities, looking to steal everyone's life comforts again. Particularly your women. He'll take them away, screaming and thrashing, and he'll thrust himself upon them and hurt them. And he'll spend himself inside of them, which is only the beginning.

"Afterward, they will change into hideous mutations of themselves, crossing humanity with the dark beings of the underworld. They'll grow horns or scales or reptilian spikes, and they will be evil. They'll love him and hate you, and they'll kill you. And they will be stronger than you. And he will do this to many, many women across the Darklands, growing an army of them. He will use them to conquer the Darklands as he's done six times before."

Lamrhath paused to huff and draw in another careful drag of air. The bits about thrusting and spending didn't help his condition. "Good Chief," he said, "Wikshen won't be satisfied until he has completely destroyed the civilization you've salvaged and adapted."

The elders' eyes bugged out, and they exchanged glances amongst themselves, followed by pointed comments. The young spear-bearers standing by shifted in various ways, repositioning their clammy hands on the wooden surfaces of their weapons, and the bare-breasted women who sat around the edges of the room suddenly found their modesty.

The chieftain's face lost a level of color. "Your Grace," he said, once the others hushed. "What can we do? We won't convert to Wikshonism." His voice turned shaky. "I will not let this happen to our wives, sisters, and mothers!"

"Which is why we're here, dear Chief," Lamrhath replied over his rambling. "How much gold do you have?"

"Not much, Your Grace."

Lamrhath shook his head and drew his face long. "Oh, dear. You see, we have spells to repel Wikshen. This is one of our faction's primary focuses. Our spells and charms take much energy, and when there is not enough energy in our bodies to generate the spells, we can fall back on drawing it out of gold. You see?"

The chieftain bobbed his head under his heavy headdress made of woven straw, black feathers, and bones. He wore the most elaborate swirling face paint.

Lamrhath continued, "Tell me now, for the safety of you and your families, what have you as far as riches and resources?"

"Well, Your Grace," the chieftain began somberly, "we have five gold chips among the whole tribe. Twenty-two silvers. Goats. Skins. Milk."

Lamrhath raised a hand, frowning. "I sympathize, Chief, and my heart is spilling its life for your situation. A tragic one. But might I propose a solution? With the donation of your gold and silver, and a weekly payment of your resources, we can work out a deal. I think my sorcerers and I can muster enough energy to cast wards around your perimeter to ward off Wikshen. We will hang charms on your doors to keep you safe inside. And we can provide a guard or two for protection, whom I will send word to after this meeting, as well as a weekly visit from a high-ranking sorcerer to make sure all is well and collect your tax."

All of the elders fell to their faces in praise. The prominent one kissed the hem of Lamrhath's cloak and praised the kingsorcerer and his generosity. This meeting had turned out quite differently than how they usually went. The tribes had always been extremely difficult, with less than half percent success. The threat of Wikshen certainly did make a difference. All Darklanders knew the tales of Wikshen.

Sigmune raised his hands to quiet them.

"My lord," the chieftain said, "surely we've not enough to pay for such a service. I am ashamed!"

"Calm," Lamrhath said. "I agree, you don't have enough to properly afford our protection, though I give it to you."

"What can we do, my lord? What can we do more for you, so you won't think poorly of me and our humble village?"

Could things get any better from here? "There's always more wealth we don't account for," Lamrhath said.

The chieftain bobbed his head. "Name it and it's yours!"

Lamrhath kept silent for a moment to draw out the anticipation as well as to tame the new wave of excitement that washed downward and added a new piercing ache to his cock. "How many virgins await marriage this season?"

The elder's droopy eyes, rising above his heavily bearded face, met the kingsorcerer's. Lamrhath kept his face unflinching, a technique he'd practiced for ages.

"I offer you another blessing, to be truthful," Lamrhath added. "This blessing doubles as another ounce of payment as well."

"We've not many eligible brides, Your Grace, only three, and they are not our most attractive yet."

"Only three?"

*Not the most attractive?* No matter, attraction didn't hold a candle to the overall relief Lamrhath needed. The phase of dominating pain and madness crept closer. In his youth, he used to thrash in his bed, screaming, begging Daghahen to find a cure. Something to soothe his pain. And most of all, to find him a woman to cancel the pain completely. Back then, one round of sex lasted him at least a week. He'd gotten worse over the years. Much worse.

He evoked the image of his favorite woman he'd seen when entering the tribe, that big-breasted honey with the pierced nipples and a cocky spark in her eyes. She must be married and not one of those unattractive eligible virgins the chief had mentioned. Even if all those sweet delicacies weren't married, they needn't be virgins like Lamrhath asked for. His request of virgins held as much political weight as his bargaining. Though he would love to bask in those voluptuous women, married or not, his high status required the demand of virgins. Lowering himself to ask for a non-virgin would ruin his whole façade by the standards of any primitive tribe.

"Three are primed for marriage," the chieftain repeated, "and there's one more. She's eleven, so she'll be ready next season."

"Eleven is old enough. Get the four of them ready and prepare a place for me to service them."

"But, my lord—"

Lamrhath raised a finger but quickly put it down to hide the shaking. "My good Chief," he said. "I'm not sure if you comprehend what I'm offering you. There is a god who lives in the fire, named Naerezek. I am the kingsorcerer, which is like a high priest to Naerezek. Our god works through me. By servicing your women, I am giving you a great blessing, and you are also giving me a great favor—a receptacle with which to pray to my god." He cleared his throat and panted. The pain building in his testicles took his breath away. His last statement wasn't a total lie; his pain might as well be a god who demanded appeasement.

Sensing his discomfort, Sigmune took over. "You should be honored!" He stood up and yelled it at the old wise men and their chieftain. He stole the focus. "Our kingsorcerer is offering you a kindness! Don't you realize if any of those women are impregnated, you'll have a god-child among you, a great leader for your future!"

Lamrhath suppressed a smile despite his pain. He couldn't have fashioned a better lie, despite its hilarity. Lamrhath was an elf, and elves couldn't impregnate human women. It had never been done, and Alkeer, where many Clanless *saehgahn* coupled with women, provided proof. As for him, never in his long life had Lamrhath ever conceived a child with a woman, nor seen a half-elf walking around the Darklands.

Sigmune reclaimed his seat and read off his notes. "Five gold chips, twenty-two silver chips, two new goats per litter, as well as four jugs of milk and two skins, plus the deflowering of four virgins upon this night. Your tribe will be granted in return: ward spells around the outskirts, a charm for every door, two Ilbith guards, and a weekly visit from a sorcerer for your protection, and the deal shall be set."

Lamrhath added, "Also, I must stress that you'll want to fly a red flag as high as you can erect it. Wikshen knows red is our color and he fears it. He won't bother you if he suspects you are under our protection."

Sigmune wrote out a copy for the village to keep, and Lamrhath sealed it with his ring and spread it before the elders to sign. They all filed in to sign their names using Sigmune's piece of charcoal. They had retained reading and writing skills from their old civilization, though the letters had evolved through the ages.

Afterward, the families of the virgins were informed, and the village granted the fourth one a hasty coming-of-age ceremony. The sorcerer named Gavor cut it short by grabbing her arm and dragging her toward the hut prepared for Lamrhath's stay.

The youngest one entered his hut first, hands nervously clasped in front of her. By now, Lamrhath panted and fidgeted in his seat on the bed. He'd waited for what felt like hours, stroking himself futilely to ease the pain.

Her voice came out shaky. "My lord…please lie back and make yourself comfort—"

He couldn't wait for her niceties and presentation. He yanked her by her arm and couldn't rip her undergarment off fast enough. Unluckily for her, she'd get his most aggressive, frantic treatment, no time to lick her between the legs first. It wasn't Lamrhath's idea to send her in first—his sorcerers had made that call.

As soon as he finished, she left him panting and sweating on the bed as she ran out in tears. He hardly noticed her departure in his moment of rebound. His state hadn't improved, regardless of what he'd done. His jaw remained clenched and shaky, and his penis refilled quickly. His sweat turned cold and flooded out of him.

The second virgin entered the hut when one of the sorcerers shoved her in. Lamrhath's pained grunting in his weak state wouldn't help her confidence. She received about the same treatment as the first girl.

The third one he could award a weak smile when she entered. His hair hung soaked by now. He extended his hand, and when she hesitated, he grabbed her arm and pulled her onto the bed. This one he kissed, though he had yet to regain the charm women usually liked. He wanted to play sensually with her, but achieving comfort came first. Oddly, the muscles within his mouth trembled in anxiety and desperation as it engulfed hers.

The tenderness didn't last long before his aggravation overcame him and he took her. He insisted she stay for a second round, and when she refused, he used force. He sent her back out weeping like the first girl. So far, she was the most attractive virgin, and he wished to bask in her. He didn't like the ferocity they sometimes forced him to use any more than they did. Back in his youth, sex had been a pleasant and invigorating sport. He wanted it to be pleasant now.

When the fourth and last girl entered the hut, he sneered and dropped his head to the pillow. None of them were the gorgeous woman he'd seen when he entered the village. Nonetheless, he needed this last girl's help as much as the previous three. He beckoned to her with a calm, serene hand which didn't shake. His cock remained erect, and this bout would skirt around normal lovemaking. After this, he should be able to capture some sleep.

Deep into the night, he finished with the last one and reclined against the goatskins, his body slick with sweat in the dying firelight, and drifted away from consciousness. Thank Naerezek for this oasis he'd found. Sleep became elusive and often impossible when the illness wracked him. He needed rest. Not that he needed much energy to hang a few red banners and pretend to cast spells around the village in the morning.

# Chapter 14
# What is a Journey through Dreams

Kalea reread the chapter on dreamwalking closely. It said nothing about fainting and dreamwalking by accident. From what she gathered, only high-level magic users could master it—besides fairies, female elves, and Luschians.

She perused the room again, trapped and smothered by the king who wanted to take her virginity. Female guards murmured softly out in the corridor, and outside lay a whole city filled with rowdy men.

Part of her hoped she was a Luschian. Visiting people's dreams might come in handy. May the Creator forgive her for using magic. The idea of her soul leaving her body sounded dangerous. Her religion warned of spirits walking around unseen, desperate to take an idle vessel. But the Creator knew of her desperation, and she used that to give herself permission. She trembled at the idea of contacting Dorhen. How ironic it would be if he saved her from here. This might lead to their reunion.

She dropped her eyes back to the page and read about how mages used dreamwalking to communicate with each other over long distances, to gather information from enemies, or to send messages to non-dreamwalkers.

After reading over the instructions again, Kalea prepared herself mentally and lay down on the bed with hands folded on her breasts, trying to remain calm. She recited the incantation the book provided, careful to remember where to insert Dorhen's name. When her eyes closed, she expected to drop out of reality as the book said.

Nothing happened. She remained in this world, wide awake. Pushing lingering, hopeful thoughts and expectations away, she started over, careful to enunciate his name. Many minutes passed, and her throat dried.

*He must not be asleep right now.* She shook her wrists out. *Oh, Dorhen, you make me so jittery! I need to calm myself, or this'll never work.*

She sipped the cup of water Kerlin left for her. A mistake could land her in serious trouble; the process needed to be done carefully. In bed as before, she tried reciting the chant with eyes closed.

"Oh no!" she said when she opened her eyes to the darkness. "Please don't be that same castle as before."

She stood and reached out to try to find a wall or something. Her hands waved through empty blackness. She found nothing, not even an indication of being inside a building or out. No sensation of warmth, coolness, breeze, or sound of any kind. She attempted to speak, to call out to anyone who might be near. Her lips moved, but she couldn't tell if her voice projected or stayed within her head. She couldn't feel a floor under her bare feet. Nothing pressed against her soles, although she assumed she stood on them.

Her hands moved faster, along with her heart. She broke into a run, but her feet made no sound against any surface. She stopped, knowing this solved nothing. She called out for someone. She cried Dorhen's name. No answer.

A faint sound arose, like deep, slow panting. She stood silent, listening to a…presence slithering closer. Her legs tensed up beyond her will to move anymore. She breathed as loudly as the presence did. It loomed over her head, mere inches away. Her arms remained free, so she rallied the courage to reach out.

Emptiness. The hissing sound remained.

*Move, legs!* She managed to turn around and reached out her arms. Nothing. The breathing sound never moved, but its volume increased.

A hot sensation steamed on her neck. She whipped around to feel for the person or creature, and her hand swiped through empty space. The steaming sensation resumed on her neck from a new direction. She turned and tried again with the same result. A whimper puffed through her throat.

A cold sensation touched her face. It might've been a hand with spindly fingers and long nails, strong like a man's. Her own hands hung heavily by her sides, too difficult to move anymore. She tried to focus her eyes, but it didn't matter. The hand and the darkness were one and the same.

The raspy breathing quickened and grew louder. The hot steam moved to the back of her neck and around to the front again. What did it want? Was it inspecting her?

The hand dragged down her face hard with spite, pulling painfully on her flesh. It developed a sense of solidity in its progression. It pressed her nose along the way, and she pulled her lips in as it moved over them. She lifted her chin as it moved down her neck and caught her collar, ripping it as it went. It continued over her chest and stomach, and proceeded along her leg, where she knew it must stop once it reached her foot.

It didn't stop. The hand maintained the same angle as it slid all the way to the top of her foot, around her toes, and to her sole. The fingers stopped at her heel, where it strangely fell away, leaving her dizzy and disoriented. Either she hung upside-down, or the hand had sunk into the floor.

The breathing began to sound human—a man's, yet it retained a level of beastliness.

"Dorhen?" she asked.

Hissing laughter erupted, like sand running through her ears.

Kalea concentrated on exiting the dream. She should've put more effort into learning how to return from a dream! In anticipation of contacting Dorhen, she'd cared more about arriving here, but this couldn't be Dorhen's dream. She must've made a mistake in her casting. Now what to do?

A force struck her across the face; an angry growl accompanied the blow. She flew backward and crumpled to the ground.

Before it all registered, a deep, throaty voice said, "You have trespassed, dreamwalker."

Kalea stuttered for a response. The side of her face relived the blow with each heartbeat.

"Get out of my realm, dreamwalking whore!"

When she finally stood, a fist clobbered her in the side. She flew farther than before and skidded to a stop, burning her arms and knees. When she moved to rise, an iron-like fist delivered a blow to her head from above. Her face banged against the floor.

"Get out of my realm! Get out!"

Kalea screamed and huddled, trying to concentrate on waking up. Something like a heavy foot struck her ribs, and she rolled for a long distance. She tried to maintain concentration.

"This is my realm. Leave this place!" Another kick sent her off again. "Never return, filth!" It released a hot roar, whooshing over her form. Kalea screamed in agony. "Leave!"

She winced at another blow.

She woke up.

When she sprang out of bed, her raucousness stirred Kerlin from his slumber. She scrambled for the candles, grabbing one to light all the extras. Even though she found solace in the renewed and comforting glow, pain radiated across her face and in her ribs. Upon inspection in Kerlin's cracked mirror, she found a large bruise decorating her cheekbone. Kerlin's gaze followed her around the room. She shook her head in disbelief at the reflection of a beaten girl in the mirror. She flipped through the book and finally noticed the part mentioning how a dreamwalker could be physically injured during the journey.

*It's real!*

"Are you all right?" Kerlin asked, and she slammed the book closed.

"I'm fine." She let her hair fall over the bruise and paused for a moment at his question. He raised an eyebrow and stretched his neck. "I'm sorry, um…husband. Go back to sleep, and I'll wake you if I need you."

He obeyed, to her surprise.

"Where did I go wrong?" She shifted her eyes and kept her voice to a whisper. "I did everything right."

Glancing at Kerlin, she reopened the book and pored over the instructions again. It didn't make any sense; she should have found herself in Dorhen's dream. Had that been a dream, or some infernal dimension? Her heart ached for Dorhen. She wished to try again, but what if she found herself in that same place?

She consulted the mirror on the wall across the room. The bruises weren't so bad, although the book stated the more beatings received in a dream, the greater the effect would be upon transition to the waking world. Did that mean each dreamwalking experience would progress in realism?

*If Dorhen can't be reached, who else can I try?* Father Liam or her parents couldn't help her here, not so far into the Darklands in a city within a forest of poison. She needed help fast…

The Dreamer. Though frightening, he seemed more amorous than violent, although he had hit her the last time they met in a dream. She remembered him well: his rich bedroom, his demonic robe. Surely he knew magic. And she'd dreamed herself to him by accident before, so she should be able to return easily enough. Despite the craziness of the idea, he could be her sole option.

Kalea lay down again. What a stupid idea! Not stupid—desperate. She didn't even know the Dreamer's real name, and a name was the least amount of knowledge one must have for this to work properly. She sat upright again. Dreamwalking without a name must be terribly dangerous! What if she entered the wrong dream or became trapped?

All necessary risks. For now, she would simply name her target "Dreamer," as he had insisted, and during casting she would picture him as she remembered, and hope it would be enough. After a few more minutes of trying, she admitted relief when her effort failed, but with continued persistence, her chanting and mental image of the Dreamer sharpened. Kalea fell asleep.

\*\*\*

A breeze swept across the long, grassy field behind her. A familiar landscape, like the Darklands after she and her companions had emerged from the tunnel under Hanhelin's Gate.

"I'm out of the forest?" Kalea muttered. She stood alone, knee-deep in itchy, waving grass. No horizon in sight. No mountains or forest canopies were visible behind the dense fog rushing past on the wind to help her guess her location. The fresh mist dampened her skin—a keen sensation.

"How did I get out of that room with the red-eyed man?" She bowed her head and rubbed her temples.

*Oh, that's right!* Her dreamwalking attempt had worked! She ran her hand over the tops of the grass. They tickled, just like in real life. The breeze settled, and so did the fog around her. She had aimed for the Dreamer's dream, but this wasn't right. She must've made an error somehow.

She took a few steps. Her feet were still bare, and dried weeds hiding in the grass snagged her chemise. Next time, she'd try to dreamwalk with all her clothes on. She'd have to study the book some more to learn how.

She didn't have to go far before she found a group of little huts made from rough branches, canvas, and animal skins. The grass lay tamped down by many feet closer to the little village's entrance. Black feathers decorated the tops of the huts and many posts erected around the perimeter. Stinking, dead animals hung about, as rancid as they would've been in real life.

As unfriendly as the place seemed, she had to find someone who could help her, if not the Dreamer. If they spoke her language, maybe she could get some help, or at least advice. She didn't want to think about what might happen if they didn't speak Lightlandic.

She set her bare feet on the other side of the subtle barrier where the grass thinned and shifted into compacted earth. Her footpads touched down on cool, moist soil laced with threads of dead grass. No people yet.

"Hello?" she called. No answer.

Suddenly, a practically naked woman turned the corner, though not to answer her call. Kalea gawked but collected herself. She couldn't be rude. Whoever these people were, they were uncivilized. The woman wore a loincloth at least, and it showed off most of her legs in addition to her entire upper torso. Swirling green paint worked to obscure her nudity.

Kalea bashfully approached the woman, who ignored her as she carried a bucket of water across the village.

"Excuse me," Kalea said, louder than her first attempt. The woman didn't stop. "Hey!" Kalea tried again, and put her hand on the woman's bare shoulder. Her hand went straight through. Kalea stopped walking and observed her hand. The bare-breasted woman left her behind, leaving Kalea with a familiar loneliness.

Another person walked by her, carrying an armful of kindling twigs. She looked exactly like the first half-naked woman. Kalea's eyes darted to the first woman and back. They were identical: same black hair, same body paint, same proud breasts sticking out far with pierced nipples.

Another woman crossed the village's center, the same woman again. And then more appeared, all of them exactly alike. Kalea's mouth hung open. She tried to touch another one, and her hand passed through. They were all specters.

*What now?* Kalea looked around, gaping and twiddling her fingers, eager to find anyone who might be different. Just more of the same woman with big breasts and supple lips to complement them.

Kalea turned to the nearest hut behind her and reached for the hanging animal skin covering the entrance. Her hand went through that object too. She ran to the next hut and tried to enter it. All of it was illusion! She decided to try them all. She attempted to touch shoulders, water jugs, a woodpile, other huts. Everything except the ground she walked on and the grass in the field proved illusory. What could she accomplish in this place? She didn't even know how to awaken.

Off to the side stood another hut, a small distance apart from the rest. She ran toward it, finally noting her leg wound was gone again. She threw open the tarp—it was solid! She practically fell into the tiny house. She stumbled into a darkness with familiar cold stones underfoot. Around a curve, sharp glowing lines of light announced a set of doors. She paused at the door and knocked.

*Enter.* Was that his voice?

Behind the door, she found what she expected: the Dreamer's bedroom as she remembered it. She'd dreamwalked before by accident, and managed it on purpose tonight. Had Kerlin spoken the truth about her being a Luschian?

The Dreamer wore a thin white undershirt and his yellow hair hung free, like a silken fountain spilling to his shoulders. As she remembered, he sat on the bed atop the dais, a bit sweaty. Light shone through the sun windows above, the only windows in the room, showering him in multicolored rays. The surrounding walls were dominated by mirrors and murals and tapestries depicting orgy scenes.

"And you've returned," he said. "Another accident?" His voice resonated huskily with fatigue.

Kalea shook her head.

"You're here on purpose?" He raised his chin to look at her better.

"I…I need help," she said, shakier than anticipated. A boiling feeling bloomed in her stomach.

"What makes you think I can help you?"

She glanced around his room. "You look resourceful. You look like you know magic." His eyes narrowed to slits. "What type of magic do you know?"

"Sorcery."

Kalea swallowed in an attempt to remoisten her throat. What an abomination, to have to ask a sorcerer for help! But Bowaen, Del, and Gaije were dead, and she had no one else to reach for. She believed Kerlin's claim because she too had eaten the fruit which took all the water out of her system. After almost dying of thirst, she'd turned out to be the unlucky one who survived it. Since she was alive, she'd have to go on. Maybe she could take advantage of this sorcerer and gain information from him as to where Dorhen and her sisters were held captive.

"And sorcerers don't work for free," he continued.

"I don't have money."

He remained silent for a moment, sitting solemnly as she'd found him. She felt as if she'd interrupted his rest or meditation. "No matter," he responded.

Kalea's heart raced. Her naked body showed through her thin chemise, she knew, and his eyes lingered on it until she crossed her arms over her chest.

Shielding herself, she put on her boldest face possible to mask her helplessness. "Where are you?"

He waved his hand, the first big gesture he'd made since her arrival. "Not important. But I should like to know how you got here and where *you* are."

"I think I'm a…" She didn't really want to tell him. "A dreamwalker."

"Of course you are. I recall telling you so at our last meeting." His voice barked.

She couldn't figure out if her visit annoyed him or not. "Well, today someone told me I'm a…Luschian."

He reared his head back. "A what?"

"A Luschian. Do you know what that is?"

His pupils focused into a fixed stare. "I do. Who told you this?"

"This is my problem. I'm trapped in a town called Valltalhiss. It's in a horrible forest."

"How did you get there, of all places?"

"I don't know, it just happened," she said, at a loss. Her voice lowered to a weak whisper, as if Kerlin might hear her speaking from the waking world. "I need to get out before tomorrow night. They are planning some sort of goddess ceremony, and their leader means to…um…mate with me."

The Dreamer's eyes sparked alive, blazing with interest, and his restful demeanor quickly expired. He slid off the bed and approached her, hanging on every word. "You need my help getting out of Valltalhiss."

"Yes. Is there anything you can do?"

The Dreamer turned around. A black mark on his back, between his shoulder blades, showed under his thin shirt. He faced her again and stared at her body glowing beneath the white fabric of her chemise.

"What are you willing to sacrifice?" Kalea stuttered for a few tense seconds before he waved his hand. "Are you willing to meet with me?"

"I have some items you might be interested in." Though she dreaded giving away Dorhen's pendant or her silver-handled washing bat, getting away from Valltalhiss might be the most important thing to her whole being.

"Fine. You'll meet with me and show me what valuables you have. We'll discuss it later. For now, you must escape."

"Thank you!" She dropped to her knees and buried her face in her hands. "My virginity is most important to me. I mean to give it to the one I love. Please tell me, sir, how can I escape?"

He watched her hard until she fidgeted, eyes darting around. She remained on the floor, and he spoke down to her. "Near you walks a sentinel from another dimension, a sanguinesent. Luckily for you, one of my people managed to summon it. You need to attract it to yourself. I can't do anything while I sleep, so I'll contact it when I awaken."

"Sanguinesent?"

"Is there a problem?"

Kalea shook her head. "I don't know what you're talking about." The lie boiled in her stomach to add to the ill feeling already dwelling there.

"You'll know it when you see it. We'll make you its target. It'll kill its way through Valltalhiss until it finds you, and then it'll escort you to me. You'll need an implement to attract its attention."

"Tell me what I have to do." Never in her life did she intend to see such a creature again, but at this elf's mercy, and in her lonely desperation, she couldn't choose better.

"If you were a mere human, it could find you easily, but you're different and will need a prop. This is where my magic can help you."

Kalea clasped her hands together.

He continued, "I can send you the item you need if I receive a prop from you of equal size and weight in return. Make it the size of your two fists, and also check how heavy it is. It should weigh as much as a cup of tea. When you find the perfect object, draw a pentagram on the floor after sunrise and place it in the center. I'll complete a spell simultaneously. When you receive my item, hold it high above your head, preferably out a window, and declare that you have desire. This will catch the sanguinesent's attention."

Against all the warnings in her gut, she nodded. "Thank you."

The Dreamer turned away from her, the side of his mouth stretching into a smirk, and Kalea's vision darkened.

She woke up.

# Chapter 15
## What is a Dead Saehgahn Rising

Kingsorcerer Lamrhath opened his eyes to the grey beams of morning shooting through the windows of the little village hut. He stretched and yawned. The memory of a conversation with a willowy girl in her chemise echoed crisply in his mind, and a furious erection pushed up against his blankets, as if the five sessions last night never happened.

He dropped his head back to the straw pillow with a sigh. That new dreamwalker had returned. He'd hoped she would. Being in such a convenient place to perform the necessary magic to help his talented new friend, he stifled his agitation at his so-soon-returned bodily need.

"Sigmune!" he shouted, knowing the man waited outside, and the skin door flap swooped open. This would certainly anger the elders, and Lamrhath would have to compensate them. "I want one of the girls from last night back."

Sigmune needed no explanation. He bowed and gestured to leave.

"Wait," Lamrhath barked before he could get away.

"My lord?"

"There's a woman somewhere in the village. I glimpsed her when we entered. She has…a nice form. Long legs, pouty lips. You'll know her when you see her."

"I probably have, my lord."

"Good," Lamrhath said. "Tell the chieftain we're taking her with us." Lamrhath closed his eyes at the wave of exhilarating pleasure mixed with pain his ailment was delivering this morning. "Just pay him whatever he wants for her."

An enormous weight crushed down on Gaije, rendering him immobile and helpless to remedy the unbelievable thirst tormenting his throat. So many agonies greeted his returned consciousness. Opening his mouth allowed in a flood of earth—not air. When he opened his eyes, they were bombarded with scratchy grains of dirt. He would soon suffocate, so he wriggled. The fear lent him some energy to do it. He forced his arms and legs to move. They barely could, but slowly the earth loosened around them.

The more he wriggled, the more space he created. Digging with his fingers, he churned the earth until they finally broke into open air. He tried to make his head follow, but the weight kept him firmly suppressed. Using his arms, he shoved the dirt away little by little until he could begin to rise. The earth held his legs down. Clawing the loose dirt away enough finally freed his face to the air. He panted and rested, cradled in a mound of loose soil.

Rain sprinkled through the canopy, and he raised his face to welcome the cool water into his mouth, but it soured his tongue. Wiping his eyes with dirty hands proved futile, especially with the introduction of the rain. He assumed the trees were to blame, by the knot cramping his stomach. The rain water must've picked up the poisonous sap before dripping off the leaves and branches. He couldn't drink it while in this forest.

"Ka…" he uttered but couldn't find the rest of her name in his exhaustion. His throat was too dry.

Needing to make sure she was alive, he forced himself to move again. He kicked his legs and scraped the earth away with shaking hands. If a female died on his watch, he feared hell, or at least shame and a beating from his elders. What would Lehomis do if he found out his own grandson had let a woman die? Not to mention his failure to rescue Mhina.

With a great struggle to support himself, Gaije crawled out of the hole, coughing up dirt and trembling his way to hands and knees. He scanned for his companions, their belongings, or his belongings. Nothing. His shoes and greaves were gone along with everything else, including his *sa-garhik*. Gaije had been poisoned, robbed, and buried alive and naked—they'd even taken his braies.

Standing up on shaking legs, he scanned for signs of anyone, hugging himself in cold or loneliness, or both. The raindrops burned as they dropped off the poisonous trees, and he had nothing on to shield against them. A persistent ache in his core drove him to induce vomiting, to rid himself of the bite of fruit he'd taken. Afterward, his mouth burned. The others might be dead. Elves were immune to most poisons, and if one bite of the fruit made him feel like this, then his friends…

But where were they? He scanned the ground again. No other fresh graves accompanied his. But footprints, many of them, were stamped around, going to and fro and leaving with drag marks behind them. If there had been people here, why would they drag the humans away and bury Gaije?

Without a scrap of clothing on, he followed the tracks. In need of a weapon and walking stick, he picked up a branch and immediately dropped it. The wet, rotting bark of the trees burned his hand. The gentle rain soon stopped, and thank the Bright One for it, because it raised red irritation marks all over him.

Gaije followed the tracks until nightfall, when faint noises led him to a dilapidated city. A crumbling wall surrounded it, with watchmen posted at every corner. Inside, folk were moving about and chattering with a level of excitement. They spoke the common tongue, but he struggled to take in their dialect. Something surprising had stirred them, by their tones. Gaije and his companions could have animated them like this. After all, the town thrived right in the center of this forest of poisonous trees, so visitors must be an oddity.

Gaije breathed in relief. His friends might be alive here. The townspeople might've buried Gaije before realizing he also survived. Perhaps they kept a good store of water to share. A dim glow lit the nearest watchtower. He went toward it, hoping his nudity wouldn't offend these people too much.

Inside the door, stairs ascended immediately to the tower and catwalk. Voices conversed on the glowing upper level. Though he intended to reveal himself, Gaije crept for now.

"Praise to Thaxyl," one voice with a strange accent said, and Gaije halted to listen. "I'll never believe our luck. Two humans and a Luschian—our mother goddess!"

"I wish I could have her."

"I want to know how they differ from Thaccilian women."

"They're better! I can't help thinking of breaching the tower tonight."

"Don't dare, fool! She is our mother goddess, and—"

"And what, meant for Kerlin? He takes advantage 'cause he is king. Wake up, stupid."

"I will after the ceremony tomorrow, when we are all walking out of here behind heaven couple."

"You dream. They are not 'heaven couple.' Kerlin is self-titled Luschian stealer."

"He is wise leader. He prevents violence among us to take Luschian for himself."

"Vlah vlah, and all your dreams. Tell yourself what is needed."

"I not worried at all. I is happy, as we will feast on human flesh tomorrow. Enough to feed us all. What miraculous Moon Ceremony it will be this year."

Gaije pressed hard against the wall, going instantly cold. They did have the humans. He aborted the idea of presenting himself. He wouldn't try to attack these men either. He continued up the stairs slowly and approached the door to the top room. Two men bickered away behind it. Their backs were turned as they watched out the window toward the black looming tower against a twilight sky. A fireplace provided plenty of light. Their firewood logs were those horrid trees, which stank as they burned. Those trees resented everything done to them.

One of the guards' cloaks hung beside the door; the other man chose to wear his. Gaije carefully lifted it and eyed a small hatchet leaning against the wall by the woodpile. He took a slow, careful step toward it, heart pounding. They wore swords on their belts, and though he could fight without one, he didn't like the odds of having to fight two men at once. Also, there might be others out on the catwalk.

Gaije stepped silently. He reached for the hatchet.

"Where you going?"

"To take piss. Relax. Your 'mother goddess' is safe from me."

Gaije slinked back down the staircase in the shadow. He placed the cloak about his shoulders and drew the hood. Stepping outside, he met the man's urine stream splattering over the dried leaves as he pissed off the catwalk. Gaije stayed pressed against the wall until he finished. Keeping the hatchet hidden beneath the cloak, he tiptoed forward.

The villagers were lighting torches and moving about the ruined buildings, wishing each other well and praising the Mother Goddess and King Kerlin. Gaije moved about them swiftly with his chin held low. In the square, they were hustling to build a large fire. Young children ran back and forth with more firewood to toss onto a massive pile. A handful of adults danced in a group, practicing the song, "Praise Thaxyl! Because of him, we will live on!"

Nearby metallic scraping sounds announced a man sharpening an array of knives. Others were erecting a few spits over an old, blackened fire pit. The citizens were obviously preparing a feast, but as Gaije looked around, he saw no animals to be slaughtered. Or even a harvest of vegetables.

Gaije pulled his hood lower, re-crossed his arms tightly to keep the cloak closed, and moved in the general direction of the main tower. He could only assume his companions were held there unless he could overhear a better clue.

He found a lonely alley, and at the entrance, a woman grabbed his cloak and called, "Strozen, where are you going?" Her hard tug on the cloak exposed his body, and she giggled. "What's on your mind now, mister?"

She attempted an advance with arms extended, and he dodged, making not a sound and pulling the hood deeper over his face.

With his cloak freed, he sprinted through the alley to leap and spring off one wall to the low-hanging awning of another. The rotted wood barely held him, and he pumped his legs to get farther up the gabled roof.

"Strozen! Strozen!" she called from below.

Roof by roof, he traversed the length of the city. He stopped on the last rooftop to size up the dark, looming tower of the decaying manor house. A narrow avenue ran perpendicular to the alley Gaije had been following from above. Lights beamed through the tiny window holes on the side wing near a large patch of wild grass. A man stood guard by the door not more than twenty paces away.

Gaije tested the hatchet's weight, practicing for his one chance. *Saehgahn* training covered bows, swords, and the body; axes were mostly thought of as woodcutting tools. The other major lesson was balance, in which Gaije excelled. He balked at the sound of footsteps scraping the gravelly road from the alley below.

"Where you been, Ravki?"

"Vloosh, brother, relax, I am here. They made me do some polishing. So much preparation. Have the humans awaken?"

"Yes, but you must stay at your station. No taunting them, they said. No need to cause them any misery before their deaths. They are providing a great blessing to us."

"Food!" Ravki said with a cheer. "I can't even remember last time I tasted such flesh. I want to see them."

"See them later, fool, I can't linger a moment longer. Take your place now!"

So Ravki assumed the first man's guard position. Blinking, Gaije could hardly comprehend what he'd heard. These people planned to…eat the humans? A shiver ran up Gaije's arms and down his spine. He could only imagine Kalea, how afraid she must be in there. That innocent look she often displayed in her eyes.

Gaije gripped the hatchet handle tighter, and set his stare on Ravki, a very unlucky person tonight. The hapless new guard groaned and moved from the spot nonetheless. He went around the corner to piss against the wall in the cover of the tall grass.

Gaije took the opportunity to drop to the dirt and sneak up behind him. As the man relieved himself, sighing, Gaije slammed the heavy, blunt back of the hatchet into his skull. Ravki fell fairly silently; the sound of his skull colliding with the axe's iron hopefully shouldn't alert anyone. One swift chop at Ravki's neck ensured he wouldn't wake up again.

Gaije bent to peek inside the glowing window hole. The inside appeared uninhabited, so he hurried around the corner to enter the door before someone could happen to stroll by. He gripped the bloody hatchet in his fist so tightly his hand went numb. A fire burned in a brazier; whoever occupied this room should return soon. A water jug sat on a table. Gaije seized it and gulped all of it down. He needed more.

A loud but muffled exchange of voices jabbered ahead. He leaned against the wall, cracked the door open, and peeked in. In a small dungeon, Bowaen and Del occupied two of the cells. The noise came from the next room at the far end. He crept in, down a set of stone stairs.

"Gaije?" Bowaen whispered.

"And what are the chances that he's naked again?" Del added blandly.

Gaije put his finger to his lips and then slowly whispered, "Where's Kalea?"

"Don't know, but our weapons are in there." Bowaen pointed to the room with the activity.

No key hung anywhere in here. Gaije sucked in some air and gingerly padded toward the next room. The men's voices were snipping at each other in a fight over something. Gaije cracked the door to spy. Indeed, two men were playing tug-o-war with Gaije's armor until one of them cut his finger on the layered blades wrapping around the greaves. He yelped and put his fingertip into his mouth.

"Fine, then," the one with the cut finger said. "I'll take the bow."

The one with the greaves dropped his jaw and scrutinized the other plucking the string in satisfaction. The candlelight glinted across the inlaid silver of the bow's horse figures. The man with his grandfather's bow also wore Gaije's tunic. The man with the greaves already wore Gaije's military mantle bearing his clan and royal insignia.

Gritting his teeth, Gaije glared at the way the cut-finger man fondled his bowstring, until he burst out, "That's my grandfather's!" and tore into the room, whipping off his cloak so he could use it as a distraction device. He brandished the hatchet in his other hand.

The man with the bow leapt in fright, and the one with his greaves exclaimed, "The creature lives! Too bad we can't eat this one!"

Gaije spared no effort, but the two held their guard positions for a reason. He flailed and whipped the cloak to distract, muddle, and faze his opponents. He didn't land any hits until the one with the greaves reached for another clay water pitcher. Gaije smashed it, along with his hand, against the table with the back of the hatchet.

"Naked creature wants to die!" the man said after a good scream.

Gaije whipped the cloak to keep the other man from making an attack, staying on the side of the broken hand to keep him at a disadvantage.

The man whirled, using his good hand to grab the cloak, and as Gaije struggled, the other used Lehomis's bow to ensnare his throat and choke him across the string.

He kicked the back of Gaije's knee, and when he dropped, the broken-handed man seized Gaije's exposed genitals to subdue him better. He laughed as Gaije howled on a shortened strand of breath.

His vision darkened. He curled up on the floor, helpless to defend himself anymore.

"Thanks, Gaije, that was amusing," Del said as Gaije sat defeated and silent in a cell of his own.

"Where is the woman?" Gaije demanded as soon as one of the guards entered the jail again.

"They won't tell us," Bowaen said as he leaned against the wall. The guard exited again after briefly inspecting the strength of Gaije's cell lock. "When we noticed you weren't with us, we were relieved. Any ideas?"

Gaije leaned his bare back against his cold cell wall. They had taken the cloak away from him, proclaiming it their property, not his.

"We have one day to find Kalea and get out of this place," Gaije said, practically in a moan.

"Why?" Bowaen asked.

"Because they're going to cut you into little pieces and eat you."

# Chapter 16
## What is a Vestal's Revolting Deed

After her dreamwalking experience, Kalea's eyes sprang open and she sat up. A glow seeped through the shutters already. She didn't have much time. Hopefully, the Creator would forgive her for taking part in casting a sorcery spell. Her eyes darted around the available objects in the room.

"Good morning, wife."

Kalea jumped at the sudden voice. She had forgotten about Kerlin and whether he'd awakened or not.

He pulled on his creased old boots and then donned a wool coat with its dye long faded. "Today is busy day," he said. "Tonight is the night I—we—shall be married."

He knelt beside her and planted a kiss on her forehead. Her racing mind hardly noticed it. What a nightmare she'd woken up to yesterday! She couldn't decide if real life beat last night's dreamwalking sessions in horror and misery.

He paused as his hungry eyes observed her face again. "What happened to your face?" he asked, and ran his thumb under her eye.

A shock of dread zipped through her. She'd forgotten about the bruises she'd collected during her dreamwalking ventures last night!

"Um." She swallowed. "I didn't mean to…"

His brow tensed as he waited for her explanation. "Your heart beats fast, but someone didn't break in here and hurt you," he said.

"Of course not." A simple lie would do, though Kalea could do nothing to control her heart rate. The truth was much harder to fathom. "I'm so clumsy," she said. "And I'm sorry I made myself look so ugly right before our wedding day." Her hand absentmindedly gestured toward the bookcase. "I was…enjoying your excellent collection of books. And I…I reached for one on a high shelf, and like an idiot, I dropped it—right on my eye. It hurt, but I'm fine. I didn't see any reason to wake you."

He studied her, a smile spreading across his lips. He laughed lightly and pulled her into a hug. She grimaced and grunted in response, hating his scent. Not that it bothered her—she didn't actually mind it, and she hated *that* fact! All of this made tears of frustration and distress gather in her eyes.

"You are an interesting and delightful creature." Her fists balled tightly when he let her go and resumed dressing himself. When he glanced at her again, he paused. "What is matter?"

"This is all wrong!"

His brow furrowed. "'Scuse?"

"I can't—I *won't*—marry you!" His jaw muscles tightened beneath his smile. She swallowed hard and hoped he didn't notice. "I mean," she began before he could say something she might find frightening, "this is all wrong. This is not the way marriage is carried out in my culture, and I demand you observe my ways if I am to observe yours!"

He stopped at arm's length away and studied her. She could see him better in the growing sunlight. He was handsome, despite his off-putting eye color. He drew his mouth wide and knelt before her, taking her hand and bowing his head over it. He rested his lips on her palm and held them there for an eternity. He might've been alluring in another time and place, but here and now, she hated when he touched her.

"Of course, of course. I live for you. What is it I can do?"

Kalea raised her chin to feign confidence as she lied, "In my culture, the groom always obliges the bride's request for a gift."

He smirked. "My limits are few. Whatever we have in this dying city, I can and will get for you. Say it."

Kalea couldn't stop her lip from quivering at what she prepared to say. "One of my companions carried a magnificent sword that shone like the moon. I demand it!" Her loud voice echoed off the stone walls. After one nod of his head, he stood. "I demand it now, right this minute!"

He responded by putting his arms around her and blatantly smelling her hair. She tensed her body to keep from shuddering.

"Yes, Mother Kalea. It's yours." He turned and left.

Amidst their chorus of hissing arguments and escape ideas at each other, Bowaen and his companions fell silent when a man in a drab purple coat stormed through the jail and straight into the storeroom where the two men from last night were snoring. He roused them with barked words in another language.

After the man stormed back through carrying Hathrohjilh, the guards went quiet as if drifting off again. Bowaen worked his jaw, staring helplessly at the man taking his sword away. Gaije shook his head slightly at Bowaen to urge him not to protest. If the two guards fell back to sleep, there might be a chance for them. They would have to let Hathrohjilh go for the sake of freedom.

The jail fell silent again for a long moment.

"Psst, Gaije," Del whispered. "You're a little leaky."

Gaije glared over his crossed arms. "Shut up," he replied. "*Saehgahn* don't cry."

"No, *you* shut up and listen. Your cell is damp. There's drainage above you. Check the door hinges. How rusty are they?"

Gaije leaped to inspect them. His eyes were wide as he returned Del's gaze. "Why didn't you say so last night?"

"Shh! Because it was dark, and you were too bloody hot-headed to think clearly."

Gaije looked again. "They've about worn away."

He jiggled the door, took one more look, and pulled against the bar with one foot braced on the side. The metal groaned and the rust flaked. He stopped to rest with a huff and tried again. Bowaen and Del cringed at the metallic noises. Gaije tried once more, knotting up every muscle in his body and gnashing his teeth before falling back exhaustedly.

"You'll have to strike it," Del said.

"No," Bowaen snapped. "Too noisy."

Del's eyes rounded the room again and again. He squinted at a spot near the ceiling of Gaije's cell. He pointed. "Up there," he whispered. "Looks like your cage doesn't meet the ceiling."

The rest of them eyeballed the gap between the top-most rail of the wall of bars and the wooden ceiling. The imperfection was due to the uneven rocky floor.

Gaije spread his empty hands to either side of his shamelessly naked body. "What do you want me to do about it?"

"What do you think, you idiot?" Del countered. "Climb up and squeeze over the top."

Gaije sneered at him. "You think I'm that small?"

Del crossed his arms. "Yeah, actually, forget I said it. I'll bet you're not strong enough to climb those bars without horizontal footholds anyway. Your little bow hands aren't strong enough to scrape any of the rotten wood from the ceiling, and you're certainly not strong enough to maneuver over the top." Del spread his lips wide.

Gaije's pale skin had flushed to match his hair by the end of Del's speech. The elf spat a big wad of saliva across the jail at Del, grabbed the bars, and hauled himself up with the sheer strength of his arms.

Bowaen watched in astonishment. Gaije did have the first door hinge to narrowly brace his big toe on, but the rest of the work he did with his arms and iron will. When he didn't have another hinge to grasp with his toes, he folded them around the bars awkwardly. He made quick work of climbing the cell. Hanging by one arm, he used his other to pick at the damaged wooden ceiling.

"What if someone's on the floor above us?" Bowaen asked.

"They're not," Del grunted.

Gaije's teeth clenched harder than they had when he'd tried to bend the bars. Soft splinters of wood rained down. Bowaen forgot to breathe as he watched. He mouthed the word "hurry."

Gaije cleared away a wide layer of wood. It still didn't appear like it would accommodate the size of his rib cage, let alone his head. His arms shook by the time he stopped. He dropped back to the floor to rest.

"Don't relax too long," Del warned.

Gaije sprang and hauled himself up the bars again. He lifted his foot high enough to place it at the narrower end of the gap where the bar ran across the top along the ceiling. He turned his head gingerly at a certain angle to put it through the opening. If he lost his grip and fell, his neck would snap and he'd hang dead. To make sure that didn't happen, he put his arm outside of the cell and grabbed the bar from there. He emptied his lungs to squeeze his ribs through, another potential deadly situation. He'd have to hurry to squeeze all the way through so he could inhale again.

Bowaen leaned toward Del in the cell next to his. "Too bad you're not in his cell. You're smaller than him."

Del shook his head. "I may fit better, but I don't have the strength he has to accomplish all this."

Every honed muscle in Gaije's body worked. He hung there in the wildest uncomfortable pose Bowaen had ever seen. A few long and painful seconds of frantic wiggling got his chest the rest of the way through. The plan was working, but it wasn't over yet. The look on his reddened face hinted at his longing to rest, but he didn't have room to balance leisurely across the top rail without suffocating.

His hips were the next daunting obstacle, since, as Bowaen and Del knew too well, his most sensitive body part hung there. Gaije did the best he could with it, wincing and hissing as he maneuvered himself over the rough iron rail. Bowaen turned away from the not-pretty sight.

Finally free, Gaije fell and landed on his hands and one knee outside the cell. The other knee he spared by placing his foot to the floor upon landing. Gaije paused to stifle his cry of pain, gnashing his teeth and hissing through them. It wasn't his knee giving him pain; he was taking the break for his genitals.

"Gaije, hurry," Del whispered, and Gaije shot him a hateful stare. "Don't go charging in there for another fight," he continued. "Find me a small piece of metal, a thin wire or something."

"I was going to snatch the key while they slept," Gaije said.

"Too risky," Del argued. "I saw scrap debris in the first room when they brought us in. Check it for some kind of thin wire."

Gaije limped around in search of what Del described. He crept up the stairs and disappeared through the doorway. During his absence, murmuring arose in the storeroom. The guards woke up!

A sudden cold sweat and pounding heart made Bowaen woozy. Ever since he'd passed the age of forty-five, his heart had acted less than predictably. No one needed to know that, though.

Gaije returned with a wad of thread-thin wire and handed it to Del through the bars. "Best I could find," he said.

Del frowned and toiled with the soft coil. It must've come off the handle of a dagger. Del twisted it over on itself and then stuck it into his own padlock.

"Can you use that to—?"

Del shushed Bowaen's question. "Of course I can," he said, working his makeshift lock pick.

Bowaen's smile beamed, despite the anxiety the voices in the other room brought. "I don't doubt ya, boy."

He turned to Gaije and whispered, "This little bastard burgled houses for their petty valuables back home. And he thought I didn't notice. I goaded him to stick around me and focus on whitesmithing and combat." Bowaen shook his head. "Not this little shithead, no sir."

Gaije stood outside their cells, waiting for Del to finish freeing himself and looking like he felt more naked than before.

The padlock clicked open. Del opened the door as narrowly as he could to keep the hinges from groaning more than necessary. They winced at every sound it made. He hurried to Bowaen's lock and repeated the process. His door screamed louder.

"They're out!"

The two guards rushed in, and as Bowaen and Gaije fought the two off, Del went to retrieve some weapons from the storeroom. Hathrohjilh was gone, so he emerged with Gaije's bow, the hatchet Gaije brought in, and his old iron pipe. He tossed the hatchet to Bowaen and the bow to Gaije, who swung the weapon around rather than fumble with arrows in their limited space.

Bowaen parried the guard's sword with the hatchet and delivered a deep punch to his gut when he found the chance. In the man's daze, Bowaen struck him in the face with the hatchet's heavy head. Nearby, Gaije disarmed his guard and strangled him.

With the two guards down, they hurried into the storeroom to arm themselves. As they rifled through the heaps of tools, weapons, and armor for their own belongings, the sound of many boots tapped down the steps into the jail. Too many men for the three to handle flooded into the storeroom.

A gang of hands grabbed Bowaen's arms, overpowering him, and wrenched the hatchet away. Folding his arms behind him, they pushed him flat and planted their knees into his back. With his head forced down, Bowaen couldn't tell if Gaije and Del were also suppressed. Del's grunting didn't sound good.

A calm voice with a foreign accent boomed above him. "Put weapons back on racks, and get their clothes off before more damage happens."

As soon as the door closed behind Kerlin, Kalea scrambled around to inspect the various objects the room offered. She needed a drawing utensil and an object similar to her fists. The torch on the wall had burned out, and the remaining charred stick should be perfect.

After drawing a crude star, she went to Kerlin's desk and found an old dry inkwell—not exactly the size and shape of her fist. She picked up the small clay cup from last night. It was weighty enough when filled with water, but the shape didn't seem right. She put it down and scanned again. The room didn't offer much. An old crate stood beside the desk, acting as a chair.

Her eyes landed on the candles from last night and the masses of warm wax they had dripped all over the desk. She peeled the wax up, still warm and soft, and squished it into a ball shape. It felt about the right size, but she held no confidence in her ability to judge its weight. The Dreamer had told her it should weigh as much as a cup of tea. She'd drunk plenty of tea in her life, but right now her nerves danced too frantically to stop and think about that.

The sunrise strengthened behind the window. At which moment would it be too late? The Dreamer would be casting his spell soon, wherever he was, and if she didn't act fast, his prop might dissipate into oblivion. She placed the wax ball in the center of the star.

A rap at the door set Kalea to covering the spell with the crate. A woman, the one from last night, politely stepped in, and Kalea sat on the crate, trying to appear calm. The woman brought a new pitcher of water and placed it on the desk. She walked in a wide curve as if Kalea were a coiled rattler. She gave a nervous curtsy and left without a word. If only some food had accompanied the water pitcher.

Kalea lifted the crate to see if the spell had worked. The wax remained. She paced now, hoping she hadn't ruined the spell by choosing the wrong object. She left the crate over it and went to the window. Opening the shutter, she spied the busy city. Many ragged people were moving and running about. In the town square, a pillar of smoke rushed into the sky. Kalea cocked her head.

Kerlin's voice echoed in the hall, yelling at the female guards and serving women again. Heart thundering, Kalea hauled the crate and placed it in front of the door in an attempt to barricade it. When the door budged, she added her weight.

"Your heart is loud! What is going on, Kalea?"

She didn't answer him. He'd claimed that the Thaccilians could hear heartbeats, and she'd already forgotten. Nothing she could do to fake her heart's activity! He pushed against the door, and she hadn't the strength or weight to keep him out. A glance over at the wax revealed it was gone!

She rushed to the pentagram as he flung the door open, slamming the crate aside. He advanced on her, and she darted away. Her hands met the new object—red, moist, and heavy. It throbbed softly in her hands.

"Oh, dear Creator!" she shrieked. Having no luxury to pause and be disgusted, she flew back to the window, held the bleeding piece of meat aloft, and screamed, "I have desire!"

Kerlin grabbed her arms and drew her back. "Shush, you can't let them hear you! Calm your heart, or they'll hear it too!"

He wrestled her away, though she wanted to say it again to make sure it worked. As he faced her and seized both her wrists, the meat slapped against the floor with a bloody spatter. He paused and sniffed the air. Breathing heavily, he licked her hand, his tongue sliding across her palm. The tickling it caused traveled straight from her hand to her abdomen. He licked her bloody finger, and then sucked it. A strange sensation, having her finger in someone else's mouth. Kalea's jaw fell open.

The glide of his tongue along her little finger slowed, and his eyes went to the meat on the floor. Dropping her hand, he pounced on the thing. "It's still warm!" He bit into the raw meat, fell into a squat, and gnawed it.

Kalea stared, forgetting about escaping as she watched him finish the whole raw thing. The blood on her hands mingled with his saliva. She thought back to her days in the convent kitchen and the deliveries from the butcher they'd prepare for all the novices. The words trailed from her mouth before she could think to alter or keep them inside.

"Was that a...a heart?"

# Chapter 17
## What is the Thaccilian People's Secret

Kerlin finished licking the blood off his hands and paused as if finally noticing Kalea watching him.

"You poor man," she said. "You must be dying of starvation. Can't your people farm?"

Squatting on the floor, his eyes grazed hotly over her. A goatee of blood wreathed his mouth.

"What are you looking at?" she asked.

He rose with a potent speed and strength he hadn't previously demonstrated, strode toward her, and grasped her face. Pressing her against the wall, he smashed his mouth hard against hers for a deep kiss. She screamed into his mouth and flailed. He took it upon himself to force her chemise ties open and trail his lips to the flesh above her heart.

At her intensified screaming and heightened heartbeat, he finally released her. Watching her crouch on the floor in terror, he took a deep breath and his face washed over with a new concern. "Sorry."

"Don't press me against the wall. Don't *ever* press m—" She put her hand over her mouth. The coppery taste of blood daubed her lips now, which she wiped across her arm.

"Sorry," he said again. "I just felt so... I've eaten now and have regained my essence. And when I look at you, I can hardly stop myself, like an animal that must fulfill its purpose."

Kalea shuddered. "Whatever you do to me, don't push me against the wall."

Kerlin bowed. She didn't like the burning in his eyes. "Better for me to leave you until time for us to mate," he said. "I'll return in a few hours." He cleaned his face in the basin, and then pointed to the sword on the floor before he left.

When the door closed behind him, the sight of the sword made Kalea's heart burn. It served as fair proof of her friends' fate. Kerlin had told the truth. How else could he have obtained the sword? Kalea took and cradled it in her arms, and a lump in her throat formed at memories of Bowaen. Hathrohjilh belonged to her now.

Forcing back the tears, she stood on her good leg, unsheathed it, and tried a few swings. She practiced for a short while, noticing its surprisingly light weight. She'd be ready for Kerlin's return. Hard to believe he trusted her with it. He truly wanted to please her. No matter.

An odd sense of confidence accompanied this sword, pushing the fear far away. She'd brave the road alone with it as her companion. Whatever had to be. Sheathing it, she sat against the wall and rested, wrapping her arms around it.

*Wake up and feed my blade, little girl.*

She opened her eyes and snapped them around for the person who spoke. "Lord Rem?" she reflexively said aloud. It sounded like his voice, but carried a load more confidence and spite. She rubbed her eyes. She must've dozed off. Sleep hadn't fully graced her last night anyway. The voice must've been a dream.

Footsteps approached the door. Kerlin! She stood and poised herself with the blade.

The door opened. He walked in. Kalea froze with the sword high over her head. His eyes sprang wide. She couldn't do it.

Her hesitance allowed him the opportunity to grab her wrists and prevent her downward swing. They wrestled for control. He pressed her against the wall to get the sword tip facing away from him, and pried the hilt from her fingers.

She limped away as fast as she could, but he stood between her and the door. He dropped the sword, raised his hands, and walked slowly toward her. She wanted to dart again, but his wide stance showed his anticipation. She tried anyway and lunged for the sword. He caught her.

"What is matter? Won't be long now and we will leave. Look." He took her to the window and opened the shutter. A bonfire raged in the square. "My people will have a feast. I won't partake because you and me, we will be over there." He pointed to a stage-like altar near the fire area. "We will do the ceremony: consummate to complete our marriage, after which we will leave." He smelled her hair. "And the hour is drawing closer, so let's go outside now. I'll wear the sword, since I know you'll use it against me."

*Where's that sanguinesent the Dreamer promised to send?* Even her inner voice sounded weak and frightened. Kerlin's strength had defeated hers in the struggle, and now he was buckling the sword girdle around his waist. He tied her washing bat to her basket of belongings, snatched her hand, and pulled her toward the door.

Down in the castle's main hall, some women put a dense, red veil over Kalea's head. "So the other men don't get too excited, Mother Kalea," the woman said. Before the veil blinded her, she caught a glance of the women in the house. They all wore tattered old dresses and similar red scarves over their hair—like vestals. Rusty swords and daggers at their belts set Kerlin's female guards apart from the regular household staff.

She could barely see anything under the veil. Kerlin guided her by her trembling hand as shadows and shapes moved behind the musty fabric. Outside, the sun lowered fast but remained bright enough to show many more humanoid shapes crowding around her. Sounds of awe and murmurs greeted her on the pebbly path moving under her feet. A fire roared in the background. All eyes were on her, she knew it. Why, though?

"Here is the altar," Kerlin said.

Kalea shook her head, afraid to say the words, but she forced them out. "I won't kneel and pray to your false god." The words drifted out numb and wan.

"Not necessary," Kerlin responded. "The god in question is you, Mother Kalea."

With his hands on her waist, he lifted her without warning. She landed on the altar, where blankets were layered thickly.

"What are you doing? This isn't right." The platform rattled as he joined her. A voice to the side rang out in another language, and the crowd around them silenced to listen. "I'm not a false god either!"

He reached under her veil and began unlacing her bodice. His hands shook as much as hers. She slapped them away. "What are you doing?"

"Shh, we'll be married now. You get undressed for the mating."

"Right here?" she shrieked. "In front of everyone?"

"Shh, yes." Kalea tried to roll away, but he caught her. The person preaching kept talking regardless of how she acted. Kerlin wrestled her. "Don't struggle—many of your followers are watching! You'll be fine."

"No! Stop it right now, I never agreed—"

Through her squirming, he tightened his grip and forced himself on her. She screamed. When she managed to tear the veil off her head, the mesmerized faces of both men and women stared at her, waiting for a show. Some of them clasped their hands together as if in prayer. A man in tattered robes used big arm gestures while preaching.

"This is wrong!" Her voice came out as a piercing squeal. Too much was going on around her, and darting her eyes made her dizzy.

Kerlin leaned in to kiss her neck; the feeling of his lips and tongue sent sharp needles down her spine. She used the moment to look for an exit or distraction. Next to the large, glowing fire pit beyond the bustling crowd, another sort of altar had been hastily built. On its platform stood three naked men, heavily guarded, bound, and hooded as if waiting to be executed. One of them stood taller and slighter, and lacked all the body hair the other two figures sported…like an elf.

"Is he"—Kalea squinted—"an elf?" Her mouth dropped open in shock.

As she stopped squirming, Kerlin pinned her and ripped her bodice laces out past her breasts, exposing them beneath her chemise. She stretched her neck over his shoulder to see the naked men better while he explored the contents of her bodice. Kerlin calmed a bit after she did.

She tapped his shoulder. "Kerlin, who are they?"

He tried to pull the veil back over her head, and she squirmed to the side. "No one. Please lie back so we can complete the ceremony. This doesn't have to be difficult." He groped her chest and bowed to her throat to taste her skin some more.

"I said no!" She pushed against his shoulders and kept him braced on the other side of her locked arms. It wouldn't stop him from violating her, though. He attempted to block her view and situate himself between her legs. "Tell me what's going on right now. Are those my companions? Is that Gaije? You've lied to me! This marriage is off!"

"Kalea," he said with agitation in his voice, "you may not recognize what is truthfully going on. You didn't even know about Thaxyl and Lusche. You'll have to trust me. After today, we'll be together, in love, inseparable."

A cold shiver ran through her. She pushed back with all of her strength. "Tell me what's going on first!"

"What's going on is you should let me bind to you, and then we'll leave here. We'll go wherever you want. I don't even know what is out there beyond forest. But first, you calm down. Your actions are scaring your people."

"No! Tell me about those three men. Who are they?"

He continued his advances, struggling against her flailing limbs, saying, "They have to feed my people, and it's my duty to marry the goddess. Without this, my people will die."

"But they're human beings!"

He paused and glared. "Exactly." That feral red flash showed in his eyes like when he had eaten the heart. "Except for the elf. He provides no nourishment and will be pushed into the fire for being difficult with us."

He added more force to his actions. Her tangled mess of skirts, torn veil, and the blankets on the altar added extra difficulty to her struggle. And the crowd stared, although by now, their expressions had phased into puzzlement. She caught a look of concern on a woman's face and disgust on a man's. The man who looked disgusted often pointed his eyes at Kerlin. The preacher kept talking throughout Kalea's struggle.

Kerlin threw her skirt up in search of her legs amongst the tangle, explaining, "We are Thaccilians and have to eat human hearts to survive. There are two humans and many of us, so their entire bodies will be divided into small pieces so each person can have a bite of nourishment. You'd be with them if you weren't a Luschian."

He tried to split her legs apart, but she kicked and screamed. Her injured leg couldn't offer much help; it ached from her overuse of it already. How could she delay her friends being slaughtered and roasted like animals?

"Help! Creator, please help me!" Kalea screamed it out loud. Her friends were alive, what a miraculous blessing!

A dreadful option dawned on her, and she slowed in her fighting to consider it. What was her virginity worth to her versus three lives? "Kerlin wait, please!" she said. "I'll marry you, I promise, but I need you to give me another gift."

He slowed his advances to listen, holding her pinned to the altar. He considered the crowd and its growing concern for their "goddess."

"Don't let them kill my friends. Set them free, and I swear I will make love to you right here however you like."

"I can't," he said, his voice huffy. His eyes took on an amorous relaxation.

"You want to please me, don't you?"

"Of course."

"Tell them to wait until tomorrow," she said. "Tell them your goddess has spoken." She wrapped her arms around his neck and breathed into his ear. "*Please.*"

He warmed in her arms, and his shoulders slackened.

She kissed his cheek, and moved to his neck. "Tell them to put the humans—and elf—back in the dungeon." He shuddered in delight and moved to open his leggings. She crossed her legs beside him. "Not until you tell them."

Contemplation showed on his face. His eyes shot over the watching crowd for another second. Kalea's new calm and warm touches to their king had made the crowd relax.

With her arms around his neck, she pulled him down to her chest and squeezed. "Tell them, and I'll lie still for you." She pecked kisses all over the top of his head while he breathed in her bosom.

He raised his head and glanced over the crowd and back to the three prisoners. He turned back to her. "No." He pushed her down, and she resumed screaming and kicking.

"Bastard!"

He used all the power of his body to suppress her and force himself between her legs. He ripped her braies and pushed her knees up. He threw the red cloth back over her head and planted his hand over her mouth with intent to suppress her screaming long enough to get the "marriage rite" over with. Kalea braced herself for what she would feel in her body in the next few seconds.

In her squirming, she managed to tear part of the veil off her eyes. As Kerlin concentrated hard on restraining her and aligning his genitals with hers, in the final moment before the first big thrust, a rusty pitchfork rose out of the crowd and stabbed into Kerlin's collarbone and neck.

Kerlin's grip weakened as a pulsing blood stream oozed into his shirt. Kalea screamed and squirmed out from under his dying body.

From the crowd, glittering eyes stared at her with a toothy, mirthful smile. The sanguinesent had arrived with a clutch of thralls wielding common tools as weapons.

*A Luschian for Lamrhath the Kingsorcerer,* said the rumbling voice of the creature in her head, too familiar for her comfort. Its five thralls, two of them women, busied themselves with clearing a path, attacking whoever stood in the way. One thrall reached for Kalea, and she batted his hand away.

*Yield to my thrall.*

"No!" Kalea said out loud. She prepared to leap from the platform. Kerlin had placed the sword and her basket nearby. A travel pack of his own waited beside her things. He must've meant for them to walk straight out of town after having sex. The Thaccilians were more concerned with fighting the monster than capturing her, giving her a slim chance to escape. There was plenty to keep the five thralls busy.

She grabbed the sword and basket and made her way toward her friends on the other platform, unsheathing it to wield it one-handed if she could manage. Any thrall who approached, she sliced and ran on, leaving them yelling and cradling their arms or shoulders. The naked, hooded figures stood near the edge of the fire, abandoned in the chaos. Some people from the crowd ignored the sanguinesent and pursued her. She was still their goddess, and the naked men were their supper.

She climbed onto the rigging, high off the ground for all to watch. Next to the prisoners stood an axe, a chopping block, and long metal poles, like skewers.

"Oh, dear Creator!" Kalea exclaimed at the gruesome instruments.

"Kalea?" said a muffled voice from under one of the hoods. Bowaen's voice!

"Yes!" She threw the hood off his head. Naked or not, she wanted to hug him in relief, but there were villagers running toward them. She used the sword to cut his bonds.

"Give it to me!" he yelled, and she offered up the sword's hilt. He faced the oncoming crowd as Kalea attended to Gaije and Del.

"Holy Swine!" Del said, once freed of his hood. "They were going to do us like geese on a hearth!"

Gaije took the axe and braced for the onslaught. They would soon be overwhelmed. A throng had formed around the platform and started rocking it. Bowaen killed any who climbed the ladder. The sanguinesent glided calmly toward them with its thralls protecting it. Perhaps it could lighten the crowd for them.

"The monster is back!" Bowaen said.

"Don't look at its eyes!" Kalea reminded. "It wants me, and will easily use you to get me."

"I can't fight with my eyes closed!" Bowaen said.

"Don't close them, avert them! You two as well!"

"Speak for the weak-willed men," Gaije said before chopping at the head of one who attempted to climb the platform. The next man climbing up wore his Norrian mantle and cloak, which Gaije grasped and yanked away before axing his head.

"We have to get back to the storage room," Gaije yelled over the roaring crowd and nearby flames. "I won't leave Grandfather's bow behind!"

"He's right," Bowaen said. "We can't walk out of here in the buff— we won't survive the Darklands. Look, the monster has most of them distracted."

Kalea concentrated her thoughts on the frightful being. *Monster, you need to clear a path for us. We need to go to the tower to collect our things.*

*Lamrhath the Kingsorcerer calls for you,* it responded without missing a beat.

*Who is Lamrhath?*

*He calls you.*

Could Lamrhath be the Dreamer?

"What have I done?" she asked aloud. She might have made a mistake, but it was a useful one. The diamond-eyed creature replaced each felled thrall with a nearby person. Tools the villagers swung at it whipped through its robe, hitting nothing but air beneath. It never made any sign of injury or distress; its bony face showed the same hideous, demonic grin. Its eyes fixed on her from below. Kalea could still look at its magnificent sparkling eyes without getting bewitched.

She said in her mind, knowing the sanguinesent heard her, *Listen to me! I don't know what you plan to do with me once you get over here, but you'd better make a plan! You have to use your slaves to clear a path to the tower!*

The sanguinesent responded, *I project there is a weakness in the city wall behind the tower.*

"Hey," Kalea said to her three naked companions, "the monster is talking to me in my head! He said there's an exit out of the city behind the tower. He'll try to grab me, so get ready to make your way over there."

A loud crack pierced their ears.

"No chance," Bowaen said. "They'll have us on the ground before then!"

The platform swayed now as its bindings loosened. The sanguinesent drew closer. Bowaen and Gaije focused their attention on clearing one side of the platform, and at the first chance they leaped off.

Kalea stood on the platform alone, staring down the long drop, which must've been as high as a small cottage roof. From below, Gaije beckoned her, spreading his arms to indicate he'd catch her. Kalea let her backside fall first to land in Gaije's arms properly.

The elf exhaled as she landed across his hard arms; he recoiled downward to soften her landing, and then placed her feet on the ground. A ripping sensation ignited in her leg at the nervous tension built in her body. She hadn't gone easy enough on her injury lately.

Gaije put Kalea's arm around his neck, similar to when they had met, to help her limp faster. She had no time to reflect on how relieved and joyful this moment made her. He might not be Dorhen, but he was someone she trusted, someone she belonged with in these days.

The same went for the other two. Bowaen marched forward without a care for his nudity and cleared the way, stabbing and slicing anyone who ventured near. He met every attacker with indiscriminate fury. Who knew what horrors these poor men had endured for the past twenty-four hours? Her limping and her worry about the sanguinesent and other attackers, thralls or not, made her forget her companions' nudity. This would be an interesting episode to reflect on later, after they escaped—if they made it out of the city alive.

The high-pitched chattering sound of the sanguinesent's throat sang over the loud disorder of the Thaccilians. Kalea glanced over her and Gaije's shoulders in dismay. The creature had left four of its thralls behind to fight off the crowd and brought the fifth one with it to chase Kalea. Gaije urged her to go faster, but she couldn't increase her speed with her injury.

"Don't look at its eyes!" Kalea couldn't help but remind again when Bowaen and Del reflexively turned to inspect the situation. They both bowed away at her warning.

"Dammit!" Bowaen yelled. "How am I supposed to…?" He aborted his question when another group of Thaccilians attacked from the side. The sanguinesent approached behind.

"I can look!" Gaije growled, and turned to meet it, brandishing the axe he took from the butcher's platform. The creature's thrall lunged to stop Gaije, and the two wrestled.

Now left on her own, Kalea fumbled to untie her washing bat from the basket strap. It might not kill anyone, but she could wallop someone on the head and possibly knock them out. She also recalled its ability to snap her friends out of the spell when they were enthralled before.

The sanguinesent drifted closer, eyes glittering in the waning sunlight, long teeth grinning with a pearly sheen above a collar of thick black feathers. Long black robes of jagged, tiered layers flowed as it moved, beneath which she saw no feet. It looked a world more surreal than it had appeared in the dark catacombs. The light danced across the thousands of tiny clustered diamond facets, an effect which made her want to stare, but the enthrallment the creature wanted her to feel didn't work.

Before she could get the bat free, a bird-like hand with two talons whipped out of the robe. From its narrow palm slid the tentacle which had entered Kalea's ear when the creature caught her underground.

The tentacle wrapped around her ankle and swiped her feet out from under her. Her scream cut short when her upper body hit the ground hard. One of the bruises she'd collected on her side during her dreamwalking journeys flared. She groaned.

*I thought you were going to help me get out of this place!* she reprimanded in her mind.

*I will take you out,* the creature grated, and proceeded to drag her across the dusty ground.

It took her in the direction of the manor, where they needed to go. The problem was, it would ultimately take her to some place she wished not to go and would abandon or enthrall her friends.

Gaije felled a thrall and gasped when he noticed Kalea being dragged away. He leaped forward and chopped at the tentacle with the axe. His attempt to cut it failed.

The sanguinesent turned around to glare its sparkling eyes at him. *An elf,* the sanguinesent said. *This one is useless and will try to foil my duty.*

Gaije tried again to chop the tentacle, but either the blade was too rusted and dull or the tentacle couldn't be chopped by such a simple weapon. As if to spite Gaije, a wiggling branch split off from the tentacle and wrapped itself around her other ankle to bind her feet together.

She wailed and worked to keep her skirt down as the sanguinesent drifted onward, dragging her bad leg over the rough, pebbly ground.

She called Bowaen's name as he finished off the last attacking Thaccilian in the group. Hearing her call, he lunged to swing Hathrohjilh at the sanguinesent. As the creature turned, Bowaen threw a hand over his eyes to avoid looking at the diamonds, yelling out strings of curses. From then on, he kept his eyes shielded and swung the sword haphazardly.

"Bowaen, try the tentacle! Hurry!"

A new horde of Thaccilians charged toward them from the main group they'd left behind. They had apparently defeated the sanguinesent's other four thralls and would easily supply him with five more.

Bowaen slashed at the tentacle, and the sanguinesent hissed out loud. The appendage flinched and dodged the blade.

*This sword's soul I am familiar with,* the sanguinesent commented.

After a few more of Bowaen's persistent swings, the sanguinesent put its other talon out, and that appendage's tentacle emerged to snag Bowaen and halt his sword.

"Del!" he called. "Get the sword!"

Del obeyed his order, but the tentacle had wrapped itself tightly around Hathrohjilh.

Tacky skin covered the thing's strong, cord-like muscles, sticking to Kalea's ankles. The Thaccilian horde approached. "Help!" Kalea called—to *them*!

Gaije's axe did nothing useful. The creature continued to drift, and Kalea found herself being dragged again. She reached her hand out behind her, toward the Thaccilians, and called for help again. A man whose red eyes held wide with concern locked gazes with her.

The sanguinesent gained speed, and the shoddy old buildings passed her by. The sky grew darker. Gaije and Del braced themselves to take on the horde.

"Hold on!" she said to them. "Don't fight them. Yet."

"Are you sure?" Del asked with a twisted expression.

"Do you want to fight the monster, or do you want to fight the monster plus an army of heart-eaters?"

Gaije and Del followed Kalea as the sanguinesent dragged her.

"Listen to me," she told them. "They think I'm their goddess, so they won't kill me." They'd do something else unpleasant if they caught her, which would be better than death. "I want both of you to run ahead to the manor," she continued. "Dodge and fight anyone you meet, but hurry to the place they've stowed your weapons."

Gaije looked at Del. "She's right. The creature is taking her there anyway." Without another word, the two ran forward, past the sanguinesent as it dragged Kalea and Bowaen toward the exit to the city.

Bowaen growled in frustration. His arms were bound to his sides, one of them in a fight for the sword with the creature's tentacle. "Great!" he roared. "Now what are we supposed to do, girl?"

"Please be quiet and wait for your moment," she told him.

"What moment?"

"Any moment you happen to find."

As he growled again, she arched her back to check the approaching mob behind her. "Help!" she called.

"The goddess needs help!" one man yelled to the others.

"Help the goddess!"

"It's taking our Mother Kalea!"

Upon their arrival, the sanguinesent took five of them as thralls to fight all the others, complicating the situation as expected. She yelled at the top of her lungs, warning them not to look at its eyes. Thinking fast, and hoping not to get stepped on in the confusion, Kalea regarded her basket. Its leather strap was still hooked on her arm, dragging behind her with her washing bat tied to it.

Amidst the chaos of thralls fending attackers off the sanguinesent, one man trotted beside Kalea and attempted to manhandle the tentacle off her ankles.

"You can't undo it so easily!" Kalea shouted. If an axe couldn't chop it, and the thing could dodge Hathrohjilh's strikes, what could mere hands do?

He gave up and continued trotting beside her. "In your great wisdom, what can be done for you, Mother Kalea?"

She pointed backward over her head while using her other hand to keep her skirt down. Her bandage was being dragged and pulled off her wound, exposing it to the harsh, pebbly road, and the pain caused a wave of nausea. "Untie my bat and give it to me!"

He frowned. "A washing bat?"

"It holds power," she said. "I'm the goddess of washing!" She just needed him to comply without question, but what would he think if the bat had no effect against the tentacle? She could at least cure some of the thralls. At her words, he gasped and jumped to the task. "And don't look at the sanguinesent's eyes!"

The creature turned around at her repeated warning and chirped in annoyance. It had already dragged her a long way. The manor appeared through the row of houses. She prayed Gaije and Del had made it there and were dressing and finding their weapons. Bowaen could do nothing but turn his head frantically to the left and right with his arms pinned down.

"This man belongs to me!" Kalea warned the non-enthralled Thaccilians. "Do not harm him!"

For now, the thralls were doing a good job of keeping the others at bay. The non-enthralled remained reluctant to kill the thralls—their family and neighbors—but as the long minutes passed, their desperation increased. They were frantic to rescue their goddess, and they were also starving and held an equally high interest in harvesting Bowaen's heart.

She turned her ear toward the man who worked on her washing bat. "Have you untied it?"

"Is knotted good," the man responded. Every once in a while, a thrall would make his or her way over to thwart his work. The sanguinesent must've telepathically ordered them to target him.

Through the manor's broken gate, Gaije and Del emerged from the side wing housing the dungeon. They now wore clothes, and both held their own weapons!

Gaije immediately released arrows into the thralls, only to have them quickly replaced with new thralls. Del lit his pipe, took a long drag, and blew the smoke at the sanguinesent. Nothing happened.

"I don't think this is the same type of creature Damos defeated back in Jumaire, Del," Kalea said.

"Had to try something," Del replied, and proceeded to swing his heavy pipe at the sanguinesent's back.

The tobacco embers fell against its robe, and a fire erupted to sweep over the entire creature, leaving undamaged fabric, flesh, and exposed bone behind. In response, the sanguinesent whipped forward to try to make Del look at its eyes. Del turned away fast.

*Tell the foolish human his fire can't hurt a being wrought from the magma of the ninetieth facet of Kullixaxuss.*

"Did you just say what I think you said?" Kalea asked the sanguinesent out loud.

"I didn't say anything!" Del responded.

"Not you!"

The sanguinesent had stated its origin as "Kullixaxuss," which meant it was a demon. Kalea shook all the way to her toes, lying helplessly on her back with her ankles tied together—touching the tentacles of this infernal abomination!

When the Thaccilian finally untied her washing bat, he eagerly handed it to her, handle-first, and she gave the tentacle the best thwack she could. It shuddered and winced on contact—a new reaction. Kalea tried again and again and again!

The tentacle loosened and winced away, allowing her to kick out of its grip. Ignoring her aches, pains, and scrapes from the long distance she'd been dragged, Kalea stood and hit the first enthralled Thaccilian to come near her.

The man blinked in confusion. "Mother Kalea?"

"Yes," she said. "Help me escape this creature. Don't look at its eyes."

She moved to Bowaen's tentacle next and chopped at it with the narrow edge of her bat. Once again, the thing winced and trembled in momentary weakness; it loosened enough for Bowaen to wriggle free and wrestle his sword away. With the sword, he spun and struck, hitting the tentacle with the blade.

The sanguinesent shrieked and reeled, then whirled to glare at him. Too fast, Bowaen's eyes connected with its diamond clusters and phased into the telltale unnerving dullness of enthrallment.

"You will accompany me back to the kingsorcerer," Bowaen said. It must've been the sanguinesent talking through him. The only way it could speak her language was in her head or through a thrall.

Without any hesitation, Kalea raised her bat and swung it at Bowaen's head. He raised his sword and blocked. She expected the blade to split the wood in half, but it held firm. Perhaps the silvery grains in the bat's wood made it strong.

Now she was in a sword fight with Bowaen, the best swordsman in the Lightlands. He blocked and parried all of her attempts, but he didn't attempt to strike her with the blade. Instead, he continuously ordered her to accompany him back to the kingsorcerer. Kalea's injured leg had gone numb and the nausea wracked her. She panted and trembled. The crowd thinned as Gaije and Del killed off thralls and non-thralls alike.

"Stop, you two!" she shrieked. It seemed like a bad idea to lose all of her followers, who kept the sanguinesent busy. With so many of their friends and family killed, the remainder could get extremely angry, even with her.

Bowaen reached a hand out for her in her hesitation, and she dodged and hit his arm with the bat. No change. He remained enthralled. Apparently, only hitting a thrall on the head broke the spell.

While their sword-versus-bat fight continued, two of Kalea's followers grabbed Bowaen from behind, one of them poised with a knife to Bowaen's throat, the other holding his arm and his head steady.

Rearing her hand back, she banged the one with the knife as hard as she could. He went down. Without wasting another second, she smacked Bowaen's head with her bat. No telling if a certain amount of pressure counted in breaking the spell yet.

Bowaen's eyes refocused. He snapped out of it and jerked the remaining Thaccilian away and took him to the ground with one arm, sweeping his heel behind the man's knee.

"Did it happen again?" Bowaen asked.

She pointed to the looming building. "Hurry and run to the manor, all of us!"

Gaije held off the crowd with his bow and some scavenged arrows while Bowaen slipped inside to dress and collect as many things as he could grab, items he actually owned and otherwise.

"There's a small door in the storage room," Del said. "Should lead into the main house. We'll get through to an exit at the back and look for the broken part of the wall."

Gaije closed the door behind them all and slammed the heavy wooden bar into place. Closed up in the cool shade of the stone building, they lost a lot of light the door would've let in. Del lit a candle stub on the table and helped Bowaen collect anything they could use.

Finally, Kalea caught her breath. The violent sounds outside kept her unnerved, however, and surely the door couldn't hold the sanguinesent out. She regarded her washing bat and kissed its old splintery surface. They might've all died without it.

All three of her friends were finally clothed, another relief. Bowaen fastened the sword girdle over his clothes but kept the weapon in his hands. Del opened the narrow door at the back of the storage room and waved everyone through. With his hand to Kalea's back, Gaije ushered her forward. He picked a knife off the table to add to his arsenal. She hurried, limping as usual, and followed Del through.

She found herself back in the corridors she'd walked earlier with Kerlin toward their marriage rites. So far, they hadn't run into any people. They must've all gathered outside to attend the goddess ceremony and feast on her friends' flesh. She shivered.

One of Kerlin's female guards, in a belted red dress and holding a notched old sword, took a stance in the next doorway. She wore a threadbare red veil over her hair, a garment spookily similar to the vestals of Kalea's religion.

"Release the goddess for King Kerlin!" the guard commanded.

"King Kerlin is dead!" Kalea shot back.

Bowaen clicked his tongue and engaged the guard. She fought with speed and skill, but Bowaen clearly went easy on her. At Kalea's side, Gaije's face drained of all its blood. His arms hung limp, holding his bow and an arrow.

Bowaen turned the sword around and knocked the guard out with the pommel. Gaije winced. She slid to the floor, and they rushed forward in search of the back of the manor.

More female guards met them along the way, either intent on returning Kalea to Kerlin, or on rescuing Kalea from her "captors." Bowaen dealt with them in a similar manner to the first, and Gaije clearly didn't like anything about the situation.

"Females in Norr don't fight," Gaije said when they were on the move again. "But since these are trying to fight us, and we need to escape, what can we…?"

"It's hard for us all, Gaije," Bowaen said, "but it's nothing we have time to philosophize about right now."

After he knocked out three more women in the courtyard, the sounds of shouting and banging sounded from the manor behind them. The horde, and possibly the sanguinesent, moved through the house. Gaije took Kalea in his arms and they sprinted on. A wall enclosed one third of the courtyard, beyond which stood the city wall where they would escape. The problem lay in getting out of the courtyard.

"There's a door!" Del pointed. "That wing should be clear."

"Too risky," Bowaen growled. "We'll take a short cut over the wall." He grabbed a bucket from the ground, and then cut the rope holding the bucket hanging above the well. "Get those old crates!"

The door slammed open, and Gaije put Kalea down to rush to stop the crowd from flooding out. "Hurry, go climb over," he told her and the others.

Kalea left him to shoving and knifing the Thaccilians trying to get outside. She limped her way across the courtyard, where Bowaen and Del were scrambling to stack anything they could find against the wall.

When she arrived, Bowaen waved to her. "You first." Kalea groaned. "I'll raise you. You can sit on the wall until I'm over. And then…"

And then she'd jump into his arms, like she had before. Her dress snagged and got in her way. Not to mention her injured leg, which she couldn't use to step on any of the boosts, making her chore a slow, painful one.

Bowaen stepped up beside her, rattling the old objects in their precarious arrangement. "I'll lift you," he said. "Put your good leg over first."

"Hurry, Bow!" Del demanded.

Behind them, Gaije struggled with the crowd thickening in the doorframe and resorted to hitting them with his bow shaft. His other hand brandished the knife he'd found in the storeroom.

Bowaen threw their belongings over the wall, counted to three, and raised her with his hands on her hips. She grabbed the top of the stone wall and hung there. She couldn't use her weak leg to brace her climb; she relied on the strength of her body to reach her good leg high enough to get it over. Once again, her lungs emptied. Her side muscles screamed and pinched as she forced them to bend, to push her leg in an unnatural direction. Her arms shook, supporting her weight. Her hands sweat. She was slipping!

"Keep it up!" Bowaen yelled. He reached to push her leg from below, but she was too high.

The female guards who had been knocked out started to come to, and a few Thaccilians broke Gaije's one-man barrier. After the first few, the rest of the crowd spilled through. Additional men broke windows and jumped through, and they all swarmed toward Kalea and Bowaen's stack of objects. Del did his best to hold them off, bashing as many heads with his pipe as he could.

*Ch-kr-r-r-r-r-r...*

The sanguinesent drifted through the door. Kalea's heart sank at the sound of its flicking throat chirp.

"C'mon, Kalea!" Bowaen ordered. "Push!"

She whimpered and trembled and pushed with sheer will to get her heel up the wall.

Success! Her heel found the top edge, and the leather of her shoe helped to grip the rough stone. She worked her way farther, farther until she lay flat on her belly on the top of the wall.

When she scooted out of his way, Bowaen jumped to grasp the edge and scrambled over, easily pulling himself up with his powerful arms. From his seat at the top, he dropped.

"Okay, now you!"

He held out his arms to catch her, but Kalea was exhausted, lying flat on the wall. Her arms were weak. She rolled off the other side, and he caught her horizontally. The two of them fell to the leafy, soft ground.

With the sun down, they relied on faint moonlight to see by. The many shouting voices and chirping of the sanguinesent continued behind the wall.

Bowaen cupped his mouth in his hands and yelled, "C'mon, Del! Don't look at the creature."

Kalea panted. She sat on the ground, unable to stand. *Yes, dear Creator, don't let him look at its eyes. I can't help him with my bat from over here.*

Del's bag of belongings flew over the side and landed beside Bowaen. Next came his pipe. He now had to climb over the wall without his means of defense. Grunting and growling sounded from over there, possibly his voice. Kalea imagined him hanging from the wall and kicking at the grabbing hands below. Bowaen fidgeted in place, baring his teeth.

Del's head appeared over the edge. Bowaen leaped forward. "Good goin'!" He stepped back so the young man could drop, and then scooped him into a big hug.

Panting as hard as Kalea, Del searched the dark ground for his things. "I need a long drag."

"Del," Kalea said. "Where's Gaije?"

He shrugged and secured his pipe strap over his arm.

She turned to the wall and shouted Gaije's name. Bowaen joined her. They waited.

She turned to Bowaen. "He was in the thick of the crowd, wasn't he?" Her lip quivered, and she covered her mouth. Her eyes watered.

Bowaen shushed her. "Gaije!" he called. In return, shouting Thaccilians and the chittering of the sanguinesent's throat cluttered the air.

"Oh, Creator." Kalea choked down her sobs. She turned away.

Another head appeared at the top of the wall. A figure dropped over the side.

Kalea ran forward. "Gaije?"

The figure grabbed her. Bowaen leaped forward and stabbed him. Kalea screamed. When he fell, his hair shone pale in the moonlight, not red. It wasn't Gaije.

Bowaen grabbed her arm and pulled her away from the wall. She cried out in pain for her leg. He scooped her up. "We gotta go!"

"No!" She squirmed in his hold. "Not without Gaije!"

As she protested, another Thaccilian mounted and jumped off the wall. Bowaen left him for Del to take care of.

"Gaije'll have to figure it out," Bowaen argued. "They'll be spilling over and coming around the side to catch us, and the monster'll be with them!"

Kalea released her tears and wailed on his shoulder. Del hoisted Kalea's basket, and Bowaen carried her as they ran along the outer city wall. They soon found the damaged area the sanguinesent had predicted. Climbing over the old, cluttered rocks, they made their way back into the forest of poison. They ran.

They left Gaije behind.

# Chapter 18
# What is Togha's New Family

Togha and the Wikshonites nestled their camp into a rocky cluster of hills. The path wound between weathered rock faces, carved long ago for the road. There may've been a reason for a road like this long in the past; today, however, they could've walked around the cluster of steep hills with less hassle. Gilda, the group's elderly leader who carried the drum, deemed it safest to camp against one such cliff face.

After eating the Clanless's confiscated food for dinner, Togha stole some private time away from the group of strange people while they chanted and bowed their heads to the ground in the night hour. He was lovingly working on combing Haggis's wooly black coat when Metta's voice drifted to his ear.

"There you are," she said. She met his gaze with a warm and serene smile.

The sight of her caused a strange pain in Togha's stomach and made his answering smile difficult. He darted his eyes, and when he looked again, her smile took on a slight lip bite that made his head light. He cleared his throat and did a few more strokes to Haggis's coat.

She made her way closer while he worked. "Why did you skip out on the worship?"

He didn't even know who they were worshipping. "I…" He told her the truth. "I don't actually know the words to those prayers."

She cocked her head in his peripheral vision. "Really? How long have you been in the faith?"

"Not long."

Silence passed between them. He could feel her eyes on him. "You don't say a lot, do you?"

Togha shrugged.

She giggled her musical laugh beside his ear. Her breath beat against his face. "Well," she said, "I guess I'll have to teach you the prayers. I can tell you all about Wikshonism while we continue our pilgrimage to Wikhaihli."

"Okay," he said, and did a few more strokes to the donkey's fur. He must've combed the same spot eight times.

As she continued to stand there, staring and smiling, he finally met her eyes and said, "Can I help you with something?"

"No," she said. "I'm here to help *you*." She revealed a little porcelain jar she'd been hiding in her black sleeve.

He looked at it, and then at her face and back.

She laughed at his confusion. "It's for your wrists, sweetie." She giggled at him again. "Sit down."

He obeyed awkwardly, finding a place to sit on one of the boulders long ago separated from the cliff face.

"I swiped this from Gilda's satchel. Let's see those hands." When Togha put his hands out, he couldn't stop them from shaking. "Why are you so nervous?"

"I don't know." He truly didn't; his mother used to do things like this for him a lot. When Metta put her hands on his, his heart pounded.

She clicked her tongue. "You poor, poor thing. How long did they have you in ropes?"

He fought to keep the shaking out of his voice. "About a week."

"I can't believe those awful Clanless would treat their own kind so harshly."

"They caught me with a scroll I wasn't supposed to have."

"Kraft Shout," she said. "I know."

"How did you know?"

She flourished her hands and cocked her head in a bouncy way, smiling constantly. "I looked in your bag."

"What?"

"I didn't mean to. I was curious about you. I didn't steal anything. Wikshonites don't steal from their own."

He chose not to point out that she'd taken the salve out of Gilda's bag. "That's fine...I guess." He didn't have much beyond his grooming brush and that scroll anyway.

The ointment she rubbed on his rope burns both chilled and stung. She spent an eternity on her task, swirling her fingers in the oily cream, holding his hand in her tiny one.

"Where are you from, Togha?" she asked after a long silence went by.

"Norr."

"Where's that?"

"South of here, on the other side of the big gate. I'm from Lock— never mind. Who cares what clan I'm from?"

She gazed up through her eyelashes. "Not when you are now a Wikshonite, huh?"

A Wikshonite. They were the first friendly people he'd encountered in the Darklands. He didn't answer her question. When she let his hands go, the ointment rubbed well into his irritated skin, she produced two black linen streamers from her belt pouch.

"You're a fledgling Wikshonite," she said, "so here's a lesson. We Wikshonites often wear black wrist wrappings as a sign of our faith. These will wrap your wounds as well as show the world who you are."

He watched, mesmerized, as she wound the strips around his arms. She'd just given him a gift. Looking at his two bound wrists, he smiled secretly.

"We should sleep now," she said.

She placed her hand on his chest, and his heart flew. Before he could comprehend it, she'd already stretched her neck to peck a soft kiss on his lips. His body went up in carnal flames. The kiss ended fast, yet at the same time it lasted long. He couldn't decide how long.

"Good night, Togha." She skipped away back to camp.

She left him sitting there, dizzy and confused. He leaned back against the rocks and viewed the dark sky with a faint moon glowing through the sheer clouds. He ran his hands over his face. That had never happened to him before. *Faerhain* didn't kiss *saehgahn* like that. His entire throat trembled in his effort to swallow.

He trailed his eyes to the campfire glow around the edge of the rocky bend. He could stay with them. He was a Wikshonite.

# Chapter 19
## What is Wikshen's Failure

Late in the evening, Lamrhath laid back against a different pillow in another small Darklandic village, snuggled in with the busty woman he'd brought from the last village. The chieftain and the woman's husband had both agreed to sell her to Lamrhath for a few extra protection services.

The woman now wore her body paint as smeared green blots and streaks after Lamrhath's handling. Initially, she had expressed her hesitance about the arrangement and fear of her new "husband," as expected, but eventually she relaxed and found her own peace in a lofty new existence beside the leader of the little sorcery pack. She had been a common woman back home. Her body paint symbolized her married status, and any mar her husband might've found on the work would mean she had been raped by another man—which would lead to a duel. They were a vain people, as primitive as they were. The body paint mixture lasted a good while with care taken; even her own husband didn't smudge it away when they carried on with their marital routine.

On the night of their own consummation, she demonstrated for Lamrhath how her people conducted their bedroom rites, a boring custom in which he lay flat while she squatted over him and flexed her inner muscles until they both came. It worked for him, but she later delighted in Lamrhath's ritual, with him on top. Her talent with those secret muscles was a specialty all its own, however, and he looked forward to experimenting with how they might blend their two styles. Lamrhath would treat this one well, as long as she behaved, and planned to keep her near his private apartments in Ilbith. Her name was *She-erk*. Or *Shrik*? It was something nonsensical like that, so he took to calling her Silva instead.

He sent Silva out of the little house they currently occupied to ask their new hosts for a bath to get rid of all her paint mess, and he lay back against the pillow stuffed with feathers and dried grass.

He took it on faith that the dreamwalking girl had found safety. Maybe all would be well with his growing kingdom after he found and slaughtered Daghahen with Hathrohjilh. Those two things remained elusive.

The Luschian who had visited his dream should've escaped, and the sanguinesent tracked her progress. If the infernal sentinel happened to fail in its mission, it would contact Lamrhath telepathically with the news. So far, so good. Maybe sometime, somehow, she'd enter his dream again. Lamrhath had last experienced one of *those* dreams ages ago, possibly sixteen years or more. He missed the ecstasy of a dreamwalker's visit. They offered special sensations he'd never known in real life sex— with the benefit of healing his ailment for a good while.

He closed his eyes and tried to release his thoughts of her. They would arouse his ailment again, despite the session he'd just enjoyed with Silva. His ailment certainly was getting out of hand.

In the morning, when he emerged from the crude little house, black banners appeared marching on the horizon toward their red ones. The black ones were rigged to look as if the Wikshonites were officially campaigning.

"There he comes," Lamrhath said, leaning close toward this village's chieftain. "Watch as we turn Wikshen away, never to harm your village."

"Bless you, Kingsorcerer!" The chieftain fell to his knees and worshipped the gold tips of Lamrhath's boots.

He and his troop of sorcerers rode out on the new horses this village had provided to meet the posing Wikshonites. Their presentation changed dramatically as he drew closer. Wikshen sat listlessly on his horse. Ropes were bound over his legs and to the horse's saddle to keep him on, and his torso was bound and his hands tied to the saddle's pommel to keep his back straight. Though Wikshen's eyes were open, his head lolled; he'd fall off if not for the ropes.

"What's this now?" Lamrhath asked, pointing with a big gesture at Wikshen for the benefit of his audience.

"He's performed his part well, my lord, and now he's out of stamina," Tumas, the first sorcerer in black, explained. "During the day, we have to tie him on or else he can't ride. He's on and off, we've noticed, but can't work out why. The beatings get him going, and he's easy to catch after he finishes a raid."

"Truly?" Lamrhath almost smiled. "So the provocation tactics work? Has he raped anyone yet?"

All the sorcerers dressed as Wikshonites shook their heads.

"We ain't seen him do it yet," another man put in.

"How...contradictory to the legend," Lamrhath replied.

"He did get a big suck-off from this vestal girl here, though." Tumas pointed to the chubby girl who'd been full of attitude back at the outpost.

Now, she sported dark circles under her listless eyes.

Lamrhath raised his voice to her. "And how was that?"

"'Bout as expected, my lord," the chubby girl drawled. She moved like a dead person who hadn't received permission to lie still yet, not missing a beat, but without the energy to do more than needed.

"She spat it out, my lord," Tumas reported. "Canceled whatever effect it might ha' done to her body."

"Pity," Lamrhath said. "You could've forced her swallow it."

Tumas shrugged. "We'll see about accommodating and studying his natural urges in time. To move things on, he's killed plenty, my lord. And he did try to escape. He's pretty angry when he's alert. Those folk you contacted weren't lying."

"How much did you lose during your encounter with the sanguinesent?" Lamrhath asked.

Tumas waved a hand. "Nothing too valuable, mostly salted fish. We retained the most important objects for you, my lord. In fact, here…" Tumas reached into a trunk and handed him a bundled package. "We got you some presents: elven scalps, several of them."

"Excellent!" Lamrhath marveled at the blood-matted package before taking it in both hands. Elven hair was a valuable and coveted asset used in sorcerous practices.

"And another thing, my lord." Tumas led Lamrhath to a wagon with a dozen large baskets tied closed. Soft sounds peeped within each. "We collected some kids from the villages. Two are from Norr. *I'm* to thank for the elf-girl. Got a boy-elf too."

Behind him, Wikshen huffed and made an angry growl from deep within his belly.

Lamrhath ignored Wikshen and gaped at the baskets. "Did you say *elf*-girl?"

Tumas smirked. "See for yourself, my lord."

He untied the basket and cracked the lid. Two big purple eyes stared back at Lamrhath from the musty wicker shadow. The eyes of a *farhah*, a real female elf of a very young age. The perfect age to teach her how to behave in their society, in which she'd grow and blossom into whatever Lamrhath might choose.

They could also harvest the elven children's hair. As of now, the female's hair fell longer than the male's. The male would have been made to wait until adulthood to let his hair grow, but that wouldn't stand in Ilbith. Harvesting the children's hair in their youth would be more beneficial for its potent magical benefits.

A mesmerized trickle of air passed slowly between Lamrhath's lips as he stared into the eyes of the pretty little thing. This one he'd make special plans for. "Tumas," he whispered, "great awards await you in Ilbith."

Tumas beamed beside him. The sorcerer replaced the lid and tied the basket closed. Lamrhath patted Tumas's shoulder firmly and pointed to the faded mountain range looming behind the distant walking cloud.

"Take them straight to Ilbith. But listen." The sorcerers in black inclined their heads closer. They couldn't huddle in too close or they'd ruin the illusion of confrontation for the spectators. "Keep up Wikshen's campaign. Split your numbers. One group takes the women and goods back home, the second group tails mine and agitates Wikshen into attacking more settlements without red banners."

Lamrhath pointed to the baskets. "As for the children, make sure they're well-fed, and do let them out to stretch their legs now and again. When you get to the Black Mountain foothills, wait for me. I'll meet you there. Go!"

On his word, a sorcerer wearing black slapped Wikshen's horse, causing its rider to lurch and sway with the turbulence. Wikshen shot him a weary glare as he went, obscured by the wind stirring his blue hair. Lamrhath made a strong pointing gesture at the procession, and the red-robed sorcerers behind him created some routine fireworks for show. Hot sparks of light flew from the stones in their red gloves. Sounds of awe and applause rose from the village.

Vivene's mouth dropped open as a few quick words expressed how they'd divide the group. "No," she accidentally muttered aloud.

A hand struck the back of her head. "What do you mean 'no,' bitch?"

She didn't answer, and he didn't pause to await it anyway. The group passed bags of food and money around, and then they drifted apart. Her group, with the wagon, children, and prostitutes, was now heading toward the mountains. Wikshen and his group split off for a different way.

She had missed her chance! Wikshen should've helped her escape, but he didn't! He was a liar! She'd failed, now too alone and helpless to escape with the children. Wikshen had never managed to make himself useful over all the days since she'd carried out his strange request to remove his boots and make a fool of herself in the process. It was over.

Over her shoulder, she watched him loll atop the horse, tied down to it, for as long as he stayed in sight. An impotent and pathetic creature who was a prisoner in his own head.

# Chapter 20

# His Fire

Another night of beatings. The lashings rattled through Dorhen's body with an odd slowness, as if he were last to know they happened. After the long tremors, a piercing pain traveled through him, giving him the rare sensation of retaining ownership of his body.

*Do you feel that, fool?* Wik's voice rumbled after several days of peace.

In their ongoing battle for control, sometimes Dorhen fell asleep while Wik controlled his body, and other times Wik fell asleep, leaving Dorhen to stagger and sway in his efforts to move. As he understood it, Wik also lost his energy and snoozed in the body off and on. He'd mentioned how they needed to stay out of the sun and they needed minerals—whatever that meant. Wik had also stressed that they needed to "join."

Now, the sorcerers were whipping him with switches and leather straps. The sharp vibrations helped Wik's strength and potency and chased Dorhen's will away with the pain and distress.

*They want us to work. Are you tired of being used yet?*

He didn't have to answer. Answering wouldn't cure his misery.

Wik's rocky, hissing laughter followed.

Outside his head, the muffled voices of the sorcerers conversed and barked orders at him throughout the lashings. Each tremor dimmed the voices and energized Wik.

*Go to sleep, fool. I can do what they want us to do tonight. No need to bother yourself.* He laughed again.

Wik was as aware of their captivity as Dorhen, or more so. He, or it—whatever this creature was—never showed any concern, fear, or disdain for their situation. *Give it time,* the pixie would say when Dorhen raised a question about it. Its ominous reassurances failed to boost Dorhen's confidence.

Dorhen focused his eyes and tried to remain conscious. He couldn't let this happen. The sorcerers moved around him. They wanted Wikshen to act for them. They'd soon release him from his bonds and raise protective magical shields to hide themselves from Wikshen as well as from the village Wikshen would attack. It lay over the next hill in the cool evening air and would soon be smoldering.

Dorhen set his determination to resist. Because once it all set off, when the leather bonds came off and the sorcerers receded from eyesight, Dorhen would have to watch himself move autonomously through the little settlement, killing people.

His vision darkened, and a slippery vapor touched his naked skin within the world of his mind before materializing into what he could only describe as the sleek, nimble bodies of snakes. In full darkness, their touch delivered a pleasure too good to resist.

But he would resist. He'd been through this before. Dorhen had made it his purpose in life to fight for his body.

*You don't know what you're doing, fool,* Wik taunted. *Too much of that and you'll regret it. You're creating a danger you'd never understand.*

Dorhen didn't listen. Resisting was all he had left in the world after losing his body to Wik. He thrashed the snakes off him. He shut the good feelings out, wriggling and writhing in an effort to sit up. He'd force his way through the wall of his mind, a thick membrane installed by Wik to keep him from taking full control of his body. He'd fight his way to the front and get back out there, to the real world.

A tremor happened beneath him. He sank a bit. What was happening?

*Don't do this,* Wik said. His voice didn't sound so sure anymore.

The snakes poured back over his lap after he'd shoved and thrown them aside. When one of them wrapped itself around him to begin the stroke, he used all the power of his mind to throw it off. He sank lower, as if whatever he sat on ripped beneath him. A brittle hammock woven of grass, perhaps. He continued, fighting off the next layer of snakes that moved in.

*You don't know what you're doing, fool!*

Dorhen ignored him. The sensation of falling through a thin floor was new and could potentially lead to freedom. Maybe he'd finally get out. He thrashed.

*Don't!*

He flailed. He kicked. He swiped his arm against the black snakes of darkness rolling at him like an ocean wave. He forgot all about the lovely tickling they used to apply. He fought to his knees, to his feet. He lunged!

He fell through the delicate floor.

He fell.

A rush of wind blew past him from below, thousands of miles per second.

He plummeted through darkness for ages, until a glow appeared below him, as if the sun rose from beneath. He passed into an atmosphere of dim morning—or evening—light.

*Splat!* He landed in a pit of cold mud. He lay there for a while, and groaned when he finally decided to move. Move? Yes, he *could* move! In fact, none of his bones had broken on impact.

He stood on shaky legs, alive. He'd survived the fall, thanks to the mud. He wore no clothes whatsoever. The good news was, he was himself again! He raised, flexed, and swung his arms. He turned and took a step, finally able to go where he wanted. Control belonged to him! He could hear clearly and smell and use all of his own senses. No more snakes. He'd done it. He smiled. He genuinely smiled; he put his hand to his face and touched his lips. He sucked in a deep breath of liberation. He was alive and free.

But where was he now? He forgot about his smile. No sorcerers were near. The landscape looked different. A massive field of mud replaced the grassy, rolling hills. Tall blue and violet rock mountains lined the background in front of a glowing orange sky. Dorhen couldn't hear Wik in his head anymore, which was enough to bring his smile back, but he had to get serious and find shelter, or at least something to wear.

Pulling his ankle out of the mud to take a step proved difficult. The longer he stayed stationary, the deeper he sank. He waded through the mud as best as he could until a stone platform appeared.

The platform displayed a big chalice on a pedestal, a golden one with deep, engraved lines filled with liquid sapphire. Studded pearls circled the rim. Dorhen climbed up the platform to inspect the treasure. The chalice stood empty, otherwise he would've gladly drunk its contents. He hadn't experienced eating or drinking since before Wik took him over. He didn't need the empty chalice, so he left it alone and descended back into the mud to look for solid land.

Shouting erupted ahead. People. Dorhen rushed forward, eager to speak to someone who could help him. The people ran toward him. Dorhen waved his arms high and hurried forward. They paid no attention to him. They were naked also, about five men and four women. Their shouts echoed, sounding both angry and frantic. They were slapping at each other in a race to get ahead.

"There it is!" the man in the lead declared. "The chalice!"

It gleamed in the dim twilight far behind Dorhen. He'd left it behind, but these people were all competing for it, scratching, punching, and elbowing each other.

The man in the lead tripped when the second man lunged and grabbed his knee. The second man scrambled over his body to steal first position. Dorhen could do no more than stand and stare. The women fought as viciously to get the chalice as the men. Their pale, supple bodies half-covered in mud bounced and jiggled as they screeched and pulled each other's hair to get ahead.

The fallen man gave a loud yelp, drawing Dorhen's stare away from the naked women. Around him, the mud swelled and fell and bubbled before a large head with naught but a huge mouth full of teeth broke the mud's surface and arched high to fall and clamp onto his back. The rest of the creature's body, one long, black, plump length, emerged from the mud to wiggle in delight as the creature—an enormous lamprey—sucked all his blood out.

The creature's presence set the remaining racers dashing with more desperation than before. A woman obtained the lead, elbowing the man in the face, only to get caught as another lamprey rose from the mud in front of her and locked its jaws onto her stomach. She fell dead, the huge black, slithery body pulsing as it sucked her life out.

The other racers reeled at the occurrence, scattered, and continued running for the chalice on the stone platform. Dorhen assumed they'd be safe once they got there.

He trembled, but couldn't help but stand stiffly and watch. Who would get the prize Dorhen had so easily deserted?

Another lamprey launched from the mud to take another down. Then another. The first lamprey finished with its victim and slithered back into its muddy home. The creature could target him next, but the spectacle held his attention. All of the runners had been caught except for one woman, a lovely redhead. She would win. Dorhen didn't notice his mouth hanging open. She approached the first step to the platform. Her entire naked bottom half wore a slather of mud, like leggings, while her top half remained clean, pale, and soft. This fiercely determined woman would make it.

The mud bubbled behind her. Dorhen shouted a warning. She didn't listen, or she didn't hear him. He took off to help her, but the mud slowed him down.

The lamprey rose high. Dorhen held his breath.

It snatched her as her hand touched the first stone step. It lifted her high, screaming, the creature's teeth stabbed into her side. After hoisting her for a second, it fell with her back to the mud, where it overcame her.

Dorhen winced and groaned, clenching his fists in helplessness to witness such an end to the fiery, alluring beauty. The lamprey's disgusting wriggling motion communicated its exhilaration at the taste of her blood.

None of the racers had won. The chalice waited alone and empty.

Too close for comfort, the mud swelled and fell again, and snapped Dorhen out of his somber funk. Now the only person left for the giant worms to feed on, he ran.

Around a bend of tall grassy thicket growing out of the mud stood another, taller platform. A large group stood at the top, laughing and cheering. From the distance, their body language indicated they were exchanging some kind of glowing money. These figures were clothed in long cloaks, most with hoods, others with what looked like fur instead of hair atop their heads. One figure patted another on the back in consolation.

They reassembled at the front of the platform. One of them counted in some other language. At the end of the count, a system of chains and gears rumbled, and a rusty old gate at the lower front of their little tower rose.

From the dark space inside, a load of more naked people scrambled out, kicking and tripping each other, shouting about the golden chalice they all wanted. They leaped into the mud, happily soiling themselves in the silty pit. The dark figures at the top of the tower cheered and clenched their money as they hung over the railing in excitement.

Dumbfounded, Dorhen watched the new race. A new round with the same people he'd already watched die! There were more people at the starting point than Dorhen recognized, but there she was: the red-haired woman who'd almost won the last race! She'd returned to life.

For a brief instant, Dorhen's heart leaped. A nagging bit of his natural instincts told him to snatch her away and take her to safety. But the passion in her eyes, focused hard above her sneering nose and lips, held him back. She wanted the chalice.

She lunged over the mud, doing well, grabbing another woman's hair to pull her back and leap ahead like a proud and spritely hind. Dorhen gawked as hard as he'd done before, despite the danger of a lamprey catching him.

And then the mud pulsed. At the center of their fast-moving group, one of the writhing black creatures jumped, tripping many as it swished along the terrain upon which they tried to run. It snagged the red-haired woman. This time, she died first.

Above, the gamblers reacted with gasps and laughter at the turn of events. Money changed hands. And there she lay, dead, as the lamprey's huge, toothy mouth clamped to her middle, sucking all her blood out until her once-vivacious naked body withered to a grey husk.

The lamprey left a shriveled mummy behind wearing circular rows of hundreds of deep puncture holes. Dorhen looked away before the urge to puke could overcome him. Nonetheless, she sank under the mud like she and all the dead bodies had done before.

The remaining bulk of the racers, many of whom he also recognized, ran on. Dorhen continued too, heading in the opposite direction before he could meet the same fate. Not twenty long, muddy lunges over the difficult terrain later did Dorhen find solid rock ground. How ironic. Why did the racers run into the deeper section of the mud pit, when they'd find safer turf in the opposite direction? Because a silly chalice with sparkling baubles stood at the center of the pit?

Instead of lingering to wonder about it, Dorhen moved on, now walking on solid ground. For all he knew, those gamblers might catch and force him to join the never-ending race.

A pathway curled and wound around a rocky area of tall plateaus with walls so high he couldn't see the top. Overhead loomed a huge black sky into which the tops of the rocks disappeared. The atmosphere's light radiated from the horizon and stretched all the way around him. The light remained consistent. As he walked for a while, he expected the sun to rise or set, but neither happened. The atmosphere remained the same with the orange light bouncing off many distant rock walls, casting reflections of violet and other warm and cool colors across the landscape. If he found any other person, he'd ask them where he was, and from there he'd form a plan to get back to Kalea's convent.

The farther he walked, the higher the path inclined. Sprouts of plant growth appeared, followed by grass under his bare feet. He made his way up a hill, where the path entered a field of ripe berries. Merry voices echoed from the top, and Dorhen hurried to meet them.

A lush field of green and purple grew at the top of the hill, and many more naked people chattered in delight, these more jolly and at ease than the racers. They moved about the garden, gorging themselves on the vine's plump, purple berries. As many women as men moved about here, also completely naked. Out of basic shame for his own nudity and his difficulty in not staring, Dorhen chose to approach a man instead of one of the women.

"Excuse me," he said, hoping these people didn't mind an elf among them.

The man stuffed one and then two more mouthfuls of berries into his face before bothering to regard Dorhen. Amazingly, the berries grew back and ripened instantly after the man picked them.

"Where am I?"

The man smiled, berry juice staining past his chin and all the way to his downy chest. "The best place in the world, my man!" he answered. "You can eat all you want and it grows back! Can you believe it? Here, try some."

Dorhen considered the fruit which grew all around him. Every one of the little berries looked perfect, large, and ripe. His lack of appetite—at least for berries—suddenly dawned on him. He could find no interest in trying one whatsoever, yet he couldn't remember when he last ate. Instead of hunger, a sadness welled in his stomach. He frowned.

The man returned to shoveling handful after handful into his mouth. He showed no interest in whether Dorhen joined him or not.

"I need something else," Dorhen said, and cast a forlorn glance over the field full of such happy people. His shoulders sagged and his feet dragged as he turned away to move on.

A scream broke the bliss of the berry field at the arrival of a terrifying rider. "Yield!" a loud metallic voice commanded through a shiny mask with deep black eyeholes.

The newcomer, an armored hunter, rode atop an animal concocted of a wolf, a lizard, and a horse in one. The animal's face showed its skull, except for the outer ranges that shifted into thick black fur that swirled down the large, horse-like body in stripes. The other prevalent planes consisted of long scaled areas, raking through the fur. Though the creature was shaped like a horse, its head and tail looked more like a lizard, with a forked tongue and bulging eyes that could point independently in any direction. The tail waved strong and thick, possessing violent capabilities.

The rider wore a pointed hunter's hat atop his silvery mask. Beneath that, his decayed chest gaped open, mostly empty, with rotted flesh hanging off jagged broken ribs. His back hunched, thick and spiny, and his limbs were armored similarly to his mask, strong and alive, unlike his chest, as he wielded several lassos to throw over the naked eaters.

As the eaters scrambled around in panic, the hunter rode through, lassoing one after another, until five naked people dragged behind his steed—free to relieve itself over the captives when needed. There was no telling if he'd catch them all or stop soon, but Dorhen didn't stick around to find out. He ran down the hill and back to the path, escaped the hunter, and continued his journey. It took a while to calm his heart.

The path with its many jagged rock formations led into a huge canyon with hundreds of intricate paths carved through it. Dorhen surveyed the complex on the horizon below the lofty hill upon which he stood. Throughout all that he'd experienced, the lighting retained the same dim sultry glow as always. Smaller rock and metal formations jutted from the ground in the area he traversed now: jasper, amethyst, bronze...

"Hello, Grandchild."

Dorhen lurched at the voice beside him, echoing metallically out of a thick, smooth wall of silver. An elf with silky blonde hair stood next to him in the reflection. Dorhen checked his side to regard the speaker, but found no one. The elf somehow existed in the silver.

"What did you call me?"

The blonde elf gave a dark, knowing grin. He stood tall with his profile showing to Dorhen, cold and standoffish. The feeling of his presence put Dorhen's nerves through his teeth, an effect like Lamrhath's but worse.

"Where am I?" Dorhen proceeded to ask.

The elf cocked his head, still facing away. He pointed, drawing Dorhen's attention to a long series of silvery pillars connected in arch formations, standing in a line going beyond his ability to perceive. The pillars stood embedded in the silver wall at this spot and others. The pole-like formations stretched to the opposite side too and, like many of the rock formations, stretched high beyond sight.

"You've found my mother's gate. Can you believe they did this to me?" The other elf didn't bother to end his eerie grin.

Dorhen had yet to hear a sensible statement out of anyone. "Who are you?" he asked.

The elf turned to face him squarely. The other side of his face was missing. His skull looked as if it had been crushed and scraped away. The raw nature of the…injury, with the moist glistening of clotted blood and exposed brain made Dorhen want to look away, but he couldn't. The elf's other side remained perfect, with long combed hair, handsome facial features, and a working eye of yellow-green. When turned the other way, his tongue moved exposed in the absence of a cheek, and most of his jaw was gone. His body only half existed too, missing his right arm and a lot of ribs on that side. He wore dusty grey robes that hung torn on the right side to go along with his damaged body. Dorhen couldn't tell if he was also missing a right leg among his long draperies.

"And congratulations," the elf added.

"For what?"

"I wore the shroud once too."

"What shroud?" The other elf wore several at the moment.

"And they used it against me," he said. "When you go back, tell 'em." Dorhen squinted at the hideous, corpse-like person. "Tell Ray and Rem they failed."

"Who?" Dorhen asked.

Disregarding his confusion, the elf continued, "Because as they should know, you can't die in Kullixaxuss! You can't die in Kullixaxuss! You can't die in Kullixaxuss!" He yelled it. The metallic, echoing voice screeched a long way through the various silver boulders and pillars. If the elf weren't merely an image on a silver wall, Dorhen knew he'd be feeling spittle on his face. The elf chanted on, ignoring Dorhen's gestures and questions in his effort to get a straight answer. Dorhen gave up and moved on. The elf's yelling echoed for a long way behind him.

Down in the valley, Dorhen entered the large complex of pathways carved into the canyon. New voices led him to a clearing with a dye-works, complete with dyebaths, drying racks, and huge clay jars of chemicals. A giant man, fat, bald, and covered with warts, worked the shop, and a few smaller creatures, though big compared to Dorhen, helped to stir the vats and hang the new, rich purple fabrics. The giant wore nothing but an enormous stained apron, and kept himself planted in a seat by the rock wall. Dorhen stayed hidden for now, afraid to approach any non-human person after all he'd seen.

A set of galloping, clawed hooves echoed through an alternate entrance.

"'Bout damn time! We're all out of dyestuffs! The lord over Skulikag demands his purple textiles," the giant roared at the newcomer—the hunter riding the strange beast, dragging at least ten naked humans from the berry patch, still alive and whining, across the rough, rocky ground. Dorhen recognized the berry-eating man he'd spoken to earlier. They'd lost a lot of skin off their backsides, knees, and elbows after the long journey from the lush, fruity hill.

Showing not an ounce of fear for the giant's anger, the hunter dismounted to release the main rope from his steed's saddle. The giant's bone-faced assistants unloaded the weeping humans from their bundle and proceeded to string them up by their ankles along the rock wall. He also remained wordless as he approached the giant, holding out his gauntleted hand for his pay, which the giant obliged with a tiny, glowing jewel from under one of his many fat rolls. The hunter mounted his steed of scales and fur and rode off the way he'd come.

Now Dorhen knew he wouldn't reveal himself. Lurking behind stacked crates and clay jars of various chemicals needed for dyeing, Dorhen made his way to the crevice in the stone at the far side. He wouldn't need to cross the main workshop to get there.

"You!" the giant roared.

Dorhen froze in cold terror.

The giant pointed to one of the lanky assistants with an inhuman skeletal face. "Wood for the fire! Gotta boil the water! Hurry!"

Dorhen lifted his foot for another careful step when the giant's next task stopped him cold. Why were all those people hanging by their feet anyway? Dorhen got his answer when the giant unsheathed a knife—a sword by human standards—and sliced off the head of the first person who hung in the line. He popped the head into his mouth and ate it while he proceeded to squeeze the man's body over a large jar similar to the one Dorhen hid behind. The man's blood ran purple out of the severed neck. The giant's big hand wrapped around the body as if it were a carrot, strong enough to squeeze it dry. He slicked his other hand over the body, using the same motion one would use to milk a cow to get every last drop of blood out.

"Marvelous!" the giant roared. "This one ate many, many berries! I'm sure the lord over Skulikag will personally wear a robe dyed in this blood!"

Dorhen's stomach churned to have to watch the body of the man he'd talked to mere hours ago be emptied of all his blood. When no more purple berry-blood dripped out, the giant slid his rope across to the other side and proceeded to harvest the next person's. Two beaked assistants took the first man down, tore him in half, and devoured the halves in a few pelican-like gulps.

Tired of seeing nothing but harm and gore, Dorhen took one sickened step toward the exit. A large hand curled around his neck and dragged him backward, chokingly, to the giant.

"What've you found? A rat?" The giant laughed and picked him up by his leg.

Upside-down, the blood rushed to Dorhen's head and the force of motion pulled on his body, wind rushing along his naked skin. The giant eyeballed Dorhen's body for a moment, and then ran his huge nose across his form with a long sniff, the suction pulling Dorhen to his nostril.

"Nope, some other kind of creature," the giant deduced, "and this one hasn't eaten any berries. His blood will be crimson. No need for crimson."

The giant dropped him, and he fell a good distance in disbelief before reality registered again, and he hit the ground shoulder-first. The side of his head hit the stone and bent his neck. Dorhen somehow lived after the fall. Certainly his neck should've broken, but it didn't. It hurt, but he survived. He could move.

Before he could make a mad dash toward one of the canyon crevices, an assistant grabbed him.

"Oh, what do I care, you stupid puke? Eat the rat and get yer ass back to work!" the giant grumbled, apparently answering a silent request of the assistant. He waved his hand and returned to his task of squeezing the headless bodies.

Dorhen thrashed in the creature's grip. Now he'd die, after all he'd been through. After all the work it had taken to escape Wik's dark snake pit.

"Whoa there, stop!" the giant roared, and took Dorhen away from the assistant with two enormous, purple-stained fingers. The clicking and chittering of a feline-like throat entered the space. "What can I do for you, sanguinesent?"

Dorhen twisted, once again hanging by his leg in the giant's hold, to catch sight of the second newcomer, another bony-faced, inhuman creature. This one's eyes dazzled like clusters of diamonds in a head like a cat's skull with mummified ears and a furry white beard on its chin. A flowing black robe covered the rest of it with a feathery black collar wreathing its neck. Its appearance came closer to the dye master's assistants than any of the other infernal creatures Dorhen had yet seen, only prouder and more sophisticated.

"Yes, sanguinesent," the giant said after what must've been a telepathic order, and he dropped Dorhen again. He slammed against the ground no gentler than before but lived through it again.

Before he could collect himself, the sanguinesent swooped in. It extended hands like insect legs and clamped Dorhen's head. From each narrow palm, a tentacle slid out and penetrated Dorhen's ears.

*This one is an elf,* a sudden voice in his head stated. It wasn't Wik's voice; it must've been the sanguinesent's. A distant chorus of similar voices murmured in response. *One cannot tell why it is here and yet unsorted. It was not officially admitted.*

Dorhen couldn't guess what or who it talked about.

*I will perform an observation and proceed with the sorting.* The voice quieted in favor of a low hum in Dorhen's head. It hurt. The longer it reverberated, the closer Dorhen got to a headache. *Much longing lies in this one, as expected of elves,* the sanguinesent said thoughtfully. *I will look further.*

The humming continued until the ache spread to the rest of his body. Surely the vibration would split him open if this continued its escalation! He'd finally die, since falling on his neck twice hadn't done the job.

*A deep yearning. Ever needing. Looking. Wanting... A deep hole has bored into this one's soul. Much unfinished business. This one has spied on the intimate moments of others in its life.*

The other rumbly voices responded in the background, *A lech.*

*Voyeur.*

*He covets.*

*Pervert!*

*Hunger.*

*Distracting libido, this one.*

The one whose tentacles explored Dorhen's head continued, *It has lusted and sinned in futile efforts to fill its emptiness. The observation is complete. I shall escort it to its proper place.*

The tentacles pulled out of Dorhen's ears, and he sighed. One of them retracted into its palm and the other wrapped around his neck, cutting off his scream with the squeezing sticky appendage.

The sanguinesent moved on through the dye-works and dragged Dorhen, strangling, along behind it. He sympathized with the berry eaters who had been dragged behind that evil horse. By now, the dye master neared finishing his work squeezing the bodies. But Dorhen couldn't breathe, much less care what happened around him anymore.

Such agony prevented him from guessing how far it dragged him. He couldn't make a sound, and hadn't inhaled since the sanguinesent finished its observation. Yet he didn't die. He remained dangling on the edge of losing consciousness, his eyes rolled up and closed, but it never happened. Death left him waiting and wanting.

The ground dragged against his naked flesh, tearing his legs and ass like the berry eaters', and he couldn't bother with the pain when he struggled to fill his lungs. Miles of earth scraped beneath him. The scenery changed, still rocky and dry, but hotter and brighter.

*We've arrived,* a voice in his head said. Now it appeared the sanguinesent could speak to his mind without inserting the tentacles.

Dorhen gasped, coughing and wheezing in the thin, smoky air when the thing finally let him go. He was too exhausted and breathless to try running away. Rolling on the ground, mouth agape, his voice creaked with every desperate effort to suck in air.

The sanguinesent wrapped a tentacle around his chest and lifted him off the ground. *This is where you belong.*

They were on a cliff overlooking a massive field of fire, more vast than the mud pit and the canyon valley. In the fiery distance, various spires stood tall and pointing, shaped like termite mounds, but big enough to house kingdoms.

*You will find your purpose of existence in the fire. Go now.* The sanguinesent dropped him over the cliff.

Dorhen freefell. His hair blew upward as the hot air beat against his exposed body. The heat intensified as he plummeted faster and farther. The closer he drew to the bottom, the hotter his skin baked. He couldn't stop it.

He was falling.

He was burning.

# Chapter 21

# His Power

Wikshen opened his eyes after a long, violent dream of hot fires and the blurred faces of dead women laughing all around him. The heat vanished and made way for a cool embrace of fresh air in the world of the living. Nightfall. The hour of delight.

He'd lost Dorhen and now manned the body alone. As expected, thin leather thongs cut into his wrists and lashed them to his ankles. The sorcerers kept him contained for now. The fool who'd lent his body had been the most resistant host he'd ever possessed and was now lost to the spiritual oceans of Kullixaxuss. A dubious situation. The host body wouldn't last long without its soul. If Wik detached from it now, it would rot.

The voices around him stirred and morphed from soft to sharp. "You're from our base in Hoxigan?"

"Yes, sir. I'm Narrick."

"Tumas. I'm in charge here."

"That's him, is it?"

"Wikshen in the flesh? You better believe it," Tumas said. "Take it in while you can. Few generations of Darklanders have seen such a sight. And if you follow my orders closely, you'll see an occurrence bitch-bloody beautiful tonight!"

The longer he spent in the sun's absence, the easier Wikshen could sit upright. For now, his head bobbed and spun. Murmuring people sat around a campfire, eating roasted sausages while watching him. Wikshen scanned for the girl who had obliged to remove his boots several nights ago. He didn't see her. Maybe she'd died while he slept.

"He's awake."

"I told you he would be. Now hurry and finish your sausage, we have work to do. Through the whisper stone, the kingsorcerer reported that a village of weavers a league south of here refused protection, so now Wikshen has to attack it."

"So he's gonna—?"

"Yep, *he's* the attacker. These stupid bumpkins'll learn soon. We'll make them learn. *Wikshen* will make them."

"He doesn't look so good, though."

Wikshen tried to groan and fell short of any sound. If only he could move away from the blasted fire!

A slap rattled his face. "Wakey wakey, *my lord!*"

*Go away, fool!* His vision sharpened after the slap. *Not this again.*

The man eating the sausage stuffed the remaining end into his mouth and put his roasting fork down. Wikshen lifted his chin and shot a glare at their eyes as they approached.

"Look at him. A thing to be looked at untiringly, isn't he? Why do you think his hair is such an odd color?"

The fool smiled down on him. The man beside him shuddered. At least ten other men moved about the camp, packing and preparing the horse they'd retained after encountering the sanguinesent.

"Don't think I could get used to looking at him, to be honest," Narrick said.

"You're going to do more than look at him. Here!" Tumas tossed Narrick a short whip.

"What's this for?"

"We have to help him wake up. Peck and I will start, and you watch until you've learned the rhythm. Jump in when I say so. Let's go, Peck!"

A harsh sting swept across his back. Wikshen inhaled at the sudden pain. His vision focused. Another wave of pain rushed across his collarbone within a second of the first. The sensation had also sharpened since the first lash. The same old rhythmic stripes of searing agony layered in, increasing in speed, each shock of pain blending into the next.

Wikshen never cried out, and ceased wincing after a moment. The pain effect and its vibrations helped to raise his energy and alertness. The sorcerers had recently caught on to the concept. This sort of treatment didn't suppress Wikshen, it did the opposite—one of the many factors that made Wikshen such a terrible force to be reckoned with. And yet, they didn't fully grasp what they did. For a while, they'd been helping him "wake up" to do their work, but with his feet now bare and the long days spent in the cover of the mists paired with long nights and reluctant mornings, Wikshen was secretly charging his strength.

"Peck, you're slacking, fool!" Tumas barked. "Remember the rhythm!"

The lashes to his back increased in strength. The vibrations registered with him, but the sting he sent elsewhere.

"Narrick, pay attention! This is an art! Certain tools provoke certain levels of his anger. The kingsorcerer also informed me how rhythm is most important! And it must escalate—like sex."

A correct assessment. Wikshen wondered how much the sorcerers knew about his own magical art of Kraft. His magical ability operated differently from sorcery, and it had everything to do with vibrations, rhythms, and escalation.

"You know," Peck said, whipping across his back, "Lord Lamrhath wants to see the monster rape someone. We were traveling with women and didn't think to let one tease him right before a raid. Now we've got none because we handed them all over to Lord Lamrhath's group. Might've made an interesting effect to try. We might not have to do this anymore if we can get another woman in our group. Who knows what we might be missing in failing to try different ideas?"

Tumas replied, "We'll finish the job tonight, and tomorrow visit Alkeer in search of a woman. Narrick, jump in now!"

The other sorcerers initiated a chant for a spell to shield them all from his violence once they untied him.

Wikshen's focus peaked. His vision could now zoom in on the stubble on the farthest man's face, a possibility the darkness brought. A few miles below roared a subterranean river. His feet, pressed to the ground before him, registered all vibrational goings-on. Minerals rose up through the rocks and soil and seeped into his footpads, and from there spread across his body. He needed the energy, he needed the stock, and a great amount of it. Harvesting minerals from the earth, absorbed mostly through his feet, was essential. This was why he had asked the dark-haired woman to take his foot bindings off. Being barefoot allowed the minerals in to strengthen him—to fill him with an invigorating newness, a relieving wash of energy and strength. And fury.

A vast potency few could dare to challenge riled him, aroused him. Using his renewed strength, he fought against his bonds.

"Hurry and finish the spell!"

*Snap!* Breaking the leather linking his wrists to his ankles, Wikshen stretched vertically in his seat after hours of sleeping and sitting curled over. Blood oozed from the gash of the sharp leather thong binding on his wrists for a few seconds before the flesh laced back together. The minerals continued to flow inside him. Reaching his bound hands to the cool and inviting night sky, he inhaled the sweet, fresh air. Sticky blood poured from the whips' gaping lacerations, but the open flesh would mend soon too.

The two idiots persisted in whipping at him, their interested expressions now replaced with concern.

"Hurry!"

His teeth were enough to tear the rest of his wrist bonds away, and then his iron-reinforced hand ripped open his ankle bonds. His ability of transitional magic, the process of taking in minerals through his skin from the earth, came easier than during any of his past lives, thanks to his host body—an elf born with this ability. Their combined efforts could make Wikshen unstoppable, if only Dorhen's soul hadn't departed.

When all of his limbs were free and he sprang to his feet, the sorcerers' glowing, fire-like shields of magic energy whooshed into place. The cowards. Others erected magic shields which blended them into the scenery. The slimy little maggots never did anything with their own hands; they preferred to appease pettygods who performed feats for them. They didn't fight head-on, they hid in the shadows and cast spells, or used mentally enthralled villagers. The weak and impotent sorcerers planned to use him like any other tool. *They* weren't about to attack a village, *Wikshen* was. And by the time they arrived, Wikshen would be so full of energy and aggression, he'd oblige. He'd rip through anyone in his path and lose himself in laughing fury. Just as they wanted him to.

A blocking spell cast by some coward huddling behind him, wearing the necessary blinding mask, suddenly cut off his magic ability. Wikshen's urge to release his Kraft, gathering in his core, withered. A number of crackling torches and metal rods charged with electrical spells jabbed toward him to herd him wherever they wanted him to go.

Wikshen ground his teeth.

*Soon.*

# Chapter 22
# What is Left in Wikshen's Wake

Hurry and go!" Dorhen called from the crowd of Thaccilians, urging Kalea to climb over the wall with Bowaen.

"No!" she screamed. "I won't leave you again."

"Don't worry about me. Meet me at the well in the forest."

Kalea retched. *He'll never make it there. I'm leaving him to die. Maybe he knows that.*

Bowaen lifted her up, leaving her no choice but to grab the wall as he bid. Kalea wept as she clung weakly to the cold, scratchy stone. "I won't leave Dorhen again. Not again!"

"Kalea!" Bowaen said. "Wake up, girl."

"Dorhen," she moaned.

"You're dreaming. Dorhen's not here."

Kalea sat up. "Dorhen!"

The fragrant smell of the poisonous fruit wafted on the breeze all around her. She didn't remember falling asleep. Bowaen sat beside her. She lay curled at the base of a tree—not one of the poisonous trees. Dawn had barely broken the darkness. Thick grass crunched beneath her elbows.

"Bowaen," she said, finally realizing Dorhen was still missing.

"Yeah?"

She shook, chilled in her sweaty chemise and half-laced kirtle. "Where's Gaije?"

"I'm here," he said, and leaned into her line of vision.

Kalea dropped her head against Bowaen's arm in relief. "I thought we left you to die."

Gaije sat in the grass, wringing his grandfather's bow in his two fists. His eyes drooped with dark circles. His quiver lay empty on the ground.

"We did," Bowaen said. "But I guess 'death' ain't in that elf's Norrian language."

"Bowaen was good enough to wait here for me," Gaije said. "I made my way to the wall to follow you, and that's when someone ripped my grandfather's bow away. I couldn't leave it. I used my knife, forcing my way through the chaotic crowd to get it back. Most of them were more interested in following you over the wall. They shouted your name. But a lot of them attacked me in anger. After getting the bow back, I found a way to climb onto the roof, which I traversed toward the broken wall."

Bowaen took over from there. "You needed rest anyway, Kalea. We lost the red-eyed people in the forest and it got all quiet, so I said we'd let you sleep so we could wait for Gaije to catch up. He did."

"That's the best news in a long time," Kalea said. She wanted to feel good in this moment, but she'd just had yet another dream about Dorhen. About her abandoning him.

A thick blanket of mist drifted through the valley below the hill upon which they were settled. The scene below their elevated position looked like some massive, whimsical lake out of a dream. She couldn't believe the company with which she sat this morning. Bowaen, Del, *and* Gaije. Alive. Kerlin had told her a disgusting lie about their deaths and she had reunited with them, but then what did she do? She left Gaije to a mob of ravenous Thaccilians and a sanguinesent. But here they were, all three. By some wild, unimaginable miracle—the Creator's grace—she found herself in their company.

Gaije stood and gathered his things. "I need arrows."

All of them trudged on, haggard, pale, and tired. They were missing articles of clothing. Gaije must not have found his tunic, but he'd taken back his traditional Norrian braies and leggings with the open hips, his clan mantle and cloak, quiver, greaves, and—after much hassle—his grandfather's bow. Bowaen wore his tabard but not the undershirt he usually donned. Del retained most of his clothes, his beloved pipe, coat, and treasured bundle of burglary tools he'd forged himself. Despite their condition, she thanked the Creator again and again they were alive. She'd come back to life again herself.

"Did you get the money Lord Dax gave us?" she asked Bowaen, who shook his head solemnly. She still had her small portion of silver and copper chips for spending in the Darklands.

Bowaen patted his vest pockets. "I left the big box behind, but I did get all the jewels out. Those red-eyed people hadn't plundered it yet."

That offered a small bit of relief: they could barter with the jewels if need be. It also must've meant he had retained the shell bracelet Dorhen gave her. She resisted asking to see it. The shells belonged to Bowaen now, and she resolved to be mature about it.

Gaije insisted they move on, and none were against getting as far away from the forest as possible, regardless of how tired they were. Gaije pointed. "Look at the smoke."

"It's not smoke, it's mist," Del said, bending over to tighten his boot strings.

"What I'm referring to *is* smoke, you fool," Gaije shot back. "Someone was raided last night." They all sprang to look out across the valley. A tall plume of smoke did rise on the horizon amidst the surly weather out of the lake-like mist.

"Do you think your sorcerers did it, Gaije?" Bowaen asked.

Gaije scowled. "Wasting two nights in that city made me angry, but it might've revealed the path for me. Let's go see who is to blame."

Kalea's party walked amongst flattened piles of smoldering ash which used to be houses. Blackened stone chimneys remained standing. Animals lay dead with their limbs harvested amidst the wreckage of domestic tools and furniture dragged out and looted. Human bodies were strewn around too, everywhere. The stench of burning flesh overpowered the burnt wood. The three humans in the party dry-heaved from empty stomachs and Gaije paced around, moving his head as if to shake off the smell.

Trying not to breathe the foul air so deeply, Kalea ordered her friends to show her any and all dead elves on site. She also looked for signs of Vivene. Holding a handkerchief over her mouth, she checked all she could find. Retching and moaning at the sights became a basic part of the process. Similar noises from her friends in their searches echoed from the farther parts of the village. She made sure to inspect the severed heads dangling about too. They kept an eye out for anything useful to take with them. Nothing. No survivors, either.

No Dorhen. No Vivene. Kalea let out a sigh but sucked it back into her lungs when Gaije shouted over the distance to reach all of his companions. She ran toward his voice. Had he found a Norr elf?

He stood beside a dead woman lying against a broken table in the village square, her dead face frowning and her open eyes half-rolled backward. This one wasn't Vivene, at least.

"I've found something," Gaije said.

"A dead person? Tell us some news, elf," Del said.

"A fresh clue." Gaije's hazel eyes took on a new fire, nearly bright enough to match Dorhen's. "Look right here."

He pointed at the woman's hands, frozen in a clawing pose. When they all leaned in to look, Kalea shrieked and covered her mouth. Dark blue strands of hair were tangled around her fingers. Every little strand caught the light and shone a brilliant blue, like a gemstone, at each looping bend.

"The bastard!" Gaije hissed. He pointed to the woman's throat, blotched black and purple, the shapes resembling large hands, one of the few bodies without missing limbs or open slashes. "He choked her to death as she clawed at his face and hair."

"That's a clue, I'll say," Bowaen said. "And this happened last night. He's not far ahead of us. Can you tell which way they went?"

Gaije's hands curled into white-knuckled fists. "Of course. North, always north."

"Let's move," Bowaen ordered. "There's nothing here but death. If there were survivors, we'd have found them by now. And none of us have seen any Norr elves." He gave Kalea the best smile he could, considering their surroundings, and she gave him back a solitary nod.

Kalea lingered as the rest turned to leave, and worked to untangle the strands of hair from the woman's fingers.

"Wh-what are you doing?" Del asked, his face drenched in disgust.

"I'm keeping the hair. It's a clue, after all."

His eyes went wider than she'd ever seen. "And you think I'm disgusting?" Del's eyebrows laced together. He didn't stick around to find out what she'd do next.

She turned her attention to the wad of hair. Blue, like Dorhen had described Arius Medallus's hair. Did the fairy have a connection to the blue-haired sorcerer? Could he and the blue-haired sorcerer be the same person?

After collecting every strand, she hesitated and looked through her basket, not sure how to store them. She pulled out her treasured *Lehomis* novel, opened it to a random spot, and dropped the tangle of hairs in. Snapping the book shut, she shoved it back into the basket and hobbled on her sore leg to catch up.

Before leaving the unfortunate ruined village behind, Kalea cast one more glance over her shoulder. So many dreams. Too many dreams that supported Kerlin's claim. The Dreamer's claim of her dreamwalking ability had been proven more than right by her return to his dream later. Whatever dark place she had found on her first attempted dreamwalk— she didn't know what it was, but it too was something real.

Overall, she'd found a big curve in the path of life, a turn she couldn't hope to comprehend. She possessed the ability to dreamwalk, and Arius Medallus might have something to do with it. Kerlin had called her a Luschian, and she now believed him after proving her ability. He'd said how Lusche, a water spirit, endowed his children with mysterious powers. Her parents had sent her to the convent at age ten for being mentally ill—with a strange connection to water. Even Dorhen had, more than once, assured her she wasn't mentally ill, and that Arius Medallus was a water spirit, one whose face she'd seen in the water for most of her life.

She wasn't mentally ill, she was something else entirely. Something not human.

# Chapter 23
## What is Togha's Heartbreak

Metta hadn't kissed Togha her last. She did it a lot. Behind Shaman Gilda's back, in the shadows of night, in brief passing when they collected firewood. And when she wasn't finding quick, cheeky opportunities to plant a kiss on his face or mouth, she was constantly touching him: his hair, his shoulder, a pinch on his arm, a nudge when they sat down to eat, or a tap of her shoe on his. Even when too far away to kiss or prod him, her eyes constantly grazed him. She reveled in her secret shamelessness and hid it under a meek smile when in the shaman's presence. She'd grin or blow a kiss when he caught her eyes. Her smile proved infectious.

This behavior didn't exist in his old society. Back home, she would not have let him know of her interest, and he would've waited for her to call him, to ask him for marriage. Oh, Bright One, he wanted her to. But she was human, and he couldn't guess what that meant for them. Pairing with human females had appeared to work out well for the Clanless members who'd held him captive. After all of her behavior, he couldn't figure out why she hadn't asked him for marriage yet. If she wanted him, what was she waiting for? Due to his *saehgahn* discipline and learning, he couldn't bring himself to show the same affection toward her, nor ask her for marriage. He continued to suffer her teasing for days and days. Sleep got harder to achieve each night.

So he did the only thing in his power to try to move their relationship along: he initiated traditional *saehgahn* flaunting methods. At the next stream they found to wash their faces and fill their waterskins, he took off all his clothes and dipped into the water. As he washed, he applied all the best poses and motions his forefathers had developed over centuries to make the display appear casual and discreet while also displaying his shapes and angles in the right ways.

He didn't have to check to see if Metta watched him. She did. Her eyes touched his naked flesh, and he didn't want them to stop. At the moment his confidence peaked, however, the shaman stomped into the water and banged his head with her drum beater.

"Stupid!" she fussed. "Wikshonites don't bathe in mixed company! Go downstream where the witches can't see you."

Togha waded to the bank with a sigh. He'd scored a technical success: Metta saw him. She watched him collect his things and dress. The warlocks present laughed at him, and one who sat next to her scowled. Come to think of it, that man had taken on a surly expression as soon as he noticed how Metta prodded Togha.

Later that night, after dinner and the prayer hour, Togha took Haggis to a quiet place to comb her down as always. A fire raged in his core. Around this hour, Metta usually came to give him a kiss. He went through his routine. Despite his heavy distraction, he couldn't neglect his beloved donkey. He did a hasty job of it. Their setting didn't help; his and Haggis's feet sank into the soft soil of this region, and the air smelled skunky. He'd have to dig the clumps of dirt out of her hooves after walking this terrain.

As expected, Metta sashayed around the thicket bend which granted Togha his privacy. And his heart raced. He dropped the grooming brush.

"Rough day, huh?" Metta asked, beaming the warm smile he'd adored since the day he met her.

"Not exactly," he said. He avoided her eye contact but waited.

"I hate it when Gilda yells at me."

"She shouldn't do that."

Metta giggled. "You flatter me so much. Why would you say that?"

He shrugged. "I don't know. Seems like a thing no one should do to you."

"Aaawww." She stepped in front of him, forcing him to look at her.

"Why does the air smell so bad?" he asked. It wasn't the best atmosphere for kissing.

"We're on the outskirts of Goblin Country," she said. "A nasty, wet swamp with dead plants and goblins—as you'd expect."

She didn't act like the smell bothered her as much. She reached up and stroked his hair like she'd done many times before. Her enamored expression made him swell with both pride and lust. She approved of him—every *saehgahn's* goal. Earlier that day, she'd seen him naked. His efforts might pay off soon. He closed his eyes at her touch. Every hair she stirred both soothed and excited.

"How's your wrists?" Her voice hummed closer than before.

He'd forgotten about his sore wrists—and his donkey, who awaited the rest of her grooming.

"You are just the handsomest creature…" Stroking his hair with one hand, Metta's other hand found his face. She turned it to meet hers squarely. "Do you know why I'm here?"

She'd come to deliver his nightly kiss, he knew that. When he opened his eyes, her own showed relaxation.

She put out a laugh. "Look at me, I'm shaking."

His body shook more than normal for some reason. Something different would happen tonight. She closed her lips and raised one eyebrow. She tugged on his poncho in a silent order to bow his head. He obeyed.

She met his lips with an open-mouthed kiss, a new experience. Togha's body flared. She slipped her tongue, a slight bit at first, to brush his bottom lip. She slipped it inside his mouth. The world around them flew away. Even the stale air vanished in favor of something sweeter his imagination forged. He touched his tongue to hers for a strange and wonderful sensation, an unearthly soft caress they shared.

Metta stepped into him; their bodies collided. He took her by the shoulders with a new endowed sense of privilege. She wandered her hands too. She kissed energetically and with abandon.

Togha couldn't stand on his own any longer. His trembling knees gave way, and they both went to the ground. Metta laughed at their fumble. He loved that laugh. Now sitting on the ground, not yet situated, she put her hand on his inner thigh. Tonight would begin a new existence for him, their new life together.

Looming over them, the donkey brayed, and Togha was pulled back to earth. "Oh, um," he said into Metta's mouth. "We should move away. She's temperamental, and she kicks."

Metta hummed a laugh, keeping their lips in contact. "Bad donkey," she cooed.

They didn't get far. Haggis brayed to warn him of the intruder. The surly warlock who tended to sit beside Metta a lot stood on their side of the thicket, watching them. At his presence, Togha's elation soured and boiled and rotted into a rage unlike anything he'd ever experienced. He leaped to stand in front of Metta.

"What do you want?" His fists clenched by his sides. If the man dared to step any closer to Metta, he'd swing one.

The man ignored Togha; he glared right past him and spoke to Metta. "So, this is where you've been going at night?"

Metta rose to stand beside Togha. "Jax, what did I tell you?"

Jax smirked. "You didn't tell me much. You just stopped putting out. I've been wondering why, and now I know."

"Jax, go away," Metta said.

"I'll do that. And I'll tell Gilda."

Togha looked from one to the other. "Tell her what?"

Jax barked a laugh. "Is he serious? Does he not know?"

"Know what?" Togha demanded.

Jax pointed to Metta and shot his glare at Togha. "You better be careful, elf. This little lady will get you into some deep trouble."

Metta ignored all that. "Fine," she said. "If you tell Gilda what you saw here, I'll tell her about *you* and what you've done to *me!*"

Togha whirled to face Metta. "What did he do to you?" Togha's hand went to his knife under his poncho. He mentally prepared himself to kill Jax the way *saehgahn* were trained to do.

"Nothing!" Metta said.

"Well," Jax said with a smile, "I guess whatever you're doing with this fellow here, you'll have to visit me right after and do the same thing. That should make it fair."

Togha growled, drew the knife, and charged.

Metta caught his poncho, and he halted. "Don't," she hissed. "Jax, listen. Togha, calm down." She took a deep breath and faced Togha squarely. "I have to tell you of an important rule in our religion, since I assume you don't know."

Togha waited.

"In our religion… The women can't have carnal relations with anyone except Wikshen, and the men can't have carnal relations at all."

Togha's face quirked. "What does that mean?"

Metta blew out a breath. "It means all those things we've been doing. Kissing. Touching. We can't do them. We'll both get in extreme trouble."

Across the way, Jax smiled. "See? She's trouble. She roped me into that shit too. Got me hooked."

Togha shook his head. He regarded Metta but didn't know what to say. It meant they couldn't get married? They couldn't do…what he wanted to do with her? He clenched his teeth. She wore a concerned expression he found beautiful and irresistible.

"Metta…" he said. He didn't know how to finish.

"I still like you, Togha." She reached for his hand but aborted the action. They could no longer exchange affections—or if they did, they'd have to do a better job of hiding it. "And listen to me, Jax," she said. "I'll stop meeting Togha at night." Her words stabbed Togha's heart. "And you won't see me again either. None of us will tell, and none of us will do this anymore. Agreed?"

Jax grinned with his teeth bared. "Sure."

When she turned to Togha again, an odd torrent of mixed emotions forced tears to his eye rims. His world shattered into pieces and now spun around him. He couldn't process Metta's explanation. He only understood the part where they couldn't kiss anymore.

She leaned in so Togha would look at her face. "I'll be a good Wikshonite, Togha, all right? And we can be friends."

That hurt so much. Togha bent over. He needed to leave. But when he considered the scene of Jax gloating and Metta moping, he knew he wouldn't leave. He'd stay. He loved Metta.

Togha survived a few more lonely days—and nights—away from the woman who'd given his life purpose and then canceled the whole thing. He could only look at her from afar, and she always met his gaze. Of course, she didn't stare as openly as she used to.

Togha distracted himself by listening more intently to the sermons the shaman delivered to learn about this way of life Metta exalted. If he learned about it, he might figure out how to stay close to her, through religious camaraderie if nothing else. At night, he made his bed as close to hers as he could manage while keeping propriety—to protect her. If he couldn't love her, he could devote his life to protecting her. That's what *saehgahn* did.

Jax continued to strut around like he was in charge, shooting smirks at Metta and Togha alike. Togha could stand it no longer. At the next chance, he caught Metta by the arm as she returned to camp with an armful of laundry from the river.

"I have to know what it meant when you said you'd be a good Wikshonite," he said.

She no longer smiled. He hadn't seen her lively smile in days. "Well, hello to you too."

Feeling like a bad person, he released her arm. "Hello."

She spread her lips deep into her cheeks, not a smile but a look of pity. "Good Wikshonites are celibate women who wait for Wikshen to call them. When I said that, I was promising you I wouldn't dally with you, but I also wouldn't dally with other men either."

"What is a dally?"

"Don't you have these words in your native language?"

He shrugged.

"It's what we've been doing—playing," she explained.

"Well, now I must know. What was Jax talking about? What've you done with him?"

She rolled her eyes high and waved her hand in a circle. "You know."

He shook his head. "No, I don't."

"I did a few…favors for him. Because I liked him."

Togha pointed to the wad of black linens in her arms. "What, you did his laundry?"

Her "no" came out as a musical whine. "It's just that I…found Jax good-looking, and I wanted him to like me. So I did things to make him feel good." She animated her free hand as if it would help Togha understand. It didn't. "We…dallied, like you and I did, and on just *one* occasion we"—she finished the sentence through clenched teeth—"made love."

Togha didn't exactly know what that meant either, but he didn't like it. Her expression melted as Togha's apparently heated up. She dropped the laundry and grabbed his arm.

"Oh please, don't be mad. I told you I wouldn't do that anymore. Please, don't make this worse than it needs to be! Besides, he and I happened before I met you!"

Her hands on his poncho alone kept him from charging back to camp to kill Jax. Her grasp turned into hugging his arm. "Togha, listen…I like you a lot more. I've never had an elf before. I can see now that having one might be a little complicated."

Before he could march away and go through with the killing, Metta took his face and pulled him into a kiss, a tender and slow one. "Togha," she sang his name as a whisper, her breath beating against his mouth. "Listen to me. The funny thing about our religion is there is no Wikshen. There hasn't been one for over six hundred years. You and I will be fine. We'll get settled in somewhere, like Alkeer or somewhere we can do good work in Wikshen's name. We'll be tight friends, you get me?" She pressed her hip against his. "*Very* tight friends."

Togha took control of his breathing. "All right. But what if—"

She put her finger over his lips. "No what-ifs."

He spoke despite her finger. "What happens if Wikshen comes back?"

"He won't," she said. "But in some other strange world where he does…I would go to Wikhaihli to serve him. I'm a Wikshonite. I love him with all my being." She tapped his nose as she said the words, "And-you-should-too."

Togha nodded.

The next morning, Gilda called the company to assembly. "Up ahead is the crossroads. One path splits off for a shortcut through Goblin Country and the other goes east to Alkeer. Since we've acquired a few who are new to this religion, I am splitting our company so you can head to Ravivill to study under Shaman Knilma, our oldest and wisest Wikshonite. You can learn far more from her than from me."

As Gilda went through, splitting the travelers to create two sensible groups, Togha's eyes darted nervously to Metta and back. Gilda sent

Togha with the group headed to Ravivill and turned Metta onto the path to Alkeer. For one split second, a panicky, longing stare connected their gazes.

Togha clenched his fist and gritted his teeth. He took Metta's words to heart, those words she had said after they shared their last kiss. He'd do as he was told. He'd live as a Wikshonite, and eventually he'd find Metta in Alkeer so they could be together as friends—the way she'd said. He promised himself she'd be all right. She'd survive. Most importantly, Gilda sorted Jax into Togha's group, and he would not be bothering Metta.

Keeping himself from looking back as his re-formed party walked away was the hardest thing Togha had ever done.

# Chapter 24
## What is Ilbith's Challenge

Wikshen."

Despite the growing night, Wikshen nodded weakly on the grass without Dorhen's soul to keep him strong.

"Wake up, freak." The annoying voice shifted to a childish taunt. "We found another village without a red flag. You know what that means, right?"

"More fun for the beast!" another idiot sorcerer behind the first shouted.

They'd made such a mockery of him: the King of the Darklands, the center of carnal worship, whom even the trolls feared, and here he sat, bound, slapped, and harassed by a load of buffoons who gladly bowed to lesser gods than he. They thought he belonged to them. They'd even marked him with their symbol some time ago, a scabby brand on his left side.

Their voices turned from muffled to sharp as the lashings increased. Wikshen dug his toes into the soil and allowed more minerals into his soles. The sorcerers would regret their actions this time. The lashings sharpened too, to piercing increments of pain heightening with each new strike. Tonight, the vibrations took him beyond alert; they carried him straight to anger.

The sorcerers raised their voices in several different chants around him. As protocol went, a few men charged up metal rods with dancing wires of lightning, while others cast spells to shield themselves from Wikshen's magic.

Before they finished their spells, he sprang to his feet and swiped a fast kick to the nearest sorcerer's face. His battleshift waved like a black flag behind his leg. In his burst of new vigor, the battleshift added gloves and leg coverings which left the palms and soles bare. Familiar black bands appeared on his biceps and right thigh.

A few voices stopped chanting, shocked at Wikshen's sudden movement, but not all. He'd spent the last several weeks in concentration, gathering the minerals he needed to lash out with his own magic, and that sweet moment had arrived. He lurched straight for the sorcerers who diligently chanted and knocked them over to stop their voices. Success for the most part; however, sorcery discipline included persevering through a chant regardless of what happened around or to them, so Wikshen slammed his heels against their heads. All chanting ended.

Three sorcerers succeeded in charging their golden lightning wands, and those earned Wikshen's specialty. He didn't need to chant to produce his superior magic. Wikshen merely breathed and focused. He flourished his arms, and at the end of the movement, he forced a blade out of his hand to slice open the nearest sorcerer who threatened him with lightning. A morkblade. It materialized as an extraordinarily sharp blade made from the minerals he'd absorbed, with long sharpened sides and various jagged, curving, and hooking corners. Morkblades flew in straight lines for as long as they could last, and cut through anyone standing in the way. At the end of their journey, they disintegrated to hardly a speck of dust, if anything.

These sorcerers had used him for the last time.

Lamrhath's company settled down to wait for the masquerading Wikshonites at the designated meeting spot. The hours stretched on so long that his companions opened their packs and passed around the carrots, cabbages, and other such produce they'd received from their new Darklandic followers.

Kaskill opened the eggs he'd been stowing gingerly in a sack packed with wool and passed them out. Lamrhath accepted one and slurped the slimy fluid through a hole in the shell. The other group was late, and they had failed to send any communications through the whisper stone.

Lamrhath tried to keep his patience as he shared the next egg with Silva. She hadn't gotten tired of cuddling close at his side, gloating at the men around them for being superior because she was sleeping with their leader. Rank turned out to be another important factor to her culture. Her husband back at her old village had possessed a lowly rank, so she considered leaving with Lamrhath her own feat of triumph over the others.

After terrorizing those four virgins with his libido the night before he claimed Silva, he expected her to exhibit similar fear. To the contrary, she surprised him with her willingness to please him. Last night, she had explained to him in her thick accent that the virgins' negative response to him was due to their young ages and his foreign love-making style. In addition to their stunted education, none of them had expected his dominant positional choice. Being an experienced and mature woman, and already married off, Silva could handle him, regardless of how sore she would get in his demanding routine. For now, he would try to go easy on her. Silva was a treasure of sorts, and Lamrhath appreciated her.

Late afternoon had shifted into a gloomy orange evening by the time Wikshen's entourage appeared over the hill, plodding along the beaten trail. Wikshen's horse walked vacant. The coiled rope which used to bind him now hung off the saddle. The shifty-eyed troop stepped carefully.

"My lord," the one nicknamed Peck said to Lamrhath's questioning expression. "He's gone."

"Gone? Why did you let him get away?" Lamrhath asked.

The whole of the caravan slowed to a stop. The sorcerers in black bent over and dropped to rest on the ground.

"Get away?" Peck parroted. "My lord, we did everything according to protocol. It's hard to explain what happened."

"Do it anyway."

"He did a terrible…"

"Dare I assume 'he' means Wikshen?"

Peck waved his arm in a circular fashion. "Please, see for yourself." Lamrhath followed him to a cart they towed, possibly a new confiscation. "Please forgive us, my lord, it's been days and we haven't slept a wink."

The wagon put off a putrid air. Peck threw aside the blanket stretched over the cargo space. Silva moaned behind him at the stronger, wafting miasma, which would make them all ill if they continued to breathe it. Hundreds of tiny wings buzzing beneath the covering billowed into the air.

Meat. Many pieces of meat covered the wooden wagon bed. One piece he recognized as a portion of a hand. Shreds of clothing were woven in and out of the bloody mess. The organs were in line with the meat chunks, cleanly sliced. The heap oozed blood, quickly coagulating and sticking to the wood like jelly.

"We thought you should see it for yourself," Peck said, his face sickly. "There's two of them in there. We tried to arrange the pieces in order."

Lamrhath never took his eyes off the rotting flesh.

"My lord, that bastard… I still can't believe it. You know how few clothes he wore… He used weapons that came out of nowhere. Our fire shields couldn't stop them. Didn't matter. And after the first blade broke through, we lost our concentration in sheer shock. The situation turned to a massacre for poor old Tumas and Narrick. What do you make of it, my lord?"

Staring at the meat, Lamrhath said, "I make of it we have a real Wikshen, lads. I want you to find and take him back to Ilbith. If he won't go willingly, we'll need to develop new spells for restraint."

He turned to the group behind him. "We'll contact Naerezek once we're home and get back to the books. Learn all you can about Wikshen. We have to control him, or we may not last."

"This is eerie, my lord," Peck said, rubbing his balding pate, the dark hair around the sides hanging long. No grey grew in the young man's goatee yet. "I've never seen the like in all my..."

The wind rushed about, and the old trees' branches squeaked as they rubbed against one another. Lamrhath slapped the top of his bald head. Peck yelped and dipped his chin to his chest.

"You're an Ilbith sorcerer!" Lamrhath scolded. "You know the ways of Wikshen." He regarded the rest of them. "We won't last another day if the lot of you are as spineless as Peck! You all have to trust me. Soon you'll be seeing dreadwitches wandering about, for holy Naerezek's sake. Wikshen won't waste any time while he's out there, running wild and free. A couple of his ungodly whores can take on an army of our best dunces *and* stand up to our most powerful spells. We'd have to summon creatures from darker pits of the netherworld than we've ever reached before to fight the dreadwitches. It's a great fortune I divided your group and sent the women and children up the mountain before this happened." He surveyed the whole company, reduced to frightened, child-like idiots, including the members of his own group, who hadn't dealt with Wikshen's escape.

"What'll we do, my lord?" Peck asked, gingerly rubbing his shiny scalp, now red from Lamrhath's ringed hand.

Lamrhath's stern look made him shrivel and sweat. "We'll put my plans into action. If this escalates into a war, so be it. Though I don't think that'll happen."

He fished through his pouch for the whisper stone with the black ribbon. "Shaman," he whispered into it, "listen carefully. Wikshen is on the loose. Look out for him in Alkeer. In the meantime, meet with my associate in an inn called the Red Ear. His name is Dyii, and he wishes to become a Wikshonite. Keep him near and he'll aid you in whatever you require. If the two of you can manage, hold Wikshen until further notice."

Lamrhath took the stone down, chose a different one, and tapped the necessary rhythm on its surface. Whispering into it, he delivered a message to the Ilbith agent named Dyii, according to what he'd told his shaman friend.

# Chapter 25
# His Eternity

The flames. The unbearable flames.

Stop it. Stop the burning!

Flesh scorched and healed.

Weakness.

No energy. Drained.

The flames burned all the way through. To his core, and then out again.

Agony.

Laughter.

Agony.

Forever.

*Dorhen.*

What does that mean?

*That's your name, sweet creature. Remember?*

The word sounded meaningless. Nothing mattered when the flames seared and moved inward, soon to come out again, leaving healed flesh behind and starting the process over.

*Awwwww, look at youuuuu,* the voice cooed sensually. Parts of those words dragged on forever and ceased to sound like a voice, instead sounding like leather rubbing against leather.

A sensation like fingers touched his eyelids, adding a cold contrast to the intense heat of the atmosphere. He'd forgotten he possessed eyelids until now; the fire raged so bright, eyelids didn't matter. The fingers dragged downward, over his face, along his neck, to his chest. It was still too hot to care.

*You remember what we did, Dorhen? Hmm?*

No. He didn't. All his awareness centered on the burning.

*You wanna do it again?*

He didn't try to answer. Too much pain. He didn't know who owned the voice, but it brought back pieces of memories. Dorhen was a name. His name. Maybe.

*If you say yes, I can put out the fire.*

*Yes!* His mind's voice shouted it, but he couldn't tell if she heard. He wanted to nod his head—if it was still there. He used the only power he realized he had for now, the power of his mind, to make a motion, to nod. To communicate. To beg for mercy, for kindness. He could offer her nothing, but he'd take on any and as much debt as he needed to escape this pain.

*Of course, my sweet little creature. I can help you. But I have to warn you, I will take you out of the fire temporarily for an unforeseeable amount of time. Our contract could last a lifetime, or possibly for five minutes. Remember? I've explained it to you before.*

Dorhen tried harder to move. To show his agreement. *Pl-pl-ease. Pl-please.* He hoped she received his message.

*And I have my price, do you remember?*

He couldn't remember her price, but he'd pay it. He'd pay any amount. He tried again to show his agreement. *Yes.*

With practice, his mind's voice came easier. He slowly began to remember himself. He was a person with hands and feet and eyes and ears. He couldn't see or feel any of those body parts now, unless she put her cold fingers on any of them.

*As you desire,* she confirmed, *we'll forge another contract.*

A bright light suddenly filled Dorhen's eyes—his eyes must've healed again. The light accompanied the horrible roaring fire all around him. A faint face hovered amidst the infernal confusion of dancing shapes.

A composition of bones rose up before him, charred black until veins, blood, and new flesh bloomed over it. His hand! Dorhen's heart rate hastened, and he worked up the strength to partially rise. That's when he saw it: his own heart, beating out in the open, before his eyes. The shock made it beat even faster, throbbing in its rhythm. Blood pooled around it in his chest cavity, and the arteries and veins grew like vines, branching out across his body to each fingertip. His flesh returned again.

Eventually, his skin grew back and covered the hideous sight of his insides at work. The flames dimmed, and the face that watched him dimmed too.

Doused in darkness, the cool air returned. Two hands appeared and stroked his hair. A cool body slid against his, trapping him to the floor. His heart beat in a different rhythm now, sending a surge of renewed blood to his new genitals. A vibrant hardness demanded a lot of his new blood, and attention. The agony of the fire had long gone, now replaced with a new agony. He needed kindness and mercy. He didn't worry too much because the person whose voice caressed his ears would take care of it. She always kept her part of the bargain.

*Is that better, sweet creature?*

Every once in a while, a set of teeth within a smile glinted and faded in the darkness. The white parts of a set of eyes. He could feel her more than see her. A large set of swollen breasts pressed and tickled along his chest, leaving wet trails behind each nipple. Everything about this person was a comfort. She was his everything. Too bad he kept forgetting about her until she showed up again, offering to stop the fires and deliver him an oasis of comfort.

*Sweet creature, you are a joyyyyy,* she drawled; a sensual drag added a pulse of extra hardness to his erection. *I'm pleased you feel so about me. I'm glad you are here. It can get boring in these long eternities, and you are a delight of entertainment.*

His confusion had vanished by now in favor of a more specific awareness. He cared solely for her, fervently and eternally. His struggle to form words and phrases changed to easily spouted moans and groans. He grew impatient. He needed her assistance. The assistance she promised. His hands searched and found her body.

"Please. Now," he whispered, already forgetting he'd ever lost the ability to talk.

As he squeezed one of her large breasts, a cool refreshing stream of nectar ran down his arm. He licked the sweet, sticky liquid off his hand. The greatest flavor in the world, and such a wonderful change from the dry inferno he'd escaped. He drank from her bounty greedily, filling his empty stomach. Such relief. The flavor and fullness satisfied for a lifetime.

A warm, wet, and tight encasement swallowed his erection, slowly sliding down until a soft body met his pelvis. Slippery and refined muscles flexed around the shaft and pulled up with soothing friction.

Dorhen let go of her breast and lay back, groaning. A stream of milk ran across his cheek and into his hair. He surrendered to the feeling delivered by a loving body come to tend his other problem. Finally. His eyes closed in total relaxation. He opened them off and on, hoping to see his mistress. He couldn't see much, but she was there, hovering over him. Her breasts sometimes dipped and grazed his chest so, so slightly. Her warmth made him feel safe. How he wanted to see her.

Her motion increased, up and down, up and down, and sometimes circular. His mistress, whom he loved and would do anything for. He'd do anything she asked. Anything. Anything. Anything, anything, anything—anything-anything-anything-anything-any—!

He released.

Collapsing back into a flat sprawl, he panted. Trembling.

A fluttery giggle touched his face with the closeness of her lips. *What a good boy, my little creature.*

Her hidden muscles squeezed a few pulses around his cock to suck it clean before releasing it to the cold air. She leaned over him one more time to kiss his mouth, but he couldn't return the kiss in his blissful exhaustion.

*I love you,* he said, not sure if the words came through his lips or not.

She didn't return his proclamation. She never did, but he didn't mind. He'd also never noticed her climax whenever they engaged in this activity. She didn't seem to care to. For the moment, she lay beside him, entwining her sleek legs with his. The unearthly nectar streamed from her nipples and between her legs.

She leaned over and flicked her tongue along his cheek. The action made his penis rise again, and she laughed at it. In the darkness, a brief image of black hair slid over a pale shoulder layered with smooth, opalescent scales.

*You're different from the others.*

Whatever she meant, he couldn't find enough interest to ask. A magnificent puzzle, his mistress.

*What can I do for you? Tell me how to serve you,* he said, managing only his mind-speech.

She laughed a bit louder. *Soon, sweet creature.*

Dorhen licked his hand again after realizing it wore a trail of leaked nectar. His stomach was full. He was complete. Satisfied and happy. But his new erection waited for its next use.

He reached out to cup her cheek, and as her face tilted, he caught another glimpse of her features. A smirking mouth corner. A dark fan of eyelashes. Even the horns growing out of her forehead were beautifully colored, like a rose, and shimmered in the faint light. Her forked tongue slithered out and teased his lips. He tried to grab it between them, but it snapped back into her mouth too fast.

Dorhen owed his dark beauty of a mistress some form of payment. He'd promised. He attempted to push her gently to the ground to mount her, but she refused.

*I'm afraid our contract is coming to an end. But don't worry, I'll return soon.* She spoke without opening her ever-grinning mouth. *Lie back now, and uphold your end of the contract.*

Smiling in absolute contentment, Dorhen obeyed. He closed his eyes and daydreamed about how he'd spend the rest of eternity with his dark mistress. His everything, his…

A piercing pain in many points tore his skin. Dorhen screamed and lurched forward to see the gaping hole in the flesh of his leg.

*Be good,* she commanded in her ever-loving, matriarchal way and bowed to take another bite—half his penis. Her sharp teeth made quick work of it before she swallowed. His blood ran down her chin. She took another bite out of his leg, sending another spray of agony to all corners of his being.

He'd forgotten about this part. She wanted to eat his flesh for her own pleasure and nourishment in exchange for granting him a few moments of sexual bliss far away from the fire. Memories flooded his mind. Details he'd forgotten returned. They'd done this countless times in the past. Thousands of sessions! She expected him to remember the terms of the agreement. She had explained to him patiently upon their first meeting how she'd take him away from the fires, to her house, a dark, cool place for relief to last "an unforeseeable amount of time." She'd included the detail of how she needed to eat his flesh, and he agreed. The fires were so hot. He was so grieved by pain that he said "yes" to her offer. The burning agony always roved over him, so intense. Knowing she'd rip his flesh off his bones and eat it, he gave her his word, so long as the burning stopped for a few minutes.

Now his screams rolled without tiring, filling the dark space with layers of echoed suffering. His shameful stupidity. Her feasting hurt more than the flames. Until he got back into the flames, then he'd figure the flames were worse. And that back-and-forth routine would continue. For centuries.

When he glanced again, fighting against all his weakness and despair, he found that she'd already cleaned off his femur and moved on to his calf. She would continue until she'd cleaned off his skull, savoring the muscles of his face and spitting out the scraps of cartilage. She'd eat his beating heart last before he finally died. He was already dead here, so it would merely be a temporary blankness before he awakened again in the fire with a new growth of skin, blood, and meat to be burned away in the chaos of immense, dancing heat.

And then he'd welcome her return.

My sweet, sweet creature. I've returned.

Pain. Agony. Flames.

Sex. Moist and throbbing ecstasy.

Hot. Fire. Pain. Make it stop! Make it stop!

Screams.


Fast, hard thrusting. She let him take control today. Gasping in pleasure atop her. Roaring in the most primal state of mind he'd ever experienced.

Echoes bounced off the walls.

She screamed in his ear, holding him tight. Breasts oozing the sweet, thick nectar against his chest.

*I love you. I love you so much.*

Screaming in the fire. He could vaguely hear other people's screams.

His tears ran profusely when his deeply coveted orgasm came.

*I love you!* His physical voice burst through. "I love you!"

*Of course you do, sweet creature.* She reached and stroked his cheek, wrapping her legs around him.

Another orgasm swept through him as he exited her flushed, supple body part. The semen spilled out and mingled with the milk she'd dripped on the floor beneath them earlier. He let out his sounds of pleasure, raising his chin high. She leaned forward and took the opportunity to lick his neck, prompting yet another erection.

Before he could coax her for another dance, she bit into his throat, sharp teeth crushing and grabbing his pipes to tear them out, severing his trachea. He could no longer talk or scream. He could only fall to the floor and allow her to take what she wanted. Eating him alive until she reduced him to a heap of bones.

He woke up again in the fire. This time he remembered the contract and the taste of her milk. The sight of his semen splashing into it on the floor. The pleasure, the pain. The pain of the flames quickly swept over him, melting his flesh. He had no choice but to surrender to it. Through the screaming and writhing, he tried to remember *her*. What was her name? He couldn't recall. Maybe she never told him. Maybe he never asked.

Days passed. Weeks rushed by. He burned, screaming. But he kept his thoughts, as difficult as it became. He kept his mind together. He tried to listen for other people behind his own screaming. Other people were here with him. In hell. She'd called this place Kullixaxuss at least once before.

Screaming in the flames. He could never hope to stop himself to listen more closely. He focused on the memories of his mistress and longed for her return. She'd arrive soon, and he'd take her offer.

More weeks passed. Still no sign of Mistress.

Another year passed. No Mistress.

Was this how long it always took? It was certainly the first time he'd stayed mindful, refusing to forget about his mistress, whom he loved and longed for. He could never please her. As intense as their love-making could get, she never climaxed. She screamed in his ear to please his ego when she gave him control. She sought to comfort him and oblige his desires, but didn't offer back to him what he offered her—what he wished so hard she would accept from him. As good as it felt, it lacked... something. He needed more than physical satisfaction. Her kisses were always empty. Her forked tongue delivered pleasure alone.

A hand settled on his head and petted his hair like an animal. *Hello, my sweet creature. Are you ready to leave the fire?*

"Yes." His voice rang out loud and eager. She'd happened to approach before his vocal chords burned away.

*My, my, you are assertive today.*

Of course. He'd struggled for years to keep his mind in check, making note of his surroundings and focusing to remember his mistress and her deal. She would offer him pleasure and nourishment and then eat him. And he'd take it. Anything to get out of the fire.

The power of his agreement could dim the flames. She never gave him anything he didn't agree to and never asked for anything without compensation. At least the situation was an honest one.

The flames dimmed, and the dark place appeared around them as it always did. It took a few seconds for his burned flesh to heal itself. This time, he didn't have to look at his own exposed heart. The black, flaky skin over his rib cage renewed to pale, supple life. His penis returned to a new rosy state of health when its charred flesh restored. It hung limp for now. It wouldn't come to life until she touched him.

A thought occurred to him. What if he tried to resist?

*You can't resist, my sweet little creature,* his mistress said. *We have an agreement.*

In his mindfulness, he could see more. A soft blue light illuminated the room, empty with a soft floor and no more than a rug to adorn it.

*Are you interested in the room or an eternity's worth of love and pleasure? Come now.*

She reached forward and ran a finger down his belly, stopping at his hairless pubis. A slight graze over his skin with her long fingernail excited him to full readiness.

Dorhen held back his urge to throw his arms around her and explore all the softest patches of flesh on her body—her nipples, the little places where her legs met her intimate area, the gossamer webbing between her fingers and toes, and all the places where pearly scales didn't grow in beautiful formation. Instead, he watched and waited, trying to make sense of all this, which he'd never tried before because the sensations had been all-encompassing during past visits.

She smiled, squatting before him on the balls of her bare feet. She didn't wear much more than a glittering anklet of gold and gemstones. The pose showed him her entire vulva, a flower slowly blooming to welcome him beyond the tiers of pink and maroon petals, soft and beautiful. Her large breasts dangled above it, already secreting the glorious life nectar from big flushed nipples, swollen to purple. He thirsted for it. Iridescent black hair draped over her shoulders in silky ripples, shading her eye sockets like eerie black pits. Her playfully curving smile showed the little sharp teeth she'd later use to take him apart bite by bite.

*Silly little creature,* she continued. *Thinking too much about your end of the bargain doesn't help, don't you know by now?*

His heart pounded and his erection ached. He put his needs aside to watch and puzzle.

She took his hand and pulled him to his knees. *I know you're hungry. Enjoy yourself before we start.*

The way she spoke without the use of her smiling mouth never used to unnerve him like it did now. The new use of his mind didn't help the situation, yet he couldn't deny his burning love for her. He wanted to please her. He wanted her approval. He wanted her.

She lay on her back before him and raised her knees to her chest, opening her flower wide, the petals curled backward to offer him the vagina within. The same sweet and satisfying milk secreted from there too.

*Drink,* she commanded.

He couldn't refuse. He plunged his tongue deep, slurping the nectar and drinking as fervently as ever before. The longer he licked and probed, the more mouth-like the opening acted, with another tongue that came forth to play with his in a long, leisurely kiss. The emptiness in his stomach remedied.

Once he filled his stomach to bursting, he couldn't stand to wait any longer to take care of his other need. His thoughts flew away. He no longer cared about his stupid brain and its constant thinking. He covered her, plunging his erection deep into the fleshy region overflowing with milk where his tongue had explored. That other tongue met his cock, and the space around it sucked him hard. Thrusting furiously into her, in and out at an extreme, rapid pace, he closed his eyes and enjoyed.

*I love you.*

By the next day, he still hadn't forgotten about his mistress, her nectar, his desirous aches, and the contract she held him to. Engulfed in the searing flames, he repeated the process of focusing his mind. Whenever his flesh grew back after burning away, he focused on his hands, watching them move and flexing them. He watched them burn away, all the while filling the smoky air with his screams.

Somehow, he managed to exist in a constant state of pain and willfulness. His focus led him to a triumphant discovery that it took about one whole day for his flesh to burn away and the next whole day for it to return. He took to counting those days, aided by the repetitive sight of his flesh melting and flaking off as crisp, charred bits.

The days passed as usual.

The months turned into years.

Damn, what a long wait it could be. His counting made the wait so much longer. Back when he had screamed obliviously, unaware she'd eventually appear and strike up a contract with him, the time hadn't felt so long.

Another two years passed.

Two more.

He waited for Mistress, doing anything he could think of to sharpen his mind, until she finally put her hand along his face.

*Are you ready, sweet creature?*

"Yes."

The cool sensation of her hands moved to grasp his, and darkness replaced the fiery atmosphere. She immediately pressed her lips to his, even before his flesh finished restoring. She wrapped her arms around him and rubbed her body against his, as if she meant to distract him before he could make any challenging thoughts. She pushed him to lie flat, and as she teased her vagina's wet entrance at the tip of his penis, he forced his brain to think of other things.

*You said "yes," my sweet creature, so you have to fulfill the bargain.*

Did she realize he sought for truth? For an explanation to this strange world? For a possible way out?

*There is no way out, my sweet creature. Kullixaxuss is eternity. Our existence is spiritual and more real than the world of the living.*

He forced his voice to work. "Are you saying I'm dead?"

She slid herself onto his erection and pushed one of her breasts into his mouth for a rapturous experience, blending the taste and nourishment of her sweet nectar with their ecstatic intercourse.

*Stop thinking now.*

*I won't.*

He filled his head with whatever idea, image, or memory he could grasp. He no longer swallowed the nectar; it soaked his cheeks. If having an empty, yearning stomach helped him not to lose himself in the frenzy of joy and love, he'd resist swallowing it all the way to the end of his sanity.

Miraculously, the effort not to swallow the nectar worked. He tried to forget the lovely feelings happening down below, and eventually his erection died and slipped out of her.

For one menacing instant, her eyes glowed in the shadow, glaring at him. The smile fled her supple, maroon lips.

Fear racked him now. He'd never dreamed of refusing Mistress before. Even worse, he'd agreed to her contract just so he could try to escape from this dark place she'd brought him to. Since she could read his thoughts, she knew all this. Could she not have anticipated his ability to resist?

He clenched his fists. He'd come into this level of strength after the sessions in which she let him be on top, as if the exercise empowered him. He thought fast before she decided to punish him. He feared Mistress's wrath, the dark flipside he knew lurked behind her love, kindness, and patience. She didn't deserve the cruelty of his deception. Sadness welled in his heart to mingle with the fear. What a horrible creature he was! He wept softly. What a piece of garbage!

At his emotion, her expression softened and her signature smirk returned. He would stop trying to deceive his one and only love! He would uphold their sacred contract, and savor the magnificent dance they performed. Her milk filled the emptiness in his body, and her love filled his soul. This world suddenly made sense. He was born, his flesh formed; he suckled, taking in the nourishment of life; he was sated, his seed ejected; and then his time came to die—to feed the greater being who lived on his flesh.

Mistress was not a mere woman. Never. She was a goddess. An eternal, loving, almighty being who cared for him. She gave him purpose. His life made sense because of her. The divine cycle they performed stood as a religion all its own, and carrying out this performance with her was his worship!

The life returned to his cock. She gave a big smile and patted his face. *Now you understand.*

She pressed him to lie back. He did. His heart pounded, reveling in the beautiful rite they prepared to perform. He stared at the ceiling, arms out to each side, waiting for the gentle caress of her benevolent lips to grace his penis.

No sooner had they delicately ringed the protrusion of his pinched foreskin did his thoughts take one more turn. Familiarity of the situation sparked. This kind of thing had happened before. With a woman. A blonde one.

*Selka*. Selka? Yes, the woman from his first sexual experience…in the ancient past.

*Kalea…*

Hearing his thoughts as usual, Mistress raised her head. And he kicked it.

Rearing his knee back, sneering, he kicked her again with all of his force, his foot smashing into the center of her beautiful face. He timed his attack precisely between two tracks of thought, the doubt about his mistress which would make her suspicious when she heard it, and the blissful celebration of her by which she'd been distracted. He'd aligned the kick after his praise of her, but right before he gave in to his own emotions and surrendered to her.

He growled in agony when one of the small horns protruding from her head stabbed his foot. Ignoring the pain, he climbed to his feet and sprinted away. Her laughter raged in the corridors behind him, echoing disturbingly. He found many winding corridors after the one she'd brought him to. She didn't appear to be following him. So far, so good.

*You'll regret this, naughty creaturrrrre.*

An area of his mind pinched. Her words hurt him. He fought the emotion. All in one, she filled the role of mother, lover, and goddess. He couldn't stand the thought of her disapproval.

*And my disapproval means you'd no longer be welcome in my house.*

More painful words. So this was her house? A spark of recognition lit his memory. He could remember. The memory came back to him with sudden, extraordinary crispness.

He had fallen into the fire when the sanguinesent dropped him off the cliff. He burned up and disintegrated long before hitting the rocky bottom, and then he'd awakened to begin the cycle. He burned and restored for a few days until she first found him.

Mistress's life routine was to wander the Garden of Fire until she found a burning soul like him. He couldn't see her very well in the bright blaze, but her cool touch soothed him, and he welcomed more of it.

*Would you like to get out of the fire?* she asked.

He agreed.

Darkness spread around him. It was a nice change from the inferno he'd suffered. Dorhen couldn't see anyone in the dark place, though. He walked through what felt like a hard, earthen corridor. His bare feet tapping on the floor made an echo, suggesting the corridor was tall, maybe grand. It was. Big windows appeared along the wall with the bright inferno raging outside for as far as he could see. Under the roar, faint screaming caught his ear and put a fearful twinge in his gut.

*Don't bother yourself with what you've left behind.* The sudden voice in his head replaced the fear with comfort. It was *her* voice, the one who'd invited him here. He was safe now. He smiled. *Come this way, come toward my voice.*

Dorhen obeyed. Why wouldn't he? He had nothing to lose in meeting the owner of this towering house. He progressed through the long corridor until it curved into a dark space with no windows. Tiny feet echoed beside his, tapping around him on the floor and up the walls.

*I was very fortunate to find you in the Garden of Fire before my sisters did.* Dorhen jumped at the voice again, surprising him out of his fascination with the little creatures he couldn't see. *Do you understand why you're here?*

Dorhen shook his head. Even though it was dark, he knew the owner of the voice saw him.

*I search the fires every day,* the voice said. It was a she. Her voice was… tantalizingly beautiful. Deep, not quite human—more beautiful than a human's could be. *I sometimes find souls like you in my searches.* Her voice had a metallic quality to it, like a ring bouncing off plates of precious metal. *Are you listening to me, little creature, or would you prefer to dwell on my voice for eternity?*

Dorhen dipped his head. "Sorry," he whispered. Speaking again without having his throat dry and burn away made this visit worth it, at least.

*Pay attention,* the voice reminded. *Since I've found you, I can mark you as my own. If I do that, you will be safe from the others. You will belong to me. Would you like to live safe in my care?*

Dorhen nodded eagerly. When he did, a glowing flower bloomed at head level before him. *I will give you a taste of life with me. You will live on me, and in return, I will live on you. Step forward.*

Dorhen cautiously obeyed. The flower's fragrance teased his nose with a delightful sweetness. The center of the flower released a gush of white fluid. Nectar. It ran down the lower petals and dripped off.

*I will ask you again, officially. Would you like to be my thrall so that I can protect you, nurture you, take you out of the fire periodically, and ultimately own your soul so you can serve me for eternity? You will know love and joy and a greater sensual pleasure than your dreams could hope to fabricate.*

While she spoke, Dorhen stared at the glowing flower. His mouth watered. With it smelling as sweet as it did, he had to wonder what it tasted like.

The voice continued, *In return, I need to collect your seed and eat your flesh for my own needs and ambitions. I am asking you for a fair trade.*

Dorhen's mouth quirked into a smile as he stared at the flower. Its petals trembled. The hole in the center expanded, releasing long, pouring streams of white nectar, wasted as it spilled on the floor.

*I would never ask for anything without compensating you in return. Do you say yes?*

"Yes," Dorhen said without thinking, or without taking his eyes away from the glorious flower.

*Good. Step forward and taste the flower. When you drink from it—*

Not even listening, Dorhen rushed in and licked one of the petals before sliding his tongue as far down the flower's center as he could reach it.

*—I will own you. You will return to the fire time and again, but no other succubus will be able to lay claim on you.*

The syrupy nectar ran down his throat in gushes of joyous fulfillment. His stomach accepted it greedily. A pair of lips and a tongue protruded through the center and kissed him, warping the world around him. What was a flower a minute ago suddenly became a woman. He stood there for hours, kissing this woman and swallowing mouthfuls of the milky, sweet liquid she generously gave. He would've stood there forever if she'd let him.

That was when he'd first met Mistress. Her generous offering called forth a deep love in his heart. With his heart swelled full and red, he gladly gave himself as her slave for life.

Now, he traversed the corridors of her termite spire again. Hundreds of tiny feet tapped against the rock walls like always. The fire outside a nearby window revealed insect-like creatures walking the walls, carrying lumps of earth in their mandibles. They constantly worked to build this place higher. The little creatures were her children. Maybe they were Dorhen's children too. These termites, about the size of cats, walked the walls, constructing the castle.

Along the bottoms of the walls, other little creatures crawled with their pale and fleshy tubular bodies, expanding and contracting like maggots. Dorhen took care not to step on them. They were Mistress's cherished larvae, with faces like tiny, chubby women and long black hair like hers.

Mistress appeared in a doorway along the curve of the dark hall, her nipples dripping with the honey-sweet milk. *You don't see the mistake you're making.* Her words sounded too much like Wik's when Dorhen had fought the snakes thousands of years ago. *Eternity is a long time, little creature,* she continued, her voice loud in his head. He paused to regard her and watched as the flower between her legs closed its petals, a sure sign of her distaste at him. *If you thought the fire painful, you are in for a surprise. With me, you'll have a home, a place to stay while you're here. After all, you'll come back here when you die, and I'll be waiting.*

She raised one knee high to flash her vulva, and the flower flicked open again. *I'll give you one chance to decide to lie down and fulfill the contract. All will be forgiven.* She stood tall on her one foot with ease and spoke as if his two kicks never happened.

Her offer tempted him, and her trembling, flicking petals tantalized his body with their dance. Dorhen turned his eyes away and ran.

The large insects rushed ahead of him, using their talents to build a wall to block off the corridor, closing it around a dead end. Mistress appeared at the center of the space with an arrangement of enticing cushions. He'd never noticed any such comforts adorning the space before. His mind had kept simple and narrow until now. He and she were all that mattered. Now, with his mind broadened, she anticipated how he would require an array of other incentives. He wouldn't back down, not after working so hard to exercise his mind and gather a store of strength for his body.

He ran straight at her as fast as he could. The air caressed his hair, waving it along the way. He leaped, foot first, for another kick. His heel didn't connect with her skull as anticipated; instead, it went through her like gelatin.

The scenery blurred. He flew into a fold of air rushing around him, more like water. A denser darkness fell.

He collapsed to the hard floor, cold like marble. Whispers sounded all around him. The echoes rang deeper and longer here. Incense. Chanting. The chanting sounded like what he used to hear drifting through the windows of Kalea's convent.

He hauled himself to his feet and walked. He still wandered naked; he had not seen a piece of fabric since the dye works. His bare feet didn't like the hardness of the floor. Eventually the floor softened, to his gratitude. His path squeezed between two lumpy walls, and he trailed his hand along one. The walls softened too, and the floor reached a point where his feet sank, squishing deep into some spots.

The chanted song continued but never changed in volume regardless of how far he ventured. A light appeared, soft and distant, which illuminated the lumpy corridor. The wall squished under his hand. The shape of one mound resembled...a woman's breast?

He squinted and leaned in, passing his fingertips over a nipple that hardened at his touch. It *was* a breast! He yanked his hand away and stepped back, his feet sinking into little mounds in the floor so soft he swore they were fatty human flesh.

They were.

Faces, many faces, and other body parts were in the floor. Part of the floor. He'd been walking on them, pressing his full weight into people's eyes and cheeks and noses. He could do nothing about it—there was no way to avoid stepping on them. He continued with no other choice. The light strengthened, revealing more faces, men and women. A few elves too. Some of them moved softly, but they were helpless to get out of the floor and walls.

Beside him, a woman's voice called out, a mindless moan of despair. Dorhen jolted and ran away. His feet tread hard over more faces as he ran.

The corridor closed in, narrowing until he squeezed through, dodging hands embedded up to the wrists, grabbing and clawing. The soft skin on the wall of many bodies pressed against his own naked flesh. Was there any chance he could become part of the wall as well? Would his foolish determination lead him to the same fate as these people?

The chanting song stalled and repeated the last few notes, over and over, maddeningly. He squeezed on, pushing past the faces and body parts and ignoring the repetitive song in his eagerness to get into the light and find an exit to this place. He didn't remember how he got here, or when. Easy to say the *when* was a thousand years ago or more. He'd grown so used to his routine with Mistress. It was a better existence than being lost out here in this creepy world. Why would anyone ever choose to be alone?

A small niggling in the back of his mind and in his genitals reminded him how much he missed her. He needed her, at least for a moment. She'd supply him with the bravery to continue like a good mother would. He sighed. Those thoughts were too difficult. If he continued, he'd cry again. His jaw trembled, but he resisted calling his mistress's name, the name "Mistress" which he'd given her.

With a wail, he collapsed and curled into a fetal position on the soft, fatty faces in the floor, frozen in an array of expressions. His naked flesh mingled with theirs. Filthy odors of the human body thickened the air. Sweat. Flatulence. Rotten teeth.

*Mistress.*

He wept. He didn't want to be lost anymore. He needed her guidance, her direction. Without her, he'd wander forever, lost. He should've taken her offer to frequent her house and bask in her presence. His soft weeping escalated into dolorous sobs. Pathetic. Alone. Stupid. He bit down on his forearm in an attempt to stop the sobbing.

He remained on the floor. For how long, he couldn't gauge. Hours? Deciding to try again, he fought his way to his feet and did his best to balance on the warped, soft floor. He resolved not to think about Mistress anymore. Too sad. If he could focus, he might find out where this passage led.

More hands appeared in the wall after a distance. Lively hands grabbed at him. He slapped them away and hurried past. One caught his exposed genitals and pulled. He screamed in the new agony and thrashed at that hand.

He fell to the floor again. Someone's nose bone crunched under his weight. He flailed against the hands holding him down. Chipped, filthy fingernails stabbed and scratched.

Snakes slithered in to join them from cracks in the floor, and many spilled out of the faces' mouths.

"No—no!" He kicked at the snakes, but more of them piled in and slithered over him. They engulfed him.

*Not the damned snakes again!* The temptation to call Mistress's name nagged. He could beg her for help and promise he'd be a good creature in the future. But he didn't.

The snakes slithered into his mouth, attempting to fill him like always before, to smother him into a dark and empty eternity.

*Hail, fool!*

That voice! Not Mistress's voice, but a deep, male voice which grated and insulted. Mistress's voice purred soft and sweet. This voice belonged to Wik.

*I see you've found your way back to your body.* Laughter like sand ran through his head. *I knew you'd return—and not a moment too soon. I can't keep your body alive forever.*

The snakes moved to his genitals and wrapped around his penis, coiling and rubbing it up and down like they used to. They'd relax him, put him back to sleep. He didn't want to sleep! He'd sooner go back to his mistress. He loved Mistress with all of his heart.

*But I can't go back!* He moaned. This eternal cycle couldn't go on. Something needed to change.

He thrashed at the snakes, kicking, slamming with his fists, and throwing them left and right. The evil entity didn't speak; instead, it watched him, if such a thing were possible in this place—sight wasn't a useful sense here. He continued his fight tirelessly. It was all in his mind, not his body. He pushed his mind to remain strong, to keep focus and not get hung up on Mistress. Where was she? He'd lost her! He'd left her so far behind. Why would he leave her?

*No!* he insisted. Slipping into a melancholy state of longing for her would be too easy.

A flash of light hinted at his success. A crash of thunder. Wetness.

The snakes lost their energy. They fell away from him.

Another flash of light followed by a crash. Dorhen's being traveled. Light! Rain pounded over his face. He found himself screaming. Screaming in his fight.

Stinging rain. All of his muscles were tensed. Cold and wetness registered in his right hand. He kept screaming. But the snakes were gone. His knees were planted deep in the moistened, grassy earth.

He was alive. He stopped screaming and fell backward, forgetting to anticipate the hardness of the ground hitting the back of his head. The shock knocked the air from his lungs. He lay there, rain pounding on him, pouring into his gaping mouth. Ordinary water. Not holy nectar—a mythical thing he could barely remember living on. He drank the water and continued trying to catch his breath. A huge black sky hung low above him. The normal sky. He'd found it.

He curled over, and then worked his way to his feet. He didn't feel miserable. This realm offered a comfortable medium between incredible pain and delirious pleasure. Confusion and disorientation bothered him now. Where was he? Two sets of memories twisted together in his head. The inferno faded into an unfathomable sliver in his emotions along with a person he used to love. What was her name?

He coughed on the water falling into his mouth. He had forgotten how water could choke him if he didn't drink it carefully. Water used to be a myth, and now here it was again, like he'd never lost it.

He took a shaky step, followed by another. An unrecognizable garment hung wrapped around his waist. At least he was no longer naked, just shirtless and shoeless, although he shivered in the chilly weather. Shelter became his next important goal. Nonetheless, the water acted as a physical representation of his flood of relief. He'd returned to the world of the living, or of wakefulness.

He was alive.

# Chapter 26
## What is in the Vibrations

Rushing vigorously through the veins of the earth like a stampede of playful sprites, the tremors rattled the compacted ground under Knilma's very bed. She shot upright from the snooze she'd recently achieved—instantly wide awake. The quick action made her old bones ache, but that didn't matter. Forgetting the arthritis, she gripped her blankets in her gnarled fists. Surely not. It hadn't happened. A dream.

A flash of lightning lit the little window, followed by a soft rumble. A storm, nothing else.

Knilma laughed and rubbed her face, her baggy eyelids stretching far. Her heart thumped heavily behind her brittle ribs. It had felt so real. Her stomach acid danced with excitement, sending a fishy vapor crawling up her throat. In her old age, thunderstorms could seem like the ethereal tremors she could only wish to feel.

"What a dream, what a dream that was," she said aloud. The cat, a village ally, curled at the foot of her bed was the only thing present to listen. It stretched its furry body and rolled over. This would be a funny story to tell her pledges tomorrow.

A tiny black speck caught her eye—a mouse running along the stone foundation of the little house. She pushed the cat with her heel, practically kicking it. "Back to work, you old skunk!"

The cat shrieked in annoyance and darted to the floor, where it shook and reoriented itself.

Laughing to herself, Knilma yawned and eased back to her flattened straw pillow. "Wake me when he *actually* returns, won't you?"

No sooner had the first snore rattled through her sinuses than another fervent, yearning, calling tremor shook her awake. All mirth gone, Knilma sprang out of bed, faster than she should have.

"My sweet, sweet lord!" She bent over as fast as her elderly body allowed and pressed her ear directly to the hard dirt floor sprinkled with straw.

A long, rumbling groan. Sad. It needed her. Immediately.

She gasped and lurched upward. Now she shook uncontrollably and stepped in place. What now? Her hands were useless balls of nerves.

"I-I..." She swallowed. "I just don't believe it!" A childlike sense of wonder filled her core. There was so much to do. What to do first?

A frantic rap at the door sounded amidst the roaring rain and thunder. *I'll open the door.* It was all she could do right now.

"Knilma! Knilma!" the woman's voice on the other side of the rough wooden barrier shouted as frantically as Knilma's heart fluttered.

"Yes!" She made her way to the door as fast as her body allowed. Her shins already didn't appreciate the shock of her sudden steps, but all her discomforts were the least important thing in the world.

She threw the latch and flung the door open to meet Paigess's wide-eyed wonderment. Knilma knew her face must look the same.

"Did you hear it? Did you hear it?" Paigess pushed halfway through the door, her younger hands searching for Knilma's.

"I did!" Her own voice shook.

"So I didn't dream or imagine it?"

"No!"

"What do we do, Knilma?"

Knilma's mouth hung open. Time to calm down and form a plan.

A louder tremor registered under her feet, a long moan both sad and brimming with lustful energy.

Paigess sucked in a huge pull of air as their wide eyes met. The two of them spouted neurotic bursts of squealing excitement. Their hands found each other and a little dance occurred between them. Knilma stumbled, and Paigess caught and eased her back to a balanced stance.

"Sorry, Knilma, I can't contain myself—I'm shocked at…!"

"It's all right. This is all too"—she fanned herself in the onset of a sweat—"sudden."

Knilma hobbled to the tree branch secured to the earthen wall and took her black kirtle off one of the stumpy cut limbs. Putting the rest of her clothing on over her linen shift might be a good first step to taking action. Paigess wore her own outer kirtle sloppily; she must've thrown it on before sprinting madly across the muddy village center to bang on Knilma's door.

"I'll tell you what we're going to do," Knilma said. "Go rouse Sammial and Tristain. They can't feel the tremors, but we'll need some warlocks for protection. And send Ernan running to Alkeer to inform Kilka."

"What about the pledges?" Paigess asked, and Knilma paused to consider the logistics.

"Bring Tamas."

Paigess scrunched her plain-looking face and cocked her head. A middle-aged woman herself, she harbored enough strength to get things done, so Knilma needed her around. "Why only Tamas?"

"Tamas is strong and hardy—and a pretty girl. I don't know what we'll encounter out there—I haven't left this village in forty years. We need people who are reliable and who won't trip us up. Those other girls are too flimsy and inexperienced for this. But nonetheless, we'll tell them the news and leave Nirnelle in charge of them. Later, they can pilgrimage to Wikhaihli to meet their Mastaren."

"I understand," Paigess said.

One more faint tremor slithered through the ground to meet Knilma and Paigess's bare feet. Another thrilling spark lit Knilma's bones, igniting a wave of emotion. Her eyes rimmed with tears and she leaned into Paigess. "Dear me, Paigess, he needs us."

Paigess embraced her. "I know, sister." The younger woman was double Knilma's height.

Knilma sniffled. "I can't believe—I didn't think it would happen again in my lifetime. You don't know how long I've waited to see him again."

"I've waited my whole life," Paigess said.

Knilma patted her elbow as she leaned away. "You're going to see him now. You were born to a lucky generation. Come here now."

Knilma and Paigess knelt before the cloth altar. "Our Mastaren, we hear you. We hear your rapturous call. Please wait for us."

Knilma's shaking hands reached out and caressed the end of the black linen cloth draped above the altar platform, a stone installation like in every house in this village. Mere hours ago, she'd faithfully replenished the fragrant offerings of herbs and fruits, and she lit the incense to carry her into deep dreams of *him*. Long-lost memories would return, filling her with the sweetness of the past. Of better days.

Knilma's prayer phased into words of the trollish language, the language of *his* dearest friends, and when she finished, she bent low to kiss the end of the black drape. Paigess followed, and then Knilma patted her arm.

"Help me up, please."

Once they were standing, Knilma pushed her toward the door. "We can't dally another minute, girl. Now go out there and wake the others. Tell them. Tell them our glorious news. Tell them Wikshen has been reborn."

# Chapter 27
# What is Disturbing Lehomis

In the stable stall where they whispered, Tilninhet grabbed Lehomis's arm as he turned to walk away. He needed to get back to tending the horses left over from the horrible raid that killed Trisdahen.

"Lass, we can't go on," he insisted in a hushed tone. Too many young and teenaged *saeghar* moved about in this area.

"Did you hear back yet?" she asked him for the third time this week. Her eyes beamed up at him, round and fetching.

"From Togha's superiors? Not yet." He gave his answer as patiently as always.

Her eyes hardened. "I know my Togha, Elder. They're going to tell you he's not there!"

Sighing, he pinched his nose bridge. "I'm sure all is well."

She closed her eyes and bowed her forehead to his chest to snuggle under his chin. "Thank you for sending the letter, Elder." It was about the fifth time she had thanked him. A seductive light sparked in her eye whenever she did.

His hands hung helplessly by his sides. He'd warned her over and over about that. He pushed her away when she attempted to touch his lapel again. "But this has to stop. We'll both get in trouble! If the Desteer find out, they'll shave my head, draw, and quarter me. They'll send pieces of me to each corner of Norr as a warning to all *saehgahn*."

"What if I send you a token?"

He grunted. "You *can't*! Don't you know the rules? I've already been married."

She sniffed. "Well, I don't see why it should matter. I'm a widow and already gave this clan a child. I should be able to marry whoever I want."

"And your child's a boy." At her blank expression, he continued, "The Desteer've been trying to get you to remarry all these years. They'd push you to keep trying for a girl."

"And now I'm finally coming around to their advice of remarrying."

He grabbed her arms but resisted shaking her.

"Ow, that bruises!"

He shushed her. "Lass," he said, trying to be calm, "you don't want me. I've only fathered boys in my day, and lots of them. Right now, we need *farhah.* Desperately. My seed is good in times of war."

"I breed for love, not logic."

He couldn't hold down a smile as he let her arms go. She pouted adorably at him. He forced his mouth to turn downward and pointed a finger at her face. "Listen, I'm going to take stock of my *saehgahn* and appoint you a permanent house-guardian. I'll send the absolute best of the group."

Her mouth dropped open. "No, Elder!"

He shushed her again. By now, the others were probably aware of a *faerhain* in the stable. Lehomis made sure no one stood too close. "Yes," he replied to her protest.

"Elder, you can't!"

"If you don't stop shouting, I'll end this conversation now."

Her expression darkened, her eyes dropping to his shoes until he turned away with his arms crossed. "Elder," she said in a soft, muted tone.

"What?"

"Will you stop by for tea this afternoon?"

"No!" He checked his volume. "We can't do that anymore. Don't you get it?"

Her pout turned to a deep frown.

"If you're going to have a house-guardian, you'll have to get used to being proper again. I'm still going to banish your brother. I'll also inform your new guardian to respect Togha's place in your house…as odd as the lad can be."

"I don't like this, Elder. And to be honest, I'd like another child. To have another *saeghar* as lovely as Togha…" A glint of moisture formed on her bottom eyelids, and she smiled gently. "I'm lonely. And of course I wouldn't mind another male child. Not at all."

"I know, Tilly."

They stood for a moment in silence.

"Elder."

"Yes?"

"My oven has developed a large crack. It loses heat. Can you please mix a batch of cob and repair it for me?" She ended her question by looking at him through her eyelashes. Why did she always put him in this situation?

"I'll be over tomorrow."

"Thank you, Elder."

Stepping out of Tilninhet's house the next day, a mixture of feelings churned his stomach. That *faerhain* had been nothing but a liability to him. She had probably been born trouble. An old twinge of grief and pity kept him agreeing to her invitations. Before leaving today, he had told her in the gravest voice he'd ever used with her that he'd never drink tea with her again. In recent days, she'd called him over to repair something—just the initial process for getting him in her house. He often wondered how many household objects her brother noticed broken and offered to fix, just to have her forbid him to touch them so she could save them for Lehomis.

Today, her cracked oven lured him over. She never lied about her need of repairs; all elves were forbidden to lie, and she was a good *faerhain* in that respect. So, naturally, the neighbors witnessed him outside, getting all muddy in his work. The oven looked good when he left.

The problem came afterward. She boiled water and allowed him to bathe the mud off, another propriety among neighbors. And then the tea was brewed. Lehomis rarely refused the tea, and over the years he'd pondered why. This time, he'd made the decision yesterday, when she commented about wanting another child. This would be his last visit.

The thing about the tea was there was an ancient ritual connected to it. For most elves, tea was tea, but once Tilninhet initiated the ritual, he faced a heavy decision. Lehomis had agreed to participate in her ritual several times over the years since her husband's death. It involved the two of them sitting comfortably, enjoying a nice warm cup, when she would suddenly stop talking. Silence initiated the ritual.

After the silence stretched on for a good while, she'd set her cup down before finishing the beverage. If he agreed to do the ritual, he would also put his cup down. His action would prompt her to extinguish the lighting, throwing sand on the hearth fire and closing the shutters to prevent the Bright One from seeing them. Then she'd sit on his lap and spread her skirt wide around them so even they wouldn't see what was happening.

The ritual was silent, quick, and required darkness and no eye contact. After it ended, they'd proceed with their normal conversing and say goodbye, never to speak or think of the incident again. Tilninhet likely thought about it far beyond what she should have.

Their first ritual begat Togha, bringing about a new happiness in Tilninhet, which made Lehomis happy. But after Togha grew tall and spent more and more time at the practice yards, Tilninhet initiated the ritual yet again with Lehomis. The first one after several years, he refused, and the second he obliged out of his own sheer selfishness. All the ones after that were out of pity for her. Today, he left her house arguing with himself about it being a good idea. He'd done her a boon if she became pregnant again.

An idea sparked. The ritual, *karra-kar-shirinhen* as it was called, "tea between widows," could be what saved his clan. He couldn't outright tell his clan widows to perform the ritual, though. It was illegal and spread through the cryptic gossip of females.

If the Desteer found out about its circulation, there would be a brutal purge: *saehgahn* heads would be lost, asses would be branded with the *sarakren* symbol, and even some *faerhain* would be made into shaven-headed examples. The Bright Purge was a proud ritual from ancient history, the Desteer's divine rite, boasting the wrath of the Bright One on their side to cleanse their society when needed.

Part of him wondered if extreme action could be taken to legalize *karra-kar-shirinhen* for certain purposes, or at least to ease the sorrow of the widows and widowers, but such a thing would take generations and lots of fierce arguing and warring to legalize. Tilninhet could possibly be encouraged to whisper her secrets and inspire a few other *faerhain* to offer the ritual to other widowers... But he knew her well. She kept her lips sealed tight, nearly to the point of a picturesque traditionalist—contrary to her appreciation for *karra-kar-shirinhen.*

Lehomis blew a breath through his lips. Proposing the ritual would be too risky. For now, he'd explore other options as alternatives to disbanding the clan, like a traditional tournament in which the clans would gather in the heart of Norr and the *saehgahn* compete in various contests to show their bodies and their strength off to all the single *faerhain*. Such an arrangement took a year or more of planning, but it could be done.

From Tilly's house, Lehomis strolled toward the town bell to give it one calm strike, a signal for a meeting among *saehgahn*. The clan males all dropped their tools, hay bales, firewood, and practice weapons to gather at the bell to hear their elder speak.

He opened his speech with caution, to work toward the real news he intended to share. "And a letter arrived from the palace," he said.

The older, married *saehgahn's* faces turned bland and ready to hurry through the meeting. The younger ones, still new to their *saehgahn* status, looked at the Elder with beaming eyes, eager for an exciting venture to break the mundane. From birth, they all developed not only a keen respect but a starry-eyed admiration for Lehomis, the ancient *saehgahn* who had escaped the troll caves and rescued the illustrious Kristhanhea from her slimy human captors. Lehomis's heart ripped in half to think how they'd react to today's bad news.

"What is it, Elder? Tell us!"

Lehomis's effort to swallow took a full three seconds. "You see, the palace is in trouble." He took a deep breath, keeping it smooth so they wouldn't notice his discomfort. "If you were to go visit their clan, you'd see how bad it is. They have no *faerhain* left—the final one married last year—and they are absolutely desolate for female company. The problem is literal."

The small group of married *saehgahn*'s faces hardened and the young ones' faces twisted. "But what does that mean, Elder?" one youth asked. His hair hadn't passed his shoulders, and others like him turned their heads to offer their best ear in absolute concentration.

Lehomis spread his hands. "The letter I got was a decree... They need to borrow *faerhain* from other villages. If they don't, their clan will be crippled as they await new *farhah* to be born and to mature. If they don't keep their marriage rituals going, their clan may fail." Which was Clan Lockheirhen's problem exactly, but because the Tinharris were the ruling clan, they took first precedence.

A chorus of murmurs arose. The older *saehgahn*'s eyes narrowed, and they whispered different words to each other than the group of unmarried.

"*Borrow faerhain?*" one of the young ones parroted.

"I think I used the wrong word," Lehomis said. At his renewed speech, the rest hushed. "Their new queen is a Desteer-queen, you see, not a mother-queen. She won't be producing any heirs, and will therefore rely on a niece or nephew to take the throne after her. Yet all of her brothers are unmarried. Their clan has no females left. The last of their common clan females has been married off, and they await the birth of more—which is the problem. They've hit a very real *faerhain*-famine."

He braced himself for the real news. "You'll have to forgive their actions, but right now they're touring Norr and *courting* females in all other clans. They will come here too, and I need you all to be cordial and patient, because we'd be wrong to get angry. So there is a good chance we'll lose a few more *faerhain* after their visit. Do you all understand?"

Pushing all that information out made Lehomis go clammy. He sucked in a large gulp of air and surveyed their reactions. The whole group stood stupefied, blinking at him. The deep silence preceded their explosion of questions, protests, and anger.

"They'll take my sister away?"

"I'll kill them!"

"We need to fight!"

"Why don't they go to the Darklands?"

"Will the *faerhain* be frightened?"

"Will they harm my sister?"

"Do the *faerhain* get a choice?"

"I feel sick!"

"There'll be less *faerhain* for us!"

"What does 'courting' mean?"

Lehomis put his hands out and shouted, "Please! Order, lads! Order, lads." Half of the group listened.

"Elder, we must stop this abomination!"

Lehomis put his hand on that *saehgahn*'s shoulder. "Listen, lads, it will be all right, certainly!" When he finally got most of them to stop shouting, he tried to explain. "No, they won't harm the *faerhain*. Yes, the *faerhain* get a choice. Garethen, your sister will be fine, but there's a chance she might find one she likes and leave with him."

He explained to them what courting meant, and all their faces paled. *Saehgahn* all desired to the depths of their souls to get married and experience love in all its manifestations, but Norrian law forbade them from trying to sway any female's decision. The whole system relied on *faerhain* studying their forms and mannerisms and then choosing one for marriage. It was a stark contrast to what Lehomis had discovered long ago in the human lands, where men went around courting and nagging women to marry them—or at least to get a quick roll in the hay. Having lived among humans for so long, he himself had partaken in human mating customs. Even when he found Kristhanhea, an elf among humans, the Norrian rule didn't apply, and therefore Lehomis pursued her romantically.

He explained his idea for a tournament, followed by his other idea about a trip to the Darklands. They could organize a campaign to find stray *faerhain* in the Darklands and steal some from the Clanless. "Lots of *saehgahn* have done this before, it'll be nothing new," he explained.

"How do you know there's *faerhain* up there?"

"Trust me," Lehomis replied.

"What about Hanhelin's Gate?" one *saehgahn* shouted from the back.

The question made Lehomis's hands drop to his sides. "I'm not sure. There must be a way, though. I'll find it. I'll find a way through because I care about you all. I care about this clan."

The whole group fell silent, no more shouting or arguing. The gleam in the young ones' eyes died. The unmarried middle-aged faces turned hard. The young dreamed and hoped for the best, while the older ones tended to accept their fate, the fate no young one would dare acknowledge. Lehomis couldn't help but think of Gaije, who had unsubtly hinted at his longing to get married. At least Gaije wasn't present. He wouldn't have to see the royal clan members reaching out and holding the *faerhain*'s hands for pleasure and not necessity, or possibly leaning in close to whisper poetic nonsense into their ears as Lehomis had observed in human lands. Even he couldn't guess what the royal clan would do.

He ended this meeting with a few harsh warnings: don't get angry, don't get violent; if something doesn't feel right about their behavior, inform the Desteer. This was a case for the Desteer to manage; it would never go on if the *saehgahn* were allowed an opinion.

Having left his two female dependents at home for half the day, Lehomis headed back and cut through the forest to get there faster. This particular trail brushed near one of the Desteer's sacred groves, where they tended a forest altar and prayed when not performing certain rituals. Whenever he neared one of these, the horrible memory of his *saehgahn* naming ceremony flashed before his eyes, an experience that had encompassed fear, awe, invigoration, and terror all in such a brief few minutes. Many a new *saehgahn* stumbled out of one of these places the most dazed and rattled in their lives, and Lehomis had been no different.

A voice on the wind caught his ear, stopping him in his tracks. "It just doesn't sit well with me, *Ahmeiha*." It sounded like a *faerhain* was arguing with one of the Desteer maidens, not an uncommon occurrence.

Lehomis's most foxlike side took over at the sound. It used to get him in trouble a lot as a *saeghar*. Using his best sneaking skills, Lehomis tiptoed closer, stepping on rocks whenever he found them to avoid the crunching leaves. He couldn't venture too close in the daylight, just close enough to listen and see if they were talking about the Tinharri Clan's imminent visit. He approached the grove wall, an intricately grown weaving of thin trees. He couldn't see anyone through the little holes in the growth, but the females spoke loud and clear.

The maiden shushed her. "The new statutes come straight from the Bright One," she told the *faerhain*.

The *faerhain* stuttered in frustration. "I thought the Bright One wanted us to watch and gauge the *saehgahn*. My daughter is ready and jumping to marry—but she's agonizing over who to pick. And now she can't go to the *saehgahn* bathing area?"

"Watching the *saehgahn* bathe is vain and vulgar."

"There's that word again, vulgar! You Desteer have been using it a lot in your sermons lately! You tell me what's more vulgar: my daughter carefully picking her husband, or throwing caution away and running off for a brief...*er* with one?"

Lehomis gasped at her choice of word. *Er* meant desire in the Norrian language. The Lightlandic language boasted hundreds of words, direct and indirect, for sex or feelings related to sexual desire. Norrian only had *er*, and no one had permission to use it.

As he expected, a loud clapping sound echoed through the waving trees. The *faerhain* didn't cry out at being slapped.

"I won't tell my sisters you used that word." The maiden's statement sounded like a warning nevertheless.

"I'm not finished, Desteer!" the *faerhain* growled. "During the last *Faerhain* Devotion, one of your *sisters* made a brief comment about the *faerhain* cutting their hair. I couldn't believe it at first, I dismissed it as having misheard her talk of punishment"—hair cutting was a common punishment the Desteer would bestow on naughty *faerhain*—"but the longer I thought about it, the more I knew I'd heard right. She wasn't talking about punishment—she said something about us cutting our hair in effort not to be vulgar!"

The maiden let out a long breath. "There are concepts you may not fully recognize," she said. "A female's long hair can have a…distracting effect on the *saehgahn*. They get a physical reaction in their bodies—"

The *faerhain* cut her off. "Now you're going to tell me what a married *faerhain* already knows?"

"Your long hair may be too much for an unmarried *saehgahn*. All of your long hair tests their self-control to a more extreme degree than you realize."

"My husband would be extremely angry."

"It's not for him to decide."

The *faerhain* growled. "Long hair is our culture! I'll not have you step between me and my husband and my culture."

"It will be all right," the Desteer maiden cooed. "Sometimes cultures change. It's the natural way of things."

"Our culture hasn't changed in thousands of years, Desteer!"

"Hasn't it?" When the *faerhain* tried to speak again, the maiden shushed her. "I'll hear no more. You are dismissed."

Lehomis ducked in his hiding place as the *faerhain* stormed, red-faced, out of the grove entrance. They wanted to cut *faerhain* hair? Males weren't permitted to attend the *Faerhain* Devotion, so this came as news to him. Who knew what the Desteer were telling them outside of *saehgahn* earshot?

"Dear Bright One," Lehomis whispered. No female under his protection would be forced to do that. Many arguments with the Desteer lay in his future.

A strange day in Clan Lockheirhen. Lehomis arrived home to find

Tirnah waiting for him at the door with Anonhet fidgeting at her elbow. Tirnah tapped a folded letter bearing the royal seal against her palm.

"What is it?" Lehomis asked, and Tirnah extended the letter in both hands.

"I'm worried there's bad news about Gaije," she said.

Lehomis took the letter and waved a reassuring hand. This one shouldn't be about Gaije... Unless the Norrian rangers had caught him and recognized him as a deserter, thus ripping him away from his oh-so-important mission to find Mhina! He tore into the letter.

*Elder Lockheirhen,*

*This letter is written in answer to your inquiry about Togha of Clan Lockheirhen...*

Lehomis sighed. "It's not about Gaije," he told Tirnah, whose expression relaxed. He continued reading. It would be nice to show the letter to Tilninhet so she too could be at ease in these strange days. He resumed the letter.

*Togha Lockheirhen has been deemed missing and is suspected of desertion. A warrant for his arrest has been distributed to all military bases.*

# Chapter 28
# His Body

One awkward step after the other carried Dorhen slowly over the field that rose and fell like turbulent ocean waves. The grass waved on the wind like ripples on the water's surface under a sky thick, heavy, and low. He could see surprisingly well in the night despite the lack of a moon, but it didn't mean he could recognize the land. It wasn't the southwestern region where Kalea's convent hid in the pines, and it couldn't be Norr. Norr was a big forest, as far as he knew. It also couldn't be Theddir, where the water sometimes rose high under the stilted buildings the citizens lived in, or the rocky canyons with mining cities like he'd seen in the southeast.

He walked for miles. Long after the rain stopped, his body shook as if chilled, though he didn't detect the sensation of cold, except in his right hand. When he wrapped both hands around his own naked torso, his nipples showed they were surely cold. If he was as chilled as his right hand, he needed to find shelter soon.

For now, he couldn't make any judgments as to his location. Being lost meant being vulnerable. Anything dangerous could meet him over one of these hills.

When the sun rose, a vague, cool light illuminated a thick atmosphere of low, drifting clouds. He didn't need the sun to rise in order to spot a heavy shadow in the distance: buildings. In the gentle valley before the settlement grazed a black speck—a person. Nothing to lose in approaching him or her. Dorhen might be an elf, but he needed mercy right now. If his presence caused trouble, at least the town jail might be warm and safe. He could possibly get a bite to eat as well.

*Mercy...* Somehow the thought of "needing mercy" made a faint sadness slither through his head, followed by an alerting spark in his otherwise numb body. He shook it away. Somehow, he'd wound up lost in this grassland with no memory whatsoever of where he'd been. He remembered no more than lots of sleeping, lots of darkness, and dreams of snakes. What a long night. There were also sexual dreams. He couldn't remember them beyond a feeling they elicited. But those dreams were normal, weren't they? And they had increased after he met Kalea, which must also be natural. Dreams were nothing but visions of what people longed for, or what they feared.

A different concern struck him. *Kalea!* He needed to find her! How could he have forgotten? In fact, as soon as her name entered his mind, so did the notion of chaos, images of young girls being raped in a convent, of fear for Kalea's safety, of fragrant smoke and dark halls and a set of hateful golden eyes. Lamrhath. Kalea might be in danger. He hurried forward.

The speck in the field happened to be an old woman humming to herself amidst the airborne water droplets beading on her black cloak and hood. Concerned about alarming her, he slowed his pace and kept a respectful distance.

He opened his mouth, but no voice emerged. His tongue flopped, thick and clumsy. He didn't realize what an effort it would be to try to translate his thoughts into words produced by his mouth. A groan escaped. His head suddenly throbbed with the newfound disorientation, unready for such a feat. How could he have forgotten how to speak? Had the numbness stunted his speech? Or were all of his nerves disconnected, cutting his mind's control over his body? What in the world had happened to him?

He swayed on his feet. The old woman's eyes trailed up his form. She was a tiny thing under his shadow. That's when he noticed how high off the ground he stood. The distance between his eyes and the ground felt wrong. He was not this tall. His perception was jumbled.

Her eyes showed both fear and awe, shining with a pale light. Her jaw worked up and down; her struggle for words matched his own.

"Mah—mah—mah," she managed. What a pair they made.

*Please don't be frightened,* he said, only to realize he wasn't successful. He tried again. "Please." It came out as a whisper.

"Mastaren?" Tears ran down her face, and she ignored them. "Oh, my—"

She dropped. Dorhen half-lunged to catch her, but didn't need to. She merely stooped to grovel at his feet, weeping.

"My lord, my lord Wikshen! My lord Wikshen!" Her bony, shaking hands rose above her head and her fingertips grazed the heavy fabric he wore. Her hands trailed and found his feet under the edge of the... kilt? Her fingers caressed the tops of his large bare feet, larger than he remembered, before her lips did the same. Her sobbing mingled with laughs of joy.

"I don't believe it!" she said. "I don't believe you are here, my sweet, sweet Mastaren!" Another rapturous laugh rang out before she calmed herself and struggled back to her feet. "What a miracle ye look, a beautiful

Dorhen wanted to ask what she meant, but he swayed dizziness. He groaned again, and her hands went to his a *I'll fall on you!*

sight for these old eyes."

Dorhen wanted to ask what she meant, but he swayed with sudden dizziness. He groaned again, and her hands went to his arm. *Let go, or I'll fall on you!*

She couldn't hear his thought. "Oh, you poor dear. You must come with me now. Hurry, before the sun rises in full."

He let her lead him by the hand toward the looming, shadowed shapes behind the wall of mist. The settlement sat at the top of a hill, and it became a chore for them both to climb it. When she stumbled, he managed to brace his hand on her back, to which she cooed and praised his generosity.

Patting his hand in her grasp, she said, "Please, Mastaren, be silent in the village and don't let them see you. Most of these folk don't honor you. Come, I'll see if the path is clear."

*Another village that doesn't like elves? Typical.*

She guided him through empty alleys; most of them were vacant at this early hour. Soft, sleepy voices murmured within the houses as Dorhen and the old woman passed by the windows. The houses were built close together, but not quite like a town. The old woman picked the tighter alleys for the sake of cover. If they were to walk straight through the center or more commonly used pathways, someone might see him. How lucky was he, to have found the one old woman in the village who didn't hate elves?

He thanked the goddess of the world for his luck before another sudden throb shot through his head, and he paused to squeeze his temples until the pain subsided. Isn't that who Kalea worshipped? A goddess who had made the world? It didn't sound right, but a firm sureness in his gut confirmed that a dark and beautiful entity, a goddess of fertility and carnal love, ruled the universe. What was her name?

"Mastaren, are you all right? Just a few more steps. My house is right around this way."

Waving the confusion away, he returned to the matter at hand. He also couldn't figure out, or manage to ask, why she insisted on calling him "Mastaren."

He ducked his head to step inside the house when she opened the heavy animal skin painted with tar which acted as a door. Her hand stayed on his arm as if *he* were the unstable one, until he was in, and then she hurried to her little hearth to stoke the embers and revive the fire.

"It's cold out there for an early summer day, isn't it?" She opened a box and retrieved a wool blanket, knitted expertly from fuzzy yarn. The fibers appeared grey because they were a mixture of black and white sheep hair.

When he took her offer to sit near the fire, she threw the blanket over his head and rubbed it over his hair and shoulders. "There you go. Get yourself dried off, and I'll find you some breakfast."

She paused. "What's this?" She touched his left side where he'd nearly forgotten about the brand he'd been given at Ilbith's hideout. "Who marked my Mastaren?" She clicked her tongue. "We'll talk later. Whoever's work this is, they'll pay."

He didn't try to speak, for what could she do about his Ilbith brand anyway? He focused on relearning how to speak, testing syllables on his tongue and trying to align them with the words in his head. His tongue flopped numbly in his mouth, but the more he worked it, the sharper its sense of touch became.

At the far side of the tiny house, the woman dragged her spinning wheel to the side and moved another animal skin away from the wall. Behind it was set an altar with cold incense and little bowls sitting on a platform beneath a tall stretch of black linen. She lit the incense, and soon the room filled with a sweet smell dancing on two playful ribbons of smoke. The smell soothed his mind and body with its warm herbal fragrance. He might be able to rest in this atmosphere.

He continued to watch her, practicing putting his tongue into the poses it would use for speech, as she opened a large clay jar and pulled out some live freshwater clams from the water within. When she opened a cupboard, a shiny surface inside the little door caught the light and shocked his eyes. She unfolded a piece of ordinary linen from a half loaf of bread. Over the fire, she hung a kettle of water, apologizing for having to reach in front of him.

"This is all I have for right now, Mastaren," she said, placing a plate with two slices of bread and a pile of slimy shelled clams on it before him. She went to the difficulty of lowering into a squat and then proceeded to bow with her forehead all the way to the floor. A string of soft murmurs jabbered through her lips. He caught a little of it. "Blessings..." she whispered. "All eternity...majesty..."

In his strange state of body, he could not tell the expression on his own face, but his narrowed vision suggested he squinted, probably frowning in his confusion too.

She raised her face and said, "Mastaren, thank you. Thank you for appearing to me. I don't know how long you intend to occupy my home, but for tonight I will prepare a feast. Anything you may need, please command me. This village has a few fetching girls. I've been grooming them. They aren't Wikshonites yet, but they've been listening to me."

Instead of trying to respond, Dorhen used his best hand to take the bread and attempt to eat it.

The old woman smiled. "My name is Linni. I'll leave you here to get some rest while I go out and gather more ingredients for tonight's dinner. I'll also see about drugging one of those girls—the prettiest one, of course."

Dorhen stopped his awkward attempt at chewing the bread and shook his head.

"No?" She bowed her head in respect. "I'll let you decide when and if you'd like to bless any girls." She made a cup of tea, took the rest of the bread out of the cupboard, and laid them before him with another murmured prayer. "Please enjoy yourself. You're welcome to all my food. There's my bed right there, and I'll be back later to do the cooking."

She threw on her cloak and hood, grabbed the basket by the doorway, and hurried out, securing the skin flap behind her. Heavy raindrops slapping against the mud outside greeted the old woman as she went out. She was getting all drenched, just for him. Why?

He blinked his eyes and they drooped. He must be sleepy already. He wasn't sure how long he had walked through the rain. All night? He couldn't remember that last blurry night very well. There was panic and screaming after a dark dream. The whole prospect of being in control of his body again was too surreal. He would've liked to know what village this was, but he couldn't just go outside and ask someone. His head fogged up in his grogginess, so he took her offer of using her bed. His feet hung off the end, so he curled up on his side and fluffed all of her thick, wooly blankets around himself. The mattress was balanced across ropes. Humans slept suspended. How strange...

He drifted off.

*Hey, sweetie. They sent me here to help you relax, so relax already.*

*Selka?*

*If you don't help me out, they'll beat me later.*

*I won't let them.*

*C'mon. Open your eyes already.*

When he did, Selka opened her robe to reveal her naked body and the hundreds of black snakes spilling out of the robe's folds. He yelped and tried to run, but they quickly filled the room and drowned him in their slithering darkness.

*No!*

Once again, he battled an army of snakes. He put the firmest mental block between his brain and his genitals he'd ever summoned. He'd never have sex again, not if he could help it. He could never fall asleep again either. Sleep made him vulnerable to the snakes' power and to…

*Hello, fool. Up to your usual stupidities?*

*Are* you *the one who's causing these maddening dreams?* Dorhen replied to the angry, grating voice, once again returned. Whatever that voice was, it had become a permanent fixture in his head.

*Only the recent one about your fetching friend at the Ilbith outpost. Should we go back for her?*

*Who are you?* Dorhen finally asked.

*You know who I am, not that it matters. Soon, you and I will fuse into one.*

*Wik,* Dorhen said. *Aren't we already one?*

Sandy, hissing laughter. *Neither you nor I are Wikshen. As of now we are two, fighting for control. We are Wikshen when we combine into one perfect blend.*

*I don't get it. Why are you doing this to me?*

*It's my divine right. I have been given your body, and I intend to use it. Wikshen must step forth.*

*Who is Wikshen?*

More laughter answered. *Wikshen is a force more powerful than you or me, a perfect being, a third entity conceived when you and I merge. All you must do is lie back and relax.*

The snakes rubbed him as they always did. These days, he could control one of his arms, and he flailed it to keep them away.

*Oh, stop it, fool,* the voice insisted. *You're making things more painful than necessary. If you're not careful, you'll slip through the cracks of this safe place I've made for you.* Dorhen stopped fighting because Wik's words had a familiar ring. *Remember what happened? You got lost in Kullixaxuss, leaving me to control your body alone. Such a thing isn't ideal. Without you to join with me, Wikshen can't arise. I'd be merely a spirit puppeteering a dead body.*

*Kullixaxuss?* The word, though strange, sounded more familiar the more he thought of it.

*Kullixaxuss is the world beyond this one, where dead souls fall. You slipped away to there. It's where you'll go when you die anyway. You were technically dead for a while, but I stayed in your body to keep it safe and alive. Good thing you made it back, or I would've been forced to discard your body and let it decay. You've accomplished a blunder none of my other hosts have ever managed—or tried.*

At Dorhen's stillness, the snakes played all over him. They couldn't seduce him as long as his mental block held, and it wavered in his struggle to concentrate. He vaguely remembered Kullixaxuss and its blazing atmosphere. Hazy images danced before him. He must've met the goddess there when he died, the one Kalea used to go on and on about. Thinking of the goddess and Kalea made him relax. When he died again, would he go back to the goddess he loved? The good feeling of the caress registered with vague memories of bliss in an unearthly woman's arms. He wanted to let the feeling continue. It would mount higher and higher until he found paradise.

*That's right, go to sleep now, you elven libertine.*

*No, I can't.* He finished his phrase with a sigh of pleasure.

*Doesn't matter how much you resist. Once I take hold, we'll become Wikshen and then the fun will begin. We'll be unstoppable.*

Dorhen flinched out of his relaxation and resumed his fighting, thrashing and twisting to get out of the pit of snakes. If he died, he died. Whatever Wik spoke about couldn't be a good thing. It sounded like he would turn into a menace on earth. If he "slipped away" again, at least his body would decay and Wik wouldn't use it to do whatever evil thing he planned. And he'd love to meet the goddess again.

He didn't slip away. His flailing carried him back out to the waking world, where he found himself in a musty old bed in a hut filled to the ceiling with earthy and herbal smells. His dreaming was becoming unbearable, an endless back-and-forth visitation between the pit of snakes and the waking world. How could he hope to help Kalea when he struggled like this? Maybe if he found her and made sure she was safe, she could help him in turn. She was spiritual, after all. Surely the goddess listened to her more carefully than she'd listen to him.

Dorhen crawled out of the old woman's bed, practically falling, and dragged himself to his feet. A slight tingling hinted at his need to relieve himself. Outside the door flap, the sun blazed orange on the western horizon; he had slept through all the daylight hours.

No one stirred outside the old woman's house, so he stood on the threshold and searched the long black kilt wrapped around his waist for an opening. A crossing string at the side of his hip tied it together. The ends hung open from above his right knee.

Slipping his hand into the opening of the black braies under the kilt, it took an extra effort to find his numb penis. It contained no feeling whatsoever, even less than his left hand. Putting his fingers around it felt too bizarre, like touching someone else's cock. The oddness caused it to scruple in its willingness to pass any urine. Nonetheless, it managed to release its arching stream. Something else beyond the numbness bothered him, however, and he couldn't resist bowing his head to look. It hung longer than it should have!

The shock made his urine stream stop, and he didn't bother to revive it. He tripped back into the house, looking at his hands. They were bigger too.

Wik's laugh rattled in his head. *Do you understand now, fool?*

Dorhen recalled something shiny and reflective in this house. He rummaged around, knocking over glass bottles and clay jars. He opened the cupboard where the old woman stored the bread.

There! A silver mirror hung secured to the inside of the door. Someone else's face stared back at him in the mirror. Big, bright turquoise eyes with a fearful roundness seemed familiar enough, but the rest... A longer face with harder cheekbones, a long nose with a strong bridge. Jagged, angular jaw. The features were basically elven and merely resembled him, but the face wasn't even the strangest part. In his earlier haziness, he'd failed to notice the long, straight hair draped over his shoulders. It was blue. The weak embers in the fireplace warmed the whole picture, but there was no mistaking the color. His hair should be brown, but somehow it had turned blue.

*It's blue because you are now half-pixie. An otherworldly power, a deity. Look behind you.*

Dorhen's eyes tore away from the silvery reflection and found the altar with the spent incense and tall black linen hanging up.

*She uses that altar to worship you. She's undoubtedly kept it for decades, long before you were born. Because she knew. She knew we would return someday. Now look down.*

Dorhen did.

*That hanging linen is a sacred shroud, woven from the same spun threads as your battleshift. A creation of the trolls, who also worship you. The one you wear is the original, a treasure I carry with me wherever I go. See how the shape of her piece is long and rectangular?*

Dorhen did notice.

*It is standing tall to represent the shadow you cast over their heads. It's long and rectangular because it's also a symbol for your sacred phallus, which holds a power all its own.*

The voice of Wik burst into laughter as Dorhen could only stare. When his gaze returned to the stranger in the mirror, tears were dampening the chiseled cheeks, the eyes rimmed red.

*Why are you crying? You have become something...beautiful.*

"I don't want this," he muttered with a whimper.

*You already have it.*

"I don't like it."

*You'll change your mind. When your consciousness blends perfectly with mine and we are in harmony, Wikshen will rise. Wikshen wields Kraft to its fullest extent. He blesses the moist, flush whores who lie down and spread for him. And he rules the Darklands.*

Emotion rattled Dorhen's entire body. Emotion he could feel, for once. It brought an awareness of nerves to his skin.

*You are Wikshen. That is your name now. It's our name.*

"No!" He sobbed and roared. He threw a fist at the silver mirror and dented the metal easily.

Under his touch, the silver fogged and turned black progressively until it disintegrated and flakes fell to the floor. A coldness ran up his arm from his hand and spread to the corners of his body.

He jerked his hand away from the withered remains of the metal in disbelief, but he couldn't deny what had happened—that the metal had gone inside of him. It flowed through him, dancing with an invigorating realism. Now full of too much energy, he thrashed his arms with a roar, and the entire cupboard flew off its brackets and crashed to the compacted earth floor.

"Mastaren!" The old woman, Linni, stepped over the threshold.

In his roaring outburst of brimming virile energy and fury, he couldn't stop himself. He didn't want to harm the kind old woman. He needed space. Wik continued laughing in his head. Linni darted to the side as he flew past her, out the door and into the night.

*Good idea. Let's see what fun we can find out here.*

Dorhen didn't intend any fun. He wanted to run toward the hills, away from the people, but Wik intended something else. The pixie controlled more parts of his body, particularly his left hand, which awoke to move on its own.

A man strolled down the path toward the village's central hall. Dorhen's left hand reeled back, and then pushed forward as if the air were thick. A hot, piercing sensation expanded on his palm. He screamed in pain and watched helplessly as a long, black blade ripped out of the center of his palm and flew the distance needed to sever the man's head.

Fighting with all of his mental capacity, Dorhen jerked his arm back and inspected his hand to see the gaping wound from the blade seal up and disappear.

*That's called a morkblade,* Wik said. *Each morkblade comes out with its own amorphous characteristic. With keen focus, you can concentrate and design them yourself. They'll cut your hand open, but the wound heals behind it. My power will heal all of your wounds quickly—which is why you need not worry about injury. No need to worry about death either. You can't die, except by fire, but the fire would have to be hot enough to reduce you to ashes. Watch this.*

Dorhen's feet picked up speed of their own volition, controlled by

Wik, and he ran at a speed he'd never seen before. The air rushed around him, stirring his hair to the roots. Wik threw his left hand to the ground, and his body followed through with a one-handed cartwheel. His black linen battleshift waved delightedly around his feet in the night air above him. Though the thing trailed long, it never tripped him; in fact, it moved away from his steps. He was weightless and graceful and unstoppable.

A thrill of delight stirred in his gut. If these abilities had been his back when he was with Kalea in the convent, he would've flattened all those sorcerers. He would've stopped the chaos in its tracks and saved Kalea and her friends on the spot. He could've been a hero to them all, rewarded with whatever they offered him. Kalea would've awarded him her love forever after.

Dorhen stopped his train of thought. *What am I thinking?* The whole thing was an abomination.

*You were right,* Wik replied. *You are now unstoppable, and the woman you want would be blessed to have you take her.*

*No, this isn't right!* Dorhen thought.

*Is it not?* Wik's laughter followed. *Oh, dear. Look, the villagers noticed what you did to that person.* Dorhen's body stopped running, but Wik wouldn't let him turn and bolt the other way from a pair of guards answering the screams of the villagers. *Let's inspire this village to embrace the faith.*

*No!* Dorhen protested, but his say never mattered.

Wik raised his palm and made another hot, stinging blade cut through his hand and fly toward the guard on the left. Time slowed as Dorhen watched in awe, half-believing the blade would bounce off the man's leather cuirass. It didn't. He couldn't fathom the sight, how the blade's movement advanced farther and farther until it disappeared, lost in the night. The man's entire top half slid off his hips and his body fell to the ground in two heavy, bloody pieces. That morkblade had zipped in its spinning motion straight across his torso and cut him in two.

The second guard, Wik used to display more strength and agility, first stunning him with a swiping kick across the face, next taking him to the ground with a sweep behind his knees, and finally raising his heel with a refined flexibility and dropping it with his leg's full weight on the man's face. A series of heavy stomps finished him off. Bone crunched under Dorhen's foot. Blood gushed out and drenched his sole, and Dorhen could feel the little tingle of iron harvested from the blood seeping into his flesh. He found how powerful his legs had become and the unnatural hardness of his heel.

*Your body will do greater damage after you absorb more metal into your blood,* Wik said. *Right now, your store is low, but after enough absorption, even a sword won't be able to nick you.*

Dorhen was finished listening. Needing to vomit after watching himself kill those three people, he focused his mind and fought to control his body. "I won't let you do anymore!" He screamed it with his physical voice.

Dorhen found a percentage of success, but his vicious fight with Wik caused more erratic movements, running, jumping, falling and writhing, twisting, and screaming. He couldn't avoid slamming into people. Wik made sure to throw out morkblades wherever he could, and laughed with Dorhen's own throat anytime they sliced through someone. Dorhen never gave up. He'd win this war if it killed him and he reunited with the goddess.

Wik steered him toward a town hall with glowing windows. Voices murmured within. A lot of people gathered inside and continued to file in. *A good place for Morkblade practice, wouldn't you say?*

"No!" All Dorhen could do was shout. He'd lost his body. Wik controlled it now. His legs moved according to Wik's will, running powerfully toward the big hall. His palms burned like boiling water with the imminent morkblades waiting to come out.

# Chapter 29
# What is Lost in the Mists

Kalea hadn't yet told her friends about her dreamwalking, how and why the sanguinesent found them in Valltalhiss, or about her probability of being a Luschian. Her mouth remained clamped as they tossed ideas back and forth about what all had gone on back there. So many questions. If she answered them with what she knew, it would only give birth to more questions. She did, however, explain to them what she knew about the Thaccilians, for their own safety. She told them to watch for red-eyed people, and that they all lived on human hearts, or at least general flesh.

"But why didn't they have you up on that stage with us," Del asked, "naked and ready for the butcher?"

"Who knows? They're crazy," Kalea said.

The next day, they spotted color in the sea of waving grass and hurried to inspect.

"Dead bodies," Bowaen said. "More dead bodies."

Gaije went straight to work plucking the arrows out of the dead, who wore yellow. Not much remained behind to salvage. No food.

Kalea stayed back away from the scene, trying not to think about it too hard, until Gaije cried out, "Some of these are elves!"

Kalea rushed forward and eagerly checked them for Dorhen. The dead elves all bore the color orange somewhere on their person, like a woven belt, a tie in one's hair, and a cloak on another. Kalea knelt and prayed for them and expressed her gratitude that none of them were Dorhen.

Bowaen and Del got to rummaging through the belt pouches and satchels.

"Eew!" Del said, and flung one object aside.

"What is it?" Kalea asked.

"Hair. Bloody hair."

Gaije picked it up. It was indeed a lock of hair with dried skin attached. "It's a scalp," he said. "These people in yellow have been scalping."

Kalea covered her mouth, not wanting to see the human scalp up close either. "Oh, how horrible," she said.

"Hold on," Gaije said. He drew attention to the orange thread wrap on the hair. "This hair belongs to elves like those. These are elven scalps."

"What would they want with bloody hair?" Del asked with a grimace.

"Trophy," Bowaen put in.

"This land has sick people, doesn't it?" Kalea said.

Another thick shroud of mist passed over them later that day. It was dark, wet, and quiet—quiet, save for the soft whir of tiny water beads settling on millions of grass blades.

The novelty of the strange weather wore off quickly, replaced by mumbled comments about how they'd catch their deaths if they couldn't find shelter. The wetness seeped through Kalea's cloak, and she shivered. Del cursed, and his movements jerked and twitched when he realized he couldn't light his pipe.

"Gotta save my tobacco anyway," he grumbled. "Runnin' out in this endless wasteland."

"Forget tobacco," Bowaen replied. "We're out of food."

"Don't say such a thing," Kalea whined, rubbing her stomach. "Dorhen told me not to fast. I'm never fasting again. My elf was wise, and I abandoned him like a heartless shrew!" She finished with a sullen groan.

"If you see any grasshoppers, eat 'em," Bowaen said. "They'll work in a pinch."

"Come to think of it," Kalea said, "Dorhen briefly mentioned something about eating insects."

Del made a *blech* sound behind her.

"Problem is, I haven't seen any yet," Gaije said. "This land hates us."

Del snorted. "Now *this* elf has said something wise for once."

Gaije ignored him. He walked solemnly behind them all with his bow unstrung. He had hurried to remove the string when the mist moved in, explaining its silk should be kept dry if he could help it. Bowaen walked in the lead with his sword drawn.

The blue strands of hair Kalea carried in her *Lehomis* book were bothersome. She wanted to check them again to make sure she hadn't dreamed all of that, as well as to make sure they were really there and they were indeed blue.

She resisted. Thoughts of the blue-haired killer weighed on her heart. The color blue created a correlation between him and Arius Medallus. Surely it couldn't be Dorhen's beloved Arius Medallus destroying villages. Was he truly a fairy at all, or a sorcerer like Gaije claimed? After seeing him in her convent's sanctuary, she thought of him as her guardian, a messenger of the Creator. Had he lied about sending her to find Dorhen?

Could he have sent her to the Darklands for a different purpose, using Dorhen as pretense?

*No, Arius Medallus is not the killer! I won't believe it until I see it.*

The urge to stare at and touch the blue hair remained, which she resisted. It next occurred to her that the blue color was like water. Blue often symbolized water. Arius Medallus was a water spirit...and so was Lusche.

When night fell, the thick, soggy atmosphere became the blackest Kalea had ever seen. They couldn't travel any farther.

"Stop walking," Bowaen ordered, "before we lose each other. When I call your name, say 'aye.' Del, Kalea, Gaije."

They all answered, "Aye."

Kalea took out Dorhen's moonstone to rub and poke it, trying to make it light up. No luck. A hand found her arm and grabbed it.

"Kalea?" Bowaen's voice. "It won't be a comfortable arrangement, but come here, everyone." As he waited for the other two to comply, he grumbled, "Stupid of me to let Damos go."

Another hand grazed Kalea's hair and jerked away. "Sorry, Kalea."

"Why are you sorry, Gaije?" They could only tell where each other stood by feel and voice.

"Okay, listen," Bowaen said. "We got nowhere in this terrain to hide and no light to see in. If we keep walkin', we could break a leg. We gotta sleep too. Gaije, bring your cloak. We're going to huddle under it for the night. We'll stay warm, and it'll keep the mist off."

"I still have everything I had packed in my basket," Kalea said, "including my quilt. We can sit on it."

"Good thinkin'," Bowaen said.

She rummaged carefully through her things to squeeze the rolled-up blanket out without dropping any of her small items. The quilt was heavy and damp, but at least a few spots were dry. The soaked grass would dampen the rest of it quickly enough.

A bumbling dance of elbows and reluctance took several minutes to get the blanket spread out, and the four of them sat extremely close to each other in a back-to-back circular manner. Kalea found herself shoulder to shoulder with Gaije and Del. Bowaen sat directly behind her. Gaije raised his cloak, and everyone took a corner to spread it over all their heads. It was made from an extremely tight elven weave which kept most of the moisture at bay. The whole underside of it was saturated in his personal scent and lots of his sweat, different from a man's. She could almost remember what Dorhen smelled like thanks to it.

Gaije's cloak, however, was the least potent thing to inhale all night. Altogether, the lot of them created a large pocket of warm body odor. The two men were absolutely foul, but they were warm, and she'd rather sleep in here than out in the wet open air.

At first, she hugged her knees tightly, trying her best to respect everyone else's personal space, but who was she kidding? If she were to fall asleep, she'd have to relax. Somehow.

With no memory of falling asleep, and no dreams to confirm she had, Kalea found herself lying crooked over Gaije's arm. Del was lying on her hip, drooling on her skirt. With a flinch, she tried to sit upright. A twinge of pain shot through her muscles, head to toe. Her movement caused the chain reaction of the others awakening. Light seeped in under the edges of Gaije's cloak.

"It's morning?" she said, and lifted the cloak from her head. The sun highlighted the persistent mist.

When Gaije sat up, he groaned and rubbed his arm. "My shooting arm."

"Worst night ever," Del said. "I slept in a pile of bodies, and most of them were men." He rubbed his face vigorously with shaking hands before moving to his pipe. After letting the pipe go again, Del cursed at the mist.

Bowaen's raspy voice growled the loudest as he stretched and winced when he knuckled the stiff spots in his back. "Me and my stupid ideas."

"It was a good idea, Bowaen," Kalea said.

The mist endured when the cool morning light rose high. They resolved not to think about their discomforts or their hunger and walked on, determined to climb out of the mist-filled valley.

Someone knocked Kalea's shoulder, and she teetered on one foot. "Del!" she growled, the ache returning to her leg at the sudden jolt. He must've been teasing. Her wound was mending well, but moments of soreness drifted in and out. She'd practiced walking without a stick, but his roughness would certainly foil her recovery.

"What's your problem?" Del responded. He slogged at her other side, slightly obscured by the mist. Bowaen and Gaije walked near him, none close enough to hit her.

She scanned the mist's depths just in time to catch Dorhen! Yes, it was Dorhen! He was running, his hair waving behind him, strong arms pumping. She called his name, and all of her friends regarded her.

"It's really him!"

She grabbed Gaije's wrist, frantic not to let Dorhen get away, though she couldn't be separated from her friends either. Gaije grabbed Bowaen's tabard in turn and Bowaen grabbed Del's arm, and they ran as a chain in the direction she insisted Dorhen went.

"She's crazy!" Del protested from the back of the line. None of them had the energy for a run, but adrenaline sparked within Kalea at the sight of her elf.

*How did he get away from the sorcerers?* A smile spread on her face. *Because he's Dorhen. He's my capable elf.*

After a long while, her smile died. *Why didn't he notice me back there?*

Ahead of her, the mist thinned and soon passed away as fast as it pleased, leaving them in the bright, warm sunlight, the first day in the Darklands they had ever seen the sky. The land opened up before Kalea, wide grassy fields with a faraway horizon, towering cumulous clouds against a blue sky, and no Dorhen.

"Dorhen!" Her voice traveled far, repeating the call for miles. She gawked and panted as her companions caught up behind her.

"Kalea, you gotta give us some warning," Bowaen said.

She turned to face him. "But I saw him. Dorhen—he came and went. I couldn't let him get away."

"Why would he want to get away from you?" Del asked, rising from his exhausted stoop. "From the way you talk about him, sounds like he wanted to get you in the sack. Men who like women don't avoid them."

Gaije narrowed his eyes at Del. "What kind of wicked *saehgahn* would want to put a woman in a sack?"

Del snorted at Gaije's question, and his mirth spread lightly to Bowaen's face.

"Look." Bowaen pointed. "See it?"

Down in another valley, a few specks could be made out, mostly obscured by the bright twinkles bouncing off the surface of water.

"I see water," Del said, "which is good enough for me."

"It's a village!" Kalea added, "Maybe Dorhen went there."

Bowaen took the lead again. "Let's find out."


A village, much like the burned one, rose from the hills. No manor house accompanied the little huts and barns of this settlement, much smaller and simpler than what Kalea would expect in the Lightlands. She scanned the rooftops for a sanctuary steeple—they didn't have one. A wooden palisade made from the thin nearby trees surrounded the settlement, and the stream flowed past before veering off and tumbling over a few short drops as the valley went.

They reached the stream and, after many greedy gulps of water and refilling their one remaining waterskin, they walked along it until they met a small group of women washing heaps of linens. The sight took Kalea back to the life she'd left behind so long ago. She almost wished she could join them in the simple, rhythmic task just for the comfort of it, but Dorhen needed her.

"Eh!" the first woman called as soon as she noticed them. "You folk look worse for wear."

"A legendary understatement," Del murmured, and Bowaen elbowed him.

Kalea rushed to the edge of the water opposite the women. "Did an elf run by here?"

The central figure of the group paused in her scrubbing. "Not that I seen."

When Kalea shot Bowaen a shocked and urgent expression, he grabbed her arm and held her back.

"We're hungry!" Bowaen said in the clearest, most friendly voice Kalea had ever heard from him. "Can you please spare some food? We have chips of money!"

"Are you sure an elf didn't come running this way?" Kalea pressed, and Bowaen squeezed her arm. He waved his hand at Kalea, who had stowed the last of the silver and copper chips with which Lord Dax supplied them for survival.

On the other side of the stream, the prominent woman stood up, and the younger ones around her followed. "We don't need money here!" the woman said, planting her fists on her hips. "What we want is news. Ya got news to share, travelers?"

"Yes!" Bowaen nodded his head along with the word.

The woman waved her hand. "Step on over." The stream flowed shallow and gentle enough to walk through. "Don't worry about yer clothes, we'll dry 'em up for ye." She eyeballed each one of them as they climbed the gentle slope of the other bank. "You got any ties to sorcery?" the woman asked Bowaen.

"No, ma'am," he said, his voice now firm.

"Good." She squinted again. "I see no signs of Wikshonism either." She paused at Kalea. "You got some hollow cheeks, girl," she finished her statement, poking Kalea's face.

Ignoring the woman's annoying prod, she asked, "Are you sure a male elf with brown hair didn't come from over that hill before us?"

The woman lowered her brow and drew her mouth tight. "Yer woman ain't right, is she?" She barked out a laugh. Gaije approached from the water after Kalea. "You got an elf right here, girl." She ran her eyes over Gaije. "With this Clanless here, I know there mustn't be any sorcery or Wikshonism among ye."

"Clanless?" Gaije asked, but the woman didn't elaborate. She led them around to the gate and banged a large branch against a metal plate dangling nearby. A gatekeeper opened the window.

"Got some new blood here," the washerwoman announced.

"No," Kalea breathed. She turned to walk the other way, and Bowaen caught her. She tried to jerk away but couldn't. "Dorhen's out here if not in there, and I have to find him!" she protested.

At her hysteria, the village women exchanged glances. Kalea writhed in Bowaen's grip until he wrapped his arms around her.

"Settle down!" he said as they struggled to pass through the gate. "We're all starvin'. We'll talk about Dorhen when we get inside with some food!"

His tone implied that he didn't believe her sighting of Dorhen, and it made her weep. Bowaen's firm grip made sure she didn't escape. She screamed Dorhen's name and reached for the outside as the gate shut her in.

# Chapter 30
# What is Dishonoring Clan Lockheirhen

Proud, blaring horns announced their arrival. The Tinharri Clan *saehgahn*. Lehomis heard them across the village but didn't bother to run and gawk at them. The *faerhain* and *farhah* did. Not too many of the Lockheirhen *saehgahn* had gathered, he'd been told, and the ones who did, did so with a cocky air of defiance and protection for their females.

That's what good *saehgahn* were supposed to do, protect the females. It wasn't wrong or unfair for a *faerhain* of any clan to choose a *saehgahn* from a neighboring clan—Tirnah had done that very thing. It was, however, deadly wrong for a *saehgahn* to try to woo a *faerhain* in any way subtle or explicit. These *saehgahn* were here to do the latter. To make sure the lads remembered, he'd called another meeting yesterday to remind his rabble not to get angry or violent—unless they happened upon a *faerhain* being harmed. But this…this would be a difficult few days.

Lehomis gnashed on his pipe stem merely a few hours later as he perched on the bottom rung of the bell tower's ladder at the center of town. He watching the colorfully dressed princes and royal cousins walk about, stopping busy *faerhain* just to introduce themselves.

One young Lockheirhen *saehgahn* approached Lehomis, shaking all the way to his toes, to report how he caught one of the Tinharri Clan touching his widowed mother's shoulder.

Lehomis sighed and bowed his head. "It's allowed, lad," he said. "Try not to think about it."

"But—but he touched her! Right in front of me, and without her permission!"

"He didn't hurt her, did he?" Lehomis asked.

The young lad stuttered for a bit. "N-no, Elder."

"Then it's okay. Now run along. Tell me if he does anything to frighten her."

The lad's pace carried him away swiftly in a pointed direction.

"He'll be back," Lehomis said to himself, "and not because of what I told him."

This would be the most difficult thing the lad's generation would face. War and death was one thing, but right now they'd have to watch their slim chances of being matched with a female slip through their fingers.

Their mothers and sisters would leave them alone here. That lad's mother was all he had.

It suddenly occurred to Lehomis how a new barracks might be in order to house all the lone *saehgahn* who'd be left behind. Other than Lehomis, who was the elder, *saehgahn* never lived alone. They lived in a house owned by a female, either as a husband, son, or house-guardian. *Saehgahn* lived to be useful, not to sit idly in an empty room. A common house for lone *saehgahn* would be well in order if the Tinharri Clan took too many females out of Clan Lockheirhen—if Lehomis didn't have to disperse the clan.

"Elder." Alhannah, the head Desteer, called him back to reality. She approached with one of the royals, this one wearing more shiny hair decorations than the rest. A silvery sheen dazzled across his dark hair in the light. A handsome and strong jaw with a wide chin went with it, as well as a set of shoulders spanning wider than any of Clan Lockheirhen's most notable male specimens. All of the present Tinharris shared similar features.

"You weren't at the reception," Alhannah continued. "This is Prince Kirnonhen. He is Queen Kelenhanen's youngest brother, and he seeks your hospitality for him and his entourage of cousins and second cousins."

The prince displayed a hard yet polite countenance as he gave a stiff bow.

Lehomis didn't bother bowing back or removing his pipe from his mouth. Better he crunch down on the bone stem than on the Tinharri prince's throat. "I knew you arrived, though," Lehomis offered. "I smelled your perfume when you got here."

The Tinharri prince's eyebrows rose in a smooth and amiable question. "'Perfume?' Forgive me, Elder Lockheirhen, but I do not have that. I am not as well-traveled as you. What is 'perfume?'"

Lehomis held the pipe in his mouth, even as Alhannah glared at him from the prince's side. Keeping his teeth firm, he explained, "It's a smelly oil ladies in the human lands put on their throats. Usually, whores use it to make themselves more attractive to the nose."

The prince's eyes showed his pondering. "Hmm." He reached into his robe and revealed a pocket-sized book with Lightlandic letters on the cover. "I have not yet read about this form of attraction. Perhaps I can secure some of this perfume for attraction of the nose."

Lehomis's bite on the pipe stem shifted to a smile he tried to suppress. "I can tell ya all about it, lad. I've been to so many different places. Come by my house for tea, and I'll tell ya about rouge."

"Rouge," the prince parroted.

"Oh yeah, the ladies in the human lands love rouge! Get's 'em laid easy as butter on bread."

"Laid?"

Lehomis finally took the pipe out of his mouth and offered the prince a smile. "It's a good thing, trust me."

"Well, I shall look into these things. Perfume, rouge, laid," he recited. He gave Lehomis a royal bow, this one deeper than at first introduction. "Thank you, Elder Lockheirhen. And thank you for opening your clan to our plight."

"*Your* plight?" Lehomis growled as the prince and the head Desteer walked away.

Alhannah prolonged her glare at Lehomis over her shoulder; her mouth shrank to a tight, downward crescent, one eye narrower than the other. The prince tucked the little leather book back into his pocket as the two disappeared into the crowd of brooding Lockheirhen *saehgahn*.

So that's what they were doing. Most *saehgahn* wouldn't be able to imagine how to woo a female—it simply wasn't in Norrian culture—so the Tinharri Clan were reading books written by Lightlandic poets. His mouth suddenly bitter, he dumped the remainder of his pipe's contents onto the dirt and rubbed his shoe across the embers.

Lehomis worked up the nerve to knock on Tilninhet's door, burdened with a duty to tell her the news. She'd been asking him every day if he'd heard back. The letter from Togha's military branch weighed heavy in his pocket. He struggled to fill his lungs with air in the few moments it took her to answer the door.

"Welcome, Elder." She smiled warmly. Today, her *hanbohik* showed the crispest edges and folds he'd ever seen her wear. Her long cherry hair tumbled down her shoulders and along her bosom, combed and styled with the care a single *faerhain* usually took.

He stifled the compliment on her appearance which impulsively leaped to his lips, almost forgetting why he'd come. He held the letter within his pocket but hesitated to draw it out.

"Are you here for tea?" she asked with a pleasant ring.

"No," he hurriedly answered. "Togha's branch sent me a letter."

Her face glowed with an excitement he knew could turn to tears in a blink. She took his arm. "Oh please, step inside, Elder! I'll brew tea."

*No more tea!* He held the exclamation in. To be honest, after he told her about Togha, he might have to accept her tea out of comfort for her. The situation was so wrong! "No, thank you, Tilly," he said.

Her eyebrows turned upward. "I don't like your tone, Elder. What's wrong? What happened to my Togha?"

Leaving the letter in his pocket, he put his hands on her arms. "Nothing. Nothing at all is wrong," he said quickly. He forced a smile. "Togha's fine! They sent him to another route, and he's happy. He does his job well and has earned at least one accolade for his hard work."

Holding a bright, fake smile on his face, Lehomis's stomach turned sour. *Did I just say that?*

Tilninhet's radiance soared higher. "That's wonderful!" She hugged him, and he allowed it. "Thank you, Elder, thank you! Oh, what a relief. How I worried for my handsome son. Oh, Elder." She turned weepy and dabbed her eyes on a handkerchief. "Are you sure you would not enjoy a cup of tea?"

If she meant real tea, he would've easily agreed to settle his stomach, but over the years "tea" had become their secret code, and he could no longer tell what she meant by it.

"No, I'm fine," Lehomis said. "Just came to report the good news."

After he bid her good day and she closed the door, Lehomis stood in shock. He'd just told a *faerhain* the worst lie he'd ever told. How in the world could she not easily find out the truth, especially if a ranger happened to show up asking about her fugitive son? Lehomis could lose his head for that lie! He'd arrived with every intention to tell her the truth, but when it came time to speak, the complete opposite blurted out. She was so fragile, and the lie made her feel so good!

He raised his fist to knock again. He didn't. He left her to her relief and happiness and moved on. He'd think about it later...and possibly take on the consequences. For now, he'd worry about his clan.

A few disgusting sights stung his eyes on the walk home. Some *faerhain* did appear bothered by the royals' intrusion.

"Please, *faerhain*, sit and talk with me," one young idiot said to a *faerhain* older than he, who was carrying two buckets of water.

"But I have to get home and boil water for the stew."

The Tinharri idiot followed her. "I can carry those for you." She squealed when he snatched one of the buckets from her hand. The helpfulness wasn't unheard of, but the incessant bothering was.

"If you must," she said. "My home is this way, but you'd better run if my father sees you."

Lehomis walked on. Another *faerhain* was sitting on a bench in the square, her knees fidgeting as another Tinharri male seated himself close to her—far too close for Norrian standards.

"Just your hand. I'd like to hold your hand," he said. "I mean no offense. Put your hand in mine, and I'll hold it for a while."

"But why?" She put her hands under her thighs to protect them.

"It's because, um, it's nice. We can talk."

"About what?"

Lehomis couldn't take any more. Rubbing his temples, he made his way home with his eyes cast on the path. The sights were painful, and not just because they were an abomination. These Tinharri males needed so many lessons. They were embarrassing themselves. Lehomis could teach them a lot...but he'd rather die.

"Elder, I'd like a word with you!" Alhannah said in a scathing tone.

Lehomis shook his head, sighing, and kept walking. "Lass, we'll have to talk later. I need a nap."

She persisted. "You can't talk to a prince of Norr like that! Elder!" She followed him.

"I'm glad Gaije isn't here to see this," he mumbled.

"Speak up, Elder."

He walked on.

"Elder!"

He finally stopped and put a hand out. "Okay, look," he began, but two people caught his eye.

Anonhet. A second glance confirmed it. She stood on the path ahead, more at ease than any of the *faerhain* he'd yet seen...with her hand in another royal's soft-handed grip. She was smiling as he smiled at her, gazing at her deeply. Too deeply. His eyes often perused her bust, tightly packed under her *hanbohik*. He leaned in too close, his smile too soft, too warm. He was trying to smell her without her noticing. Anonhet might not have realized that, but Lehomis couldn't help but notice it, considering his experience.

"Elder," Alhannah pressed, but he ignored her.

"Anonhet," Lehomis called as carefully as he could.

Their trance broke, and Anonhet's smile dropped. "Yes, Grandfather?"

"Please go in and make me a cup of tea to help me sleep."

Bobbing her head to Lehomis, she avoided the young royal's eyes and took her hand away to run off toward the cliff face with their front door in sight. Shooting the Tinharri *saehgahn* his most piercing glare, Lehomis turned to follow her, ignoring Alhannah.

"Elder," the royal *saehgahn* said, "I should like to visit Anonhet for tea at an hour of your best judgment—Elder?"

Lehomis walked away.

# Chapter 31
## His Followers

"How much farther, marm?"

"What do ye mean, how much farther?" Knilma rubbed her tired, baggy eyes. "He's Wikshen, so we'll walk as far as he needs us to, Sammial, never forget that!" She grasped the sides of her sedan chair, her knuckles creaking under the pressure. "Gentle, now! Walk smoother! You want to toss me right down the hill?"

The young man gave a grunt and held his tongue.

"I thought so. Now, as I told you little muttonheads, the voice echoed from the southwest, a strong vibration. Shouldn't be far now."

They'd been walking for five hours since Knilma awoke to the voice vibrating on a sharp line through the earth to her room in Ravivill. She'd retired there forty years ago. Her old heart thumped heavily. The idea of Wikshen's voice through the earthen vibrations seemed too surreal as of today, that familiar, sensual, inspiring command she'd been trained to listen for and had devoted herself to heed. Against any doubt, she'd heard it—at the same time as Paigess.

Paigess rode Togha's jenny donkey while Knilma used her old sedan, a simple seat on two poles, carried by the other two warlocks. They'd met Togha on the road soon after setting out. He and a few other young Wikshonites were headed to Ravivill when Knilma met them on the road. Togha, an elf and the oddest one in the group, had a quiet reserve about him. He possessed a good meditative personality for Wikshonism, and he eagerly turned in his tracks to head back east at Knilma's request. That elf had devotion.

After finding Wikshen, Knilma would return to work in Wikhaihli under the new Wikshen's rule. At the thought, her heart fluttered and returned to its heavy, slow throb. Wikshen returning to reign.

"Who knew I'd live to see another Wikshen?"

"Isn't it exciting?" Paigess said from the jenny's back. "I've stared at drawings of him in books all my life. What do you think he'll look like in this generation?"

"I think he'll look strong and quick," Knilma said. "They're always strong and quick." Knilma was the last living person to have seen a Wikshen in the flesh six hundred and fifty years ago. The mere memory of his image energized her. "Sammial! Tristain! Jax! Walk faster! You too, Togha, keep up!"

The three human warlocks groaned in response, and Togha kept as quiet as he always did.

The village's gate hung open. A dead man lay beside the road. Knilma smiled at him. "Wikshen did come here. Go up the hill. Let's see if he's still here."

The sedan bobbed onward with the young men's steps. They stopped groaning and their legs quickened; the sedan moved more easily through the dark village. Dawn would be here soon and no clouds clotted in the sky, which wouldn't do. Wikshen hated the sun. It didn't kill him like it did his trollish subjects, but it blistered him on the hottest of days, and usually made him tired and irritable. Like the pixie side of his soul, Wikshen thrived in the dark.

A frantic crowd gathered at the village center, around the main hall. At first, no one noticed their little black-cloaked group, but when they did, someone shouted, "Witches!"

The sedan chair landed with a jolt as the warlocks leaped to engage a handful of approaching men. Paigess slid off the jenny's back, whipped her drum around to the front, and released its beater from her belt.

"Stay close to us, Tamas," Paigess ordered the tall, bronze-skinned beauty they'd brought from Ravivill.

The two most experienced warlocks took three practiced steps toward the men, scraping their feet through the dirt. After sucking in deep breaths, they threw their fists forward and shouted a short, crisp *ha*!

The approaching group scattered back as if knocked with a giant hammer. One man's body burst into a few bloody pieces because Sammial's skill was more advanced than Tristain's. The spectacle kept the rest of the villagers at a respectful distance.

"We're shamans!" Paigess corrected the bystanders with a voice stronger than Knilma's. "And if you behave, you'll live. One of us will be assigned to your village for spiritual guidance!" She slammed her drum once, and the beat tremored through the area in a wide radius.

A sorrowful wail in Knilma's head tugged at her shriveled heart. "He's here!" she said, and pointed to the largest building, the town hall.

Forgetting the sedan, she hobbled the rest of the way over, Paigess and the warlocks forming a protective barrier around her. Up the path, a young girl sat on the grass, weeping softly, her face dirty and battered. Knilma caught her eye briefly, but a more important urgency waited.

The town hall's doors were barred and nailed shut on the outside.

Men scurried about, throwing twigs and hay against the wall. Men with torches shared flames with new torches. A stack of firewood and kindling ignited after the first torch's contact. On the other side of the building, men and women hastily finished stacking flammable materials and called for a torch to use.

Paigess rushed forward and pounded three drumbeats. The ground shuddered and rocked the villagers off their feet, and they dropped their torches and additional kindling. The last booming beat opened a small cave in the ground, and two men and a woman fell in.

Sammial approached the fire with the sacred shroud they carried and smothered it before it raged out of control. Togha approached with a found pitchfork and pried the boards off the doors at Knilma's order.

When the doors opened, a male scream ripped through the darkness within. Stepping inside, Knilma grabbed a bronze medallion dangling on her belt and tapped it with a tiny bronze mallet. A blue flame kindled at the medallion's center, and she pointed the disk toward the hall's cooling brazier. The flame reacted, jumping into the brazier and dancing like a normal fire. The blue flame worked better for Wikshen to function in, but Knilma couldn't help squinting to see in its dim light.

"Damn these old eyes! Paigess, bring a torch—just one!"

A heart-wrenching moan echoed through the empty building. Behind her, the warlocks held off the crowd. Their Kraft Shouting killed a few more, and the remainder of the crowd lost their confidence.

"Let me through! I'm a shaman too! My name is Gertrude."

Knilma turned slightly with her feet, unable to twist her spine. Another middle-aged woman stepped forward and raised her wrist high to display its black ribbon wrapping, a subtle sign of her devotion to Wikshen.

"Let her through, Sammial. I know her."

Gertrude pushed past the two warlocks when they lowered their hands. Knilma had exchanged letters with Gertrude. The woman kept her shaman status secret in this particular village because of its hostility, unlike Knilma's successful conversion of Ravivill to Wikshonism. Gertrude wrapped her wrist with the black ribbon, but wore normal farming clothes instead of the usual black garments. Some places accepted shamans and their talents, and some condemned them. In upcoming days, more villages would learn to accept the Wikshonites. They would have to, or the sorcerers would get them instead.

Gertrude stood beside Knilma as Paigess arrived with the torch, wincing at the next roar from the dark corner. "He's been screaming like this for the last three hours," Gertrude said. "It was worse before. He must be tiring out."

"What happened?" Knilma asked.

"Earlier today, a big meeting was assembled here when Wikshen arrived at the village. Linni, an elderly witch, found him first. He emerged from her house, killed a few, and made his way into the hall." Gertrude fanned her glistening face. "What a sight! He lunged around, swinging a big axe he'd found outside—one-handed! He leaped atop tables and threw grown men against the walls. But he suddenly paused and collapsed into convulsions and screaming, allowing us to escape with our lives. I don't know what's wrong with him."

Knilma frowned, her eyes squinting into the darkness. "Let's go ask him. Bring the torch."

Hobbling up the steps to the elevated floor, Knilma ventured closer. The screaming pierced her ears. At least they were still in good working order...for now. The scream morphed into a painful moan, sending a needle of sad agony through her heart. This was undoubtedly him, but she had never known Wikshen to sound like that. He should be proud and virile. The sounds drew her deeper into the shadow, nagging at her caring instincts. If death stalked her right now, it would have to wait until after she took care of his distress.

She softly spoke the ancient term of address reserved for Wikshen, "Mastaren," and was answered by an intensified moan of agony grasping her heart. "I'm here now."

With a few more daring steps into the shadow, the light revealed a large form huddled on the floor, twisting around to his back and then to his knees. He rose and bolted, slammed into a thick timber post supporting the ceiling, and crumpled to the floor. The big wooden building shook. He stayed there, grasping at his own hair.

"My, my," Knilma said. "You have blue hair this time, which means you'll avoid people. You prefer solitude."

He tried to rise again, but fell limp as if his muscles didn't communicate with his brain properly.

"Calm down, Mastaren! I'll help you relax. Listen to this."

He roared another scream and clawed at the floor, leaving deep, blood-filled trenches in the wood. He had destroyed his own fingernails with this sort of behavior. She selected another medallion from her belt, a smaller one, and tapped it with the little mallet. A pleasant vibration sang out, and Wikshen fell limp, panting on the floor.

"You're a tall one. And what's this? You're also an elf! Well, now." She hobbled closer, despite the other shamans' reluctance to try. "Approach, ladies, and pay your respects." They obeyed. "Paigess, hold the torch back a bit."

Knilma reached toward his clammy face. "Let's have a look at you." She brushed his mystical hair aside and found an empty stare. He practically laid his face in her hands like a dying animal. "Aww. These black lines trailing off your eyes like beauty marks, they're short, which means you won't live long. But don't you worry, Mastaren, we'll fortify Wikhaihli and keep you safe. Whatever it takes, we're here to protect you. And oh, what a pretty face you have. Look at this nose, long and pointing...means you've got a cock to please the girls all day long." She burst into a laugh.

Wikshen's expression didn't change beyond a slow blink. He raised one trembling arm, sat up, and seized his wrist with his other hand, gnashing his teeth. A bellowed growl of pain erupted as a blade emerged from the center of his palm.

Gertrude, the youngest shaman present, snatched his wrist also and jerked it toward an empty corner so the morkblade flew into the wall, ripping through the wood. Wikshen cradled his hand, bleeding all over himself.

"Oh, you poor thing. You're so green, you haven't absorbed enough minerals and know-how to use the morkblades properly. Without any practice, it may feel like—well, a knife through the hand. Here, listen to this."

She tapped the small medallion again, and he relaxed further. Now, as he lay calmly on the floor, she resumed stroking his hair. "We're going to take you home now, Mastaren, don't worry another minute. You're in good hands."

She turned to the others. "Togha, hitch Haggis to a cart."

The elven warlock's face showed pallid, nearly grey with emotion after seeing their deity for the first time. When he strode away, she lowered her chin and thanked Wikshen in prayer for Togha, their newest recruit. His donkey would come in handy to carry Wikshen home.

"Mastaren," Knilma said, "can you walk?" He blinked, breathing a bit fast, and worked his lips. "C'mon, out with it."

"Runnnnn..." he whispered, and fainted afterward.

"Tristain! Help gather up your deity!"

The warlocks packed the cart with straw and layered blankets, and then placed the Mastaren neatly on top. At least he slept peacefully now. They covered him over with a sacred shroud, a deity cloth Wikshonites carried around and worshipped in the Mastaren's absence, the finest weaving in all the Darklands, made with special wools and flax, and dyed black with a specific mixture. Covering him head to toe would protect him from the sun. On the long road to Wikhaihli, Knilma intended to do everything in her power to restore his energy and wits.

Knilma boarded the cart and planted herself by his head. The warlocks loaded her sedan on a confiscated pack donkey along with other confiscated supplies and then took the animals' reins. The other shamans walked beside the cart with Tamas, whose beautiful young eyes lingered long on Wikshen's form under the shroud.

As Wikshen's entourage filed out of the village, a filthy young girl ran up the path toward them. Paigess grabbed her drum beater, ready to send an earthen tremor under her feet if she meant any harm to their deity, but Knilma raised her arm to prevent it.

"You're the weeping girl from earlier. What do you want?"

"I want to go with him!"

Knilma smiled and lifted an eyebrow. "Do you now? What's your name?"

"It's Myrtle," Gertrude answered for her. "This girl was on trial for witchery when Wikshen stormed into the hall. She's not a witch at all, though. A boy from this town had fallen in love with her. He kidnapped her from her hermit-father's cabin and brought her here for marriage. But his parents didn't like her. They accused her of being a witch who had cast a love spell over him. The townspeople were working through the issue when it happened—"

"I have to go with you, or they'll kill me," Myrtle said, on the edge of hysteria.

Knilma studied her face, heart-shaped with a button nose, her chin held low. "You first said you wanted to go with *him*, not us."

Frowning, Myrtle nodded sharply. "I do. He...he saved my life. They sentenced me to an immediate death right before he appeared in a violent rampage. He saved me, and I love him!" The girl's eyes flashed, bright and maniacal.

Knilma laughed and patted her chest when it began to ache. "Good answer, girl. This is how it happens. Wikshen inspires new followers wherever he goes, a fascinating concept to witness. You'll have to tidy yourself. You might be cute under all that grime. Come on, if you want. You'll walk behind him and do lots of pondering. You'll learn the prayers while you walk too."

Myrtle bowed, and Knilma showed her palm. "Hold on." She pointed downward. "Take your shoes off. Wikshonites don't wear shoes."

The girl furrowed her brow. "Seriously, marm?"

"Seriously."

She bent and untied the straps from around her ankles and tossed her little leather shoes away.

Knilma pointed to the lumps of Wikshen's feet under the shroud. He looked like a dead body under there. "He doesn't wear shoes, so why should you? Your feet'll be bleeding long before we get home, but you'll get used to this life. Now off we go!"

The cart rolled forward. Casting a quick glance over her shoulder, Myrtle trotted at the cart's pace.

Kalea lay in bed, drained and lethargic. Ignoring the murmurs of the strangers in the dark room, she stared at the moon through the window. Dorhen wasn't in this settlement they'd found. But she *knew* she'd found him back there—and lost him again.

The door creaked open, and Bowaen crept in. "How is she?" he asked.

The village woman answered, "I imagine she's awake. She's been staring at the window for the last hour since I came back in here. Does she have a habit of sleeping with her eyes open?"

"No," Bowaen said, already headed to her bedside. "Hey, girl," he said softly. "How you feelin'?"

Kalea blinked her eyes for the first time she could remember and shrugged into her blanket. She kept staring at the moon.

Bowaen cleared his throat. "The doyen of this place likes us," he said. "He says we can stay for a while." A nervous, one-beat laugh followed his statement. "We'll…we'll rest here as long as you need."

Kalea didn't care to talk right now. She had been dragged in here kicking and wailing, crying herself to dehydration and exhaustion. They'd left Dorhen out in the grasslands. He was out there, and she lay around in here. It should be Dorhen kneeling at her bedside right now…

"Um," Bowaen continued, "I'm not good at this sort of thing. I never even done this for Del when he was a kid." He slowly leaned forward, pecked a fast kiss on her forehead, and then leaped to his feet. "If you're hungry or something, these ladies will be in here with you. Ask 'em for anything you might need." He exited the room.

Kalea released a long breath. Bowaen didn't believe she saw Dorhen in the mist. He might be correct, but she'd certainly seen someone or some*thing*. Unless she really was mentally ill and had managed to hallucinate him. Either she wasn't mentally ill and was a Luschian, or her Luschian-ness made her mentally ill. Whatever the fact was, it had to be the reason her parents put her in the convent.

A thought suddenly struck her. Did Kalea's parents know of her Luschian identity? Could they be Luschian too? Or just her mother?

Didn't Kerlin say only women were Luschian? Her mother had never mentioned such a thing. Her household kept faithful to the One Creator. The One Creator was all she ever knew. When she'd entered the convent, could the convent personnel have known? Father Liam? If so, why didn't they tell her? Did Dorhen know about Luschians? Could that be what attracted him to her?

All of this was just speculation. She'd never seen anything, in all the books she'd ever cracked open, of Luschians in ancient lore—besides Kerlin's old book, of course. She was Luschian, but apparently no one knew that. They saw her symptoms and wrote them up as "mentally ill."

*I am Luschian,* Kalea conceded to herself.

Suddenly her heart bounced, fluttered, and then hammered at the revelation that back in the convent, when Dorhen had started acting desperate—when he kissed her in the cellar—now she realized what it all meant. Why hadn't it struck her sooner?

She sat up too fast and her head spun. She needed some food. She whined.

"Miss? You okay?" one of the two attending women asked.

"Can I have some food?" Kalea replied.

"Of course."

They both went out, to Kalea's relief, leaving her alone in the dim light of the moon and the fireplace. She needed a moment to herself. She rubbed her chest where her heart pounded. Her throat had gone dry, nearly to the extreme the poisonous fruit had caused. "Oh, dear Creator," she muttered, "why? Couldn't You, if not anyone else, have warned me?"

Dorhen. Back in the convent.

"I had dreams," he'd said when they stood on the cliff with the old well, pouring their hearts out. His voice echoed loud and clear in her memory. He'd said the dreams were "so real, more real than this."

Dorhen's dreams of Kalea. Her dreams of him. They were the same dream.

Kalea's lip quivered. All at once, she wanted to weep, scream, and beg the Creator for His mercy. She'd done a wicked thing. Many wicked things! Kalea had dreamwalked into Dorhen's dreams and virtually seduced him. He'd never cast love spells on her; she'd been doing that to him! Her dreamwalking shenanigans had teased him to the point of sneaking into her convent cellar, spilling his emotional truth all over her, and begging her to let him love her. In her fear, she'd dashed his moonstone to the floor and run away. It was all her fault. What other evil magical abilities did she possess?

Should she try Dorhen's dream again tonight? The too-recent

memory of her earlier mistake chilled her spine. She'd only succeeded in dreamwalking on purpose to visit the so-called Dreamer. She could return to his dream to ask him questions and report her escape from Valltalhiss, but dreamwalking again would be a sin. She'd already done enough of it to poor Dorhen. She'd cast a spell for the Dreamer and dealt with the sanguinesent too. If Kalea hadn't been on her way to Kullixaxuss before, she was bound there now. She would also now owe the Dreamer for his help, and she didn't want to accompany the sanguinesent back to him. Dorhen was most important.

She would avoid the sanguinesent, never visit the Dreamer's dream again, and find Dorhen. To hell with finding Remenaxice's brother, Adrayeth! She didn't have time for anyone beyond the ones who suffered under the sorcerers' cruelty. When she found Dorhen, she would right the wrong she'd done him. She'd apologize for all her dreamwalking, and then give him every bit of herself until her penance to him was paid.

# Chapter 32
# What is a Struggle with the Red Kingsorcerer and the Black Shadow God

Kalea ran her comb through her damp hair for the ninety-ninth and one hundredth strokes. The candlelit air warmed her clean skin, lovely and soft for the first time in over two months. Earlier, the village doyen's wife had taken her stitches out; now, her leg wore two wide stripes of puffy pink scars with more healing to do yet. She'd spent most of the day sleeping, something she'd never done in her life, neither at the convent nor on the road. A surreal calmness and refreshment graced her being today, and strangely mingled with her lingering guilt for Dorhen.

"I must be losing my grip on reality," she whispered, absentmindedly running the brush through her hair for the one hundred and fifth stroke.

During her bath, she resolved not to mention her Dorhen sighting again. Either she had seen him yesterday or she imagined it. Things had been a little too strange lately. To be honest, all the strangeness originated with Dorhen's first appearance in her life. Today, she donned a new skin. After all the processing she'd done in bed under the moonlight, she'd come to terms with her new Luschian self.

Last night, the doyen's wife gave her tea that made her fall asleep, and she awoke in a shroud of mental mist, her memory of seeing Dorhen both hazy and unlikely, while her older memory of luring him into dreamwalking seduction sharpened in its new reality. Her feelings for him would never change. She loved him, and she wanted him.

Since she missed dinner last night, she ate some bread before taking her bath, but tonight's dinner would begin soon. She left the water in the wooden wash tub dark and filthy. A heaviness weighed on her heart as the water, tainted with her shed grime, reminded her of an important piety.

Kalea put the brush down and turned to the dim sunset beaming through a window. She knelt under the light and prayed, "My dear Creator, I've done terrible things…" Her voice caught. Confession was usually difficult, but she'd never committed a sin as horrible as casting sorcery spells before. "I don't even know where to start. I must go as far back as Dorhen. That's when I stopped confessing. I understand if You're angry with me."

She paused to consider her personal revelation of being a Luschian. What did it mean to her religion? According to Kerlin, a god named Lusche made the Luschians for such a bizarre purpose: to neutralize the Thaccilian race. Did it mean she should pray to Lusche instead? She dipped her head and made a dry breathy sob. Her heart hurt. She couldn't pray to another god. She loved the Creator. She hated to make the thought, but...

*Does the Creator still love me?* She bit her thumb to stop her tears. With her head bowed, she tried again, "My Creator..."

A shudder surged through her entire body, halting her prayer and rattling her so violently her hands separated from their pose. A rumble followed, rolling through her ears: *Koorrroorrr—calls for you—oooorrrrr.*

Rising on her knees, she froze in shock and listened hard. The sounds vanished as fast as they came. "What was that?"

The door creaked open, and she jumped a mile high. "C'mon, girl, ye ready for dinner?" one of the village women asked.

Kalea leaped into a stand and caused a dull soreness to shoot through her healing leg. "I'm more than ready to eat," she said. She shook off the queer fright. A new awkwardness replaced it, and she added, "But I'm naked." She spread her hands helplessly. They'd taken her clothes to wash them.

"I brought this for ye." The woman handed her a length of dark grey fabric with ties and helped Kalea figure out how to wrap it around herself. All the other women wore the same wrapped dress bound over the breasts with the ties winding over the shoulders and across the back. Her collarbone, shoulders, and arms were naked, which did nothing for Kalea's comfort.

She hugged herself along the walk from the bathing stall to the big house's center. A slight soreness registered in her leg with each step, but she could finally walk on it again. She'd had to go without her staff since losing it in Valltalhiss.

This house was big because it belonged to the village's doyen. The entire village ate together there. Near the large fire, all of their clothing hung to dry. Kalea's friends were also wearing Darklandic clothes courtesy of the villagers. A jovial roar met her in the large room; everyone had already assembled to begin their feast. A large, roasted goat off the spit lay carved on the table. Gaije was refusing a slice when Kalea took a seat next to him.

"I forgot. You Clanless don't eat meat," the serving woman said. "Haven't met with your kind in a while. Good thing we got carrots and cabbage." She moved along to the next person.

"Elves don't eat meat?" Kalea asked him.

"We eat fish sometimes," he said. "Haven't you noticed I always refused the dried jerky Bowaen would offer me?"

"I assumed you simply didn't want any."

When the next serving woman approached with a pitcher of mead and filled Gaije's cup, he slid the cup away. "I need water instead."

The serving woman rolled her eyes and slid his cup over to Kalea before walking away, mumbling curses.

Kalea hid her giggle behind her hand, a giggle despite her heavy heart. "So elves don't eat meat and they don't drink alcohol," she said.

Del, who sat at Gaije's other side, added, "They're barrels of fun, aren't they?"

Kalea laughed again. She basked in the atmosphere of this place's warmth, food, and hospitality, a nice change to what had become normal in her life. She kept her mood in check and ignored how hard the local women eyed her after the show she'd put on yesterday, crying and worrying about Dorhen.

Doyen Carnan, who sat next to Bowaen, rambled excitedly about their arrival, but Bowaen kept the man's ideas at bay.

"No," Bowaen said, smiling and also working at a wad of meat between his teeth. "We can't stay, sir. We're looking for some people."

"You'll return soon, though!" the doyen said with a jolly ring in his voice. "My village could use some more strong men, and your woman, she appears better today. I will arrange for her to marry my son, Carnan the Second." He motioned to a sturdy man at his shoulder, a younger version of himself with thick bones and a single eyebrow shading his eyes instead of two. The doyen's son leaned over the table to nod and smile at Kalea.

Bowaen choked on his gulp of mead and exchanged glances with her.

The doyen continued, "Even the Clanless can stay."

"You mean Gaije?" Bowaen pointed to their stoic, red-haired companion.

"Yes, yes! The Clanless elves are strong and duty-bound—I know this. But he can't marry any of my women. That's the condition."

"Why not?" Bowaen asked, which would relieve the rest of their curiosity too.

"Because my village needs people, man!" He clapped Bowaen firmly on the shoulder. "You see? No new people comes from a union of human and elf."

Kalea's mouth dropped open. "Really?"

The doyen nodded his head deeply with a sincere tension in his lips.

Gaije shrugged at Kalea when she regarded him. "You've nothing to worry about, Doyen Carnan," Gaije said. "I'm leaving as soon as the sun rises."

Kalea couldn't let her sad thought go. "That means Dorhen and I…" Her voice trailed off. Then again, she was Luschian now. What did *that* mean for her and Dorhen? Could she create a family with him if she, in fact, wasn't human? There was no way she could find out beyond trying. Even if she were to turn around and go back to ask the Thaccilians about it, who knew if they'd know anything?

Bowaen caught on to what she mumbled about; his eyes rounded at her. He turned back to their host. "Doyen Carnan," he said, "we appreciate your hospitality for tonight, but we gotta go tomorrow. No joke."

"Not a good idea," the doyen said, keeping his proud, happy countenance. "You say you come from the far south, so I assume you don't understand this land."

"We don't," Bowaen said.

"There are factions in many places, hiding in the hills and the mountains and the forests, and many cities."

"What kinds of factions?"

"Factions who tame lightning and other elements of nature. Factions who speak to the dead and make bodily relations with evil entities from the bowels of Kullixaxuss."

Kalea perked up at the word "Kullixaxuss." The doyen took several more gulps of his drink, leaving her in suspense. Back in the Lightlands, most folk called it "hell;" Kullixaxuss was the ancient name for it, spoken so easily by none other than the sanguinesent. At the beginning of time, the One Creator had emerged from that evil place and rescued His children. He created the world as humanity knew it so they could all live out their lives, and then He created a paradise their souls would move on to after they died. Otherwise, they'd all go back to Kullixaxuss—unless they happened to drift away from the Creator's grace, in which case they'd return to Kullixaxuss anyway.

Her group exchanged glances. Doyen Carnan continued, "These factions…They try to intimidate us. But my village fights. My village farms and herds and breeds and *fights!*" When he yelled the last word, the whole hall, men and women, raised their cups and cheered. "That's why we need lots and lots of people. We will grow our domain and resist the factions and cults who want to tame us."

"Doyen," Bowaen said in all seriousness, "do the factions wear red?"

The doyen's cheerful smile turned blood-thirsty at Bowaen's question. "Yes! Red! Yellow! Purple! Black! They wear these colors—there are lots of different factions! But my village kills them!" The whole room cheered again. "We will not bow to the red kingsorcerer *or* the black shadow god! We'd sooner die!"

Bowaen asked before he could yell again, "What will your king do about them?"

The doyen barked out, "King? King! My man, Darklanders have not bowed to a king in seven hundred years or more. Where've you been?"

At Kalea's side, Gaije mumbled to his plate of boiled vegetables, "On the better side of the gate my ancestors built."

"The black shadow god," the doyen said, "he kills all our kings. Every time. Every time the Darklands breeds a king, man, the black shadow god tears him down and eats his bones!"

Kalea reared her head, clamping her mouth shut.

"We Darklanders, we never forget." Carnan's voice mellowed after another deep gulp. "We teach our children reading and writing and history, as well as how to kill, farm, and herd." He beat his own chest with a firm, flat palm. "It's us against them in this world. Us good people. Some are like my fine settlement here, and some prefer to move around like our nomadic neighbors—they are our friends. We fight together against those who dabble in unnatural forces one should not dabble in."

The doyen chugged the rest of his drink and pounded the empty tankard on the table for a refill. Before Bowaen could ask another question, the doyen grabbed his shoulder, his speech beginning to slur. "My friend, we Darklanders exchange news. My fine women told me you'd give me news, so give it."

"We found some bad stuff along the way here," Bowaen said, caution dragging at his voice.

The doyen's lips tightened. "Mmm. Yes, indeed."

Bowaen continued, "A village got destroyed."

Carnan's eyes hardened. "Where?"

"South and west."

"South and west!" the doyen repeated. "This is bad news. They are our neighbors we trade with. Fine people, very fine! Did anyone survive? How many died?"

"Um," Bowaen began carefully, "a lot of people lay dead. We don't know how many escaped, but many dead people cluttered the place. We didn't find any survivors."

The doyen stood and waved his arm. "Take action! He says the Weavers were attacked!"

Most of the town hall jumped up and ran out the door. A frantic bell rang outside in the stirred commotion. The ones who remained inside rushed around, boarding up the windows and stashing spices and furs under certain rough-cut floorboards.

The doyen reseated himself at the banquet table. "This is what we do. When we hear news of attack, we prepare. You are all safe here."

Gaije remained silent, but his eyes turned wide and his neck extended.

"We can't be locked in here," Bowaen said with an edge of doubt creeping into his voice.

Carnan remained calm in his burgeoning drunkenness. "You're safe in here, do not fear. You see, we live in days of trial. Some Darklanders choose the red kingsorcerer and some choose the black shadow god, but we Herders, we choose *freedom*!"

All of his people who remained in the hall cheered again.

"Now listen," he said, turning back to Bowaen. "Tomorrow, you will go with some of my scouts. Show them the ruined village you found. We can salvage their tools and bring the survivors home if any of them returned. Did you see any clue left behind? Any at all to try to pinpoint which faction made the attack?"

Bowaen's eyes bounced back and forth among his friends. "Someone we are tracking," he explained. "A sorcerer with blue hair. We found blue hair strands on one of the victims."

Carnan shot to his feet again. He might've wobbled, but he wasn't quite drunk enough yet. "That's Wikshen! The black shadow god!"

Bowaen squinted. "Who?"

The doyen grabbed Bowaen's shoulders. "We've already got news of his return! Wikshen! Why in the world are you tracking him?"

This time, Gaije stood. "Because he took my sister away."

The doyen's eyes rolled over to Gaije, and he offered a helpless smile. "My good man, you've lost someone, and I'm sorry for you, but listen to what I say. She's lost."

Gaije stiffened. Kalea poised to put her hand on his arm. Nobody needed his hotheaded rashness right now. "That's not true," Gaije replied, more calmly than she expected. "He has her, and I have to take her back home to her mother."

The doyen shook his head gravely. "She's gone, Clanless. I'm sure the shadow god ate her for breakfast long ago."

Gaije lunged forward, and Del caught him before any violence could be incited in this man's house.

Kalea put herself into the confusion. "Doyen," she said, "I'm looking for the blue-haired sorcerer too."

Carnan pointed at her. "Why? Are you one of his whore-witches?"

A string of futile no's popped out of Bowaen's mouth in an attempt to calm the scene. "He has our loved ones, doyen. We gotta find him. Can you tell us where he might be going? Where's his lair?"

"All of you must leave here! Wikshen lovers!"

Kalea shrieked over all the noise and shouting, "But can't you understand, we have to rescue some innocent people?"

"I'll have none of it!" the doyen roared. "You want to go find him? Go! But don't come back here and expect the security I provide. My offer has expired."

"Where can we find this Wikshen?" Bowaen tried again.

"I don't know. I don't go looking for such abominations! Try Alkeer—those people are corrupt enough!"

"Alkeer," Bowaen repeated. Gaije pulled Kalea away from the table as the doyen grew more hostile and insistent for them to leave. Before he could yell anything else or act, a handful of his villagers roared into the hall.

"What is it?" the doyen demanded. "Wikshen?"

"Monster, sir, monster!"

Kalea's eyes popped and found Bowaen's doing the same. The sanguinesent's chattering resonated from outside the door before a set of tentacles slithered through the cracks and tore one side of it off the hinges.

"Sanguinesent!" Kalea shrieked.

"What in the Swine's asshole?" Bowaen barked.

"It's tracking me!" Kalea explained as Gaije pulled her toward the back rooms. "It's had some kind of mental connection to me ever since the caves, and…" She stopped herself before getting into the long story about the Dreamer and dreamwalking and casting spells. "Remember when it was talking to me in my mind back in Valltalhiss?"

"I reckon we're leaving now!" Bowaen yelled at their group.

A full collection of the sanguinesent's thralls banged their way into the hall and engaged the confused villagers.

Del snatched their clothes off the lines hanging by the fire, and they all scrambled to collect whatever else they owned. They were forced to keep the new clothes the doyen had let them borrow. Shoes in hand, they left the doyen's people to keep the sanguinesent busy while they slipped out one of the back windows. A gap broken into the palisade wall marked the monster's entry point. It proved the closest and fastest way out of the settlement.

The sanguinesent's mental voice rumbled in Kalea's head as they dashed through the hole to freedom. *The kingsorcerer calls.*

# Chapter 33
## What is in Lehomis's Heart

Anonhet returned later than usual from her music lessons in the Desteer hall. She almost didn't notice Lehomis sitting by the oven under the kitchen's pavilion as she hurried by.

"Oh, hello, Grandfather," she said with a tiny shake in her voice.

"Have a good afternoon?"

She dipped her chin. "Yes, thank you. I...I finally mastered the ending of 'Leaves are Falling in Summer' on the flute."

He forced a smile. "Good. You should play it for me later."

"I will." She wrung her flute in her hands, practically dancing in place.

"Talk to any Tinharri *saehgahn* today?" He blew a smoke ring at the end of his question.

Her face swelled like a ripe tomato. "Only for a few minutes. You know how they are. They go all around with their incessant chatter."

A smile curled his lips. "Like a bunch of *shi-helah* mother-in-laws, huh?"

Her hands tightened around the flute. "Um, Grandfather, where's Tirnah?"

He let his smile go. "She's inside, setting the table."

"Thank you." She gave a hasty curtsy and hurried away.

Letting her go, Lehomis bit his lip. It was none of his business. The lass had come into adulthood a year ago; she could choose anyone she desired. He'd give her a long few minutes before going in to dinner.

The next day, he joined the lads at the creek for a bath. Less of them showed to bathe than normal because most of the *saehgahn* insisted on staying in the village to keep an eye on the Tinharris. The mood thickened the air with a somber quietness. Those who did talk to each other kept to whispering, usually to grumble about how much they hated the royals, how smug the royals were, and what they'd like to do to them.

Lehomis warned them to keep the complaints low because the royals' presence in the clan hadn't killed the *faerhain's* interest in spying on their bath. In fact, their visit had intensified the *faerhain's* scrutiny and might possibly speed their decision-making process. They were now tasked with weighing the Tinharri males against the Lockheirhen ones. Luckily for the Lockheirhen males, they outnumbered the Tinharris.

Lehomis instructed them to smile and stand up in the water often. They heeded his advice and started their usual games and contests designed for showing off. Petty wrestling matches among friends were a great way to show spying females their strengths. Lehomis sat on the bank and cleaned his long hair in sections, smiling and laughing at the antics.

*The faerhain will make their choices*, he thought. *They'll choose the* real saehgahn *who uphold traditional laws and customs.*

Lehomis's suspicion that plenty of *faerhain* were watching was proven correct when a chorus of high voices bickered in commotion from a short distance up the bank, hidden behind a wall of wild hydrangea in full bloom. A sharp, commanding voice cut through the distant voices.

The *saehgahn* paused in their games. Lehomis stood up, naked as the day he was born, and went to investigate with his long hair draped over an arm.

"Alhannah!" he snapped when he stepped into the thicket where the *faerhain* were hiding. She stood with a stern gesture poised at the younger females. "What's the issue here?"

"I caught these childish little pigeons watching you."

Lehomis spread his hands. "We know they were watching. What's the actual problem?" A clutch of other naked *saehgahn* crowded behind him.

"It's no longer allowed. You know this, Elder. We've talked about it. And won't you all cover yourselves?" She threw her shawl at the group of males but didn't have much more to lend them. The shawl fell to the muddy, foot-trodden ground.

"Lass, I'll tell you again. Looking at their form and physique helps the *faerhain* choose the best of them."

"And I'll tell *you* again, Elder. The Desteer have long ago decided that this practice is vulgar and unfair."

"Why? Because we're better built than those Tinharri royals?"

A series of sniffs and snorts from the other males followed. Alhannah narrowed her eyes, and Lehomis couldn't miss the redness flaring along the outer rim of her ears.

He leaned forward and squinted. "Question: what clan did you say you were from, Alhannah?"

"I didn't, Elder."

"You're the single maiden not born to this clan. And funny how you happen to be older, more experienced, and more talented than our own

Desteer maidens—putting you snugly in the highest chair of the hall. Where were you before you were traded to my clan?"

She raised her chin and kept her eyes firm on his. "I was traded here as a gift to your clan."

Lehomis wound his free hand in the air with his other arm supporting his hair like a draping black sash. "A gift from…?"

"The royal palace."

"The royal palace, which is the home of the…"

"Tinharri Clan."

"There ya go, lass!" He snapped his fingers. "Tell me somethin', do the Tinharri Clan males all keep their clothes on around female folk? Are they as proper and decent as you Desteer are trying to make *us*?"

Alhannah frowned and kept silent until Lehomis crossed his arms.

Lehomis continued, "They're dying out, I hear, so I'm guessing they're as eager to flaunt their prowess and their bodies around as we are."

Besides the confrontation itself, this meeting was giving the collection of six present females an up-close gander at the eight *saehgahn* standing behind Lehomis. The females all looked about as interested in Alhannah's answers as they were in the males' bodies—maybe more so.

A slight glint of moisture now showed on Alhannah's painted face. She stood firm and silent until Lehomis laughed and waved a hand.

"Look, I know the Tinharris' plight. I've seen this happen before, though not in my clan. Sure, for now, the Tinharris are bending the rules and asking females for marriage instead of the other way 'round. But listen to me. You *won't* change my customs and laws so your Tinharri cousins can get a leg up in the competition. This has to be fair. The *faerhain* can still choose any *saehgahn* they desire. If none of them choose your Tinharri, that's fair too. Whatever happens, I'll expect you not to whine and pout about it."

He noticed how hard he pointed his finger at her after his speech ended. He lowered it and waited for her response.

"Yes," she finally said, "I'm Tinharri too. I will talk again with my sisters about the changes to decision-making protocol. But, Lehomis…" Now she pointed her finger at him. "You have to relax and let things take their course. After they leave, we can have more meetings to find out how to help Clan Lockheirhen."

"Thank you. Isn't it nice to talk things out?" He turned. "C'mon, lads, finish your bath. And smile…the *faerhain* are hiding in this thicket."

Bright One help him, Lehomis didn't trust a word Alhannah said. He'd try to be civil and keep a stiff upper lip if any amount of *faerhain* left the clan with new Tinharri husbands at the end of the week, but he struggled with trusting anything she promised.

Along the walk home, Lehomis took a short path through the brush. Murmuring voices caught his ear, and the strained sounds sped his feet to a dead run. Branches caught his fresh, clean hair. At a small clearing off the path, he stopped fast.

"Grandfather!" Anonhet said, her face beet red. She jerked her hand away from the Tinharri male she was with, the same *saehgahn* as the last time.

"Anonhet, is he bothering you?" Unmarried *faerhain* and *saehgahn* weren't supposed to meet alone in the forest unless they had exchanged the marriage token and officially made the decision—or in the case of emergency.

"No, Grandfather," she stuttered, and put her hands behind her back.

Lehomis made a conscious effort to close his mouth. "Oh." He pulled his pipe out of his robe pocket and put the stem between his teeth. "Then what are you doing?" Surely they weren't going to perform the marriage rites here! It was a terrible spot; they'd have to pick some place more private.

"I…I didn't know you'd take your bath today."

"But today's Thursday."

Her eyebrows narrowed. "Is it?"

"Anonhet, are you all right?"

She put her hand against her forehead. "Yes, of course."

Her Tinharri suitor stepped forward, "Elder, please allow me to—"

Ignoring his words, Lehomis snatched the little poetry book from his hand. He'd been fingering the thing the whole time. It was a different size and color than the one the prince kept in his pocket.

"Elder, please!"

Lehomis dodged his hands with ease and focused his eyes on the book. If this lad was a Lockheirhen, he would've been fast and precise enough to snatch the book back. "Look how slow he is, Anonhet. The Tinharris are so engrossed in books they don't get near as much practice."

"Elder, we practice five hours a day at our physical abilities."

"That's funny, lad." Though he considered the lad's words a joke, Lehomis didn't laugh. When he moved to open the book, the idiot was still too slow to take it back.

Lehomis was eager to read a line of its ridiculous poetry aloud, but the pipe fell out of his mouth instead. In his shock, he failed to collect it. A picture met his eyes instead of a page full of words. He turned the book upside-down and back over. The drawing in the book diagrammed female genitalia, labeling all of its points and suggesting what to do with them.

An illness roiled up in Lehomis's stomach. The Tinharri lad's face shifted to white.

"What's the matter, Grandfather?" Anonhet's ignorant curiosity showed clearly.

Lehomis snapped the book closed, forced a smile, and sighed through his nose. Legally, he could kill this lad, right here and now. He'd tell the Desteer how and why he did it later, only to be excused, go home to supper, and enjoy sweet dreams for the rest of the night. But this was the Tinharri Clan. The royals, the governing clan who were dying out. They deserved it if they were so weak that they needed such a book to cheat the marriage rites. If a *saehgahn* couldn't satisfy his *faerhain* on the marriage pelt, the marriage would be rejected by the Desteer the next morning, and all the neighboring *saehgahn* would laugh at him and rejoice for the *faerhain's* extended availability.

He tossed the book back to the lad, its pages fluttering loudly. "Oh, nothin'." He paced around to the side. The lad's face didn't regain any color when he got his book back. "I told Alhannah I wouldn't interfere."

He leaned over a fallen log to see the bundle of things the Tinharri lad had brought, part of which consisted of a wooly white ox pelt, rolled and bound with twine. It was dry and lacked the raw smell of blood. Lehomis pointed. "Did you buy that?" *Saehgahn* were supposed to kill the white ox, skin it, and then arrange the place where the marriage rites would occur.

The lad didn't answer the question, but Lehomis knew anyway. He drew his mouth wide in effort not to let his anger show. "That's fine." He picked up his pipe from the ground and put it back in his mouth. "Good, good." He shoved his hands into his pockets. He wouldn't bother asking if the lad held a marriage token. Why would he follow that rule and none of the others?

He regarded Anonhet. "See ya." As he walked away, a new rise of murmurs flowed behind him.

"But please," the Tinharri's voice whispered harshly.

Another string of bickering. Lehomis turned around to see Anonhet jerking her hand away from him again. She shoved the lad in annoyance.

"Grandfather?" she called, pattering up the path to join him.

*Good lass.* Lehomis smiled and offered his arm. He'd kill the lad with his bare hands if he tried to follow. The Tinharri stepped onto the path but stopped halfway. Lehomis threw a pointed finger at him as a silent warning, and then he took Anonhet home.

***

Anonhet didn't talk about the Tinharri lad much along the walk back, and Lehomis didn't pry. She acted as frazzled as he'd ever seen her.

"He was a know-it-all," Anonhet said after a long several minutes. "Drove me crazy."

Lehomis laughed through his nose and immediately turned serious. "Did you send him the marriage token?" he asked.

Anonhet frowned at him. "No. He just... He nagged me to marry him until I agreed. I felt guilty for skirting the rules." She sighed, and Lehomis mimicked her.

"You did right in the end, lass."

Another stretch of silence passed.

"Grandfather, why do we have this custom? Why do the *faerhain* have to make the decision?"

"Because if it were left up to the *saehgahn*, they'd all kill each other until a meager few remained alive."

She cocked her head in his peripheral vision. "If that happened, there would be an even number of males and females."

Lehomis kept his eyes forward as he smiled. "Sure, but we wouldn't have enough strong bodies to defend our clans and country."

"Imagine all those funerals."

He nodded once. "*Laugaulentrei* wouldn't be a lake anymore, it would be a giant mound of ash."

"That would be so sad." She mewed the statement. "Makes me glad the onus is on the *faerhain*. It keeps the peace between the *saehgahn*."

"It's nice and fair, isn't it?"

"Yes. I never thought about it before. I always thought we *faerhain* were lucky...or spoiled. But it's a hard decision."

"We all have difficult roles, don't we?"

"Mm-hmm." She surveyed the forest landscape in the waning daylight. "I sometimes worry about their feelings."

"Whose feelings?"

She shrugged. "Everyone's. The *saehgahn*. And...Gaije's."

Lehomis kept quiet, giving her as much room to speak as she needed.

"At my *gaulaerhainha* ceremony, when I set out on my walk to the center of town...my heavy feet weighed me down. I'll never forget the silence of the village. Some of the *saehgahn* looked...stressed, to say the least. I tried not to look at anyone individually, but I remember red faces and tears on one or two. Most of them were bowed in prayer, faces practically in the mud. It was so odd to know I caused such tension... I especially didn't look at Gaije when I walked past him, but I think he stressed over it too. I could feel it."

Lehomis listened hard. It was not his place to ask questions, but he'd certainly hear anything she wanted to tell him. The empathy she had felt on the day of her coming-of-age ceremony was a strong sense all *faerhain* had. It came stronger than that of human women. The stronger the sense, the more suited to the Desteer a female elf would be. Hearing her story rekindled his own memory of suspense. The same phenomenon of tension and emotion occurred every time *farhah* transformed into *faerhain*.

"I'll admit, Grandfather, I thought about the Desteer hall. What would happen if I became one? Where would I end up? Did I have enough talent to perform Desteer duties?" She smiled in his peripheral vision. "I still can't guess. On the other hand, I pondered if I could be selfless enough to be a wife. Could I really develop enough strength to run a household? To make hard decisions? To go through childbirth? And I knew very well how life went for Tirnah and Trisdahen. She rarely got to see him.

"And I remember Mhina's birth. I was eleven. Several Desteer maidens rushed about the house, pushing me out of the way but also insisting I watch. I could feel Tirnah's pain, but whenever we made eye contact during her labor, she smiled—always trying to send a message that she was fine, or that everything would be okay...eventually.

"Afterward, the Desteer lectured me about how painful it was—for both parties. If I decided to become a wife, I'd be in Tirnah's place. If I chose to be a maiden, I'd be delivering babes around the village. And she made sure to tell me about the deaths I'd see too. Such a confusing and long night."

By now, Lehomis could only look at the ground moving under his feet, becoming darker as the sun set.

She continued, "The same heaviness and confusion returned on the day of my *gaulaerhainha* when I walked to the center of the village."

"What made you choose the home?"

"Tirnah." Anonhet inhaled long through her nose. "I wanted to be like her. And to be honest...I want you to be a grandfather to my children."

Lehomis couldn't suppress his smile or his urge to squeeze his arm around her shoulders as they walked. "You got it, lass."

They arrived back at home to find it empty. "Tirnah's not in her room," Anonhet said, trotting back through the rough-cut corridor of Lehomis's cave-like home.

Lehomis suppressed the twinge of fright threatening to stir his heart. "What all places did she say she'd go today?"

"I know she went to trade for some medicinal herbs earlier," Anonhet offered, "but she should've been back by now."

Lehomis turned back to the door. "I'll check the apothecary—and her old house. For all we know, she may have dropped back by to put out a tear or two."

The widow who kept the herbal garden confirmed Tirnah's visit and pointed in the general direction she had gone upon leaving. "She didn't say where she'd go next or mention what else she might've needed," the elder *faerhain* said.

Lehomis thanked her and walked away, gaining more speed in the low-sinking sun. Around the bend, off from the Desteer hall he found her. With a Tinharri *saehgahn*.

The shock of such a sight stopped all his senses. The other *saehgahn*'s fingers slid into her honey-gold hair, a smile plastered on his face. The world around them vanished, and so did all of Lehomis's rational thoughts.

Lehomis charged forward with a roar and tackled the other male, who also gave a yell. Tirnah screamed, and soon the air filled with all manner of voices. The patter of feet crowded in around them, but all Lehomis knew was an awareness of himself and his opponent. This Tinharri would leave in a jar, bypass the palace, and go straight to *Laugaulentrei* to battle forevermore with Trisdahen's ashes.

Unadulterated vigor pulsed through Lehomis; he was as young and alive as he'd always been. Aside from longevity, his curse endowed him with everlasting strength and youth, and now this royal buffoon would see the extent of his potent *saehgahn* fury. Every knock of his fist against the lad's royal face sent a loud message.

He barely noticed his own body being dragged off the young royal's. The Tinharri lad scrambled to his feet to try to collect whatever measure of dignity he could, but all Lehomis wanted to do was sweep him onto his ass again.

"Sorry, Elder," a voice said by his ear. A pair of his own Lockheirhen *saehgahn* had pulled him off the Tinharri.

"Desteer's orders," the other lad said in his opposite ear.

With a deep breath, Lehomis's vision expanded. His heart continued its hard throbbing. A large group of elves, male and female, had gathered around to gawk.

"Is Tirnah all right?" one of the murmurs asked.

"The Elder sure is angry," a child's voice rang out.

A pair of teenaged *saeghar* were smiling and elbowing each other, pointing at the Tinharri with the bloodied face.

Lehomis hadn't paused to gauge the Tinharri's impressive height. He had always been on the short side of the *saehgahn* scale, himself. He didn't care. He could kill this brazen lad—easily.

"What in the Bright One's radiant eye is going on here?" Alhannah stepped into the circle of people with her arms out wide to prevent any more action. She surveyed all the younger Lockheirhen *saehgahn* until her eyes settled and narrowed on Lehomis.

"I was viciously attacked, *Ameiha*, by your village's elder," the Tinharri said, addressing Alhannah in the formal way, and pointed to Lehomis.

Alhannah approached Lehomis, who shook out of the others' grasps. "Elder, is there a reason for such violence? A good one?"

Her voice hardly registered through the blood pounding in his ears. He threw a pointing finger at the Tinharri. "I saw him touching Tirnah!"

Alhannah crossed her arms, her long sleeves draping to the ground. "Was Tirnah in distress? Was she crying? Or trying to pull away?"

Off to the side, Tirnah kept her chin low and her eyes too. Other *faerhains'* hands were gracefully stroking her sleeves.

Lehomis stuttered for a moment. "I'm sure she was," he managed to get out. He couldn't piece anything together in his memory. All he remembered was searching for Tirnah, and in the next moment, he was pummeling someone's face. He wanted to pummel the lad's face some more.

Alhannah approached Tirnah and took her chin in her long fingers. "Was he disturbing you?"

Tirnah's face flared red, and she shook her head.

"We were out for a walk, *Ameiha*," the Tinharri lad said. "She agreed to walk with me, during which she gave me permission to touch her hair. I made sure to ask her first."

Lehomis's eye twitched in his desperate effort not to turn around and attack the lad all over again.

"Is this true?" Alhannah asked Tirnah. The Desteer's hand caressed her face before settling on the side of her skull. She was using a gentle version of *milhanrajea* to catch the truth.

Without much to say, Tirnah nodded her head in short rapid motions. When Alhannah turned back toward Lehomis, her eyes were dull.

She gave a sigh before saying, "Lehomis." Her mouth quirked into a bored frown. "Tirnah confirms that nothing amiss happened here. Why did you attack her suitor?"

"Her *suitor*?" Lehomis stepped forward. His clawing fingers balled into tight fists. The other *saehgahns'* hands grazed his shoulders again.

Alhannah stepped before him with her arms out. "You have to calm down. Can't you see how stressed you've made her? She doesn't need this drama in her current state."

Lehomis waved a hand at the bloody-faced Tinharri lad, "Your royal cousins need to be told which *faerhain* are off limits! We just got back from *Laugaulentrei*. Tirnah is a new widow. Can't you give her a little time?"

Alhannah drummed her fingers on her opposite sleeve until Lehomis finished talking. "In this time of crisis, I'm afraid things might be different. Since the Tinharri Clan is in reproductive famine, and Clan Lockheirhen recently survived a brutal attack, I'm leaving it up to the widows and single *faerhain* to decide if they are ready."

Alhannah turned again to Tirnah, and Lehomis cringed. "Tirnah," she began.

Lehomis put his face in his hands. He couldn't hear this.

Alhannah asked her, "Are you ready to remarry?"

Tirnah raised her bright eyes, rimmed with moisture, and shifted them between Lehomis and her Tinharri "suitor." She licked her lips and worked them. No words followed. She lowered her face.

She ran. Away from the crowd, from the Desteer maiden, from the suitor, and from Lehomis, who couldn't bring himself to follow.

# Chapter 34
# His Sleep

Five days. Five days, Wikshen slept under the sacred shroud on the wagon bed with Knilma sitting beside him, and he showed no signs of awakening. After the first two nights, worry overcame her and she peeled down the shroud in the moonlight to see the peaceful expression on his face. His chest rose and fell easily, his nose clear for the air to pass through. He was merely asleep, nothing to worry about yet. So she let him sleep.

"Will he rise soon, marm?" Tamas asked her when they stopped to rest by a river. A big elder tree grew beside it, shielding Wikshen from the sun in addition to his shroud.

Knilma grazed her old fingers across the shape of his forehead. "When he's ready, girl."

Tamas's big, dark eyes took on the appearance of a starving child hopelessly waiting for a big holiday meal. She trailed her sight along the length of Wikshen's great form.

Knilma had worked on Tamas since the girl's stringy preadolescent age. She'd tutored all the children in Ravivill on the wonders of Wikshen: how beautiful his majesty was, how powerful he was, how he killed the tyrants and blessed his followers and empowered his lovers.

Tamas had been one of the difficult ones, but she came around eventually. She had left the village with Knilma in shocked awe at the news of Wikshen's return. Knilma had lived a long life. She'd seen how most believers didn't actually believe until they saw some form of concrete proof. Any religion was just another faction of people banding together for one purpose or another, and the main flock fell in line simply because it was part of their upbringing. Things changed when miracles turned out to be real.

Even the warlocks tagging along in their group had changed in ways since the night they found their deity, the most notable effect being their renewed respect and the lack of words young men tended to liberally dispense. They no longer snorted and joked and complained like they used to. With Wikshen returned, many other things would change. Not one person who encountered him would be quite the same.

Most of Wikshen's entourage chatted and bickered at the water's edge, drinking heartily and filling their skins. Myrtle, their newest member, ascended the hill, running like the youth she was, to kneel at the back of Wikshen's cart. She'd finally gotten the chance to wash her face and hair.

"Not bad," Knilma said with a smile. She handed the girl her comb. "Fix yourself up as much as possible. We should have fresh clothing waiting for us at Wikhaihli. You're a pretty thing, so I'll make sure you get a place in Wikshen's tower."

Myrtle smiled and bowed her head low. "Thank you, marm."

Knilma turned back to Tamas. "You too, Tamas, have grown into a lovely dark rose. I selected you to accompany us because of your exceptional qualities, both physical and faithful. You will also have a place in Wikshen's tower."

Tamas's face brightened as she lowered it to share a smile with Myrtle. The two girls were extremely different, Tamas with her graceful height, strength, and bronze Darklandic skin; and Myrtle with her fair skin, petite stature, and cute round face. Over the next few months, Knilma would be eyeballing a lot of girls to put in Wikshen's sight. Each generation of Wikshen came with his own different tastes, she understood, so she scrutinized the best of each type to stock his tower. She herself used to have warm auburn hair in her youth, which her Wikshen had not favored despite his own fiery locks, redder than hers. Not that it mattered, since she was a natural-born shaman, and shamans didn't enter into carnal rites in Wikshen's chamber. Shamans stayed celibate altogether, so mostly by vicarious interest did Knilma enjoy the blessings of Wikshen.

Knilma filled her lungs in a long drag through her nose as the day turned to night. They'd been on the move again for the last four hours after stopping by the river. Soon, they'd arrive at Alkeer. That little itch of worry entered her heart again for an instant when she snaked her hand under the shroud to touch Wikshen's hair. He had suffered such anguish when they'd found him. What if his dreams were disturbed? She'd taken to stroking his hair last night and speaking softly to him, especially at night.

"What is he like?" Myrtle asked softly as she walked beside the cart. "His personality?"

Walking beside Myrtle, Tamas perked up to benefit from the question as well. Jax, the warlock walking closest to the cart, also appeared to await the answer.

"Besides divinely right in acting however he wishes?" She chuckled at herself, sighed, and considered a more helpful answer. "Wikshen is the same person in every generation, but wearing a different body each time, so naturally there's bound to be variations. How extreme or slight,

I don't yet know. But he's a passionate and beautiful soul. Others would see him differently from me. Some would see him as a cruel beast who rapes and kills."

"But does he?" Myrtle pressed.

Knilma spread her hands. "You saw what he did in your village. And yet you practically jumped onto this cart and begged to be brought along with him, didn't you?"

Myrtle lowered her chin.

"I'll tell you something." Knilma raised her index finger and paused for effect. "*Nothing* Wikshen does is random." She let another pause follow the statement. "He's not a senseless killing beast. Everything he does has calculation to it, and that's what we'll remember as we observe his antics, won't we?"

Sammial piped up, "And his calculations lead to…"

"Victory," Knilma filled in for him. "Wikshen is a deity who *must* rule. Though you may catch him enjoying sweet desserts, a woman or the scent of a flower, Wikshen has a greater purpose. He also enjoys things we may not, like the cascade of blood or a woman's screams in his ear, battle. If we stand with him, we'll be standing on the side that will prevail over his, and our, enemies. We'll be the ones to survive."

The others nodded. Togha kept his head turned forward as he drove the cart, pulled by his own donkey.

Knilma continued, "But you'll see… There's beauty in his chaos. He doesn't typically stay in his tower at Wikhaihli. He likes to be out here, in the misty hills. I loved it when he'd come home, though." Her eyes wandered along the darkening hills around them. "I quickly got used to his voice screaming through the corridors. He'd yell, 'Knilma!' and I'd run to please whatever serious or petty request he had." Mimicking his call in her hissing voice brought the memory back to the forefront of her mind with a sharpness she hadn't known in a long time. "'Knilma!' He wanted his breakfast. 'Knilma!' One of his concubines angered him, and he wanted me to beat her. 'Knilma!' He…" Her smile dropped. The younger people leaned forward in anticipation. "He suspected Grella was plotting to kill him…"

"Who was Grella?" Tamas asked.

"His favorite concubine. The First Sister for every generation of Wikshen for as long as the title existed. She lived for many ages on Wikshen's blessing. She came to reclaim her title every time Wikshen was reborn, and he always chose her."

Knilma shook her head. "I could never figure out what was it about that tart Wikshen couldn't resist. Her passion and intensity matched his.

Two souls too much alike. He used to get so angry and beat the bloody hell out of her, and she'd smile like a wealthy harlot as I cleaned the blood off her face.

"'He loves me,' she said one day. She spat her blood in my face. Oh, she hated me. It's all coming back to me now. She hated me for some reason, and found flaunting her status as a way to hurt me. As if I'd be jealous of their sacred rites. I'm a shaman. I was a shaman back then too. How could I ever be a threat to her high status?"

Myrtle cocked her head. "The First Sister's rank is higher than a shaman's?"

"Oh yes. All the concubines outrank the shamans. That's why Grella never made sense to me. In fact, before her, Wikshen carried out his sacred rite publicly, on his throne or in his room with the doors open and shamans present. Once Grella gained a certain level of power, she closed the doors and made it a secret ritual."

"What happened to her?" Tamas asked. Knilma had told some of these stories to Tamas before in her efforts to convert the girl to Wikshonism, but there was still so much to recount.

"She died, hopefully. Wikshen's blessing keeps women alive for a long time, but not forever."

Myrtle shook her head, squinting in the bright sunset. "Wikshen's blessing being…?"

"His seed, girl. The sacred rite I'm talking about is sex. He chooses those who are worthy of it. That's why I say he's not simply a killing, raping monster, despite how he appears to outsiders. He's a beautiful deity with a vision for how the Darklands should be shaped. He'll conquer all of this." Knilma waved her arm as far as she could, considering her sore joints. "Things are going to change in this land, and if he chooses you to join him, you are lucky. Take my words to heart." Knilma leaned over the cart's rail toward Myrtle and clenched a fist as if she hid something wonderful within it. "The blessing of Wikshen is *power*."

The girls walked in thoughtful silence for a while. Paigess, the other shaman, walked behind the cart, nodding her head in agreement.

"And when we get to Alkeer, you'll all be educated on it," Knilma added. "It takes tremendous faith and devotion to become a concubine. If you ask me, you two girls are fine candidates."

Tamas smiled and Myrtle's chest swelled.

Sammial cleared his throat. "With all due respect, marm, you said Grella must be dead. And we all know there hasn't been a Wikshen in the world for more than six hundred years, and you said yourself—"

"That I knew him? And you want to know why I've lived this long?"

Knilma said.

Sammial cocked his head. "Yes, marm."

"Well, you're right. I knew him. And I'm still alive, but look at me. I could die any minute. But haven't you noticed how much tea I drink?"

"Um, yeah, but—" Sammial answered.

"I have a few secret ingredients I put in it. I call it my 'live-long brew.' The secret herbs are rare and powerful. The tea won't keep me alive forever, I assure you, but it has worked for a long time."

"What's the secret ingredient, marm?" Sammial asked.

Knilma grinned and put a finger along her nose. "A *very* special ingredient. Just I and a few others know it." She shot Myrtle and Tamas a smile. "We'll brew it up and share cups with you girls when we get to Wikhaihli."

"Will Wikshen drink it too?" Tamas asked.

"He doesn't need to," Knilma said. "The pixie inside of him keeps him alive for as long as it takes to conquer the Darklands." Knilma paused and next gave Sammial a growl. "Now look what you've done, you idiot, you've taken me off the subject of our Mastaren!"

"So then… Grella," Tamas cut in. "Did she—Grella—really kill the last Wikshen?"

Knilma's eyebrows narrowed and her throat caught. "She did." Knilma would say no more about it.

Wikshen stirred beside her. A soft moan sounded beneath the linen shroud, and her attitude perked.

"Mastaren?" Knilma folded the end of the fabric over. It was safe to do so at twilight. Wikshen breathed differently now, closer to wakefulness. Another moan slid through his pale lips.

"Mastaren," Knilma whispered, getting as close to his ear as her creaky old bones allowed.

"Kah—" he muttered. "Ka…lea."

"I don't understand, sweet Mastaren."

"Ka—lea," he said again before falling into a rhythm of gentle snoring.

"He's coming around," Knilma said, looking up to regard her companions. Their faces now displayed various versions of wonder.

They stopped to camp soon after. No walking clouds were in sight, so the moon and stars lit the landscape. The warlocks got straight to work clearing a spot in the tall grass for a fire while Paigess and the girls tediously hand-picked dried grass blades to use in place of firewood. It wouldn't burn long, but they might get some water boiled for tea to help Knilma sleep. She stayed with Wikshen on the cart, parked a fair distance from the fire out of respect for him. If he was to gain his strength back and awaken, he needed darkness.

When Paigess handed her a teacup, she held it close to Wikshen's nose. Wikshonites always carried herbs of as many varieties as they could pack. They made sure to carry the ones Wikshen favored. This tea combined the strong elements of spearmint and dandelion. Nevertheless, he didn't budge at the aroma.

"On this spot, we will build an altar," Knilma said. "We'll commemorate this moment in history: the seventh Wikshen's journey home. His reign will begin soon. He'll slaughter the sorcerers and make the Darklands his own kingdom again."

She snapped her fingers. "Togha!"

"Yes, marm?" His flat voice sounded from the shadow beside the cart. Togha was a quiet boy, had been since she met him. He walked a wide circle around their Mastaren, avoiding looking in his direction, to answer Knilma's call.

"We passed rocks about half an hour ago. Follow our trail backward and get a big one. More than one if you can manage."

"But Haggis is—!"

"Is what? Tired? She's a donkey, you idiot! What's a donkey in the eyes of Wikshen?"

Togha pouted at her with his pretty face, his eyes dark despite their usual light grey color.

"Bah!" Knilma waved her hand. "If you're so worried about Haggis, *you* can carry the rocks!"

Togha trudged away, stepping awkwardly through the tall grass. It could take him half the night on foot! Knilma snorted. Dismissing his stupidity, she inhaled the steam rising from her teacup.

Beside her, Wikshen twitched and rolled his head to the side. "Kah—leahhh…"

Knilma awoke at sunrise to the shouting of her name.

"Knilma?"

"Mastaren?"

She shot upright from her bed in the grass. As much as she hated leaving his side, she needed to move her legs and stretch out to sleep on the ground. Wikshen could use the space anyway. He hadn't shouted her name, however: another newly arrived warlock runner had. This might be a return runner from Kilka.

Panting heavily, the man reported, "Kilka says to go to Alkeer."

Her supposition had proved right. Knilma reared her head back with a frown. "Alkeer is too dangerous, boy. Besides, the Mastaren would benefit greatly if we went straight to Hathrohskog."

The warlock shook his head, letting his panting calm down. "That's the thing, marm. Hathrohskog isn't what it used to be."

Knilma's frown deepened. "You're joking. What could be wrong with it?"

"No one knows, but it's dead. The trees are skeletons, and they can no longer shield the Mastaren from the sun. The whole forest is a bog in a hole, marm."

Knilma lowered her eyes. "Have I been away that long? Even though I've lived in Ravivill for seventy years, I never dreamed a forest as formidable as Hathrohskog could...die. Especially in that amount of time."

"Much has happened in seventy years, marm. The Clanless are flourishing, though they fight against Ilbith. They've taken over the strongest towers in Alkeer, and they warn people away from Hathrohskog."

"So no one goes there anymore?"

"Not many. The Clanless have exterminated a large part of the goblin population and built roads winding through Goblin Country, so no one needs to cut through Hathrohskog anymore."

Knilma took in all the young man reported. Hathrohskog would've been the best place to take Wikshen in his hours of weakness. Dense minerals he could absorb into his body rested in the forest's soil. The flesh-eating soil used to take many lives and enrich itself for Wikshen's feet.

"Kilka says to take Wikshen to Alkeer," the warlock repeated. "She's preparing a new lair for him, where he can regain his strength. She says to keep him in Alkeer. Don't let him leave."

"But the danger—"

He cut her off. "Although the Clanless have control of most of the city these days, there are many of us Wikshonites there too. We'll meet you outside the wall and disguise your caravan. We'll smuggle him in."

Knilma raised an eyebrow. "Alkeer then."

# Chapter 35
# His Blood

Like the warlock runner had reported, Knilma and her companions encountered no trouble sneaking Wikshen into Alkeer under the notice of the Clanless *saehgahn* who patrolled Alkeer's entrance. Inside the city, there were a number of Wikshonites who did little to hide their faith; sorcerers from any faction were more scarce.

The runner shared updates on how the city had changed as they made their way through the noisy streets toward the port district. "No more boats, you'll notice, marm."

Knilma raised her eyebrows and dropped her mouth corners as she surveyed the distantly familiar scenery. The docks were rotten in many places. The most important sections for foot traffic showed signs of regular repair.

"We've lost all contact with the islands," he continued.

"How odd," Knilma said. "My Wikshen used to love this area. He was a fisherman before becoming Wikshen, you know." She took in the salty air, now laced with wood rot, garbage, and dead fish. "I accompanied him back to this place many times."

The warlock nodded. "Yes, marm. That's why Kilka rallied one hundred warlocks, myself included. We commandeered the Sword Swish, ran the old owner out, and claimed it for the new Wikshen. We're going there now. She's ordered a safe haven for him inside. It's a good place to cook and provide all the best services to our lord."

She put her hand on his shoulder and squeezed. "You're a good man. Is Kilka inside now? We have a lot of catching up to do and plans to make."

"No, marm, she set things in motion here and took off for Wikhaihli to prepare our Mastaren's home."

Knilma drew her lips tight. "Mmm. I expect it's not in its best order either."

The warlock spread his hands. "It's been so long. There hasn't been a Wikshen for centuries. None of us believed Tristain's words at first when he burst into our hideout with the news. I'm ashamed to admit, we laughed at him."

The warlock's eyes darted to the cart they were walking beside.

Knilma had taken to walking since entering Alkeer. From here, neither of them could see Wikshen under the sacred shroud.

Knilma put her hand on one of the bundles of dried grass they'd stacked around him to throw off any Clanless guardsmen upon entering the city.

"You'll see him soon, once we've got him safe in the darkness."

Knilma couldn't hold back her tears as she entered the old tavern on the dock. The Sword Swish, Wikshen's favorite. By some miracle it had survived the ages and apparently stayed in business. The Wikshonites had blackened the windows with tar, and it smelled strong enough to raise the dead, and possibly the Mastaren too. Many candles were lit to see by in the dense darkness. Knilma warily allowed Wikshen to be carried in on a stretcher amidst so many hazardous flames.

"We're about done with everything," Scayetta, an Alkeerian shaman, said. "We'll switch to Kraft Fire soon." Kraft Fire was a heatless blue light Wikshonites had discovered long ago in a certain magical vibration. It supplied a safe light to use when needed, particularly in the presence of Wikshen, so his followers wouldn't trip over each other in his dark halls.

The ceiling arched overhead with many crossbeams to hold it up, perfect for hanging black banners and the huge black drape used to section off the stage.

"Wikshen's sacred altar is up there." Scayetta pointed to the stage. "We're setting his table now. He has all the luxury we could find in the city in there, with enough room for a few beauties to keep him company. And we can open the curtain for worship when he's ready."

Knilma wiped her nose on her handkerchief. "Good work, Scayetta. And good work to Kilka. This is an excellent effort in so short a time, but there's room to expand. We'll conquer the entire port, if not the entire city. Tell me now, is there any ink and paper handy to write Kilka a note?"

"There is," Scayetta said, and guided Knilma to a cozy little office where the building's original owner had left his business materials and money behind in his hasty exit.

No sooner had Knilma finished her letter and leaned back from the page did Scayetta dart into the office. "He's awake."

Knilma hurried out to the main hall of the tavern, full of smoke after the candles were snuffed out and replaced with the metal dishes bearing Kraft Fire. Knilma reached out and tapped one of the young witches on the shoulder. "Incense," she ordered.

A normal part of Wikshonism, certain herbal scents benefited Wikshen in various ways, evoking certain moods in him. Before writing to Kilka, Knilma wrote an order of such herbs and sent it out with a warlock to alert their foragers. The bottom of the list stressed pennyroyal, lots and lots of pennyroyal for his libido. It worked versatilely in moving him into other charismatic moods when combined with other herbs. Placing the last inky dot on the page, a sense of familiarity came over her. She was thirty-five years old again, doing business under her Mastaren.

She took the steps to the stage one by one and entered the enormous black canopy which housed him like a comfortable nest of luxuries. Food had recently been placed on the table, still steaming. The smell made her stomach rumble in confusion with her excitement. The finest silver tableware she'd ever seen glistened in the blue lighting. Many fluffy cushions supplemented his bed, a large mattress on the floor. Before allowing her Mastaren to be laid upon it, she interrogated the local witches, asking whether they'd stuffed the cushions with the finest down Alkeer could provide, and how fine were the sheets, and had they been stored in lavender and calendula? The bed hid under its own canopy, draping from the rafters. Like Scayetta said, it could accommodate a few more bodies than Wikshen's own.

He sat at the edge of the bed, his back turned to her. His mythical hair trailed down his back like a long, silky waterfall. Outside the curtain, the other shamans argued softly about who was worthy enough to brush it and tend to other such doting duties.

Knilma would put first priorities first. "Mastaren," she tried. He didn't answer. He didn't move either. "Are you comfortable?" His bare shoulders rose up and his hands came around to either of his arms. He shivered. "Are you cold?"

He said nothing. Knilma tiptoed closer. Wikshen was characteristically unpredictable. He could kill as easily as he could laugh and ask for a flatcake and a tankard of extra-sweet mead. She knew his moods very well and how to deal with him. Approaching this new Wikshen was a risk, but one she'd willingly take. She had lived long enough to see him reborn. Happiness returned to her old bones.

Because of her short stature, she didn't have to stoop to reach his head level. She couldn't sit on the floor, or she'd have trouble getting back to her feet. "Mastaren," she tried again in her softest tone.

He kept staring at the curtain. His rounded eyes were unblinking.

"Mastaren… It's me… Knilma." She put her hand on his shoulder.

His eyes turned to her but went straight through. His sadness was infectious. What could one such as he be so sad about?

He opened his mouth. "Why's it so dark?" His lost whisper pierced her heart.

"For your benefit, Mastaren." She bravely reached her hand to stroke his hair. The turquoise light in his eyes glowed so beautifully. "There's good food over there, cooked for you alone. Flatcakes. Eggs. Pies. Oysters. We're all here to make you comfortable. You have shamans, witches, warlocks, and pledges—we're all here to protect you with our lives. You can rest easy and enjoy yourself. You have two attractive girls out there too, waiting for your call. All you must do is call."

"Where am I?"

Knilma reared her head back. He used to sense the vibrations and magnetic activity in the earth to orient himself. They weren't far from the sea—he should be able to smell the salt mingling with the old wood of the tavern they were in. He should know it well.

"You're at home in Alkeer," she answered, barely able to hear her own voice through her throbbing heart. "It's your favorite tavern, in fact. This place used to make your favorite dishes. You'd come here and eat and bless and kill at your leisure. Many, many dreadwitches were born here. You wouldn't have people you disliked in here." The blue strands of hair running between her fingers were silkier than her old Wikshen's hair, an elven trait. "It's all yours now. We've converted it into a temple to your majesty, and will fill it with people who serve you."

A tear streaked down his face, catching a twinkle of light for an instant before disappearing.

"Mastaren?" Knilma's voice shook.

She removed her hand from his shoulder when he shuddered. "That doesn't make sense."

"What doesn't make sense?"

He closed his lips, and the bottom one quivered. The tears ran freely. "I don't know where I am. What am I supposed to do?"

What did he mean? Wikshen should know exactly what to do. If not for her shaman's instinct, she'd question his authenticity. But this was Wikshen. He even wore the battleshift—the same one Knilma remembered! It radiated with Wikshen's energy, sending sharp sparks of memory to Knilma like an old debt finally paid. This was Wikshen… and suddenly he didn't know where he was or what to do with himself?

Knilma cleared her throat. They'd take it as slowly as he needed. She wouldn't tell anyone about this. If any of the others outside the curtain inquired about his confusion or gloom, she'd shut them up and send them on a task.

"You won't have to worry about anything," Knilma told him. "You'll leave it to me, your old friend Knilma. Just call my name. Remember how you used to call my name?"

He closed his eyes and swallowed.

"Come to the table and eat, Mastaren. You'll feel better. I'll be right here with you, on the other side of the drape. Come on now." She stepped back, but he made no move to rise. "Just call my name if you need anything. It's Knilma."

Stepping past the canopy flap, she fought back her own emotion. She patted her chest. She'd seen Wikshen in a great variety of his moods, but she'd never seen him cry before. It was too much for her to handle at once. In a few moments, she'd organize a group prayer session at the foot of the stage, accompanied by his most rousing of incenses. Maybe he'd pull through after that, and also after he ate.

When the old woman left, Dorhen glanced around his dark, unfamiliar surroundings. The dark did nothing to mar his vision or his sharp comprehension of the layout. Massive black curtains hung around him. Eerie, murmuring voices prayed on the other side. Regardless of what the old woman had said, this wasn't his home, and the word "Alkeer" meant nothing to him. How far was that from Kalea's convent?

A pain in his chest slithered up to his throat and emerged as a soft sob. He put his hands over his mouth to stifle the sound. A lot of people were out there, listening and watching. What did they want from him?

He didn't remember how he got here. He vaguely remembered when he last wandered. People screamed in his memory. The sound of his own voice, shouting and laughing beyond his control, echoed with them. He'd lost himself. He'd been in a fight with his own body to make it stop moving on its own, to make it stop killing. And he lost.

And it would happen again.

He rubbed his forehead with his good hand and fought the emotion, the confusion. How long since he'd seen Kalea? Since he'd known peace? His last moment of peace occurred outside Kalea's convent, looking at the big row of windows along the wall where the candles glowed after sunset. As the novices went to sleep, their candlelight gradually dimmed until the glass went dark. He couldn't sleep that night, even if he wanted to. He spent a few hours waiting, daydreaming about her. The memory of her hand tickled his palm. Her voice echoed in his thoughts while he sat there on the ground, burning with joy and anticipation for the moment she'd come out of the big house and stay out. She'd chosen him. She'd chosen him over her home, her convent family, and her Creator.

A dream. His life had become too much a whirlwind to ponder what a dream the whole thing was—that he could be so lucky to have someone like her leave her safe confinement to be with him instead. It was too good to be true. Dorhen was not lucky. He was a damned soul. The ever-unobtainable vision of himself with Kalea had been a cruel prank of Kalea's creator-goddess. His life was meant to be nothing more than a web of suffering, whipping him from one bad existence to another.

The moment of the convent's attack marked the end of his life. Ever since the fateful incident, when her voice screaming his name ripped through the many other sounds and he rushed into the building, breaking a window, breaking a door—after that point, his life slipped beyond his control. The world scrambled into a jumble of faces and voices and... opium smoke and dark halls, blows to his face, pain, musty smells, a woman's mouth in the dark, and his uncle and... His father. Somewhere in all that mess, he found his father. Or his father found him. He'd learned he was the scum child of a bastard. Born into suffering. Dorhen remembered his father's loathsome face in those last moments before his own life ended. His father had made him a monster.

Dorhen's head spun, unable to control his thoughts, his memories, or his actions. And now look at him. He'd lost time and place. And Kalea. He'd soon lose his body and also his mind.

For now...he retained a small bit of himself, but it wouldn't last long. Before the horrors continued, he could end it. He could end it before he killed again. He couldn't let himself go back for Kalea. Somewhere in his jumble of confusion and memories, he'd hoped to find her again, but that hope expired. A terrible idea. He now owed it to her safety to do something about himself. He owed it to anyone near him.

He crawled to the little table. It squatted low to the floor with a cushion to sit on. The smell of the food registered amidst the various potent fumes in the air. His sense of smell was heightened too, he noticed. Hot tar and incense tried to muffle the fresh flatcakes and roasted bird on the table.

His left arm reached out to take a slice of bread. Dorhen wasn't hungry; the arm moved of its own will even though the other voice in his head slept for now. This wasn't the first time it had moved on its own. In disgust, Dorhen batted it and forced it to drop the bread. A sickening dread drenched his mind. He no longer possessed his left arm. Wik owned it now.

Another sob racked him, rattling his throat. He was trapped. Numbness riddled other parts of his body too. He lifted the stout silver pitcher. Glistening beads of condensation covered the surface like tiny crystals. He wiped across the wetness and checked his reflection again. The same stranger stared back from the silver surface. His hair still showed a blue hue. The reality of the nightmare lived on.

He wouldn't do it again. He would not let that demon in his head take over and go on another rampage. Beside the roasted bird lay a sharp silver knife.

A slight clatter of dishes roused Knilma's attention. "Are you all right, Mastaren?" she asked from her crouched pose in front of the covered stage.

She regarded her companions, who bowed with her. "Keep going," she whispered to them. This would be Myrtle's first prayer session as a Wikshonite—and how perfect that Wikshen was present for it!

Standing up, she hobbled around the stage to the steps and curtain opening. The voices murmured the long-drawn prayer syllables she'd initiated.

On the stage surface, the Kraft Fire in Wikshen's sacred space glowed at full strength. He sat at his table, hence the sound of dishes, but something was amiss. Did his misery persist? Perhaps a nice steamy bath would soothe him instead of food.

"Mastaren," she said as she came around the table. When he didn't move, she hurried to his side. The outside murmuring stopped as the others reacted to her calls. "Mastaren?"

He stared into oblivion. The beautiful blue-green glow in his eyes had dulled to nearly black. His lips were partly open, and blood from his throat ran all over the surface of the table, pooling around the dishes and food, and flowing down the tablecloth.

She cried out loud and staggered. "Drums! Bring the drums! Damp cloths! Incense! Hurry!"

It took more than an hour for Knilma to swab the blood off his face and body. "A flesh wound as little as this can't kill Wikshen," she explained to her two young protégés, Myrtle and Tamas. "The pixie inside him keeps him alive. It holds his soul and prevents its escape. Soak this cloth and pass me a new one."

The other shamans tapped their drums gently around him to lend their Mastaren strength. He had sliced deep into the side of his neck and severed a major artery. It didn't make sense, not for Wikshen. Didn't he know only fire could kill him? Everyone but him knew it, apparently.

When she had his neck all cleared away, the blood flow had stopped and signs of healing showed as the two ends of the cut fused back together. One of the most common aspects of Wikshen's lore was his fast healing ability. As she understood it, even if his head were cut off, his neck could be fused back together and he'd return to life.

On several occasions already, she'd dodged her companions' questions as to why he'd do that to himself. "He needs time," Knilma told them in more than one way. She wrapped his wound loosely with a clean linen cloth and called the warlocks to carry him to his bed.

Clamping her mouth shut to any more questions about Wikshen's suicide attempt, she wrung her hands all the way to the office to write a letter detailing the incident to Kilka. Along the way, she grabbed the wrist of one of the warlocks, one whose name she didn't know. "Prepare a cart and get a load of warlocks ready. We're leaving. We're going to Wikhaihli."

The warlock lowered his brow and flashed a serious mien. "Wikshen has to stay here," he argued. "Kilka's grave orders."

Knilma pursed her lips at the insolent boy. "And why, might I ask, should Wikshen stay here?"

"She didn't go into detail," he said. "She stressed, with the fires of Kullixaxuss in her teeth, how important it is to keep Wikshen here until further notice."

"Wikshen can leave whenever he wants."

He shrugged. "Kilka's orders."

Before she could throw a finger in his face and tell him where he could stuff Kilka's orders, Tristain burst into the temple. "I just heard…" He panted heavily. "They sent me running here…"

Turning her stare to the newly arrived warlock, Knilma said, "Out with it, you idiot!"

"A sanguinesent!"

Knilma frowned. "Did you say 'sanguinesent?'"

"Yes," Tristain said from his bent-over position. "They spotted one in the Longwalk. Southwest."

"Oh, dear."

"What's a sanguinesent, marm?" Myrtle asked.

"A friend of the sorcerers," she answered. "Sanguinesents are demonic entities from a layer of Kullixaxuss. I know the sorcerers like to contact beings like those."

"How did it get here?" Paigess asked.

"How else?" Knilma said flatly. Not much surprised her anymore. "The sorcerers can summon them. It's not easy, I've heard, so it must've come from one of the higher factions."

Paigess spread her empty hands. "Ilbith?"

Knilma didn't answer. Instead, she turned and continued toward the office. "I'll include that tidbit in my letter to Kilka."

Paigess and a number of others followed like ducklings. "Knilma,"

Paigess said, "what will we do? What does this mean?"

Knilma kept her respiration slow for the sake of her old heart. "I'm nothing but an old woman."

"You're the most experienced Wikshonite among us!"

"But still just an old piece of bread in this scheme. We need our Wikshen. He alone can lead us in times like this. So many people and groups of people would have us destroyed. We are a group who rallies around Wikshen. Without him, we're nothing."

"But something is wrong with Wikshen," Paigess pressed.

Knilma didn't stop shuffling toward the office or bother to look back. "He is our sole focus. If we can help him, he can help us."

When she'd gotten the others and their questions off her rear end, written her letter, and sent it back out with Tristain, she returned to check on the Mastaren.

He writhed on the floor, huffing and grunting as he wrestled with his own battleshift. He was tugging on it, kicking inside of it, and trying to pull the cords out.

"Mastaren," Knilma said, "are you trying to take off your battleshift?" This could be the oddest thing she'd ever seen a Wikshen do—odder than seeing him weep. He grunted and growled, saturated in emotion. The sight made her jaw drop and threatened her old heart.

"Why won't it come off?" he roared. Feet and shoulders against the floor, he arched his back high.

Knilma shook her head and realized her mouth gaped. She shushed him. "Please don't shout such things. Your followers are…"

Knilma bent over to pant when her heart skipped and fluttered. She regarded him again. "Mastaren, you can't take it off. It doesn't come off." He ignored her. She stepped toward him. "Mastaren, please calm down." She extended her hands. "Only a special person can take it off, a person of your choice. But you have a lot of contemplation to do before—"

He roared to compete with the most fearsome of beasts before collapsing to pant in exhaustion…and then he went at it again.

"Mastaren, you have to stop. They can hear you out there. Your followers need you to be strong. Difficult situations are arising."

He didn't listen. Once again, she found herself tempted to question the authenticity of this Wikshen. Knilma's stomach soured as if she'd eaten rotten eggs.

She tried again. "Mastaren, you can't take your battleshift off. You need it!"

The fabric took on a life of its own—a living entity in itself—and avoided his hands. The ties moved like snakes, slithering away from his grasp. Its liveliness showed proof enough of his legitimacy. It was all the proof they'd ever need.

Clicking her tongue, Knilma stuck her head out of the curtain opening and observed the startled faces of Wikshen's followers. "I need a chime bowl," Knilma said, "a big one."

"Which big one?" Paigess asked, her empty hands fidgeting.

"The biggest one we have here."

The biggest chime bowl in their new temple spanned about the width of a barrel in diameter. The chime's hammer was big enough to work as a weapon. Knilma let Paigess do the honor of making the sound because of her younger age and her strength.

"You leave us no choice, Mastaren!" Knilma called on the opposite side of the curtain from where his struggling was clearly audible. At Knilma's signal, Paigess reared the heavy metal hammer back and swung forward.

*DONG!*

The mighty chime rattled the whole building and Knilma's brittle teeth. People around her winced and covered their ears. A chorus of warlock voices moaned. Sammial rubbed his ears. Many of these Wikshonites were young and new to the religion. They hadn't heard the variety of chimes, bells, and drums that were important to their worship. Sounds and vibrations like this came in handy for communication with Wikshen, as well as their magical discipline of Kraft.

On the stage, behind the black curtain, the ruckus ceased after a few thumping sounds of Wikshen's limbs hitting the wooden floor. It had worked. He passed out in the intense vibration. For Knilma and the others, the sound was merely uncomfortable, but Wikshen would feel it down to his bone marrow, possibly deeper.

As much as using that bowl in such close proximity hurt her Mastaren, it hurt her more. It didn't matter how involved with Wikshen she'd been before—everything about this situation was strange and unexpected to her, to her companions, and to written history. It took a hell of a lot of courage to re-enter his canopy.

Knilma spent the evening at his bedside, keeping to a meditative state of mind. Paigess was right, Knilma was the most experienced Wikshonite. She might be useless to lead the lot of them, but at least she could keep her emotions in check when in the public eye and stay strong to set an example. She'd spend the coming days close beside him to try to make sense of his erratic, dare she say...unwilling behavior. For now, as she sat beside him, she wept.

He'd been neatly tucked in by his followers. He breathed easily again, like when he'd ridden on the cart. He wasn't as she remembered, neither in appearance nor personality. She missed *her* Wikshen, but she put the thought out of her mind and doused her emotions. Duty remained most important. She might not recognize him and he might not recognize her, but he was Wikshen.

She reached out to take the linen bandage off his neck. Like his battleshift showing a mind of its own, his healing ability couldn't be faked either. The wound had disappeared as if it never happened.

His breathing rhythm changed at her prodding, and he sat up suddenly. He neither yawned nor stretched.

"Mastaren?" she said.

He slowly turned his gaze to her, his pupils shrinking. His brow narrowed. "Knilma," his voice rumbled.

Her heart jumped for the hundredth time today. She gave a hopeful smile. "Yes, Mastaren."

His eyes perused her. "You look like hell. What happened to you?"

"I aged, Mastaren."

A smirk lifted one corner of his mouth. "You're old now. Where've you been?"

Both of her hands flew to her mouth. The tears accumulated in her eyes. Despite nearing the edge of breaking down, she replied, "The question is, where've *you* been?"

He let out a long breath through his nose. He looked down at himself and then perused the room. "Bring me flatcakes."

# Chapter 36
# What is Going on in Alkeer

Tall towers and steeples of many heights speared through the walking cloud ahead.

"I think we've found Alkeer," Bowaen said, and Kalea grabbed his arm in excitement. An unspoken relief encompassed their group. Two days had passed since they'd eaten at the settlement, and today they were all starving again.

On an old, beaten road carved through the tall waving grass, herds of people on foot lugged bags and crates, and spared hardly a word for Kalea's party. The people pushed against their course in long spurts, as if Alkeer bled out its citizens. The crowd thickened closer to the city walls. The flood of bodies cramming themselves out through the portcullis blocked the path.

On either side of the portcullis stood a *saehgahn* on guard duty, helping to dislodge and usher people through. He and those similar to him wore mismatched armor pieces all unified under the color orange. This one wore an orange sash about his waist, and his companion across the way wore an orange-painted helmet.

They approached one such guard, and Bowaen asked for an explanation.

"Don't go in!" the guard yelled over the roar of voices, busy pulling and pushing people on their way.

"Why? We're starving!" Bowaen replied.

"Wikshen!" the *saehgahn*-guard said. He dislodged a skinny man from the crowd under the portcullis, and the man flailed like a doll at the elf's manhandling. Paying the crowd and his work no mind, he continued, "The Clanless recommend turning around and going the other way. Though traditionally Wikshen grants amnesty to our city, this one's new, so there's no telling what he'll do yet. You'll find most of these folk camped fifteen leagues to the southwest. Go there instead!"

"We're looking for a missing *farhah* and a blue-haired sorcerer," Bowaen said, and the guard stopped and gaped.

"Missing *farhah*?"

Gaije stepped forward. "My sister. She was taken from my village, and I've tracked her this far."

"Dear Bright One," the guard said. "We haven't seen a *farhah* in the Wikshonites' care, and if we had, we'd be fighting them now rather than doing this. But I'll tell my clansmen what you've said, and we'll divide our priorities."

"Her name is Mhina," Gaije said. "Where is the blue-haired sorcerer? Have you seen him? He's an elf too, or so I think."

"You're talking about Wikshen. Look for him inside." The guard fetched a spear with a bright orange ribbon tied to it, leaned against the wall of the barbican, and used the spear's shaft to herd the crowd to make a path for them to slip through the gate.

Once inside, the town wasn't quite falling apart as they expected. A large number of citizens walked about casually. Music drifted in the air. Corner taverns bustled with drinkers and whores. Many people were clad in black robes, bearing bells and wearing black ribbons on their wrists, and some elderly women carried drums on their backs like shriveled old turtles.

More elves like the ones at the gate patrolled around. Despite their admirable discipline, their mismatched armor and tattered clothing failed to impress. Once again, they all wore an orange accessory. They clearly weren't associated with Norr. They also sported a symbol depicting an orange leaf broken in two on their backs, either painted or stitched, like the elven clans of Norr.

After an hour of wandering the streets, the path opened to reveal the best thing they'd seen in a long time: a market square. Though its food and supplies were exhausted due to the panic, Bowaen bought the first loaf of stale bread he found and broke it into four. After scarfing it down, they asked around for Wikshen.

"Great Sea, no! Keep 'im away from me!" the first woman to receive the question shrieked.

A man standing outside a small mill by the canal told Del, "Try the street with all the damned black cloaks and bugger off now!"

"Fool!" an elf wearing an orange bandana spat in Bowaen's face. "Take your woman to the camp out in the Longwalk!"

"Oh, dearie," a woman working a depleted butcher shop responded to Kalea's inquiry, "you're such a pretty thing. Don't go letting him rip into your body now—because he will!"

They finally decided to acknowledge their exhaustion at sunset. Better to sleep and face Wikshen later. The stars had appeared in the evening sky before they found a shoddy little inn on Scouel Street not brimming with patrons. Music filled the dark, smoky air, a bawdy song of lutes and other instruments strung too loose to sound like music. The audience clapped along nonetheless. The patrons here commonly sported primitive pierced ears and noses, painted faces, and heavy fur pelts.

When the noisy musicians finished banging away on their stringed instruments, a girl younger than Kalea danced on a table by the fireplace singing a filthy song, earning crude comments and whistles. Kalea had attracted attention as well since they entered. She clung to Bowaen's arm to appear spoken for. Bowaen kept his free hand on Hathrohjilh the whole night. Del watched the dancing girl intently, and even Gaije's posture relaxed as they chatted around the table for a few hours. Locals called him "Clanless" in here too.

"There's that word again. Why are they calling you that, Gaije?" Kalea asked.

"Seems the Clanless are *saehgahn* who abandoned Norr. At home, we call them *deserters*." Gaije deflated before them and didn't bother to say more. She didn't ask.

Once upstairs in their room, they lit a few candles to talk in a quieter setting, despite the raucous noise from downstairs. Kalea opened the *Lehomis* book Father Liam had given her in a feeble attempt to regain a feeling of familiar comfort. As she casually turned the pages, she spotted a few strands of hair sticking out of the top. She opened it to examine the mess of hair she'd collected from the dead woman's hand. She held them close to the light.

They were still blue—she wasn't completely crazy. How could something so beautiful have come off a creature so evil? She almost wanted to see the source of the hair in person, just to see how it looked on someone's head. Could he be any worse than the Dreamer?

She caught herself staring at the smooth blue hair and quickly stopped fondling it before any of her friends noticed. She closed it back into the book.

Togha inhaled deeply over the raspberry tea he'd ordered at an inn in Alkeer. He and the Wikshonites had finally arrived to deliver Wikshen to the new base at that poor other tavern the cult had seized.

Wikshen. The fabled deity Metta had promised wouldn't return. After six hundred years, what were the chances of it happening in this lifetime? Many people had probably stopped believing in Wikshen and written him off as a story, not a real living deity.

For Togha, this meant the end of the world. How would Metta feel when she found out? Could she have caught wind of it yet? Would she keep her word to be a "good Wikshonite" and devote herself to this blue-haired freak?

Wikshen disrupted everything. Togha's plan of fitting in with the Wikshonites and forming a plan to win Metta over had toppled over and crashed into a fast-paced, unpredictable set of tasks to fill each miserable day. As of now, he'd finally found a moment to break away and be by himself.

He warily lowered his hood, considering the public place in which he sat. All the Darklandic places he'd visited so far didn't seem to mind elves, although some didn't appear to care much for the Clanless. And though his Wikshonite companions had raised their guard when entering the city, the public attitude toward them also felt lax here.

"Oh, look what I've found, my friends. A smear of shit on this establishment's chair."

Togha winced and gritted his teeth at the familiar voice. That's who he'd hoped not to run into in this city. Before he knew it, a swarm of other *saehgahn* closed in around him—trapping him.

"And here we hoped he'd die out there in the grasslands after casting a cowardly Kraft spell and escaping," another elf said from beside him.

The group loomed over him. This would not end well. Togha kept his teeth tightly together.

The group's leader, Riminhen, leaned over close to Togha's head. Orange rooster feathers tied in his hair brushed the table. "Why did you come here, shit stain? Why did you not die out in the wilds like you were supposed to do?"

"I guess the Bright One hasn't called me yet," Togha offered, keeping his eyes on his hot teacup. The thought of throwing it in the other *saehgahn's* face occurred to him, but he wouldn't be able to fight the rest of the group plus the one he'd scald.

"This isn't good," the first *saehgahn* said. "Now you're here again, to dirty up our city with your shameful behavior and wicked magic."

Togha shook his head slightly. "You've misunderstood me."

One of the *saehgahn* behind him shoved the back of his head, causing Togha's face to bob dangerously close to his hot tea. "I think I saw this lousy creature enter with a bunch of Wikshonites!"

Whatever they were thinking of doing to him, it would be worse than how they'd treated him during their last run-in. They should go ahead and get it over with. He would invite them to finish him off and spare him of this nightmare his life had twisted into.

"Well, we must fix this," Riminhen said. "We can't have a tainted elf strutting into town with his fellow faithfuls."

Togha's hands curled into fists on the table. "I don't worship Wikshen!"

"Of course not. But you do ride around with his people and carry their ungodly books on your person."

"That's because—"

One of them swiped his head from behind, sending his hair over his face.

"Here's what we're going to do." Riminhen cleared his throat and motioned for another *saehgahn*, who brought a large tankard of ale from the bar. "Because you're an elf, we agree that you deserve a certain level of respect." The other elf set the tankard loudly on the table in front of him. "So we're going to give you the honor of taking yourself out of this world. You'll drink this whole cup and more until you die. If you do it, you are an honorable *saehgahn* who is worthy of redemption. If you don't drink it and instead try to escape, we'll catch you outside the door and kill you in the street—like a sniveling street urchin. The choice is yours."

"What if this tankard doesn't kill me, and I have no money for others?"

At his question, the prominent *saehgahn* emptied his coin purse on the table. Several copper chips rang out. "It's my pleasure to help you on your way, *saehgahn*."

Togha huffed and took a few moments to stare at the foamy tankard. It stank. His voice slid out as a whisper. "Who'll take care of Haggis?"

Riminhen snorted. "You still have that donkey? Don't fear, we'll put it to use in your absence."

"And Metta… What about her?"

"Who's Metta? A woman you adore?"

Togha sniffed. *Metta,* he sang her name in his head. A spark of hope had lit him up when Knilma caught his group on the road and announced they were going to Alkeer. He'd gladly accompanied the old shaman. He had yet to find Metta here, though. He would look for her in the temple—if he managed to escape his current predicament. But Metta…

"I can offer you this morsel of comfort," Riminhen continued. "If your Metta is an average and innocent citizen, she'll fare much better after your death. If she's a Wikshonite…" The whole group chuckled among themselves. "I think she'll be a lot more interested in fornicating with her deity than with you."

That stung Togha's ears and his heart. Amid all the laughter, the lead *saehgahn* nudged the tankard closer to Togha, took his teacup, and flung the liquid into the nearby brazier with a steamy hiss. The group moved toward the door.

"I know you'll make the right choice, shit stain. But if you're stupider than I think you are, don't bother exiting through the back either."

Togha focused on the tankard. He put his hands around it. Those

Clanless bastards were right. He no longer stood a chance with Metta. Not with Wikshen returned. He pulled the tankard closer, its pewter bottom grinding against the old wood of the table. All that was behind him. His plans had incinerated before his eyes. He could never compete with her devotion to Wikshen. There was nowhere else he could go, nowhere else he wanted to go, and the Clanless wanted him dead anyway.

Instead of lifting the big cup, he bowed his head over it and put his lips on the rim, tasting the residue of the bitter, coppery flavor.

Kalea waited until her friends exited their inn room before basking in the privacy to don her kirtle. She laced herself up tight; she didn't want to look like all the loose women walking around outside. She also tucked Dorhen's pendant snugly beneath her layers for fear of thieves.

She went down to join her friends in the main hall, ready for a full day of scouring Alkeer, the largest city she'd ever seen, for signs of Dorhen and her sisters. It seemed as good a place as any to run into the workings of the sorcerers who'd kidnapped them.

The inn lulled quietly today, except for the sound of two male voices yelling. If she didn't know any better, she'd think someone had "dishonored" Gaije again. Maybe he'd finally snapped and gone off on Del.

She was right about Gaije, but Del wasn't involved. Near the central hearth in the great hall, Bowaen and Del stood back to watch a fight. A barmaid watched too, wincing and wringing her wooden tray.

"What happened?" Kalea asked the woman.

"I wouldn't know. I don't get in the middle of two elves having it out. Must be about a stupid woman. Nothin' like a woman to set two elf-men biting at each other's throats. I've mopped up blood in the past because of their nonsense. They better hope they don't break somethin'!"

Indeed, in the corner, Gaije pummeled what appeared to be another elf dressed all in black. When Kalea stepped onto the scene, Bowaen and Del turned their eyes away from the action to acknowledge her.

"What's going on?" she asked them.

Del managed to grin with his lips around his pipe, and Bowaen snorted.

"Gaije seems to know this fellow," Bowaen said.

"He's gone hotheaded again," Del added.

The noise and violence sickened her stomach. "What did the other elf do to him?"

"He met Gaije's eye contact and said 'hello,'" Bowaen said, and he and

Del shared a laugh.

Shaking her head, Kalea marched over and grabbed Gaije's tunic to haul him away.

"I-swear-to-the-Bright-One-if-you-break-my-nose…!" the other elf yelled when he had space.

In Kalea's care, Gaije relaxed. "I don't think the Bright One will mind what your nose looks like when He takes you!" Gaije spat at him.

She couldn't blame the stranger: he had a beautiful face, despite the blood and puffiness Gaije's fists had caused. His thick black hair slid along his shoulders like heavy satin. His hair hung slightly longer than Gaije's, which suggested he had probably been *saehgahn* longer.

Kalea put her hand brazenly on Gaije's hair and stroked it. "Be calm now," she said. "Tell me what's the matter here."

Her gesture slowed Gaije's huffing. "This is my *distant* cousin," Gaije said. "His name's Togha." He spat again.

Togha winced and grimaced at his projectile of saliva. He grunted, collected himself from the floor, and slogged over to a table where a lone tankard of ale waited. He put his hands along the cup's sides.

"What are you doing?" Gaije asked, stretching his neck to study Togha's action.

"Go away," Togha mumbled, keeping his eyes on the tankard.

Kalea took it upon herself to sit at his table. Togha didn't bother looking at her. He played his fingers along the sides of the vessel, as if he didn't know if he should drink or not.

Kalea twisted around to regard Gaije, who quietly stared at the spectacle. "Gaije, I thought elves couldn't drink ale."

"They can't," Gaije confirmed again.

She turned back to Togha and puzzled at him.

"Will you please not stare at me?" Togha asked without looking at her. "I'm trying to make an important decision. It's what I was doing before your friend attacked me."

"Why are you thinking of killing yourself, Togha?" Gaije asked.

At his question, Kalea's heart sank, and she cupped her mouth. Though all words and gestures pointed to that explanation, she hadn't wanted to acknowledge her supposition.

"It's none of your business."

Another long few seconds of silence passed. The central brazier crackled, and the sound of the morning bustle chattered outside.

Gaije crossed his arms and stepped closer. "It's probably better this way. You've always been such a dishonorable flirt, always looking to get your head cut off one way or another. Looks like you deserted your post, and I'm willing to lay money that you stole the queen's service beast."

"Haggis is *my* donkey!" Togha slammed his hands on the table, paused, and settled back down. Kalea jumped at his sudden action.

"So what happened?" Gaije asked. "I see you wandered all the way here… Are you now one of them? A Clanless?" He didn't have anything orange on him like the other "Clanless" elves walking around town.

Togha snorted. "They won't have me. Strict for a load of misfits, they are."

"Misfits—because they deserted?" Gaije asked.

"Deserted, convicted, *sarakren*, maimed. Yet they won't have someone like me."

"Why?"

Togha sighed as he took his hands away from the tankard and sat back in his chair. "I can't drink this sour piss," he grumbled.

Bowaen stepped forward and took the tankard. "I'll give it a good home, how 'bout that? If you still want to die, just ask Gaije." Bowaen buried his top lip, whiskers and all, into the sinking foam head.

With the ale gone, Togha looked around at their group, mostly Gaije. "Out in the Darklandic forests, I found a spell scroll stashed in a tree stump when I was digging roots and picking mushrooms to eat. Later on, I met the Clanless and they found it on me. They beat me to a pulp, though they didn't break my nose. I escaped their custody and ran into a group of Wikshonites soon after. They assumed I was one of them, and I allowed their belief. I joined them."

"You're one of those Wikshonites?" Bowaen said. Kalea braced herself, thinking he and Gaije would both dive across the table to strangle Togha.

Gaije narrowed his brow at his distant cousin. "Did you just say you follow *Wikshen*?"

"Technically."

"Togha," Gaije said, his face turning nearly as red as his hair. He shook his head with his hands spread out. "Wikshen found his way to Norr and ransacked our home! Didn't you know?"

Togha's eyes widened. "Why didn't you say so sooner?"

"Why didn't you ask? You're rude and selfish! Your little pettygod took Mhina, you fool. I want to know where he took her!"

Togha went silent. His face might've paled, but it was too flushed with bruises and puffiness to tell.

"Where did he take her?" Gaije pressed.

"I don't know! I didn't see her. I've only seen Wikshen in his state of catatonia and deep slumber. Do you think I'd be sitting here staring at a tankard if I'd known she was under my nose?"

Gaije slammed his palm on the table, rattling it and everything on it, causing Kalea to reconsider her choice of seat. "Time to stop being suicidal! The Bright One led you to the Wikshonites so you could help free her! You can start by helping me! I'm going to find one or the other. You're the fool who follows that bastard, so tell me where to find him. Folk were telling us all day yesterday he is in town. Now what's *your* answer?"

Togha bowed his head. "I know where he is."

"Where is he?"

"Can you do something for me as well?"

Gaije made an *ich* sound from deep in his throat. "What could be more important than rescuing a lost *farhah*?"

"It's not *more* important!" Togha shot back. "It's also important to me." The four of them waited. "I have a lover, a seamstress girl I met in the Darklands. If you happen to see her, can you please"—he sighed—"check on her? I haven't seen her in town since my return; she might've gone straight to Wikhaihli. In fact, we were on a pilgrimage to Wikhaihli until the plan changed."

His head dropped lower. "I don't want Metta to be there when he takes complete power. I don't want her to give herself to…*him*. I joined the cult to be with her. Now, I want to escape the cult and take her with me. I found out too late that warlocks are supposed to be celibate and Wikshen has all the mating rights. This doesn't work for me."

Kalea grimaced. "What kind of religion is that? Why would she…?"

Togha eyed her. "You must be from the Lightlands too. Darklandic women find allure in the Wikshonite faith. There's something about Wikshen they can't resist. I don't understand it."

"She must be very special to you," Kalea said.

"Who am I to lay any claim on her?" Togha's expression drooped by the end of the question.

A long silence passed before Gaije stepped forward. "I suppose"—he clicked his tongue—"in the Darklands, we can pursue women…if—if we desire."

Togha's eyebrows leaped in his brooding, but he didn't raise his eyes from the moist ring the tankard had left in the wood grains. "*Er*," he said—the forbidden Norrian word. "I want her to leave the cult, but she won't leave easily. As a favor to me, can you check on and talk to her for me, try to convince her to leave the cult, or to come and see me? Or at least talk of me to put me back into her mind? That might help, and I'll aid you any way I can. I'll tell you how to find Wikshen's tavern. And if Wikshen has Mhina, I'll do all I can to help save her."

Bowaen swung the empty tankard on his finger. "How the hell are we supposed to get into the Wikshonites' hive to find these girls?"

Togha's eyes darted to Kalea. "Lots of people are joining the faith. I guess you all are hoping to join as well."

Kalea's head went light, her brain void of all the thoughts and questions and comments she previously wanted to say. *Join the Wikshonites?* Instead, she shook her head.

"What an asinine idea," Bowaen said for her. "I'm pretty sure all of us here…" He shook his head also.

"I didn't say you'd join for real," Togha replied to all of their grumbling words and grudging body language. "Just get in there, feign interest in the religion, do your snooping around for what you need, and get out. It's much easier for a devoted follower to move about in their ranks than it is for a person who would snarl and judge and persecute them for their faith."

"As disgusting as it sounds…he's right," Gaije said. All bodies turned to him. "Togha may be a flirt, a sneak, and a deserter, but his antics could suit the type of mission we're on."

Kalea sighed and buried her face in her hands, elbows braced on the table. "Now I'm pretending to be a Wikshonite. How many Sovereign Creators and lashings will it take to undo all the lies *plus* converting to a pettygod religion? We'll all need some serious confession after this."

Gaije narrowed his brow at Togha. "Why won't you accompany us to the tavern?"

"I'm in a tight spot right now. That ale your friend drank was supposed to kill me. It's courtesy of the Clanless *saehgahn* who caught me this morning. If I don't drink it and die in here, they'll kill me as soon as I step out the door."

"Oops," Bowaen said, putting the empty tankard back on the table.

Kalea took her hands away from her face. "How will you escape?"

Togha snapped at the barmaid as she passed by with her dirty rag to wipe off the surrounding empty tables. "I'll need a room with a window and five more ales." He tossed a jingling bag of coins to her and turned back to their company. "I'll lock myself in a room and pretend to drink in there. The staff here will tell the Clanless that I took a few tankards up with me. At night, I'll slip out the window and leave the door locked. Tomorrow morning, when the Clanless ask the innkeeper to open it, they'll find five empty cups plus this one, and a body-shaped mound under the blanket." He drummed his fingers on the table. "And I may not be able to accompany you to Wikhaihli either. The Wikshonites keep me busy."

"What do they have you do?" Gaije asked.

"Run messages around." He kept his somber countenance as a laugh lurked behind Gaije's gentle smile. "What's so funny?"

"Yes, Togha, I'll see if I can find Metta. Now tell us where Wikshen is at this moment."

# Chapter 37
# What is Another Confession

Kalea couldn't help but notice the lack of One Creator sanctuaries in Alkeer. She'd seen at least one steeple rising over the many rooftops, leaning a bit in its disrepair. It might've been a cathedral long ago, but up close they found it a rundown shell, partitioned off to house hundreds of families who needed shelter.

A Clanless member in a bright orange tunic stood guard outside of it. That's what the Clanless did here. Togha had briefly explained to them this morning that no government ran Alkeer. Various factions who warred for control constantly took sections of it away from each other—sometimes finding time to improve the city in between. City ordinances changed like the weather. These days, the Clanless controlled most of the city's largest towers and districts.

It was the best case scenario in a land such as the Darklands. The Clanless stood for basic Norrian principles and safety for the innocent. They protected women and children first and foremost, and sought to make life in Alkeer better for them. They wanted Togha dead because they didn't trust his morals after catching him with a spell scroll. Just like back in Norr, the Clanless harbored little tolerance for off-putting male elves, for fear of the Overseas Taint.

Following Togha's rough instructions, Bowaen led the way through the thick crowds, navigating by landmarks; few street signs could be found. The city was a world more vast and complex than any Kalea had ever seen. Togha had given them directions to Wikshen's tavern in the port district. Locating the port wasn't as easy as looking to the sky for seagulls either. Some districts were blocked off with garbage dumps, shanty houses, or barricades put in place by gangs less friendly than the Clanless. The Clanless were also something to be wary of, except in Kalea's case. Her sex could easily earn their sympathy, but if her male companions did anything to make themselves appear threatening before the Clanless, they could wind up dead on the spot.

Despite Togha's warning, Gaije might as well have been their group's pass in the eyes of the Clanless. Along the way, a few other *saehgahn* clapped him on the back and greeted him with proud acknowledgement. After the first two instances, Bowaen laughed and pointed at how Gaije's orange hair made him blend in with them, to which Gaije made a bitter face.

In the market, dark canopies hung about the area to shelter the sellers, mostly animal skins painted with tar. They proved most useful in shielding the vendors from flash showers rather than the sun. After one quick downpour, an old woman with a black shawl and drum on her back mumbled to the general folk standing around, "There'll be a walking cloud moving in today."

"Oh, great," Del said to his companions. "We better hurry and find the port, or we'll lose it in that damned cloud."

Bowaen gestured for their attention and pushed farther along through the busy throng. On the sidelines of the market, nestled between any nook and cranny available, men and women lounged around with pipes in their mouths and vacant stares in their eyes. A great number of them slept. An alert person passing by tugged the shirt right off one of the lounging men's backs. A woman swooped by and took the shoes off another man who lolled in confusion—the last one in sight who retained his shoes. The patrolling Clanless members were fairly adamant about kicking the members of this group in the ribs as they passed. The loungers hardly noticed, but bore large varieties of bruises.

Deeper into the shady alleys, the loungers sprawled more vacantly than the group in the sunlight. Some hardly breathed, their protruding ribs bulged, and Kalea didn't want to pause and worry over whether they were dead. The alley smelled densely of illness and waste. She buried her nose in her cloak and hurried along behind Bowaen.

Emerging from the dark hole of an alley, they found another busy avenue with more people selling anything they could find. A piercing shriek caught Kalea's ear with familiarity. *Kee-erp*, it called. Kalea paused and exchanged looks with Bowaen.

A silver bird glided overhead and landed on someone's arm. Bowaen mouthed the word "Damos," and Kalea nodded her confirmation. Bowaen pushed forward with more urgency than before, disregarding the upsloping road they were supposed to take.

At the other end of the block, Bowaen called Damos's name. The young man looked up from under his hood, and his pretty blue eyes widened in alarm. He bolted the other way, causing his parrot to launch off his shoulder and make her own way from perch to perch along the buildings.

"What about Wikshen's tavern?" Gaije called across several heads to Bowaen, who didn't pay any mind.

Gaije took Kalea's hand and pulled her along as they dashed across the street, through clumps of standing people and in front of rickety rolling carts, following Bowaen. Leaving this city with both Damos and Mhina would make things convenient, although Kalea still faced the matter of the sorcerers and locating her own friends. Since entering the city, she had seen no red gloves, nor any other strangeness that might point to the sorcerers. Among all the elves she'd seen, none were Dorhen.

"Damos!" Bowaen shouted, his voice booming and echoing over the casual chatter of the crowd.

The young man led them on a merry chase, far off their course. They wound around curving avenues, tripping over broken cobblestones, and trudged muddy streets laced with urine and feces, human and animal.

They also found themselves in another alley filled with drugged people sprawling around, some murmuring and yelling incoherently. Gaije took Kalea in one hooked arm to keep her away from a raving man who reached out to snag her hair. Gaije shoved him roughly against the wall; his head hit and he crumpled to the ground. Too shocked and unprepared to react, she allowed Gaije to lead her on after Bowaen.

Out in the sunshine again, Bowaen, with Del at his elbow, gained a wide distance on Kalea and Gaije. As the two in the lead ran on, Kalea saw Damos slip into the narrow, sunken door of a cozy pub.

She pulled away from Gaije's grasp. "Stop!" she said.

"Bowaen and Del are leaving us." He paused to wait for her explanation.

"Damos is in there," she whispered.

"I'll get the others." He turned, and she grabbed his cloak.

"No! Wait out here. I'll see if I can talk to him. Bowaen will only make him want to run again."

Gaije's face went hard. "I'm not letting you go in there alone." He crossed his arms at the end of his statement.

"Then can you enter quietly and watch me from a distance? And not bother Damos?"

His eyes trailed and his mouth straightened as he considered. "Yes."

"Okay, let's go." Kalea made her way across the street toward the pub.

Gaije grumbled behind her, "We may lose Bowaen and Del."

She twisted around. "Well, you're welcome to stand outside and wait for them to retrace their steps."

Gaije shut his mouth and entered the pub after her. Why did he worry over her so much? In the same way that the Clanless were said to operate, Gaije insisted on watching over Kalea simply because she was female—ever since they first met. Apparently, all the relation to her he needed was for them to be simple traveling companions.

Could Dorhen's reason for liking her be something that simple? Her stomach still tingled at the thought of Dorhen and his antics, like the way he'd grin in his own private delight whenever she granted him a little of her attention. He gave her such a grin after they had prayed together. She remembered the heat coming off of him while they bowed in close. Creator help her, she needed him.

But had he claimed her just because she extended her aid and forged some vague acquaintanceship first? Surely not. Why did Dorhen choose her, and not some other woman from Tintilly? Why Tintilly? If he wanted to dote on a woman, he could've chosen one from anywhere in the Lightlands. He could've encountered countless charitable women along his travels. For that matter, he could've chosen a prostitute who would've been easier to win than Kalea, and who would've shown him greater appreciation for his gifts.

Kalea stopped herself and banished the thought. The image of him forging a relationship with a prostitute drenched her mind and the back of her throat with a bitter acid. Better not to think about who he'd consorted with in the past, or who he could hypothetically consort with.

Once inside the crowded pub, Kalea motioned for Gaije to stay back. He scowled as he did so. If he had his way, she'd be clinging to his arm. If she did, Damos would never talk to her.

Leaving Gaije on the ground floor, Kalea climbed the stairs to the loft where a row of rooms could be accessed. From this vantage, she peered over the heads below for a grey hood or a crown sprouting silvery blonde hair. Damos's grey parrot must've been outside, perched on a rooftop or something.

From below, Gaije's eyes stayed plastered to her. He didn't like the distance and all the bodies standing between them. If she were to get in trouble, it would take a while for him to push his way through the crowd. When she met his eyes, he pointed. She turned around and found Damos standing next to her. She jumped.

"Is your friend down there going to try and catch me?" Damos asked.

Kalea hastily shook her head. "Gaije doesn't care about you. He's on an important mission to rescue his sister."

Damos let out a breath and braced his arms on the rail overlooking the main floor. "Where are your other friends?"

"Out in the streets…looking for you."

"Are you going to turn me in or try to convince me to go back to the Lightlands?"

"Not at all," she said. "I also have a different reason for being here. I've lost a loved one—many loved ones, actually."

"Look," Damos said, lowering his eyes to the wooden rail, smoothed from years of hands. "I'm sorry I ran off on you back in Norr."

Kalea smiled. "You don't have to be sorry about that." She turned completely toward Damos, away from Gaije. Damos's eyes dropped, and she asked, "Are you all right?"

He huffed and turned his eyes away.

"I wanted to check on you," she said. "I won't tell my companions I found you. Gaije won't either. He's only worried about my safety."

"He's right to be. This place is horrible, so much worse than Sharr."

"That's right, you're native to Sharr, aren't you?" He nodded. "Why are you here, if it's so bad?"

"I'd heard it was good," he said, "that a sect of valiant elves patrolled the streets."

"Well, they do in fact."

"It's still not quite what I'd hoped for. I came here mostly to restock my supplies, and I'll depart soon. I'm looking for the best place to live out the rest of my life."

Smiling, she crossed her arms cozily on the rail and lowered her chin. "But you're so young. You have a long life to look forward to."

"How would you know?"

"Aren't you?"

His face flushed. "Not that young," he mumbled. "How old are *you*?"

"Twenty."

He frowned and turned away.

"Forget what I said, okay?" She cleared her throat. "Why did you come to the Darklands?"

"I can't tell you."

She reached out and put her hand on his shoulder. He might've walked away by the look of his body language, but he paused to inspect what she'd done. The situation was too delicate for her to make any mistakes. "Remember when I mentioned confession back in Norr? I know much about redemption in the eyes of the Creator because of my station."

"Which is…?"

"I'm a vestal." He checked her garments in the next instant. "Yes, I know, I'm not wearing the habit, but I *am* a vestal. I'm a Sister of Sorrow from the Hallowill convent. I have a knack for reading people inside and out, and a strong intuition endowed by the One Creator." She didn't believe that, but she couldn't lose this rare chance to gain information on Bowaen's target.

"But—but I saw you dancing at the inn in Jumaire before the sprott attacked."

Kalea pursed her lips, trying to keep level. Her face warmed. "Yes, I danced because a bad man threatened my life. I'm not proud of what you saw me doing."

"Sorry." He blew a breath out over the crowd below. "You're right about what you said. My heart *is* heavy," he confirmed.

Kalea made a deep bow of her head, a gesture Father Liam and the other priests used to show how sincerely they listened. "Damos," she said softly with a well-placed feminine touch. "Although it's not a vestal's place, I've heard confession before from other people. I have a talent for it."

"You do?"

She made that deep, priestly bow again. She'd lied and would have to confess it later; she was terrible at hearing confession. Using the tactic was important today, though, and she'd certainly be able to handle Damos's confession better than she had Dorhen's. Damos, for one, had never peeped at her in the bath, and she harbored no suppressed affections for him. This situation's circumstances were better by far.

Damos rolled his lips in, staring hard at the wooden grains of the rail. "Can you hear my confession right now?"

"Of course. It will be an official confession, privately between us. I will not repeat what I hear. I can also help you figure out how to make amends with the Creator."

She put her hand on his shoulder again and guided him along the catwalk to a quieter corner near the back. Her patronizing gestures came awkwardly; she certainly was impersonating a priest. "We should stand shoulder to shoulder without looking at each other. You face the crowd down there, and I'll look opposite at this wall. You can speak softly in my ear."

They situated themselves as she bid, and he began. "I pray the glorious One Creator forgives me for the sin I am about to confess."

Closing her eyes, Kalea made the deep nod again. "What have you to confess, child?"

He trembled at her shoulder. He must've told the truth about his heavy heart. "I've done a terrible...terrib—"

After a long silence, she offered, "There is no sin too deep for the Creator to forgive. None in the whole world."

He bowed his head in her peripheral vision. "All right... An escalation of events at home caused me to run away."

Kalea listened hard, narrowing her focus to one crack in the wall and sharpening her hearing to his soft voice. Another long silence. "You've run away from some important duties," she said.

"No. Well, yes. My running away isn't the confession."

"Go on." She couldn't tell how often in his life he'd practiced confession, but she knew as well as anyone how difficult it could be. Everyday practice did not guarantee ease if one carried true guilt.

"I have many heavy duties. Important ones," he explained.

"Such as…"

"I'll exclude such details from my confession, but I will tell you that I come from a lofty family. Like many other nobles, I entered the Wistara college to study magery—not entirely important, but there's that detail."

"Mm-hmm."

He cleared his throat, and when he spoke again, a dryness resonated. "I'm guilty of the sins of lust…and murder."

"*Murder*," Kalea repeated absentmindedly, and then checked herself. The Desteer maiden in the ruined village had acted so disgusted and cold toward him after performing *milhanrajea* on him. So he'd murdered someone…

Damos clamped his mouth shut for the moment. "My college held captive a woman. They questioned her, beat her. She'd been dabbling in dark magic, but I felt sorry for her. She met me with a sort of special eye contact whenever I entered the dungeon."

Kalea's heart beat faster at the provocative story. Lust and murder, no wonder the Desteer got so offended. What a record Kalea had created for herself as a confessor! First Dorhen, whose confession was a little too personal for propriety, and now this.

"On one occasion," Damos continued, "my superiors left the dungeon. I should've walked out on their heels…but I lingered. I shouldn't have." He struggled with his dry throat some more. "She…called me over to her cell. An open weaving of wrought iron bars made the door. And…"

Kalea waited.

"Things happened."

Kalea's throbbing heart sped up. She didn't want to hear about it. This would be the end of her confessor's career, she promised herself. No more clients after this one!

"What happened exactly?" She hated herself for asking, but necessity demanded it. In confession, it was important to state what you'd done, or you wouldn't earn complete forgiveness from the Creator and become fully healed on the inside—plus, it might help in Bowaen's cause.

"It began with a kiss," he said. "The kiss got a bit…hot. She gave me my first kiss. I figured at the time, by the moment she pulled her lips away, I loved her." He scoffed. "I was stupid. I don't know if you've ever kissed for the first time yet, but when you're a man—and a virgin—you think your first kiss is written on the wall of eternity."

"Well, it is a landmark," Kalea said. "It's writing on some kind of wall in your life."

He smiled in the corner of her eye, not a happy smile. "Well, in my stupidity, I believed I loved her and she loved me. I interpreted the eye contact she'd granted me as us falling in love. I'd fancied her for a long while anyway."

For Damos's sake, Kalea did worry about the length of time they'd been talking. "So what happened next?"

"The lust," he said.

"All right, so with the kiss, you lusted after her."

"No. Not—not quite."

Kalea waited, a billow of illness swirling around in her stomach. She preferred happy stories with nice endings, not horrible stories worthy of confession. After today, she'd stop announcing her vestal status to people. She'd already renounced it anyway when she kissed Dorhen on the mouth and promised to let him protect her. She'd chosen him over the Creator.

"The kiss ended only to advance to a more…" He swallowed. "She opened my codpiece and did a sexual act on me." He paused to bite his lip. Kalea's mouth hung open. "She made me feel like I'd climbed to the top of the universe. I was in love. I chose her. I enjoyed every minute of it, and I hope the Creator will forgive me for that."

"He will."

"But my confession isn't over. She…well, stopped doing the act before I was ready. She brought me to climax's doorstep. As I braced against the bars, ready to fall over in relaxation but aching with need, she smiled and said I'd get the rest of it after I helped her escape."

Kalea's mouth dried like an old tome. *Please let that be the end of the story!*

"Naturally—and I hope you can understand, seeing how you're not a *male* priest—naturally, I was upset, yearning, and sore—physically. You can't start something like that and leave it unfinished. With all my physical discomforts, I became emotionally sore. And I set my mind to fulfill her request. After all, I had already decided I loved her anyway, so I knew our love would be completed, and I'd do whatever required." He buried his face in his crossed arms. "God, I'm an idiot!"

"Shhh," Kalea said, "don't swear during confession."

"Sorry." A moment of silence passed.

"You also mentioned murder," Kalea prompted, hoping to move

along to the end of the confession. She'd go out and splash her face in the horse trough after this.

"Yes, well… You see, I ran to the Darklands because I am a criminal."

"Hmm." That's not how Lord Dax and Lord Rem had acted when they asked Bowaen to retrieve Damos. Then again, maybe they never planned to tell Bowaen about Damos's crimes. But it didn't make sense regardless—why *not* tell Bowaen he was chasing a criminal to bring back to face justice?

"Having it firmly set in my mind that I loved this woman and needed her to provide my deeply coveted release, I helped her escape the college. I smuggled the key, and I used my own knowledge and ability to lower the spells cast over her prison, and the two of us made it out to the Wistaran forest. And I wanted what she owed me. But when I finally developed the nerve to try to initiate another kiss, she pushed me away and asked me to take her to Sharr.

"Getting to Sharr required a full two days of walking and a ferry ride across the strait before another few days of walking to reach the city walls. Keep in mind, she was now a fugitive and I'm a noble who could easily be recognized. The trip was hard. Keeping a low profile proved difficult too, but I got her there. And I aimed to take care of her. She caught an illness along the way, so I found her a nice cozy spot in an old shed in the city. Made her a nice straw bed, got some blankets."

He paused to swallow again. A peek at him revealed his reddened face. "Her illness was the new excuse not to give me what I was owed." Damos turned his head to give Kalea a hard stare, which she couldn't help but return. "I promise you, I'm not an animal!"

Kalea didn't think that at all, but Damos gave her no opportunity to respond.

"I'm just a young idiot! I'm a new man with an eagerness to become a *full* man. As I said before, since you're not an actual priest, I'm not sure if you'll underst—"

Kalea shushed him softly. "You have my sympathy. Keep going. It's my job to see you through your confession." *And please make it brief!*

"Well, this woman"—Damos shook his head—"had the art of lying mastered. She had eaten an herb from the ground along our way to make herself mildly and temporarily ill, so I could see for myself her wan skin and feel her fever. She acted all pitiful, but she neither planned to give me my release nor to be my wife or my lover, or whatever else I'd hoped!"

Damos bowed his head, raised it, and curled his lips in. "I returned to the shed the next day to find her missing. She caused me such worry. I put my college uniform back on, instead of the plain travel clothes I'd set out with, and went home to the—to my manor I lived in. That's when I heard the news."

"What news?"

"My father lay on his deathbed. Someone had poisoned him."

Kalea crinkled her nose and formed her next question.

Damos spoke faster than she. "I never would have guessed, but they'd caught her. *My* lover! The woman I had let touch me, helped escape, then nursed back to health and hoped she'd touch me again. She had infiltrated my home dressed as a maid and used her knowledge of herbs to poison my father."

"He's dead?"

"I didn't stay around long enough to see him die. One page noticed my return. He told me the news and was the witness of my presence. As soon as he finished speaking, I spun on my heel and walked out. I ran. I had brought Azrielle with us from Wistara, and she and I...we disappeared. I was ashamed, scared, and still aching in my loins." Damos laced his hands together and lowered his forehead to the rail. "I assume my father is dead by now. I murdered him."

"You didn't," Kalea said. "She murdered him, and you're an innocent victim in this."

He shook his head without raising it from the rail. "She would've pointed the finger at me. I'm sure she did. Even if I'm not a murderer, look what a disgusting thing I did. A disgusting thing that got my father killed."

"M-maybe he's not dead," Kalea offered. "They might've found an antidote for the poison and saved him, but you didn't stay around long enough to find out. If only you'd—"

"No."

Their confession stance was no more; now they talked face to face. Damos's wet and red eyes knocked at her heart. She put her hand on his shoulder. "Oh, Damos."

"You know what she turned out to be?"

"Evil?"

Well, yes. But she wasn't just a hearth witch with a knowledge of herbs."

"What was she?"

"A sorceress."

Kalea's entire body went cold.

Damos shuddered as if her chill had jumped over to him. "And I knew all about her affiliation to a sorcery faction before I let her out of the dungeon. The College of Wistara is trying to root out the prominent sorcerers in the Lightlands. They search for their hives."

"Well, I can tell them there's one in Carridax Cathedral," Kalea said, blandness creeping into her voice. She could no longer stand the word "sorcerer." Her homeland had ceased to feel like home after her Carridax experience.

Damos turned his eyes back to the jolly crowd on the ground floor. "It's bad, Kalea." He let the phrase stand for several seconds. "I held a place of importance back in the Lightlands. I bore a duty because of my station to help with the sorcery problem…and I ran away."

The last part came as a whisper. A few silent tears ran out. Her own heart breaking, Kalea wrapped her arms around him without thinking. He stiffened for an instant, then proceeded to slide his hands around her waist.

"The One Creator hears your confession and grants you forgiveness. Your penance may be the heaviest I've ever heard of…"

He pulled away to look her in the eye. They weren't supposed to make eye contact, much less hug. "What is it?"

"Thought," Kalea said. For some reason she didn't need to weigh his options for penance; the words flowed freely from her lips. "You must think about what is right, and then you must do it. That's your penance."

His brow furrowed, and he absently scanned the crowd again. He chewed his lip. "That *is* a heavy penance."

"Penance is never easy. It's no easier than confessing."

He sighed through his nose, looking more mature than ever before. He reached out and took her hand, squeezing. "Thank you, Kalea." He touched his lips to her knuckles. When he gazed at her again, a new intensity shocked her from deep within the cold blue. She took her hand away.

"Good luck, Damos." She stepped backward.

"After hearing my story, you're not going to turn me over?"

"To who?" she asked. "The Creator knows where you are, and I'm busy. I have my own sorrows."

She whirled around and tapped down the wooden stairs to rejoin Gaije. Hopefully, she'd done it. Bowaen might not have to capture him. Maybe Damos would do the right thing and return to face his shame. After a while, she'd consider checking on him through dreamwalking and relay the news to Bowaen. She hadn't forgotten her ability. She feared it to a healthy extent, but if it was so important for Damos to go home, dreamwalking made a great tool for communication on such matters.

After Kalea and Gaije hurried back outside to find their friends, the group re-formed inside a thick shroud of mist which "walked" into the area just as the old woman in the streets had predicted. A lot of arguing and cursing about the mist ensued, as expected.

Kalea dreaded Bowaen's anger at her and Gaije's absence when they slipped into the pub, but the guilt pressed deeper into her when she lied about not seeing Damos. Gaije's back stiffened more than usual as they played dumb, pretending they had looked for Damos and not found him. Gaije would've told them the truth at once, had Kalea not begged him to keep his mouth shut beforehand. He let her do all the talking, but keeping silent must've been hard for him.

They left it all behind them when they moved on in search of Wikshen and Gaije's sister. Once they found the port district, a deserted place, Kalea anxiously stretched her neck the closer they drew to the ocean. The heavy mist covered the ocean view. Seagulls ran about the street in search of food and finding little. Not many people had been here for a day or so. The pier was kept up with new wood here and there, but no ships were docked. A pole sticking out of the water a ways out might have once been a mast. One fishing boat bobbed on the waves, knocking against the dock. Abandoned fishing rods lay along the edge of the pier.

No locals could be found, except perhaps a drugged person lounging on the side.

A ragged old man came out of the dense wall of mist and grabbed Bowaen by the shirt and pulled his face close. "Turn around, boy!" he hissed. "Wikshen's here! Turn around now and walk away or he'll kill ya!"

Kalea visibly shuddered at those words. Her stomach hadn't recovered from hearing Damos's confession, and this new course worsened it.

Bowaen asked, "Which building?"

The man pointed to a tall tavern on a sturdy foundation of stacked stones with its windows blackened out. Most of it was structured from wattle and daub, with extra-thick support beams. The gabled roof soared high. The old man let go of Bowaen and ran off, leaving them to stand in a circle staring at each other for a moment.

"This is it," Bowaen said, his face as sober as Kalea had ever seen. She allowed her fear to show on her face. "We're all pretending to want to join the cult. Got it?"

"What do you think they'll make us do?" Kalea asked.

"No way any of us can know that," Bowaen answered gravely, and turned toward the building with tarred windows.

They proceeded tensely forward across the empty street. An old sign swung in the salty wind with chipped paint showing two swordfish crossing their bills as if in a duel. The smelly tar polluted the air.

Bowaen paused at the door. The word "knock" was scratched fresh into the old wood. Bowaen obliged the carving, and the door quickly cracked open.

An older woman stuck her nose out and studied each of them. "This tavern is closed."

Bowaen leaned in closer. "We want to see Wikshen. Is he here?"

The old woman scanned them over again. "Here to pledge yourselves?" He cautiously nodded. "Wikshen has received enough pledges for today. Got any money?"

"Of course."

"Good." A wrinkly old hand reached through the narrow opening and beckoned Kalea. "You'll come in and see him."

Bowaen's mouth dropped open as he spun to regard her, his eyes wide and worried.

Kalea pointed to herself. "Me?" The ocean waves were whispering gently and the seagulls called; no other voices were left on the pier. "W-w-why me?"

"He won't see any more men but is most often willing to see attractive women…even when he thinks he's done with them." Her mouth corner quirked.

Kalea sent her best pleading face toward each of her friends. Sometime since the witch had invited her in, Bowaen had taken her wrist. He squeezed it. Even Del's expression melted into pallid concern.

"What'll happen when I go in?" she asked, turning back to the woman.

"Whatever he wants, my dear."

*Whatever he wants.* Kalea turned those words over in her mind more than once.

Bowaen mouthed the word "no."

Kalea turned back to the old woman. "Will he answer my questions?"

"Only if he desires."

Kalea regarded her friends again. "Gaije… I'll do it for Mhina."

Bowaen squeezed her arm tighter and told the old woman, "We'll go in with her."

"Not a chance," the woman replied, and widened the door as she rang a bell hanging from her belt.

They couldn't see much of the inside with the windows blackened out as they were. The bell tone summoned two men in black tabards, similar to the way Togha dressed, but these had shaved heads on one side, and their remaining hair had been dyed black and hung long over their left shoulders. They stood to block Kalea's friends from entering the building after her.

She didn't look back, especially at Bowaen, and before she knew it, the door slammed behind her. Kalea stood alone in the dark among many strangers wearing black. In a split second, she'd cut herself off from her friends. She'd ignored Bowaen's silent protests.

The old woman stopped her in the foyer, took away her washing bat and basket, and grasped both her breasts. "Can't hide much in bobbies this small, can ya, girl? Eh?" The old woman cackled out her laughter. She turned Kalea around and stuck her hands up her dress to grope her legs, presumably for whatever could be strapped to them. "Skinny, aren't ya?" she said.

Kalea made it a point to keep her respiration steady and deep. She ignored the strange woman's hands. "I can't see a thing in here, ma'am," she responded. How could all these people get around? The darkness froze her in place like marble, and the woman's groping old talons made her shiver.

"You'll get used to it. Wikshen is the incarnated god of the dark and will not have any light in his dwelling."

Kalea's heart couldn't pump much blood to her head for the moment. The air thinned. Dizzy enough to topple over, she turned her face away so the old woman couldn't see her fear and weakness.

The woman dropped her basket along with her belt, since it could also work as a weapon. "What's this?" the old woman said, snapping her attention down. She was rummaging through the contents of her basket and had found the blue lock of hair Kalea kept stowed in her book.

What could she say in return? Nothing. In this moment of horror, Kalea couldn't fathom what to expect or what to say about that particular item.

"My, my," the old one continued. "How blessed you are, and how lucky. Lucky, lucky, lucky girl...to have been chosen by *him*."

# Chapter 38

## His Visitor

"Um…What did you say?" Kalea's voice peeped. Wikshen had…*chosen* her?

A big, crooked-toothed smile cut into the old woman's cheeks as she glanced up from her squat on the floor. "Hurry now. Take your shoes off. Let's not keep you from him any longer."

"But I—I…"

Why was it so hard to say "I've changed my mind"? She couldn't keep the trembling out of her gestures. The medley of tar and herbal incense blended in her throat, making it scratchy, and mingled in her lungs. She held it in her mind how important it was for her to be in here. She wasn't truthfully here to join the Wikshonites or to…do whatever they thought she was going to do with their deity, she'd come here to find out about Mhina. Gaije needed information about his sister, and Kalea turned out to be the one to do it. Outside the door, he must feel guilty right now. Her chest hurt for him. But she'd also come for herself. If she paid attention, she might glean some information about Dorhen and her sisters from the convent.

*I have to find out where Dorhen is,* she thought. *I'll endure whatever Wikshen intends. Whatever it takes.*

The strange incense burned her nose with its heavy aroma. Kalea's eyes adjusted to the darkness as well as they could. No light breached the blackened windows, yet small shoots of light darted here and there through many cracks in the old building. The incense smoke swirled around in the beams like long, graceful snakes. Merely a few days ago, this place had functioned as a tavern. The smell of mutton and spilled ale lingered under the layers of occult smells. The bar stood abandoned, now used for storage and business. A hooded person bent over a large book, writing in it. Soft noises echoed from the kitchen, where they still prepared food. The cooks might be afraid to make much noise.

The old woman herded Kalea to the right side of the room and forced her to her knees before a black sheet hanging on the wall. "This is our altar," the woman said softly. "Kiss the platform beneath it and ask it to spare your life. Then you will be a proper pledge."

*Oh no. Please.* Kalea cringed and shook her head involuntarily, the motion subtle enough to go unnoticed. She couldn't bow to a false idol, much less a silly length of fabric!

The old woman dropped a handful of coins in the brass bowl at the base of the setup. "I found these in your pack. You must always bring an offering when paying homage to Wikshen. Food and certain herbs are also good, but metals are best."

She jumped at the old woman's hand on her shoulder. "I said, bow your head." She pushed Kalea's head down until her lips brushed the cloth lying over the stone base. "Three times," she continued, and proceeded to push her head down twice more. "Once for the pixie, once for his host who lent his capable body, and again for Wikshen."

Now Kalea wanted to vomit out the substantial breakfast she'd enjoyed this morning. She'd just worshiped a false god!

The woman pointed to the back of the room, where the stage stood covered in layers of more tent-like black draperies. Kalea could barely tell anything was there in the darkness. She squinted until the old woman produced a dish from her pocket and tapped a metal object to the rim. A chime echoed softly, strange and flat, and a small blue flame sparked to life in the dish.

*She's a witch!* Kalea had handed herself over to witches. She now stood at the beck and call of a monster posing as a deity. And soon she'd join him, to be cowed around and ordered to do Creator-knew-what with him!

Bearing the new light, the witch hurried forward and entered the shrouded stage. Silhouettes sprang up in front of the new glow. The witch-woman put the flame on a low-standing table, at which a large, slim figure sat motionless and confident. No words were exchanged between the old woman and the figure.

"Is..." Kalea paused to swallow. Her throat muscles stopped, and she fought through it. "Is that him in there?" she whispered as the witch returned.

"Shh, don't ask stupid questions. Go in now and do whatever he bids you."

The witch pushed her with a firm, confident arm. If Kalea felt strange before, now she couldn't feel her body at all. The scenery moved past her, so she must've been walking. She managed to ascend the steps without tripping and pass through the heavy drapes without getting tangled.

"Remember," the witch said before leaving her alone with Wikshen, "do *whatever* he tells you to do."

The light from the little dish in this heavily shadowed space overwhelmed her eyes, blocking out who or what sat on the other side of the table. A naked bent knee could be made out, emerging from a covering like a robe or sheet. And an arm rested on the table, wearing a glove with exposed, relaxed fingers angled toward her.

She waited. For something, anything. To be called. Invited. Greeted. Ordered. None of that happened. Her lungs trembled when she breathed—she hadn't known such sensations were possible. When her parents left her at the convent, it hadn't terrified her nearly as much as this. She was utterly alone. She stood at the mercy of a powerful monster, surrounded by his fervent worshippers.

She couldn't stand the silence any longer. "I…" she tried, but he still made no sound. She reminded herself about the mission which rested on her shoulders. "I'm not here to pledge myself."

"Of course not. You came to kill me," responded a smooth, deep voice. It wasn't Arius Medallus's voice. His blue hair had made her worry that Dorhen's beloved fairy guardian also happened to be Wikshen. This meeting felt nothing like Arius Medallus's appearance in her convent.

At his words, whatever she would say next flew away. "What did you say?"

"I know why you're here." The hand lifted from the table and made a slight gesture. "Sit with me."

She slowly moved forward, but couldn't see him any better. The table was set with silverware, a black tablecloth, and various types of skillfully prepared food. The closest thing to him was a platter of fresh fruit.

"Why do you think I will…kill you?"

He didn't answer, nor did he indicate he would. He didn't move. The voice, running dark and smooth, rang out suddenly. "Thinking has nothing to do with it. When I lay on the floor at the sorcerers' lair in a puddle of piss, you appeared to me in a vision, most likely a memory belonging to my host."

"I don't underst—"

"I recognized you in the forest, and now I'm seeing you for a third time, eliminating all possibility of coincidence. You're here because you mean to be. You are persistent, and that's why you are worthy."

"Since I'm here now, wouldn't you kill me first?"

Silence. Maybe he was smiling at her, thinking her stupid. "It's my objective to survive as long as I can, as you would expect. But I don't want to kill you. You are my choice." He turned his hand over on the table. "Place your hands on the table. Palms up."

She hesitated for long, agonizing seconds.

"Don't be afraid."

She slowly did so, her hands trembling. He placed one of his large, hot hands over one of hers. An uncomfortable tingle happened in the middle of her palm and ran up her arm, turning it to ice. It travelled across her chest, and she wheezed for a moment. Her voice rattled out in an involuntary moan. The cold made its way to her other arm and down to her hand.

Tiny gold nuggets, like seeds, seeped out of the skin of her palm and flooded her grasp, spilling onto the table and then to the floor. They bounced across the wood in all directions, tapping into the dark corners beyond her scope of vision. She let out a louder, jittery moan, ready to panic from the prickly sensation until the eruption wound to an end.

Panting, she rubbed her chest in an effort to bring the heat back into it. The tiny nuggets left her hand sore, as if she'd been pricked with hundreds of needles.

He took his hand away, now ice cold. At her sounds, many voices on the other side of the curtain murmured and made impressions of awe.

"There, see?" Wikshen said. "I can't channel through just anyone. Only my concubines."

"Your wha—?" Her voice lost its strength. This was too much.

"And I can't buy you." He batted the nuggets out of her hand, causing them to spray against the wall at the back of the stage. "But you might be bargained with for my body."

"You make no sense!" She slapped her hands on the table, and instantly regretted it because of her sore one. Her heart leaped and fluttered. She might die of a heart attack at any minute, but for now she stood her ground. Speaking calmly proved hard. "What are you—?"

She stopped herself and took a deep, long drag of whatever air she could find in the strong cloud of incense. She formed her words carefully. "Wikshen," she said, "I want to ask you some questions."

He crossed his arms.

She drew her hands back into her own space. "You kidnapped a *farhah*—a little girl elf in Norr. Where is she right now?"

He stood up. The black drapery he wore around his waist fell over his exposed knee and cascaded to the floor in several long fabric ripples. With it flowed a long vest, leaving his thick, sculpted biceps bare.

Kalea stood also. When he was not directly behind the light, more detail of him showed. His fabled blue hair hung to the small of his back, silky with every beautiful strand in place. He fit Gaije's description exactly, and Kalea recognized him, eerily, as the dark entity who had groped her when she staggered through the Norrian forest—the incident Wikshen had mentioned earlier.

"You can go now," he said.

Go? So easily? She had expected horrors beyond imagination. Her bodily reaction to this meeting had been worse than the meeting itself. He wanted to be difficult. She hadn't come here to participate in his magic trick and listen to a bunch of cryptic words about why she was here and whatever his body had to do with it!

She widened her bare feet on the floor. "No."

"Would you like to stay? I've failed to produce a blessing so far, but you may be the one." He trailed his fingers across his navel as he spoke.

"I would like some answers."

His hands dropped to his sides. "I'm bored now."

Her fists balled, fingernails digging into her palms. "Listen here, do you know what you've done, kidnapping that child? Don't you have a care, or shame, or sense? Do you understand sin?"

When he turned around, the light hit his face. His cheekbones were high, his nose broad. His eyes were shadowed and ominous.

"Did you stop to think about her mother? That you'd stolen her only daughter?"

"No," Wikshen said. His left hand resumed caressing his naked, sculpted belly. What did he ponder?

"Is the girl alive?" Kalea pressed despite her distrust of the way he touched himself and stared back at her from under the shadow hiding his eyes. "Tell me!"

The curtains rippled and the old woman's voice rang out, about to end her audience, but Wikshen stamped a foot on the wooden stage, and the witch fell off after a precise tremor he sent her way. He turned back to Kalea like a looming shadow with thick hair, heavy on his head, staring at her as if to silently beckon.

"Is she alive?" Kalea asked again.

"Keep yelling at me."

"You—you evil…!" Her brain didn't register it, but she stormed at him, fists raised. He stood firm, welcoming her threats to his body. He put his arms out to each side and stared her down. "Is she alive?"

"Maybe," he whispered.

"Answer me!"

He licked his lips. A smile curled both sides of his mouth. His teeth gleamed in the blue light. One long one on the side resembled a fang.

"What's her condition?"

"Not good."

She thrust her palms into his solid, unyielding stomach, and he took a step backward, though he remained unfazed. The voices roared outside the drapes, and Wikshen stomped his foot again and again to keep the witches and warlocks out. He possessed some kind of magical grasp on vibrations.

Wikshen kept his eyes trained on her. "Ask something else," he said.

Something else? Why couldn't he answer her question about Mhina? Though she could barely think anymore, if she could at least get him talking, the conversation might backtrack to Mhina.

The question which occurred to her next made her guts churn. "Why did you 'choose' me?"

His head cocked. A muscle in the side of his face moved in the dim light—he smirked. "Good question. How could I choose someone with such a wiry frame and no tits?"

"I'm serious, you—!" She reared back and grabbed a knife off the table, lying next to the butter, and threatened him with it. "Don't try to fool me. Answer my next questions. Were you involved with the raid on my convent?"

"I know nothing about this."

"Sorcerers raided my convent! Were you one of the sorcerers?"

The corners of his mouth turned downward. "Don't insult me, or I'll let the shamans have you."

"How's that an insult?"

"I am *not* a sorcerer. And I wasn't at your convent."

"But you rode with the sorcerers."

"The sorcerers are a boil on my scrotum. What's your next question?"

"I'm looking for an elf named Dorhen. Do you know what happened to him?"

"I might know something."

"But do you know *him*?" She marched forward with the knife poised. She backed him against the wall. He grinned faintly as he watched her.

"You must know where he is," she said. "I know you were in the Lightlands when you took the *farhah*! You were with the sorcerers! You were in their camp with Vivene! What have you done with Dorhen? Did you kill him?"

She thrust the knife against his neck. He whipped his hand and grabbed the blade without a care for its sharpness.

Kalea lost her balance and stumbled. She caught herself, momentarily confused as to why the knife weighed less than before. The blade was gone. When he had grabbed the blade, it melted and disappeared into his palm, sinking into his skin. He absorbed the metal.

She couldn't fight him. She stood helpless. Her stomach churned. She gaped up at him, holding the empty wooden handle. She opened her hand, and it dropped to the floor uselessly. Her heart pounded like nothing she'd experienced before. Her body quaked. She opened her mouth and her jaw shook.

He leaned in close to her. His hair half-veiled her face. His breath beat against her jaw.

"Yes, I did." He whispered it. With both hands, he took her face and held her close, playing his nose around her ear. He smelled her hair and whispered, "I killed him, and he screamed and he begged for my mercy. And then I pissed on his face."

Kalea went numb. Her trembling ceased. She blinked. Her lungs stopped. Hovering beside her ear, he brushed his tightly smiling lips against her cheek. He pecked a kiss.

Her tears ran and her throat ached. Tensing every muscle she owned, she sprang for his neck, to grab it and squeeze as tight as she could before he inevitably killed her in self-defense. But her knees gave way and she leaned against him instead, grasping his vest along with locks of his blue hair. She cried. She sobbed against the bare skin between the lapels. She worked her jaw and throat a bit before she could get the word "why" out. She couldn't form another thought besides that one. *Why?*

Wikshen slid his hands around her—groping her again, she supposed, but she couldn't feel it. She could feel nothing besides the pain of her heart ripping in half. Who knew what he'd do to her now? She'd gone weak, and now relied on Dorhen's murderer for support. He held her. She no longer heard her own wailing. She'd vacated her body. Her consciousness had stepped out to watch the scene from a more comfortable distance away. There they were, in an embrace, Wikshen's head bowing over her as she huddled into his chest like a trembling, traumatized cat. The ends of his blue hair rested on her shoulders. This could very well be Kalea's last moment as a virgin, and she wouldn't even notice. She would be too weak and powerless to stop it, and she didn't care. The best she could hope for was for him to kill her afterward. Maybe he'd piss on her face when he finished.

A hand came out of nowhere and yanked her hair backward, and she instantly and dizzily returned to her body. A bulbous jute sack hit the side of her face with a thick puff of airborne powder.

"Cover your face, Mastaren!"

Kalea coughed, barely noticing herself being ripped out of Wikshen's arms. The grainy dust rushed through her nose and into her lungs. Wikshen lurched but let her go as she collapsed to the floor, becoming dizzy and coughing uncontrollably. In her spinning vision, Wikshen staggered into the shadow. He made a sick sound and heaved.

"What's the matter, Mastaren?"

"No!" Wikshen's voice roared weakly after spitting.

The numbness creeping through Kalea's body grew wider by the second, but she could sense her arm being pulled. A witch was trying to drag her away. Another, stronger hand landed on her chest.

"Leave her here!" His voice lost its cool edge. "I want her here!"

The chaotic voices rolled all around Kalea. "Mastaren, she has dishonored and tried to harm you!"

"I don't care—obey my order! I want h…"

The sounds faded.

# Chapter 39
## What is Locked Away

Vivene gaped in awe at the ancient tower materializing from the heavy Black Mountain smoke. They'd finally arrived at their destination. All along, the sorcerers had given her no idea what to expect about where they were going or how long it would take.

Following the "kingsorcerer's" order, they met back up with his group at the foot of these dreadful, smoky mountains and continued together. The kingsorcerer was not a jolly person, even compared to the sorcerers she'd been traveling with. The sorcerers she'd gotten to know would offer a smile or a joke now and again—to each other, not to Vivene and the other captives. All she got were slaps on the back of her head and orders.

She kept her best distance from their leader. Luckily for her, a leggy Darklandic primitive woman kept him occupied. He never bothered to give Vivene a glance. He did, however, harbor enough interest to open one certain basket to look at or speak to the child trapped within. Vivene shook her head at the sight. *Those poor kids.*

Now, her awe glued her eyes to the rugged black spire rising from a massive pit of misty nothingness. Hundreds of windows dotted the curved walls, some lit. Several pointed shapes looming faintly behind the main tower suggested there was more to the structure than was visible at first.

"Welcome home, lads," Lamrhath said, stepping briskly past Vivene. A small shiver rattled through her as he did. His statement garnered replies of cheer and relief from the other sorcerers. Lamrhath's primitive woman's awe mirrored the other women's.

Just because they'd seen the tower didn't mean the journey was over. A mile or more of trekking around a winding cliff lay ahead. The path sloped downward as they spiraled closer to the colossus standing in the pit of mist. A bridge never appeared around the bend as Vivene expected. She wrinkled her nose and resisted asking how they would get into the tower. In truth, she didn't care how she'd get in. She knew by the ache in her gut she'd never get back out. Besides, questions were illegal in the Ilbith faction.

At last, the trail stopped at a little landing with miles of drop-off all around. No bridge, no ladder, no water or boat. At this low point in the canyon, the cliff still loomed impossibly high. No bottom could be seen under the mist below. She could only tell water flowed down there from the faint sound.

One of the most prominent sorcerers under Lamrhath took a shiny plate he'd kept under his tunic from around his neck and angled it to make the sunlight glance off. He flashed the medallion side to side at a specific wing in the tower. Studying his motion, Vivene recognized a pattern. He was doing more than getting someone's attention, he was communicating in an advanced alternative language.

It took a few moments' wait for him to stop his flashing and put the medallion away, and then a surge of lightning split the air, eerily similar to what had happened on that fateful night at the convent. Bright, dancing wires of light formed a U-shaped hole in the air, and a dark corridor could be seen inside the shape, a stark contrast to the misty daylight outside.

"Hurry now," the sorcerer said, ushering everyone through.

The kingsorcerer went first with his woman, followed by sorcerers carrying the baskets, and then Vivene and the other women. All the goods were loaded in behind her, and the last few sorcerers filed in. The portal closed swiftly after the last person.

A sinking feeling washed over Vivene as she stood among the crowd, getting straight to work in the new setting. She had arrived. For the rest of her suffering life, she'd be here: in Ilbith. All thanks to that bastard, Wikshen, who hadn't helped her escape while they were together. From here, she would focus on finding out what had become of the other novices, and then later try to cope with this brand new life she'd been given. There was no telling what she'd have to do, how she would be treated, or how miserable it would be.

She watched the sorcerers unpack the crates from their horse and wagon. They'd landed in a cave-like setting, expertly carved and wide. Other horses were kept here in stalls, making the place smell like a proper stable. But many red-robed men walked around, ordering drab-looking people around and approaching to meet the newcomers. The drab people moved about, caring for the horses and sweeping the floor, which was set neatly with crisp new bricks. Vivene would most likely be slotted to join them in their work. This place must have cooks and servants.

The children's baskets were quickly carried away at Lamrhath's order. Vivene's stomach sank as she watched them go, and then the kingsorcerer himself walked pointedly away with his primitive lady-friend.

Her new home. It occurred to her quickly how Father Superior had traded the novices to this place. She'd gone from having a promising future as a vestal…to this. The corruption in the convent must've run as deep as the sea. Her parents had paid good money for her to live as a vestal—it wasn't merely a charity to house crazy and deformed girls. And look what they'd done to her! She'd thought she would live a holy, celibate life, and already she'd lost count of how many cocks had entered her body after the first week!

Now, a new life awaited—not under the blessings of the Creator but under a lecherous kingsorcerer in the Darklands.

Up several winding flights of stairs, Vivene's captors led her to a squalid room where her fellow novice sisters lived. She ran into their many arms, and all the girls huddled together in a tangle of tears and words of welcome and ever-present sorrow. That's what they were: the Sisters of Sorrow. The tears escaped Vivene's eyes after all those weeks of her iron will forbidding it.

When they all calmed down, Vivene surveyed the group. "Where's Eronia?" she asked.

The girls around her sulked. Some broke straight into more weeping.

"Dead," Millie answered. "The sorcerers tried to make her inhale that flowery smoke when we got to this tower. She just wouldn't calm down. The smoky stuff triggered her asthma. She died right there."

"What a waste!" Vivene shouted, and the group shushed her.

"Just as well," Millie said. "Every time they'd rape her, her breathing would drag and wheeze. I guess it would've happened sooner or later. Better that it occurred sooner."

"And where's Tanya?"

Millie huffed. "You know how much her heart troubled her?" Vivene didn't need too much explanation, but Millie told her anyway, "All the walking involved with getting here, paired with the rape and foul treatment, strained her heart to its last struggling beat." Millie shrugged. "Her bad heart was the reason she got put into the convent. All the peace of quiet hours, prayer, and contemplation did her a lot of good. If only this hadn't…"

Millie trailed off into a frown and put her hands over her mouth. Vivene scooped her into a hard embrace.

"Well, now *I'm* here," Vivene said. She didn't bother to explain the proclamation. There was nothing she could do to help any of them or herself, but she'd stand strong for them.

"And Kalea's not here, of course," Millie said when she'd regained her composure. "We're hoping she's still alive."

"She is," Vivene said. "If she's not here with us, you know she got out."

"I heard someone break the door, but how could she…?"

"Didn't you see the elf?"

Millie spread her hands and met the other girls' eyes. "We were all terrified and screaming. I recall a man's voice shouting and fighting the sorcerers, but an elf?"

"Yes," Vivene said. "She kept an elf as a lover. He got in and helped her escape. He got captured with us, though. I was hoping he'd help us out, but he's gone now."

"Well," Millie said, her voice dragging low, "all that is over now—"

Rose piped up. "Kalea did get out." The girl stepped forward, her funny round face smiling. Her face was dry, unlike everyone else's.

Vivene sniffled. "Rose, you made it too, huh?"

"Kalea got out," she said again.

"Did you see her?" Rose shook her head. "So how do you know she got out?" Vivene asked.

"She's coming here."

"How do you know?" Vivene's voice shouted again, despite the possibility that sorcerers outside in the hall could hear. She'd never been able to muster as much patience for Rose as Joy and the others had. Rose had been born different from everyone else. Aside from ugly, she was dumb in a lot of ways, but at closer inspection she seemed to fathom things on a completely different level from everyone else.

Rose's innocent smile beamed on. "The Creator told me."

Cupping Silva's face in both of his hands, Lamrhath pulled his lips slowly away from hers. They were standing in her new room, located close to his own. She smiled more smugly than ever. Not too long ago he'd had her, and now he already fought a full erection. The illness crept into his abdomen and the ache hit fast, but he wouldn't bother her again today. She was the best treasure he'd found in the Darklands in ages. She was not only obedient and beautiful, she liked being with him. She recognized his greatness and appreciated the high status he offered her. Not many did.

He opened a wardrobe to show her the assortment of fine dresses she now owned. As soon as they'd entered Ilbith, he'd sent a sorcerer running to prepare her room, and to gather these dresses from their stock of long-collected spoils.

"And this," he said, opening a box to reveal a gold and ruby necklace. "Wear it all the time. It displays your status and will keep all the other sorcerers from bothering you. You are to be solely with me." Her eyes sparkled at him and pored all over the glittering piece of jewelry. "Prettier than the body paint, isn't it?" he asked with a smirk.

She gave the bow they had taught her to do. "My lord," she said.

He took her face again and kissed her forehead. "You'll be my wife." At his proclamation, she melted into him, and he resisted his urge to return her affection, which would escalate into another unceremonious romp. Instead, he took her hand and kissed her knuckles. "Get some rest. I'll see you tomorrow."

She curtsied, another move they'd taught her. "Where will you be tonight, my lord?"

He paused along his way to the door. "Visiting my other wife."

Duty required Lamrhath to stop by his grand office to catch up on business inside of Ilbith and out. He took a few moments to close his eyes and listen to his collection of whisper stones bearing messages from various corners of the Darklands and a few from the manors and sanctuaries around the Lightlands.

*Wikshen has been acting strange by comparison to our deep-rooted lore,* one of the stone voices said.

He spoke back into the stone. "Study him hard, his every movement. Take down notes and send them to me."

He sent replies to the other sorcerers, answering questions and delivering new orders. He had finished his last response when the door swung open and Talekas strolled in, sporting a questioning expression.

"Welcome home, my lord."

Lamrhath waited until he noticed Talekas also waited for something.

"Um," Talekas said, "where is Wikshen? I assumed he'd be at your side."

Lamrhath dropped a heavy book onto the other side of his desk to clear space. "Wikshen. Escaped." He didn't look up from his petty toiling, and cracked open a different book to peruse its headings and jot page numbers on a leaf of paper.

"Escaped?" Talekas echoed.

"Not to worry, because he's already been found. Wikshen thinks he's a god, Talekas. It'll be hard to keep him on our leash, but we'll find a way. In all reality, he's merely a pixtagen: a mortal whose mind was conquered by a pixie. He's a simple pettygod. In fact, his cult may prove to be his most valuable asset, more than his power."

"You're not worried?"

Lamrhath shot him a smirk. "Why should I be worried?" He scribbled the title of a book that occurred to him after his perusal. "I'm horny, that's what I am. Here." He tapped a corner of the paper. "Dry this ink and then take it down to the library to locate these texts. For now, I have to retire. It's been a very long journey."

Talekas bobbed his head. "Yes, Kingsorcerer. I'm so sorry to hear of your misfortune in the portal castings."

"It's over." Lamrhath hurried out of the room.

Lamrhath barely made it to his chamber on his own feet. As the door slammed behind him, he keeled over and moaned. The cold stone floor froze his cheek. He panted and struggled to his hands and knees as one of his concubines approached. This was bad. His illness was reaching new levels of torment like never before.

"My lord!" the concubine whined, and put her hands on his arm to comfort and help him up.

"Prepare me a bath," he said, his voice running ragged and strained.

Now on his feet, he bent over to hug his stomach. His other hand ventured to feel the tightness of his erection. When would it end? He'd taken a moment with Silva mere hours ago when they stopped to rest along the canyon trail! Even the exhaustion of travel couldn't stopper his lust. How could he ever get anything done when his libido caused such pain and suffering at all hours of the day? A lot of his sorcerous duties required long hours of meditation and chanting. Some rituals lasted three days straight. How could he ever get through another one of those without stopping to have sex?

By now, two of his other concubines had come running, and the first darted away to order a bath from the maids. While they heated the water and filled the tub, he ordered a release by mouth from one of his attending concubines.

Afterward, he could enjoy his bath in peace. A bath always preceded a visit to his wife. He wanted to look his best for her, to be fresh and clean—not that she ever appreciated his efforts. At least this time, he'd released before the visit, which meant he wouldn't have to attack her like an animal on first glance. He bore important news to share and wanted to make this evening perfect.

His first wife lived in her own apartment as well, a bit grander than Silva's. This particular wife, however, required being locked inside. Her meals were passed through an opening in the door.

"Orinleah," he said, gazing at her magnificent face.

She was robed all the way to the floor in one of the special garments he had commissioned for her. The flash of a brocade floral pattern woven into the red silk dazzled his eyes. The neckline swept deep across her shoulders to expose her collarbone and throat, which sparkled with the greatest jewels his faction could acquire. Her gowns were expertly crafted in the finest fabric imported all the way from Sharr through his intricate sorcery network. Anything in Kaihals he wanted waited at his fingertips.

He drew attention to her particularly special necklace. "Do you wear these jewels every day?" he asked.

Her face stayed bland save for the narrowing of her brooding eyelids, her mouth straight and firm. "I do it because I'm supposed to. What do you want?"

She knew what he wanted. They'd been married for sixteen years already. She was also made to bathe, dress, and prepare for his visits. Her silky, dark hair made him shudder with a tingly thrill that sparked his cock. He'd brought along a leather satchel, and now he focused his thoughts on it to restrain his libido.

"I came to see the one I love."

"You don't love me, you fool," she scoffed, and turned away. "Just do your business and leave me alone." She sat on the bed—a great, fluffy bed built just for her—and crossed her arms.

Lamrhath frowned. "I've been gone so long, and you've nothing to say to your husband?"

"I haven't seen my husband in sixteen years. You killed him. You told me so yourself."

Lamrhath scoffed at the thought of Daghahen. Yes, he'd killed him—as far as *she* needed to know. As of now, Daghahen and the sword, Hathrohjilh, were still missing, and soon he'd have to send more agents out to locate them.

"Does it matter?" he asked. "Daghahen and I were twins. The same flesh, divided into two, and I'm the better half. So why can't you accept me?"

She rolled her eyes, keeping them averted. She crossed one leg over the other. Long and sleek, it emerged from the high slit in her dress; her legs were nicer than Silva's. "Hurry and get it over with." She moved up the bed and laid herself out stiff and straight, like a dead body in repose.

Lamrhath frowned, fingering the satchel in his hand. "I guess you don't care to hear the news of your son, Dorhen, do you?"

She sat up. Her eyes took on a new light, a fierce light. She didn't speak quite yet.

He had planned to share the news with her over the dinner they'd eat together in her chamber. A pleasant evening was all he wanted, dinner and lovemaking. And as a gift to her, he'd tell her about Dorhen.

"We found him," Lamrhath said.

She got off the bed and hesitated, choosing to cross her arms instead of storm him for answers as he expected. She scowled. "What do you mean, you found him? You can't find him."

"Oh yes, I can. And I did." His voice came out soft but gruff.

"No." She shook her head. "My son is beyond your grasp."

Lamrhath cocked his head. Now he expected an explanation. "What do you mean? As much as you've praised and talked of him, you've never mentioned anything like that before. You don't know where your son is."

She raised her chin with pride. "I don't know where he is, but I know he's safe from *you*. And I'm telling you now to catch you in your lie—of which you have many."

"Explain."

"On the night you snatched me out of my own house…"

Lamrhath focused on listening, his ailment forgotten for now. "Yes?"

"I went to the creek where the mist gathered in the sultry air."

This was interesting. She'd never let on about any knowledge of her son's status or location. She'd told him little past Dorhen's departure with his father to dig potatoes—besides what a strong and fierce *saehgahn* she expected Dorhen to grow into. In the weeks following Daghahen and Dorhen's disappearance, when Lamrhath's scouts had spotted Daghahen in the human lands, he didn't have his son with him. During their sixteen-year search for Dorhen, Orinleah offered no help, but she spoke of the lad often and usually in delirious reverie.

She continued, "Down there, I met a friend of mine, a fairy who'd watched over me since I became a mother." She kept her stern disposition as she strolled over to the small window, the only one in her room. "I asked my friend to take Dorhen away, should anything happen to me. And I knew he'd be the best guardian for my child—a fairy, of all people."

After all his experience with spirits and other worlds, Lamrhath easily believed her claim. "Why did you do that?"

"I agonized for weeks about my Dorhen. I didn't trust my husband with him. As soon as the two departed, I dashed for the creek and sealed the deal with the fairy. On that very night, if Daghahen was planning to harm him, the fairy would've intercepted. It meant I would lose my son regardless, but he'd survive. I gave over my Bright One-endowed ownership of him as his mother to the water spirit I trusted more than my husband. Earlier that night, I felt a grave twisting inside of me." She made a firm fist at her abdomen. "I knew something would happen, but I couldn't have anticipated it being *you*, instead of my husband, who caused the danger."

Lamrhath lost his cool façade. Now he stood amazed at her. "What were the terms of the deal you made with the fairy?"

"That he would take Dorhen into his care. He would keep Dorhen safe for all time and never harm him, never mistreat him. The fairy told me he would bestow a blessing on my son. He agreed to my terms. We sealed the deal, and I returned home to wait for Dorhen. You came instead, and your threat put the deal into effect."

"So you're the guilty party," Lamrhath said, unable to suppress a smile. "You were the reason he was so hard to find. You gave him to a *fairy*."

Orinleah pursed her lips. "I'd do it again. I should've given myself to the fairy as well."

Lamrhath slid his fingers through his freshly washed hair. "You were the reason I set out to find him at all."

"Why would you go looking for my son? He's of no value to you."

A little laugh burst out of Lamrhath's throat before he knew it. "You know I love you, darling, but you're wrong. He's of value because I have his mother here, refusing to accept her marriage to me."

She shook her head and turned away from the window and the deepening sunset. Soon the candles would provide the romantic lighting for their evening together. "I still don't accept it, because *you* are wrong. He is under a fairy's protection."

Her constant attitude stung him during their every meeting. "No fairy protected him when we found him. In fact, he was a dirty little scamp who spent his evenings knobbing human girls in a convent when we found him. Your little *saeghar* is all grown up, and I can show him to you."

She hissed the words, "You're a filthy liar."

Lamrhath shook his head and opened the satchel. "See for yourself. We captured him and my artist drew him for you." He caught a slight glint of doubt in her large, round eyes as he took out the charcoal drawing of Dorhen's face and handed it to her.

She snapped the drawing from his hand and studied it for a long moment until she finally snorted. "You're such a lying fool." She'd always been a brazen one, despite the beatings she'd sometimes earned. This was one *faerhain* who didn't fear death or pain. "This is not my son." She shoved the mounted vellum panel back at him.

"Careful, don't smudge it!" He held it out, enticing her to look again.

"That's not my son; he doesn't smile like that."

"How would you know how he smiles? You haven't seen him since he was six!"

"I know my son, and that's not him."

He pushed the drawing closer. "I wouldn't be so sure."

Orinleah sat on the bed. Her eyes lingered on it. He stood over her, offering the drawing until she took it. Her mien softened, though he couldn't gauge whether she was coming around or not.

"I'd planned to bring him to you so you could be together again."

At his statement, she glanced up and back at the drawing.

He continued, "It has been my great desire for you to look into my eyes and tell me things I'd like to hear."

She snorted. "Like what?"

"Like 'thank you' for once… But for now, there's been a delay with Dorhen's arrival. Nonetheless, I've made it my duty to bring him here. He's my gift to you, as I know you miss him. Can we be friends again?"

Without taking her eyes off the drawing, she growled, "We were never friends in the first place."

"We were when we met."

She glanced up at him once more, her face painted with doubt. They had first met on the day of Dorhen's birth. How she smiled at him then, and chatted with him, and invited him to return for a future visit. All the while she held Dorhen, naught but a breathing new mound of flesh swaddled in her arms.

For one precious moment, Daghahen had left the room, and there Lamrhath sat with Orinleah and her son. The three of them. He knew how happy that worthless whelp, sown by the wrong seed, made this *faerhain*. If he could reunite the two… If he *could've* reunited the two before Daghahen ruined it all…maybe Orinleah would smile at him again and say "thank you" or "welcome." Maybe she'd let him into her life for once. Maybe she'd let him back into her dreams like she used to.

Swallowing thickly, he whispered, "Let's get along for once."

He ventured to put his hand on her exposed leg, hot and smooth under his hand, and his breath caught in a sudden new whirl of emotion. His erection pulsed to its full stature, ready again after such a short period of rest. Orinleah set it on fire with the feel of her skin, the resonance of her sensual voice, and even her cold, defiant expressions.

He wanted to do it right this time. He wanted her to appreciate him. Tonight was special. He'd finally found Dorhen, and Orinleah would eventually see the real thing, although such a major drawback had occurred with the lad's possession. Dorhen should've been his gift to her after all those years, so she could finally appreciate him and his efforts to please her. Instead, because of his stupid brother, all he could offer her was this drawing and a promise that she'd see her son soon. They were supposed to be a family, the three of them.

Lamrhath nudged her to lie down, and she did so absentmindedly while studying the drawing. She held her eyes on it as he parted her legs to find her reluctant intimate area unguarded by any undergarments. She was made to dress like this for all of his visits. He would do this right. She should like some tenderness once in a while.

At the sight of her most secret body part, his body raged with excitement. He suppressed his thrill with all of his willpower. The ache crept in fast and would be agony soon. He parted the fleshy lips between her legs and slicked his tongue between them. The taste was too much, and the feminine scent taunted him…

His heart pounded at an alarming new speed. His ailment introduced nausea to his own mix of feelings, discomforts, and emotions. Skipping this portion would be unfair to her. He truly wanted her approval. He wanted her to like it. When not practicing his magic, he fornicated all day long with some of the most gorgeous creatures his faction could bring him, but for some reason he *needed* Orinleah to approve! For once!

His cock sent pulses of agony to the rest of his body. He could stand it no longer. Even with his tongue shoved into her moist, fleshy opening, he groaned in pain. The thought crossed his mind to take his cock out and massage it to orgasm as he worked on her, but masturbation never removed the pain. His hand never accomplished what a woman's body could.

Orinleah finally dropped the drawing when he surrendered to his anguish and crawled on top of her. She'd shown no impression at his tongue work.

He thrust into her with both a groan of agony and a sense of relief, knowing the pain would soon stop. The caress always promised he'd get his relief. Each vigorous thrust eased his agony until it was no more.

Orinleah didn't make a sound. She lay there, waiting for it to be over—she always did! Her eyes trailed back to the drawing beside them on the bed. He made more noise than she ever would, and he hated it! He hated his ailment, but it trapped him! An all-enveloping urge held him every bit the prisoner that she was.

Tears he barely noticed emerged as he worked. Alone. This whole situation isolated him with his illness. Her being there beneath him didn't matter. He was alone. And he hated himself for it. Why did he do this? Why did he put himself through this vigorous vortex of pain and pleasure with a woman he futilely wished would love him? Why did he try? The same thoughts passed through his mind whenever he found himself in this situation—in this *faerhain*'s bedroom, jabbing his aching penis into a hidden realm of shame that made him feel as ill as his ailment.

The room disappeared. She disappeared. And there he remained, moving to please the master that was his pain until he appeased it like the god it was. Orinleah was his offering to it.

He left her room moments later, long before he'd planned. He was supposed to spend the night in there. He left the drawing with her and paused outside her door, feeling as stupid as she always claimed. It was always her. He had many, many women at his disposal, but she made him feel this way—and yet he kept returning. He wanted her. After all the things he could get away with doing to her, he still felt as though he didn't have her.

Putting Orinleah through that came with perks, though. It staved off his pain for longer periods than any of his other sexual partners. She brought him back to a level state of comfort and health. Sometimes, he'd feel no pain for a week before needing another screw. The act of doing it, however, whenever he engaged in it—with anyone—took him a step closer to becoming a monster.

# Chapter 40

# His Presence

Kalea shivered in the new spring wind rustling the trees. She was already sick of the cold. She counted the days on her numb hand before shoving it back under her arm inside the shawl she'd brought from the convent.

"I'm back." Dorhen approached from behind.

She turned to regard him, standing there with a lifeless smile, holding two fish he'd speared from the river with a sharpened stick. More fish. Dear Creator, why couldn't she have a warm bowl of oats for once? She used to take that old breakfast routine for granted. Sighing through her nose, she gave him a nod of approval.

Eventually, she'd have to make amends with him. The knowledge of how hard he tried didn't get past her. Ten days, about a week and a half since she'd left the convent with him. That's as long as it had taken for their inevitable falling out to happen.

He got straight to work, gutting and cleaning the fish for the little fire she'd been feeding twigs into. She listlessly watched the blood cake on his hands. An apology poised on her lips, but for some reason she couldn't speak it. The blood all over his hands stood for something they were probably both thinking about.

His lips parted while he stared hard at his work. "Hhh…" he tried and gave up. A few seconds later, he tried again. "H-how's your wound?"

*It's not a wound, you idiot!*

Kalea took a deep breath. "Fine. And I told you, it's not a wound." She turned her face away. There was so much he didn't know. She hadn't been in the mood to explain it to him yet.

Even in her annoyance, she couldn't look away from his broad shoulders and strong hands too long. The wind swept his hair over his face, and he let it. He kept his head down in concentration.

Despite their joy and excitement on their first day, they had yet to consummate their relationship. Lately, Kalea couldn't stop second-guessing whether they were in a relationship at all. How tightly he gripped her hand when they had set out, and she gripped his back. The passing days loosened that grip. As of today, she might as well have been a runaway and he a hired ranger guiding her through the woods.

Since they embarked on their journey, he'd become nothing but a tight wad of orders and warnings. *Stay close. Don't speak while walking. We can speak when we stop to camp. Don't eat any mushrooms or berries unless I say it's okay.* Kalea didn't want to eat unidentified forest vegetation, and his rules and sternness didn't actually bother her; it was other things that happened too fast for her comfort.

On the second day, he woke her up before the sun rose, stripped off his clothes and dipped into the freezing stream water—and he expected her to join him! Her refusal prompted a long conversation about Arius Medallus's wisdom, but Kalea could hardly care, she wasn't ready for... that! She wasn't ready on the third day either. Or the fourth.

Now they were about to start day ten, and she had yet to bathe with him. The members of her convent never bathed as often as he did. *Arius Medallus says you must shed your bodily scents,* he'd argued. If dangerous people were to find them, they could easily go by smell. Though she couldn't argue with his logic, she wasn't entirely convinced they were in danger. Dorhen, however, spent a good amount of his energy worrying about such things: danger lurking behind every tree, bad people. Until he could prove bad people did indeed stalk them, Kalea would keep her clothes on. His blunder of spying on her once through the convent's window didn't matter. She didn't want him to see her naked again. Not yet.

So after all that arguing, the conversations stopped. All of them. He continued to wake her every sunrise—to her disdain—strip naked, and bathe in the stream without a care for her gaping eyes. He'd tromp out of the water a few minutes later with parts of him smaller than when he went in.

She pulled her shawl tighter around her shoulders. She'd gladly skip breakfast and hurry to set out and let the warmth radiate through her body. The cold would drive her insane if she suffered it another day. She'd grown sick of walking too.

"Dorhen." He raised his eyes briefly from his work and then returned them. "What would happen if I decided to settle down with a man in town? What would you do?"

His hands stopped moving. She couldn't see his face through his curtain of hair. His shoulders rose and fell. "I'd live somewhere near your house...and I'd guard you."

She blinked. "Why?"

He dropped the fish and his knife, huffed out a breath, and wiped his face on his sleeve, careful not to get his filthy hands on anything. He picked the knife up again and cut more scales off the fish's body.

"You don't know why," she mumbled, knowing he heard her. She sat in the awkward silence for a while, listening to the sound of his blade slashing at the slimy little creature he'd stabbed out of the water. She cleared her throat. "I don't want to walk anymore."

He kept working.

"I don't want to be cold anymore either. Women don't like to be cold; they can't withstand it like men can."

He threw his knife down and stood. "I'll get more firewood."

"Wait!" she said, shooting to her feet before he could storm away. "Don't. That's not what I mean."

He slowly returned to his work with the fish. "Then what do you want?"

"A house. I want to live in a house with a hearth and a bed."

"Well, there's a place called Evarville not far away. A village with lots of forest land around it. You can look for a husband there tomorrow." The anger in his voice made her wince.

"Dorhen."

"What?"

She paused. She didn't like how he'd stopped looking at her. "I don't want to get married. I just want a house."

He took a deep, calming breath. She deemed it important to tell him she didn't truly mean to marry someone else. "I'll build you one," he said.

"Do you know how?"

"No... I'll figure it out."

"Dorhen," she whispered. "Do you love me?"

He stopped working. He met her eyes with a deep focus and held them for a longer period than he had for days. "Yes, I do." He stared at her. He was waiting for her response.

*I love you too.* The words passed through her head repeatedly but never came out of her mouth. She did love him. But things were so difficult. It was so damn cold out here! She'd never noticed, before living in the woods, how long the cold air lingered in spring.

After a long while, he returned to his work. Her silence hurt him, she knew it.

"So maybe you can imagine how much I worry about you," he said. "You still haven't shown me your wound. Where is it?"

She shook her head, "Dorhen, you don't underst—"

"I picked some yarrow to make a salve for it. It'll stop the blood flow and ease your pain too." He jerked his head to the side to indicate one of the leather pouches hanging on his belt. "What happened? Did you fall on a sharp stick? Were you using my knife?"

She put her hand out. "Look, it's not what you think."

He took his attention away from the fish again. They were nearly ready to skewer and put over the fire.

Her jaw tensed in her effort to give him the next statement. "Those bloody rags you caught me washing in the river… They weren't from a wound. They were from my cycle."

He narrowed his eyes. "Cycle?"

"Mm-hmm. I have a cycle. All women have it. It might also be the reason I snapped at you earlier in the week."

He squinted further and shook his head. "I don't understand…"

Her face went instantly clammy. "I am bleeding in a place I can't show you—but it's not a wound! All right? It's normal." He'd been so upset since he caught her washing her rags, it took an effort to calm him down, which led into one area of their overall fight, and today she'd have to be careful not to distress him again.

He blinked his eyes rapidly. She could almost predict what he'd say next.

"Listen, it's okay. I'm fine. In fact, it means I'm healthy. You've been feeding me well, and I've gained a little weight."

"How can that be healthy?"

She sighed and covered her face. "It just is. It has to do with reproduction." By now, he'd forgotten about the fish. "You know, as in having babies? It means I'm healthy enough to have babies."

His eyes spaced. She could see on his face how he processed through what she was telling him. She wasn't sure if she'd chosen the right words or caused him more confusion. "But I don't see how…"

She groaned. "Neither do I, to be honest." She gave him the first smile in many days, a forced smile, and it eased his pose to a degree. "Here's the thing: this is going to happen every month."

"What?"

"Yes. Every month—unless I get pregnant." Dorhen's face paled as she spoke. "So I don't want you to worry. The way we live right now prevents me from having the privacy I normally would, so you'll probably see me washing bloody rags in the creek every time. And you might find me irritable for no reason. And if we were to ever…get married, I would be off limits for a week out of every month."

Now his eyes darted side to side.

"It's a bit complex, I know. You'll have to bear with me. It's not a convenient routine, but just know that it *is* a good thing. No more worrying." She gave him another smile for the sake of his reassurance, and he smiled back with a predictable level of confusion. The color didn't return to his face very quickly. "Thank you," she added. "For everything you do."

Later that night, they bedded down after bypassing Evarville. She had made a special effort not to be tempted to stop there for any reason, even for supplies. She wanted to reassure Dorhen that she wouldn't brush him off and marry some other man. They left Evarville far behind.

Their beds were laid side by side, close together for security. She shivered, wrapped tight in the quilt she'd stolen from the convent while he slept deeply in his bedroll beside her. He could always fall asleep much faster than she could. His head must be blissfully empty, while hers always whirled round and round with thoughts about this and that and the day's events and what might happen tomorrow. The muscled lines of the edge of his arm and shoulder glowed in the moonlight as he slept on his stomach—he always slept on his stomach. He also had an amazing ability to sleep in practically nothing, while she put on everything she owned to ward off the chill. According to Dorhen, sleeping without clothes prevented too much body odor from collecting in them—which would tip off the bad people who might be tracking them. Every day, he carried out his disciplined routine of bathing, putting on clothes, and shedding the clothes before going to sleep. Meanwhile, she stank up her own clothes all night long and skipped bathing every morning. She could smell herself, which could also be keeping her awake at night.

And then he started to shudder in his sleep, followed by the whimpering. His bad dreams had returned. He'd slept in peace on the first two nights of their togetherness, and then the nightmares occurred every night since their fighting began. It was those witch dreams again, the ones he'd told her about. The witches in the dreams always held him down, cut open his chest, and squeezed their cold hands into his wound as if searching for something. He usually awoke in cold fear, shivering, while Kalea feigned being asleep.

Now, he suffered them once again. She exhaled through her lips, watching the twinkling night sky. She'd listen to his sorrow no more. She'd not sleep cold anymore either. She peeled back her blanket and slipped into his. She dragged her quilt over on top of his bedroll to combine their beds into one.

He shuddered awake at her movement and her brush against him. He sighed in relief at escaping the dream, and then a new alertness took him when he noticed her plan. He sighed again, and she felt his smile through it. He put his arm around her and planted a kiss on her forehead. They would sleep together from now on.

*Sleeping with Dorhen.* She'd never done such a thing before, the idea wild and uncalled-for in her mind as she settled in. They still couldn't consummate though; she couldn't predict when she'd be ready for that step. But the warmth—the heat—of his mostly naked body was the best thing she'd experienced since they first set out.

He sighed again in utter bliss at her gesture, and she could've mimicked him. Instead, she closed her eyes and nuzzled into his throat as he showered her with touches of his lips to her hair and kisses to her temple.

Kalea woke up. The voice from her dream hovering over her face didn't go away, as if the dream continued in the waking world. Her consciousness half-registered what went on around her. She struggled to regain her wits. A familiar darkness replaced the dream's memory with an unfavorable reality. She'd been drugged as she yelled at Wikshen. One of the witches had released a plume of fragrant powder in her face from a loosely woven bag, making her numb all over and forcing her to fall asleep. The realization made her mope and whine. Why couldn't her dream of Dorhen be reality?

Someone wept over her. She tried to turn her head, but it didn't happen, as if her brain had disconnected from her body. Lips brushed her hair, then a nose that inhaled long and slow. Her dream hadn't quite washed away yet, apparently.

"Why would you come here?" the voice whispered through the weeping. A big arm squeezed tight around her. "You shouldn't have."

Kalea couldn't respond to the voice. A heaviness dragged her eyelids down against her will to stay awake and investigate. A tear rolled out of her eye.

A soft, masculine sob erupted into her hair. The arm around her trembled. "You have to leave this pl…"

She fell back asleep.

Knilma stood at the entrance to Wikshen's canopy, watching as he cuddled and caressed the insolent girl who'd been weeping and screaming at him before her sedation. His interest in her was a bizarre and miraculous surprise. He'd shown no such interest in any of the women he'd seen so far, and many within Alkeer came to greet him. At Knilma's insistence, he'd let a few prod and stroke him, and yet nothing inspired him to produce a blessing. The first smidgen of care he'd shown for the opposite sex surfaced for this one.

Knilma tiptoed closer to the scene. "Wikshen," she said, "does this girl please you?"

In response to her question, he tensed up, raising his shoulders high and bowing his head low protectively over the sleeping girl.

"Go away," he rumbled.

Stepping back in alarm, Knilma made the best curtsy her body allowed. His sudden emotional surge for this girl was strange, but his aggression in the sexual situation wasn't. Knilma would give him as much space as he needed. That stupid girl could emerge from the canopy as First Sister at any time. Perhaps Wikshen would be fine after all. If he desired her, she'd learn to accept it after he blessed her. Things often went that way. It didn't matter how much she protested or how hard her companions outside had banged on the door to retrieve her last night. Their insolence got them what they deserved.

Knilma hastily left the stage and drew the curtains tightly closed. She put her finger to her lips when the other shamans approached for her update. "Just wait and pray," she told them. "Wikshen has made his choice."

Kalea awoke to the faint seagull calls outside. It took effort to piece together that she was in Alkeer, on the dock side of town…and in Wikshen's temple. She tried to move and slowed at the stiffness in her muscles. Her joints popped. She groaned, and suddenly remembered to be quiet and aware. Daylight flared through the various cracks in the building's structure, especially from the high, rickety ceiling above her.

She found herself in Wikshen's bed, all fluffy and decadent around her, as ugly and dark as it was. But Wikshen wasn't there. A sad hurt bloomed in her empty stomach while she lingered, remembering last night's dream.

A candle burned on the table next to a plate of fish and a tall cup. Her stomach ached in hunger. She hadn't eaten last night, despite Wikshen's invitation to join him. What had she done with him? She checked herself. She still wore all of her layers. The knot on her bodice stayed firm, the way she always tied it. Her braies were tightly in place. He must not have taken advantage of her while she slept in her drugged stupor. Odd. Fortunate, but odd by all likelihoods. She'd assumed that's why the witches had ushered her into this dark space: to be Wikshen's plaything.

Alone in the complex of black drapes and canopies, she crawled to the low table on hands and knees and sank her teeth into the fish's skin, lukewarm and sprinkled with pepper. Her lip quivered to eat it. Dorhen had once caught a fish for her, cooked it, and taken it into the heart of her convent so she wouldn't go hungry. According to her dreams, he would've done the same for her every morning had they managed to keep their plan.

They wouldn't ever manage to get away now. Wikshen had killed Dorhen.

Choking in her grief for the loss of her love, Kalea reached for the goblet to wash down the oily, peppered meat she could no longer taste. It contained a fruity, non-alcoholic beverage. Out of sheer necessity, she gobbled more fish, and it filled her belly. It was a nice, big catch, fresh out of the nearby ocean. Eating as much as she could hold, she kept an eye on the drapes' entrance. She'd deal with Wikshen in stride if he caught her eating his breakfast.

With the urgency of hunger remedied, she slowed her chewing and listened. Distant voices chanted. She couldn't see beyond the black veil of Wikshen's tent-like partition, but she heard no one lingering immediately outside of it.

Her attention finally found a collection of objects on the far side of the table. Her washing bat, with its silvery wood grains shining in the candlelight, leaned against her basket. Stretching her neck in curiosity, she found her shoes and all of her belongings!

*Bowaen? Surely not!* Yesterday, the shamans had barred her friends from this temple, despite their proclamations of being pledges. Her thoughts immediately trailed to Togha, Gaije's cousin and clansman. He was a Wikshonite. He must've gathered her items and put them here for her to find. Maybe he couldn't stay to help her, but had done what he could.

Nibbling the fish and picking bones out of her mouth, she moved to that side of the table. Beside her shoes was a scrawled symbol on the floor in chalky lines.

"K," Kalea read the first symbol. Beside it, two other letters appeared to have been written with more difficulty, R and N. "R... N," she said, and repeated the letters faster. "R-n, r-n..." She put the two letters together. "Rn. Run." Beside the awkward writing, a drawn pictograph showed a door with the sun shining on the other side. This was her chance to run. Kalea stuffed the rest of the fish meat into her mouth and strapped on her shoes.

*Bless that Togha!* Kalea thanked the Creator five or six times for her chance to escape. The silence on the other side of the curtain seemed promising. She chugged the rest of the fruity drink—a lovely, sweet liquid—and gathered her belongings.

Tiptoeing her way to the edge of the stage, Kalea peeked out of the curtain to find her path clear. No one occupied the main hall at the moment. Wherever they'd gone, they must be with Wikshen. The sound of soft drums and chanting echoed from one side of the tavern and possibly below her. They all must be in the cellar. It sounded like a worship session went on, which made Kalea shudder in disgust. It certainly sounded creepy compared to the happy songs the vestals used to sing to the One Creator. The Wikshonites' sounds and antics made the memories of yesterday rush back: the murderer, Wikshen, and his dark, wordless presence. She didn't need to hear his voice among the others to know he was down there.

A chill flared in her spine as she made her way to the front entrance of the tavern. She bypassed a narrow corridor with stairs to the cellar, where the sounds echoed loudest. The chanting stopped abruptly as she passed. Someone was vomiting.

"Mastaren, are you all right?" an older woman's voice murmured in the distance, followed by a big commotion. A medley of objects clattered. A drum hit the floor with a deep reverberation. Kalea took that as a cue to rush right out the door and dart into the first crowd of regular-looking townspeople she could find on the next street.

Kalea stood on Alkeer's busy street. *Now to find Bowaen.* Her heart sank lower on the tail of that thought because she didn't know where to start. They hadn't exactly made a plan for what to do if the cult threw Bowaen and the others back into the street. If Bowaen didn't come along soon and find her, she'd remain lost in Alkeer. Alone. She'd never remember how to find the inn they'd slept in on the other side of the massive town.

She decided to walk casually with the flow of the crowd and keep her eyes peeled. "Bowaen!" she called, stretching her neck for any sign of him. Gaije's coppery hair should be easy to spot.

A hand grasped her shoulder, and she whirled. "Bowaen?"

It wasn't Bowaen. Togha found her instead. His pretty grey eyes with heavy black lashes burned hard, and his lips made a straight sort of frown.

Kalea smiled. "I'm so relieved to see you!"

"Come with me," he ordered, wrapping his fingers around her arm. A zap of fear stabbed her in the gut when she realized he could drag her back to his cult. He guided her through the crowd the opposite way from where she came.

"Where are my friends?"

Glancing back at her with an air of seriousness she couldn't stand to face, he said, "Gaije and your other friends tried to break into Wikshen's temple last night to save you."

"What?" Kalea's teeth chattered. "And what happened?"

"Needless to say, they made a mistake. They were taken to die in Hathrohskog."

She tried the word, "Hathroh…"

"Hathrohskog," Togha said in his signature flat tone. "It's a forest north of here. Past that, you'll find Wikhaihli—where Metta should be. Mhina might be there too, especially if you didn't see her in the temple." He paused to regard her.

"I didn't see her," Kalea reported. She followed up in a murmur, "I didn't see much, though. How long will it take us to get to the forest?"

"It would take *you* a few hours at best," he said, "maybe two if you run. I can't go with you. They've got me running around here, and if I shirk my duties, they'll sacrifice me to Wikshen."

He practically dragged her along the road. Her arm hurt as he ripped her through the tighter crowds. She'd never brushed against so many strangers in her life.

"I'll be going alone," she said, mostly for herself. She'd hardly felt as adult as she did in this moment. The responsibility rested on her now to find a young elf-girl, plus a grown woman, two grown men, and a *saehgahn*. But Dorhen… If she made it to the forest to find her friends dead, she'd be utterly alone.

Togha took her all the way to the edge of the city and pointed to the gate, guarded by a Clanless member he dared not approach. He took her by the shoulders with a force she'd never expect from a new acquaintance.

"Go through the gate and turn immediately to the right," he said. "You'll be walking north." His assertive ordering vaguely reminded her of the dream of Dorhen she'd experienced last night. "When you get there, don't drink the water and don't eat any berries. Find your friends and cut whatever ropes are binding them."

"They'll be tied down?"

"Don't let the soil touch your skin."

"Okay," Kalea said, her eyes round and receptive to the sternness he was sending her.

"Once you've found them, keep going north. Wikhaihli is on the other side of the forest. You can infiltrate it like you did this temple."

Kalea's stomach pitched. She hated pretending to be a Wikshonite, but she would have to do it again soon.

Togha continued, "And don't forget Metta. She's a beautiful girl with black hair. Cropped like this." Togha put his finger across his eyebrows.

"I'll find her." Kalea's voice came out weak. When Togha turned to walk away, she grabbed his black poncho. "Togha."

He turned and waited.

"Thank you. What you did in the temple to help me escape, getting my belongings back from the witches… It thoroughly helped. I wouldn't have gotten far without my shoes and my bat."

Togha squinted. "I didn't do that."

Kalea's nose wrinkled. "You—you didn't?"

He shook his head. "I haven't been in the temple today. You'd better hurry." He turned and rushed off, disappearing fast into the sea of flowing people.

Wikshen leaned, bent against the wall. He spat again.

"Mastaren," Knilma said when he didn't answer her the first time. He bowed again and poured the rest of the feast he'd eaten last night onto the cellar floor. She watched in cold, tense bewilderment. He'd been sitting calmly on the altar, listening to their soft drums and chanting, with a bell to separate the verses. She had caught his eyes trailing to the ceiling. Something he'd left upstairs distracted him.

Now he stood amidst the mess he'd made, his eyes blazing at her before looking to the ceiling again. "Where's the girl?" he asked.

"You have two of the best I've ever seen right here, Mastaren." Knilma spread her hand to indicate Myrtle and Tamas kneeling on the floor without clothes, their smooth bodies oiled and fragrant. They'd been made into two official offerings to their deity. Their faces showed mystified stares.

"Where's the other one? The one who screamed at me?"

"She's upstairs in your bed. She gave us no choice other than sedation."

One of the witches who'd been cleaning and tidying the temple padded down the stairs. "The Mastaren's woman has gone!" she reported.

"What do you mean, gone?" Knilma replied.

"I knew we should've tied her down," Paigess said beside Knilma.

Wikshen sneered in annoyance, vomit painting his chin. As if the pixie inside of him flew into a rage, he snatched one of their drums and threw it against the wall with a long, reverberating *k-toom*. Pausing, he put out a gruff rush of hot air and then stormed into the shadow behind the hanging sacred shroud and disappeared—as if he'd walked through the wall.

The shamans and witches waited in silence. Wikshen had left them, mid-rite, with no way to tell where he'd gone.

# Chapter 41
## What is Eating Away at Them

Lady Kalea!" A high male voice rang out behind her. "Please wait, madam!"

Kalea turned. "Damos?"

The young man dodged the inflow of people to Alkeer, darting past the sleepy Clanless member standing guard at the gate. "Kalea!" he called again.

She waited for him, itching to hurry on. A good long walk divided her from her friends in need.

Damos's parrot flapped from the top of the wall after Damos and alighted on his shoulder as he stopped beside her to pant.

"What are you doing?" she asked.

"You're going out there alone?" he countered.

"I have to. My friends were snatched up by Wikshen."

Damos's face melted into a disgusted concern. "Wikshen?"

Kalea resumed walking at a swift, stiff pace. "Yes," she said. Damos kept up beside her. "Shouldn't you be back there, contemplating going home to face your justice?"

"I can contemplate my penance as I accompany you," he said.

Kalea gave a pithy laugh. The temptation to remind him of Bowaen's mission came over her, but she held it in. Right now, Bowaen needed help, and Kalea could use all the aid the Creator would bless her with. She told him her friends were in Hathrohskog, and Damos reared his head while he walked.

"Dear Creator," he said. "Alkeer folk hand out generous warnings about that forest. 'Don't go north,' they say. 'Nothing up there but a wicked forest and witches.'"

"Those witches captured my friends," Kalea said. "By all means, go back to town if it's so bad in the north."

She didn't turn to regard him in his hesitance to answer. She wouldn't—either he wanted to come along or he didn't. She'd appreciate his company and aid, but Bowaen needed to capture Damos or simply make him wear Lord Dax's ring. She'd already given the young man one chance to escape, and now he'd returned. Best to let him choose his own fate. They were all here in the Darklands for a reason, and Kalea needed to find her sisters and…her convent sisters.

Kalea's throat closed up. She turned away from Damos; if her face turned red with her caged sadness, she didn't need Damos to see it and be concerned. Yesterday's news burned away at her soul, rekindling every time something reminded her of it. She couldn't think about it. She stifled the name she used to love saying aloud and inside. There was much to do, people to save, and no time to stop and mourn the dead. *Dead.* She didn't like that word either.

*Bowaen, Del, and Gaije. Mhina. Rose, Vivene, Tanya, Millie…* She ran all those names through her head. A great duty to many people settled on her shoulders. She couldn't spare a moment to stop and suffer a selfish thought—to shed selfish tears—when so many people depended on her.

"Damos," Kalea said, after a stretch of silence. "Your bird can turn into a ravian, can't it? Can we fly to Hathrohskog?"

Damos hissed through his teeth. "I flew on her all the way to get to Alkeer. She needs a rest, but…" He took the bird from his shoulder to his hand with a command to step up. "Azrielle, *chiror-argull-ik.*"

A pale stone ring on the hand the bird perched on flashed and faded. Damos pushed his hand forward to bid the parrot to fly off, and as it did, it shapeshifted. Its head and beak grew to the proportions of a horse, its tail feathers extended from its original fan-like formation to long ruby streamers, and its body shifted into that of a lithe, energetic lion, something Damos could easily ride. The little parrot became a huge, silvery beast, one she'd seen before when she spotted them flying over Jumaire and Hanhelin's Gate.

Damos pulled her arm. "Hurry and get on. She hasn't rested for long enough. We need to make this quick, or she'll lose the transformation midair and we'll plummet to our deaths." At Kalea's hesitation, he said, "Don't worry, I can read the signs of her spell wearing off."

The ravian was every bit the mythical creature she'd read about in the Creator's Word. As he helped her to mount behind him, she held back her tears. If anything, the sight of the creature strengthened her faith in her beloved Creator and diminished the doubt she felt when considering that she might be a Luschian. She didn't care what sort of non-human she turned out to be, she would not abandon her faith in the One Creator.

When Damos noticed her sniffling behind him, he asked if she was all right, to which she explained her momentary feeling of awe.

"She's magnificent, I know."

Damos leaned forward to stir the silver feathers on the side of Azrielle's cheek, at the corner of her black beak. The ravian stood on four legs, like a massive lion, but thinner and scalier, with talons on each paw. The elongated body, covered in a mixture of short hairs and soft feathers, offered enough room for the two of them to ride. Azrielle's visible eye relaxed at Damos's touch, silver with a hint of yellow, like a sunny morning sky. It could twist its head around to the back like its original bird form could do.

At Damos's word, the ravian took off. In exhilarated fear, Kalea squeezed her arms around Damos's torso. Not liking the idea of rising so high into the sky, or the spell's potential to run out of energy at any moment, Kalea clenched her eyes shut and huddled in at the back of Damos's neck.

"Don't be afraid," Damos cooed, though he didn't show any sign of disdain at her closeness.

Now looking to disrupt her dreadful thoughts of falling, Kalea asked Damos in his ear how his pet bird could shapeshift at all.

"I told you I attended the college in Wistara studying mage craft, right?" he said.

"Yes."

"I was there because I showed a talent in magic from an early age. When you're born into my family, they hurry to figure out how useful you are, and then you go to training for it. Not that it was odd for me to do mage craft. It's actually an important thing I'm *supposed* to do." Damos cut his casual chat off at the end of his statement and made no hint he'd say more.

Kalea couldn't help but identify. "I went into the convent at ten years old. I know it's not exactly the same as being talented in something—I'm not talented in anything—but maybe it's a similar situation."

"Close enough," Damos replied. "To answer your original question, my talent made Azrielle change into a ravian. It's a high-level, practically fabled ability. The ravians belong to the Creator."

Kalea knew that much. The Creator rode on a ravian made of light when He wanted to travel. He also sent beautiful ravians to escort the souls of the dead back to His palace.

"The sages couldn't believe what I could do," Damos continued. "I couldn't fathom it either."

"How does it work?"

"Azrielle, the parrot, serves as a medium. The ravian is a separate entity who comes from another dimension, and Azrielle lends her body for the ravian's entrance into this world. It's hard to explain how I can do it though. I sort of…spiritually figured out how to call the ravian, and the word I used works as a funnel to channel all the necessary energy, thoughts, and communication I need to make the call. I made the word up, borrowing meaningful syllables from an ancient language we mages are made to learn. To put it simply: I invented the spell."

"You're so smart!" she said, talking over the roar of the wind. "You certainly are talented."

Damos didn't respond. He was an extremely promising student—and he'd run away from it all. His talent must be the reason Lord Dax had asked for his return. Damos might be a vital component to the fight against sorcery in the Lightlands.

*Damos, go home.* Those words passed through Kalea's mind, and she held them in. She'd tell him to go home eventually, but not now. Not until he got her all the way to Hathrohskog to rescue her friends.

Damos didn't say much along their way after their conversation about the ravian. He clearly came from an upper class family; his eloquence and respectful demeanor showed it. The silence wasn't awkward; Damos was easy company. Maybe he sensed her mood. Her thick silence built a wall between them, regardless of how intimately she clung to his back with her hands clasped around his stomach.

They managed nearly an hour of flight before the forest emerged from the heavy mist of a walking cloud below them. Kalea gasped and pointed, not expecting to see the forest so soon, but of course Damos saw it too. Their ravian flight must've halved their travel time. As luck would have it, the bird's body beneath them trembled and sank in the air.

"Whoa!" Damos said to it. "Land, Azrielle."

The ravian obeyed his command. The lion-like body shrank throughout the bird's efforts to put them safely on the ground. The three of them descended into a sea of fog with no way of telling how far down the ground was. When they reached it, Kalea and Damos hastily dismounted, and the ravian skipped a few yards with wings outstretched, shrinking back into an ordinary flapping parrot. Azrielle, the parrot, waited for Damos to pick her up from the grass, her beak opening and closing as she panted.

With the bird perched on his arm, he scratched her head, brushing the feathers forward. "She's all out of energy now. Should take weeks for her to be able to shift again." Azrielle nuzzled her beak into Damos's palm.

Kalea gave a weak smile. "And here I thought your trip through the Darklands was a carefree flight to wherever you wanted to go."

"It's not so simple," Damos said. "Magic, I must say, makes life more complicated, not more convenient."

Kalea took Damos's hand and met his eyes. "You certainly made things easier for me. Thank you, Damos. And thank you, Azrielle."

Taking her hand in return, Damos kissed her fingers. Something about the gesture, its softness or slowness, set it apart from the last time he did it.

Blushing hotly, Kalea took her hand back and gestured to the black tree limbs poking through the cloud wall. "I have to go. You don't have to go into the forest with me."

"Nonsense," Damos said. He stepped up beside her. "I can't let you go in there alone."

"Then let's hurry." She rushed forward with one hand on her washing bat and her other hand supporting the old laundry basket hanging off her shoulder. Damos's feet tread through the grass behind her.

An abrupt shift in atmosphere happened as soon as they stepped into the forest. Damos moaned behind her. "Bog land isn't far off," he said.

Kalea's feet sank deep into the earth with each step. "Togha said not to let the soil touch your skin."

"That won't be easy."

She relied on her pathetic little leather shoes and wool stockings to protect her feet. Her dress would pick up a lot of mud, so she tucked the hem into her belt, leaving her chemise visible above her ankles.

Black moss grew everywhere among other unsightly plants, and most of the trees were dead. The landscape sank inward, as if they were walking down a gentle hill slope. The silence hung heavy.

"Bow-a-en!" Kalea called. If her friends were nearby, it shouldn't be hard to hear them call back.

No answer. They could be dead already. Swallowing to keep her throat from thickening in sadness, she forced the thought away. She couldn't think about death right now. Not until she found proof.

She and Damos trekked deeper into the depressing grey tangle of vines and moss. They stepped carefully from one patch of grass to the other, as the mud all around became wetter along their progression. They certainly were walking downward too, as if the whole forest grew in a crater. The smell of the atmosphere didn't improve.

"It's like a miasma," Damos said, keeping close behind her. "A wrongness inhabits this place."

"I guess the people in Alkeer knew what they were talking about," Kalea responded.

"Strange enough how close to Alkeer this forest is," he said.

She hummed in thought. "At least this forest is honest about its evil."

"Hmm?"

Kalea explained, "There's another forest near Hanhelin's Gate with sweet-smelling fruit trees. The fruit looks just like apples but can kill a person if eaten."

She shuddered. As odd as her time with King Kerlin had been, he did save her life after she ate a bite of it. Those Thaccilians had saved Bowaen and Del's lives too as an ironic twist of fate. What odd experiences she'd already been through since coming to the Darklands.

The grass lumps on which they tread ended before an intricate field of large stones they had to traverse instead. Finding a path across the stones became tricky after a while. Kalea stumbled when her foot slid off one stone. Damos lurched and hooked his arm around her.

"Ah!" he hissed, noticing he'd put his foot into the mud. It caked all over his boot. At least his footwear was larger and better made than Kalea's.

"Thank you," she said.

"Of course." He motioned to his feet. "We'll see how well these boots can stand the wicked sludge this place is covered in."

"We'll look for water to wash our shoes."

Damos hummed a flat tone. "Probably not a good idea either."

Before Kalea took another step, she paused to regard Damos's hand on her shoulder. He hadn't broken the contact since catching her. He finally let her go.

He cleared his throat. "Lead the way, my lady."

She did. The anxious fear for her friends churning her stomach didn't mix well with whatever embarrassment Damos caused her.

She studied the path they followed. "They can't be far," Kalea said. "Togha told me they were brought into this forest as a sort of execution. Wherever the 'execution' site is, it shouldn't be far. Why would they travel so deep into such a horrid place? Especially when the soil could harm them too!" Her voice echoed far through the silent air.

"Their clothing must be better for it than ours," Damos offered.

His words made sense. All the Wikshonites wore black garments made from a specific fabric. However, all the Wikshonites she had seen so far walked barefoot.

The forest closed in around them tighter as they progressed, until they found a tread path. Footprints were stamped and dried into some of the flatter patches of earth, to her relief. Following this beaten path should show them exactly where the Wikshonites went.

Azrielle had been flying about from tree to tree throughout their trek, and returned from where she'd flown ahead, squawking.

Kalea looked to Damos in alarm. The noise could give away their position to any Wikshonites in the area.

"She's upset about something," Damos said. He pointed. "Hurry.

Let's go straight that way."

Kalea rushed forward and, within a few moments, heard a distant moan. A man's voice. Kalea whirled around to Damos. "Bowaen," she said, hoping.

She rushed forward where the earth declined in a steep slope and found them. They were indeed tied to the ground, half covered in the soggy earth.

"Damos!" she called, running forward without regard for the mud seeping through her stockings. Her legs stung. The soil was trying to eat her.

"Wake up!" She went to each one, shaking them. Gaije was the one moaning. Waking the men proved difficult.

Damos got to work cutting their ropes, and the three of them finally ventured to move and groan and scratch at their skin. If her skin burned, the others were worse off; she needed to wash the mud off of them, but this boggy land offered no clean water. A murky pond stood nearby with its bank seamlessly transitioning into the muddy ground they walked on. Strange frog songs croaked from their hiding places among the rotten logs and dead plants cluttering the water—at least, she hoped they were frogs.

Her friends' moaning escalated to yelling as they continued to scratch at their skin. They were suffering worse than she. She rushed to the nearest one, Gaije, and used her handkerchief to wipe the blistered side of his face of the mud caking it. His clothes were wearing away; his cloak bore more holes than she remembered. She groaned at their suffering.

Bowaen crawled toward the water where the frogs chirped. The water didn't look safe, so she scanned for a way to help them. When he reached a tangle of vines growing at the edge of the murky water, the vines grabbed and held him away from what he wanted—as if they meant to.

Kalea leaped to his rescue. The vines didn't catch her as strongly as they held Bowaen. She leaped past him and went to the water's edge to find it dank and scummy.

*Dear Creator, I need this water,* she prayed as she reached toward it, and all the algae and scum floated away from her hands as they submerged. The occurrence brought back the memory of when the fake priest made her stick her hand in the bowl of blood.

Cupping the water in her hands, she threw it on Bowaen's exposed legs where his leggings had thinned and torn along their journey. She wiped as much mud away with her wet hands as possible. For the most part, his clothing had shielded his skin, and the seep-through caused less irritation than the direct skin-to-mud contact. The more she inspected, however, the more obvious it became that the soil would've eaten through the fabric.

She moved with determination, fetching water and rubbing it on Bowaen's skin. The water helped. A realization crossed her mind: he needed her. Her life situation had transitioned to a strange new stage after meeting Wikshen. Now that she'd lost Dorhen, she would have to decide what to do next. She didn't have to agonize over it any longer. Her new life's goal was set, though unsaid. She would see Wikshen burn. Her teeth clenched to think of it. The menace to her, her friends, and her friends' loved ones would die. It didn't matter whether she or Gaije killed him, so long as they made it happen. A sob escaped her tight throat while she dwelled on the thought, furiously working to help her friends.

The water continued to clear itself for her hands, and she never paused to ponder the phenomenon. The great and powerful Creator answered her prayers, no mystery about it.

Bowaen relaxed and nursed his sore skin while Kalea rushed to tend the other two. Though her little leather shoes had worn thin, Kalea disregarded her own safety.

Once most of the mud was washed away, bloody sores dotted her friends' exposed flesh. Scratching at the areas had opened bleeding lacerations on their skin. All of their eyes were dampened in a glassiness of pain and exhaustion. They moved to the driest spot they could find, a thick bed of black moss.

"Look who I found, Bowaen. It's Damos," Kalea said, trying to be upbeat.

Their bags were strewn about, all their money gone, of course. Damos couldn't do much but gather their things from the ground and wash them in the water Kalea had purified. At her introduction, Damos paused and bowed.

Bowaen made a weak smile with a breathy laugh. "I'll be damned. Damos. You got a knack for showing up on the oddest occasions."

"How could I not, when the lady needed me on this occasion?" he asked, and returned to his work.

"My grandfather's bow," Gaije said, half groaning.

Kalea looked around. "I don't see it." Her lip quivered. Losing the legendary bow was a shame, but she had a lot to be troubled about. She'd found her friends, barely alive. They'd be nursing their sore spots for a while, but here they were. And still, she'd lost so much.

"Hathrohjilh's gone," Bowaen added, throwing a clump of moss into the mud.

Kalea surveyed the dense forest around them. She felt lost. The grey sky made it impossible to tell the hour, much less determine east from west. Did the time of day matter anymore?

All eyes moved to Gaije, a natural forest-dweller, for direction. His eyes slowly turned toward Kalea, red, round, and moist. "What did he say about my sister?"

The question caught Kalea off guard. He must've meant Wikshen. She nodded to him and whispered through quivering lips, "She's alive." She threw herself at him. He caught her weakly and held her steady. "But Dorhen is not!"

After Kalea calmed down, the five of them sat in silence, leaning into a circle, each facing out. Damos made sure to sit beside Kalea. The weak light faded, as the sun must've been setting. The black trees sprouted no leaves; only the rare patches of green moss provided color. The air stank like burning hair or flesh, though no fires could be found. Bowaen and Del couldn't manage to kindle one of their own because the damp, rotten wood crumbled to mush in their hands. Mold supplied the other present stench.

"Gaije," Kalea said, finally ready to talk after a long recess of weeping followed by silence. In the comfort of all her friends, she'd found the liberty to weep over Dorhen. "I remember the mention of a place called Wikhaihli. It's Wikshen's home, and his followers gather there. I think it's safe to assume Mhina's there right now. I heard nothing of her presence in the Alkeer temple."

"That's our next lead," he replied with a sober tone lacing his scratchy voice. "Do you know where Wikhaihli is located?"

"Somewhere around or in this forest, I think." She dropped her heavy head onto Gaije's shoulder. "We're going to find your sister."

Everything about her whole being stood flipped upside-down. Her life in the convent and the contentment of a normal, predictable routine was long gone. Even her humanity was replaced with the word "Luschian." Would she ever feel normal again?

She drew her knees up and hugged them, leaning on Gaije. Damos, sitting at her other side, hugged his knees too. She had asked them for a moment. For now, she couldn't muster enough motivation to stand and walk.

Luckily, the mist thinned, and a glow from the sun behind the clouds fell over the forest. A shimmer in the brush followed a faint moan. Sucking in a gasp, she slid out of the pile they had all formed for a pathetic sense of security. She strode across the soft soil toward the nearby brush where the shimmer of light winked, and the sorrowful moan called to her again.

Hathrohjilh, the sword, stood stuck in the earth among a collection of other things. Gaije's bow lay beside it! In fact, everything they owned of value was here. A dead man's hand also stuck out of the mud.

Grimacing, Kalea used her cloak's corner to wipe away a large clump of soil to reveal the dead man's face. A Wikshonite. By the look of it, this warlock had probably helped tie her three friends down, robbed them, and tried to make off with the loot. Somehow, he was caught in the thorns and wound up in the mud too. He'd died faster than her friends would have.

Despite the horrible sight, she smiled at their good fortune. "We thought you were gone for good," she said to the brilliant, shining sword.

She reached for the worn, leathery handle, and finally noticed a pair of eyes staring at her from the brush. A hideous creature crouching beside the sword with a viciously possessive demeanor reared up and shrieked a piercing noise at her. Its mouth dropped open, and the eye sockets widened to empty black pits after the eyeballs vanished.

# Chapter 42
## What is a Tryst with the Darkness

Kalea staggered back, grabbing her ears, and the men sprang to their feet in defensive stances.

An old woman with a face like a piece of gnarled meat, her skin brown and creased, stood up next to the sword and stared Kalea down. Deep clusters of enlarged pores dotted the corners of her features. Her wispy white hair contrasted strongly against her baked skin. Atop her head sat a pointy black stocking cap with the tail hanging over her shoulder, and she was dressed in black rags bound with rope, accentuating her thin proportions. Her eyes were back in place again—likely an illusion, a fantasy brought on by Kalea's shock.

"How dare you touch that sword!" the old woman squawked.

"The sword is ours," Kalea spat back, widening her stance and stiffening her spine.

"This is Wikshen's territory. Get out, or the forest'll eat you alive."

"It already tried and failed," Bowaen said, tromping through the soggy earth to join Kalea.

The old woman eyed him. "Pity, is that. This forest needs all the meat it can find. Ye can see how it withers in hunger. I'll let the forest take you for itself, so go ahead, go free."

Kalea marched forward. To her surprise, the witch-like creature shrank before her. Kalea thrust her index finger into her face and got quite a grimace out of her. "I'm taking the sword, try to stop me! In the name of the Creator, I'll fight you!"

Kalea grabbed the handle and lifted it out of the dirt as the loathsome old woman watched. Her hideous, gnarled hands fidgeted. If she had teeth, she'd be baring them.

A sense of great relief rinsed Kalea's head when she held the sword in her possession. A tickle in her palm grasping the handle didn't go unnoticed. On her stiff walk back to the group, she shot the others a leery expression. The old woman had vanished upon second glance.

Another one of those walking clouds rolled over the forest with a density like none they'd seen yet. Kalea could hardly see two feet before her. One tiny morsel of hope sparked when they found an old piece of arrow-shaped wood lying on the ground with the word "WIKHAIHLI" scratched across it. It was dislodged from its post and lying on the ground, so none could tell if they actually walked in the right direction. To make things worse, nighttime approached, and the mesh of forest encircling them grew thicker.

"We may have to sleep in a pile again for security," Bowaen mumbled.

At this point, Kalea didn't mind such a suggestion. They'd done it before, and these men had become her best friends in the last several weeks. They were gaining the lead over the closeness Kalea shared with her convent sisters.

They attempted to cut their way through the brush, but the forest would have none of it. As dead and rotten as it appeared, it remained sturdy and full of vigor. They would have to tear their own bodies through for miles until they found the exit.

"I'm sorry I caused us to waste the day," Kalea said to the group, twiddling her fingers as the men trudged about, attempting to create a livable camp for the night hours.

Without looking at her, Bowaen put his hands up. "Hey, we get it," he said. "We've all had our bad days."

Del attempted to light his pipe, but Bowaen leaned over and punched his arm.

"What the hell do you want?" Del asked. Whenever things got uncomfortable, he lit his pipe or at least fidgeted it in his hand. The length of the thing ironically kept him physically distant from the others.

"I want you to save your flint and help me with the fire! Hard to believe you have any tobacco left."

"I traded for some in Alkeer," Del grumbled. Slinging the pipe's strap back on his arm, he resumed the fruitless task of looking for dry twigs to start a fire.

"Doesn't matter," Gaije said, his voice dragging as he focused on salvaging any dried rations left in their muddy bags. "We can't wander far or we'd never find our way back, especially after dark."

Bowaen didn't listen. He stubbornly skirted around their camp's perimeter in search of anything useful.

"Don't worry about flint," Damos piped up. "I can summon electricity. Small amounts of it are good for starting fires on kindling."

"Bless you, Damos," Kalea said from across the way.

His eyes sprang from the dab of ointment he was rubbing on his arm to meet hers. He didn't speak. His deep blue eyes sent her some kind of message she didn't know how to read. He was a handsome young specimen with his smooth olive skin. His face, framed in locks of fair hair swirling past his jaw, possessed good angles. With his ability, he'd be a great addition to their party. He could help them rescue Mhina and the convent girls, and then the whole lot of them could go back together. Damos should eventually decide to go home and face whatever responsibilities he'd left behind. He hadn't mentioned anything about joining their group, but Kalea assumed he'd stay, especially after insisting on accompanying her into Hathrohskog. Whether he'd go back to the Lightlands with them after their missions remained to be seen.

"No, bless *you*, Kalea," Damos replied.

Kalea reared her head back and pointed to herself.

Damos dipped his head deeply, almost a bow. "Yes," he said. "You're the one who saved these men. How did you purify the water?"

Kalea scrunched her nose. The others stopped to listen to her explanation. She hadn't thought about it. It happened suddenly, and then it was over. "I prayed…" She opened her mouth as if to say more, but she had nothing. She studied her hands. She really had purified a section of the water. The men even filled their waterskins with it after they regained their composure.

"I don't know," Kalea continued. "That's it. I just prayed. I didn't save them. The Creator did."

Bowaen grinned at her through the prickly scruff on his face. "You said at the beginning that washin' is your skill. Well, you washed us."

Still smiling, he bent down to continue with the fire pit he'd built in the earth, arranging the stones. His arms exhibited intense red scratch marks and lacerations from the irritation the soil had caused. Del and Gaije wore the same markings.

As Damos moved about camp, stacking questionable firewood or laying out his blanket on which to sleep, Bowaen's eyes targeted him a few times. He would put his hand in his pocket, clearly tempted to give Damos Lord Dax's ring. At one point, Bowaen raised his hand with Damos's name poised on his lips, hand in pocket, but Kalea took his arm and pulled him away.

"No, Bowaen," she whispered.

He gave her a glare unlike anything before. He'd never lost his patience with her, but tonight could easily be a first.

Before he could protest, she leaned in to his ear. "This is a delicate situation. Don't you think he'll get suspicious if you hand him an expensive ring for little or no reason?"

Bowaen sighed. "What am I supposed to do?"

"We have other work to do before we take him back. If he joins our group of his own will, we'll be that much stronger—he's an extraordinary mage. Please trust me on this. Besides, he…"

Bowaen waited. "He what?"

"He likes me." Her memory of Dorhen's longing face with pleading eyes zapped her mind and body. Dorhen had liked her enough to risk his life, and he barely knew her. Dorhen had died for her.

Bowaen didn't seem to notice her new somber expression. "Well, I hope he likes you enough to go along with your rescue mission and fighting the sorcerers in the process."

Getting choked up, Kalea shook her head.

"Does he know yet what we're up to—the extent of it?" Bowaen asked.

Kalea swallowed and patted Bowaen's chest. "If he has a care, he'll help us. It's the best we can hope for."

The darkness fell fast over the dense mist. Night bloomed inside the thick atmosphere long before the sun set on the outside world. This misty forest was its own separate world.

Kalea squeezed her knees together as she sat on a mossy rock, waiting for the men to finish their tasks and pass around some food. Several times, she fought the urge to turn around and make sure someone wasn't watching her from the dark tangle. She needed food. She needed… something. Her body shook. Her nerves were raw, causing her heart to pound. Goosebumps rose in waves over her flesh, and for some reason her nipples pushed hard against her tight bodice. A restlessness kept her fidgeting, probably from hunger. Her breathing deepened. She also needed to step away to answer a call of nature.

She stood up. "I'll be back."

"Where ya going?" Bowaen asked.

"Do I really have to explain it?" She didn't mean to snap at him, but they commonly excused themselves from the party for such moments.

Del explained for her, "That means she's going to hike her skirts and squat behind a bush for a nice long, girly piss."

Without thinking, she reached down, picked up a rock, and chucked it at him. The rock clipped his shoulder. He didn't react as much as she'd expected. He murmured, "Damn bitch," and rubbed his shoulder. Her conscience stung her immediately after, but she'd have to apologize later.

Bowaen pointed hard at Del. "Shut up!" He turned to Kalea. "Kalea, don't go far, understand?"

She understood, but it did nothing to fix her mood. She fought back her tears. She wanted to cry, in addition to answering nature's call, and her blood danced inside of her. That odd black shadow in the thicker forest surrounding their clearing appeared to inch closer, but stopped and receded from the firelight, only to try to venture forward again.

She clicked her tongue at Bowaen. "But I don't want any of you to see me."

"I don't care. We can't risk you getting lost, girl."

"Well, why don't you sing, and I'll follow your voices to get back?"

"We've almost got a fire here."

"Good," she said. "I'll see the glow *and* follow your singing."

When Bowaen opened his mouth to argue some more, Gaije beat him to the floor, singing in his native language. His voice rolled over the syllables in a somber tone. She couldn't understand what he said, but the tune bore an array of sad notes. No one else bothered to speak, and Kalea took it as her chance to go.

"I'll be just around this bush," she told Bowaen.

"Hurry back."

Gaije's singing kept on in the background as she did her business awkwardly in the heavy darkness. Who knew what manner of thorns or sharp sticks hung behind her to poke her in the rear end should she move wrong? She would find her way back easily, though, because the crackling of flames eating thin twigs mixed in under Gaije's song with a rise of joy from the other male voices.

She didn't exactly hurry back after she finished. Crying in front of them all was embarrassing, and she didn't want to do it again. Their lives were complicated enough without her constant moaning and weeping over Dorhen—burdening them with her personal issues. She took a few steps deeper into the darkness, sniffling in sadness.

Putting her hands out before her, she wandered until they landed on a large rock with moss growing on most of its facets. She leaned against it for a moment, deeming it okay to cry again. Why not let the tears out if that's what she needed? She took Dorhen's moonstone out of her bodice to fondle, hoping to see it glow again. Its light would be a big help in a place like this; unfortunately, the stubborn stone refused to shine.

Kalea only managed a few tears. That frolicking sensation in her blood distracted her. She dropped the moonstone to let it dangle around her neck. She'd somehow found a warm spot amidst the general cool and damp air. The mist hung around though, somehow, and it slid over her skin like hot hands.

Her blood raced downward. A feeling of delight replaced the strangeness. With her chin raised, she sucked in deep, relaxing against her perch. She'd long forgotten Gaije's song drifting from her camp's direction; the blood pulsed through her ears with a loud, whirring energy. A long, released breath took her voice with it as a weak moan. A patterned vibration, like a voice amid the roaring in her ears, made her gasp and jolt. Someone else's voice, but she couldn't make out what it said.

Her skin beaded over with moisture. The rock's curve supported her deepening backward bend. She spread her stance, in need of something, but found it too overwhelming to puzzle out. Her mental processing spaced and became difficult to retrieve, like trying to catch snow flurries on a breeze. Her hand moved to the laces on her bodice in a sudden need to cool off, and a trembling arose in her legs.

What was it about this darkness? It tightened around her, locking her in. Her lips had been parted, and she finally realized it. Her eyes were closed. She leaned back farther, pushing her breasts forward.

"Kalea," a voice called.

She jumped, and the spell broke. She found herself leaning against the rock, one heel braced against it. Her skirt was hooked around her knee! The carnal need persisted, even when she watched her friends bicker and scurry around.

Kalea," the voice said again, not too loud.

"Yes!" she called back, shoving her skirts down and smoothing the fabric over. Her bodice strings dangled untied; she finally noticed and yanked the cords to put them right again.

*Dear Creator, what's happened to me? I'm quite the lonely, pathetic woman!* Her heart pounded fiercely now. Regardless of the darkness's cover, she prayed her companion didn't see her splayed across the rock with her skirt up and her legs open.

"There you are." Damos's voice. "You were gone a while, and they were worried."

"Sorry," she said, working to compose herself. "I was crying. I didn't want to bother you all."

"Aren't you hungry?" His voice hummed closer.

"Yes."

A faint glow in the mist highlighted Damos's figure. "Kalea." His voice softened considerably. His hand met her shoulder and slid down to her hand. He squeezed it. "I'm so sorry." His whisper slid past her ear and into her hair. "I'm sorry about your loss. It's a terrible thing to lose a loved one."

She put her arm around him and rested her chin on his shoulder. "Thank you."

"If there's anything I can do, let me know."

She sighed and relaxed against him, closer than before. The throbbing still stirred her thighs and between her legs. "I appreciate your friendship."

Hugging her in return, a laugh escaped his throat; his chest rattled against hers. "I'm glad we met. I know it was through horrid circumstances, but I'm fond of you." She could hear the smile in his voice. "Sorry I made that comment about your dancing. I…I sincerely enjoyed your dance. You're a talented, graceful, and knowledgeable woman."

She didn't respond, and a long few seconds passed between them; neither made a move to end the hug. She hadn't refuged in such closeness since the convent. Back there, she could count on many friends to hug her when she felt sad. She faced the journey alone until she could locate her lost sisters.

Damos's breath tickled the side of her neck. He turned his head so slightly that it barely mattered…except for how it aligned his lips with her neck as he pressed them ever so slowly and cautiously, testing her reaction.

She gasped in surprise at the surge of renewed energy to her lower body, and when she exhaled, her voice trailed out. His tongue slipped past his lips to graze the skin on her neck. Those sensations returned in full, and now another body pressed against hers.

Damos tilted her head so he could press kisses along her neck, and her panting and moans of yearning egged him on. She squeezed him closer to her and pressed her pelvis against his hip, which exacerbated her aching need. She didn't stop to wonder why.

Her will had weakened and fallen away during her moment with the darkness. She had developed a keen need, and now she had someone to fulfill it. Or else she'd have to face her torturous grief alone.

His breathing became heavy like hers. Damos turned forward and pressed her square against the rock, the hardness within his leggings taunting her desire. Tempting her. She put her hand on his hip where a section of his leggings were tied in place. She could rip his laces open. Playing with the idea for a moment sped her heart along.

He slid his tongue between her gaping lips for a long, wet venture of exploration. His hand found her breast between the kirtle she'd failed to tie all the way and her chemise.

A new voice shortened their progression. "Kalea? Damos?"

Damos huffed in aggravation. He leaned back and answered, "We're fine! Give us a moment!"

A light laugh found Kalea's lips at the instant he attempted to reestablish the connection. She took his hand out of her bodice, smiled, and pecked one last kiss on the front of his mouth. The disappointment soaked into his eyes as she did so.

"Let's go eat, handsome, before they inhale it all."

A new broad smile beamed on Damos's face in the faint firelight as she took his hand and led him back. Entering the firelight was like reentering reality, and the embarrassment struck under their friends' eyes.

"So what were you two up to?" Del asked through a sharp smirk.

Kalea dropped Damos's hand and tucked her chin. Sheer panic smothered her arousal. Her face radiated hotter than the sultry air she'd shared with Damos. She worked her jaw for a pathetic lie.

"The lady was upset," Damos said with a note of hostility in his voice. "Have a little respect."

Del laughed anyway.

When they passed out the food rations, Damos handed a large amount of his own share to her. "Thank you," she said, hesitation lacing her voice. He didn't attempt to sit next to her, but he wanted to, she knew it. A part of her wished he would.

As expected, a great guilt hit, and she ceased all eye contact. Now finding herself wanting distance, the embarrassment returned. His eyes trailed to her often with an air of new, silent panic which she tried not to notice. She didn't want to be rude, but now she had a lot to process.

*What about Dorhen?* The thought made her want to cry, this time more fully. She couldn't help wondering about his soul. Could he see her behavior from the place of his afterlife?

Another thought registered after: What *about* Dorhen? He was gone now. She no longer had him or the prospect of him. She was twenty years old, out of the convent, and yet unmarried. Most laywomen got married at around age fifteen, sometimes thirteen! She'd already missed so much time to sort out her life and decide who she could or should match up with. That area of her processing made her sad.

She attempted to swallow her emotions with a wad of jerky they'd handed out for dinner. Her life would go on, but after she mourned for him properly. The elf she loved. Kalea stopped chewing and put a hand over her mouth. She cried right there, with Damos staring at her. He stayed in his seat, regardless of how concerned he appeared. The rest of the men kept their seats too, eating awkwardly, unsure how to deal with her erratic emotions. She wouldn't have wanted them to coddle her anyway.

Whatever that was with Damos in the brush…it would have to wait at least a short while. With Damos a part of their group, she could take the opportunity to get to know him.

When she calmed down, she finally looked over at him and smiled, reigniting hope in his eyes. "Thank you, Damos," she said again. She'd leave it up to his imagination to decide whether she meant thanks for the extra food or for the kiss.

***

An hour or two later, Kalea rolled over in her bedroll to the left and right. With night fully set in, the dark hung heavier than ever before like a sort of mist itself, thickening the air. Their little campfire showed dimly from where she lay, filtered by the dark mist—or miasma, in Damos's words. He must've been right about his choice of word.

Though the surreal dark veil in the air made for a curious oddity, she ignored it in favor of the sheer, hot, sexual need which had struck sometime after they all retired to bed. She'd never fall asleep at this rate. Her pounding heart made it impossible to lie still.

Damos lay a short distance away. More than once, she'd considered waking him up and asking him for…

She sighed and grunted. That would be stupid. She'd already gone over it at dinner—she hardly knew him! It would change things to such an extreme degree. What if they both regretted it later? What if they didn't get along in the long run?

Even worse, what if he took it as his own selfish conquest and skipped off, back to his life as a rich nobleman attending college, and never thought of her again? What if he told all his friends about the peasant girl he'd boffed in the Darklands? She didn't want to do anything to make her feel like a harlot for the rest of her life! She wanted a good man who would love her. She wanted security and structure, not this…this fleeting frenzy of sex her body begged her to partake in!

Stealing a peek at Damos in the dimmed firelight, he didn't exactly convince her he slumbered either. Boy, she'd given him a good teasing this evening—and after hearing his confession about his grim past. He was too vulnerable for her behavior. And what a line of decency she'd crossed as his confessor, knowing about his own lust and tempting him like she did without a care for his feelings.

Turning her face away from him, she beheld the impenetrable blackness bowing over her face. No sky, just black. Her legs trembled uncontrollably. Strange ideas entered her ponderings, like how she desired to open her chemise strings and let the mist graze her naked chest with its airy fingers like it did against her face. If she were alone, she might have tested that idea. Another strange thought: she could excuse herself to the dark forest again and take all of her clothes off, just to see how the mist felt against her. To see how the mist would graze against her most intimate parts.

Her senses roved back in, and she shunned herself for such bizarre thoughts. *What's wrong with me?* She should be in mourning for Dorhen, and all she could think about were her own body parts and how to appease them.

A new question crossed her mind: did the mist have the same effect on her friends? They were all irritable, but anyone could be irritable in this heavy forest. All around her, they snored steadily, definitely asleep, save for Damos. Damos had an excuse to be sleepless.

Despite knowing her logic had flown right out of her head, she crawled out of her bedroll, tiptoed over, and put her hand on Damos's shoulder. Wide awake, he turned to regard her with a hopeful light in his eyes.

"I want to talk to you. That's all," she said, fighting the natural reproductive instinct from which she suffered. Laying some ground rules with Damos might be a good way to avoid any slip-ups. Also, a short recess away from the radiating fire heat might help to cool her body and her urges. "Let's step into the shadow and talk," she continued.

He wrestled out of his tangle of blankets. Azrielle, his beloved pet, slept on a tree branch with her head tucked down backward. Their stirring didn't wake her.

Despite her intentions, Kalea's excitement picked up more when they stepped into the shadow. Damos's hand found her shoulder, and she grasped it, pushing his chest away with her other hand to keep him from getting too close for decency. Some darker side of her mind called her crazy. She needed him, or anyone, to tend to her needs. She sucked in a deep pull of air and released it slowly. She'd never felt so carnally natural in all her life, at least not so intensely. There hadn't been much in the convent to arouse such desires of nature.

"What's the matter?" Damos whispered.

"I want to say sorry for kissing you earlier."

A long silence. "Oh," he finally said.

"You're a very nice man, Damos, and I'd like to get to know you more. But that was too fast, too soon."

She couldn't see him in the darkness beyond a few faintly highlighted edges. He sighed. "I'm sorry as well. I was too forward."

"Don't be. I can't blame you."

"Yes, you can," he said. "I acted rashly. The last thing I want to do is dishonor you. I acted stupidly... And right after sharing my sympathy for your loss. How insensitive."

Now Kalea felt bad for making him feel bad. She couldn't help but put her arm around him. Her body flared. By now, a great amount of moisture had formed in the fibers of her braies, and she couldn't believe how intensely her feminine area ached.

Once again, all those bad ideas returned to the front of her mind for her to reconsider. How bad could it be?

The longest silence of her life followed.

*I'm going insane. Creator, forgive me for what I might do.*

She put her hands on his sides. His slim body, slightly bigger than hers, radiated sultriness beneath his moist undershirt. Her fingers found the strings on his leggings again. She played with them, and his breathing increased. She pulled the string and released the knot's tension. Damos's hands were trembling when they chanced a feel of her sides in return. She shouldn't have shed her kirtle before bed. Now he had a better feel of her contours beneath her chemise. They trailed slightly upward to find the lower curves of her breasts. Their mouths drew near each other again. Their breaths mingled.

"Kalea," he said.

"Hmm?"

"I absolutely respect whatever you want to do, but you're killing me."

"Damos, I…" She pressed her middle against him.

*Enough of this. This has to happen, or I too shall die. I'm going to have sex with this man.* The thought was so foreign even as she processed it, scandalous. She'd never considered such a statement before. *I'm going to have sex for the first time—right now, right here in this rotten, evil forest.*

She trailed her fingers along Damos's handsome face and down his body; his form was noticeably thinner and shorter than she remembered Dorhen's. He didn't have tight, muscled arms and wide shoulders. Damos was softer because he'd spent most of his life reading books and practicing magic, but he was sweet and he apparently cared about her. She should just get it over with to end her suffering—both of their suffering—and then they could go their separate ways if that's how things fell out. At least they should both be able to sleep after this.

She let Damos go, and he released an exhalation of disappointment. He likely couldn't see her actions when she pulled her gown up past her belly, over her head, and off her arms. She stood before him, naked except for her braies. She could hardly believe what she'd done.

"It's all right, Damos," she whispered.

Venturing closer to him, she found his hands and put them on her bare breasts to show him her intention. He took her in his arms, surprising her with his speed and excitement. He kissed her, and his hands wandered. One of them slid down the back of her undergarment to cup her naked bottom. He shook all over, possibly more than she did.

"Oh no," she gasped the words.

"What's the matter?" he asked, and spread his hot mouth across the side of her neck, causing her to groan.

"We can't lie on the ground. It'll hurt us."

Her words slowed his advances. She also wore her shoes and stockings to protect her feet from the mud. The ground around them was too dark to see if enough moss to lie on covered it.

"I know," she said, "I can lean against that rock from earlier. Can we do this quickly and hurry back to bed?"

"Yes, my lady. We'll have more time later. I will romance you in much better settings in the future."

His promise made her tingle as much as his groping and kissing. He'd romance her. She'd like that. They stumbled together in the general direction of the big rock. She leaned back against the cold thing and didn't even notice the discomfort. An intense nervousness shook her, aside from all the overwhelming feelings of arousal. She had to wonder if it would hurt, or if she'd scream in passion and wake their companions. How embarrassing it would be if they were caught in the middle of their deed!

He pressed her against the rock, kissing her hard. He trailed his kisses down her body.

*What happens next?* She thought about removing her braies for him, until his hands carefully peeled them down and he planted a wet kiss far below her navel.

She arched backward and moaned, eyes closed, hardly remembering to keep quiet. Her nipples pointed upward in the open air, and the darker side of her liked it. The idea of being naked in the forest, vulnerable to whatever would happen to her and in danger of being caught, enticed her. The darker side of her promised she and Damos would make a nightly tradition of this.

"Hurry," she panted. "I need this so bad."

He huffed a lecherous sound and fiddled with his clothing. She kept her back-bending pose while she waited, not caring who saw her naked breasts, not caring if he wandered into her braies or ripped them off and did whatever he was going to do. She put her heel against the rock and spread her thighs as far as she could.

"My lady?" Damos said.

"Hurry, Damos, or I'll pounce on you."

"No, really, Kalea, what is happening with your necklace?"

"Hmm?" She opened her eyes, and a bright light bombarded her pupils. Dorhen's moonstone glowed again! Of its own will!

She could see Damos bright and clear now, and he could see her as well. With this light, they'd definitely get caught. She blinked her eyes. What to do with it? She still needed Damos's help. She regarded him, at a loss. The longer it glowed, the more her senses returned and the sillier she felt. She closed her legs and sat upright on the rock.

"I'll put it under our clothes so it doesn't give us away." As her hands moved to lift it over her head, the guilt of her remaining loyalty to Dorhen registered. But Dorhen was dead and she could move on. He'd been murdered by Wikshen.

Damos waited patiently, his eyes studying her pendant's persistent glow. He'd already opened the front of his leggings when the pendant's disruption occurred.

Two long, black arms hooked around Damos's shoulders and dragged him backward.

Kalea shrieked in fright, dropping the pendant back to its place between her breasts. A creature—made of the darkness—roared with loud and eerie ferocity and yanked Damos to the ground, where it hauled him away, ripping him through the soggy earth and unforgiving thorny brush.

Kalea screamed and called Bowaen's name. She ran after Damos without a thought for her nakedness. His body flailed fast along the ground, and Kalea collected plenty of scratches and scrapes following. She kept running as her friends' voices echoed behind her.

"Help! Help us!" she yelled. She screamed Damos's name. The light of her moonstone lit the way so she could avoid falling into a deep pit of mud, as well as allowing her to keep sight of Damos's pale-colored clothing gaining distance. All the way, the darkness grazed her bare flesh. A sense of awareness in the darkness bit at the edges of her consciousness.

She caught up to Damos, who frantically reached for her, and she grabbed his clothing and pulled. The invisible force dragged him downward now, into an extra-soft patch of soggy earth. She managed to get his hand, and he gripped hers in return. She pulled with all of her strength and quickly lost hold. Too slippery. She got his shirt as his hands searched to take her arm.

He sank into the mud. Deeper. He let her arm go when she too began to sink. She roared a doleful call. No matter how much she pulled, he wouldn't budge. He kept sinking, powerless to fight the force which dragged him down.

His head went under, leaving his arm and most of one leg out in the air. His grip on her hand weakened. She reached in with her other arm, plunging it into the painful soil to try and hook his neck and pull his head up. Despite her effort, he sank deeper, too deep to accomplish the feat.

Bowaen pushed in beside Kalea and took Damos's leg. Distressingly, pulling his ankle accomplished removing his boot. He dropped fast, and Bowaen resorted to digging his bare arms into the soil despite suffering its damage earlier. They came out empty.

Damos's hand, now sunk to the wrist, no longer gripped Kalea's. No matter how hard she pulled it, worrying she'd hurt him, it was no use. The thick mud had the best hold on most of his body.

Kalea wept, scrambling to pull his slippery hand until it disappeared under the mud, prompting her to fish for it. As she tried again to dig into the mud, the stinging earth soiled her bare arms. "Hurry, Bowaen!" she screamed.

Bowaen tried again. "Nothin'!" he yelled.

When she persisted, her arms penetrated deep. She immersed to her chin, but could no longer feel any sign of Damos.

Bowaen dug deep too, once more, and then took a hold of her and pulled her away from the mud. "That's enough," he said, shushing her wailing and removing his cloak to wipe her arms. "Don't get yourself injured."

Bowaen finally noticed her nudity and his eyes rounded like saucers. "Kalea," he said, and absently handed her his cloak so she could wipe herself off. "What were you and he—?" He stopped himself.

Del and Gaije's voices shouting through the trees announced their arrival, and their difficulty in finding Kalea and Bowaen after a long stumble through the dark. Before they could notice her state, Bowaen ushered her to put the cloak on.

Kalea forced herself to stop crying and the hiccups took over. She nodded her head, and the motion too easily turned to trembling. "Yes," she said between sniffling. She couldn't lie about what they'd been up to at this point. The mud's irritation registered fast. "It's as you'd think. I liked Damos. A lot." Her eyes trailed back to the mud pit, now Damos's grave.

Bowaen huffed and stepped back. "That kid," he said. "We've lost him!" He roared it and kicked furiously at the ground. "He was the reason I'm out here! Shit!" He kicked again. "Fuck my fucking life!" He finished by burying his face in his hands, and aborted the act because of the mud on them.

Kalea sobbed freely. First Dorhen, and now Damos. "Damos," she said through her sobs. "He was good! He was a good man, and a promising mage!"

Del eyeballed the muddy spot where Damos went in. "What happened?" he asked. "Why were you so far away from us?"

Kalea gestured at the mud. "Something dragged him!" She spoke through her sobs. "Damos and I were together, and he was…snatched by two big arms! He got dragged away, and I followed. And now he's in there." Her explanation bled into a torrent of tears and anguish.

Bowaen crouched, burying his face into his arm. He'd brought Hathrohjilh with him.

As she carried on, weeping and moaning, a slither of ethereal movement crept into her borrowed cloak to graze her body and provoke her sexual need again. She stopped crying. The effect was supernatural. It wasn't her, it was this forest—this darkness! The darkness itself aimed to seduce her, and Damos had merely been unfortunate enough to be the one she lured into the black miasma!

Kalea went cold and numb, but stirred up once again with that ache in her loins. Her body was being bewitched despite all her trauma and mourning. It had caused her to put Damos in danger. It killed him. She raised her wary eyes to survey the black forest around them. The light from Dorhen's moonstone faded.

"Oh no," Del groaned at their fading light. Without the light, they'd be stranded.

Gaije stormed forward as the light died and took Kalea's shoulder. "We have to stay together and try to make our way back to the camp."

She leaned into him, into the warmth of Gaije's body radiating against hers. Her darker side urged her to snake her hand into his open braies and feel the smooth contours of his muscular, hairless ass.

Kalea fought the temptation of this malevolent darkness. None of this was her own doing. If Del were the one standing close, she would've been tempted by him. Same for Bowaen. If she gave in to the darkness, she would couple with any of them! Earlier, Damos was the unlucky, convenient stud, especially with his own desire for her. That's why her carnal urge overpowered her more necessary mourning for Dorhen: she suffered an enchantment! And the spell persisted. She shivered in disgust in addition to the yearning. She'd have to fight it all the way out of this forest.

The company now stood in a tight group, enshrouded in darkness. "We'll hold hands and make our way back to the campfire glow," Bowaen said.

Kalea shook in a medley of different bodily effects as she clung to Gaije's arm. "There's something wrong," she said.

Gaije stepped away from her. "I feel it too." The stretching of his bowstring groaned.

"Someone else is here with us, I know it," Kalea said. She reached out for Gaije again.

"Let go," he said. "I'll need my arm to shoot."

"But how will you aim in this darkness?"

"I have more than my eyes. I sense the stranger too."

She stepped away as he bid, trusting his skill as an elven archer not to hit one of his own.

A shaky breath escaped his throat and a murmur she didn't catch. His arrow erupted in flame and illuminated a face in the darkness beside them. The person's eyes were heavily shadowed over a broad nose and smirking lips.

Wikshen.

Startled, Gaije released the arrow, and the looming enigma swiped a hand to deflect it. The arrow landed on the ground, and its flame died. Once again in the dark, a strange voice laughed at them. A cold blue flame ignited and floated beside the stranger's shoulder, like the one in the dish on Wikshen's table.

"You three pricks should've stayed in the earth," his deep voice rumbled, the shadows hanging heavy on his face.

Now surprisingly calm, Kalea couldn't help but stare.

"Are you the one who killed Damos?" Gaije asked.

"This is my home, and I didn't want him here."

Kalea wailed in sadness, the shock of Damos's death so fresh. At her sound, Wikshen regarded her and smiled.

"Like we told your witch," Bowaen said, "your *home* failed to kill us. Would you care to try?" His hands were locked tight around Hathrohjilh's handle, wringing it in his eagerness for revenge.

"You might exit this forest unharmed," Wikshen replied, causing the four companions to raise eyebrows. "If you leave me an offering."

"Well, what do you want?" Bowaen asked.

"I want what is mine."

When Wikshen reached his long, muscled arm toward Kalea, she shrieked and stepped behind Gaije.

"Leave her out of this," Bowaen snapped.

Gaije stepped forward. "And what of my sister?"

"You'll have to be more specific," Wikshen said, pacing slightly to the left. His eyes scanned for Kalea as he stroked a lock of hair from his face to behind his tall ear.

"You don't remember the elven child you stole?" Gaije roared and released another flaming arrow, but Wikshen leaned away from it with an amazing speed and grace. The arrow flame died with a hiss when it collided with the mud.

"Give us the child!" Bowaen demanded.

Wikshen's grinning teeth glowed in the strange lighting. "Perhaps we can make a trade." He gestured toward Kalea again, standing naked and shivering under Bowaen's cloak.

"Not gonna happen," Bowaen said.

"Then I'll take what's mine after you all die."

He pointed a clawing hand toward Del and, as if throwing strings, his fingers grew into five prickly metal wires shooting out and wrapping themselves around him. They lifted him into the air.

Bowaen dashed forward, and Wikshen used his other hand to create sheets of metal acting as shields against Bowaen's sword. Del struggled against the wires until one wrapped itself around his mouth. His feet kicked helplessly far above the ground.

It didn't matter where Bowaen tried to strike; Wikshen waved his hand and blocked every hit with appearing and disappearing metal plates. He looked like a tree with his arm raised high, sprouting branching wires with Del tangled in the mess. He remained stationary, fending off both Bowaen's sword and Gaije's arrows. Gaije could fire arrows rapidly, and Wikshen deflected all of those too. He used his free hand to swat the arrows and one foot to create flying blades to ward Bowaen off. His long, black kilt waved wildly with each kick. When Bowaen managed a strike between the blades, the fabric deflected the sword.

The wire spell expired, and Del plummeted to the ground as Wikshen stepped aside. Kalea ran to Del's aid and helped him limp away; he favored his wrist. With his hands and feet free, Wikshen moved about. His toned arms and legs worked gracefully in his fighting style, and his long kilt didn't burden him.

Wikshen raised his hand, and out of the flesh of his palm, a curved blade emerged, bringing back Kalea's memory of the tiny gold nuggets seeping out of her own hand. Unlike those nuggets, this piece of metal was huge and sharp. Each limb could create an ethereal blade to throw when needed. Neither Bowaen nor Gaije could touch him.

Kalea watched him in hatred. Togha's sweetheart worshipped this person? What sort of woman could she be? Kalea would never let herself be spellbound by such a creature! She wouldn't...

Hathrohjilh clashed against the blades springing out of Wikshen's hands practically every ear-deafening second. Sweat beaded on Bowaen's brow. How long could he last? If he made the slightest mistake, a phantom blade would cut him open or sever an appendage.

Kalea dropped Bowaen's cloak and ran into the darkness in little more than her skin. She'd left her washing bat at their camp, and if she could find it, she might be of better use to her friends armed, despite her lack of clothing. The thick darkness slid over her body like airy gelatin, as if groping and feeling her. It unfathomably seemed to…taste her.

Sheer hope guided her in the general direction of their camp. She lifted her moonstone and squeezed it. Its light fluttered to life and struggled to stay aglow. It gave barely enough luminescence for her to avoid hitting a sudden black tree in the dark.

The orange embers of the campfire provided the relief she desperately needed. She picked up the washing bat, its silvery sheen reflecting both the fire's orange and her moonstone's blue. She tore back into the miasma, still without clothes.

The effects of desire—Wikshen's desire—continued to rack her. The living darkness tried hard to entice her to join with it. Her breasts bounced with each step, and the darkness relished them. It really had been touching and exploring her, begging her to remove her clothes and submit to it. A foul spell of Wikshen's, nothing more. Even as the sounds of clashing blades and angry voices reached her ears again, Wikshen simultaneously enjoyed her through his dark miasma. She'd stand it no longer.

A sudden hunch urged her to try something with the bat. Maybe Arius Medallus had known she would encounter Wikshen. She might be able to fight him with it.

Following the shouting sounds of her desperate friends, she arrived to find Bowaen panting deep and hard, trying to beat Wikshen's speed. Wikshen kicked Hathrohjilh from Bowaen's hand and lunged to grab his throat.

Kalea's heart skipped. A menacing delight lit Wikshen's glowing blue-green eyes. He could crush Bowaen's throat with the twitch of a muscle.

His long fingers pressed deep, and Wikshen didn't flinch when Gaije's arrow pierced his shoulder. He flattened his palm to make another black blade and snatched it out of the air when it completed its growth. He gripped it hard and pointed the fine tip of it at Bowaen's face.

Racing toward them, Kalea hit Wikshen with her washing bat, right on the back of the head, before he could plunge the blade into Bowaen's eye. Wikshen balked and turned a slow, menacing look at her while Bowaen wriggled away.

Another arrow sank into Wikshen's flesh with a punching sound.

Wikshen growled more in anger than pain as he tore both arrows from his body. The blood spilled over his sculpted curves, and he chased Gaije. Kalea stood near Bowaen, watching in horror as Gaije ran, narrowly escaping his flying blades. Wikshen didn't run, he walked after

Gaije. Taking a chance, Gaije paused to shoot at Wikshen, and then repeated the process. Wikshen pulled the new arrows out, painting his body with more blood.

Looking toward Kalea, Wikshen opened his mouth and spewed a long fall of vomit that mixed with the blood covering his chest. Ignoring his own sudden illness, Wikshen launched into a greased run toward Kalea.

Gaije and Del dashed in her direction, too far away to beat Wikshen. Kalea froze; terror clouded her mind too much for rational thought, ogling the fast-approaching dark entity.

In the brief moment of his arrival, his eyes widened as if in surprise. Kalea covered her head, and Bowaen launched to her defense. Wikshen veered off beside her and rammed into Bowaen.

They fell into a chaotic tangle of three bodies. The force knocked the wind out of her, though Bowaen took most of the hit.

A hard punch to a meaty surface sounded in her ear, and she cried, "Bowaen!" She lay pinned to the ground, motionless for the moment, gasping.

With a better grasp on her breathing, she lifted her head. A big, hot hand cupped her naked breast. She shrieked and crab-walked away from Wikshen.

Grunting, Bowaen crawled out from beneath his limp body. Hathrohjilh's blade stood erect from Wikshen's back, penetrated all the way to its guard. The blood pooled in the mud around him.

Del and Gaije came over, and the four of them stood in silence, staring at Wikshen. Dead. The light of the blue flame faded, along with the supernatural darkness. Kalea's moonstone deserted its effort to stay lit. Stars appeared in the sky, and the moon now lit the forest as the One Creator intended.

"He's not actually dead, is he?" Gaije asked.

"I killed him," Bowaen mumbled. "Serves him right for killing Damos."

Del moaned in pain. "The bastard broke my wrist when he dropped me!"

Wikshen's body held Kalea's stare.

Gaije turned to Bowaen. "Get your sword, and let's leave."

"Agreed," Bowaen said. "I'm not staying here another minute."

Gaije knelt to turn Wikshen over so Bowaen could pull the sword out. Kalea turned her eyes away but didn't think to cover her ears from the moist sound of the blade sliding through flesh and blood. Instead, she crossed her arms over her breasts as the shock of all the events wore off.

Once the adrenaline dissipated, the soreness in her leg reawakened after all her running.

Gaije collected his stray arrows while everyone else gathered their things, and they ran from the site as fast as they could. They returned to their campsite in the moonlight to gather up all of their belongings. They also took everything Damos left behind except for his parrot, which wasn't to be found.

All packed and dressed for travel, the four of them hurried on. It didn't matter how exhausted and sleep-deprived they were, getting out of that wicked forest took first priority.

# Chapter 43
## What is Tirnah's Curiosity

Thank the Bright One, the day of the royals' departure dawned. After refusing to greet Clan Tinharri at their arriving procession, Lehomis made sure to attend their parting ceremonies, especially so he could count the damage they did to his clan.

*Two faerhain. Three. Four. Five!* At least five young *faerhain* accepted the Tinharri males' courting. The sight pierced Lehomis's eyes. His clan couldn't afford to lose so many ripe females.

Prince Kirnonhen himself left the village without a *faerhain* to accompany him home. He rode atop his fine horse—Lockheirhen bred—with the same proud posture as when he arrived. Maybe he wanted his subordinates to get a chance to gain a wife before him, an honorable gesture. Several clan villages lay ahead for them to visit, after all.

Lehomis grinned bitterly, baring his teeth with *saehgahn* fierceness at any one of them who looked his way as they rode or walked past.

Tilninhet walked among them.

"Tilly?" he said, at first assuming she was merely moving her position in the watching crowd. But no, her hand held the arm of a shining royal *saehgahn* in his mature years.

Her eyes met his with a matter-of-fact, though caring, light. Not quite stopping, she hesitated and stretched her neck to deliver the message, "You brew tea well, Elder."

His heart sank as he watched her walk on. Off to a brand new beginning, truly a great outcome for her. She deserved it, regardless of his confused feelings about how he might sometimes miss her. He had told her repeatedly to get remarried, and now she followed his advice.

Before she got too far away, he called out with another bold lie to support the first one he'd dealt her, "I'll send word to Togha!"

She stopped and inclined her head with a genuine smile. A happy smile.

The events of the day weighed heavily on Lehomis as he trudged home. It was over. Now he could put that old shame behind him and focus on the future, on taking care of the females in his house and preparing for Mhina's return. The thought of Anonhet getting married and leaving him hurt enough. Thank the Bright One tenfold he hadn't seen her walking in the procession! She wouldn't choose a Tinharri male, though. The lass was thoughtful and loyal to her own clan.

Speaking of Anonhet, he passed her on the way home as she ran out to the herb garden. Catching her arm, he said, "Lass, I'm going to eat dinner in my room tonight." He needed some alone time, just for tonight.

"Yes, Grandfather."

He trudged that way. He hadn't seen Tirnah at all today. He didn't ask about her. If something were to go wrong, Anonhet would tell him.

*Faerhain,* he thought. If it wasn't Tilninhet jumbling and confusing his emotions with her tea ceremonies, Tirnah and her grief would keep Lehomis busy with worry.

He didn't make it to his bedroom. On his way into the house, Tirnah burst out, bumping his shoulder, her face red. She halted and turned, but failed to deliver the apology he guessed she meant to give.

"Are you all right?" he asked.

She didn't answer. She ran.

"Where are you going?" All those days which had passed since the embarrassment Lehomis and the Desteer caused her, and she still acted as raw as ever. It could be more of the usual mourning stuff today. He followed her when she turned in the opposite direction of town. She headed to the forest, where the river flowed.

"Are you following me?" she cried, halfway to the river.

"Of course I am. Where are you going? I'll make sure you get there safely. What do you need?"

"I don't need you!"

His head ached dully. He preferred the solitude of his room right now, to lock himself in for the rest of the night and only be bothered when Anonhet brought his dinner. Regardless of how thoroughly the *saehgahn* ranged the Norrian forest, they couldn't keep it perfectly safe for their sacred females to roam alone. Even if Tirnah didn't get mauled by a bear or wild boar, she could twist her ankle and fall into a troll chasm and be lost for too long. He intended to let her have her space, but by the Bright One, he'd make sure no harm befell her. His clan had already lost six *faerhain* today!

His protective instincts flared when she stepped into the water to grab one of the little gondolas they used to travel the river. He'd seen *faerhain* in mourning throw themselves into the river before, and he'd be damned to hell if he allowed this one to do that.

Running to beat her, he took control of the gondola and asked, "Where are we going?"

"Go away, Lehomis," she said. A warning laced her tone.

"No."

"I want to be alone."

"How about I row, and you pretend I'm not there?"

As he untied the boat, she climbed in and he boarded after her, pushing off into the river's gentle flow.

"Which direction?" he asked. "Want to go see Harimeiha?" Harimeiha was one of Tirnah's friends who lived up the river. "She's going to give birth soon. She might like to see you."

Tirnah sat in the bottom of the gondola, hugging her knees. "I don't want to see anyone."

Shrugging, Lehomis rowed on in the direction of his choice. He rowed downriver, away from Harimeiha's house, toward the place where the river slowed and widened out. Tirnah should enjoy the peace and quiet. Apparently, she just wanted to float around and think about things. He'd enjoy the serenity as well.

The late afternoon sun glittered on the river's surface. A lot of pink water lilies bloomed along the river's edges of this slow-moving section. Lehomis took the gondola along beside them in case she'd like to look closer.

With her back turned, he couldn't tell her reaction. Her honey-blonde hair draped over her shoulder and spread across the lavender *hanbohik* top she'd chosen today. She'd been refusing Anonhet's offers to style her hair, and he couldn't help but notice her wardrobe change. She had already put aside her dark-colored *hanbohiks* for the bright colors single *faerhain* used to announce their status. Did she genuinely mean to remarry soon? Lehomis doubted greatly she truly wanted to. She'd been so erratic and emotional; single *faerhain* looking for a mate were supposed to be reserved and observant.

As far as he could tell, she stared at the lilies. He stopped rowing and let the boat drift listlessly along the flowery area. He sat on one of the seats and listened to the peaceful forest sounds.

After a few long minutes, he said the words he'd been meaning to say for a while. "I'm sorry, lass."

A long pause. "About what?"

"Hitting your Tinharri friend and causing a scene. I don't know why I did it." Her shoulders bobbed at his words. He continued, "I've wanted to say it. Didn't know how and when, though."

A longer silence followed. Now he'd made an awkward stumble in their space of serenity. He needed something to say to smooth it over, anything. "If you like, we can visit the next clan, and you can talk to the

Tinharri there."

She shook her head, her hair shimmering like the lake.

"You had every right as *faerhain* to talk to them," he went on.

She turned halfway around. "I don't want to." Her face showed straight and blank, no tears or other sign of emotion.

"All right." He hugged himself and gazed out at the setting again.

Unprovoked, she offered, "You didn't have to be concerned about my talking to him."

He replied, "I know."

She turned halfway again, reluctant to look at him. She told the salmon-colored blossoms, "At the time, I decided to let that Tinharri woo me a little... I had no intention of choosing him or any of them."

Lehomis kept listening. Why did his heartbeat increase?

She shot him a brief smile with rounded eyes. "He read me a line of poetry from the human lands, and then he told me I was pretty... I liked it. Is that odd?"

"Not at all. Humans use similar tactics to woo their females."

"Well, it was nice. Very nice. The humans, they have intriguing customs. How different it is for a male to shower a female with such niceties—frivolities."

"It's different, but not all that lovely, actually—" He stopped himself. It might be better to let her enjoy her fantasy than describe the smoky taverns with busty bar wenches and fornicating couples rubbing together in the back alley. That was his experience with human courting rituals.

She continued, "In Norr, we spy on the *saehgahn*, pick one out, have a stern meeting with the Desteer, and then seal the marriage on the ox pelt. For however long it lasted"—she sighed—"I wanted to be wooed. And praised. And lavished."

Lehomis smiled and took up the oar. "All you had to do was ask."

She twisted around with a newfound light in her eyes. Her mouth hung open until a bright laugh burst out. "Scandalous!" She put her hand in the water and swiped a splash at him.

Chuckling, he pushed the gondola along. As she turned back around to face the bow, smiling, he didn't miss how her free arm wrapped around her middle.

# Chapter 44
## What is Wikshen's Cult

I'm glad you escaped Hathrohskog."

Kalea turned. "Lord Remenaxice? Is that you?" They were standing in a misty Darkland field.

"Yes, my dear." He smiled.

Kalea couldn't shake her confusion. "How are you here?"

"This is a dream."

She studied her hands. She was solid and clear-minded, but certain facts didn't make sense. Where were her other friends, and how had Rem found her out here? "This is a dreamwalk?"

He bowed his head, his pale hair gleaming in the soft light. His long tabard and mantle looked as clean and pristine as she remembered, unlike her clothing.

"You can dreamwalk too?" she asked.

"It's one of the few things I *can* do. I can't contact my brother. I need you for that."

She put a finger to her chest. "You knew I could dreamwalk?"

His smile faded. "Oh, I'm sorry. Was I not supposed to know this about you? Humans have such notions of secrets and privacy. I don't mean to infringe on yours."

"No, I mean... I myself didn't know I could dreamwalk."

"Is that so?" His smile returned. "I would've told you before, but it didn't cross my mind. My mind is so, so busy. Nonetheless, here we are now. I'm actually visiting your dream at this moment. Your ability to dreamwalk means you can receive me well. Non-dreamwalkers can get too confused for communication, but if you work with them, they get used to it."

"Rem, I have to report what happened. In fact, I plan to look for Lord Dax in his dream soon...to tell him Damos has died."

Rem cocked his head; his smile didn't fade. "Really now?"

Kalea bobbed her head. "We're all at a loss. No sooner did we break out of Hathrohskog's border did Bowaen announce he'd head back home. Gaije had to convince him to keep going forward to look for Mhina. Bowaen reluctantly agreed because of the promise he made weeks ago to help Gaije in exchange for his aid in finding Damos. But now Damos is gone. I hope Lord Dax will be able to recover things in the fight against sorcery…in the face of this tragedy."

Rem shook his head, smiling. "Don't let Bowaen stop searching."

"For Mhina and my convent sisters?"

"For Damos."

Kalea stuttered. Lord Dax had talked about Remenaxice's questionable mind. "Keep searching for Damos," she mimicked, unsure what to do with the advice.

Lord Rem nodded his head with his eyes closed. "You'll find him."

"But we saw him die," she whispered.

"And don't forget to look for Adrayeth, my brother. He can help you in many ways."

"A-all right." As she spoke, Lord Rem dissipated into the mist. "Wait, Rem!"

The dream dissolved.

Kalea retained Rem's words in the waking world, but they did nothing to ease the grief weighing down her shoulders. They had failed to take Damos back home. Bowaen showed obvious upset about his failure, and she couldn't blame him. *She* was the one responsible. *She* had ruined Bowaen's chance to earn his fortune! And Damos… That poor boy had been so nice to her. He'd rescued her when she was poisoned and bleeding, and he accompanied her into Hathrohskog, a generosity in itself. And yet her mind kept trailing back to Dorhen.

She resisted telling Bowaen about Remenaxice's message in her dream. She didn't want to burden herself with Remenaxice anymore. He wanted her to meet with his brother, Adrayeth, and Kalea couldn't do that. She couldn't imagine why meeting him might be so important, but it wasn't important enough to her. Gaije, Mhina, and her sisters were important to her now.

Bowaen probably wouldn't believe her anyway. No one knew about her dreamwalking ability yet. Rem's advice to "keep searching for Damos" made her feel absolutely stupid. She and Bowaen had watched together as Damos sank into the deadly mud. As many times as they'd plunged their naked arms into the painful, flesh-eating earth, he slipped beyond them. The soil would've destroyed his flesh, if not suffocated him first. A breathy little sob escaped her at the thought. She flipped her thinking to something else.

"I'm sorry you all saw me naked last night," she said after an hour of walking the Darklandic grasslands along a steep cliff overlooking a misty ocean. It was more like looking at a wall of grey than ocean. Seagulls called in the distance but never showed themselves.

Del snorted. "You're apologizing for that?"

"Yes. I didn't intend to create such a scene… He died because of me."

Bowaen turned. "Not true." He turned forward again.

"I lured him into the shadow, away from the fire. The fire made us safe."

"Some vestal you are, huh?" Del's words jabbed.

"I'm not a vestal," she whispered. Her behavior on that night bothered her as much as Damos's demise. Why did she feel so guilty in regards to Dorhen? Feeling guilty about getting Damos killed made sense, the other did not. Just because she'd promised to run away with Dorhen didn't mean they were married or anything!

*I live to serve you. Will you let me?*

*Yes.* Her exchange with Dorhen touched her memory. Maybe they *had* gotten married in that moment. Marriage was an exchange of vows, after all. She'd promised to let him serve her. That's why her attempt to seduce Damos came off so wrong. But a big change had occurred. Dorhen had died.

"I have a question for you all," she said, and they all turned their ears. "Last night, did that heavy black fog make you feel different?"

"Made me feel smothered," Bowaen said.

"I longed for the stars," Gaije answered.

Del made no gesture. "Nope."

"Didn't it make you feel strange, though? Particularly different…in your bodies?"

Her friends responded with head shakings and shrugs.

"No," Gaije said.

So the black mist didn't affect them the way it affected her. The memory of the vaporous fingers grazing her body lingered close to her consciousness and tingled her even now. Wikshen's power had put her under a spell, and then he killed Damos. It was over now, though. They'd killed that bastard.

Before long, a massive dark shape with a tall spire emerged from the mist.

"This must be Wikhaihli," Bowaen said. About two hours' walk separated Hathrohskog from Wikhaihli. "Don't talk to anyone when we go in there. Leave it to me. Don't even look at anyone."

"Won't that look silly?" Del asked as they stared down at Wikhaihli's walls from the hill they'd climbed. A walking cloud poured over it and rushed past and through; the tall tower and shorter roofs appeared and disappeared in the foggy stream. The seashore whispered close to the complex at the bottom of a long drop from the bluff upon which Wikhaihli sat. Its vast, grey horizon faintly showed behind the layers of atmospheric mists.

Del continued, cradling his broken wrist and shaking from the pain, "And won't they know what we did? I mean, they're witches, aren't they?"

Bowaen's face held stiff. "Possibly. Let's try to assume we can get by for a night without them suspecting anything."

Del pointed to Bowaen's tunic. "You're covered in his blood."

He shushed Del harshly. "Well, I woulda bought a new one, but I didn't get the chance to buy one in Alkeer." His fists were clenching as if he desired to scream. He'd cursed plenty since they left Damos behind in his muddy grave. Bowaen's anger, whenever it bubbled near the surface, elicited Kalea's shame and grief. He needed to relax, or they wouldn't survive a night in Wikhaihli. A good bite to eat should do wonders. They hadn't filled their stomachs since the inn in Alkeer.

Gaije put his hand on Bowaen's shoulder. "It's all right. Listen," Gaije said as Bowaen turned to him. "I've been rethinking our arrangement. This is my task. I can't ask you three to accompany me."

Kalea stepped closer to Gaije. "It's our task." His eyes dropped to her from his height. She explained, "Dorhen may be gone, but my work is mounting higher. I'll find my sisters, and I assume your sister isn't far from them."

If she spoke any longer, she'd burst into tears. Also, she did not want to give Gaije the chance to say no. She turned away to hide her emotion. The wound of Dorhen's death would be raw for ages, and she didn't want Gaije to know how much it actually affected her. The same went for Damos's incidental death.

Bowaen shook his head, keeping his face low. "I made a deal with you, Gaije." Thankfully, he diverted the attention to himself.

"Thank you, Bowaen…and Kalea." Gaije turned back to the misty city below. "So how do we deal with the witches in there?"

Bowaen sighed. "Back in Alkeer, we told them we were pledges."

"So?" Del said, earning Bowaen's stare.

"*So* the tactic worked. And I'd like to bite off my tongue for saying this, but they favored Kalea—she's the one who got in." All eyes returned to her.

Her brow tensed. "Do I have to say it again? Think I can just prance back to my convent or my parents' house with all those sorcerers moving into our cities? Think I'll move on and forget about Dorhen, my sisters—and Damos?"

"Calm down," Gaije said, and patted her back. "I see your position.

Listen, after this, if you've no other plans, you can go home with me."

She blinked her eyes. "What?"

"I know you don't want to go back to your home. My grandfather can take you in. He has a soft spot for human women. I'm sure he'll be more than happy to accommodate you."

She couldn't hold her tears in any longer. She threw her arms around him, and though he stiffened up, unsure how to react, she hugged him tight and sobbed into his smelly cloak.

"What did I say wrong?" Gaije asked the others.

"Nothing, must be that time of the month," Del said.

"Which time of the month?" Gaije asked, and received no answer.

"Kalea." Bowaen's hand grasped her shoulder and gently shook her. "We have to move before the witches see us standing here. The fog is lifting. Straighten up; you have to act for us."

She released Gaije and wiped her tears on her own cloak. She had an important purpose and intended to see it through. And after they completed their mission, she would have a home to go to.

"Kalea," Bowaen said, stepping to meet her squarely. He rummaged through his pockets. "I might've abandoned my lockbox in Valltalhiss, but I didn't let my valuables go."

Opening a drawstring bag, he fished out her bracelet. The pearly shells shone and sparkled. Her heart sank at the sight of it. "Here." He held it out to her. "I don't need it. Not anymore."

Kalea frowned and covered her mouth. The bracelet Dorhen had made for her—she'd thought she would never see it again. She hesitated before taking it, unable to believe his gesture. "Oh, Bowaen!" She cried on his shoulder.

Outside the gate to Wikhaihli, Bowaen faced Kalea with an air of doubt like back in Alkeer. "Listen…" She caught a quiver in his lip. "I want you to be careful in there."

She tightened her mouth. She'd gotten her crying out and resolved to cry no more. She had work to do now. "Of course. Don't worry about me," she told him.

The stiffness didn't leave his shoulders and jaw. Bowaen banged on the heavy wooden door secured to Wikhaihli's surrounding wall.

"This place might've been a monastery for the Sanctity of Creation at some point," Kalea said while they waited for a response. She needed something to say to control her jitters. The scenario back in Alkeer would apparently repeat itself. They'd let her in after she showed them the lock of Wikshen's hair, and she'd act like a pledge. She held it in her hand as they stood outside the walls, its strands itching her sweaty hands. "That tall tower looks like the main chapel of a monastery."

No one responded to her comments. She stepped closer to the door, rehearsing the words in her head to get them into the cult.

When Bowaen banged again, a tiny shutter on the door finally swung open. "What you want?" a low, resonating male voice hummed through the carved hole in the door. She could only see his black hood through the opening, with a hint of his mouth.

Kalea swallowed. "I wish to serve Wikshen." The words spewing out of her mouth soured her tongue; she put on her best expression anyway. With Wikshen already dead, finding Mhina in there might be easier, at least. Her novice sisters' whereabouts would remain in question. "And my friends too. We want to pledge our loyalty."

The black hood tilted up, and a set of red eyes met Kalea's. *A Thaccilian!* Out here? Why not, though? Just because a lot of them lived trapped in Valltalhiss didn't mean *all* of them were accounted for there.

Kalea's trembling intensified. The red eyes narrowed, and then the shutter slammed closed. Kalea jumped at the loud sound.

The big doors groaned open on their rusty hinges, and the black-cloaked man with red eyes met them squarely. He took his hood off, which confirmed Kalea's suspicion. He resembled King Kerlin down to the intensely hungry stare. Red eyes, blonde hair, except his hair was cut short around his crown with longer strands lying over his shoulders from the base of his head. Fringes of cropped bangs hung over his red eyes, which lingered on Kalea, taking her discomfort to the limit.

He smiled at her. "You'll impress here," he said. He even sounded like a Thaccilian.

She extended her hand to show the blue lock of hair. "Wikshen has chosen me."

He waved his hand. "Bah. Come in now. You look not very comfortable. You need food and water."

So far, he was the least interested in her lock of blue hair. She put the relic back into a little wooden jewelry box Bowaen had donated to the cause. It made a grander show than pressing the lock into her old *Lehomis* book. From there, she held the box between her hands to act as if it were a sacred relic with holy powers. Earlier, Bowaen had coached her to use confident body language and a haughty voice—to act more important than those in the complex because of what they'd said in Alkeer: *Wikshen has chosen you.*

Paying no mind to Bowaen, Gaije, and Del, the Thaccilian guided Kalea with a hand at the small of her back into the bustle of the complex.

Allowing his guidance, Kalea cast more than one glance over her shoulder to make sure her friends were still there. They followed as warily as expected. She couldn't guess what might happen in this place, if they'd be killed or kicked out, or if any of these people would somehow know they'd killed their deity last night in Hathrohskog. Before approaching Wikhaihli's gate, they had stashed their weapons and other things among the rocks and grass out in the field, to be collected later. They couldn't risk their weapons being confiscated.

Walking across the wide courtyard confirmed Wikhaihli's ancient history as a monastery, now in disrepair. Everything expected of a Sanctity of Creation monastery could be found: a stable, dormitory buildings, a kitchen with a tall pillar of smoke rising from the chimney, a bell tower in the central courtyard, and a grand chapel. It all took her back to the days in her convent.

A lonely chicken pecked at the ground along the path. The people outside were sparse and those present walked with purpose, dressed all in black, and quiet if not for a bell or two dangling from their belts. So far, everyone they met carried a bell or a drum. Old women walked around with the drums on their backs like some they'd seen in Alkeer.

Kalea and her friends stayed quiet. Too quiet? Part of her itched to make conversation. "We're hungry. And can we bathe?" Kalea suddenly said, hoping it would delay her process of converting to the Wikshonite faith.

"First, you talk to shamans," the Thaccilian said.

"Are you a warlock?"

"Technically, but can't do Kraft magic. So I handle mundane duties, more mundane than other warlocks."

His nonchalance comforted her. It might've slowed her heart if not for the looming dark tower drawing closer with every step. He acted more relaxed than the Wikshonites at the Alkeer temple.

He moved his hand to her shoulder and steered their course toward a door beside the main chapel, under a shoddy gallery in desperate need of repair. Her heart sped as they drew closer.

"You don't want to pledge yourself—not actually," he whispered, putting Kalea's nerves over the edge.

How in hell did he know? "I have to," she whispered back with her best effort to steel her nerves.

"Tell them unflattering things about you," he whispered. "Anything. If they find reason to believe you imperfect, they slot you as a lowly servant. Is better."

He might've offered good advice, but she needed to gain access to the deepest crevices Wikhaihli possessed. How much range did a lowly servant have? It could be a little or a whole lot. The option teased Kalea's brain. She'd have to gain her audience with the shamans and figure it out from there.

He squeezed her shoulder hard, and they all stopped. Turning, he gave a signal to her companions not to venture any closer. "You three, accompany me to different office. I'm not holy enough to go forward into this one."

He walked Kalea to the door and knocked for her. The hinges creaked, and a fat, middle-aged woman peeked around the edge of the door.

"What now, Dyii?"

"Girl showed up at gate," he said calmly in his odd dialect. "She pledges herself. Ugly creature, if you ask me."

The woman opened the door wider and eyed Kalea. She raised an eyebrow. "I'll be the judge of whether she's ugly or not."

Before letting her go, Dyii squeezed Kalea's shoulder one more time. Kalea resisted looking at him for whatever he was trying to tell her. She was on an important mission. Somewhere in this complex, she'd find Gaije's sister and possibly the convent novices. The deeper into the cult she could poke around, the better.

The fat woman pulled Kalea through the door by her arm. She stumbled and watched Dyii's longing red eyes as the door closed between them.

"I'm Kilka," the woman said, "head shaman here until Knilma returns."

"I love Wikshen, and I want to join this community," Kalea burst out.

Kilka patted her back and sat at the desk in the cozy room with old tapestries covering the stone walls. "Of course, girl, and I'll find out where you'll be most useful."

Kalea presented the lock of blue hair within the open jewelry box and placed it on Kilka's desk.

Kilka stared at it for several long seconds. "Where did you get that?"

"Wikshen. He chose me."

Leaving the hair where it sat, Kilka shuffled through various papers in a lockbox. She took out a list, dipped her quill, and said, "Spell your name."

Kalea did.

After writing her name, Kilka added a note after it, which Kalea couldn't read from her angle. "How old are you?"

"I turned twenty about two months ago."

"Bit old, but you qualify for the running." Kalea didn't ask what the "running" was. Kilka jotted down her age and then stood. "Arms out."

Kalea raised her arms as ordered, and Kilka pinched the fatty flesh on the back of one. She frowned and twisted Kalea's arm around to inspect her elbow. "Bony thing, aren't you? And dirty."

"I've traveled a long way on foot—because I love Wikshen so much."

*Don't overdo it, you idiot!*

Kalea clamped her lips and allowed Kilka to continue the inspection. The woman groped both her breasts like they had done in Alkeer, and then she groped in new ways. She braced one hand on Kalea's back and pressed her other hand against her belly before digging her fingers in hard enough to bruise.

"You're not pregnant?" Kalea shook her head. "Been with a man lately?"

"Never." Her last memories of Damos's face flashed in her head, bringing with it a sorrowful pain in her gut. That pain amplified what Kilka's fingers did. Nevertheless, her words were the truth. It hadn't occurred to her, however, that making love to Damos might hurt her chance to infiltrate Wikhaihli.

Kilka knelt down in front of Kalea. "We'll see, won't we?" She raised Kalea's skirts to look at her knees. Kilka clicked her tongue as she dropped the fabrics. "You wearing anything under your chemise?" Kalea nodded. "Remove it."

*This is for Mhina. It's absolutely necessary. Whatever it takes!* Kalea recited to herself as she reached under her own dress and pulled off her braies.

Kilka put her hands under her dress and groped her thighs. "Skinny, skinny, skinny." Kilka shook her head and clicked her tongue again. Her fingers trailed higher, where she prodded around Kalea's hips. "As I thought, you got some bony hips, girl." Her hands touched all around the knobby bones jutting at the sides, and around to her buttocks. "This won't be good for Wikshen. Do you understand? We make things comfortable for him here. Your body must cushion and caress his, not jab and poke him as he's trying to give you the blessing you demand."

The mental picture her words painted made Kalea nauseous. Nonetheless, she mustered a smooth façade. "But please listen. As I've told you, I walked a long way with little to eat."

Kilka squinted at her. "You'll get a fuller evaluation later to see if you deserve the concubine status. If you're deemed worthy, we'll see about sparing some milk and fatty foods for your diet to soften you up. If not, this emaciated condition you've gotten your body into will work fine for a maid's status."

So her crossroads forked between a concubine and a maid. Whichever one could access more of the complex, she'd reach for it. Luckily for her, if they made her a concubine, she wouldn't have to worry about "comforting" Wikshen—not when he lay dead in Hathrohskog.

Kilka's exploration continued, to Kalea's dismay. "Widen your stance." She groped her inner thighs and prodded all the way up. Slipping her fingers into Kalea's intimate crevice, she put one finger up too high.

Kalea squealed, and her jaw tensed to compete with the religious statues in her convent. "What are you doing, please?" Her teeth chattered.

Kilka's finger wiggled around but only penetrated to the first knuckle. "You still have your hymen. Good on you. And behold, you told the truth about your virginity, even better."

"Of course I did!" Kalea braced herself on the desk.

Kilka took her finger out and, at last, took her hands out of Kalea's skirts. Wiping her hand on her own skirt, Kilka shushed her. "Keep your calm, especially if you'd like to meet Wikshen."

Kalea wanted to laugh through all her anger and embarrassment. She'd already met Wikshen! Bowaen stabbed the bastard! Kalea retained her calm, though. With the evaluation ended, it was time to move forward.

Bending over the desk to jot some more, Kilka said, "Being a virgin isn't mandatory. If Wikshen likes you, he likes you, but it's a rare trait we like to offer him. You're eligible for his inner chambers."

At that, Kalea stifled her feelings and squared her shoulders. She was in.

# Chapter 45
# What is the Black Cloth Devotion

The corridors after Kilka's office grew deeper and narrower as they ventured.

"We're entering Wikshen's private realm," Kilka told Kalea, guiding her by candlelight through the complex. "There are several areas of Wikhaihli where only Wikshen and his most devoted can go."

"Who would be considered his *most* devoted?" Kalea asked out of genuine curiosity.

"His concubines and his top shamans. Knilma is the highest ranking shaman and I come next. There are a few spaces even we aren't worthy to tread."

A lonely hand bell chimed in the distance, keeping a slow rhythm, several seconds separating each chime. Walking these silent stone corridors with the music of a somber bell ignited memories of the convent where Kalea grew up. They used a bell to shift into new prayer verses. In here, murmuring or singing did not accompany the bell like it did back home.

"It's so dark," Kalea noted as they descended yet another staircase.

"Of course it is."

The final stretch of walking brought them to an open space, lit mostly by an unnatural blue flame in a dish, like she'd seen in the temple at Alkeer. At the center of a large space, a group of women wearing nothing but narrow black panels at their fronts and backs, positioned in rows, all held the same uncomfortable-looking pose. None of them moved. Though the pose made Kalea's back hurt to look at, it was graceful. Their bodies were arched backward, one graceful arm raised in the air, poised on one knee with the opposite leg straight out, bracing one toe on the floor. The display might as well have been a motionless dance.

"We generally call that *position*," Kilka said when she noticed Kalea staring. "It's a worship routine for higher level witches. There are many positions, and each one requires a body with perfect strength and balance acquired over years of refining."

Kalea couldn't quite say her thoughts aloud, nor did she want to acknowledge to herself that the motionless dance was beautiful. As they walked the circumference of the group, the sight of the figures and their limbs turning created cascades of repetitive movement despite the women's static positions. Uncannily beautiful.

Kilka patted her shoulder. "You'll learn that soon, but for now you've too many basic necessities to catch up on."

An older woman in black sitting to the side chimed the bell again, and the posing women flourished their limbs into a new position. Kalea caught the dance-like transition before Kilka tugged her onward.

She stopped Kalea's progress at a black panel of linen hanging on the wall—another altar like the one they made her bow to in Alkeer. "Take off your shoes and kneel," Kilka whispered, pressing on her shoulder.

Groaning on the inside about having to bow to a false idol again, Kalea sank to her knees. The stone floor beneath her was worn to perfect smoothness.

"The lock of Wikshen's hair you have, put it in the dish and tell him you've arrived."

Kalea gladly parted with the horrid artifact. She placed the whole box in the metal dish. "I have arrived," she recited. At the same time, she told the Creator repeatedly in her head that she didn't mean anything by her action. She did it for Mhina and her sisters.

Next, Kilka bid her to bow and kiss the edge of the linen. "Now take off your clothes," Kilka said.

Kalea swallowed. They hadn't asked her to do that in Alkeer. When she hesitated, Kilka swiped at her bodice laces in sharp jerking motions until Kalea took over. She hesitated again in her chemise, and the shaman tugged it off to render her completely naked. She reasoned with herself that she could put aside her modesty for now. Only women occupied this space anyway. Standing naked in the dark felt too similar to her night in Hathrohskog, how the living darkness touched her and frolicked with her through the forest branches. All these experiences with Wikshen were happening too close together.

"And what's this?" Kilka asked. Her attention gravitated to Dorhen's moonstone and the bracelet Bowaen had recently returned to her. Kalea couldn't keep the alarm from her expression. "No jewelry here," Kilka said, and reached for the pieces.

Kalea fought, squeaking and slapping her hands away. Her shrieks echoed through the cold stone halls.

Kilka shouted with authority, "Obey, slut!" and slapped Kalea's face. Her strong hand sent a thunderous tremor through her skull. Kalea fell, her face vibrating for the moment.

As soon as she sprawled on the floor, naked and chilled, Kilka pounced on her. In their struggle, the string on her bracelet broke and the shells scattered in all directions, tapping far into the dark underground chamber. The shaman ripped the pendant over her head and pocketed it.

Even after getting her way, the woman took a chime from her belt and tapped it. The chime's vibration entered Kalea's body and pierced her back as if she'd just been lashed. Kilka tapped a few more chimes, and Kalea screamed at the sharp, ethereal pain.

"Keep screaming, Wikshen likes that sound," Kilka said with a smile. Throughout the commotion, the other women in the cave paid no attention. "On your knees, you little hussy!" Kilka ordered.

Kalea obeyed, and the woman gave her one more vibrational sensation to sear her back. "Look to the cloth! Apologize for your insolence and ask it to spare your life and come into your body!"

*One Creator, I call You instead!* Kalea bowed her head and forced out the words Kilka wanted to hear.

When Kalea returned to her feet, Kilka's expression cooled. She hovered in close to Kalea's ear. "You're not a Wikshonite yet. See that tunnel entrance?" She pointed to a black crevice in the rocky wall. "You will walk its entire length, through the dark, on your own. I'll take a different route and meet you on the other side to deliver your next task."

How hard could this task be? Completely naked and shaking from the fear and painful resonance of Kilka's spell, Kalea approached the mouth of the dark tunnel. It was narrow enough for her to brace her hands on both walls and guide herself through. She couldn't imagine anything scarier than spiders lurking inside. Eager to get all this over with, she walked right in.

The tunnel stretched on for a long distance. The dim, glowing entrance soon disappeared behind her and left her alone with the darkness. Walking through it, her senses dwindled to nothing but the blackness and the feel of stone under her feet and against her trailing fingers. No sounds occurred beyond her heartbeat and inhalation.

She walked for so long she lost track of the time and distance. The silence intensified to a maddening scream of nothing, and the darkness pressed on her eyes. When she closed them, more darkness.

The intangible pain of Kilka's ethereal lashings vanished. In here, it truly was her and the darkness. The best she had to judge the distance was the exhaustion of her feet. Pain turned to numbness in her soles. She swore the floor shifted into different materials, like metal or compacted dirt. When she curiously crouched to find out, she found the same old smooth stone. Her imagination had caused the confusion.

The floor dipped down, farther into the earth, and down again. How deep did she go? How deep *would* she go? All those buildings crammed together on the ground above were the surface veneer. The rest of Wikhaihli, its most important parts, lay underground in any number of burrows and dens.

The path stretched on. Loneliness set in. She missed the sound of her friends' voices bickering. Del poking fun at Gaije, Gaije not getting most of the jokes because they were foreign to his own culture. Her ears screamed in madness in the silence. She tried to hum, but she hardly heard herself.

She slapped the wall with a flat palm, wishing she could find a door to escape the dark confinement. No doors, only solid stone walls. She ran. The sooner she could get out of here, the better. She ran for a long time. Her bare feet slapped and stung against the hard floor.

Slowing down, she panted. Her hands were numb from grazing the wall. They'd be raw later, but she couldn't stop trailing them along, or her face might eventually collide with a curved wall. There might also be a chance she'd get turned around. Thank goodness the tunnel stayed singular; she didn't have to choose any forked passages. Just one long, deep, and dark path.

Every step she took which didn't reveal an exit to the tunnel brought her closer to tears until she could stand it no longer. A loud burst of a sob preceded a stream of steady weeping. She collapsed and gave in to the emotional urge. Her voice filled her ears like an unreal, loud, and abstract noise. How loud her screaming got, or how long she spent on the floor in a fit escaped her comprehension. How easily she regressed to the state of childhood when she'd throw a tantrum, screaming, whining, and begging to get what she wanted until her father gave in. In here, her father couldn't step in to coo at her, give her an extra biscuit, and read to her from the *Lehomis* book.

The reality of aloneness set in. So utterly and completely alone. She no longer had Dorhen's moonstone with its temperamental decisions to light up and remind her of the elf who loved her. The darkness was her solitary possession. Actually, it possessed her.

A breeze brushed past her clammy skin. Or was it a breeze? She stopped crying, partially coming to her senses. Crying would not get her out of the tunnel. That breeze was the first sensation beyond her own bodily discomfort she'd sensed in ages.

She resumed walking. Her feet throbbed and she limped on them. For all she knew, they could be bleeding. Another breeze brushed past her.

Hands.

No, that couldn't be right. Her imagination ran wild again. No one was with her.

Hands in the dark. Many of them. All of a sudden, she didn't feel so alone, but logic insisted otherwise. Step by step, she moved forward. Did it matter if she arrived? Maybe not. Nothing mattered anymore. Her mind numbed and her steps continued autonomously.

"Kalea," a muffled voice rang in her ears. "Kalea."

Someone shook her?

Her mouth had dried long ago, her throat too. She needed water.

More shaking. Hands gripped her shoulders. The air moved around her skin like heavy cream. Her eyelids fluttered.

"Kalea, snap out of it." That was Kilka's voice.

Fingers squeezed her face. A blue light registered. Her limited sensibilities told her she was awakening from sleep, yet she was standing. Her numb feet had vacated her awareness. Her lips were dry and flaky when she attempted to put them together, and her dried tongue couldn't help them.

"Water," Kalea rasped.

Kilka patted her face. "You've done well, girl. You walked all the way through the tunnel. We didn't have to go in and retrieve you."

*I did it. For Mhina.* She laughed out loud. Mhina was a girl she'd never met. She had done it for Gaije, to be honest. Her good friend. She'd do anything for him.

"What's so funny?" Kilka asked.

She didn't remember walking that last long stretch; somehow her body had done it for her.

"I did it," Kalea said. "I love Wikshen." That statement came out easily. It didn't feel like such a lie as it had back in Kilka's office. Her fuzzy head struggled to discern the real world around her. She remained aware of the darkness filling the tunnel exit behind her, a darkness she had spent a long time with.

Kalea was turning to reenter the tunnel to be with her new friend when Kilka took both her shoulders and turned her toward another shrine on the wall. It was similar to the first, except a small fountain nozzle stood out from this one, trickling between two lengths of black linen.

"Water!" Kalea sang deliriously when she finally noticed it. She'd forgotten to note all the sights and sounds in this new space. More witches and shamans walked about. One of them placed a cone of burning incense in a little bowl before the fountain altar. She hurried to the fountain, and Kilka slowed her.

"Approach with respect," she said. "Squat down here."

Kilka guided her into position, which Kalea needed because she couldn't control her wobbling and swaying. She'd love to collapse and sleep on the floor right on the spot, but she wanted to drink the water even more.

"Squat over the incense. Let the smoke touch you. Here, put your feet on these bricks," Kilka instructed, and helped Kalea to place her feet on two clay bricks embedded into the floor. Her feet settled into grooves carved by centuries of other people's feet. "Brace your hands here."

Two recesses for her hands were sculpted into the wall. An abstract mingling of shapes and carved lines decorated the area around the nozzle. The shapes resembled one human body at first, but at a second glance it became a medley of many people in a tight composition.

Kalea's position, with her back arched in her squat, allowed the warmth of the lit incense to radiate against her lower body. Without any more thought or direction, Kalea tilted her head close enough and let the cool water from the nozzle fill her mouth and run down her throat. She drank heartily. It filled her stomach, but she couldn't get enough. Much of the water ran past her chin and her neck, between her breasts, and beyond. The cool liquid running between her legs mixed playfully with the smoky incense heat.

Such a relief to get a drink. She didn't pause to wonder if this was some form of worship. It might as well have been, but she was so thirsty and hoped for food. She stuck out her tongue to enjoy and lick the soft stream of water; she let it stream over her body wherever it wanted. She came alive again after such a long period of withering in the tunnel.

"Good." Kilka took her arm.

Kalea wasn't ready yet. A new heat bloomed between her legs, and she enjoyed the act to a new extent.

Kilka pulled her to standing and took her face in both hands. "Welcome," she said, and kissed her forehead. Some other women wearing black filed along her path to the door, and each one called her "sister" before adding a kiss to her forehead.

"You are a Wikshonite," the last woman said, opening the door for her.

Kilka accompanied her through the door, where hot, steamy air hit her naked body, a stark contrast to the cold state she'd gotten used to.

Feminine giggling echoed around the numerous corners they turned until they arrived at a large, steamy bathing area. A tiled recess in the floor was filled with milky, opaque water and a dozen naked young girls chatting and laughing. Many of them seemed younger than Kalea.

"Get in there and wash yourself," Kilka said. "We wash every single day for our Wikshen because that's how he likes it. When you're done, we'll evaluate you under the light to decide if you're a good candidate." Kilka turned on her heel and walked away.

Actual flames lit this room, lots of them, so she could see more than she'd seen in the chambers past. The light brought a shallow wave of awareness back to her. A hot meal and a bed should fix her up the rest of the way.

Feeling as grimy as ever, she didn't hesitate to step into the bath recess and immerse in the hot water. How did they make it so hot? Kalea rubbed her arms and legs under the soothing liquid's caress, dipped her hair, and then reached for the herbs in the baskets the other girls were using. Mimicking the other girls, she took a few stems of lavender and wrapped them in a towel twisted over her hair. She sat on the step and rubbed her body down with the herbal soap. This process wasn't too different from how she used to bathe in the convent with other girls present. In this case, the bath was bigger, and they could all use it at the same time.

Kalea lowered herself into the water once again to rinse. A slim pair of hands slid around her collarbone.

"You're new, aren't you?" The voice hinted the mouth was smiling. "Welcome, sister." A wet pair of lips stamped her cheek.

Kalea whirled around to find a pretty young woman with large breasts floating on the chest-level water. She didn't have her black hair bound in a towel like many others did. Her bangs were cropped across her eyebrows and her hair hung to her shoulders.

"My name is Metta. What's yours?"

*Metta?*

Kalea stuttered for a while, gawking at the very woman Togha had sent her to find. She had swum right up and announced herself. "Kalea," she finally got out. "My name's Kalea."

Metta smiled. "Nice to meet you." She took Kalea's hands and held them to her swelled bosom. These women were a world more touchy than the novices and vestals she'd left behind. "I'm from Alkeer. I'm a seamstress, been practicing all my life. And my ma taught me witchcraft from a young age too, although my ma isn't a Wikshonite like I am. How about you?"

"Um." Kalea's mind raced with the awareness she'd lost in the tunnel, now reunited with it. "I'm from the Lightlands." Kalea stopped herself. Did it matter if this woman knew where she came from? "I'm good at washing. I used to be a vestal in a convent dedicated to the One Creator. I would wash clothes every day."

Metta cocked her head. "Who's the One Creator?"

"He's God. He made the entire world… Didn't you know?"

Metta's face remained uncomprehending, but she held her pleasant smile. "The whole world?" Kalea nodded. "Was made by a creator?"

"Yes."

"I never heard anything like that. Sounds like a lot of taradiddle."

Kalea frowned in instant offense, then quickly calmed herself. No sense in getting angry at another ignorant Darklander. Ever since stepping onto this side of Hanhelin's Gate, she had seen no sanctuary or slightest indication any folk here worshipped the One Creator.

"Bet that's why you joined the Wikshonites, huh?"

"Um…sure." Kalea averted her eyes. Finding Metta presented yet another difficulty in convincing her to leave here, or at least think of Togha.

Metta hugged her suddenly. "You made such a good decision." Her naked body pressed hard against Kalea's. Kalea made an effort to subtly wiggle out of her hold.

"I'll catch you up on everything I know," Metta said with a beaming smile that flashed in her eyes. "You don't have to know witchcraft to be a Wikshonite. A lot of these girls are just regular women—pledges. Did you know Wikshen set his foot on the earth recently?"

"Y-yes. Yes, I'd heard," Kalea said.

"His majesty lured you all the way here from the Lightlands." Metta put both her hands to her heart and rolled her eyes to the ceiling. "He's so magnificent. He can literally have whatever and whoever he wants. And he's called you from so far away—I can't believe it. He called me too, you know."

"Of course," Kalea said lifelessly.

"Kalea," Kilka's voice echoed from around the tiled corner. "Stand up here. Let's have a look at you."

"Good luck," Metta whispered while patting Kalea's shoulder.

Kalea's embarrassment returned as she dragged herself out of the water. The soothing water had taken her sore muscles to a relaxed phase.

Kilka shook her head at the sight of her body. "As skinny as my hands projected, though it is fixable… But what's this?" Kilka leaned in closer to inspect the thick red scars on her leg where Chandran had scratched her in his beast form.

"Accident," Kalea explained. "It happened during my travels."

"It would take a lot of care to repair this hideous damage," Kilka said. "You're probably not worth the effort. Turn around."

When Kalea did, Kilka shouted, "Hold on!" She grabbed Kalea's shoulders from behind and eyeballed her back. "You've been lashed!"

"I thought those healed well," Kalea offered.

"Not well enough. They're too visible—and too old to repair. Were you a slave in the past? If you were, they allowed you to keep your virginity."

"They're from my old religion."

"What kooky religion would do such a thing to otherwise beautiful skin? Other than these horrible stripes, you don't have a mole or boil anywhere to mar your near-perfection. Even your limbs are in graceful proportion, and you're taller than a lot of girls." Kilka paused to huff. "This is a shame. You might've made the perfect playmate for our deity after a few weeks with a better diet, but this ruins it. This is all wrong. Your old religion ruined you."

*And thank the Creator for it!* Kalea thought, smiling inside.

"You'll be a maid," Kilka said. "You almost earned a cushy existence in Wikshen's chamber, but instead you'll be cleaning."

The smile inside Kalea died. She wouldn't get full access?

"I'll tell you what I'll do, though," Kilka continued. "You'll be a black maid. We are all devoted Wikshonites, but black maids are both high-ranking Wikshonites and servants. As a black maid, you'll be put to work in Wikshen's tower, and therefore you'll be in his sight. If he wants to choose you, he will. Uglier girls get the lower maid rank, and they cover duties in other parts of Wikhaihli."

So Kalea would still have a decent level of access in Wikshen's tower...

"When you're done here, report to the housekeeper on the first level of the tower." Kilka stormed away, grumbling about Kalea's bony, scarred ass.

All the women finished their bathing and went for the towels as Kalea used hers, feeling like a chewed piece of meat after Kilka's ridicule.

Metta draped one arm around Kalea's shoulders. "Don't worry, being a maid is fine. Being in the tower with Wikshen is all that matters."

Kalea couldn't manage to fake any pleasant emotions.

"Let's get dressed. I'll show you where to find the housekeeper."

After she dried off, a young woman in black approached Kalea with a set of folded clothing. "You're the new black maid?" she asked.

Kalea nodded.

The new clothes the girl handed her weren't too different from the dress she'd received in that Darklandic village which had showed her party brief hospitality. Metta helped her wrap the straps around her body, crisscrossing them properly and tying them at the back. The garment was too...open. It came with no chemise to wear underneath, her shoulders and arms were left bare, and the braies consisted of a tiny piece of fabric tied around her hips with string. She also got a fresh kerchief for her hair. Everything was crisp and new. No shoes, though—hardly any Wikshonites wore them anyway. After the main garments, all she could put on her arm was a black ribbon Metta bound around her wrist and tucked in the ends.

"This ribbon is a sign of our faith," the girl explained. "We all wear one, and sometimes we add bells to it."

She and Metta were outside crossing the courtyard to get to the main tower when they paused at a commotion. Drums were beating slowly amid flat-toned bell chimes. In the distance, the largest gate closed and a great wail erupted from every person present, except Kalea. Metta darted off to join the commotion, wailing along with them, and left her gawking.

Two strong warlocks with half-shaven heads toted a litter across the courtyard, draped heavily in black sheets which hung stylishly and were graced with herbs and flowers. Beneath it lay a long, unmoving form. A small troop of girls in black dresses, decorated with bells at their wrists and ankles, ran out of a side building to join the procession, where they performed a practiced dance around the dead body.

Sweat beaded on Kalea's temples despite the cool breeze. Her hands clenched in her strange blend of nerves and anger.

"They don't know," she told herself. "We didn't kill Wikshen." This spectacle made her want to leave, to abandon her mission right away, but she couldn't. She continued watching the madness. She'd helped kill Wikshen and stood proud with the knowledge.

A tall, middle-aged woman with a drum on her back approached her. "You're the new black maid? Come along," she said to Kalea.

"But—" Kalea scanned around for any sign of her friends among the roaring crowd. This would be a good time to meet up with them for an update.

The woman pulled her by the hand. "Don't worry about the Mastaren."

The procession disappeared into the main tower, where Kalea was bound.

# Chapter 46
# What is the Duty of a Black Maid

Kalea met the housekeeper who oversaw the troop of maids at the entrance of Wikshen's manor, and she led her down into the bowels of the building after the wailing funeral procession cleared. The housekeeper, seemingly a witch herself, ogled Kalea with a smirk.

"Hmm." She scratched her warty chin. "Odd to see one like you here. But then again, those who don't pass uppermost inspection are handed to me. If you don't wish to make this position and its duties your life's ambition, you'll work in chains, and it gets worse after that. Got it?"

Kalea nodded. Some of the other maids waited behind the housekeeper, obviously less pretty than the women in the bathhouse. They at least sported common moles on their faces which might've failed the beauty inspection. Luckily, Kalea had her lash scars in addition to being on the skinny side.

"We keep the prettier maids closer to the Mastaren," the housekeeper continued, "so you'll be in the chapel and inner chambers. Follow me."

The chapel was the soul of Wikshen's manor. The grand nave opened before them through a narrow little corridor leading from the basement levels where the maids lived.

Kalea gasped at the familiarity. Before her loomed a massive sculpted ceiling. Tall blackened windows lined the outer wall, and a long rug ran across the lengthy area, leading to a shrine. This unholy chapel to Wikshen used to be a sanctuary to the One Creator. These filthy witches had converted a divine dwelling of the Creator to a dark, hollow hole. They'd changed the nave into some strange blend of throne room and worship chapel. The ceiling soared, showing black-painted sections of plaster where once there must've been murals. Pitiful glows of struggling daylight made their way through certain openings. Musky, swirling incense smoke danced in the weak sunbeams and around braziers with blue fire. Frescos probably used to decorate the walls, by the look of some of the arched spaces, but had since been plastered over and made into black cloth altars like the one she'd stripped naked for.

Kalea's stomach churned. She swallowed numerous dry gulps. She couldn't let the witches think she was sick, or they might turn her out. They'd ruined such a marvelous tribute to the Creator!

The long, black rug ran from the main entrance to a throne, which should've been an altar where offerings were left to the Creator and pilgrims knelt for the daily blessing. The installed throne surprised her with its simplicity. It stood on a four-tiered dais, which was grand enough but not ornate. No ornamentation adorned the space. The whole drab place suppressed the spirit, rather than inspiring it like it would have if it still belonged to the Sanctity of Creation. The throne's height seemed most important about it; otherwise, it consisted of a cushioned wooden platform resembling a bed more than a chair, which stood at nearly a person's full height so Wikshen could sit above everyone's head.

It stood empty now because no ruler lived to occupy it, and yet a line of about ten people walking on their knees formed behind the rope isolating the throne. A large, black cloth lay draped over the throne and rippled down the steps and under the rope where the pledges, dressed in ordinary peasant clothing, were instructed to kiss the edge, pray to it, and move on.

In a symmetrical fashion, more deity shrines with hanging cloths were arranged around the room. A weeping woman currently occupied one of these side shrines, letting her tears fall onto the hem. Every few seconds, a clinking sound announced one of her coin offerings falling into the bronze bowl next to the cloth.

A whip slapped down Kalea's spine with the sound of a sharp chime as she stared in disgust at the ruined sanctuary. The stinging vibration made her wince back to attention.

"If I catch you slacking or misbehaving, you'll get a series of chime whips. Understand?" Kalea's new position would be worse than she thought.

"Are you listening?" The housekeeper pointed to the long rug. "In the morning, we roll up the rug to clean beneath it. The floor is of first concern to the maids, as it's part of our devotion to go barefoot. The stones in the floor are made of earth, and we walk on it always."

They approached the rug to find it woven with jagged rocks. The pledges were all made to remove their shoes and stride the whole length toward the throne on their knees. Kalea couldn't decide if her rite of passage through the long dark tunnel was worse than this or not.

In the courtyard behind the chapel-manor, Kalea glanced around for some indication of her friends before a maid handed her a bucket, rag, and brush. No one occupied this place besides a few other maids. The woman showed her the proper strokes used to clean Wikshen's floors and sent her off to work in one of the side wings. The housekeeper warned that the strokes must be precise, or she'd be beaten with a magic chime again. She received two more when she made a wrong move.

Soon, she began to grasp the scrubbing technique. She learned to sit straight on her knees on the floor and scrub it in straight up-and-down strokes. This cult favored discipline most of all, right after obedience. The motion exhausted her back and thighs. It stirred the pain in her healing leg. Despite the difficulty of her new routine, she put her best effort forth, reminding herself of her mission. She needed the housekeeper and other maids' trust. The more her new mistress and sisters trusted her, the more freedom she'd have.

When the sky turned orange at sunset, the large tower bell tolled, startling Kalea as she stooped to dump her filthy water bucket in the back courtyard.

The housekeeper approached from behind, pushed her into a kneeling position, and forced her head down in prayer. All the workers around them were doing the same. "Stay like this for the remainder of the bell. Do this at each bell."

The housekeeper took the same pose beside her and murmured the chant, "Wikshen, father of the darkness who lives in the shadow, your presence is beautiful, your cruelty inspiring. We assemble to watch your delight in chaos, your anger at disbelievers, your destruction of opposing civilization. We assist you in any way we can. And though we laugh when you destroy our enemies, we savor the pain you do to our bodies as well. We are alive to serve you, until you decide otherwise."

She repeated those lines until the tolling finished. The woman stood again, looked at Kalea, and said, "You have much religious study ahead of you, girl. You're more than a maid, you're a Wikshonite."

And here Kalea had assumed being a maid would excuse her from having to stray too much from her own religion.

"You look confused," the housekeeper said, and Kalea shrugged. "You mean you traveled all the way here and you don't even—?" The housekeeper sighed. "Wik is the God of Darkness; you could say he *is* darkness. Every few generations, he chooses a host to possess so he can enjoy our earthly pleasures with us and against us.

"But every time he comes, he finds displeasure. Things like reigning kings, disbelievers, music, and arrogance stir his anger. Wikshen's anger is beautiful. It cleanses the earth of these foul deeds. Casting judgment makes him happy. He likes the energy which moves in chaos, the sound of screams and pain. He looks for this.

"Over the generations, we've found what he likes and what he doesn't. We've made a comfortable home for him here. We may escape his violence, or we may not. He's unpredictable, and will pass judgment on us as he chooses. We welcome it because Wikshen doesn't make mistakes."

Kalea clamped her mouth shut and stifled a frown. She wanted to say no, she wanted to scream and protest and storm out! But she couldn't. She had to be willing, to feign interest, and later, she'd save Mhina and the novices so she could return with Gaije to her new home in Norr.

"You have to make yourself available," the housekeeper said. "If Wikshen likes you, he will take you. This is considered a blessing. If he takes your body, your status will elevate to the highest level of Wikshonite. All the girls dream of this."

Kalea ground her teeth. They feared his violence, yet welcomed his violence to their bodies and expected Kalea to do the same? The sooner she could find Gaije's sister and get away from these barmy people, the better.

"Stand up," the housekeeper ordered, and Kalea realized she was still kneeling. Rising to her feet again proved a challenge. "You've done well on your first day, considering. You may go to the dining hall and have your supper. Afterward, you may retire early."

Kalea hurried away at her word. They had been gracious enough to give her a few crackers and a small square of cheese when they realized her intense hunger. She couldn't tell yet if they still intended to fatten her up to make her more comely. But now her stomach growled again, and she couldn't get to the dining hall fast enough. She vaguely remembered how to find it from the brief tour of the complex from earlier today.

All day long, aside from trying to get her scrubbing form right, she'd spent the rest of her mental energy memorizing the layout of the place. Knowing every nook and cranny and corridor and office would be important for the sneaky work ahead of her. Although she'd use her maid status to hide in plain sight, knowing all the best hiding places was a good idea.

On her way back through the nave, she stopped to gawk at two of the pledges who'd reached the front of the line. A man in fine clothing was kneeling before the empty throne-altar with his beautiful daughter. He pushed a large bag of coins under the rope where Kilka stood and listened to the two's words of deference. Nearby, three servants in attendance knelt beside a load of crates and sacks, among which were stacked several cages with chickens, clucking and scratching.

"News of the new Mastaren has traveled a long way to reach my ear, madam," the man said to Kilka.

Kilka crossed her arms. A load of newly arrived pledges were filing in behind this pair, despite the late hour.

"My daughter, Brielle, and I have traveled a long way to pay our respects. I am the owner of many lands and serfs to the northwest, and wish for Wikshen to know that he has my and all my people's alliance."

Kilka inclined her head, seemingly reluctant to soften her face with any gesture of friendliness.

"In addition to this fifty gold chips and these goods," he continued, "I pledge my daughter to our new deity. I pray he uses and enjoys her to the fullest extent of her worth."

Kalea's mouth dropped open and her empty stomach twisted.

"She's the most beautiful woman on my lands," the man added.

"Wikshen accepts your gift," Kilka said. "Let me look at you now."

Brielle didn't act at all like the situation distressed her, as horrified as Kalea felt for her. A smirk quirked her stunning face. Her eyelashes were long and dark, her lips blood-red without the use of rouge, and her pale blonde hair accentuated those colors.

Kilka ducked under the rope to join them on the other side. Without any words or hesitation, she grasped the girl's lapelled dress and pulled both sides open to inspect her naked chest. Brielle acted cool throughout Kilka's public procedure.

"Mm-hmm," Kilka hummed. "Take your arm out of one sleeve." When Brielle obeyed, she inspected the softness of her arm like she had with Kalea early this morning. "Excellent," Kilka said, and knelt to stick her arms up Brielle's dress for a brief pelvic exam…in front of all those people. "Virgin," Kilka continued.

"Yes, of course, madam." Brielle's father beamed with pride.

Brielle smiled and exchanged a smug look with her father, who reached over and patted her shining hair.

Kilka finished her inspection and hastily rose to help Brielle put her sleeve back on. "Flawless as far as I see," she said. Kilka's new smile beamed. She put her arm lovingly around Brielle, and the two now faced her father.

"Can I be guaranteed my Brielle will receive a high station in Wikshen's kingdom?"

Kilka caressed Brielle's shoulder. "I'll certainly see about it momentarily. Regardless, she'll be taken care of."

The man bowed low. "Thank you, shaman."

Kilka stepped aside with Brielle hooked in her arm and allowed the girl's father to crawl to the black Wikshen fabric and kiss its edge under the rope. He touched his forehead to it and prayed for a few seconds after. Before walking proudly out of the nave, he gave his daughter one last, gentle kiss on her forehead.

A man gave away his daughter to Wikshen. Just like that. The warm, salty smell of supper stewing on the hearth in the dining hall did nothing to entice Kalea now. She'd eat for necessity's sake, but the scene she'd witnessed ruined her appetite, possibly forever. What made it worse was how she'd done the same thing: she'd given herself away to a false deity and joined a cult of lunatics. Somehow, seeing someone else do it made it all the more real than when Kalea had gone through the gestures.

Kalea absently approached the hearth, where another old woman in black stood with a ladle. Eating was important, regardless of her nausea and dread.

The woman smirked at her. "What do you want?"

"Some supper, ma'am. Please."

Snickering, the woman swirled the ladle around in the steamy stew. "My pleasure, miss. Hold out yer hands."

"Excuse me?"

"How else do you expect to eat yer stew when you forgot to bring a bowl from the kitchen with you? You must have some pretty callused hands!" She burst out laughing.

Kalea hadn't seen the kitchen yet. No one had explained the dinner routine yet. She had wondered all day if she'd get to eat with her companions, but she saw no sign of any of them.

When she opened her mouth to ask the cackling hag where the kitchen was, a hand touched her shoulder and she jumped.

A blonde-haired man she barely remembered after her long day hovered over her. "Shut up now, Mimara." He pointed his red eyes at Kalea and smiled. He handed her a bowl and spoon. "I brought her one."

Kalea froze at his stare. The Thaccilian she'd met this morning. What was a Thaccilian doing in Wikhaihli? So many other questions waited to pop out of her mouth at any inappropriate time. After she accepted the bowl, barely realizing it, he removed his hand from her shoulder with a reluctance Kalea couldn't miss. He gestured to Mimara, and Kalea handed the smirking woman the bowl he'd given her.

"And after you finish, take the bowl out back and wash it. Ya need help figuring where 'out back' is? Eh?"

"That's enough," the Thaccilian said, and guided Kalea, once again with his hand on her back, to choose a seat at one of the two long tables. A handful of people in black were already seated, a diverse collection of women, young and old, and men, some with half-shaven heads and some without. "This dining hall fills fast, so hurry and get a spot of your favor."

"Thank you," Kalea said awkwardly. "I forgot your name already. It was a long day. Sorry."

"Nothing to be sorry for. My name is Dyii."

Kalea scrunched her nose. "As in 'death'?"

"Yes, I know, it sound like the word 'die,' but it's from northern Darklandic culture where I grew up in brothel."

"I see." Kalea picked a spot at the end of the table, the most isolated seat. She couldn't look forward to having to sit among a large crowd of Wikshonites. "Dyii," she said, lowering her voice, "where are my companions right now? Will they be eating in here?"

Dyii hissed. "Shhhh. Don't ask about them and don't seek them. In this place, males and females don't associate with each other in more than casual passes, and that's why I can't sit and answer your questions, as much as I'd love to. But, Kalea…there's something…"

She watched him from her seat. "What's the matter?"

"They made you black maid today?" Kalea glanced down at her little black maid's dress. He sighed and lowered his voice to a whisper. "This is good. It mean you still have chance."

"What chance?"

He squeezed her arm like at their first meeting. "Stay away from him," Dyii said. His instruction came out in a breath. "I try to see you again. Goodbye." He dashed off before she could ask anything else.

Tearing her eyes away from Dyii's hasty exit, Kalea noticed the woman with the ladle, Mimara, raising an eyebrow at her. Kalea shivered, feeling the deepest bout of loneliness to strike her since she got here. It sounded like her friends wouldn't be joining her, and Dyii didn't seem to want her to get near Wikshen. What did it matter anymore, when Wikshen was already dead? He posed no more threat to her and her friends.

She dipped her spoon into the thick, lumpy liquid. Clam stew? It was as salty as she expected and came with flakes of green herbs harvested, no doubt, from the grassy field outside.

"Kalea!" a shrill voice sang across the hall.

Kalea felt how her body's aches and stiffness increased after a few moments' rest when she attempted to twist in her seat.

Metta sprinted across the way from the door to sit beside her. "How was your first day as a black maid?"

Kalea squinted. "Metta? Are you all right?" The last she'd seen of the loopy girl, she was running off, wailing, to walk and cry behind Wikshen's dead body along its procession into the tower.

Metta sighed through her nose, her face washing over with a new serenity. "I am. I paid my respects, then went into the practice hall to stretch and breathe. I did two positions in the course of two and a half hours. I am filled with *his* dark love, and ready to be myself again." Her eyes rolled in euphoria at the end of her statement and her smile spread wide, showing the teeth beyond her canines. She smelled extra-fresh, as if she'd taken a second bath, though her hair wasn't wet.

"Positions?" Kalea said. "You mean those poses?"

"Yes," Metta said. "Kraft Positions. We should do them together sometime."

"I don't know any of them."

"I'll teach you."

Kalea bit her lip. "They look hard."

"Sure, they can be," Metta agreed. "It takes focus and practice." At Kalea's silence, Metta's smile died. She reached and put her hand on Kalea's forehead. "What's the matter? Are you worried about the Mastaren?"

"The Mastaren?"

"That's what we call Wikshen. It's like saying 'my lord' or 'your grace.'"

"I'm not worried," Kalea answered flatly.

A warm smile widened Metta's pink lips. "Good. But I sense a somber mood hangs around you. You lost a friend?"

Kalea's throat stuck for some reason. "I haven't been well lately," she said, yearning to be honest. Not that she wanted to blow her cover; she just needed a friend. Metta should make a good candidate because of Togha's request to find this woman. Befriending her might help in convincing her to leave Wikhaihli. For now, Kalea wanted someone to talk to. "I lost some friends recently."

Metta's eyes and mouth rounded. "Oh, Kalea." Her voice dragged softly. The attention made Kalea's emotion worse. "Were they Wikshonites?"

"No." Kalea removed the black kerchief from her head and wiped her nose. "An elf I used to love." The pain pierced her heart at the thought of Dorhen. How far she'd gotten from him, and now she found herself in this strange environment with strange people. She should be with Dorhen right now.

Metta covered her mouth with both hands.

"Before I came here," Kalea said around the emotion waiting to burst from her lungs.

"Is that why you follow Wikshen now?" Kalea could only force her lie by nodding her head. "You're looking for guidance and comfort in the Mastaren?" She nodded again. "Poor thing. You'll learn to forget this elf you've lost, because the Mastaren is your lover now."

Kalea stifled her sob and resisted shoving the stupid girl away. She bit her tongue to keep from asking what the cult would do now with Wikshen dead. Too much she could say would get her in trouble.

"I had a brief affection for an elf too," Metta said, rubbing her back.

Kalea faked her surprise. "You don't say!"

"I did. His name is Togha." The girl's cheeks flushed red. "For a brief moment, I thought what a nice treat it might be to dally with him for a bit. He's such a pretty thing. But the whole thing was wrong. Togha is too pretty—if that makes any sense—and my interest in him was fleeting and vain." She ended with a sigh.

Thinking back on how Togha spoke of Metta, he had displayed a certain sincerity. He must not have thought of their relationship as "vain." And Metta's story didn't hold a candle to Kalea's sad story. Her love for Dorhen was anything but vain. It was deep. He loved her. She knew he loved her, and she had obliged to allow his love into her life. She wanted it. She needed it—today more than ever. And then Wikshen stole it from her in one swift night wind.

Metta continued her musings. "A few moments of having aching loins for a regular man—or elf—can't ever stand against the deep, deep ache in my heart"—she slid her hand into the lapel of her wrapped dress and cupped her left breast, as if it were important to demonstrate the elimination of the fabric barrier between her hand and her heart—"that I feel in my service to Wikshen. I regret never saving my body for the Mastaren."

"So you and Togha have already..." Kalea waved her finger when she couldn't find the right words.

Metta laughed out loud. "Heavens, no. I could never have been with Togha because of my religion. I just liked a lot of boys before my new life here, that's all. And I regret my foolishness...because Wikshen is the ultimate."

Kalea wanted to ask what was so great about him. She stopped herself. As a new cult member, she supposedly loved Wikshen too, and carried the same basic religious understanding Metta believed. Since Wikshen had died, the religion would apparently live on until the next generation of their living deity showed up, as Kalea understood it. But she wanted to ask *something*! There must be some kind of sense buried somewhere in all this zealous raving.

Kalea cleared her throat. "Metta?"

Her new friend raised her eyebrows and waited. Kalea stalled because she didn't really know what to ask or how to ask it.

"As you know, I'm new to this religion, having come from a different one." Metta waited patiently for the rest of Kalea's question. "What does it mean?" Kalea waved her hands in a round motion, as if to indicate the whole dining room. "I've never s-seen Wikshen before. And yet, I…"

Metta lunged forward, close enough for their breaths to mingle. "Feel a sensation in your body? A hunger, a longing, a devotion? An answer to his call?"

Kalea swallowed as she considered Metta's input. Hunger and longing? Yes. Sensation—one hundredfold yes. But not so much the devotion… Or…maybe she was wrong and Metta was right, which was why she sought to ask the girl about it.

Metta's hands were warm, practically hot, as they took Kalea's free hand. The spoon in her other hand remained forgotten. Kalea's heart accelerated to pounding. Her body wanted to know, but her brain didn't want to hear it—or be here. Her logic told her to dash outside and sprint straight back to the Lightlands and pretend this had never happened. She'd shut the memories out of her head and focus on the One Creator like she used to.

But Metta spoke anyway. "There's an ancient legend. You know about Wikshen's six previous lives prior to this one?"

*Wikshen is dead!* Kalea thought, biting her lip to keep the words from emerging from her mouth.

Metta's gaze on Kalea's eyes deepened. "Wikshen conquered the Darklands. Every. Time. He. Returned. So you know he'll do it again."

Was conquering the Darklands so hard? Kalea hadn't seen much of anything beyond a settlement or two and a ruined city full of Thaccilians since crossing the gate.

"The sorcerers," Metta continued. Kalea hadn't thought about the sorcerers since being immersed into this wild new culture. "The sorcerous factions are growing in this age. In previous ages, kingdoms, great cities, and wealth abounded. And Wikshen came and flattened all of it. He used to be thought of as a monster, until the Darklanders finally realized the difference between a monster and a true god."

Kalea cocked her head, "What *is* a true god?" In her head, she continued with, *If not the One Creator?*

"The difference between truth and lies," Metta said. Speechless, Kalea waited for more. "The ones who would go on to establish Wikshen's religion realized the truth: Wikshen wasn't a monster. He was the one we were supposed to follow, not some spoiled rich king wearing gold! When Wikshen returned again and again and again, it became obvious that he was our destiny. Was he violent? Yes. Was he cruel? Yes. But we learned how to serve him. We made his will our way, and so we followed his way. And as we continue to carry our faith and grow the religion, a greater, more permanent establishment will take root in the Darklands. We'll never be pestered by tyrants or sorcerers again."

Kalea resisted the inclination to ask her next question: but isn't Wikshen a tyrant? Instead, she asked about what Metta mentioned earlier, the one thing which worried the deepest pits of Kalea's being. "What did you say about bodily sensations, though?"

Metta's smile glowed brighter than the oil lamps in the dining hall. "It's the call to blessing." Kalea blinked and opened her mouth. "In our religion, women have power, Kalea, great power. Haven't you noticed who's in charge behind these walls?"

She had. Shamans—female ones. They bossed around the warlocks in all aspects of everyday living. Dyii had told her himself how he couldn't enter Kilka's office or go into Wikshen's inner chambers. Only women could.

"Wikshen favors us above all else," she said. "Even the black maids! You, my friend, have access to the most private chambers in the Darklands because Wikshen chose you. You'll have a high seat in his kingdom."

"Why does Wikshen prefer women?" Kalea asked.

"Why do you think?" Metta's smile closed into a smirk, and her cheeks turned pink to match her lips. "We're his counterpart. He has no use for men beyond working them like oxen. Look around you."

Now Kalea finally noticed it. Even though both men and women bustled in the hall, the men sat at the opposite long table on a floor level lower than the ones the women occupied. Kalea had previously assumed that the step in the floor was built to accommodate the sloped terrain.

Metta hugged herself, rubbing her hands along her own arms. "Sacred things happen between Wikshen and his women. Wondrous, miraculous things."

"Like what?"

The girl's flirty smile beamed. "Sacred things." Her hands shifted to gripping her own upper arms while she spoke. Her fingers pressed hard until they turned white.

*Sacred things.* Kalea shuddered, afraid to ask for any more details, and tried to recover by taking her second bite of stew, now cold after all their chatting. She chomped on a large, chewy clump. The stew helped to settle her stomach. "Mmm," she said, "these clams are huge."

Metta giggled behind her hand. "Of course they are. They're geoducks."

"What's that?"

"A type of clam. We eat this every night."

Once again, she was reminded of the convent and its repetition of the daily meals. Of course, her old convent didn't have access to the sea, so this repetition was new. As pleasant as the geoduck stew tasted, she could already tell how mundane it would become eventually. Kalea eagerly tossed down five more bites before noticing Metta's lack of a bowl.

"Where's your bowl? Do you need to get one from the kitchen cupboard?"

That sweet smile beamed below Metta's nose again, her eyes twinkling under the shadow of her straight, cropped bangs. They maintained the relaxation they'd taken on while she told Kalea about Wikshen's "miraculous blessings."

"Nope," Metta said. "I've been summoned to a sacred ritual tonight and will eat there. I'm so excited."

"What's so exciting?"

"I've been selected for concubine candidacy."

# Chapter 47
## What is Kalea's Devotion

Kalea's head ached and spun when the housekeeper shook her awake at dawn the next morning. She had wasted hours last night trying to dreamwalk into Bowaen's dream and then Lord Dax's, to no avail. She should've stolen that book she'd read in Valltalhiss. Regardless, she'd been certain she followed the steps correctly, and yet she failed. Surely Bowaen was all right. This place favored women over men, but men were still permitted to be Wikshonites and move about the complex. So long as Bowaen, Gaije, and Del succeeded in convincing the Wikshonites of their loyalty to Wikshen, they should still be alive.

Straight from her bed, the housekeeper sent Kalea and the other black maids to the bathhouse after first visiting the fountain shrine again. In her clearer state of mind, she felt one hundred times more foolish to strip, squat, and drink from the stone nozzle.

On this trip to the bath, she learned the lesser maids didn't have the right to use the grand bathhouse. The black maids really were an elite rank, despite some of the humble jobs they performed. The regular maids bathed in the back courtyard. No men could access that area, so they got naked and did their constitutions in the open daylight with cold well water. Kalea didn't envy them.

When Kalea stripped off her sleeping gown and stepped into the water with the other black maids, Metta caught her arm. "Oh no, Kalea, come bathe with us!"

Blinking her eyes, Kalea grabbed her black garments and linen nightgown before following Metta to the other side of the steaming pool. Lowering herself into the hot water after sleeping on a chilly floor all night was tedious, and as soon as she regarded her present company, she immediately felt out of place.

"So you could've been one of us, if not for your slavery scars?" a brunette asked, leaning against the side of the pool with one arm resting on the edge.

Kalea cocked her head. "Slavery scars?"

Metta hooked her arm around Kalea and shot back, "She's as devoted to the Mastaren as we are and deserves to bathe on this side of the pool!"

The brunette smirked.

Metta turned to Kalea. "Don't mind them, they'll grow up someday. That's Nan, whose father is a scholar, so she thinks she knows more than we do."

Nan stuck her tongue out at Metta.

"See what I mean?" She flourished a hand at Nan. "Childish."

"Metta," Kalea whispered, "let me get this straight. Were these girls also chosen to be concubine candidates?"

"Right," Metta said, smiling despite the dark circles around her eyes. "Last night challenged our bodies like never before, but we made it, and we're ready for the next step."

"What did you have to do in the ritual?" Kalea asked.

"We can't tell a lowly maid our business!" a girl with flowing red hair said before spitting a wad of saliva at Kalea, which missed and floated away on the cloudy water's surface.

"Forgive Casslin, please," Metta said, "but she's right. Our sacred rituals as upper-ranking Wikshonites are private."

Kalea stiffened her lips. Who cared what these harlots were doing late at night in a pettygod's chapel? The tip-off about how there were private areas she'd never get to explore made her heart sink for Mhina, though. Metta might also prove too hard to persuade to leave her lofty place in the cult.

Kalea changed the subject. "Does your father serve Wikshen too, Nan?"

"Nah, I ran away from his house. Couldn't stand all the studying and rules. By chance, a shaman found me after I made it to Alkeer."

She didn't like her father's rules? Kalea resisted asking why she didn't mind the many rules in Wikhaihli. Kalea perused her eyes over the large group of Wikhaihli's finest—fifteen of them, not counting Metta, all of whom sported a cocky expression and a beautiful body. Kalea suddenly realized how insufficient hers was. Such a thing hadn't mattered back at her convent; it welcomed short girls, chubby girls, and others who were born with glaring imperfections. Here at Wikhaihli, looks seemed to be everything.

"So you've met Nan and Casslin," Metta mused, and then she hummed thoughtfully, recounting the rest of their names. "Brielle arrived last night. Her family is wealthy."

Kalea tried to keep her face from looking shocked. She'd witnessed Brielle's arrival and barely recognized her this morning as she splayed herself along the edge of the pool, her blonde hair soaked down, holding her nose high. She featured the cutest face and milkiest skin with the brightest pink points of them all. She was more luminous than the redhead.

Metta moved on. "And Tamas arrived last night too with the head shaman and Myrtle, who's right over there."

Tamas displayed a broader frame and longer limbs, but also a seductive grin and skin which almost glittered like real bronze, especially when wet. Metta ran through the rest of their names, with help from the girls because some of them she'd only known since last night. "And on the end is Hetael."

Finally noticing the quietest one, Kalea made a conscious effort to close her mouth and not stare at the spectacle they called Hetael. That one's face could seduce as well as the others', but it couldn't have been the reason she was chosen to be in this group. Hetael's breasts were amazingly large, and Hetael knew it by the way she leaned both of her elbows back on the edge of the pool and allowed them to float far out before her, always jutting them forward, no matter how she moved or which way she turned. She didn't care who stepped in front of her or how long they stared.

Last night, Kalea underwent horrified sympathy for Brielle, whose father offered her up like a sacrificial animal to this cult's pettygod, but all those feelings washed away like the dust from Wikshen's floor she'd scrubbed and rinsed yesterday. None of these girls were sorry to be here. They, in fact, were in competition with each other and must've been vying for attention last night at the ritual, eager to prove who was prettiest. Metta herself couldn't have been much different. She boasted a combination of a lot of the traits all the other girls displayed. Metta also flaunted breasts larger than Kalea's, hair blacker than Tamas's, and skin as pale as Brielle's. Kalea liked her kindness best. She also had a lovely voice, and must've been good at singing, though she hadn't mentioned anything about it yet.

Kalea recognized her foolish feelings of inadequacy and did her best to shake them. She smiled limply at all the girls' chatter. She'd return to bathe with the black maids in a heartbeat if Metta weren't so clingy and insistent.

The housekeeper took her on a tour of a new wing in Wikshen's tower, where Kalea was finally left alone to clean a garderobe on the ground floor. She'd endured another long lecture, this one about how to clean the jakes properly. Though it smelled atrocious, she thanked the Creator for the moment of solitude.

A tap rattled the shutter, and an eye appeared between two wooden slats.

"Yes?" she answered, opening it slowly. "Del!" He must've heard her voice before the housekeeper left her. "Where've you all been? Are Bowaen and Gaije well?"

"As can be expected," Del said. "Ever since we set foot here, we've been put to work, digging geoducks out of chest-high mud at the beach."

"Sounds rough," she said. "You look so tired."

"Yeah, well, it isn't easy with a broken wrist. They wrapped it up, but won't hear any complaints from lowly workers like us. Gotta dig geoducks even if we are on our deathbeds. Anyway. Gaije wants to know if you have any news."

"Only that these people are going to hell faster than—"

He shushed her. "Listen, my gob-nobbin' wrist can't handle any lock picking in the outer buildings, but that doesn't matter when you're in a better position. Here."

He passed his bundled tools to her through the window. Luckily, her apron possessed a large patch pocket and the tools were rolled in a common pouch for knitting needles, so hopefully it wouldn't be inspected if found.

"What am I supposed to do with them?"

Del's brow tensed into a seriousness she'd never seen. "Get in and check every room. Gaije wants to know exactly where his sister went, even if you just see her name written on papers. Or look for other keywords like 'elf.' Right now, he's sayin' prayers to his bright god for having put you in this situation."

When Kalea cooed in sympathy for Gaije, Del brought her back to attention. "Now look. The picks have different shapes and sizes. Let's hope all the locks in there are similar, so when you find one that fits, keep it apart from the others where you can easily find it."

"I've never picked a lock before."

He rolled his eyes. "Obviously. Just stick it in and try to feel if it's a snug fit. If it is, carefully twist the pick so it acts as a key. Sometimes you might try a circular motion. If it gets a good hold, the lock should move."

Kalea nodded firmly, hoping to remember all this.

"And then—listen, remember this—to avoid being caught, you have to lock yourself out again when you leave. If they're noticin' locks undone, they'll be sure to pick you, the newcomer, as their first suspect."

Kalea bit her lip and stuck her arm out the window to catch his sleeve before he walked away. "Del." His eyebrows elevated. "I'm sorry I threw a rock at you."

He waved his hand. "Forget it."

"And, Del… No matter what they say, don't pray to their deity. It's the worst thing you can do. And please give my message to the others."

With a smirk, he went on his way.

Kalea closed the shutter softly and put the roll of tools in her pocket. A sudden shudder hit her with a low rumbling sound in her head, like the echo of a voice. She gasped and threw the shutter open again. Del was no longer around. She couldn't see anything else out there beyond a stone wall adjoining to her wing of the tower. Heavy clouds obscured her view. This window pointed east, behind Wikhaihli. Looking outside didn't matter anyway; the sound had occurred in her head. She trembled in fright. The sanguinesent had the ability to talk in her head.

*Be careful, Del.* She had no choice but to trust her friends to stay safe from the monster. Teeth chattering, she pushed herself to go back to work.

The housekeeper later set her on a long corridor lined with doors and arches to new spaces. On hands and knees, she crawled and cleaned, and when she reached a door, she peeped under the crevice at the lit room on the other side. The windows in these small rooms remained free of tar, but the corridor was quite dark.

Seeing no feet and hearing no voices behind the door, she checked to either side for people who might pass by. She tried the door. Locked, of course.

Her heart hammered as she reached for Del's tool pouch. It held at least twenty picks of different lengths and shapes, some expertly made while others looked to be rigged from eating utensils. Few were particularly apt for this lock, and when she found one that fit all the way inside, she winced at every sound it made before it broke off, echoing through the corridor. Frantically scrambling her fingers, she managed to pull the broken part out of the keyhole and put the pieces away, then went back to cleaning the floor.

Snoring sounds grated behind the next door. Peeking under the door revealed a cozy room similar to the last, with cool daylight shining through the window. Surely there wasn't an elf-child held in there. Kalea skipped that one as well.

She skipped the next one due to three stern-faced shamans hobbling through the hall. Behind them walked two younger women, none of whom she had met in the bathhouse. One of the younger ones kicked her bucket over, placed it over Kalea's head, and laughed with her young companion as they strolled away.

"Witch," Kalea grumbled. Now she faced a huge puddle to mop

up and she needed more water, so she headed to the well in the back courtyard.

The water level in the well was low for such a damp region. She found a surprising level of comfort in looking at the glinting distant water, like she had back home. Frogs croaked down there. She delayed for a bit, letting the cool air waft against her face—until a set of fingers grazed the back of her hair.

She whirled around to find no one there.

"Better move on," said a voice from the corner of the yard. Another maid sat on a stool, washing clothes in a wooden tub, currently scrubbing muddy, coppery stains off white rags. "If they catch you resting, you'll get yer ass beat."

"Was someone behind me just now?" Kalea asked.

"No, girl. Why ask?"

Dropping the subject, Kalea lowered the bucket into the well, refilled her cleaning bucket, and hurried back to the corridor, grabbing a fresh rag along the way to mop the spill.

As the sun set, the corridors filled with more witches and shamans going to and fro, so Kalea resisted picking any locks. With patience, she'd do her diligent chores and learn all about the basic flow of this building's routine. Midnight might be the best time to sneak around because all the worshippers would be in the chapels by then.

For the sake of good impressions, Kalea made it her mission to finish the last corridor she'd engaged in scrubbing, even if she completed her work by candlelight. So she did, and scooted her candle along on her knees, back aching, swishing her rag back and forth over the slate floor.

A load of weepy voices murmured behind one of the doors, and Kalea couldn't resist peeking through the open crack where a soft blue glow seeped through. A hand hung limp over the side of a bed. She squinted to see in the thickening darkness.

An exceptionally old shaman stood in her view, her gravelly voice making various inquiries in a hushed tone Kalea couldn't make out. Other shamans polluted the space with their different conversations.

"Just the other day…"

"Knilma, you've been away so long, so you'll have to…"

"So beautiful…this blue hair."

"I've already sent Yasmin to fetch…"

The voices murmured on like that.

Kalea found it hard to look away. *So this is…Wikshen's body,* she thought. They were preparing it for the funeral. One of the women took the limp dead hand and placed it on the bed.

"Well, of course it fell off," the oldest woman in the room said. She placed a thick, folded cloth into a narrow rectangular box and locked it. She handed the key to another woman. "Gives us a good chance to wash it down in the catacombs."

"Yes, Knilma."

Knilma continued, "Anyway, when he died, a brief separation of the two souls occurred. When Wik lost his grip on the body, so did the battleshift." Knilma's voice cracked at the end of her statement, and she wiped her eyes. A younger woman sniffled, followed by a few weepy whimpers.

A short moment of silence passed over the group until Knilma patted the locked chest. "Wash this in the underground spring."

At Knilma's order, a middle-aged woman hoisted the chest and exited the door with another woman carrying a basket of soiled rags like the ones that were being washed in the courtyard.

"Who's this?" the woman with the basket asked.

Before Kalea could scramble away, a third woman swept through the door and hissed, "Damn your light!" and slapped Kalea's face with a clap that echoed long through the hallway.

Skull rattling, Kalea lurched backward. The wind from the woman's swing put her candle out, and the door closed and locked beside her.

*Me and my stupid curiosity.* Kalea cradled her face and stood up in the dark. Stars danced before her eyes to blind her further in the new darkness. No cleaning would ever get done in this darkness; she'd have to return in the morning to finish her work.

She had bent to gather her bucket and rag when a slight dizziness passed over her. Not a good sign—she might fall down the stairs unless she could regain her balance. She was standing on hands and knees waiting for her eyes to adjust when it happened. The wind thickened in her lungs, and the darkness coagulated in the air around her. Crawling to the side where she remembered the wall to be, she found it and attempted to climb to her feet.

Venturing upward, the darkness slid over her naked arms as if she were swimming. It billowed and gathered around her, attracted to her. She leaned against the wall and panted heavily. Her heart picked up with a familiar excitement and sent little twinges of feeling to her nipples and intimate area.

"Uuuuhhhhhhh." She slid back to the floor, raised her chin, and moaned out a few more long calls of need. Sorrowful, if she could be the judge of such a thing.

The air grazed her quickly warming skin. Not the air, the darkness did it. The living darkness. Vibrant. Energetic. It wanted her.

Her thoughts flew wildly about; the ones about her duties and her sneaking were lost, thrown out. No longer important. The thick caress of the atmosphere…touched her. She needed more. Her legs, they could no longer support her, so she reclined back, arching her spine. She raised her knees. Moans slipped out of her throat beyond her notice or care.

She untied the strap of her apron and threw it aside before tugging at her lapel to let her breasts out. She moaned again, on the verge of screaming when the air touched her pointing, tingly nipples.

The darkness grazed along her flesh like fingers and lips. She stretched out on the floor, moaning, and touched her own breast, looking for those invisible fingers. She found no more than her own ready body. Her legs and abdomen tingled in an exuberant thrill, wanting and waiting. She was alone, but nowhere near lonely. The waiting hurt more than the sexual need. Her eyes stayed closed as she pulled at her skirt in a feeble attempt to raise it. She found her simple, scanty braies and untied them before peeling away the side and opening her legs to the air.

And the darkness moved in.

Touching.

Licking.

Kalea squealed and arched her back. Raising her knees high. She moaned and moved as it stroked her, but it wasn't enough. It wouldn't be enough. She needed more.

The door creaked open and a flash of blue light beamed out of the nearest room.

Kalea groaned, ignoring the interruption, wishing the darkness to do more. But the soft blue light fought it away. The darkness receded.

An old woman laughed. "Bless you, child, bless you!" She laughed again as if Kalea were adorable.

The light's presence pushing against the darkness somewhat helped to bring Kalea back to her senses, but not enough. She still didn't care what state this woman saw her in, and she *needed* the tender help of a man—any man.

The old woman stooped to retie Kalea's undergarment. Kalea groaned now in both annoyance and intimate pain. She pushed back on the old woman weakly.

The old one laughed a few more beats. "You're a true Wikshonite, aren't you?" She patted Kalea's face when her eyes closed.

Kalea didn't want to rejoin reality. A tear leaked out of her eye and into her hair, but she had no idea why.

The old woman continued to straighten her clothing. "What's your name, girl?"

A whisper was all she could manage. "Ka-lea." A strange sob followed—she couldn't fathom why she made such noises, much less stop herself from making them. She moaned when a new shock of thrill touched her belly and traveled south.

The old woman's laughter faded. "Look at you... Kalea? That's how you say it?"

Kalea made no attempt to rise or let the old woman help her up. She continued to sprawl, legs open, knees high, crying.

"I know what it's like, Kalea. It's a wonderful and amazing thing. But it's not Wikshen, it's merely a signature of his aura. And it can hit any one of us—well, not the shamans—but girls like you, of course. Come on now."

She pulled Kalea's skirt back down and pulled her dress's lapel back over. She took a striker out and relit Kalea's candle. In the new flame light, Kalea's episode dissipated quicker. Her loins continued to throb, but her thoughts and reasoning rushed back. Somehow, her braies had become soaked.

"I'm Knilma," the old woman said. Kalea could, at last, focus on her amused face illuminated in the candle light. Her cheeks bunched under her eyes, but her grin didn't touch them. Her eyes maintained a strange coldness. "Head shaman of the Wikshonites," Knilma continued. "I arrived today." Knilma squinted at her in the helpful new lighting. "You look familiar."

Kalea blinked her eyes and turned her face away, but Knilma grabbed her chin and forced her to face her. A smile cracked on her wrinkled lips. "You're *her*."

"Who?" Kalea asked in defiance, but she knew what the old woman meant.

"The one at the Alkeer temple. The one he..." Knilma sucked in a long drag of air through the nose. "Did you not run away from your destiny?"

Kalea shook her head. "I had something to do... My mother needed me. I intended to return swiftly."

"And you came all the way to Wikhaihli to find your Mastaren again." The smile on Knilma's face warmed. She examined her again. "I see you're"—her eyes lingered over Kalea's body—"a black maid? Why did Kilka not slot you as a concubine candidate?"

Kalea fussed with her hair to put it back in line, out of breath and flushed. Her desire for a long, hard wallow in bed with a man nagged her. "Because of my scars." She paused to rub her face. "I have faint scars all over my back. Kilka didn't like the way I looked naked."

"I see," Knilma responded. "So by chance, you are a black maid. Just because a girl isn't perfect, doesn't mean she can't serve in Wikshen's house. That's why we have black maids slotted to clean this place. They too can be extremely devoted Wikshonites—and better they stay in here too, away from those dirty warlocks outside who might be tempted to break their celibacy. Although I must say, an ecstasy to your degree can be a bit...let's say distracting, when you got floors to scrub and surfaces to dust."

Knilma paused to look at her again. A smile creased her face and lit her eyes too. "Let's take a walk to get you back to your senses. You're a lucky girl, Kalea."

Kalea tried to stand on her shaky legs. They didn't want to cooperate, but she forced them. "What do you mean?" Her voice trailed weakly.

The end of the ecstasy brought on a longing sadness, as if she'd been promised something but didn't get it. The emotion receded in favor of a new pang of returned need. Kalea moaned and bent over, bracing herself on the wall.

Knilma raised her chin and beheld the shadowy corridor. "It's persistent to have you tonight—Wikshen's shadow," Knilma said. "It's watching you, lurking in this corridor, blocking the moonlight. Crying shame the Mastaren is dead."

*Indeed,* Kalea thought. Knilma took her arm and helped her to keep standing. The darker side of her desired to continue writhing on the floor, hoping for sexual bliss to grace her, but the return of her old sensibilities battled it.

"We would've had quite a good worship ritual this night if he were with us."

"Pity," Kalea replied in a breath, and even she couldn't tell if she were serious or being sarcastic.

"I'll trust Kilka's judgment in placing you with the maids, but that ecstasy you underwent..." She shook her head. "It means big things."

Kalea stood on her own strength again, and the idea finally turned a sour edge in her mind. How could it not have before? If the idea of taking off her clothes and rolling on the floor disgusted her now, why didn't it disgust her a few minutes ago? Wikshen managed to bewitch her, even in death, and Knilma considered it a religious ecstasy.

She cleared her throat and asked Knilma, "What ecstasy?"

"It means Wikshen chose you."

Kalea's vision blurred. There were those words again. Even Wikshen had confirmed them. Why?

"You belong to him. He's already claimed you. Congratulations."

"That can't be…"

"Why?" Knilma probed, narrowing her eyes.

*Because Wikshen is dead. Because I'm not a Wikshonite. Because I hate him!*

"Because I just arrived here the other day. I'm new, and I know very little about this religion," she said honestly.

Knilma shrugged her tiny, hunched shoulders. "Does it matter? The fact is, you're here. You traveled a long way, I know."

"What does it mean that Wikshen chose me?" Kalea asked. She needed some straight answers once and for all.

"It's why you traveled here, regardless of whether or not you know why. You may not realize he chose you. Maybe you didn't choose *him*—most of us chose this religion, but you didn't. And yet you're here, aren't you?"

"So why?" Kalea demanded. "How and why did he choose me?"

"He must've found you pleasing in some way." Knilma said. "Wikshen surrounds himself with women. He likes pleasure. He likes women. Can you blame him? He is a creature of nature. He enjoys the basics of nature, hence our extensive recipe list for his love of flavors. And to him, women are one of those natural things he indulges in.

"It gets more complex from there, however, because he also conquers the Darklands every time he returns. So he chooses women, and then allies himself with them. They fight alongside him as his greatest weapon—a fearsome and indestructible force they are. We shamans are nothing but old hags with drums compared to the force of women Wikshen chooses. And that's you, girl. You are a blessed creature."

"So you saw me. You know…my secret. Can you tell me what"—Kalea swallowed and stuttered—"wh-what happens to me next? What does it mean? Will it get worse?"

Knilma drew her wrinkled mouth tight and winked an eye, studying Kalea. "Hard to say if it'll get worse. It might. The good news is, there's no reason to be embarrassed. The other girls will envy you, along with the common witches, the most talented concubines, and even some of the shamans."

"How can I make it stop?"

"By all means, don't try to self-soothe when this happens. You must be patient and wait for your Mastaren. Only *he* can make it stop." Knilma's gaze trailed to the door, behind which Wikshen's body lay cold and naked. "The ecstasy is what happens when he calls to you and your body answers."

Kalea's stomach dropped. The rest of her residual arousal vanished.

Knilma raised one finger. "This is significant, girl, so let me explain. A ritual was conducted last night, which yielded sixteen exquisite concubine candidates, two of whom experienced an ecstasy like yours, although theirs lasted two to three seconds, no more. A scant three seconds of the feeling you just experienced, and none of them dropped to the floor to open their legs for their Mastaren like you've done, my dear."

Kalea's face went long, her mind blank and lost. She couldn't offer any words of any kind, not even a boastful lie about her devotion.

"By all proper calculations," Knilma continued, "you should've been in that ritual. If you had been, you would've emerged top tier." Giving Kalea a grandmotherly smile, Knilma patted her hand. "Top tier, as in the most important and praised concubine. The one he would, most likely, bless first—which is the highest of all Wikshonite honors." Giving a mysterious smile, she ran her fingers along Kalea's hair. "We shall see."

She pointed to Kalea's bucket. "Gather your things and go on to bed. We'll talk again soon." Before leaving Kalea alone, Knilma paused to add, "And please, girl…from now on, limit your time outside this house. You wouldn't want another ecstasy to hit you outside and in the wrong company."

# Chapter 48

# His Return

At the morning bathing hour, Kalea joined Metta bashfully. She resisted thinking about her torturous episode of arousal the previous night, despite Knilma's words overloading her head. As usual, the feeling of foolishness at her behavior lingered. She was a vestal, not a Wikshonite.

Keeping focus on her most important task, she proposed questions in hopes of gaining any slight hint she possibly could. "Are there any elven Wikshonites?" she asked.

Metta raised an eyebrow. "Togha and our Mastaren, but none else, of course not. I hear there's a new elven male with red hair who arrived recently."

Kalea relaxed to hear about Gaije. She followed up, "What about *faerhain?*"

Metta threw her head back and laughed like a horse. "The Clanless keep elven girls hidden deeper than a miser's vault. There are no *faerhain* here."

"You've heard nothing of any coming through here? Not even of children taken from villages?"

"We get the occasional child-pledge but no elves. Why so interested?"

Panic crept into Kalea's blood for not having designed a pretense more creative than curiosity. "I saw a…drawing hanging in Alkeer. A missing person poster. It appeared that our…Mastaren…um…*whisked* an elven girl from her village along his travels. I worried about her and wanted to know if she was safe here."

Metta put a hand on Kalea's naked shoulder. "You are a virtuous woman, Kalea, and admirable. The Mastaren will admire you too, I think."

"Who's *your* Mastaren, Metta?" Brielle asked as laughs echoed around her. "Mine is Wikshen, the murderer, the rapist, the conqueror. The living deity, embodiment of Wik."

Metta frowned. "Mine is the same—and he's more than what your simple brain can imagine! And soon we'll see him."

A wave of interested murmurs and sighs washed over the girls, prompting them to hurry their washing and rinsing.

"I wish you could be there, Kalea," Metta said. "If you didn't have those trivial scars on your back, you'd be included in tomorrow's Solemn

Exhibition."

"What's that?" Kalea asked.

"It's like an introduction. After the shamans evaluate us, they select who's worthy enough to attend the rite." Metta looked into the air and flourished her hands gracefully when she explained, "We approach Wikshen's platform. He looks at us, and then we are allowed to look at his eyes. He hears our names, and from then on, he knows us."

Brielle piped up, "And Kilka is sponsoring me, so all of you stand back." The girl's eyes were large, like a cat fixed on a mouse.

"Shut your mouth, it's too small anyway," Nan said, and Brielle launched a splashing war between them until it escalated into an actual fight. Some other girls close by, Hetael and Senna, split them up.

Metta caught Kalea shaking her head. "Is something wrong, Kalea?"

Kalea wanly watched the two girls fighting. "But Wikshen's dead." It slipped out. Nonetheless, these girls had to be told. But didn't they already know? After all, they'd all cried and screamed behind Wikshen's body's procession, just like Metta had.

"Dead?" Metta repeated as if she were hearing it for the first time. She burst with laughter. "Oh, Kalea—" Metta was cut short by the escalation of the girls' scuffle.

"Damn you!" Hetael shrieked, cupping her melon-sized breasts. Two bright scratch marks marred one now, near bleeding. "I was going to accidentally slip out of my dress tomorrow when bowing to him."

"Guess you'll have to expose your ass instead!" Nan said.

"He'll see mine long before yours!"

And the fight started again. Never in her life had Kalea heard such language—especially from women! Being amongst a troop of such shameless girls made her feel no more at ease than it had yesterday.

Knilma's words echoed in her memory. Apparently, due to the length and intensity of her ecstasy, Kalea was superior to them.

When the bickering died down, Kalea opened her mouth to resume her conversation with Metta to tell the girl that Wikshen was indeed dead, but the loud voices echoed their last off the warm tile walls and attention drifted to the murmurs Helga and Velle exchanged.

"I heard them clear as a bird's whistle," Velle said. She settled her eyes on Kalea. "You're a black maid, right?"

"Yes," she said.

Velle turned back to Helga and whispered in her ear.

"What's all this about?" Nan demanded, storming toward them in a wave of fragrant, opaque water. She put her arms around the two others as if the three of them would share the secret. The rest of them gravitated in, and Kalea found herself in that pull too.

"This morning, in the kitchen, Kilka and one of the others thought they were alone," Velle repeated in a whisper to the lot of them. "Remember what happened at the ritual?" She smiled. Only Kalea lacked that bit of information. A solemnness broadcasted through Metta's body language.

Velle continued smiling, purposely drawing out the anticipation. Brielle smacked Velle's shoulder. "Ow!"

"Hurry, before one of them comes in here. What did you hear?"

"Okay," Velle said. "I couldn't hear too much, but last night Knilma caught one of the black maids…"

Kalea's mouth immediately dried.

Velle gave that mischievous smile again, to all of their annoyance. Kalea would prefer she stop at that point. Velle waved her hands intricately as she searched for the words. "A dark ecstasy struck her."

"No," Brielle spat. "Not a stupid black maid!"

All eyes turned to Kalea, who teetered at the edge of panicky madness.

"It was the biggest ecstasy Kilka had ever heard about," Velle continued, pulling the attention back to herself. "She took off all her clothes and rolled around on the floor—completely naked. It lasted for hours! When Knilma found her, the girl was screaming because Wikshen's dark essence was…" Velle pulled in her lips and rolled her eyes up. "You know. It was…having sex with her."

"Can it do that?" Brielle shrieked.

Kalea could barely hear any more under the thundering of her heart in her ears. She jumped when Metta's hand landed on her naked shoulder. The room spun.

"Did it take her all the way?" Mirral asked.

"Nearly, but when Knilma brought a candle into the hall, its light chased the shadow away, leaving the girl unsatisfied," Velle answered.

"Kalea?" Metta said.

Another girl asked Velle, "Did Kilka say which maid?"

"Did you hear about this, Kalea?" Metta asked.

All eyes returned to her, and Kalea shook her head frantically.

"Knilma didn't tell Kilka who it was," Velle said.

"Did anyone act strange in your dorm last night?" Metta asked Kalea.

"I…um…" Kalea cleared her throat. "No. None of the maids talked about it." She breathed easier when the other girls released her from their stares.

"That little bitch," Brielle said. "When I find out who…" She squinted her beautiful eyes and shook her head with pursed lips.

"Well, you have nothing to complain about," Nan told her. "You got your ecstasy the other night."

Kalea stared at her after that slip. Brielle was one of the two Knilma mentioned who had experienced the same phenomenon she did—but to a much smaller extent. Who could the other girl be?

Kalea steeled her nerve to ask, "What is an ecstasy?" Just as fast, she drew all their stares again. Of course, she knew by now what it *was*. She wanted to find out what it meant. These girls might produce more information than Knilma dispensed last night.

"None of your business, maid," Brielle said, and stuck her tongue out. "And if you are wise, you'll go back to your basement and find out who had it."

"I'll tell you what it is," Metta said, acting cooler than ever before. "An ecstasy is power."

Right after her bath, Kalea got straight to work like a good maid, no matter how much her muscles screamed at her after yesterday's effort. Her eyes adjusted to the dim light of the afternoon, but as the hours passed on, they registered less and less.

At the back of the tower, on the first floor, a sliver of light glowed under a door at the end of the corridor. She'd been trying to unlock doors all day with hit-and-miss results. The doors she'd managed to open showed her little more than uniform rooms with a bed, basin, and wardrobe full of black skirts and shawls. She tiptoed toward this room at the far end, careful not to stub a toe on the uneven stones in the dark floor.

"Ma'am?" she tapped at the door. "Are you in?" She tapped again. "Ma'am?" She listened against the door. Silence.

Dropping to hands and knees, she confirmed the room's vacancy. Alone in the corridor, she reached for Del's tools, shifting through several before resolving to try the one she'd broken yesterday.

*Del is going to curse me.* If it got her in and she found something useful in there, she'd use that as pleading material. She inserted the small, thin rod into the keyhole. This tool had flat sides. When it stopped moving, she carefully twisted it. *Click.*

Gasping in disbelief, Kalea swung the creaky door open. The waning sun in the window lit the room. This woman, probably a shaman, had a decent bed, a writing desk, fireplace, and a huge strongbox. There were papers stacked on the desk that Kalea couldn't resist reading. One listed the newly recruited witches.

*Nan—19—non-virgin—pledges 10 silver chips / 8 bottles of ink.*

*Senna—22—non-virgin—very limber.*

*Casslin—15—virgin—pledges 2 skeins of yarn.*

*Helga—17—virgin—pledges 1 silver chip.*

*Hellebora—19—virgin.*

*Aesh—20—virgin—pledges 2 silken cloaks.*

*Mellise—18—virgin—pledges 1 goat.*

*Hetael—21—virgin—exquisite breasts and legs.*

*Metta—19—non-virgin—pledges 2 silver chips / fine bronze scissors.*

*Carazella—16—virgin.*

*Velle—17—virgin—exquisite lips / thighs.*

*Mirral—16—virgin—pledges 1 sack of potatoes.*

*~~Kalea—20—virgin—comes bearing Wikshen's hair.~~*

*Brielle—17—virgin—pledges 50 gold chips / 10 bolts of silk / 17 chickens / 40 salted ham hocks / 7 sacks of vanilla / 18 sacks of salt / 10 sacks of sugar.*

*Tamas—18—virgin—pledges 1 pearl / 2 fishing rods.*

*Myrtle—16—virgin.*

*My choice for First Sister to be presented to Mastaren is Brielle, the best possible candidate and most generous pledge, though as usual Knilma is slow to agree.*

Kalea gaped at her own name, but soon it made sense. Kilka had slotted her as a maid after she found Kalea's scars. So far, nothing about Mhina.

Kalea glanced at the door for anyone who might catch her here. She sifted through the various lists and found a letter.

*Dear Kilka,*

*Glorious news! Wikshen lives again. I felt his voice through tremors in the earth! We're setting out to retrieve him. Return to Wikhaihli and prepare his chambers as soon as possible.*

*Signed,*
*Knilma*

Another letter lay under it.

*Dear Kilka,*

*We've found Wikshen after he vigorously ransacked a pitiful village with his divine hands. He is elven this time, and more beautiful than I could have imagined. He's struggling to fill his energy store, however, and has fallen under a deep spell of sleep. He often murmurs syllables on his breath I can only imagine are a woman's name—no one I used to know in the past. We're letting him rest for now, as he rides in a wagon bed. Don't forget to stock Wikhaihli's larders well with fresh oysters, fish, flour, and eggs. If I recall properly, Wikshen loves sea fish flatcakes.*

*Signed,*
*Knilma*

*Dear Kilka,*
*We went to Alkeer at your recommendation. Please come back. Wikshen finally woke up, but he doesn't eat, sleep, or take any women to bed. Has regular nightmares and screams in the night. Pushes women away who try to comfort him. Vomits regularly and seizes. Bring proper herbs to treat such ailments.*
*Knilma*

*Dear Kilka,*
*Wikshen cut his own throat with a piece of common cutlery. Later, I caught him trying to remove his own battleshift as if it ̶w̶e̶r̶e̶ bothered him somehow.*

Knilma had forgotten to sign the last one. The story was odd enough, but none of the papers talked about an elven child. She didn't want to miss anything, but each moment spent raised her anxiety.

One more thing. Checking the strongbox briefly before leaving could be important. Any valuable clue might be found inside, so she went through the tools and hastily stuck random selections into the padlock. Her hands shook, but she had to check this too if she was to be thorough.

She held her breath until the lock clicked open. She slowly lifted the lid. Jewels glittered all around the interior, pieces confiscated from the new pledges, no doubt, and some were rough stones. A grimoire with a pig's face on the cover lay tucked under multiple folds of silken shifts. Other rough-cut stones were treated with better care, sorted and cushioned in raw cotton. One of them put off a slight hum.

Kalea picked up the humming one, a sparkling pink crystal, and put it to her ear. When she concentrated hard enough, she deciphered a voice.

*Take Wikshen to the sanctuary stone at the crossroads.*

Kalea pulled the crystal away. Listening didn't feel right. She dropped it, but another one caught her eye. Her moonstone. *Dorhen's* moonstone!

She snatched it up and held it to her heart, trying her best to stifle the swelling emotion. The tears streamed down her cheeks. She huffed out a heavy breath instead of the sob of grief she wanted to cry for her lost love.

"Dorhen," she whispered.

Dorhen woke up in the flames.

He shielded his face from the roaring wind of intense heat. Rocks, hot iron scraps with wriggling bodies impaled on their shafts, and broken statues that were no longer recognizable waved in the heat. He had returned. He must've died. He couldn't remember how or when he arrived back in Kullixaxuss, but seeing it now was instantly familiar, as if he'd never left.

The heat registered quickly and rose higher and higher until he could stand it no longer. He crumpled to the ground and wailed, enduring the flames. He could do nothing else in this place. His naked body burned away.

And then it restored to continue the routine.

Alone.

Hot.

Pain.

Agony.

He belonged here. On his last visit, the sanguinesent had properly sorted him into the Garden of Fire. His destiny.

The days rolled by. Sometimes he counted them. Sometimes he didn't bother. A year. Three years. Six years. Sixteen years. Thirty-six years. Sixty-nine years. Did counting all the years help? No, not when he knew they'd keep rolling on for eternity. He'd found his way home. Tomorrow would begin year seventy, and that's when he'd stop counting.

A tiny leap of hope entered Dorhen's heart at the touch of a voice inside his head. *Oh, look. Look who inevitably came back.* A purring voice. A beautiful voice. *Did you sincerely think you'd escape your destiny, my little creature?*

"Mistress?"

*Yes.*

She appeared inside a broken stone arch, fully lit by the sea of flames. Her black, iridescent hair remained untouched by the fire; it hung heavy like a silken cloak to the floor, and its iridescent shine blazed green, blue, and purple. The heat proved no match for her pearly-grey skin either, shimmering with scales along her arms and at her sides and hips. She wore no clothing, as usual, but when he'd enjoyed her company long ago, she used to wear a single gold anklet. Since their last encounter, she'd added sparkling gold chains draping up one leg and attached to a piercing on her navel. Another chain draped around her hips with tiny drops of glowing crystals.

Dorhen planted his palms on the blistering stone floor beneath him and bowed his head, but he couldn't keep his eyes off this oasis of love and comfort for long. The vision of her raised his cock.

*Do you like my new decorations?* she asked. *You left so suddenly and disappointingly last time, and long before you could learn anything about life in this realm. You, as you know, are one of my thralls. As you rely on me for comfort and relief, I rely on you for nourishment and status.*

"Status?" he said.

*Yes. I'll explain it to you and give you one chance to redeem yourself, or else you'll be cast down deeper into a more uncomfortable level of Kullixaxuss.*

Mistress stepped closer and squatted in front of him, giving him a reminding view of her vulva, a literal flower which used to bloom before his eyes. His memories of drinking its nectar with careless greed pulsed through his blood. To his sadness, her flower remained closed. Who knew if she'd ever let him feast again? Her breasts remained dry too.

She explained, *It is my aim to eat, and you are one of many who oblige my need. When I eat, I get a link closer to raising my status among my compatriots.*

Dorhen kept his mouth shut, listening to anything and everything his beloved mistress wished to share with him. But the sight of her shining body filled his erection to bursting, even as it crisped in the scorching air.

*Are you listening?* Mistress asked. *The more I eat, the more links I can add to my chains—the more jewelry I add to my body. I am not here to make you suffer or take advantage; I merely need you to give your word and complete the arrangement with me. I keep a record of which of my thralls are most obedient and pleasing. Once I've collected all the jewels of one person, I own their souls. With more souls, I can raise my status and increase my palace, taking my best thralls in to serve me there.*

Dorhen panted, soon to lose his lungs to the heat. They were drying from the inside. "Palace?" he managed.

At his question, Mistress pointed to the tall steeples of the termite mounds looming over the fires. *When we carry out our contract, I also collect your seed, which I use to make sons and daughters. My sons build my palace taller, and my daughters metamorphose into glorious succubae like me.*

She reached out and stroked the side of his face, to which he closed his eyes and inclined his head for more. *With patience and obedience, you would leave the flames and move into my palace permanently. You'd still have duties, and I would go out again to find more thralls in the fire to continue the process of collecting jewels.*

"Where do you get these jewels?" Dorhen ventured to ask in a dry voice; she would at least catch the question from his thoughts after his throat burned away.

Her hand caressing his face traveled downward to point at his chest with its blackening skin, crisping and drying, peeling and rising off his baking muscles. *From deep inside your heart, when I eat it,* she answered.

Dorhen bowed his head again. His strength drained away as he neared the moment when he'd collapse into a living corpse and bake beyond a pile of ash like he did every day.

*I don't find many elves in the Garden, but they have more exotic and valuable hearts. I need to eat your flesh, and in return I'm promising to take you out of the fire for good. Won't you agree, be patient, and accompany me to a better place?*

When Dorhen raised his eyes again, he beheld her beautiful chiseled face with those entirely black eyes, sharp little teeth in a sexy grin, and shimmering little red horns. She drew his attention to her vulva, blessing him with the sight of it blooming, finally. The outer petals curled back, followed by its beautifully colored inner petals. From her vagina peeked her innermost petals, little throbbing muscles that used to kiss him back and milk his penis for all of his seed—what a euphoric thrill it would deliver!—and out from that slithered her secondary tongue, a sleek little pointed muscle with a peachy, bright pink color that used to dance and play with his. It wiggled in flirtation at him before whipping back inside, and then out poured her holy nectar in welcome of him.

His heart sang. For her, his testicles swelled, tight and full and past ready to disgorge his love at her command. He loved this creature with every ounce of his heart. His mistress. His goddess. The word "yes" poised on his lips. He wanted to say it fast, but he also wanted to savor the sight of this magnificent creature who offered him a better eternity than what he'd been living. Of course he'd say yes! Of course! He'd clean the floors of her palace with his tongue if she'd let him live with her!

His lips quivered in absolute rapturous glee, humbled and near bursting with emotion at her kindness and beauty. That she'd choose a wretch like him to serve her! He opened his mouth to speak before his tongue burned away.

A roar of cold black air rushed over both of them, snuffing out a wide radius of the surrounding fires. *Damn you, vile, squeaky little worm! You fool! You weak idiot!*

The new voice was male, raking and booming. Thunder rushed through the earth under Dorhen's hands and knees. A figure materialized in the black cloud, a tall, fierce-eyed, bearded male with a face eternally void of mirth.

The newcomer reached a massive, strong arm out to snatch Mistress before she could dodge, before Dorhen could grab her to hold and protect.

Mistress released a piercing scream that tore Dorhen's heart. She wriggled in the tall, black figure's hand like a small animal snatched from the forest. She continued to yell and squirm until she disintegrated in the greater figure's hand, floating away on the windy confusion of hot and cold that now spun around them.

At Mistress's departure, an earthquake shook the ground, and one of the spires in the distance crumbled and crashed down.

Paying no mind to the chaos behind him, the large figure pointed a thick finger with a sharp nail in Dorhen's face, now lost and afraid without his mistress. *Fool! This will all end! Don't you remember where you're supposed to be?*

He remembered nothing except his mistress. The agony of her loss welled within him. His eyes burned with tears.

*Your antics got us stabbed with a very powerful sword, fool! You died! And now you're here again—wasting your time, in your weakness believing that you love a pathetic little succubus! What did I tell you about complying with me?*

At this point, Dorhen waited for the heat to finish him off so he could die again, to sleep in ash and mourn for his mistress. "Why?" he whimpered.

*Why what, fool? You'll return back here when you die anyway, and I'm sure you'll be found by one of her maggot-spawn to continue your futile cycle of madness. You must return with me while you can, or else we'll both lose your body to the worms. Might as well enjoy power on earth before you spend an eternity as a slave down here.*

He didn't wait for Dorhen's response. He grabbed his arm in his huge, black hand, and Dorhen's flesh immediately restored at his touch; new flesh spread across the rest of his body. His hair sprouted out of his head again. All of this should've taken an entire day. The formidable spirit dragged Dorhen deep into its accompanying black cloud. They moved toward the sound of a large tolling bell and left the fire behind.

Being led by his arm through a thick atmosphere of cool darkness, Dorhen closed his eyes. Relief. He was free. Mistress was gone. But it wasn't over. Wik's warning echoed of how Dorhen would return to the fire when he died. He wouldn't live forever. Eventually, Wik's aid and control would end and Dorhen would die—of old age if nothing else. His inevitable return to Kullixaxuss would haunt him. And upon his return, he would meet another succubus just like Wik said.

Dorhen swallowed at the sudden wave of dread. He was a damned soul in this world. He needed help. Who could help him?

"My poor Dorhen," Kalea cooed on the floor of Kilka's chamber. The sun was setting out of the window's view, probably a good time to quit for now. She was satisfied enough with getting her pendant back, and had yet to find any document hinting at Gaije's sister. She'd keep trying. She closed the chest, clicked the padlock in place, and exited to work on relocking the door. Her bucket and rag waited against the wall out in the corridor.

As she fiddled with the lock, the echo of footsteps set her into desperation. Voices approached. Kalea's new, terrified trembling disrupted her motor skills. When the little *click* happened among her frantic picking, success or not, she fumbled the lock pick into her cleavage and dropped to the floor with the rag to feign hard work.

Her heart was hammering by the time two shamans walked past, neither interested in her. They hurried up a narrow staircase in a corner Kalea finally noticed, hauling a sense of urgency. Their murmurs came short and urgent, words such as "poor child" and the like.

She followed with her bucket and rag, thankful for being barefoot, although her toes knocked a few of the rough stairs, and by now they ached from treading the hard surfaces all day.

The shamans ascended two floors. The stairway landing offered a door leading into a long dark corridor. One room on this floor was lit, and the door hung open. Several voices murmured inside.

Kalea dropped to her knees and pretended to clean, shuffling closer and closer to the door. She willed away the pain in her knees acquired from kneeling for so many hours. Perhaps Mhina was the "poor child" in there. After a fleeting glance, she could report to Gaije about his sister and they would formulate a plan to rescue her.

A loud bell tolled and gave Kalea a mighty spook in her concentration. She covered her mouth and tried to slow her heart.

The speaking changed to humming and moaning in harmony with growing intensity. Kalea crawled toward the door, forgetting the bucket and rag. She peered around the doorframe.

Candles lit the small, humble room, along with a few dishes of the blue Kraft fire. Six shamans stood around a bed, and atop it lay the dead body of Wikshen, looking pale, nearly grey. His lips were blue to match his hair, and he was now thoroughly clean of all blood and grime. And he lay naked, his black shift arranged over his lower body and legs instead.

The oldest shaman, the one she'd met last night, sat on the bed with him while Kilka stood sternly at the foot, her voice loudest. A younger shaman stood on the other side with rags and water at the ready.

The tolling bell through the open window rattled Kalea's head. The intensity of the ritual held her fast and drew her closer, her head now inside the room. Another shaman stood in the corner, tapping a metal object against a bronze bowl at certain points in the chanting.

How many tolls rang? Six?

On the seventh, Wikshen roared to life, gasping as if awakening from a nightmare, red rushing into his face. Kalea jumped in terror and covered her mouth to prevent a scream.

Wikshen awoke from the dead. The bastard lived to commit more terror.

His eyes bulged, staring beyond their surroundings; his mouth remained open in shock. He lurched forward, and the shamans threw their hands on him to restrain as well as to calm. His hand shot to his chest where Hathrohjilh had pierced, to find no trace of the injury.

The old shaman took his hand away from the former wound site. His eyes roamed across each of the shamans in delirious disbelief, and Kalea recoiled in fear to escape his gaze.

The women shushed him tenderly, stroked his hair, and patted his hand until he began to relax. Kalea leaned forward again, fixed on the scene. He panted, finally letting his eyes blink slowly, and lay back down. Tears glistened on his cheeks, pouring without reserve. He breathed with his eyes closed for a while. One shaman dabbed the sweat beading on his forehead.

The invisible pins stabbing into Kalea's spine faded. She lowered her brow and watched in utter curiosity. This was her fourth sighting of Wikshen and the first time he'd appeared like just a person. Not a shadow deity or a bloodless, demonic menace—a person, a sympathetic creature who could feel pain.

"Shoo, shoo!" A shaman had caught her staring and whipped a cloth at her face until she backed into the corridor.

When the shaman closed the door, Kalea ran, abandoning her cleaning implements in favor of getting as far away from him as possible, especially before another ecstasy could befall her.

The black maids slept on woven straw mats on the floor. While a dozen other girls snored around her, Kalea got out of bed and groped at the stones under her knees, remembering the wide gaps between some of them when the sunlight shone in. She folded up her skunky old mat and prodded the stones underneath. One of them moved with a heavy groan. Wedging her fingers in the crack around it, she pried the stone up.

She couldn't see a thing in the dark room and wasn't terribly curious about feeling around in the hole with her bare hand. She used her handkerchief to poke around to make sure the hole didn't drop too far. Old, flattened dirt lay at the bottom. She took Dorhen's moonstone from around her neck and wrapped it in the handkerchief. She couldn't allow it to be confiscated again, and jewelry would be a hard thing to hide considering this place's public nudity policies.

To keep the stone from crushing the pendant, she dug a tiny grave in the dirt with her fingers. Ripping open her mattress a little, she took a handful of its straw stuffing for extra cushion to protect Dorhen's precious relic. A tear rolled down her nose bridge as she went through this whole process. Putting the floor stone back in its place, she replaced the mattress corner over it.

Lying back down, she couldn't fall asleep so easily. Resting on her back, thinking of the moonstone beneath her bed, she thanked the Creator for guiding her back to it and asked Him what to do next. Wikshen lived again. That thought put all of her nerves to the outside of her flesh. How could they possibly deal with a person who could survive being skewered all the way to Hathrohjilh's hilt? No matter how exhausted, she couldn't keep her eyes closed. Not while Wikshen dwelled a few floors above her. How could she manage to explore his manor now? Not to mention her anger. Wikshen lived again and Dorhen remained dead.

The housekeeper roused Kalea—far from ready to face Wikhaihli today—before sunrise. With the same sadness dragging heavily behind her aching heels, she went straight to work after the whole morning regimen of visiting the fountain shrine and bathing in the hot water. The housekeeper ordered her to tend some of the bedchambers, emptying chamber pots, airing out the mattresses, and collecting sheets due for washing. All of these tasks she knew very well from the convent.

The sun struggled to shine through the tarred windows, and the grief pressed on her head and shoulders. Longing for the light, Kalea made her way back to the garderobe and stuck her head out the window to find Del waiting for her. She asked about the well-being of Bowaen and Gaije, and told him she had seen no sign of Mhina. Gathering her nerve, she broke the news of Wikshen's return from the dead.

"Bloody hell..." he uttered. He cradled his wrist, bound in a linen strip.

"Don't worry yet," she told him. "I'm going to continue in my sneaking."

He nodded and trudged away, and Kalea returned to her work. Curiosity took her upstairs again. Did it indeed happen, or did she dream it?

A cool glow lit the polished stone floor from the open door of the room from last night. Whispers drifted out. She wanted another look. She tiptoed along the wall toward the door.

"Open the windows," rumbled a male voice, soft and familiar.

An old woman's grating voice answered, "That won't do well for your energy, Mastar—"

"Open the shutters!"

Kalea froze and sucked in a breath at the frightening boom of a voice. The shamans must've stared as Kalea did. Kalea foolishly took another step. Another. Morning light flared through the room and into the corridor. Kalea peeked around the doorframe.

Wikshen was sitting on the bed, his head drooped, blue hair draped and running down his chest, the handsome shape of his face silhouetted against the backlighting. The wind blew into the room through the open windows and stirred his hair.

"Mastaren," one of the other shamans said, "stand, please, and dress in the battleshift."

Bowing his head, he rubbed his face before rising from the bed, stumbling a bit. With no clothing whatsoever, he took long-legged strides toward the window where they waited, sinews and muscles working beneath his flawless skin. The graceful lines of his leg muscles flexed in the gentle window light.

The shamans each held an end of a long black cloth. Showing not an ounce of concern for his nudity, he raised his arms as the women ceremoniously wrapped the cloth around his hips in a precise fashion.

The older one let go of her end, and the cloth took on its own life, slithering into place and lacing itself in a diagonal fashion from his right hip to the front opening. His right leg slid through it as he took a step. As the "battleshift" finished securing itself, his posture gained starch, and like magic, a pair of fingerless gloves and open-toed socks materialized on his limbs.

"Maid, what do you need?"

Kalea caught herself staring again. The younger shaman's hands were on her hips, and she tapped her foot.

Kalea kept her eyes low and clasped her wrist with her hand meekly.

"I came to tend the...the Mastaren's bedding."

The shaman rolled her eyes and motioned toward the bed with its rumpled blankets and flattened mattress. Kalea awkwardly made her way past Wikshen. Knilma watched carefully, one side of her mouth tensing in interest. Wikshen stood like a cocky pillar, arms hanging, head set forward.

An uncanny sense of nakedness struck Kalea, and she couldn't help checking to make sure she wasn't. Despite the intensity of her bewilderment and attention, Wikshen paid her no mind and didn't oppose her eyes on him. Did he recognize her from the Alkeer temple? And the forest? She approached the bed to do her work, and when she stole a glance back, the shamans were taking his arms and ushering him out of the room.

# Chapter 49
# What is Lamrhath's Treasure

After a long leisure period spent locked away in his apartments, Lamrhath emerged, finally ready to rejoin his faction. There were new whisper stone messages to listen to, letters to write, texts about Wikshen to decipher, and spoils to sort. He shook his head at the line of girls they'd recently bought from the little forest convent. He recognized one or two from the audition at the outpost.

"Ugly lot," he said bluntly. "This may not've been worth losing three sorcerers over. I'd hoped for enchanting little virgins with bright eyes and luminous complexions." He paced down the line, shaking his head. A few other sorcerers and a guard stood in attendance. "Although we did find Dorhen among them for a fortunate twist…while it lasted," he continued. "Might as well ask while I'm here: why was there a virile twenty-two year-old elf in your bedchamber?"

None of the girls answered.

"He wasn't dressed like a member of your religion. Was he boffing all of you, or just one?" He crossed his arms and waited. When no one answered, he said, "Does it matter that I ask this? You won't be in trouble for it, not here. I'm simply amused by the story."

The girls shifted their eyes. Some wrung their hands.

"We don't know," the sobbing voice of one of the younger ones rang out.

"How could you not know?" Lamrhath clicked his tongue. He drew a dagger from his belt and snagged the ugliest girl in the group by the back of her neck.

The others shrieked and cried the girl's name. "Rose!"

"Tell me, or I'll kill this one!" He pressed the dagger to Rose's throat.

"Stop!" The fattest girl stepped out of line. "I know why he was in there."

Lamrhath tightened his lips and released the ugly, quiet one. "I'm waiting."

"The elf was…*boffing* just one of us. He broke in to protect her."

He widened his mouth. "Sounds extremely likely. Which one? You?"

"No, sir." The fat girl put her hands across her chest.

"I remember you," he said, leaving the ugly girl behind to approach the fat one. "You were traveling with my sorcerers. What's your name?"

"Vivene, sir."

"Don't call me 'sir,' call me 'my lord.'"

"Yes, my lord."

He pointed his finger across the line of scared, homely girls. "Which one was screwing the elf?"

"She's not here, my lord."

"Where is she?"

"Died. She's dead, my lord."

He narrowed his eyes. "Did she die on the road?"

"Yes."

"How?"

"Asthma."

This time a real smile spread across his face. "I can believe that." He turned his back to exchange glances with one of his sorcerers. "But it's funny."

"What's funny, my lord?"

The nearest sorcerer whipped her back with a cane, and Vivene yelled and arched.

"No questions," Lamrhath reminded her. "The funny thing is, the convent's superior promised us fifteen young novices. We soon got word of one who died in a structural accident and were promised fourteen instead. I was told two died on the road. There should be twelve girls standing here. There are eleven. Where is the twelfth girl?"

Vivene lowered her blinking eyes to the floor. She shook her head.

Lamrhath leaned in closer. "Where is she, Vivene?"

"Dead...I guess."

Lamrhath inched his face closer to hers. "Who is she, Vivene?" His hand moved to his dagger to unsheathe it again. "Vivene," he pressed. The blade scraped against its sheath.

"Kalea!" another girl with a wet, red face shouted.

Lamrhath put his dagger back and gave her his attention. "Who's Kalea?"

The crying girl stuttered. "Please don't kill us!"

"Who is Kalea?" he asked again.

"She's—she's—she's the one who's not here."

Vivene hissed at that girl.

"Is Kalea dead?" Lamrhath asked.

"I—I—I—I don't know. I don't know!" The crying girl shook her head and sobbed into her hands.

"That's not true—Kalea wasn't a novice, she took her vows!" Vivene shot out at the whole room.

The crying girl gestured strongly at Vivene. "But Kalea slept in our dorm that night! Besides, I knew she was sneaking around lately, talking to someone in the courtyard—a man—and not Father Liam—a younger man!" The girl gnawed on her sleeve as she wept.

"Maggy, what's the matter with you?" Vivene yelled.

Lamrhath put up his hand to silence her. "Maggy," he said, "where is Kalea now?"

Maggy shook her head. "I don't know. Maybe still at the convent." She wiped her face on her sleeve.

Lamrhath stepped back and nodded his head. He'd be sending his next whisper stone message to the convent. If he could locate this girl, Kalea, she might prove to be a valuable tool in leashing Wikshen. Elven males, when bonded to a female, tended to carry a deeply passionate fire for that female, a fire which could make him march proudly to his death if required. Who knew how much of his original elven host would remain in attendance? Studying Wikshen, thoroughly learning how he operated, could be the rarest treasure trove of knowledge anyone could grasp. Ilbith could do just that. How interesting it would be to collect this girl named Kalea to find out how much Wikshen would remember her... and what he'd do to her if they were locked together in the same room.

Lamrhath fished through his pocket and approached Maggy, who eyed his gesture in horror. He presented to her a tin coin. "Here, Maggy," he said. "This is what we call a 'favor token.' We give it to servants who deserve a reward. You can use it, only once, to get a new garment—a cozy pair of stockings, perhaps—or an extra helping of supper, or a chance to excuse yourself from your sexual duties...for one occasion."

Not wanting to touch her grimy hands, he flipped the token into the air and let her catch it in a bumbling display.

*Kalea.* He played the name on his tongue as he walked out of the servants' quarters. His list of missing persons had grown a little longer after Wikshen and Daghahen.

Lamrhath's men led him to another wing where some of the other spoils were kept. Talekas joined his entourage along the way. "They ate their oats and fish, my lord. All of them are well, no snots, no fevers," Talekas reported.

"Good. They've been getting their fresh air and exercise?" he asked.

Talekas flourished his hand as he walked beside Lamrhath. "We've tidied the east courtyard and let them out every morning."

Talekas opened the door to the nursery where a dozen children had made their new home. Two nannies manned this room; one of them sat in a chair with a child on her lap. All the other children stopped cold in their bickering and running about when he entered. Ten human children and two elves.

Lamrhath scanned for the latter. A group of little ones huddled around the one he'd come to see. When he approached that group, the little elven *saeghar* ran forward, yelling a war cry.

"No!" the second nanny shrieked, and lunged for the lad.

A sorcerer caught him instead and slapped the boy hard along his shaggy head. Though fazed, the young elf fought on. Growling like a rabid animal, he fought as the sorcerer held him away from Lamrhath.

"That one's name is Bairhen," Talekas said. "He's from the same clan as the girl, so you can imagine his natural sense of protection for her."

"We'll have to separate him from the rest of the group," Lamrhath said. "He'll be our special little project, won't he?" Lamrhath cast a fake smile at the lad. "After we've disciplined him properly, maybe Orinleah would like to have him in her apartment as a present from me—to fill the position Dorhen should've filled."

Leaving the wild elven child to face the wrath of the sorcerers, Lamrhath turned toward the corner, where the other children scattered and bounded to the opposite corner like a box of trapped rabbits, leaving one radiant little creature to stand on her own.

Kneeling before her, he reached and took her hands down to reveal big purple eyes in a soft little face, recently cleaned. Her hair had been brushed before his arrival. Its exquisite gold color would glitter within the fibers of his new magic-blocking vest when harvested. They would test their new elf-hair garments against Wikshen's morkblades.

When Lamrhath touched the girl, Bairhen raised his volume and spouted angry Norrian words behind him until the sorcerers were forced to deliver harder hits.

The *farhah* kept calm and challenged Lamrhath's eyes without fear. He touched her silken hair, sparkling like gold in the daylight from the window. Lamrhath made another smile, this one closer to genuine. Simply looking at this precious creature made him feel extraordinarily calm.

"Hello again, Mhina," he whispered.

# Chapter 50
# His Name

Kalea didn't see Wikshen again during the day. She thought about him, though—she couldn't help it. She did her chores as faithfully as she would at home. Actually, she performed these chores better to satisfy Wikhaihli's flawless discipline.

No one bothered to punish her for her antics last night, when she had spied Wikshen rising from the dead. Knilma, the shaman who knew about her ecstasies, hadn't spoken to her since. Kalea resisted stopping her in the corridor at one point to ask more questions about her episode. She couldn't entertain that bizarre supernatural effect. If it happened again, she'd force it away with all the willpower she could summon. She'd call on the One Creator to stop it. And during the daylight hours, she would push Wikshen from her cloudy mind and try to think of Mhina instead.

A thick walking cloud moved in and blocked out the sky. With it, a wretched drizzle spread over the complex right as Kalea received the miserable task of carrying dishes through the weather from the kitchen to the manor. It didn't help much to walk through the cloister; the cold rain blew in sideways in addition to the cloister's disrepair. Geoduck stew and stale bread served all the Wikshonites daily while a wealth of flavors and recipes were reserved for Wikshen. Meats, soups, fresh-baked bread and pastries, berries, and flatcakes of different styles all teased her nose as the dishes warmed her hands.

Her heart thundered to beat the sky for each trip she made to his private dining room, located down the hall from the room he stayed in. She stretched her neck toward it, desperate for another look at him—for some reason. Would he recognize her?

After the last trip, the shaman barked hasty orders at the black maids. Knilma approached Kalea with a vial of oil. "Bend down, my dear." When Kalea obeyed, Knilma rubbed a strong-smelling oil on her throat. "This smell arouses him," she explained. "Pennyroyal. You'll be dousing yourself in this a lot."

Kalea swallowed and trembled. Knilma wanted to entice Wikshen to attack her at his dinner table?

"No need to fear, girl," Knilma said, taking note of her shivers. After finishing with her throat, the old woman shoved her hand between

Kalea's legs and wiped the remainder on her naked inner thigh. She pulled the strings on her skimpy little undergarment and yanked it away. "You won't need this."

She turned to the other maids. "That goes for the rest of you. Remove your braies!" The other maids followed her order.

Kalea closed her mouth and breathed slowly through her nose to slow her heart. No luck.

Knilma flattened her palms and motioned to the maids. "Get in place now. He'll be ready soon." She guided Kalea to the front of the line of maids to kneel beside the door. They all bowed their heads.

In the last few moments, the shamans handed out damp cloths for the girls to tidy their faces. One of the shamans arranged another maid's hair. Looking their absolute best for Wikshen happened to be a large part of their religious devotion, especially for his first formal dinner at home. Though they were mere maids, they also acted as important instruments to entice Wikshen's desire. Why was it so important to arouse him? So much about this cult's customs confused her.

Knilma placed a black glass pitcher in Kalea's hands. It might've put off a fruity scent, but Kalea could hardly tell over her stinky perfume. "Listen, girl," Knilma said. "He'll eventually order his punch refilled, and that'll be you."

Hearing her plan, Kalea swallowed a thick lump in her sore throat. Knilma put her hands on Kalea to fix her posture until she'd achieved a straight-backed, head-bowed pose which apparently made her look attractive. She didn't feel attractive. The sweat on her back irritated her skin and the oil made her want to sneeze, not to mention the fear of Wikshen mauling her when she shuffled in to fill his cup.

The shamans blew out the candles after lighting pennyroyal incense sticks. They waved the smoking sticks around ceremoniously, struck solitary drumbeats, and whisked into the dining room to kill the candles in there and place the incense.

At the sound of the drum, a door at the end of the hall opened. Unable to stifle her terror, Kalea stared openly. Wikshen didn't emerge. A long line of black-robed people filed into the hall and toward the dining room. As they walked, a shaman struck a drum in a slow, steady rhythm: *dtoom…dtoom…dtoom…*

The robed people wore hoods and black masks over their mouths and noses. A brief sense of relief touched Kalea when she caught Metta's eyes under one of the silky black hoods. These were the concubine candidates. In her state of religious concentration, Metta didn't smile or attempt to make communication with her eyes. At the end of the line, Kalea recognized Brielle's eyes, which narrowed. Beneath her mask, she sneered at Kalea, who decided to bow her head until they all disappeared into the dining room.

When all the girls disappeared into the dark dining room, the drum stopped and Kalea's heart fluttered at the realization of who should show next. She promised herself she'd be safe. Everything would be fine. She'd refill the cup as needed, and Wikshen wouldn't bother her. Why would he want her anyway when she was all skin and bones with her faint flagellation scars striping her back? She'd get through this tense moment, and then after his meal, she and the other black maids would clear the dishes and return to their dorm. Regardless of her self-reassurances, keeping from trembling was impossible.

A shaman stepped lightly toward the bedroom where Wikshen had sprung from the dead last night and knocked on the door. "Mastaren? Are you ready to eat?" She waited in silence. "Mastaren?"

She knocked again and tried the knob. It didn't open. She fumbled for her key ring, calling for Wikshen. Kalea raised her head to watch.

The shaman opened the door and stuttered. She ran into the room. "He's gone! Where did he…?"

The maids all shot to their feet, and the other shamans joined her in the bedroom. Kalea ventured closer to peek inside. The window hung open, and the surrounding stones were dampened by the incoming rain. The shamans rang bells and banged drums to alert the entire complex.

Wikshen never turned up, so the Wikshonites carried on as normal, assuming he'd decided to leave. Kalea helped clear the table and recover the dishes, which were dispersed to his various shrines out in the region, to her disappointment. All that delicious food. Apparently, they cooked for him every day, regardless of whether he showed up to eat it or not. If not, they sent the food out to the shrines as offerings to him. Wasteful bastard.

At nightfall, Kalea made her way to the witches' dormitory to collect their dirty laundry, behind in her chores after having to help search for Wikshen earlier. Her slow-moving limbs ached by now. The young premier witches poured into the hall, chattering and giggling, groomed with smoky black soot around their eyes. Metta's black hair coiled around the back of her head stylishly with two ponytail ends hanging to her shoulders, her eyes spaced and her mouth smiling dreamily.

"Kalea!" She ran up and hugged her. Pulling Kalea by the arm, they entered the little cell where Metta slept. Kalea couldn't decide if this living situation was better than the maids' or not. At least Metta had some privacy in her small compartment. Her bed, though still a mat on the floor, looked thicker than what Kalea slept on.

"He's back." Metta leaned against the door after closing it, her eyes rolling in bliss before her lids closed.

"Where did he go?"

"I don't know. We all got ready and went to the private chapel for the Solemn Exhibition, and he came! He…" Metta's voice took on a panting of some sort. "His glorious, magnificent, dreamy presence appeared for us."

Kalea cocked her head. "And did you really…exhibit yourself?"

"Yes, of course. I came here to make myself available for him." She hugged Kalea again and pulled her to the floor, where they sat facing each other on the bed, a softer bed than Kalea's sleeping mat.

"He has such a deep voice. And you know what?" Kalea's wide eyes followed Metta's every exaggerated movement. "Since Brielle has Kilka's sponsorship, she stood first in line. Kalea, let me tell you, when she approached him, she did the proper bow and took her chance to look into his eyes one-on-one. And you know what he said?" Kalea shook her head. "Brielle over-acted at being graceful, of course, and Kilka recited all of her merits: wealth, grace, dancing ability, and then he said in return—listen to this—he asked what the word 'eloquence' meant, and a shaman defined it for him. And then she had to explain to him how the commerce of Brielle's father's lands worked and how it would benefit his kingdom if he kept it functioning." Metta smiled. "How refreshing—his honesty and humility. He's a delight, Kalea, easy to talk to. But that's not the best part.

"Brielle recited her own speech, and at the part when she declared she'd stay in his protective establishment for as long as he'd have her, he stopped her and said, 'No. You're wrong. There are no safe places anywhere. Especially in my care.' And Kalea, her face"—Metta laughed into her black cloak—"the way she rapidly blinked her eyes. She got so flustered at his dismissal of her speech, she turned and went the wrong direction, and bumped into Knilma. Knilma got so angry, she hit Brielle in the butt with her cane!" Metta roared with laughter.

Kalea tried to make an entertained face for her sake, but in reality she'd gone numb. What could she say? What should she feel?

Metta kept talking. "My heart pounded so loud I could barely hear my own voice. And when I found myself face to face with this…this deity… How can I put this?" The laughter washed out of Metta's face at an incredibly odd speed. "He gazed deeply when he met my eyes." Metta's breathiness continued, and now she grabbed at the air, staring as if fireflies floated around her. "The ages locked inside of him, and…and…

Do you know how many lives he's lived?"

Kalea's voice barely made it out. "No."

"This is his seventh life. He's new but also ancient. He is so cool and in control, a presence who knows all, so I don't have to. I trust him to the extent of my being, Kalea." Metta's mouth remained open as she shook her head. "His eyes had a glowing nature to them I cannot describe, like turquoise. I sensed neither peacockery nor jest—he frowned and never gave a smirk, just pure truth and sincerity and wisdom. Even what he said to Brielle was wrapped in sincerity... Kalea, I'm going to see if he'll meet you too."

Kalea shook her head. "You—you will?" She'd already met him. Would anything be different if she met him again? The way Metta talked about him now made the whole situation seem different.

"Oh yes, you must meet him," she said. "I need to tell someone my wish, my urge. Kalea, I desire..." Kalea's eyebrows rose in anticipation. "To make love to him. To be beneath him for any brief moment would be enough."

A tear rolled down Metta's cheek, twinkling in her cell's soft lantern glow. "I've thought about it most nights, and now I'll dream of it." Metta was crying genuine tears. Kalea stuttered and shook her head. "How beautiful it would be. I would make it my mission to soothe the ancient wounds he carries. It would comfort me to comfort him."

"Metta," Kalea said, "in the bathhouse and other places, I heard them say he rapes. Aren't you afraid?" She couldn't deny her own memory of him kissing her cheek and telling her he...had killed Dorhen. Feelings of contradiction rose in her gut. Dorhen didn't feel so far away anymore. His presence emanated from somewhere, like it had back at the convent when he lurked in the forest outside the wall waiting for her.

"No, no, of course not! He doesn't rape, he *blesses*!" Metta said. "And it's our duty to be ready and willing when he calls."

"How will you get the chance to...do *that* with him?" The thought of the two of them wound together in passion made Kalea ill. It couldn't happen. It was wrong.

Metta smiled through her tears. "Time will tell. I'll make myself available, and one day he'll call me... For once, my life has meaning. I have a purpose." Metta closed her eyes and hugged herself. "I've found religion."

Kalea opened her mouth, but only air escaped. She wanted to say, *Metta, let's go back to Alkeer for a while*, but couldn't. How could she now? It was the worst moment to say it but the best moment to act on it. Kalea also wanted to cry. Why did she care that Metta wanted to lie with Wikshen? It was none of her business, and yet a sense of coldness stabbed Kalea at every mention of it.

Metta threw her arms around her and hugged her tight for the next several moments. The girl cried openly, and when she pulled away, she wiped tears from Kalea's face with her sleeve—tears Kalea hadn't realized she'd made.

"Will you stay the night in here?"

*No!* She wanted nothing more than to be alone after this. Kalea shook her head with her mouth hanging open. "Um, I don't think I'm allowed."

Metta sniffled. "Oh, well, I'll let you go before the housekeeper gets angry."

Kalea stepped cautiously into the dark, rainy night, arms limp by her sides, her head blank and a bit dizzy from exhaustion. If she were home at the convent, she would've been asleep hours ago. The wind blasted her face with a misty rain, and she hugged herself as she made her way toward the manor.

She paused at the realization she'd forgotten the sack of laundry she was supposed to retrieve from the witches' quarters. Instead of turning around to encounter those crazy witches again, she sighed and walked on. She'd worry about it tomorrow along with whatever punishment her mistake would cause. Tonight, in bed, she'd push Wikshen out of her mind again along with the mental picture of him and Metta together, and tomorrow she'd try to insert Togha into their conversations. She missed her friends. If she could sneak out to the beach, she might find them early one morning where they supposedly dug geoducks.

Footsteps scraped the stone walkway behind her.

"Bowaen?"

The person didn't answer, but a sliver of lantern light outlining the form suggested a male figure. He launched after her. She ran too, shrieking in hopes of alerting someone. She stumbled over the uneven stones in the path and waved her arms to right herself. She managed to continue running, though he gained on her. His panting huffed right behind her head.

"Stop!" a deep voice ordered.

She didn't listen. She had encountered enough strange men in alleys at night to know this wasn't right. She needed to alert someone. She remembered the many bells hanging around the complex. Where could the nearest one be? Thinking became impossible!

By sheer luck, she found a dangling rope along a wall beside a door. It might or might not be attached to a bell, but she gave it a yank anyway.

*Clang!*

Split-second relief flooded over her before two strong arms closed around her and locked her in. The man shushed her. She screamed, and a hand covered her mouth.

"Please quiet yourself! It's me! It's Dyii! Remember Dyii?"

Of course she remembered him, but why did he chase and restrain her? Her feet lifted off the ground. She kicked her legs as hard as she could and accomplished little.

"Please quiet, please." He kept his voice hushed. A darker shadow than the open sky engulfed her as he half-carried her into an alley between the dining hall and one of the general offices where warlocks were allowed to go.

The alley ended at the big outer wall, where it split and ran between the wall and buildings. Only one exit besides the one they'd entered presented itself. A big heap of old junk blocked the opposite alleyway. Her eyes adjusted in the weak glow of a window's light. She panted harder than her kidnapper.

He released her body but retained her wrists. His sculpted face showed fear. The dim lighting flashed in his red eyes like a fire burning into her. He pressed in close to her so she couldn't dart away.

"I can't explain…Kalea." His shaking hand ventured to her heart. She cringed in anticipation of what he might do. "There's a feeling I have for you. The sound of your heart, it's a rhythm I've never…"

"Is it because you're a Thaccilian and I'm a Luschian?" she asked.

He reared his head back. "You know the race that I am?" She nodded her head with her mouth hanging open, panting. "But what is this thing you say about yourself?"

He held her wrists in his strong grasp when she tried to jerk away. "Let's talk about this tomorrow," she pleaded.

He trapped her. She couldn't move. "Can't talk now," he whispered. "Listen. You have to leave this place. It's not safe."

Kalea blinked, pausing in her tangled thoughts of how to escape.

"I can arrange a—"

An odd, animal-like chirping sound resonating from a dark corner made him pause. *KrrrRRRrrrRRRrrr…*

"Shit," Dyii whispered, and squeezed her hand. He tensed his body around her and pressed her hard against the wall, which triggered the hysterical terror she'd suffered from after Kemp the farmer had attempted to rape her. Kalea's tremors took over; she would run wildly as soon as she could.

A sanguinesent drifted into view. Its eyes glittered with a familiar brilliance. Its four long, cat-like teeth were clamped together until they parted to let out a tongue like a snake's to taste the air. The thing glided in its black robe, as if it didn't need feet to get around.

"This isn't a good time!" Dyii hissed at the creature.

Too surprised and on the edge of insanity, Kalea failed to warn him not to look at its diamond-cluster eyes. When Dyii turned back to her, his Thaccilian eyes had gone dull.

"You'll accompany me back to Ilbith now," he recited blandly, lacking the exotic accent and life his normal voice should have.

"No!" Kalea screamed and jerked away, hurting her own shoulder.

"You have made a pact with the kingsorcerer and must fulfill your promise," the sanguinesent explained through Dyii's mouth. "It is my duty to sort you."

"The kingsorcerer?" She'd definitely heard that word before.

Dyii's hands clamped hard on her, harder than before his enthrallment. With her trapped in Dyii's clutches, the sanguinesent moved in closer. Kalea closed her eyes. She didn't have any breath to scream with.

An extreme force jerked Dyii backward, and his hand was swiped off of Kalea's wrist. Confused and off-balance, Kalea stumbled and fell, unable to stand on her own in her lightheaded state. Pushing herself up, she strained her eyes.

A taller figure slammed Dyii to the ground and punched him repeatedly. The meaty sound of a fist against flesh *thunked* over the sound of pouring rain and the sanguinesent's irritated chirp. Leaving Dyii knocked out in restless sleep, he rose to his full towering height and slowly came into focus.

Wikshen.

Kalea squinted at the scene, at Wikshen, who'd beaten the man who had pinned her to the wall. Familiarity resonated. They were even in an alley, like the day she'd met…

Why did Wikshen care, though? Why was he here? Had he heard her ring the bell?

He engaged the sanguinesent squarely. The creature's chirping intensified. Without a thrall, it didn't have much defense beyond its fangs and tentacles. Wikshen showed no concern for either, nor did he become enthralled.

The sanguinesent's tongue flicked out with a sense of attitude; it tested the air and aura of its opponent and continued its chirp. So far, its voice stayed out of Kalea's head.

Wikshen widened his stance and flexed his arms. Tonight, he wore two armbands around each bicep and elbow-length fingerless gloves with the long drape around his hips as always.

Without warning, Wikshen grabbed Kalea's arm and yanked her up like a ragdoll. She yelped. He put himself in front of her. His manhandling aggravated her dizziness.

The sanguinesent revealed its two-clawed hands from its black robe, and the tentacles emerged. Wikshen caught one in his hand, and the rest of the length wrapped around his arm. The other tentacle got his other arm.

Kalea wailed in dread. She searched around for her washing bat, but she didn't have it! She rose to her feet and pressed her back against the wall. If she could squeeze by, she could run through the alley and back to the dorm.

Wikshen kept his hold on the tentacles while they held him in return, and he whipped the sanguinesent around with ease. Kalea remembered too well how strong the tentacles were, but they were no match for Wikshen. His clenched teeth flashed in the light with ferocity at the creature. One tooth grew a bit long on the side, like a fang.

In defiance of the monster's hold, Wikshen walked forward and grabbed the sanguinesent's skull-like head. Its chirp took on a rumbly slowness, like dread or anger. He walked the sanguinesent and its tentacled mess to the alley's nearest exit, or at least to the awning's edge where the misty rain dripped. Wikshen pushed and held the creature's head under the pouring water, and *vfoom!* The sanguinesent disappeared in a puff of black smoke.

Wikshen turned back to Kalea, and she caught a hint of his tensed brow and tight jaw. He marched toward her. She froze and stared. The scene slowed in her brain.

He reached his hand out fast as if to grab her, and she had a flashback of Dorhen reaching his hand out after rescuing her from Kemp. She winced when Dorhen's image vanished, replaced by Wikshen.

Before they made contact, the sanguinesent reappeared in a cloud similar to the way it had disappeared. Water somehow made it go away, but not permanently. Kalea jumped and pointed, having lost the ability to speak during the frantic situation.

Wikshen whirled around to face it again. He lunged straight for its bony face and caught it again in his large hand. Using the eye sockets and other bony formations, he yanked the creature's head forward and slammed his other hand into the back of its skull with an angry grunt that put a spark in Kalea's abdomen.

Wikshen's hard strike somehow made the sanguinesent's eyes disperse, releasing their hundreds of small diamonds to shower all over the ground in glittery chaos. With the diamonds gone, the rest of the creature's head and body turned to ash that settled all over the ground and drifted off to wherever the slight breeze took it.

Wikshen dusted his hands and rose stiffly to his full height, fists clenched by his sides. Without turning his head, he eyed her. "Go back inside," his voice rumbled, and then he turned to leave.

The spark reignited in her gut at the sound of his voice. That voice, familiar once again. Kalea's heart beat harder at it. She scrambled to her feet, willing her vision and strength to return. Whatever was going on in her body, she prayed for it not to be another ecstasy. That sensation, mixed with her dizziness and fear, overwhelmed her. She couldn't help but remember this person lying in the bed with shamans all around him, how the tears streamed down his face. He was more than a monster. He was...

No. She couldn't entertain such crazy ideas! She leaned against the wall, gingerly moving forward despite all her temporary illnesses. But she had to! She...!

"Wait!" Her voice burst out for the first time since the panic set in.

He didn't. He took a step.

"Wait, I said!"

He ignored her and stepped farther away. He was leaving. Dyii snored on the ground nearby. If she were to try to speak to Wikshen, she needed to act fast before he came to.

Kalea let the wall go, stood on her two feet, and squared her shoulders. She took a deep breath. "I know who you are!"

He stopped.

*He stopped.* The words trailed surreally through her mind. She'd tried those words in experimentation. Her eyes widened, staring at his muscled back with the cascade of long blue hair trailing down his moist skin. Her effort to breathe slowly did nothing for her nerves. The phantom taste of peppery fish spread across her tongue. She had eaten it in his room in the temple. The word "run" had been chalked with difficulty on the floor next to it. Metta had told her how he struggled with a big word when she met him. This creature! This intimidating, seductive creature couldn't spell "run" or understand what "eloquence" meant?

Everywhere she'd gone where she'd met Wikshonites, they'd informed her that Wikshen had chosen her. Someone else had chosen her too, months in the past!

*You might be bargained with for my body,* Wikshen had once told her. This was too unreal.

*Say something else,* she urged herself before he could decide to disappear again.

She took slow steps toward him. "I…" She cleared her throat. "I won't pursue you anymore if you don't want me to. But before you go, I have to tell you something."

He waited, keeping his back turned. He listened to her. Could it be…?

"I'm sorry," she said. She dragged in a slow pull of air. Her lungs hurt, especially after all the running. Her next selection of words slid out as if she no longer retained control. She needed to say them. If she couldn't venture through this conversation, she wouldn't be able to sleep tonight—or any night. "I'm sorry I abandoned you," she said. "I didn't want to run out on you. I've regretted it every day since."

There. She'd said it. She approached his side, and he finally turned his head to look at her. The glow from the window barely illuminated the side of his face and the outer rim of his pointed ear.

He glanced at her and returned to staring into the rain beyond the awning. His gaze melted downward, to his feet. "How did you know it was me?"

Now she shook uncontrollably. *No. That's not what he said. He didn't say that!*

If this conversation felt surreal before, now she floated above her body, looking down on herself as she stood there talking to…him!

She pulled herself back to reality and focused. Tomorrow, she'd wake up and find out she had dreamed or dream*walked*. Until then, she'd play out the scenario.

She answered his question with another question. "You think you can fool me, Dorhen?"

*To be continued . . .*

Kalea dreamwalks by accident.

The sanguinesent appears.

Togha meets Metta.

Dorhen no longer recognizes himself.

Kalea gets an audience with Wikshen.

Lehomis bids farewell to Tilninhet.

# Glossary and Pronunciation

**A Note on Elvish pronunciation:** You'll find a lot of H's in Elvish words. Oftentimes a male elf's name contains the suffix "hen," it's the masculine suffix ("ah" or "het" being the female counterpart). Usually the H in "hen" his pronounced. Other H's found in elvish words tend to be "swallowed," such as the first H in "Daghahen" (Dag-uh-hen). How to pronounce the H's in Elvish words will largely be based on your own instincts. I, personally, tend to swallow the H in "Dorhen."

## <u>Characters</u> (* main characters)

**Alhannah:** (Ahl-hawn-ah) the head Desteer maiden in Clan Lockheirhen.

**Anonhet:** (Ah-non-het) A young elf woman who works in Lehomis's household. Gaije is in love with her.

**Arius Medallus:** (Air-ee-us Meh-dahl-us) A fairy who used to watch over Dorhen. He sent Kalea to find Dorhen, by following the sword called Hathrohjilh.

**Bairhen:** (B-er-hen) A young elf boy who was abducted from Clan Lockheirhen alongside Mhina.

**Bowaen:** (Bō-ay-en) A rugged, middle-aged swordsman and runner for the Wistara White Guild. He was employed by Lord Dax to find and bring home Damos, the Grey Mage. Kalea travels with him because of the mysterious sword he carries.

**Brielle:** (Brī-el) A young woman whose wealthy father gave her to Wikshen as an offering.

**Chandran:** (Shan-der-an) A sorcerer from the Ilbith faction who had kidnapped Kalea in the past. He summoned the sanguinesent and also transformed into a monster before dying by Bowaen's hand.

**Damos:** (Day-mōs) a young Grey Mage born to a noble house in Sharr.

**Del:** (Dell) A skilled thief and lover of tobacco. Bowaen's apprentice.

**Gaije:** (Gāj) A young elf, talented archer, and debut *saehgahn* from Clan Lockheirhen in Norr. Lehomis's grandson.

**Gavor:** (Ga-vôr) A sorcerer in the Ilbith faction.

**Hetael:** (Het-tāl) A member of the Wikshonites.

**Kaskill:** (Cas-kil) A young sorcerer in the Ilbith faction. Wikshen bit his finger off.

**Kerlin:** (Kur-lin) The king of Valltalhiss.

**Kilka:** (Kil-kah) A shaman and prominent member of the Wikshonite cult.

**Knilma:** (Nil-mah) A shaman and the oldest member of the Wikshonites.

**Kristhanhea:** (Kris-tHan-hā-ah) Lehomis's legendary wife who lived and died long ago.

**Lamrhath:** (Lam-wrath or Lam-er-hath) The current kingsorcerer and leader of the Ilbith sorcery faction.

**Liam, Father:** (Lee-ahm) A priest Kalea used to think of as a father.

**Orinleah:** (Or-in-lee-ah) Dorhen's mother and member of the Linharri clan.

**Paigess:** (Pī-ges) A shaman and close friend of Knilma's.

**Lehomis:** (Lay-ah-miss) A legendary elf, master of archery, writer, and elder of Clan Lockheirhen. Gaije and Mhina's ancestor.

**Maggy:** One of the kidnapped novices.

**McShivvy, Daghahen:** (Mik-shy-vee, Dag-uh-hen) Dorhen's father and Lamrhath's twin brother.

**McShivvy, Lambelhen:** (Mik-shy-vee, Lam-bell-hen) Lamrhath's original name. The twin brother of Daghahen.

**Metta:** (Met-uh) A fetching young member of the Wikshonites. Togha's sweetheart.

**Mhina:** (Mēn-ah) A seven-year-old elven girl who was kidnapped by Wikshen. Gaije's younger sister.

**Millie:** One of the kidnapped novices.

**Mirral:** (Mir-ôl) A member of the Wikshonites.

**Myrtle:** A young woman who pledged herself to Wikshen.

**Nan:** (Nan) A member of the Wikshonites.

**Peck:** (Pek) A sorcerer in the Ilbith faction.

**Remenaxice, Lord:** (Rem-en-ak-sis) A mysterious elf in Carridax. Also known as "Rem."

**Riminhen:** (Rim-in-hen) A member of the Clanless elves of the Darklands. Togha's enemy.

**Rose:** Kalea's friend and one of the kidnapped novices.

**Scayetta:** (Sky-et-tah) A Wikshonite shaman.

**Selka:** (Sel-kah) A chamber mistress at Ilbith's Lightland outpost who gave Dorhen his first sexual experience.

**Senna:** (Sen-nah) A member of the Wikshonites.

**Sigmune:** (Sig-myoon) A sorcerer in the Ilbith faction.

**Silva:** (Sil-vah) A woman from a Darklandic tribe of nomads.

**\*Sufferborn, Dorhen:** (Suffer-born, Door-en or Door-hen) An elf who fell in love with Kalea. He was kidnapped by the Ilbith sorcerers during Kalea's convent raid. A mishap involving Daghahen and the sorcerers caused him to fall to the possession of the pixie, Wik.

**Tamas:** (Tam-us) A young woman of primitive Darklandic heritage who pledged herself to Wikshen.

**Talekas:** (Tal-ek-as) A sorcerer in the Ilbith Faction.

**\*Thridmill, Kalea:** (Thrid-mill, Kah-lee-ah) An ex-vestal from the Hallowill convent. She had planned to run away with Dorhen before he disappeared while trying to rescue her when the convent was raided. Now she's out looking for him and the kidnapped novices.

**Tirnah:** (Teer-nah) Gaije's mother.

**Togha:** (Tōg-uh) Gaije's distant cousin and an official Norrian letter carrier.

**Trisdahen:** (Triz-dah-hen) Gaije's father. He was killed in a raid led by Wikshen.

**Tumas:** (Toom-as) A member of the Ilbith sorcery faction.

**Vivene:** (Viv-een) A friend of Kalea's, and one of the kidnapped novices.

**\*Wikshen:** (Wik-shen) The flesh embodiment of the pixie, Wik. A living deity worshipped by the Wikshonites. Also known by the unofficial titles: "The King of Shadow," "King of the Darklands," "The Black Shadow God," and the Wikshonites call him "Mastaren."

## Places & Things

**Alkeer:** (Al-kir) The largest known city in the Darklands.

**Azrielle:** (Az-ree-el) Damos's pet parrot.

**Battleshift:** A sacred shroud, made by the trolls, woven with a special blend of fibers, and dyed black with a specific formula. Wikshen wears it around his hips like a kilt. It's usually the only garment he wears and comes with various magical abilities. The battleshift is also a physical representative of the pixie, Wik.

**Black Maids:** An order of servants within Wikhaihli who rank higher than all the others and whose duties entail keeping up Wikshen's inner chambers. Black maids are characterized by their uniform black dresses (unlike the common maids who tend to wear leftover rags of undyed linen or wool).

**Blinding Mask:** An invention of the Ilbith sorcery faction which aids a sorcerer's effort to block another person's magical ability.

**Braies:** (brā) Underwear usually made from linen. Also refers to a piece elves wear with their *sa-garhik*.

**Bright One, The:** See "Lin Yilbarhen" in the Elvish/Norrian language section.

**Carridax:** (Cair-i-daks) A city in the Lightlands established by two noble houses, the Carri's and the Dax's.

**Chips:** A motley assortment of valuable metal scraps used as currency in the Darklands. The Darklands have no official government and therefore no official mint. Chips can range anywhere from foreign coins or coins left over from old Darklandic civilization, to thin "chips" or nuggets, to broken jewelry.

**Clanless, The:** A ragtag clan of Norrian misfits who've gathered and organized in the Darklands. Each individual has opted not to return to Norr for his own reason.

**Creator's Word:** The official religious tome of the Sanctity of Creation.

**Darklands, The:** The northern side of the continent of Kaihals, consisting mostly of wild lands and territories, famous for being overrun with disreputable ruffians, warring tribal peoples, cults, and evil creatures.

**Dendrea:** (Den-dree-uh) the official Lightlandic currency.

**Desteer, The:** (Des-tīr) See "Desteer" in the Elvish/Norrian Words section.

**Dreamwalking:** A magical practice in which the dreamwalker enters another person's dream to communicate with them.

**Dunce:** A slang term for a certain league of minion in service of the Ilbith sorcerers.

**Elder:** The male leader of any Norrian clan, whose position is complemented by the head Desteer.

**Gaulice:** (Gôl-iss) A city in the heart of the Lightlands.

**Goblin Country:** A large boggy region at the heart of the Darklands.

**Grey Mages:** A faction of mages who train in Wistara and serve in the Kingdom of Sharr.

**Head Desteer:** The female leader of any Desteer chapter of the Norrian clans, whose position is complemented by the elder.

**Hael:** (Hāl) One of the five pixies favored by the Ilbith sorcery faction.

**Hanhelin's Gate:** (Han-hel-ins gāt) A huge fence, made of a metal that looks like iron, running across the entire continent. It was built to end a war with the Darklands and continues to protect the Lightlands today.

**Hathrohjilh:** (Hath-row-schil or Hath-row-jill) A mysterious sword Bowaen won from Daghahen in a game of dice.

**Hathrohskog:** (Hath-row-skog) An ominous Darklandic forest located between Alkeer and Wikhaihli.

**Ilbith:** (Il-bith) The most powerful sorcery faction, known for their ability to cast portal spells and their appeasement of five powerful pixies. Also a tower located in the Darklands.

**Ingnet:** (Ing-net) One of the five pixies favored by the Ilbith sorcery faction.

**Jumaire:** (Joo-mer) A city in the Lightlands where Kalea first met Damos.

**Kaihals:** (Kāls) The name of the continent.

**Kingsorcerer:** (king-sorcerer) The leader of the reigning sorcery faction in the Darklands within a network of many warring factions.

**Kraft:** (Craft) The magical discipline practiced by Wikshen and the Wikshonites in which one's own bodily energy is channeled to accomplish various feats. Focuses on (but is not limited to) transitioning minerals and humors, and channeling vibrations.

**Kraft Fire:** An ethereal blue flame accessible through Kraft magic.

**Kraft Shout:** A Kraft spell which uses vibrations of the voice to achieve various supernatural effects, most commonly in the earth.

**Kullixaxuss:** (kul-iks-aks-us) The underworld where unearthly beings dwell and originate, also known as Hell.

**Leho's Bow:** (Le-hōs bō) A legendary weapon wielded by the famous Lehomis. It has magical abilities.

**Lightlandic:** The most prevalent language in the Lightlands. The official language of the Kingdom of Sharr. Also considered the common tongue.

**Lightlands, The:** The southern side of the continent of Kaihals, shared by the Kingdom of Sharr and the Sovereign State of Norr.

**Lockheirhen:** (Läk-air-en) An elven clan in Norr, established by the legendary Lehomis Lockheirhen, whose primary function is raising and trading horses. Gaije is a member of this clan.

**Longwalk, The:** A large area of grassland located at the lower eastern side of the Darklands. Darklanders call it as such because it takes a long time to walk across it to access any of the neighboring cities and settlements.

**Lusche:** (Loosh) A benevolent pixie of legend who was the enemy of Thaxyl.

**Luschian:** (Loosh-ē-an) A child of the pixie, Lusche.

**Mastaren:** (Mas-tar-en) A variation of the word "master." The official form of address for Wikshen.

**Miktik:** (Mick-tick) Lehomis's favorite horse back in ancient legend.

**Morkblade:** (môrk-blade) Wikshen's signature Kraft spell. Only Wikshen can master it.

**Naerezek:** (Nair-e-zek) One of the five pixies favored by the Ilbith sorcery faction. Lamrhath's patron pettygod.

**Norr:** (Nôr) The Sovereign State of Norr. A large forest in the northern Lightlands and also the country of the elves, consisting of a union of many clans.

**Norr elves:** (Nôr elvz) the most common term for the elves who originated from the region of Norr. Note: no other type of elf is known, but the Norr elves' own cultural worries point to there being others.

**Norrian:** (Nor-ē-an) Of the Sovereign State of Norr. The language of Norr.

**Overseas Taint:** A genetic corruption in the Norr elven bloodline said to have been brought from overseas and bred into the population via foreign elves.

**Pettygod:** (petty-god) Any of various stray spirits (ghosts, fairies, demons, etc.) to have inspired cult followers whose appeasement of such spirits can often evolve into actual religions of various sizes and popularities. Pettygod cults are often hostile and their practices are frowned upon or condemned by normal society.

**Pixtagen:** (piks-tah-gen) "Pixie-taken" A new being created as the result of a pixie taking possession of a human (or elf's) body. Wikshen is a pixtagen.

**Portal:** Any of various spells which can create magical doorways for long-distance travel.

**Ravian:** (ray-vee-an) Giant mythological birds of brilliant colors and benevolent demeanors, possessing faces and feathers like parrots and bodies like lions. They are said to have once existed in greater numbers long ago. A few are still accessible through magical practices.

**Ravivill:** (Rav-ee-vil) A village in the Darklands that has accepted Wikshonism.

**Sacred Shroud:** A black linen cloth, made in the likeness of Wikshen's battleshift, the Wikshonites use as a worship symbol.

**Sanctity of Creation, The:** The belief in a single master architect, known as the One Creator, who made the entire universe and rules over all he created. The official religion of the Lightlands.

**Sanctuary:** A building used for worship of the One Creator.

**Sanguinesent:** Sentinels from Kullixaxuss, whose main duty is to sort resident souls and keep things orderly.

**Scouel:** (scowl) A malicious birdlike creature with black feathered wings and bodies like that of a dog. They are extinct on the continent of Kaihals, but are still said to exist in Kullixaxuss and are accessible through magical practices.

**Sharr:** (Shä-r) A large island south of the Lightlands and also the name of the ruling kingdom of the Lightlands (excluding Norr).

**Sharzian:** (Shär-zē-an) Of the Kingdom of Sharr.

**Sister Scupley's (or Vivene's) Love Manual:** Actually titled, *An Exploration of Love in Three Forms: Poetic, Symbolic, and Carnal,* Sister Scupley, the Mistress of Novices in the Hallowill convent, owned this forbidden book. It detailed the mechanics of sexual intercourse. Vivene used to like to thumb through it when she was supposed to be tidying up.

**Sorcery/Sorcerer(ess):** Any of various magical practices which involves the appeasement of otherworldly spirits in exchange for magical tokens, spells, and favors.

**Sprott:** (Srät) A minor type of fairy who can easily be captured and controlled (usually by sorcerers). Kalea and her companions fought a sprott at the inn of Jumaire.

**Swine, The:** A supremely powerful demon, who resembles a pig and dwells in Kullixaxuss. Often used as a swear word ("holy Swine" etc.). He's also a pettygod and founder of the most common dark magic practice. Spell books with his face on the cover can commonly be found in all regions.

**Sword Swish, The:** A very old tavern in Alkeer the sixth Wikshen used to frequent.

**Taradiddle:** Pretentious nonsense.

**Taulmoil:** (Tôl-moy-l) A small town in the heart of the Lightlands where Kalea is from.

**Thaccilians:** (Thak-shee-lee-uns) A race of people, characterized by their red eyes and light-colored hair, spawned by the power of the pixie, Thaxyl.

**Thaxyl:** (Thak-sill) A once-great pixie and pettygod.

**Theddir:** (Thed-deer) A town built on stilts to tolerate frequent flooding located immediately to the south-east of Norr. The last town in the Lightlands where elves are welcome.

**Tinharri:** (Tin-ärē) The ruling clan in Norr.

**Tintilly:** (Tin-til-lee) A town located on the edge of Hallowill forest where Kalea met Dorhen.

**Troll:** An ancient race of beings who live underground.

**Valltalhiss:** (Val-Tal-hiss) An ancient, decrepit city located at the center of a forest of poisoned trees.

**Vandalyns, The:** (Vand-uh-lins) A faction of sorcery in the Darklands and rival of Ilbith. Known for their use of curved blades which can channel magical lightning.

**Vestal:** A celibate woman whose life is devoted to worshipping the One Creator.

**Warlock:** A male who practices any of a variety of magics. The common male followers of Wikshonism, who don't practice magic, are also referred to as warlocks.

**Wexwick:** (Weks-wik) A rundown town on the west coast of the Lightlands, north of Ravian Cove, where bandits and thieves tend to hide out.

**Whisper Stones:** Magical stones the sorcerers use to communicate over long distances.

**White Owl Guard:** The personal guard of the reigning king or queen of Norr. Gaije's father served as a White Owl and Gaije had been drafted to train for the guard before he deserted.

**Wik:** (Wick) A powerful pixie and pettygod. One of the five pixies favored by the Ilbith sorcery faction.

**Wikhaihli:** (Wick-hay-lee) "Wik Haven." The main hub of the Wikshonite cult.

**Wikshonism/Wikshonites:** A religion centered around Wikshen, which focuses on waiting for his next return and then submitting to his violent will. Followers of Wikshen are called "Wikshonites."

**Wistara:** (Wist-ahra) A peninsula between the greater Lightlands and Sharr, serving as common passage between the two land masses.

**Witch:** A female who practices any of a variety of magics. The common female followers of Wikshonism are referred to as witches.

### Elvish/Norrian Words

*Aahmei:* Informal "mama."

*Ah:* "Yes."

*Ameiha:* Formal "mother." Often used to address Desteer maidens and queens.

*Amonimori:* "Good morning."

*Caunsaehgahn:* "Coming into service." A coming-of-age journey male elves must complete before they can graduate to full adulthood.

*Daghen-saehgahn:* "Guardian-servant" a husband.

*Desteer:* "Whisperer." The largest spiritual order in the Norrian religion. The Desteer members are always female and referred to as "maidens."

*Fa:* "She"

*Faerhain:* "Life carrier" adult female.

*Farhah:* "Soon to be life carrier" young female.

*Gaulaerhainha:* "Choosing her fate" a female's coming-of-age ceremony in which she chooses the "hall" or the "home."

*Ghaish:* "Hot." This tends to be an exclamation the elves shout out when they are burned by something hot.

*Guenhighar:* A pet name for a young boy.

*Guenhihah:* A pet name for a young girl.

*Hanbohik:* The traditional Norrian dress, worn by females, consisting of a long skirt that fastens over the breasts with a collection of thin underdresses, long sleeves, tied lapels, and small jacket or hip-length tunic worn over top.

*Harranhennhi:* "Thank you."

*Laugaulentrei:* "The lake of the dead tree," the final resting place for deceased elves.

*Lin Yilbarhen:* "The Bright One." God of the elves and the official religion of Norr. Seen as the "light" who leads his children through the wilderness.

*Milhanrajea:* "Mind Viewing." The practice in which a Desteer maiden uses her psychic ability to delve her sight into the mind of an elf to see their thoughts, intents, problems, and/or desires.

*Pahkahen:* Formal "father."

*Pawbhen:* Informal "papa."

*Sa:* "He"

*Saehgahn:* "Servant." An adult male. Also an official, sacred order to which all male elves must join and adhere.

*Saeghar:* "Too young to serve." A young male.

*Sa-garhik:* Traditional leggings, worn by males, consisting of two separate pieces for the legs fastened to the braies, a garment that covers the pelvic area. *Sa-garhik* is similar to human culture's leggings, except for their open design, often exposing the hipbone and the sides of the buttocks.

*Sarakren:* "He is forbidden." *Sarakren* is a status given to *saehgahn* who are forbidden to marry. This status comes with a brand on his left buttock (always visible between his braies and leg coverings) to warn *faerhain* away.

*Shi:* "Old" or "elderly."

*Shi-hehen:* A retired and elderly *saehgahn* who no longer has to answer the call of *saehgahn* duty, except in dire village or family emergencies.

*Shi-helah:* An elderly *faerhain* who's household workload has decreased and been taken over by younger females.

*Tok:* "No."

I'm so glad you've returned for
*Unwilling Deity*!
If you enjoyed the experience, please consider leaving a review at your favorite retailer. Leaving a review is the best thing you can do for your favorite books and authors! It not only helps other people to make the decision to buy, it causes the retailer to show the book sooner in search results and in those "just for you" suggestions.

Let me tell you, writing books is NOT easy! It has been my dream ever since 1998 when I was a lonely, unpopular thirteen-year-old girl hiding away in my bedroom, surrounded by my hundreds of colored pencil drawings and stacks of rock and roll cd's. This story is something I've planned and developed ever since then. It was the steepest mountain of my life. I can honestly say that these characters, particularly Dorhen and his ladylove, Kalea, have been every bit a part of me as my shy personality, my odd fashion sense, and my love for metal music. When I finally reached the finish line of publishing the book of my dreams, I found life to be harder than ever before—not easier. That's why I'd like to ask you for your best, honest, kindest review. I love hearing feedback from readers and I do remember what they say and consider their advice while writing future books. You don't have to say a whole lot in the review, just that you liked it, or that the book was at least adequate—hahahah!

For more information, news of future installments, art, and merchandise, please visit www.jchartcarver.com.

Made in the USA
Middletown, DE
04 August 2022

70521847R00298